D1443412

FATE OF THE COUNTRY

FATE OF THE COUNTRY

The Civil War from June to September 1864

Don Lowry

HIPPOCRENE BOOKS
New York

Copyright © 1992 by Donald S. Lowry

All rights reserved.

For information, address:
HIPPOCRENE BOOKS, INC.
171 Madison Avenue
New York, NY 10016

ISBN 0-7818-0064-1
Library of Congress Cataloging-in-Publication Data is available.

Printed in the United States of America.

*"We all feel that upon Grant and you . . .
the fate of the country depends."*

Senator John Sherman
to his brother,
Major General William T. Sherman

CONTENTS

PART THREE—ATLANTA

PROLOGUE

This book takes up where my first, *No Turning Back*, left off. However, it could stand on its own as a chronological narrative of a very interesting and somewhat neglected period of the Civil War.

The summer of 1864 was the psychological nadir of the Union cause. Although the military situation was actually better for the North than it had been during the three previous years of war, it was not so perceived by most civilians, politicians, or even many military officers at the time. Hopes had been high when Grant took over as the Federal general-in-chief in March, but after a series of indecisive battles that had apparently produced nothing but depressingly long casualty lists, he seemed to be stalled outside of Richmond and Petersburg. Sherman seemed to be equally bogged down in Georgia, and the Rebels were soon up to their old tricks of threatening Washington and the North by way of the Shenandoah Valley.

This perceived lack of progress was dangerous to the Union because 1864 was a presidential election year, and the Democratic party might very well take advantage of war-weariness to elect a candidate on the promise of putting an end to the war, even if it meant either letting the South set itself up as an independent country or allowing it to dictate national policy to a reunited federation in which majority rule would be a thing of the past. Some dramatic event, some obvious evidence of substantial progress, was sorely needed in order to inspire the North to see the war through to ultimate victory, and Sherman's capture of Atlanta, after many hard battles and weeks of frustration, proved to be just that. It is, therefore, the climactic event of the present volume.

This is not, however, strictly a history of the Atlanta campaign, but ties it to events taking place over the same three months in other theaters of war. That campaign was, in fact, not only an integral part of, but the essential element in, Grant's overall strategy for winning the war. It was the campaign he would have undertaken himself had he not found it politically necessary to personally take charge of the war in Virginia that summer. His overriding concern throughout his own campaign against Lee was to ensure that the latter could send no units to reinforce the Confederates in Georgia. To borrow George S. Patton's colorful description of his own WWII tactics, Grant took on the job of holding the

Confederacy by the nose, while Sherman kicked it in the behind. It was a blow from which the Confederacy never recovered.

All quotes in the text are presented with the same spelling and punctuation as in the sources noted. For instance, the correct spelling of Spotsylvania is with one *t*, but if a source spelled it with two *ts*, I have left the second *t* in. With a very rare exception or two, only quotations have been foot-noted.

I would like to thank my wife, Julie, and my son, James, for their continued help and encouragement through this second volume.

PART ONE

PETERSBURG

"Grant's army is across the river."

Major General W. H. F. Lee to his father,
General R. E. Lee

CHAPTER ONE

An Unseen Battlefield

14 June 1864

Major General William Tecumseh Sherman placed field glasses to his eyes and studied a group of Confederates on the slope of Pine Mountain some 800 yards away, who in turn were using their own binoculars to study Sherman and the other Union soldiers around him. "How saucy they are," Sherman remarked to one of his corps commanders. "Howard, make 'em take cover. Have one of your batteries fire three volleys into 'em."[1] Without waiting to see the results of his order, he turned and rode away.

The Civil War was a couple of months into its fourth year on that cool, cloudy morning of 14 June 1864, and Sherman was the commander of all the Federal forces between the Allegheny Mountains and the Mississippi River. Wielding three field armies of unequal size, drawn from the three geographical departments that comprised his Military Division of the Mississippi, he had already, in a bit over a month, maneuvered his Confederate opponent from near the Tennessee-Georgia border southward about three-quarters of the way to Atlanta, a vitally important Southern railroad and manufacturing center. The largest of the three forces that Sherman led—all named for rivers—was the Army of the Cumberland, commanded by his old friend Major General George H. Thomas. It consisted of three corps of infantry, the 4th, 14th and 20th, and three divisions of cavalry. The smallest of the three armies was the Army of the Ohio, commanded by Major General John M. Schofield. It consisted of only one corps of infantry, the 23rd, and one division of cavalry. The remaining force, the Army of the Tennessee, commanded by Major General James B. McPherson and containing the 15th, 16th and 17th corps, had briefly been Sherman's own before he had been named to command all three. Before Sherman, it had belonged to his good friend Ulysses S. Grant.

Sherman's Southern opponent was General Joseph E. Johnston, commander of the Department and Army of Tennessee. Johnston had ridden with two of his four corps commanders to the crest of Pine Mountain that morning to survey the situation. Lieutenant General William J. Hardee was the commander of the 1st Army Corps of Johnston's army, and Lieutenant General Leonidas Polk was the commander of a force known as Polk's Corps, or the Army of Mississippi, recently brought from that state to reinforce Johnston. Both men had been corps commanders in this, the South's main western army, since it had been formed two years before, except for brief exiles whenever they had run afoul of its former commander, the infamously and infinitely querulous General Braxton Bragg. It was a quarrel with the latter that had sent Polk to Mississippi, but he had been called back, along with many of the troops in that department, after Johnston had replaced the unsuccessful Bragg. Hardee still had a brigade of infantry and a few batteries of artillery stationed on Pine Mountain even though the Confederate army's main line had recently been moved a bit farther south, and he was worried about the safety of his units in this advanced position. It was at his request that Johnston had come to Pine Mountain with Hardee and Polk to see for himself.

Major General Oliver O. Howard was the commander of the 4th Army Corps in Thomas' Army of the Cumberland. He had passed on Sherman's order about firing on the Rebels to Captain Hubert Dilger, an artillery expert who had left the Prussian army in 1861 to come to America for some practical experience. Dilger was known in the Federal army as "Leatherbreeches" because of his habit of wearing doeskin trousers. Now he personally sighted his rifled field guns at the clump of Confederate officers a half-mile away, saying in his German accent, "Shust teeckle them fellows," as he gave the signal to fire.[2]

Dilger's first shot killed the horse of a staff officer riding with the Rebel generals on Pine Mountain. Johnston and Hardee moved quickly away, but Polk, who was older, more portly, and perhaps more concerned with his dignity than the other two—before the war he had been the Episcopal bishop of Louisiana—moved a bit too slowly. The third shell struck him in the chest, tearing out his lungs. "My dear, dear friend," Hardee cried. Tears streamed down Johnston's face as he whispered, "I would rather anything than this." In the bishop-general's tunic was found a book of poems with a mark by the stanza, "There is an unseen battlefield, In every human breast, Where two opposing forces meet, And where they seldom rest."[3] For Polk, bishop and general, the battle, external as well as internal, was over, but for his comrades and their Northern opponents it had barely begun, and many would join him before it ended.

The Federals soon knew the results of Dilger's marksmanship. Union observers who had broken the Confederate signal flag code soon read a message which was wig-wagged from the Rebel position. It said, "Send an ambulance for General Polk's body."[4] The loss of General Polk was no great disaster to the Army of Tennessee, as far as his military ability was concerned. Just about everybody, except possibly his old friend Confederate president Jefferson Davis, conceded that Polk was no military genius. As one Southern soldier put it, "He was a very nice man, but of not much use to the army."[5] Yet he was a sentimental favorite among many of his men. When Federal troops occupied Pine Mountain a couple of days later they found a crudely lettered sign there that proclaimed accusingly, "You Yankee sons of bitches have killed our old Gen. Polk."[6]

Sherman had troubles of his own just then. The terrain in northern Georgia was very wooded and very rough and the weather had been extremely wet, turning the roads and fields to sticky mud. Advances had been hard to come by lately. And, on that same fourteenth of June, Sherman received bad news from another part of his domain. His three armies were dangling at the end of a railroad supply line that stretched back through northern Georgia to Chattanooga, thence across middle Tennessee to Nashville, and ultimately up through Kentucky to Louisville and across the Ohio to Cincinnati. "Our profoundest admiration goes to the way Sherman keeps up his railroad and our rations," a soldier of the 73rd Indiana Regiment recorded in his diary that very day.[7] However, this lengthy artery was vulnerable to attack, both by sabateurs and small guerrilla bands and, most especially, by the hard-riding troopers of the Confederate cavalry, who had raised the raiding of Yankee supply lines to a fine art.

The true master of the craft, the "Wizard of the Saddle," as he was called, was Confederate Major General Nathan Bedford Forrest. Based in northern Mississippi, Forrest had recently been conducting a series of raids into western Tennessee and Kentucky that had taken him as far north as Paducah, on the Ohio River. Sherman feared that Forrest would soon turn his attention to the Federals' vulnerable supply line. "In anticipation of this very danger, I had sent General Sturgis to Memphis to take command of all the cavalry in that quarter, to go out toward Pontotoc, engage Forrest and defeat him," Sherman wrote in his memoirs, "but on the 14th of June I learned that General Sturgis had himself been defeated on the 10th of June, and had been driven by Forrest back into Memphis in considerable confusion."[8] The next day Sherman wrote to Secretary of War Edwin M. Stanton in Washington: "Forrest is the very devil, and I think he has got some of our troops under cower. I have two officers at Memphis who will fight all the time—A. J. Smith and Mower . . . I will order them to make up a force and go out and follow Forrest to the death if it costs 10,000 lives and breaks the Treasury. There will never be peace in Tennessee till Forrest is dead."[9]

Major General A. J. Smith was the commander of two small divisions known as the Right Wing of the 16th Army Corps, and Brigadier General J. A. Mower was one of Smith's division commanders. Sherman knew them both well from past association. Smith's force, then including a small provisional division of the 17th Corps, had been loaned by Sherman to Major General Nathaniel Banks, commander of the Department of the Gulf, for an unsuccessful campaign up the Red River through Louisiana and back. More than once these veteran troops had saved Banks from disaster, but their return to Sherman had been delayed when unusually low water in the Red had left the gunboats of the Union fleet stranded by the rapids at Alexandria. Banks had stayed to protect the fleet until dams could be built to float the gunboats over the rapids. He had then been superceded by Major General E. R. S. Canby. The troops from the 17th Corps had preceded Smith to Memphis, and some of them had been with Sturgis during his recent defeat by Forrest.

There had been thought of either bringing Smith's and Mower's 16th Corps troops to reinforce Sherman's main force or loaning them to Canby for a campaign against Mobile, Alabama, the South's largest remaining port on the Gulf of Mexico, but instead Sherman now had orders sent to Memphis to have Smith or Mower "pursue Forrest on foot, devastating the land over which he has passed or may pass, and make him and the people of Tennessee and Mississippi realize that though a bold, daring and successful leader, he well bring ruin and misery on any country where he may pause or tarry. If we do not punish Forrest and the people now, the whole effect of our past conquests will be lost."[10]

Sherman's army, and all the Union armies, had enemies even farther to the rear than Forrest could reach. The people of the North were by no means united behind the war effort. They could in fact be grouped into about six categories: There were the hard-war Radical Republicans,

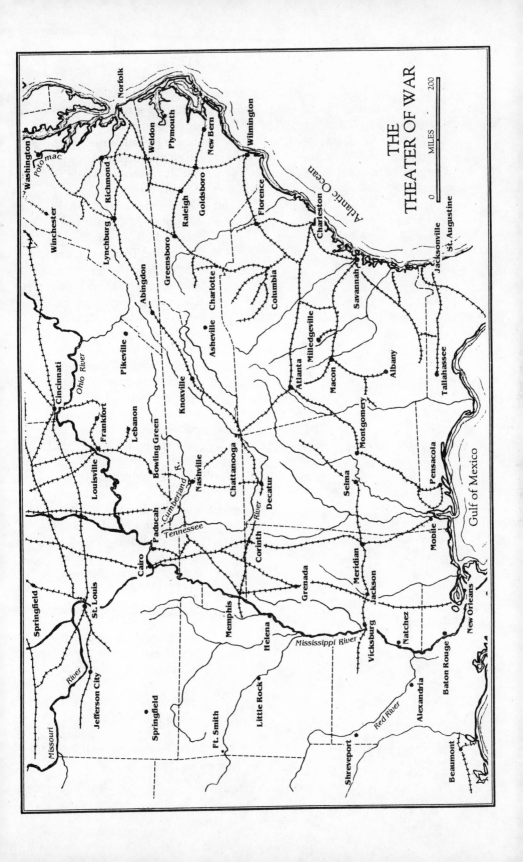

THE
THEATER OF WAR

0   MILES   200

who wanted to use any means to win the war, to eradicate slavery, and to treat the South as conquered territory without rights. There were the members of the loyal opposition—Democrats who supported the war but only for the purposes of restoring "the Union as it was [including slavery in the South], the Constitution as it is." There were also Peace Democrats—those who preferred peace at any price, even Southern independence. And there were even some who did, or would, actively support the Confederate cause. Finally there were those, both War Democrats and moderate Republicans (including President Lincoln), whose primary goal was to restore the Union—although not necessarily as it was before the war, for the war itself had already wrought many irreversible changes, including the liberation of many slaves—but unlike the Radicals had no agenda for remaking the South, or taking revenge upon it or its leaders once the war was over.

There were, of course, many shadings and much overlapping among these groups. There were, for instance, Radicals in Lincoln's cabinet. An especially gray area was the boundary between Peace Democrats and Confederate sympathizers. Square in the middle was a series of secret societies with members throughout what today we call the Midwest, but was then known as the Northwest. These groups went by names like the Knights of the Golden Circle, the Order of American Knights, and the Sons of Liberty. While the rank and file membership, which ran well into the thousands, was probably made up mostly of those who merely wanted peace, the leadership was actively allied with the Confederate government for the mutual benefit of both parties. At any rate, any opposition to the prosecution of the war by the United States was bound to give aid and comfort to its enemies.

A case in point was that of Clement L. Vallandigham. He had been an Ohio congressman until he had been defeated for reelection because his district had been gerrymandered to include a strongly Republican country. In and out of office he was a prominent leader of the peace-at-any-price wing of the Democratic party. In 1863 he had run afoul of Major General Ambrose E. Burnside, who at that time had commanded the military department whose area included the state of Ohio. Burnside had arrested Vallandigham because he had given a speech highly critical of the government and the war, despite an order published by Burnside forbidding such activity. The politician had then denied that the army had the right to make such an order or to try civilians for breaking it, but the civil courts had refused to consider his application for a writ of habeus corpus. A military tribunal had promptly condemned him to imprisonment for the duration of the war.

The Vallandigham case, of course, had caused an uproar throughout the country. Horatio Seymour, the governor of New York and a leading Democrat of the loyal-opposition stripe, had summarized the situation well when he had said that what Lincoln would do about this arrest would "determine in the minds of more than one half of the people of the Loyal States, whether the war is waged to put down rebellion at the South, or destroy free institutions at the North."[11] It had indeed been a sticky situation for Lincoln. If he had sided with Burnside, he would have lost the support of many good men and have made of Vallandigham a political martyr who would have haunted him constantly from his cell, wherever that might have been. If, however, Lincoln had overruled Burnside and freed the politician, that would have been a clear signal that anyone could oppose the war, obstruct the draft, encourage desertion, even aid the enemy, and get away with it. "Must I shoot a simple-minded soldier boy who deserts, while I must not touch a hair of a wily agitator who induces him to desert?" Lincoln had asked. "I think that, in such a case, to silence the agitator and save the boy is not only constitutional, but withal a great mercy."[12]

The president had neatly avoided both horns of this dilemma and had turned it against the Peace Democrats by changing Vallandigham's sentence from imprisonment to banishment. The "wily agitator" had been sent to the front in Tennessee and handed over to the Confederates, thus neatly identifying him as a friend of theirs in the popular mind. The spectacle of the martyr clambering to return to the despotism he had so ardently disparaged had defused the crisis. The Rebels had received the Ohio Democrat solely "in the capacity of a destitute stranger," and had been only too happy to be rid of him when he had caught an outbound blockade runner for Bermuda. He had told his reluctant hosts that if they could only hold out until the presidential election of 1864, Lincoln would be defeated by the Democrats. However, the Confederate official who interviewed him noted that "Mr. Vallandigham had said nothing to indicate that either he or the party had any other idea than that the Union would be reconstituted under Democratic rule."[13]

The exile had worked his way to Canada, where he had been greeted as a hero, and had settled down at Windsor, across the river from Detroit. By then his fellow Democrats had nominated him for governor of Ohio—both candidate and issue embodied in one person. The Republicans had countered by nominating a War Democrat, one John Brough. With the help of enthusiasm engendered by Union victories at Gettysburg and Vicksburg, plus the resentment stirred up by Confederate general John Hunt Morgan's untimely raid into Indiana and Ohio that summer, Brough had won decisively. Vallandigham had continued to be the darling of the peace-at-any-price set, however, and, although still in exile, had become the official leader of the Order of the Sons of Liberty, the latest of the pro-Southern secret societies generally lumped under the sobriquet of "Copperheads," due to their use of liberty-head pennies as a badge of recognition.

In this new capacity, Vallandigham had held secret meetings with the Confederate commissioner to Canada, Jacob Thompson, who had been the U.S. secretary of the interior in the Democratic administration of President James Buchanan, Lincoln's immediate predecessor. The exile had assured Thompson that the Sons of Liberty were almost ready for an uprising in the states of Ohio, Indiana, Illinois, Missouri and Kentucky. Arms, he had said, were being acquired, and the members were being drilled in infantry tactics. The Confederates had agreed to finance this effort, and the date of 20 July had been selected for open revolt. There was, in addition, the presidential campaign to consider. The Democratic national convention was scheduled for 4 July in Chicago, and Vallandigham had asked for and received Confederate financial aid to ensure that both the platform and the candidate emerging from that convention would be anti-war, if not pro-Confederacy.

Lincoln, it was thought, might not necessarily be adverse to running against a Peace Democrat. Congressman Fernando Wood, former mayor of New York and an ardent Peace Democrat, had recently called on Lincoln with the suggestion that Vallandigham be allowed to return to the country. Wood declared that "these War Democrats are scoundrelly hypocrites; they want to oppose you and favor the war at once, which is nonsense. There are but two sides to this fight—yours and mine, war and peace. You will succeed while the war lasts, I expect; but we shall succeed when the war is over. I intend to keep my record clear for the future."[14] There was a good chance, Wood indicated, that the Democratic party might split again in 1864 as it had in 1860—this time over the issue of war or peace—and again allow Lincoln to win without a majority of the votes. Lincoln had made no commitment regarding the exile's return, however.

So now, on the night of 14 June 1864, Vallandigham put on a false mustache, blackened his reddish eyebrows, strapped a pillow under his trousers and vest, and caught the ferry from Windsor to Detroit. Despite the disguise, he was recognized on the train heading south. A passenger bent down and whispered to him, "I know your voice but you are safe from me."[15] The next day he appeared unexpectedly, without the disguise, at a district convention of the Democratic party at Hamilton, Ohio. He was greeted with enthusiasm and promptly named a delegate to the upcoming Democratic national convention. He was perhaps somewhat disappointed that no soldiers showed up then or later to arrest him again and cause another wave of anti-Lincoln feeling which might sweep the Democrats into power. When a newspaper correspondent happened to mention Vallandigham's return in Lincoln's presence, the president said, "What! Has Vallandigham got back?" The reporter answered that it was common knowledge. "Dear me!" Lincoln replied. "I supposed he was in a foreign land. Anyhow, I hope I do not know that he is in the United States; and I shall not, unless he says or does something to draw attention to him."[16]

Shock waves of the war had begun to reach even more distant shores that day. On that same fourteenth day of June the USS *Kearsarge*, a steam sloop of war of 1,031 tons, entered the harbor of Cherbourg, France—a port that 80 years later would be liberated from the Germans by Americans. The captain of the *Kearsarge*, John A. Winslow, was pleased to find that the message he had received two days before from the U.S. minister in Paris was correct. Here in Cherbourg he did indeed find the famous Confederate commerce raider, the CSS *Alabama*, a ship that had eluded him for months.

The officers and crews of the two American vessels looked each other over carefully but could do little else there in a neutral port. Then Winslow took the *Kearsarge* back out into the English Channel to wait for the Rebel ship to come out. He would not have long to wait. The *Alabama's* captain, Commander Raphael Semmes, wrote to the Confederate agent in Cherbourg asking him to notify the U.S. consul that it was his intention to fight the *Kearsarge* as soon as he had made some necessary repairs. "I beg," he said, "that she will not depart before I am ready to go out."[17]

---

1. Lloyd Lewis, *Sherman: Fighting Prophet* (New York, 1932), 373.

2. Ibid.

3. Samuel Carter, III, *The Siege of Atlanta, 1864* (New York, 1973), 152.

4. James Lee McDonough and James Pickett Jones, *War So Terrible* (New York, 1987), 176.

5. Ibid., 177.

6. Carter, *The Siege of Atlanta*, 153.

7. Lewis, *Fighting Prophet*, 373.

8. William T. Sherman, *Memoirs of Gen. W. T. Sherman* (New York, 1891), vol. 2, 52.

9. Edwin C. Bearss, *Forrest At Brice's Cross Roads and in North Mississippi in 1864* (Dayton, 1979), 137.

10. Lewis, *Sherman: Fighting Prophet*, 370.

11. George Fort Milton, *Abraham Lincoln and the Fifth Column* (New York, 1942), 168.

12. Ibid., 174.

13. Ibid., 179.

14. Ibid., 225.

15. Carl Sandburg, *Abraham Lincoln: The War Years 1864–1865* (New York, 1926), vol. 3, 545.

16. Ibid.

17. Clarence Edward Macartney, *Mr. Lincoln's Admirals* (New York, 1956), 225.

CHAPTER TWO

The Key to Petersburg

14–15 June 1864

"I wish, when you write or speak to people," President Abraham Lincoln told a friendly newspaper correspondent on 14 June, "you would do all you can to correct the impression that the war in Virginia will end right off and victoriously. . . .As God is my judge," he said, "I shall be satisfied if we are over with the fight in Virginia within a year. I hope we shall be 'happily disappointed,' as the saying is; but I am afraid not. I am afraid not."[1]

The pontoon bridge the Federal army built across the historic James River of Virginia on that fourteenth day of June 1864 was said to be the longest built since the emperor Xerxes of Persia laid one across the Hellespont to invade Greece some 20 centuries before. Working from both shores, the Northern engineers put the floating bridge together in only seven hours. It was 13 feet wide and 2,100 feet long, spanning a stream about 80 feet deep, depending on the tide, which could make a difference of 4 feet. It required 101 pontoons to support the plank roadway, held in place by three big schooners that were anchored in midstream above the bridge and attached to the midsection with cables. It took days for the Union Army of the Potomac to cross, including its hundreds of pieces of artillery, thousands of wagons and 5,000 or more beef cattle—rations on the hoof. Then the bridge was taken apart. The only recorded casualty of the crossing was a milk cow named Mildred belonging, by right of conquest, to General Grant's headquarters mess.

Only a little over three months had passed since Ulysses S. Grant had been promoted to the three-star rank of lieutenant general—the first in the U.S. Army since George Washington—and had been made general-in-chief of all the Union armies. He had refused, however, to confine himself to an office in Washington, but had instead left his predecessor, Major General Henry W. Halleck, to handle the paperwork there with the new title of chief of staff and had made his own headquarters with the Army of the Potomac. This was the largest and best equipped of the Federal forces, and perhaps the least successful, until his arrival. It had once come within sight of the spires of Richmond, the Southern capital, only to be beaten back by the hammer blows of Confederate general R. E. Lee. The latter, and his Army of Northern Virginia, had remained its nemesis through two years of seesaw campaigning.

When Grant joined the Army of the Potomac he had not displaced its regular commander. Major General George Gordon Meade had been in command for almost a year, since just before the battle of Gettysburg, where he had won a defensive victory over Lee but had failed to pursue him to the death. Grant had retained Meade in his post to handle the administration, the logistics and much of the fighting of that army so that Grant could concentrate on the strategy not only of Meade's army, but of the overall Union war effort. Grant had won his laurels in what was then styled the West—the area beyond the Allegheny Mountains—and he was succeeded there by his friend and trusted subordinate, William Tecumseh Sherman. It had fallen to Sherman to undertake a campaign into Georgia against Joe Johnston, the Army of Tennessee, and Atlanta, while Grant led Meade and his army against Lee, his army, and the Confederate capital, Richmond.

Meanwhile, Grant had directed that other Union forces must do their part to keep the Rebels in their own fronts too busy to reinforce either of these main armies or to otherwise get into mischief, and all Federal armies were to advance in early May. It had been Grant's desire to send forces from General Nathaniel Banks' Department of the Gulf against Mobile and up the Alabama River to get into the rear of the Rebels opposing Sherman. But Banks had already begun a campaign that Halleck had dreamed up, sending him in the opposite direction, up the Red River toward Shreveport. Banks had let his forces get strung out on the road, and the head of his column had been defeated by Confederate major general Richard Taylor, son or former President Zachary Taylor. Banks' retreat back down the Red had then been complicated and delayed by unusually low water in the river that had almost trapped the accompanying fleet of Union gunboats at Alexandria.

Another Federal force had been aimed at the rear of the Confederate army opposing Meade. Two army corps drawn from Federal garrisons in Union lodgments along the coast of Virginia and North Carolina were formed into a new Army of the James under Major General Benjamin Franklin Butler, a pre-war Democratic politician who was now allied with the Radical Republicans. He had considerable administrative talents but insufficient military experience to handle such an army in the field. But the forces collected and their objectives were within the geographic limits of his department, and he insisted on commanding the army in person. Grant would have preferred to have left that job to Major General W. F. ("Baldy") Smith, commander of one of the two corps involved, but Butler was too politically prominent to ignore or to remove.

Butler had begun well, sailing his army up the James River, dropping off garrisons along the way, and had landed his main force at Bermuda Hundred. This had put his army on a peninsula bounded by the James to the north and its tributary, the Appomattox River, to the south, and squarely between Richmond on the James and the smaller town of Petersburg on the Appomattox. Between the two ran a railroad that was a critical supply line for both the Confederate capital and Lee's army. However, Butler had then frittered away his chances in hesitation, advancing timidly, first toward Petersburg and then toward Richmond, until the Rebels had gathered enough reinforcements from farther south to counterattack under General P. G. T. Beauregard. Despite much blundering on both sides, Beauregard had driven Butler back to a line of defenses which the latter had previously prepared across the Bermuda Hundred peninsula.

Meanwhile, Grant and Meade had crossed the Rapidan River in northern Virginia and had collided with Lee's army in a bloody, confused engagement in the thickets of an area known as the Wilderness. After two days of heavy combat that ended in a tactical draw, Grant sidled to the southeast and so did Lee. The two collided again near the small county seat known as Spotsylvania Court House. This time the fighting was more prolonged and, if possible, even more intense, featuring, instead of thickets, well-constructed earthworks that presaged the trench warfare of World War I. One corps-sized Federal assault had broken through a salient in Lee's defenses and had captured most of a Southern division, but Lee had pasted together a new line. Grant had then moved farther south to draw Lee out of his trenches, only to run into more entrenchments, this time with their salient point protected by the North

Anna River. Grant had declined to attack this formidable position and had again moved to the southeast. Lee had again moved to stay between the Federal army and Richmond, his men again throwing up intricate earthworks. In early June, after bringing W. F. Smith's corps from Butler's army to reinforce Meade's, Grant tried to break Lee's lines near a crossroads called Cold Harbor and lost 7,000 men in a matter of minutes.

Three small columns had meanwhile advanced from the Federal Department of West Virginia. A cavalry division, under Brigadier General William W. Averell, and an infantry division, under Brigadier General George Crook, had both crossed the Alleghenies from the Kanawha River valley to raid the railroad that connected Virginia with Tennessee, while Major General Franz Sigel had advanced with a division each of infantry and cavalry southwestward up the Shenandoah Valley until he had been defeated at New Market by Confederate major general John C. Breckinridge. While Sigel had retreated, Breckinridge had taken his small force to reinforce Lee at the North Anna, but Sigel had been replaced by Major General David Hunter, who had led another advance up the Shenandoah while Breckinridge was away. Joining up with Crook's and Averell's divisions, Hunter had marched all the way to Lexington. Lee had to detach first Breckinridge's small division and then one of the three corps of his army, the 2nd, under Lieutenant General Jubal Early, and had sent them toward Lynchburg to head off Hunter.

Hunter's Union army left Lexington on 14 June, heading for Lynchburg. On the fifteenth his force crossed to the east side of the Blue Ridge, and one brigade of his cavalry, riding in advance, occupied the town of Liberty on the Virginia & Tennessee Railroad, only 24 miles west of Lynchburg. Grant had meanwhile sent most of the cavalry from Meade's army, two divisions under Major General Philip H. Sheridan, to destroy the railroads connecting Richmond with the Shenandoah and to link up with Hunter, but Confederate cavalry had headed him off. After a drawn battle, Sheridan had decided that he would not be able to get through to Hunter, so instead he had turned northeastward to draw the Rebel horsemen away from Lee while Grant was making his move across the James. On the morning that Early had left for Lynchburg, Lee had discovered that Grant had begun what looked like another short move to his left, to the area between the James on the south and a swampy tributary called the Chickahominy on the north. In reality this was a feint, under cover of which Grant had shipped Smith's corps back to Butler and had moved the Army of the Potomac to the James, and across it on the great pontoon bridge, for a strike at Petersburg.

W. F. Smith had carried the nickname "Baldy" since his West Point

days. He was a man of considerable competence, but his fatal flaw was
his inability to work as part of a team. He considered himself superior
to just about everyone, and could never give wholehearted support to
any plan that was not his own. It had also developed, during the course
of Butler's recent advance toward Richmond, that he was rather easily
intimidated by an aggressive enemy or by the sight of well-constructed
defenses. After its brief attachment to the Army of the Potomac for the
battle of Cold Harbor, which Smith considered had been bungled by
Meade, his 18th Corps had been put back on transports, shipped back
up the James River, and returned to the Bermuda Hundred peninsula.

From there his two divisions marched, on 15 June, to a smaller pontoon bridge that Butler had laid across the Appomattox River near its
junction with the James, a few miles to the northeast of Petersburg.
Smith was joined on the south side of the river by a Union division that
had been occupying the small port and railroad terminal called City Point
at the tip of a small peninsula that jutted into the confluence of the
Appomattox and the James. This force consisted entirely of regiments of
so-called United States Colored Troops (U.S.C.T.): 3,500 black soldiers—mostly runaway Southern slaves—with white Northern officers.
Altogether Smith had perhaps 14,000 infantry with which he was supposed to capture the lightly defended Petersburg. His vulnerable southern flank was covered by the small cavalry division of Butler's army,
which was commanded by Brigadier General August V. Kautz, and he
had Grant's reassurance that the leading corps of the Army of the Potomac, the 2nd, would soon march up the south bank of the James to join
him, followed ultimately by Grant and the rest of Meade's army.

However, things had gone wrong from the start. Some of Smith's
troops had been landed at the wrong place and had found it necessary
to march several miles before reaching Butler's bridge over the Appomattox. Brigadier General Edward W. Hincks' division from City Point had
also been delayed, because it had to wait for Kautz's cavalry to move to
the front and clear the way. Then, about a mile and a half south of
the river, one of Smith's divisions encountered Rebel skirmishers, and a
brigade had to be deployed into line of battle to push them back. Next,
the Federals came under attack from a battery of artillery that would fire
a few rounds and pull out when the Union infantry got too close, only
to unlimber and fire again from a few hundred yards back.

Farther south, one of Kautz's cavalry regiments came upon a line of
rifle pits running along a ridge with obstructions, known as an abatis,
out front. These defenses were manned by dismounted Confederate cavalry and contained four pieces of artillery. The Union horsemen gave

way to the division of black troops, and Hincks' two brigades were formed in line of battle, one behind the other. Then they advanced to begin their first combat.

They entered dense, marshy woods that were full of fallen timber, and as they did so the Confederate cannon began firing cannisters of iron balls as if they were giant shotguns, "inflicting considerable damage."[2] The woods broke the advancing regiments into isolated groups, and the first of these to get clear of the trees charged alone and unsupported across the 400 yards of open ground that led up to the Southern defenses. Artillery and rifle fire drove them back to the woods, leaving 120 dead and wounded men behind and spreading panic and confusion among some of the other groups. The second brigade, thinking this was a Rebel counterattack, fired into the first. One of the regiments in the second line was a brand new cavalry outfit serving as infantry. Already "discontented and spiritless because it was not mounted," this unit broke and ran when it saw the first brigade retreat.[3]

But the two regiments on the right side of the first line, the 22nd and the 5th U.S. Colored Troops, made it through the woods in reasonable order. The Confederate artillery fire made it impossible for the Federals to stay where they were, so the colonel of the 22nd ordered the two regiments to charge. They advanced across the open ground shouting, "Remember Fort Pillow!" (Black soldiers had reportedly been massacred at that Tennessee fort by General Forrest's Confederates a couple of months before.) There would be no massacre here on either side, however, for the Rebels pulled out, leaving one cannon behind. When the celebration around the captured gun was broken up and the dead and wounded were taken care of, Hincks got his men moving again. The Rebel horsemen and their battery continued to harass the Federals as they advanced, and a mile farther down the road the latter came to a halt at the sight of the defenses of Petersburg.

The Rebels had been working for a year and a half to build and improve the semicircle of earthworks that stretched from the Appomattox east of the city, ten miles around to the same stream west of town. Known for its designer as the Dimmock Line, it included 55 square earthen forts, called *redans*, which were connected by breastworks six feet high and twenty feet thick at the base, with a ditch six feet deep and fifteen feet wide on the outside. In front of this dry moat was an abatis made of felled trees, pointing toward the front with their limbs interlaced and sharpened to dangerous points. There were rifle pits in front of the abatis, in which skirmishers could be posted to prevent a surprise, and there were narrow lanes through the abatis so the skirmishers could come and go. In front of all these defenses the ground had been cleared for a distance of half a mile, giving the defenders a clear field of fire at any attacking troops. There was only one weakness to these defenses: there were not enough defenders. The city's commander, Brigadier General Henry Wise, had only about 2,200 men, about one for every four or five yards of entrenchments, while Beauregard had estimated that it would take about 25,000 to adequately man the entire line. Wise eased his deficit somewhat by manning only the eastern half of the line, but he was still woefully short of men.

Throughout the afternoon Kautz's Federal cavalrymen skirmished with the Confederates near the southeast bend of the defenses and tried to capture the entrenchments there, but the Rebel artillery fought them off, killing Colonel Simon Mix, commander of Kautz's 1st Brigade. Around 5:30 p.m., when his men were running low on ammunition, Kautz pulled them back and put them into bivouac far to the rear. Meanwhile, Colonel Samuel Duncan's 2nd Brigade of Hincks' division skirmished with the Rebel defenders farther north, where two roads came together just before entering the works from the east. Three times they managed to capture the rifle pits in front of the main line, but each time they were driven out by counterattacks. Wise shifted more of his sparse defenders to the critical northeast part of his line and called on Beauregard to send help from north of the Appomattox.

Meanwhile, the rest of Smith's men worked their way forward in the cruel heat to advanced positions, only to "lay five hours, suffering much from the well-directed fire of the enemy."[4] Smith had already proven, during Butler's tentative advance toward Richmond a month before, that he was not eager to send his troops forward against such prepared defenses. Since then he had seen, at Cold Harbor, just how deadly Rebel cannon and rifles could be when firing at massed attackers from behind such protection. Finally he decided to put his advance on hold while he made a personal reconnaissance of the eastern end of the Confederate defenses in search of some weakness which he could exploit, drawing sniper fire whenever he showed himself. "I was obliged to make it alone on foot," he recorded, "and sometimes on my knees, and it occupied nearly two hours."[5]

Smith found that the defenses were the strongest he had ever seen and that there was plenty of artillery in the Rebel works, but there didn't seem to be much enemy infantry present. He decided to send his troops forward in successive skirmish lines, the men spread out enough so as not to make good targets, but in sufficient strength to overwhelm a weak defense when they got through the abatis and the ditch and over the earthen wall. By the time he had looked over the defenses and made his plan, most of the afternoon was gone. He set the hour of 5 p.m. for the beginning of a coordinated attack by all three of his divisions, to be backed by the fire of all his artillery. Unfortunately, while he had been reconnoitering his chief of artillery had ordered all of his horses to be unharnessed and watered. Unwilling to have his infantry attack without artillery support, Smith angrily moved the time for the attack back to 7 p.m.

At that hour Smith's guns began to rain shot and shell on a salient in the northeast corner of the Confederate works and the blue-clad infantry started forward, Martindale's 2nd Division on the right, Brooks' 1st in the center, and Hincks' division on the left. Smith, in his afternoon reconnaissance, had spotted an undefended ravine that ran between two of the redans on the east face of the salient. A hundred Federals fought their way through the outer rifle pits and then penetrated the main line there. When they fired a volley into the Confederate rear the defenders began to throw down their arms. A Federal captain found himself the proud possessor of a Rebel lieutenant colonel's sword and 227 prisoners, and the battle flag of the 26th Virginia was soon captured. At the same time, the 13th New Hampshire leaped into the ditch outside the front of the salient. From there it was "some thirty or forty feet to the top of the parapet," one of them wrote, but the Yankees climbed the sloping dirt wall "on bayonets stuck in the sand, grasping grass and weeds to assist in climbing, striking their boots into the gravel."[6] The commander of a battery of four guns surrendered to these New Englanders when they came clambering over his works.

To the west of the salients, one of Martindale's brigades drove the Confederates from another redan and captured a pair of guns. South of the salient, most of the 1st U.S.C.T. of Hincks' division and part of Bell's 3rd Brigade of the 3rd Division, attached to Brooks' 1st Division, captured another redan, known as Battery No. 6. And a bit to their left, four companies of the 22nd U.S.C.T. reached the cover of the ditch in front of Battery No. 7 and worked their way around to the rear of the redan, capturing three more cannon. Then the two black regiments, the 1st and the 22nd, turned to their left and swept down the Confederate entrenchments "across a deep and swampy ravine" where they "wavered at first under the hot fire" and then drove the Rebels out of Battery No. 8.[7] The Confederates fell back to Battery No. 9, reformed, and counterattacked. The two Union regiments managed to hold on to Battery No. 8, but could advance no farther for they were out of ammunition. However, the 4th U.S.C.T. and two companies of the 1st came up and pushed on through heavy brush and fallen timber to drive the Southerners out of Battery No. 9 and then No. 10 as well, capturing another gun. The Confederates abandoned No. 11 without a fight.

More than a mile of entrenchments had been taken with relative ease. Nine of the redans were captured along with sixteen guns and 300 prisoners, Hincks' U.S. Colored Troops taking the lion's share of each as well as most of the casualties. One instance was recorded of white Union troops having to protect Southern prisoners from blacks who wanted to retaliate for the Fort Pillow massacre, although they were too late to save one Rebel who died when a black soldier "came up to him . . . and ran his bayonet through his heart."[8] Hincks wanted to push on into the city itself, but Smith would not consent. By then it was nearly 9 p.m. and he knew that Lee was reported to have detached a large portion of his army for dispatch to the south side of the James that afternoon. Those veteran Rebel troops could already be on hand and might counterattack at any moment. He told Hincks that they should prepare to hold what they had captured until the reinforcements from Meade's army arrived.

It was more than two hours, however, before Meade's troops began to appear. They belonged to the 2nd Army Corps, commanded by Major General Winfield Scott Hancock. The latter had had a bad day. At dawn he had received orders to wait on the south bank of the James for rations for his men, which Butler was supposed to send down the river for him. He didn't need the rations, he had brought his own, but he followed orders and waited. However, the rations did not come. At 7:30 a.m. Meade decided that Hancock could depart without the expected rations, but just as the troops were about to march he got word that the long-expected boat had arrived, so he told Hancock to wait. The boat turned out to be carrying something other than the unwanted rations, however, so again Meade decided to let Hancock go. But the boat on which he sent word of this decision ran aground, and it was 10:30 a.m. before Hancock received the message and got his men on the road, five hours behind schedule.

That was not the end of his troubles. "I spent the best hours of the day on the 15th," he later complained, "in marching by an incorrect map in search of a designated position which, as described, was not in existence or could not be found."[9] What should have been a march of sixteen miles turned into one of almost twice that length. What's more, no one had bothered to tell him that he was expected to do any fighting that day, at least not until after 5 p.m., when he received a note from Grant's headquarters saying that Smith was attacking Petersburg and that Hancock should hurry to reinforce him. That was followed by a note from Smith that said, "If the Second Corps can come up in time to make an assault tonight after dark, in the vicinity of Norfolk and Petersburg railroad, I think we may be successful."[10] Hancock had ordered his men to pick up the pace, then he had ridden forward. His men had heard the sound of firing ahead as they trudged on under a bright moon. One remembered how "the booming of the cannon cheered us. We were tired, hungry, worn with six weeks of continuous and bloody fighting." But they understood the strategic situation, and "we wanted to push on and get into the fight and capture Petersburg."[11]

Hancock found Smith at about 10:30 p.m., but by then Baldy had changed his mind about a night attack and merely requested that Hancock's men replace his own in the captured works. Hancock was the senior officer and could have ordered an attack—he was known as the most aggressive and most competent corps commander in the Army of the Potomac—but he was tired and was suffering from a wound that he had picked up at Gettysburg the summer before which had now reopened. He willingly deferred to the judgment of Smith as the man on the scene. The latter was himself suffering "from the effects of bad water, and malaria brought from Cold Harbor."[12] Smith knew that both his own and Hancock's men were exhausted, while Hinks' black troops, "intoxicated by their success . . . could hardly be kept in order."[13] He figured that a night's rest was essential and that the morrow would bring two more corps from Meade's army, making a force that certainly ought to be able to handle whatever Rebels Lee had sent down this way. By 11:30 p.m. two of Hancock's divisions had replaced Smith's men in the captured defenses. After being allowed to cook and eat a belated supper, they were put to work for most of the night in revising the entrenchments to face the other direction. Hancock's other division, Barlow's 1st, had still not arrived because it had taken a wrong road in the darkness and had marched nearly to City Point before turning back. Meanwhile Smith fired off a message to Butler: "Unless I misapprehend the topography, I hold the key to Petersburg."[14]

General Pierre Gustave Toutant Beauregard, who commanded all Confederate forces between Richmond and South Carolina, would certainly have agreed with that assessment. "Petersburg at that hour was clearly at the mercy of the Federal commander, who had all but captured it," he wrote later, "and only failed of final success because he could not realize the fact of the unparalleled disparity between the two contending forces."[15] Most of Beauregard's own men had previously been sent north of the James, either to Richmond or to reinforce Lee. All he had on hand that fifteenth day of June, besides Wise's 2,200, was a division of maybe 6,000, under Brigadier General Bushrod Johnson, which was holding the defensive line that kept Butler from moving eastward out of his Bermuda Hundred trenches. When Smith's corps was reported to be south of the James and marching toward Petersburg, Beauregard had sent a wire to the Confederate War Department in Richmond: "We must now elect between lines of Bermuda Hundred and Petersburg. We can not hold both. Please answer at once."[16] The reply from General Braxton Bragg, nominal commanding general of the Confederate Army—nominal because President Jefferson Davis made all the real decisions himself—merely stated that Major General Robert F. Hoke's Division was being returned by Lee to Beauregard. The latter shot back that that did not answer his question, but Bragg made no further reply.

Hoke's troops arrived at Petersburg in time to join Wise's in working on a second line of defenses inside the line that Smith had captured. Hancock's men, working on the captured entrenchments through the night, heard the whistles of the trains that brought in Hoke's men and "reflected that every carload of Rebels is so much the more for us to contend with."[17] Hoke's reinforcements brought the strength of the city's defenders up to about 8,000 men, but by then Beauregard had received word of Hancock's approach and knew that the odds would still be heavily in his enemy's favor. He could assume that the Federals would attack the next morning and that they would overwhelm his small force, take the city, and thus cut most of the railroad lines into Richmond from the south. He had by then moved to Petersburg himself from his headquarters north of the Appomattox. Since the War Department refused to tell him which was more important to defend, the Bermuda Hundred line or Petersburg, he would have to decide for himself. He sent off a telegram to Bragg saying, "I shall order Johnson to this point. General Lee must look to the defenses of Drewry's Bluff and Bermuda Hundred, if practicable."[18] Johnson was told to evacuate his position, leaving campfires, pickets and skirmishers to bluff Butler as long as possible, while the rest of his men were to march as fast as possible for Petersburg.

---

1. Bruce Catton, *Grant Takes Command* (Boston, 1968), 390.

2. Thomas J. Howe, *Wasted Valor: the Petersburg Campaign June 15–18, 1864* (Lynchburg, 1988), 23.

3. Ibid.

4. Ibid., 31.

5. Ibid., 29.

6. Ibid., 32–33.

7. Ibid., 34.

8. Ibid., 35.
9. Catton, *Grant Takes Command*, 287.
10. Ibid.
11. Howe, *Wasted Valor*, 36.
12. Shelby Foote, *The Civil War: A Narrative* (New York, 1974), vol. 3, 432.
13. Howe, *Wasted Valor*, 36.
14. Foote, *The Civil War*, 3:432.
15. G. T. Beauregard, "Four Days of Battle at Petersburg," in *Battles and Leaders of the Civil War* (1887–1888), edited by Robert Underwood Johnson and Clarence Cough Buel, vol. 4, 541.
16. Foote, *The Civil War*, 3:433.
17. Howe, *Wasted Valor*, 40.
18. Foote, *The Civil War*, 3:434.

CHAPTER THREE

If It Takes Three Years More

15–16 June 1864

At 2 a.m. on 16 June General Robert E. Lee was wakened in his tent at Riddell's Shop to receive a message from Beauregard saying that he had pulled Johnson's Division out of the Bermuda Hundred defenses. "Cannot these lines be occupied by your troops?" Beauregard asked. "The safety of our communications requires it."[1]

Lee had spent the fifteenth concentrating what was left of his army in the area between White Oak Swamp, which is a tributary of the Chickahominy, and Malvern Hill, which is on the last loop of the James before it is joined by the Appomattox. With two of his cavalry divisions, under Hampton, off chasing Sheridan's Union troopers, Early's 2nd Corps on its way to Lynchburg, and Hoke's Division on its way to the south side of the James, all Lee had left were the three infantry divisions of the 1st Corps, under newly promoted Lieutenant General Richard H. Anderson, the three infantry divisions of the 3rd Corps under Lieutenant General A. P. Hill, recently recovered from a debilitating illness, and one cavalry division under his own son, W. H. F. ("Rooney") Lee. The latter, at least, had been temporarily augmented by a small brigade of cavalry under Brigadier General Martin W. Gary from the Department of Richmond, which was a small independent command charged with the immediate defense of the Confederate capital.

Captain Paul of Beauregard's staff had visited the elder Lee on the morning of the fifteenth with pages of figures to show how desperately short of manpower his department was. But Lee hated paperwork and had ignored the figures. Besides, with Early and Hampton gone, Lee was desperately short of troops himself, and he had already moved Hoke's Division to Drewry's Bluff, in the southern defenses of Richmond. Anyway, Captain Paul had not known at the time that Smith was already south of the Appomattox, nor that any portion of Meade's army was south of the James. Nevertheless, Lee had sent orders to Hoke to report to Beauregard and he had requested that General Bragg send Brigadier General Matthew Ransom's large brigade south from the Department of Richmond and call out the local reserves to take his place. Also, Lee had ordered the construction of a bridge across the James River below Chaffin's Bluff, on the north bank, to provide a shorter line of communication between his own forces and those of Beauregard. However, Lee and his army had remained relatively quiet throughout the fifteenth and in total ignorance of the Federals' great pontoon bridge and of the crossing of Meade's army out of his department into Beauregard's, and even of Smith's attack on Petersburg. "Thus," wrote Brigadier General E. Porter Alexander, chief of artillery in the 1st Corps of Lee's army, "the last, and perhaps the best, chances of Confederate success were not lost in the repulse at Gettysburg, nor in any combat of arms. They were lost during three days of lying in camp, believing that Grant was hemmed in by the broad part of the James below City Point, and had nowhere to go but to come and attack us."[2]

Meanwhile, Major General Ambrose E. Burnside's 9th Corps of Meade's Army of the Potomac had crossed the James on the great pontoon bridge on the fifteenth, while Major General Governeur K. Warren's 5th Corps had prepared itself to follow. Major General Horatio Wright's 6th Corps had waited on the north bank, where it and Brigadier General James H. Wilson's 3rd Division of the Cavalry Corps protected the army's rear from the prying eyes of Rooney Lee's Rebel horsemen. Grant himself had ridden a transport up the James that day and had set up his headquarters at the little port of City Point northeast of Petersburg on a high bluff overlooking the confluence of the James and the Appomattox, and there he found time to pen a note to his wife Julia. "About one half of my troops are now on the south side of James River," he told her. "A few days now will enable me to form a judgment of the work before me. It will be hard and may be tedious, however I am in excellent health and feel no doubt about holding the enemy in much greater alarm than I ever felt in my life. They are now on a strain that no people ever endured any great length of time."[3]

So, at 2 a.m. on the sixteenth Lee sat up on his cot and read Beauregard's message. It completely failed to explain the emergency at Petersburg that had lead to his withdrawal of the troops from his Bermuda Hundred defenses without prior notice. For Lee there was no time now for questions, nor for anything else but action. Quickly the sleeping soldiers were roused, and by 3 a.m. one brigade of Pickett's Division was on the march. The rest of the division was soon to follow, and Anderson, commander of the 1st Corps, was to go along and take whatever action was needed to secure—or, more likely, recapture—the lines, that Beauregard was abandoning, that protected the direct road, telegraph, and railroad connections between Richmond and Petersburg. A. P. Hill, commander of the 3rd Corps, was left in charge of the defensive line between Riddell's Shop and Malvern Hill, for Lee and his staff were themselves on the road to the new Confederate bridge over the James at Chaffin's Bluff before daylight.

Around 10 on the night of the fifteenth, the lieutenant colonel in command of the Union picket line on the right of Butler's Bermuda Hundred line detected movement in the enemy's entrenchments. He crawled forward on his hands and knees at several places between 2 and 3 a.m on the sixteenth and discovered that a large number of Confederates had been withdrawn and that the movement was still going on. He reported this to Brigadier General Alfred Terry, commander of Butler's only remaining corps, the 10th, and at daylight the latter captured many of the Rebel pickets and, against some resistance, part of Johnson's main line and a large number of prisoners. Terry then advanced his forces and took possession of the enemy works.

About dawn on the sixteenth Barlow's wayward division of Hancock's Union 2nd Corps began to arrive at Petersburg after its unintentional detour during the night. There the bedraggled Federals passed the walking wounded of Hincks' division, making their way to the rear. Black soldiers were still a rare sight, and a Federal colonel took note of the fact that "they were in no panic and, to my amazement, each man seemed to bring his gun with him. I have never seen wounded men come out of a fight as they did."[4] Smith's 18th Corps held the right of the Union line, northwest of the captured salient. Gibbon's division of the 2nd Corps was on Smith's left, then Birney's. Barlow's exhausted men moved in on the far left. Around 6 a.m. Gibbon and Birney began to reconnoiter the

Southern positions to their front, which they had not previously seen in daylight. Then Hancock ordered a reconnaissance in force to find the best spot for an attack to be made once Burnside's 9th Corps arrived.

At 7:45 that morning Butler wired Grant at City Point that the Confederates had abandoned their works opposite his Bermuda Hundred lines and that he would advance and try to reach the Richmond & Petersburg Railroad.

The job of making Hancock's reconnaissance in force was given to Colonel Thomas Egan's 1st Brigade of Birney's 3rd Division, which was hit by Rebel artillery fire even before its regiments could be put into line of battle. But the troops were formed up in some fallen timber, and then the two lead regiments moved forward across a broad field in the face of artillery fire of "extraordinary briskness."[5] However, the men in one of the supporting regiments had only a few days left on their enlistments and, having no desire to get killed now, when they were so close to making it home alive, they failed to advance and merely took what cover they could find.

Meanwhile the men of Ransom's Rebel brigade had marched the twenty miles from Richmond through the heat of the night, and they arrived at the new Confederate line of defenses "wet with sweat," then had to run, "getting to the works before the enemy reached there" and "just in time to meet their charge, and drive them back."[6] But Colonel Egan, whom one of his soldiers characterized as a "third rate idiot," would not give up. He reformed his men and tried again. They managed to capture Battery No. 12 on the old Dimmock Line but could not reach the new line the Rebels had dug overnight just beyond a small tributary of the Appomattox called Harrison's Creek. Egan himself was carried to the rear with a wound near his kidneys. "If any tears were shed," his disgruntled soldier wrote, "they were tears of joy, mingled with the hope that his wound will keep him away till our terms end."[7] Egan's attack, however, prompted Beauregard to send a message to Lee at 9:45 a.m. that said, "The enemy is pressing us in heavy force. Can you not send forward the re-enforcements asked for this morning and send to our assistance the division now occupying the trenches lately evacuated by Johnson's division, replacing it by another division?"[8]

About 9:30 a.m., a half-hour behind the tail of Pickett's column, Lee crossed the river to the formidable defenses at Drewry's Bluff, designed to keep the U.S. Navy from ascending the James to Richmond. From there he sent off a telegram to Beauregard that said, "Please inform me of condition of affairs. Pickett's Division is in vicinity of your lines front of Bermuda."[9] This crossed with the wire to him from Beauregard asking him to forward to Petersburg whatever division he had presumably sent to replace Johnson's in the Bermuda Hundred lines. This airy assumption that Lee's troops had arrived in time to replace Johnson's before Butler's Federals broke through, and that Lee had countless divisions to spare from his primary job of protecting Richmond from Grant's and Meade's army (still presumed to be north of the James), as well as the vagueness about what enemy was pressing him and in what force, must have puzzled, if not irritated, the gray commander. At 10:30 a.m. he wired Beauregard, "Your dispatch of 9.45 received. It is the first that has come to hand. I do not know the position of Grant's army, and cannot strip north bank of James River. Have you not force sufficient?"[10]

It was soon learned that Butler's Federals were blocking the turnpike and railroad between Drewry's Bluff and Petersburg. Lee only found out later that Bushrod Johnson's pickets and skirmishers fell back to their second line of defense at 10:15 a.m. and that they were then pushed out of this and forced to retreat toward Petersburg. The entire length of the defenses abandoned by Johnson's Division was soon in the hands of Butler's Union troops, who pressed on to the west as far as Chester Station and to the southwest to Port Walthall Junction, both of which were on the Richmond & Petersburg Railroad, whose track they were now busily ripping up.

Meanwhile, Smith's 18th Corps skirmished with the Confederates at the northern end of the new defenses at Petersburg, and some of Hincks' men were put to work digging earthworks on the top of a hill so that artillery could be put in place to counter a Rebel battery on the north side of the Appomattox that was in a position to enfilade any Union advance near the river. The head of Burnside's column began to arrive about 10 a.m., and at 10:15 a.m. Grant sent a message to Meade, still at the big pontoon bridge, for him to send Warren's 5th Corps to protect the Union left flank and to come forward on a steamer himself and take charge at the front. At 10:30 a.m. Grant ordered Smith to find the best point on his sector for making an assault but to hold troops in reserve, ready to reinforce the left in case of a Confederate counterattack. Then Grant left City Point and rode forward to assess the situation.

When Meade arrived at the front about noon he met Grant, who was riding back from his look at the captured defenses. The lieutenant general was in good spirits, and he told Meade, "Smith has taken a line of works there stronger than we have seen this campaign! If it is a possible thing I want an assault made at 6 o'clock this evening."[11] By 1 p.m. two of Burnside's divisions, Potter's 2nd and Willcox's 3rd, had arrived, but the troops were exhausted. "It was pitiable to see the men," wrote Lieutenant Colonel Theodore Lyman of Meade's staff, "without water, broken by a severe march, scorched by a tropical sun, and covered with a suffocating dust."[12] The temperature stood near 100 degrees and many men, unable to keep up with the marching column, were scattered along its wake. Those who had kept up would not be fit for much for quite a while, and "when our lines were formed," one of them wrote, ". . . the corps was but a skeleton compared with its former strength."[13]

At 1 p.m. a message from Anderson informed Lee that with Pickett's Division alone he could not drive the Yankees back into their own lines. Lee quickly sent off an order for another of Anderson's divisions, that of Major General Charles Field, to hurry across the river and for the third to stand by at the north end of the bridge. Early in the afternoon another wire from Butler to Grant announced that he had captured the entire line of Confederate works on the Bermuda Hundred front. By then Grant had already ordered two divisions of the 6th Corps to be sent up the James on transports to reinforce Butler's penetration. But when Pickett attacked the northern edge of their position, Butler and Terry took counsel of their greatest fear, that the wily Lee and his vaunted army would fall upon their weakened forces now that Meade and Grant were no longer keeping those renowned Rebels busy. Terry ordered his men to fall back. Field's Division arrived during the afternoon, and by dark Anderson had succeeded in recovering Johnson's second line of defense and in reestablishing Confederate control of the direct links between Richmond and Petersburg.

Meade was now in charge of Union operations at Petersburg, but he was unfamiliar with the ground, so he sent two officers to find the best place for an attack: Brigadier General John G. Barnard, Grant's chief engineer, and Lieutenant Colonel Cyrus B. Comstock, one of Grant's aides. At 3:45 p.m. Barnard recommended that Barlow's 1st Division of Hancock's 2nd Corps should make the attack on its sector, to be preceded by an artillery bombardment, and supported by the 9th Corps. Meade then conferred with Burnside and Hancock while his chief of staff, Major General Andrew A. Humphreys, and Barlow made a further reconnaissance.

By 4 p.m. Meade had decided upon a somewhat larger attack. Barlow's four brigades, supported by two from the 9th Corps on their left, would assault the defenses on high ground near the southeastern corner of the Confederate position, where the Dimmock Line merged with the new second line. In addition, Birney's 3rd Division of the 2nd Corps, supported by Gibbon's 2nd Division, would attack the new line farther north on some high ground around the Hare farm, west of Battery No. 9. Also, Smith's 18th Corps would make a strong demonstration on the

Federal right to tie down the Rebels in that area, and Kautz's small cavalry division would move around to the south toward the Jerusalem Plank Road to threaten the Confederates' right and protect the Union left. In accordance with Grant's wish, the attack was set for 6 p.m., giving the commanders two hours to get their men formed for the attack and the artillery moved into firing positions.

By mid-afternoon Lee had received a message from Beauregard that included the equivocal statement, "We may have sufficient force to hold Petersburg."[14] This was followed by a report that Confederate signalmen had counted 47 Union transport steamers on the James River in the last few days. To this Lee replied at 4 p.m., "The transports you mention have probably returned Butler's troops," which assumption was, of course, correct. Then he asked the key question, "Has Grant been seen crossing James River?"[15]

At 5:30 p.m. Butler informed Grant that his forces had destroyed three miles of the Richmond & Petersburg Railroad, but that the captured defenses could not be held by his small force. Night attacks by Anderson's Confederates succeeded in recapturing part of Johnson's front line of earthworks.

At the designated hour of 6 p.m. the Union artillery opened fire on the Confederate defenses at Petersburg. "As the sun declined," wrote one witness, "the air, full of dust and powder smoke, gave a copper hue to the scene."[16] When the cannon fire slackened the infantry moved forward. On the Federal right, troops from Smith's 18th Corps advanced to within 75 yards of Brigadier General Johnson Hagood's Brigade of Hoke's Confederate division. There was close fighting for an hour, but Hagood characterized the attack as a "feeble effort."[17] Men of the 13th New Hampshire, occupying high ground near the salient in the Dimmock Line that they had helped to capture the night before, had a rare view of what one of them called "a grand but terrible spectacle."[18] To the south they could see units of Gibbon's, Birney's and Barlow's divisions moving across the valley of Harrison's Creek and into the ravines in front of the second Rebel line.

Most of Gibbon's division was kept in reserve. One brigade alone, which had joined the Army of the Potomac from the defenses of Washington only a few weeks before, went forward. Its men, deployed in line of battle with skirmishers out front and the largest regiment in reserve, were protected somewhat by woods for most of the way. But when they emerged from the trees they met a destructive fire that wounded their commander, Colonel John Ramsey, among others.

They hit the dirt and began to dig in, some within 30 yards of the Confederate line.

To the south of Gibbon's division, Birney sent in two of his four brigades, one behind the other. "It was a magnificent sight," one of them remembered, "to see the long lines advancing with gleaming bayonets, even though to almost certain death." Some of the Federals "had not advanced more than a hundred yards when we were met by a terrific fire of musketry from the enemy directly in our front," as one recorded. "The fire was returned, and then began a battle royal which lasted until ten o'clock in the evening."[19] Like Gibbon's men, they went to earth close to the Rebel lines and began to dig, except for the color guard and about 30 men of the 1st Massachusetts Heavy Artillery (serving as infantry) who made it to the base of the Southern defenses, where, unnoticed, they hung on, their feet in the water of Harrison's Creek, until darkness allowed them to slip back to their regiment.

South of Birney's attack, Barlow's entire division went forward where the new Rebel line connected with the old Dimmock Line, defended by Bushrod Johnson's division and Wise's Brigade. Colonel James Beaver, commander of one of Barlow's four brigades, led his men through a shower of artillery fire until one shell buried itself at his feet and then exploded, tossing him into the air with a severe wound. This threw his brigade into confusion, and most of his men retreated, although a few of them continued forward to the protection of the ravines in front of the Confederate works, where eventually about 500 men of the 7th New York Heavy Artillery surrendered. Loss of leadership also hampered the other brigades, and they too ground to a halt after capturing some forward rifle pits and fortifications. On Barlow's left only one brigade of the 9th Corps went forward in support of the 2nd Corps attack. It captured some rifle pits and then skirmished with the Rebels until nightfall.

Although there were some 50,000 Federals on hand versus 14,000 Confederates, the limited nature of the attack and the disproportionate advantage of the defensive in Civil War tactics kept the Southern line intact. However, the Confederates considered the Union lodgements near their works to be a serious threat, and after dark Beauregard launched several vigorous attempts to drive the Northerners back into their original lines. These attempts failed, but they kept the Federals off balance for the rest of the night. Meanwhile, Beauregard set his engineers to designing and building a third line of defenses between the second line and the city. By midnight the leading elements of Warren's 5th Corps of Meade's army came marching in, and the rest of that corps continued to arrive during the early hours of June 17.

The failure of the Union attacks at Petersburg has often been attributed to a loss of morale due to the heavy casualties taken at Cold Harbor and in the weeks before, but while there is little direct evidence of such demoralization, there is plenty for a simpler explanation. Meade told Grant that "our men are tired and the attacks have not been made with the vigor and force which characterized our fighting in the Wilderness." An officer in Barlow's division reported his men as "utterly used up," saying that "the utmost exertions of the officers were almost ineffectual in keeping them in a wakeful condition." A soldier in Birney's division said he "fell asleep just where I was lying," in spite of "a battery of twelve-pound Napoleon guns . . . firing over our heads."[20]

Beauregard's answer to Lee's key question was sent at 7 p.m., but it was self-contradictory. It said, "No information yet received of Grant's crossing James River. Hancock's and Smith's Corps are however in our front."[21] The obvious intent of Lee's question had been not to find out whether Grant had personally crossed the James, but whether Meade's army, by then commonly called Grant's, or any sizable part of it, had crossed. If Hancock's troops were present at Petersburg then at least part of Grant's army must have crossed the James. And yet Beauregard had not seen fit to mention this key fact until now. It did not necessarily mean that all of Grant's army had crossed, however. On the other hand, it was quite possible that it had or would. "Lee was in a furious passion—one of the few times during the war," one of his generals observed. "He was mad because he could not find out what Grant was doing."[22]

On the other hand, the Northern commanders had pretty good information about what Lee was doing. At 7:10 p.m. Butler received a message from Union admiral S. P. Lee. Sailors on Federal gunboats had seen what they overestimated as from 40,000 to 50,000 Confederates crossing the James from north to south. This information was passed on to Meade and convinced him that the bulk of Lee's army had not yet reached Petersburg. He therefore determined to make another attack that night and assigned the job to Burnside's 9th Corps. However, because of the time involved in planning and preparing for the assault, it was decided to put it off until dawn.

That night Meade sent Lieutenant Colonel Theodore Lyman of his staff to City Point to report to Grant. After hearing Lyman's account of the disappointing results of the day's action Grant just smiled and said, "I think it is pretty well to get across a great river, and come up here, and attack Lee in his rear before he is ready for us!"[23]

President Abraham Lincoln was in Philadelphia that sixteenth day of June 1864. He spoke at a banquet that evening at the Great Central Sanitary Fair, which was raising funds for the Sanitary Commission, a volunteer organization somewhat analogous to the modern Red Cross. After commending the efforts of such organizations, he raised and answered the question, "When is the war to end?" He said he did not want to name a particular day, or month, or even year "for fear of disappointment, because the time had come and not the end." But he added, "We accepted this war; we did not begin it. We accepted this war for an object, a worthy object, and the war will end when that object is attained. Under God, I hope it never will until that time." He was interrupted by what one reporter noted as great cheering. "Speaking of the present campaign," he continued, "General Grant is reported to have said, I am going through on this line if it takes all summer. [More cheers] This war has taken three years; it was begun or accepted upon the line of restoring the national authority over the whole national domain, and for the American people, as far as my knowledge enables me to speak, I say we are going through on this line if it takes three years more."

To this sobering thought he added another. Hinting that he might soon call for another wave of volunteers and, if necessary, another draft, he asked, "If I shall discover that General Grant and the noble officers and men under him can be greatly facilitated in their work by a sudden pouring forth of men and assistance, will you give them to me?" When this was answered with cries of "yes," he answered, "Then, I say, stand ready, for I am watching for the chance."[24]

Far up the James River from Richmond, Hunter's Union Army of West Virginia moved through the town of Liberty Court House toward Lynchburg that day, with one division tearing up track on the Virginia & Tennessee Railroad as it advanced. Rebel cavalry had burned the bridge over the Big Otter River, and it took all day for the Federals to lay a pontoon bridge. Based on reports from fugitive slaves that Lynchburg was lightly defended, and reports in the Lynchburg papers of frantic efforts to evacuate that city, Hunter reasoned that it would not take him long to capture the place and put to the torch all the Confederate supplies and facilities there. He therefore ordered his wagon train of extra rations, fodder and ammunition to turn in the opposite direction and precede the army toward the Kanawha Valley of West Virginia. He had heard that Sheridan's cavalry had turned back from its attempt to link up with him, and he did not propose to linger in the area alone.

Confederate Major General John C. Breckinridge had arrived at Lynchburg on the fourteenth and had joined his two infantry brigades with the cavalry that had been hovering in Hunter's front. But even counting the local reserves, some artillery, hospital convalescents, and the cadets from the Virginia Military Institute, he could only field about 5,000 men. Jubal Early's 2nd Corps of Lee's army reached the Rivanna River, near Charlottesville, on the sixteenth, still some 65 miles northeast of Lynchburg. But the railroad had been repaired between the two cities, and Early began rounding up locomotives and cars to carry as many of his men forward as possible. Early got in contact with Breckinridge by wire. Among other things, he told the latter that his "first object is to destroy Hunter, and the next it is not prudent to trust to telegraph."[25]

---

1. Foote, *The Civil War*, 3:434.
2. J. F. C. Fuller, *Grant and Lee: a Study in Personality and Generalship* (Bloomington, Ind., 1957), 227.
3. Bruce Catton, *Grant Takes Command*, 290–291.
4. Howe, *Wasted Valor*, 43.
5. Ibid., 44.
6. Ibid., 44–45.
7. Ibid., 45.
8. Clifford Dowdey, *Lee's Last Campaign* (New York, 1960), 337.
9. Clifford Dowdey and Louis H. Manarin, eds., *The Wartime Papers of R. E. Lee* (New York, 1961), 784.
10. Ibid., 784.
11. Catton, *Grant Takes Command*, 291.
12. Howe, *Wasted Valor*, 49.
13. Ibid.
14. Dowdey, *Lee's Last Campaign*, 338.
15. Dowdey and Manarin, *Wartime Papers of R. E. Lee*, 785.
16. Howe, *Wasted Valor*, 52.
17. Ibid., 53.
18. Ibid.
19. Ibid., 53–55.
20. Ibid., 60.
21. Dowdey, *Lee's Last Campaign*, 339.
22. Howe, *Wasted Valor*, 58.
23. Ibid., 60.
24. Roy P. Basler, ed., *The Collected Works of Abraham Lincoln* (New Brunswick, N.J., 1953), vol. 7, 396.
25. Frank E. Vandiver, *Jubal's Raid: Early's Famous Attack on Washington in 1864* (New York, 1960), 34.

CHAPTER FOUR

What Has Become of Grant's Army

16–18 June 1864

Down in Georgia on the sixteenth of June, Joe Johnston abandoned Lost Mountain and pulled back the left half of his line so that it ran north and south, just to the east of a stream known as Mud Creek. The next day, as rain began to fall again, Sherman's forces advanced to explore this new line. Both divisions of Schofield's 23rd Corps, also known as the Army of the Ohio, reinforced by Geary's 2nd Division of Hooker's 20th Corps of Thomas' Army of the Cumberland, attacked Major General Patrick Cleburne's crack division of Lieutenant General William J. Hardee's Confederate 1st Corps, inflicting heavy casualties on the Rebels and wounding Brigadier General Lucius E. Polk. This Polk was the nephew of the Leonidas Polk who had been killed three days before, and this, his fourth wound, put him out of the army for good.

When Meade assigned the next attack at Petersburg to the 9th Corps, General Burnside chose his 2nd Division, commanded by Brigadier General Robert B. Potter, to make the actual assault. Brigadier General James H. Ledlie's 1st Division of the 9th Corps and Barlow's 1st Division of the 2nd Corps would support it. Potter in turn gave Brigadier General

Simon Griffin, commander of his 2nd Brigade, the job of planning the attack. High ground known as Hickory Hill was chosen as the objective. This was the location of the house and outbuildings of the Shand family. It was at the southeastern end of the Confederate second line, connecting with the older Dimmock Line at Battery No. 15.

The Federals planned to exploit an inherent weakness in this position, namely, that within 100 yards of its front was a ravine through which a small tributary of Harrison's Creek ran roughly parallel to the Rebel lines. The Union soldiers were ordered to muffle their canteens, cups, etc. and, under cover of darkness, to file silently into this ravine. By 1 a.m. on 17 June both brigades of Potter's division were in place. Griffin's 2nd Brigade was on the northern or right flank, near the point where the small stream joined the creek and opposite the buildings and orchard on Hickory Hill. Colonel John I. Curtin's 1st Brigade was on the left of the Union line, nearest to Battery No. 15. Each of the brigades was formed in two lines, and each had three regiments in its front line. Griffin had four and Curtin, three in their second lines. The exhausted soldiers lay quietly in the ravine for a couple of hours, getting a rare chance to rest as they waited. Curtin's men crept forward to within 40 yards of the Southern defenses in the dark. When they accidentally knocked a fence rail to the ground the noise drew a few shots from Rebel pickets, but the Federal soldiers were not detected, and quiet returned.

The Confederate defenses on Hickory Hill were defended by the five small Tennessee regiments of Bushrod Johnson's old brigade, commanded by Colonel John S. Fulton since Johnson had been put in charge of the entire division. In addition, there was one battery of artillery in the redan known as Battery No. 15, and there was another one in an orchard just north of the Shand house.

Just after 3 a.m. the first light of dawn began to appear. With muskets loaded but not capped and with bayonets fixed, the Northern soldiers began to move "noiselessly, swiftly, powerfully . . . upon the sleeping foe."[1] On Griffin's front only a single Confederate managed to fire his gun before the defenses were overrun and all Rebels who resisted were bayonneted. In Curtin's brigade, despite the plan, the 36th Massachusetts stopped to fire a volley. This alerted the defenders and a "hot flash of musketry and smoke of cannon" met the advancing Federals "without a shrub to shield them from the withering blast."[2] One of Curtin's regiments, another cavalry outfit serving as infantry, broke and ran, but the 45th Pennsylvania moved up from the second line and took its place.

Despite an enfilading fire from Battery No. 15, as well as the resistance to the front, Curtin's men took their objective almost as quickly as Griffin's did. The 48th Pennsylvania captured the colors of the 44th

Tennessee, recaptured the flag which the 7th New York Heavy Artillery had lost the day before, and took more prisoners than there were men in the Union regiment. Then, led by its commander, Lieutenant Colonel Henry Pleasants, the 48th charged another 100 yards and took Battery No. 15. There they captured two brass 12-pounder Napoleon guns. More Confederate artillery soon drove the Federals out of the redan, but they took their prizes with them. Altogether Potter's division captured 4 guns, 5 colors, 600 men, 1,500 muskets, and a mile-long section of the Southern works. What was left of the defenders retreated to a line farther west, and the South Carolina brigade of Brigadier General Stephen Elliott advanced to block any further penetration.

Ledlie's 1st Division of the 9th Corps was supposed to support Potter's left. However, Ledlie let his men sleep until it was time to advance. Then they had to move a half-mile, mostly through a thick pine forest where the Confederates had carefully cut the trees three feet above the ground so the Yankees would have great trouble advancing either over or under them. The branches had been trimmed to sharp points, and Ledlie's advance slowed to a crawl. "We were ragged enough before we struck that," one of his men remembered, "but when we finally got through that slashing our clothing was hanging in tatters."[3] By the time they had penetrated these entanglements, Ledlie's men were too late to exploit Potter's breakthrough. Barlow's division of the 2nd Corps was supposed to support Potter's right, but its men were also allowed to sleep. Some of them did advance on Potter's right, but they did not apply much pressure to the Rebel defenders.

Potter's division pursued the retreating Confederates but, lacking support, could not go very far without exposing its flanks. Potter put the 7th Rhode Island to work turning the defenses of Battery No. 15 to face the enemy and sent skirmishers out as far as possible, but that was about all he could do alone. However, as one of his men said, "had a single . . . corps been on the ground in position, or had the divisions which were ordered to support us been ready to advance . . . the long, tedious, wasting, bloody siege of Petersburg might have been avoided."[4]

Around daylight Warren's 5th Corps began to arrive, and its leading division, Brigadier General Lysander Cutler's 4th, took position on Burnside's left, entrenching within 600 yards of the Confederate line. By the middle of the morning the rest of the 5th Corps had reached the front. Its men, like those of the other corps, arrived in an exhausted condition. Meade expected Lee and his army to show up any time now and the Southerner's record as a highly effective counterpuncher made it advisable to protect the Union army's one exposed flank, the left, so he placed the entire 5th Corps on the defensive there.

Birney's 3rd Division of the Federal 2nd Corps advanced during the morning, with the support of part of Gibbon's 2nd Division on its left. It pushed across Harrison's Creek and took the eastern side of the Hare house hill against only light Confederate resistance. But that was the end of the 2nd Corps' advance. Hancock felt it was unwise to persevere because the 9th Corps on his left had stalled and could not protect his flank. Throughout the day sharpshooting was kept up by both sides up and down the line. In the 2nd Corps sector, where the opposing lines were very close to each other, it was death to expose one's head above the earthworks.

At 6 a.m. the first 2,000 men of Wright's 6th Corps arrived at Butler's front on the Bermuda Hundred line. And at 6:30 a.m. Butler wired Grant to ask for instructions. Grant replied that he wanted Butler to use two divisions of the 6th Corps to hold the Confederate line of defenses which he had taken, preventing direct communication between Richmond and Petersburg, but by 10:30 a.m. Anderson's Confederates had retaken that line except for a stronghold still being held by the Federals near Clay's house. Lee moved his own headquarters from Drewry's Bluff to near the Clay house so that he could oversee the reestablishment of the Rebel defenses. Among these was a battery of heavy guns overlooking a stretch of the James River called Trent's Reach. When Johnson's Division had pulled out, the big guns had been buried and their location camouflaged. The Federals had failed to find them, and now they were dug up and remounted.

At 9 a.m. Lee received another message from Beauregard in which he still reported only Smith's and Hancock's corps in his front. He again asked for reinforcements from Lee, but this time he wanted them so that he could take the offensive and drive the Federals away. No sooner had Lee finished reading this than he received another dispatch from Beauregard telling of his loss of Hickory Hill and asking for reinforcements to resist the overwhelming Union attack that he expected at any moment. If he could hold out until dark, he said, he would pull back to a new, shorter, more easily defended line. But he needed "reinforcements to resist such large odds as are against us. The enemy must be dislodged or the city will fall."[5]

At 11 a.m. Warren sent a message to Meade by field telegraph that Burnside was preparing another division to attack and that his own 5th Corps was ready for action. Meade replied with an order for Warren to extend his left as far as possible to explore the ground and the enemy's strength and positions.

At 11:15 a.m. Lee received another message from Beauregard, whose nimble mind had taken yet another tack. A member of the Union 5th Corps had been captured but professed not to have any idea where his corps was. Instead of taking the prisoner's presence as evidence that the 5th Corps was in his front, Beauregard used the prisoner's alleged uncertainty to leap to the conclusion that Grant must have sent the 5th Corps in pursuit of Early's Confederates, then on their way to Lynchburg. Based on this ill-founded assumption, and the weakening of Meade's army that it seemed to imply, Beauregard again asked for reinforcements to undertake an offensive to "crush the enemy in our immediate front."[6] However, Lee did not feel he had troops to spare for either defense or offense at Petersburg. At noon he replied that "until I can get more definite information of Grant's movement I do not think it prudent to draw more troops to this side of the river."[7]

The second division that Burnside was preparing for an attack was Brigadier General Orlando B. Willcox's 3rd of the 9th Corps. Its two brigades were brought forward to the ravine in front of the Shand house, where they were protected from Confederate artillery fire, and arranged in attack formation. There they waited in the broiling midday heat for the order to attack, while Confederate artillery kept up a sporadic bombardment. At 2 p.m. Brigadier General John F. Hartranft's 1st Brigade moved forward in two lines with Colonel Benjamin C. Christ's 2nd Brigade following, and Brigadier General Nelson A. Miles' 1st Brigade of Barlow's 2nd Corps division in support on the right. As the front line reached the top of the ravine where the attackers had been sheltering, it was met by a "hailstorm of shot, shell, grape, cannister and minie balls." Miles' brigade rushed forward against heavy rifle fire and one of its regiments, the 5th New Hampshire, took some high ground that overlooked the Confederate line to its front. From there it "maintained such a rapid accurate and deadly fire, that the enemy could not rise above their breastworks."[8]

However, there was no Union artillery support and there were no friendly units protecting Hartranft's left, and from that direction a battery of Rebel guns enfiladed the advancing line. The Federals pressed on, however, and the Confederates were on the verge of breaking when they were saved by confusion in the Federal ranks. The leftmost regiment in Hartranft's front line had originally been aligned facing the wrong way and as the brigade advanced, the various regiments began to overlap. Their officers tried to correct this by moving them more and more to their right, but they soon became confused and disoriented and turned sharply to their right. This brought them perpendicular to the Southern defenses and presented their left flank to the enemy. With a yell of derision the Rebels poured in a devastating fire and the attackers "melted away in a moment."[9] The Federals broke and ran for the rear. Coming up in support, Colonel Christ saw what happened to Hartranft's brigade and ordered his men to lie down and dig in. He was soon wounded and his successor, Colonel William C. Raulston, found that the Confederate fire was so severe that his men could neither advance nor withdraw, but could only hug the earth.

By 3:30 p.m. Lee was finally tired of working in an intelligence vacuum. At that hour he wired his son, commanding the cavalry on the north bank of the James, to "push after enemy and endeavor to ascertain what has become of Grant's army." At 4 p.m. an attack by Anderson's corps drove Butler's troops from their last toehold in Johnson's old defenses, the Howlett Line, opposite Bermuda Hundred. Then Lee heard from Beauregard again. The latter had received a report from a civilian who had seen a huge body of Yankees crossing the James, and a Union prisoner had estimated that there were 30,000 more Federals on their way to Petersburg. Lee sent a telegram to A. P. Hill, commanding the infantry still north of the James: "General Beauregard reports large numbers of Grant's troops crossed James River above Fort Powhatan yesterday. If you have nothing contradictory of this move to Chaffin's Bluff."[10] Even this move would still leave his 3rd Corps north of the James, but at Chaffin's Bluff it would at least be at the north end of the new bridge that connected with Drewry's Bluff on the south side.

Burnside still had one more division to throw at the defenses of Petersburg, Ledlie's 1st. Since forcing its way through the slashed pine forest, it had been occupying Batteries 15 and 16. Now it was moved to its right and placed in the ravine west of the Shand house, with Colonel Jacob P. Gould's 1st Brigade on the right, Lieutenant Colonel Joseph H. Barnes' 2nd Brigade on the left, and Lieutenant Colonel Benjamin G. Barney's 3rd Brigade forming a second line. Confederate artillery hit this new threat as it formed up, killing or wounding 32 men before the attack even started. Once in the ravine the Federals were fairly well protected from ordinary fire, so the Rebel gunners started firing low and letting their shots bounce along the ground, which at least forced the Yankees to keep their heads down. While the men lay in the ravine dodging these bounding shots, someone decided to deliver their mail to them. The men teamed up in pairs, one man reading his mail while the other watched for ricocheting cannon balls.

At last came the order to attack, and at 6 p.m. the two front brigades advanced, with Barney's brigade following about 100 yards back. Ledlie himself, however, chose to stay behind so as "not to expose his precious life," as one of his officers put it.[11] He had consumed a great deal of liquid courage, but it didn't seem to help. Colonel Gould took command of the attack. With strong artillery support, the men of the first two brigades charged out of the ravine and 200 or 300 yards across the Shand and Avery farms, past hundreds of dead and wounded comrades from the other divisions that had charged that day. Heavy artillery and rifle fire staggered the front line and forced it back, but the second line forged ahead and the first line reformed behind it and returned to the fray. Suddenly the 23rd South Carolina of Elliott's Brigade of Johnson's Division broke and ran, and the Federals exploited this opening to drive two other Confederate regiments from their defenses west and southwest of the Shand house. By dusk the Northerners had formed a salient driven into the Rebels' second line. From their position farther north, members of Birney's division watched the fight, tracing the positions of the contending forces in the gathering darkness by the flashes of their rifles. They saw the Confederates south of the breakthrough retake their lost position, only to lose it again, retake it again, and lose it again.

Brigadier General Samuel Crawford's 3rd Division of the Union 5th Corps advanced on Ledlie's left, but not far enough to connect with that division. At 8 p.m. Meade urged Warren to use his entire corps to exploit Ledlie's gains, but a half-hour later the army commander changed his mind and told Warren that, unless decisive results could be guaranteed, his attack should wait until morning. Warren was happy to wait.

North of Ledlie's position Barlow led his 2nd Corps division forward, but most of his men were stopped by the entanglements of the Confederate abatis. A small portion of the defenses in that sector were captured by the 66th New York and held until 9 p.m., when lack of ammunition forced these Federals to withdraw. About that same time Christ's brigade of Willcox's division moved up to support Ledlie's, and his 1st Michigan Sharpshooters captured part of the Rebel works from the 35th North Carolina, along with that regiment's colors and 89 of its men. But the Confederates continued to counterattack, and Ledlie's men were also running low on ammunition, even though some of them had crawled among the dead and wounded, gathering cartridges from the fallen.

Under a bright moon, Ransom's Brigade of Confederates moved into some woods just west of Ledlie's salient about 10 p.m., then charged. A savage hand-to-hand fight ensued, where "the bayonet and butts of guns were freely used, as there was not time to load and fire," one North Carolinian remembered.[12] Seventy-eight men of the 1st Michigan Sharpshooters were surrounded and captured. Then, about 11 p.m., another Rebel brigade, Gracie's Alabamans, charged "over the crest with fierce cries, leaped over the works, captured 1,500 prisoners, and drove the enemy pell-mell from the disputed point."[13] The Federals relinquished the captured Southern defenses but held onto a position well in advance of the one they had held that afternoon.

At 10 p.m. Lee received a message which Beauregard had sent at 6:30, stating that he would hold his present line until dark and then fall back to a shorter line closer to Petersburg, but that he feared the town would be captured unless he received reinforcements. He proposed to retreat across the Appomattox River and to defend the line of Swift Creek just north of it. Lee then sent orders for the third of Anderson's divisions, Kershaw's, to march south from Drewry's Bluff to Petersburg, and for A. P. Hill to bring his 3rd Corps across the James as far as the Petersburg Turnpike to await further orders. This would at last put all of Lee's infantry south of the James. At 10:20 p.m. he received definite word from his son, Rooney, commanding the cavalry on the north side, that "Grant's army is across the river."[14]

At about sunset Brigadier General Thomas Neill's 2nd Division of the Federal 6th Corps had arrived at the Petersburg front in the same exhausted condition as all the other Union divisions which had arrived in the past two days. Meade used these men to replace Brooke's division of Smith's 18th Corps, which was being sent back across the Appomattox to rejoin Butler. Martindale's division of the same corps would remain in place on the Federal right because its proximity to the Confederates made it dangerous to withdraw. Hinks' division remained in reserve behind the Union right. Wilson's 3rd Cavalry Division had crossed to the south side of the James but was badly in need of rest after covering the army's moves from Confederate probes for the previous five days. Many of his horses had not been unsaddled for three days. That night Hancock, weak and suffering from his reopened wound, turned over command of the 2nd Corps to his senior division commander, Birney. The day's results had again been bloody but indecisive, due mainly to the tendency of Meade and his corps commanders to throw in their divisions one or two at a time. There were still two more corps that had not been used at all, the 5th and the 6th, although most of the latter was still on Butler's Bermuda Hundred front. Grant had remained at City Point most of the

day, where he received word from Butler that part of Lee's army had
been sent to defend Lynchburg from Hunter's advance.

By 7 a.m. on the seventeenth enough rolling stock had been gathered
to carry one of Early's divisions, that of Major General Dodson Ramseur, plus one brigade of Major General John Gordon's, to Lynchburg
from Charlottesville, while the rest of the Confederate infantry marched
along the tracks, ready to board the cars as soon as they came back
empty. The artillery and the wagons moved by road. About 1 o'clock
that afternoon Early stepped off the train in the threatened city, glad to
see that Hunter's Federals had not yet captured the place. He found that
Breckinridge was in bed, suffering from an injury received in a fall when
his horse had been killed under him at Cold Harbor. Two other generals
were in town, however. One was Major General D. H. Hill, without a
job because he had so displeased Confederate president Jefferson Davis
some while back that the latter had withdrawn his promotion to lieutenant general before the Senate had confirmed it. Hill, however, had refused all assignments offered him in his previous grade. He had served
as a volunteer aide to Beauregard while the latter had fended off Butler's
feeble moves against Petersburg and Richmond during the month of
May. The other general on hand was Brigadier General Harry Hays,
who was there to recuperate from a wound he had received at Spotsylvania. Both generals offered their services to Early. Two more generals
arrived from Richmond later that day. Major General Arnold Elzey had
been sent to command Breckinridge's two infantry brigades, and Major
General Robert Ransom had been sent to command his four small cavalry
brigades, which had been temporarily merged into two commands, one
under Brigadier General John McCausland and the other under Brigadier
General John D. Imboden.

Early rode out with Hill and, after a quick survey of the situation,
found that the defenses constructed for the small force then present were
so close to the city that enemy artillery would be able to fire into the
town. He ordered a new line of defenses laid out two miles west of town
for the defending force that was soon to be enlarged. A half-hour after
Early's arrival, Duffié's 1st Cavalry Division of Hunter's army approached Lynchburg from the west and ran into strong opposition from
McCausland's troopers. The other Union cavalry division, Brigadier
General William W. Averell's, led Hunter's main force toward the city
from the southwest, and at about 4:30 p.m. reported enemy artillery and
dismounted cavalry in its front, five miles from the city.

Averell's cavalry and Crook's infantry charged and drove Imboden's
Confederate horsemen across Blackwater Creek and into their main de-

fenses, capturing 70 men and one cannon. They were joined by the other Union infantry division, Brigadier General Jeremiah Sullivan's, but Early blocked their path with Ramseur's infantry. Soon the fighting died down and both sides settled into bivouac. During the night Federal pickets could hear the whistles of locomotives pulling into Lynchburg with the rest of Gordon's Division, as well as loud cheering and the music of military bands. Most of the noise was made by one engine running a few empty box cars back and forth through the city. Early wanted Hunter and his men to think that the defenses were being reinforced.

The next morning, the eighteenth, with Rodes' Division still waiting for a ride and his artillery still on the road between the two towns, Early correctly guessed that Duffié's advance from the west represented a diversion and that the real attack would hit him from the southwest. Therefore he left the cavalry and part of Breckinridge's infantry to block Duffié's path and massed the rest of his available infantry and most of the guns of Breckinridge's command to stop the main thrust. Duffié did manage to push the Rebel horsemen back across the Blackwater, but found the crossing of that stream guarded by earthworks containing both artillery and riflemen. Meanwhile, Hunter sent Averell's cavalry to his right to menace the other Confederate flank. He intended to make his main attack with Crook's 2nd Infantry Division against the left of the Rebel line, but before he could launch it Early sent his own infantry forward and attacked Sullivan's 1st Infantry Division on its own left flank, driving these Federals back across Blackwater Creek. Sullivan counterattacked, and his 116th Ohio captured the outer line of Southern defenses, but because it was not supported, the Confederates drove it out again about sunset. In the meantime, Hunter called off Crook's attack and instead ordered that division to cover Sullivan's flanks. Late that afternoon the trains brought the rest of Early's infantry into Lynchburg, and he sent them to reinforce McCausland against Duffié. Early had always been an aggressive, hard-hitting brigade and division commander, and now that his whole force, except his artillery, had arrived his subordinate generals expected him to order an offensive that evening, but he was new to independent command and as such a bit cautious. He decided to wait until morning.

Hunter, meanwhile, conferred with Crook and Averell. Confederate prisoners told the Yankees that Early had 30,000 troops on hand. Even if this were an exaggeration (and it was; even when his entire corps had arrived Early did not have more than 15,000), the capture of Lynchburg was obviously not going to be as easy as it had seemed a couple of days before. The Federal Army of West Virginia was a long way from home and short on supplies. It could not forage around for food and fodder in the face of a sizable enemy force like Early's, and what little it still had in its own wagons had been sent off to the west on the sixteenth. Besides, it did not have enough ammunition left for a major battle with a large enemy force.

If Hunter's army could not stay and fight, what was it to do? If it retreated back down the Shenandoah Valley, Early might use the railroad east of the mountains to get ahead and cut it off from its source of supplies, namely the Baltimore & Ohio Railroad. However, there seemed to be a more viable route of retreat, westward over the Alleghenies to the valley of the Kanawha River, where Crook had left a cache of supplies before moving on to connect with Hunter's main column. Also, supplies might be brought up the Kanawha by steamer to meet the army. Furthermore, West Virginia was friendly territory, being inhabited mostly by Union-loyal people, while the Shenandoah was predominantly Southern in its sympathies. So about 9 p.m. on the eighteenth the Army of West Virginia slipped away from its camps and began marching toward its namesake state.

By the time the Federal movement was reported to Early, it was after midnight. He considered a night attack but decided against it since, as he later wrote, "It was not known whether he was retreating or moving so as to attack Lynchburg on the south where it was vulnerable, or to attempt to join Grant on the south side of James River. Pursuit could not, therefore, be made at once, as a mistake, if either of the last two objects had been contemplated, would have been fatal."[15] Sometime during the eighteenth Early must have received the telegram that Lee sent to him that day. It said, "Grant is in front of Petersburg. Will be opposed there. Strike as quick as you can, and, if circumstances authorize, carry out the original plan, or move upon Petersburg without delay."[16]

---

1. Howe, *Wasted Valor*, 65.
2. Ibid., 66.
3. Ibid., 68.
4. Ibid., 69.
5. Dowdey, *Lee's Last Campaign*, 345.
6. Howe, *Wasted Valor*, 74.
7. Dowdey and Manarin, eds., *Wartime Papers of R. E. Lee*, 788.
8. Howe, *Wasted Valor*, 77.
9. Ibid.
10. Dowdey and Manarin, eds. *Wartime Papers of R. E. Lee*, 789.

11. Howe, *Wasted Valor*, 94.
12. Ibid., 97.
13. Ibid., 99.
14. Ibid., 102.
15. Jubal Anderson Early, *War Memoirs* (Bloomington, Ind. 1960), 376.
16. Dowdey and Manarin, eds. *Wartime Papers of R. E. Lee*, 791.

CHAPTER FIVE

Nothing but God Almighty

18–19 June 1864

At 1 a.m. on 18 June, Beauregard's defenders of Petersburg quietly pulled back to another new line of earthworks. Two days before, the Southern general had ordered Colonel D. B. Harris to lay out this third line of defenses on the eastern side of the town, roughly 500 to 800 yards west of the second line, and to mark its key points with white stakes. During the daylight hours of the seventeenth, staff officers from both Hoke's and Johnson's divisions had been sent to familiarize themselves with this new line and the positions that their commands would occupy in it, so that they could serve as guides when the move was made after dark. Campfires were left burning and pickets remained in front of the old lines to deceive the Yankees as the men were moved to the new defenses. Some of the men found that these were "being constructed by negroes who had been at work for some time. We pitched in," a member of the 34th Virginia recorded, "helping them with bayonets, tin cups and anything we could throw dirt with."[1] Other units were not so lucky and had to start from scratch.

At about the same hour, the first of three staff officers sent by Beauregard arrived at Lee's headquarters tent near Clay's house on the lines opposite Butler's Bermuda Hundred position. The last arrived at 3 a.m. Each brought prisoner reports confirming that a large part of Grant's army was confronting Beauregard at Petersburg. The third courier, Major Giles B. Cooke, told the gray commander just what his chief had instructed him to say: that without reinforcements "nothing but God Almighty can save Petersburg." The profoundly religious Lee replied solemnly, " I hope God Almighty will save Petersburg."² In accordance with Lee's previous orders, Kershaw's Division of Anderson's 1st Corps began to march for Petersburg at 3 a.m. At 3:30 a.m. Lee ordered that Field's Division should follow, and that A. P. Hill's 3rd Corps, already south of the James River, should also march for Petersburg as fast as possible. Pickett's Division would hold the Howlett Line opposite Bermuda Hundred. Lee also sent a message to the superintendent of the Richmond & Petersburg Railroad, asking, "Can trains run through to Petersburg?" And adding, "It is important to get troops to Petersburg without delay."³

Major General George Gordon Meade, commander of the Army of the Potomac, ordered the commanders of his 2nd, 5th, and 9th corps to organize "strong columns, well supported" for a "vigorous attack" to be made at 4 a.m. on 18 June, the fourth day of Federal attacks on Petersburg.⁴ Martindale's and Hincks' divisions of the 18th Corps, and Neill's division of the 6th were to be ready to support the attack or to launch assaults themselves. Burnside answered that Ledlie's division was so shot up that there was "scarcely anything left of it," while his other two divisions (his 4th Division, composed entirely of regiments of U.S. Colored Troops, had been left behind to guard the great pontoon bridge) were "much wearied," and he asked, "Shall I attack with them?" Meade replied, "I want the attack to go forward as ordered with all the force you can put in."⁵ When 4 a.m. came the attack was not ready, and Meade, who was famous for his temper, was in what Colonel Lyman of his staff called a "tearing humor."

At 4:30 a.m. Union skirmishers moved forward, followed by the main force in heavy columns. Martindale's division of the 18th Corps advanced on the Federal right, with Neill's 6th Corps division on his left; then came Gibbon's and Mott's (formerly Birney's) divisions of the 2nd Corps, then Willcox's division of the 9th Corps, with Potter's following, and finally Brigadier General Samuel W. Crawford's 3rd Division and Cutler's 4th Division of the 5th Corps, the latter carrying entrenching tools. As this huge line moved forward it was met by a profound silence. The puzzled Northerners soon discovered why, when they reached the Confederate second line of defenses and found it empty of living defenders. The dead were there in plenitude, however. Where the 1st Michigan Sharpshooters had fought the 35th North Carolina the evening before, "the dead were literally piled one upon the other."⁶ The men of Ledlie's division came forward to bury their fallen comrades. Meanwhile patrols were sent out to discover the Rebels' new positions.

At 5:30 a.m. Meade reported to Grant that "the men require rest, and it is probable, unless some favorable chance presents itself, that we shall not do more than envelop the enemy." Nevertheless, at 5:55 a.m. he ordered all his commanders to push forward, "keeping up prompt communication with the troops on their right and left."[7] Beauregard's newest line ran more to the southwest than his previous two, so that the Federals on the left had farther to go to approach it than did those on the right. The 9th and 5th corps troops had to advance over a mile under fire from Southern guns through difficult terrain laced with ravines full of dense undergrowth. Meade knew from captured Rebels that Lee's army was still not at Petersburg, and he tried to impress upon Burnside and Warren "how important it is to push our advantage before Lee gets up." At 7:20 a.m. he told Birney, now in command of the 2nd Corps, "If we can engage them before they are fortified we ought to whip them."[8] But it was very difficult for the Northern units to maintain their alignment while advancing through the woods and ravines, and this took time. At 8 a.m. Burnside reported that he still had not been able to connect his right with Barlow's left.

At 7:30 a.m. Kershaw's Division of Lee's 1st Corps, after what one of his men said had started as a forced march and later turned into a run, crossed the Appomattox, where it was greeted by the cheers and waving flags of the residents of Petersburg. It marched on out of town and moved up behind Wise's Brigade and Johnson's battered division on the Confederate right. Some of Wise's men were withdrawn from the defenses. For three days they had "had practically nothing to eat, almost no water to drink, and no sleep at all except such little as we could snatch from the few short intervals of calm," as one of them put it.[9] At 9:30 a.m. Field's Division crossed the Appomattox and was sent to the far right of the new Rebel line, where it connected with the old Dimmock Line at Battery No. 25 near the Rives house.

Martindale, now in charge of Neill's division as well as his own, reported to Meade that he could not advance until the 2nd Corps connected with his left. Birney, however, claimed that it was Neill's division that was holding up his advance. At 10 a.m. Meade asked Martindale and Birney to set a time when they would be ready for a joint attack, warning them that "there is too much time taken in preparations, and I fear the enemy will make more of the delay than we can."[10] At 10:20 a.m. Birney reported that his right, Gibbon's division, and Neill's left had at last linked up. However, Barlow's division was still advancing and not ready to attack.

At 10 a.m. Warren reported that Crawford's and Griffin's divisions were ready to attack, but Cutler's and Ayres' divisions were still pushing across difficult ground, against heavy opposition from Confederate skirmishers and artillery. At 10:30 a.m. Warren suggested that the attack be set for noon. Meade acquiesced in this and at 11:34 a.m. outlined his plan. Martindale, Birney, Burnside and Warren were all to move their men forward, "endeavoring to have them advance rapidly over the ground without firing till they have penetrated the enemy's line."[11] Meade wanted dense columns to hit the Rebel defenses, hoping to simultaneously penetrate the Southern works at several different points.

For some reason, Brigadier General Robert McAllister's 2nd Brigade of Mott's division of the 2nd Corps attacked ahead of schedule and alone against a formidable crescent-shaped section of the Confederate line that McAllister described in a letter to his wife as "built to lead us into a death trap." His men stepped off sometime between 11 a.m. and noon and were soon hit by a fire "that cut our men down like hail cut the grain and the grass."[12] After advancing about 100 yards his men hit the dirt and started to dig in.

At midday, Beauregard and Lee stood together on Reservoir Hill southeast of Petersburg, surveying the scene below them. Knowing that Lee's entire army was on the way, Beauregard's mercurial temperament turned optimistic again, and he suggested putting everything into an attack on the Federal left flank that he envisioned would push Grant's army back against the river, where it would be crushed. Lee, however, decided that such an attack would be far too risky and chose to stay on the defensive. Meanwhile the march of Hill's 3rd Corps "became pretty much a free race for Petersburg." One of Hill's men remembered that the heat of the day and the frantic pace reduced regiments "down to the size of companies" because so many men could not keep up, and that "brigades would stretch for miles" as the faster men at the front outmarched the slower ones farther back.[13]

To the right of McAllister's position, Martindale's, Neill's, and Gibbon's divisions advanced promptly at noon. Martindale's men captured a weakly held advanced line several hundred yards west of Harrison's Creek, along with 40 Rebels who were too slow about getting out of the way. The attack ended there for lack of support when Gibbon's men ran into a "perfectly murderous fire of musketry, canister and spherical case which swept the open field in front."[14] Like McAllister's men a few minutes before, Gibbon's went to ground and started digging.

To McAllister's left, the 9th Corps' leading unit, Hartranft's brigade, had just reached a ridge topped by the Taylor farm at noon. The Federals drove Confederate skirmishers through fields of oats and into the long trench that contained the Petersburg & Norfolk Railroad tracks. Here the 37th Wisconsin stumbled over telegraph wire that the Rebels had strung between stumps hidden by long grass at the end of this cut. A withering volley struck the Northerners while they were entangled in the wire. To Hartranft's left, Crawford's division and part of Griffin's, both of the 5th Corps, charged into the railroad cut a little after noon and drove the Southerners into their breastworks.

However, to continue their advance the Federals needed to climb up the other side of the steep trench, in some places twenty feet high. They had to hack steps out of the dirt bank to reach the top, only to find that any man showing his head above the cut immediately became a target for Rebel skirmishers a few hundred yards away in the ravine of Poor Creek, and snipers in the main Confederate line beyond. Even worse was the fact that, to the north of Hartranft's position, the Rebel line turned at an angle and crossed both the creek and the railroad tracks. From there, Southern riflemen and one cannon fired straight down the railroad cut, turning the trench into a slaughterhouse, until some of Hartranft's men frantically tore up rails and ties and built a breastwork across the cut to protect themselves. Captain Jacob Roemer of the 34th New York Battery meanwhile defied the Confederate fire to push two of his guns forward by hand, and the accurate fire of his gunners soon forced the Rebel artillerymen to retire. Hartranft's right was exposed in the first place because Barlow's division of the 2nd Corps had received no order to advance, and refused to do so without orders. In response to Hartranft's pleas for help, Potter sent Curtin's brigade forward, but it merely joined Hartranft's men in the cut, thus becoming part of the problem, not the solution.

By early afternoon, Meade's grand assault had ground to a halt. The new Rebel line had not been penetrated anywhere, and only Gibbon's men had come close to it. On the Federal left, Cutler's division of the 5th Corps had stopped to repair bridges over the Petersburg & Norfolk Railroad. It had farther to go anyway and was not in position on the ridge opposite the Confederate line until 1:30 p.m., by which time all the units on its right had run into trouble. Ayres' division was even farther back, and part of it faced to the south as protection against a

flank attack. At 1:55 p.m. Birney reported to Meade that Gibbon had
not broken the enemy line, but indicated that the 2nd Corps would try
again. Meade replied that it should do so "with the least possible delay."[15]
Five minutes later Warren reported that he had not yet attacked the
Confederate main line because the 9th Corps could not advance to protect his right, because it in turn was already more advanced than the 2nd
Corps and was being enfiladed from its own right flank. Warren advised
that it "would be safe for us all to make a rush at, say, 3 p.m."

Meade's famous temper reached the boiling point—he had experienced
similar problems with his corps commanders at Cold Harbor—and he
shot a dispatch back to Warren: "What additional orders to attack you
require I cannot imagine. My orders have been explicit and are now
repeated, that you will immediately assault the enemy with all your
force." He added that "if there is any further delay the responsibility
and the consequences will rest with you." Burnside was given a dose of
the same medicine. With Birney, new to corps command, Meade was a
little gentler when he sent a message at 2:30 p.m. saying that he found
it "useless to appoint an hour to effect co-operation." He told Birney,
"you have a large corps, powerful and numerous, I beg you will at once,
as soon as possible, assault in strong column."[16]

A new attack, however, had already started. About 2 p.m. Martindale
sent his own two brigades forward on the army's extreme right with
Brigadier General Frank Wheaton's brigade of Neill's division advancing
on the left and somewhat farther back, and a single regiment formed in
column moving along the bank of the Appomattox. When the Northerners came within 300 yards of the Rebels, the latter fired a destructive
volley that shattered the regimental column and caused the main line to
break and run. The Federals reformed and tried again, but with similar
results. They dropped to the ground, partially hidden by growing grain,
some seeking cover behind their fallen comrades, and began to dig in
with their cups and bayonets in the stifling heat. Wheaton's men had
hardly advanced at all before they also stopped and began to entrench.
At 3:35 p.m. Martindale reported to Meade that his attack had failed
because of enfilading fire from his left and no further attacks would be
possible without the support of Gibbon's and Mott's divisions on that
flank.

At 3 p.m. both Warren's and Burnside's corps started forward. Cutler's division of the 5th Corps had formed up behind the protection of
a rise almost a half-mile from the Rebel defenses, its two brigades placed
one behind the other. On Cutler's right was Griffin's division, with its
right in the railroad cut. On Cutler's left was Ayres' division. Both
Cutler's and Ayres' divisions were already beyond the railroad, which

curved to the southeast there, but they would have to cross Poor Creek to get to the new Confederate line. When Cutler's leading brigade, Colonel J. William Hofmann's 2nd, advanced over its protecting rise it was hit by rifle and artillery fire. Just before it got to Poor Creek, most of its men broke and ran back to its starting place. About 200 continued on and took cover in the creek bed, but even there they were taking fire. All seven of Hofmann's regimental commanders were either killed or wounded.

The other half of Cutler's division, what was left of the famous Iron Brigade, commanded by Colonel Edward S. Bragg, followed Hofmann's men and was also hit by a storm of infantry and cannon fire. While descending the sloping ground, Bragg's men could see what one called the spires of Petersburg about two miles away. They also took cover in the ravine of Poor Creek, although a few scattered groups went on to within 75 yards of the Rebel defenses. Cutler said he "lost in killed and wounded about one-third of the men I had with me." The commander of one of Bragg's regiments wrote that "our brigade was simply food for powder."[17] Ayres' division, assigned to guard the army's left flank, merely advanced to the high ground between Poor Creek and the railroad. Part of it manned the old Dimmock Line facing south, while the rest dug in facing west.

To the right of Cutler's division were the 5th Corps divisions of Griffin and Crawford. Between them and the Confederate lines was a rise, a ravine, another rise, and then another ravine, this one containing Poor Creek, and finally a long slope up to the earthworks. Crawford's men also had to cross the railroad cut, many of them tumbling into it before they knew it was there. Then they crossed the first rise, where they were struck by a deadly fire from enemy artillery, and they promptly hit the dirt.

Between Crawford's and Cutler's divisions was Griffin's division, with two of its brigades deployed side by side, Colonel Jacob Sweitzer's on the right and Colonel Joshua Chamberlain's on the left. They had a hard enough time just getting to the first rise, and when Chamberlain saw what lay beyond it, he questioned the order to attack, but was assured that the order stood. He called his regimental commanders together for precise instructions and ordered two batteries of artillery forward. These he located so that they could just barely fire over the first rise, and when they opened up, it did wonders for the morale of Chamberlain's infantry. More encouragement had come when Chamberlain had his men instructed on the exact target of their assault. "Our line responded to a man," one remembered, "and went forward with an enthusiasm hardly ever witnessed in battle."[18]

Chamberlain's men crossed the first rise just after 3 p.m., and immediately "began to melt away under the merciless storm of iron and lead" as they crossed the first ravine and the second rise and came down the slope to Poor Creek. Just then Chamberlain, leading from the front, was hit by a bullet that smashed through both his hips, shattered his pelvic bone, and grazed his bladder. He propped himself up with his sword and continued to urge his men forward until he collapsed from loss of blood. Many of his men pressed on, crossed Poor Creek and drove the Rebels from their defenses, "only to be hurled, broken and bleeding, back to the base of the hill" by a counterattack.[19] Two of the Federal regiments, however, dug in on the west side of the creek. About then Sweitzer's brigade crossed Poor Creek and pushed to within twenty yards of the Confederate works, just north of where Chamberlain's had struck. Just as the Rebels there were about to retreat, those who had repulsed Chamberlain's men poured a destructive fire into the flank of Sweitzer's brigade, which broke and ran for cover.

At 4 p.m., Birney began organizing another attack force to hit the most easterly portion of the new Confederate line. Many Federals in the area were in a mutinous mood, refusing to advance over ground where attacks had already been repulsed with great loss. Mott's brigade, now under Colonel Daniel Chaplin, felt this way, except for the 1st Maine Heavy Artillery Regiment, which was too inexperienced to have lost its enthusiasm. Veteran infantry throughout the Army of the Potomac had thought it a great joke when Grant had pulled such heavy artillery regiments away from the relative ease and safety of garrison duty a few weeks before. The veterans had made fun of their inexperience and their unthinned ranks, calling them heavy infantry. Now they yelled to General Birney, "Let the 1st Maine go!"[20]

That was Chaplin's own regiment and he formed its three battalions in line of battle one behind the other in the protection of a sunken road with two other regiments of his brigade farther back for support. To its left was what had been Egan's brigade, now under Colonel Henry Madill, with Mott's other two brigades backing it up. Gibbon also provided two supporting brigades. At 4:30 p.m. all these Federals began moving forward into an open field and were hit by Rebel fire in front and flank. Madill's men took cover behind a barn but more than 200 of them were killed in just a few minutes, nevertheless. The veteran units of Chaplin's brigade also took cover, leaving the relatively inexperienced heavies on their own. Within ten minutes a couple of hundred of them were streaming back to their starting place. The other 632 were left behind, dead or wounded. This was the highest casualty rate of any Federal regiment in any single action of the entire war. "Many of the men who had not been wounded," the regiment's historian recorded, "had their garments tattered and torn by bullets and shell." A tearful Colonel Chaplin offered his sword to Mott, saying he had no further use for it. Then he berated the veteran regiments of his brigade for not supporting his inexperienced heavies. "There are the men you have been making fun of," he told the old soldiers, "you did not dare follow them."[21]

By 5 p.m., most of Willcox's division of the 9th Corps had joined Potter's in the railroad cut, and at 5:30 p.m. Willcox's men and Curtin's brigade of Potter's division clambered up the steps that they had cut into the west embankment and rushed across open ground to Poor Creek, driving away some Confederate pickets who had been using the creek for cover. Then, about 6 p.m., Hartranft's brigade of Willcox's division and Curtin's brigade of Potter's advanced up the hill between the creek and the main Rebel line. They got to within 125 yards of the Confederate earthworks before being forced to hit the ground and start digging. Curtin was severely wounded in the attack and was succeeded by Lieutenant Colonel Pleasants—the same who, with his 48th Pennsylvania, had captured Battery No. 15 two days before.

Just as this final assault wound down, A. P. Hill's Confederate 3rd Corps arrived in Petersburg, led by the 12th Virginia of Mahone's Division, most of whose men came from that city. They were greeted warmly by old friends, although, as one woman wrote, their faces were "so thin and drawn by privation that we scarcely knew them. It made one's heart ache to look at them."[22] They were marched to the front and put in the old Dimmock Line between the Jerusalem Plank Road and the Weldon Railroad.

Meade called a halt to all attacks at 6:30 p.m. and ordered Warren and Burnside to straighten their lines and make sure of the connections between their forces. Although he was greatly disappointed with the day's attacks, he told them he "was satisfied we have done all that it is possible for men to do, and must be resigned to the result."[23] At 7 p.m. Warren told Meade that he and Burnside wanted to make another effort just as it got dark, although actually Burnside was skeptical of the idea and had only consented to provide support for a 5th Corps assault. But a half-hour later Meade told Warren to forget it for, even if the 5th Corps was in shape to attack, the rest of the army was not in condition to follow up any success he might have.

At 9:45 p.m. Meade summarized the day's events for Grant at City Point and expressed his belief that Lee had reinforced Petersburg. Grant replied that he too was satisfied that all had been done that could be done, and added that "we will rest the men and use the spade for their protection until a new vein can be struck." He told his staff that he would make no more assaults on the defenses of Petersburg, but would extend his forces to his left in an effort to cut Lee's lines of supply to the south while "confining him to a close siege."[24] The positions of the opposing lines east of Petersburg did not change substantially for the next ten months, although the defenses became ever more elaborate. On the east side of the town, at least, it became primarily a war of snipers, mortars, siege guns, dirt, lice and boredom.

Down in Georgia that day, 18 June, Confederate general Joe Johnston decided that his ten miles of entrenchments were too long for his army to defend without being stretched too thin somewhere. Therefore he fell back two miles to a heavily entrenched six-mile-long line anchored on Kenesaw Mountain, still blocking Sherman's route down the railroad through Marietta to Atlanta. Sherman, meanwhile, was happy to receive a message that day from Major General C. C. Washburn at Memphis, saying that his wishes had been anticipated and that A. J. Smith's corps-sized force was already preparing to go down into Mississippi in an attempt to defeat Forrest, or at least to keep the pesky Confederate off Sherman's supply lines. Sherman seems to have had even more confidence in Smith's principal subordinate, Brigadier General J. A. Mower, than the considerable amount he had in Smith. In his reply, he told Washburn to "say to General Mower that I want him advanced, and if he will whip Forrest I will pledge him my influence for a major-general, and will ask the President as a personal favor to hold a vacancy for him." Sherman then wired Lincoln that Smith and Mower had been ordered to "pursue and kill Forrest," and asked that a second star be held for Mower, whom he described as "one of the gamest men in our service."[25]

---

1. Howe, *Wasted Valor*, 108.
2. Ibid., 109.
3. Dowdey and Manarin, eds., *Wartime Papers of R. E. Lee*, 791.
4. Howe, *Wasted Valor*, 106. 5. Ibid.
5. Ibid.
6. Ibid., 111.
7. Ibid., 112.
8. Ibid., 114.
9. Ibid., 115.
10. Ibid.

11. Ibid., 117.
12. Ibid., 118.
13. Ibid., 117.
14. Ibid., 118.
15. Ibid., 122.
16. Ibid., 123.
17. Ibid., 127.
18. Ibid., 128.
19. Ibid.
20. Ibid., 130.
21. Ibid., 132.
22. Ibid., 133.
23. Ibid., 134.
24. Horace Porter, *Campaigning With Grant* (New York, 1961), 210.
25. Bearss, *Forrest At Brice's Cross Roads*, 149.

CHAPTER SIX

And She's Headed Straight for Us

19–21 June 1864

There was a slight haze on the English Channel, although a soft wind was blowing, when Sunday 19 June 1864, dawned on Cherbourg, France. The sea was calm, the air somewhat cool for June. Raphael Semmes, captain of the CSS *Alabama*, considered Sunday to be his lucky day, and so he had delayed until now his promised encounter with the USS *Kearsarge*. He had kept his men busy clearing the ship for action, and cleaning and oiling her guns. At 9:30 a.m. the *Alabama* weighed anchor and got under way, making for the open sea. News of the impending battle had been in all the papers for three days, and there was not a hotel room to be had anywhere in town. As the *Alabama* passed the entrance to the harbor she was greeted by cheers from throngs of spectators standing on the mole, many of them waving little Confederate flags that had been hawked by enterprising vendors. The *Alabama* was at that moment the most famous warship afloat. For almost two years after slipping out of Britain, where she had been built, and taking on her armament and her Confederate officers in the Azores, the Rebel raider had roved the seas eluding the Union navy. She had captured, burned or sunk over sixty Yankee merchant ships worth millions of dollars, plus one Federal warship, a converted excursion boat on blockade duty that had been no match for her.

The *Kearsarge*, however, was as perfect a match for the *Alabama* as could have been found. "The combat no doubt will be contested and obstinate," the Rebel captain recorded in his journal, "but the two ships are so evenly matched that I do not feel at liberty to decline it."[1] Both were three-master ships powered with steam engines. The Union vessel was 201 feet long and displaced 1,031 tons. The *Alabama* was 212 feet long and displaced 1,016 tons. The *Kearsarge* carried a crew of 163 officers and men, while the *Alabama* had 149. The Federal ship was three years old, the Confederate, two. The *Kearsarge* mounted seven guns throwing a total weight of 430 pounds. The *Alabama* carried eight guns throwing 360 pounds. Most of the Union ship's punch would come from two 11-inch Dahlgren smoothbore guns mounted on pivots, one fore and one aft, so they could fire to either side, supplemented by the much smaller 32-pounders of each broadside. The Rebel ship also carried 32-pounders in broadside and two large pivot guns, in this case an 8-inch smoothbore and a 7-inch (100-pounder) Blakely rifle. Although the Confederate's pivot guns were somewhat smaller than the *Kearsarge's*, the superior range, accuracy and striking power of its rifle might be expected to make up the difference, at least at longer ranges.

The *Alabama*, however, had disadvantages caused by her long stay at sea that were not readily apparent to any but her own officers and crew. Her maneuverability was hampered because her bottom was badly fouled and needed to be scraped and recoppered, and her boilers were beginning to leak at the seams. Perhaps worst of all, her ammunition was no longer reliable. The state of the percussion caps and powder in the shells for her guns was questionable after months at sea in various climates, and lately some of them had been failing to explode. The *Kearsarge*, on the other hand, had been refitted only three months before. Moreover, the Union vessel held an advantage known only to those on board her. She had a net of iron chains bolted onto each side of her hull from scuppers to below the water line and hidden by boxes of 1-inch planking. This might not stop a solid shot from a heavy gun, but the more common exploding shells—at least those of the smoothbore guns—would probably bounce off or break up before penetrating the chain and the hull. Of course, her bow, stern, and upper deck remained unprotected.

The *Alabama's* highly destructive cruise had not only made the Confederate raider the most famous warship on the high seas but had also made Captain Raphael Semmes one of the most famous naval officers of the time. Captain John A. Winslow of the *Kearsarge*, on the other hand, was unknown outside of limited naval circles. Semmes was a 55-year-old

Maryland-born Catholic who had moved to Alabama. Winslow had been born in North Carolina two years later than Semmes, but came of Boston Puritan stock and had moved back to the Bay State at an early age. The two officers had once been messmates aboard the USS *Cumberland* during the Mexican War. Semmes was slender, tall and easily recognized by his large, pointed, handle-bar mustache that led his men to call him "Old Beeswax." Winslow was heavy, balding, going blind in one eye, and wore a fringe of graying whiskers. He had briefly commanded an ironclad gunboat on the western rivers earlier in the war, but for the past year and a half he had been stalking the *Alabama* and other raiders with the *Kearsarge*. Months of frustration and disappointment at his failure to catch any of them were about to come to an end.

Winslow was reading the Sunday service to his crew when a lookout cried, "She's coming out and she's headed straight for us!"[2] The Rebel was escorted by a French ironclad frigate and an English yacht. The Union captain closed his prayer book, had the drum beat to general quarters, and turned his ship about to run for deep water well beyond the three-mile limit of French sovereignty. He didn't want to cause an international incident, and he didn't want the *Alabama* to be able to run for the safety of the neutral port if Semmes found he was getting the worst of the fight. The French ironclad turned back at the three-mile limit, but the yacht, the *Deerhound*, tagged along to watch the fight from close range.

Seven miles northeast of Cherbourg the *Kearsarge* turned and made straight for the oncoming Rebel, two miles away. Semmes continued straight on, and when the range was down to a mile he turned to his executive officer and asked, "Are you ready, Mr. Kell?" Lieutenant George Kell said that he was. "Then you may open fire at once, sir," Semmes told him.[3] The Blakely rifle roared but struck only water, kicking up a geyser well short of the oncoming *Kearsarge*. Two minutes later a second shot went tearing through the Union ship's rigging to fall behind it. The Southerners' 32-pounders soon joined the fray, but their shots were also high, as the gunners failed to compensate for the closing rate of the two ships.

The range was down to half a mile before the Federals replied, but their first shots fell short. Winslow tried to maneuver his ship astern of the *Alabama* to rake her, but Semmes sheered off to port, and the two ships began to steam in concentric, ever-tightening circles from about half a mile to a quarter of a mile apart, pounding away at each other with broadsides from their pivot and starboard guns as the three-knot current bore them westward.

The Southerners drew first blood when one of their shells exploded on the Union ship's quarterdeck and took out three members of the guncrew for the after pivot gun. As it turned out, these were the only Federals to be seriously hurt during the entire battle. Later, a shell from the big Blakely rifle lodged in the *Kearsarge's* sternpost, but failed to explode. Another Rebel shell exploded in the Federal ship's hammock netting and started a fire, but this was quickly put out by a damage-control detail. Many Confederate shells were stopped by the *Kearsarge's* chain armor. Semmes, observing the effects of his fire through his glass, called to his first officer, "Mr. Kell, use solid shot; our shell strike the enemy's side and fall into the water."[4] Kell made the switch and then began to alternate the two types of projectile.

The Alabama was firing about twice as fast as the *Kearsarge* but with less accuracy, while the Yankee gunners took their time and struck their target about twice as often. Winslow had his 32-pounders sweep the Confederate decks while his two big pivot guns fired at the hull. "The effect upon the enemy was readily perceived," the surgeon of the *Kearsarge* wrote, "and nothing could restrain the enthusiasm of our men. Cheer succeeded cheer; caps were thrown in the air or overboard; jackets were discarded; sanguine of victory, the men were shouting, as each projectile took effect."[5] One Union shell disembowled a gunner at the *Alabama's* 8-inch gun and then exploded, taking out eighteen more men. Other crewmen threw the dead overboard and removed the wounded, but the gun could not be manned again until a shovel had been brought to scrape up the worst of the remains and sand had been thrown on the deck to provide footing in the gore. Another Union shell struck the carriage of the 8-inch gun and spun around on deck until one of the men picked it up and threw it over the side. A shell from one of the big 11-inch Dahlgrens penetrated the raider's coal bunker, throwing up a dense cloud of coal dust. Others struck near the water line and either blew up inside or passed clear through the Rebel ship.

Soon the *Alabama* slowed and then began to list to starboard and to settle slowly by the stern, although without slackening her fire. As his ship went into her seventh circle, Semmes, who had been wounded in the hand, ordered Kell to make sail and head for the coast of France, thus righting his ship and bringing her port guns to bear. But the chief engineer then came on deck to report that his fires were out and he could no longer work his engines. Kell went below to have a look, but when he reached the wardroom, he was met by an appalling sight. "There stood Assistant-Surgeon Llewellyn at his post," Kell wrote, "but the table and the patient upon it had been swept away from him by an 11-inch shell, which opened in the side of the ship an aperture that was fast filling the ship with water."[6] Kell reported to the captain that the ship could not remain afloat another ten minutes. "Then, sir," Semmes replied, "cease firing, shorten sail, and haul down the colors; it will never do in this nineteenth century for us to go down, and the decks covered with our gallant wounded."[7]

Winslow wasn't sure whether the *Alabama* had struck her colors or they had been blown away, and fearing a ruse by the wily Rebel, he ordered another broadside while maneuvering to cut across her bow and rake her. Soon, however, a white flag made it clear that the Confederates were surrendering and Winslow ordered fire to cease. The Confederate wounded were placed in a boat that had escaped major damage, and Kell ordered the rest of the crew to jump overboard with spars to keep themselves afloat until they could be picked up. Semmes threw his sword away and then took a life-preserver. Kell took a wooden grating, and both officers joined their men in the water. The *Alabama* soon gracefully lifted her bow and quickly sank by the stern, just 90 minutes after she had opened fire.

The boat full of wounded rowed to the *Kearsarge*, where the master's mate in charge requested that boats be sent to rescue their shipmates now floating in the water. The Federal ship only had two boats left that could float, but Winslow sent both of these after the Rebel survivors, and once the first load of wounded was taken on board the Federal ship, the Confederate boat was sent back for more as well. Winslow also used his speaking trumpet to call upon the British yacht, still hovering nearby: "For God's sake, do what you can to save them!"[8] The *Deerhound*, which had been built in the same English yard as the *Alabama*, lowered her boats and began fishing the sailors out of the water, including Marine Lieutenant Beckett Howell, who was Jefferson Davis's brother-in-law, as well as Semmes and Kell.

A cutter from the *Kearsarge* pulled alongside the boat where the Rebel commander lay exhausted on the sternsheets. "Have you seen Captain Semmes?" a Federal officer called out. Kell, who was wearing the cap of a crewman of the *Deerhound* and was gripping an oar, replied, "Captain Semmes is drowned." When they reached the yacht the Confederates were given coffee and rum to counter the chill and asked where they wanted to be landed. "I am now under English colors," Semmes replied, "and the sooner you put me, with my officers and men, on English soil the better."[9] Before dark they were in Southampton, where they received a hearty welcome. Winslow, after clearing his decks and assembling his crew for prayers of thanksgiving, steamed into Cherbourg, where the *Kearsarge* was greeted by boatloads of enthusiastic people, many of whom had probably cheered for the *Alabama* a few hours before.

When word of his victory reached the United States, Winslow received the thanks of Congress and a promotion to commodore. The section of the *Kearsarge's* stern-post with the *Alabama's* unexploded shell stuck in it was eventually cut away, and was exhibited at the World's Columbian Exposition at Chicago in 1893. Semmes was wined and dined in Britain, presented with a gold sword by officers of the Royal Navy and other admirers, and promoted to rear admiral in the Confederate navy. However, he never commanded another ship. "I considered my career upon the high seas closed," he later said, "by the loss of my ship."[10]

Semmes did not accept his defeat gracefully, but complained for the rest of his life that it had not been a fair fight because Winslow had not only used chain armor, but had hidden it—not that the Rebel commander had ever given any of his multitude of victims, mostly unarmed merchantmen, a fair fight. Of course, Semmes had been free to make similar use of his own store of anchor chains, had he thought of it. At any rate, it had not been Winslow's duty to give Semmes a fair fight, but to put an end to the depredations of the *Alabama* by any means that would not embroil the United States in a war with a European power.

The escape of Semmes to England after he had surrendered, and by means of an English yacht, at that—not to mention the warm reception he received there—further increased the ill feeling in the United States against the British, who had built the ship, provided most of the crew, and allowed it to put to sea in the first place. After the war, an international tribunal ruled that Great Britain owed the United States $15,500,000 in damages for its part in the *Alabama's* career.

In Virginia, at daylight on 19 June, Confederate lieutenant general Jubal Early finally knew for sure that Hunter was retreating and in what direction. He sent his own 2nd Corps troops to follow on the heels of the main column; Breckinridge's infantry, now under Elzey, to follow Duffié's cavalry; and Ransom, with McCausland's cavalry, was sent to try to cut the Federals off at Liberty, 25 miles west of Lynchburg, or at the pass over the Blue Ridge called Peaks of Otter. Imboden's horsemen were to move to the south, where some of Averell's cavalry had been seen the night before, before turning west. At 9:30 a.m. Early sent off a wire to Lee in care of Bragg, saying, "Last evening the enemy assaulted my lines in front of Lynchburg and was repulsed by the part of my command which was up. On the arrival of the rest of the command I made arrangement to attack this morning at light, but it was discovered that the enemy were retreating, and I am now pursuing. The enemy is retreating in confusion, and if the cavalry does its duty we will destroy him."[11]

As this message shows, Early distrusted his cavalry. He had commanded in the Shenandoah the previous winter, and his experience with the Valley troopers left him doubtful of their reliability. His inability to appreciate his cavalry or to make the best use of them was one of Early's principal flaws. About 4 p.m. the Confederate advance overtook Averell's horsemen, who formed the rear guard of Hunter's army, near the town of Liberty. There followed a sharp skirmish, but with darkness the firing gradually died out. Ransom's cavaliers had lived down to Early's expectations. Imboden had not received his orders, and McCausland's command had taken the wrong road and didn't reach Liberty until after the infantry had pushed the Federals through the town.

From there Hunter would have the choice of three routes, north to Buchanan on the upper James, northwest to Fincastle, or west along the Virginia & Tennessee Railroad to Salem. On the morning of the twentieth, Early sent Ransom via the Peaks of Otter to get ahead of the Federals, should they turn to the north, and he led his infantry westward to continue the pursuit. Then the tail of Hunter's column was seen to disappear into Buford Gap on the road to Salem. The Federals deployed artillery at the top of the pass to command the road where it went through a gorge so narrow that a regiment of infantry could not deploy into line. "We tried to throw forces up the sides of the mountains to get at the enemy," Early later wrote, "but they were so rugged that night came on before anything could be accomplished, and we had to desist, though not until a very late hour in the night."[12] Hunter's infantry, meanwhile, was put to work destroying as much of the railroad as possible.

Some 130 miles southwest of Buford's Gap on that twentieth day of June, Confederate brigadier general John Hunt Morgan and the thousand or so remaining troopers of his command reached Abingdon, Virginia, not far north of the Virginia-Tennessee line. They had thus completed their retreat from the most recent of the notorious Kentuckian's celebrated raids into his home state. Eight days before, they had been attacked and defeated at Cynthiana by Federals who had turned back from an intended invasion of southwestern Virginia to overtake the Rebel raiders. He did not know it, but Morgan had made his last raid.

Another cavalry raid was ending on that twentieth of June. Major General Phil Sheridan, with the two divisions of horsemen he had led west from the Army of the Potomac after Cold Harbor, had, since colliding with Wade Hampton's two divisions of Rebel troopers at Trevilian Station eight days earlier, been circling back to the east. The day before, the Union troopers had crossed to the south side of the Mattapony River, one of the two streams that flow together to form the York at West Point, Virginia. The Federals were moving toward White House plantation on the Pamunkey, the other river that joins to form the York. The plantation had descended through Martha Washington's family to R. E. Lee's son, Rooney, but it had been Grant's supply base during his recent operations east of Richmond, until he had crossed to the south side of the James.

Sheridan's troopers heard cannon fire in the distance as they moved south, and soon dispatches from Brigadier General John Abercrombie, in command of the base, informed Sheridan that it was about to be attacked. However, advance scouts brought back word that the Rebels had already been repulsed, so the weary horsemen continued their march at a leisurely pace and camped that night on the north bank of the Pamunkey, across from the base.

With them had come about 2,000 escaping slaves, who, along with Sheridan's prisoners and wounded, had been sent on down to West Point, escorted by a couple of regiments. "Where all the colored people came from and what started them was inexplicable," Sheridan later wrote, "but they began joining us just before we reached Trevillian—men, women, and children—with bundles of all sorts containing their few worldly goods, and the number increased from day to day until they arrived at West Point. Probably not one of the poor things had the remotest idea, when he set out, as to where he would finally land, but to a man they followed the Yankees in full faith that they would lead to freedom, no matter what road they took."[13]

On the 21st, Sheridan's two divisions crossed the Pamunkey, and Hampton's Confederate troopers, who had been threatening the base at White House, withdrew to the west side of the Chickahominy River, where they covered the approaches to Richmond.

At the foot of the Blue Ridge on the morning of the 21st, it was the infantry that gave Early problems for a change. Major General Robert Rodes did not receive his orders to take the lead that morning, and it was long past dawn when his men were finally on the road. By then, all that could be seen of Hunter's Federals was a cloud of dust disappearing to the west. Nevertheless, Early pushed his weary, hungry men along the hot, dusty road. Up ahead, later that day, something appeared which must have at first seemed to be a heat mirage or a fevered dream to the suffering Southerners. "We noticed several ladies standing on the side of the road," remembered a member of Gordon's Division. "And when we came nearer we saw two beautiful young ladies and their maids and near them were two huge washtubs. The young ladies gave us an invitation to come forward and partake of some ice water and brandy julep. The men needed no second invitation," the young Rebel added.[14]

Around noon Early finally had some good news from his cavalry. McCausland had cut into the Union column and captured several cannon. He hadn't been able to hang on to all of them, but he had spiked five and carried off three. Later in the day, Early received word that Hunter had turned aside from his route along the railroad, which would ultimately have led him down into Union territory in east Tennessee, and was instead making for Lewisburg, West Virginia. Early knew that the Federals would find no provisions in the mountains and so could not stop until they reached the valley of the Kanawha. The Army of West Virginia was marching right off the board, so far as the war in Virginia was concerned.

That day, Sherman asked Secretary Stanton for authority to send guerrillas and malcontents out of the country: "Honduras, British or French Guiana or San Domingo would be the best countries but they might object to receive such a mass of restless democrats. Madagascar or Southern California would do." He added that, "Our civil powers at the South are ridiculously impotent, and it is as a ship sailing through the sea— our armies traverse the land and the waves of disaffection, sedition and crime close in behind, and our track disappears. But one thing is certain, there is a class of people, men, women and children who must be killed or banished before we can hope for peace and order, even as far south as Tennessee." To his commander in Kentucky Sherman said, "If they won't live in peace in such a garden as Kentucky, why, we will kindly send them to another, if not a better land, and surely this would be a kindness and God's blessing to Kentucky."[15]

---

1. Foote, *The Civil War*, 3:381.
2. Macartney, *Mr. Lincoln's Admirals*, 230.
3. Foote, *The Civil War*, 3:384.
4. John McIntosh Kell, "Cruise and Combats of the 'Alabama,'" in *Battles and Leaders*, 4:608.
5. John M. Browne, "The Duel Between the 'Alabama' and the 'Kearsarge,'" in *Battles and Leaders*, 4:619.
6. Kell, "Cruise and Combats of the 'Alabama'," 610.
7. Ibid.
8. Browne, "The Duel Between the 'Alabama' and the 'Kearsarge'," 621.

 9. Foote, *The Civil War*, 3:388.
10. Ibid., 389.
11. Vandiver, *Jubal's Raid*, 54.
12. Early, *War Memoirs*, 377.
13. P. H. Sheridan, *Personal Memoirs* (New York, 1888), vol. 1, 428–429.
14. Vandiver, *Jubal's Raid*, 57.
15. Lewis, *Sherman: Fighting Prophet* 396–397.

CHAPTER SEVEN

However Bold
We Might Be

21–24 June 1864

"At City Point there was a level piece of ground on a high bluff, on which stood a comfortable house. This building was assigned to the chief quartermaster," Lieutenant Colonel Horace Porter, one of Grant's aides, recorded, "and General Grant's headquarters camp was established on the lawn. The tents occupied a line a little over a hundred feet back from the edge of the bluff," Porter wrote. "In the middle of the line were General Grant's quarters. A hospital tent was used as his office, while a smaller tent connecting in the rear was occupied as his sleeping-apartment. A hospital tent-fly was stretched in front of the office tent so as to make a shaded space in which persons could sit. A rustic bench and a number of folding campchairs with backs were placed there, and it was beneath this tent-fly that most of the important official interviews were held." On each side of Grant's quarters were other tents, each holding two officers of his staff.

"A wooden staircase was built reaching from the headquarters to the steam-boat landing at the foot of the bluff, ample wharves, storehouses, and hospitals were rapidly constructed, and a commodious base of supplies was established in the vicinity. On the day the wharf was completed and planked over," Porter remembered, "the general took a stroll along it, his hands thrust in his trousers pockets, and a lighted cigar in his mouth. He had recently issued instructions to take every precaution against fire, and had not gone far when a sentinel called out: 'It's against orders to come on the wharf with a lighted cigar.' The general at once took his Havana out of his mouth and threw it into the river, saying: 'I don't like to lose my smoke, but the sentinel's right. He evidently isn't going to let me disobey my own orders.'"[1]

On 21 June a white steamboat chugged up the James and nosed into that wharf at City Point. Aboard were President Abraham Lincoln and his young son, Tad. According to a letter that Colonel Porter wrote to his wife a few days later, "We were sitting in front of the General's tent when there appeared very suddenly before us a long, lank-looking personage, dressed all in black, and looking very much like a boss undertaker. It was the President. He said, after shaking hands with us all, 'I just thought I would jump aboard a boat and come down here and see you. I don't expect I can do any good, and in fact I'm afraid I may do harm, but I'll put myself under your orders and if you find me doing anything wrong just send me right away.' Gen. Grant informed him bluntly that he would certainly do that."[2] In his book written 33 years later, however, Porter said Grant and his staff met the boat at the wharf. There he added that when Grant inquired after the president's health, the latter confessed to a bit of seasickness caused by rough water on Chesapeake Bay. One of the staff officers, seeing a chance to make points with the president, suggested champagne as a sure cure for seasickness. "Mr. Lincoln looked at him for a moment, his face lighting up with a smile, and then remarked: 'No, my friend; I have seen too many fellows seasick ashore from drinking that very stuff.'"[3]

At any rate, the general offered the president a tour of his lines and a chance to see and be seen by the men, which was promptly accepted. Lincoln, Grant, Assistant Secretary of War Charles A. Dana, Porter and two other staff officers rode among the troops of both Meade's and Butler's armies. "The soldiers rapidly passed the word along the line that 'Uncle Abe' had joined them, and cheers broke forth from all the commands," Porter wrote, "and enthusiastic shouts and even words of familiar greeting met him on all sides."[4]

After a while Grant suggested they visit the black troops of Hincks' division, to which the president readily assented. He had heard good reports of their behavior at Petersburg. "I was opposed on nearly every side," Lincoln remarked, "when I first favored the raising of colored regiments; but they have proved their efficiency, and I am glad they have kept pace with the white troops in the recent assaults." When Hincks' men saw Lincoln, their enthusiasm knew no limits. They shouted, cheered, laughed, cried, and sang hymns of praise. "They crowded about him and fondled his horse;" Porter wrote, "some of them kissed his hands, while others ran off crying in triumph to their comrades that they had touched his clothes. The President rode with bared head; the tears had started to his eyes, and his voice was so broken by emotion that he could scarcely articulate the words of thanks and congratulation which he tried to speak to the humble and devoted men through whose ranks he rode. The scene was affecting in the extreme, and no one could have witnessed it unmoved."[5]

Operations had not ceased on the Petersburg front just because Grant was busy with Lincoln's visit. In fact, on that 21st of June, Burnside's 9th Corps extended its right to connect with Smith's 18th, relieving Birney's 2nd and Wright's 6th Corps for a move around to the south of the city. Warren's 5th Corps connected with Burnside's left and extended the Union line down to the Jerusalem Plank Road. The 2nd Corps was put into position on the left of the 5th Corps, and that night the 6th Corps bivouacked behind the 2nd, ready to move out in the morning. In addition, Brigadier General James H. Wilson was ordered to prepare his own 3rd Division of the Army of the Potomac's Cavalry Corps, plus Brigadier General August V. Kautz's Cavalry Division of the Army of the James—in short, almost all the cavalry still with Grant's armies in Sheridan's absence—to move out at 2 a.m. the next morning for a raid on the railroads south and west of Petersburg.

Lincoln spent the night on his boat, and the next day, the 22nd, about 8 a.m., he went farther up the river for a visit with Admiral Samuel P. Lee, commander of the Union ships in the James, and with General Butler. A pontoon bridge that Butler had thrown across the river the day before at a place called Deep Bottom was opened in the middle to let the boat proceed. "Mr. Lincoln was in excellent spirits," Porter remembered, "and listened with great eagerness to the descriptions of the works, which could be seen from the river, and the objects for which they had been constructed. When his attention was called to some particularly strong positions which had been seized and fortified, he remarked to Butler: 'When Grant once gets possession of a place, he holds on to it as if he had inherited it.'" Soon after returning to City Point, the president started back for Washington. Porter felt that Lincoln and Grant "parted from each other with unfeigned regret, and both felt that their acquaintance had already ripened into a genuine friendship."[6] As Lincoln was leaving, Grant told him, "You will never hear of me farther from Richmond than now, till I have taken it. I am just as sure of going into Richmond as I am of any future event. It may take a long summer day, but I will go in."[7]

That day Birney's Federal 2nd Corps was directed to swing forward, pivoting on its connection with the 5th Corps, on its right, until it reached a suitable distance from the Confederate lines, there to entrench.

Meanwhile, Wright's 6th Corps was ordered to proceed about three miles beyond the Jerusalem Plank Road to Globe Tavern to cut the railroad running south to Weldon, North Carolina, where it was to intrench while connecting with Birney on its right. Since the two corps were to advance through densely wooded thickets in different directions, they were not expected to maintain connection. Until both had reached their objectives, they were to protect their own flanks individually. However, so much opposition was encountered from Rebel skirmishers that the 6th Corps was only able to advance halfway to its objective that day. Of the 2nd Corps divisions, Gibbon's, on the right, having the least distance to cover, reached and entrenched his portion of the new line, Mott's position was reached but only partially entrenched, and Barlow's division was not yet completely in position. Moreover, Birney's left flank was not protected as it was supposed to be.

Lee, meanwhile, sent A. P. Hill with two of his divisions, Wilcox's and Mahone's, supported by Johnson's Division of Beauregard's command, down the Weldon Railroad to try to block this move against his supply lines to the south. When the Federal 2nd Corps swung to the north while the 6th Corps moved westward, Mahone saw an opportunity to exploit the gap between them. Before the war this diminutive Confederate general had been a civil engineer for the railroad and had surveyed much of this area. He proposed to take three of his brigades and one battery of field artillery by a concealed route to attack Birney's flank while Wilcox blocked Wright's path. Hill and Lee agreed, and Mahone quickly led his men through a ravine and into dense woods unseen by the Federals, then deployed them into line of battle behind a heavy skirmish line.

With a yell and a volley, Mahone's Rebels burst upon the flank and rear of Barlow's Yankees, taking many prisoners and driving the rest back to their starting place. Mott's division, seeing its own flank uncovered, also returned precipitately to its starting point. This in turn uncovered Gibbon's left flank and his division also retreated, abandoning a battery of four guns that the Rebels soon turned against their former owners. The greater part of several of Gibbon's regiments were captured with their colors. Hill then sent Wilcox's Division to exploit Mahone's success, but it arrived too late. In an hour or less, Mahone's surprise attack had chased Birney's 2nd Corps over a mile back into its defensive works. These Mahone attacked at several points, but unsuccessfully. Gibbon counterattacked, also without success. Soon Mahone realized he in turn was now in danger of being flanked or surrounded. At about dusk he ordered his men to gather up the 1,742 prisoners, eight flags, four guns, and numerous small arms they had captured and to return to their own entrenchments.

Four railroads led into Petersburg on the south side of the Appomattox River to connect with the short Richmond & Petersburg line that funneled all their contributions into the Confederate capital. There was a very short road coming in from City Point to the northeast and a somewhat longer one coming in from Norfolk, Portsmouth, and Suffolk to the southeast. Both of these lines were already completely under the control of Grant's forces. Of the two remaining, one ran almost due south to Weldon, North Carolina, and points south. This was the line which Mahone's flank attack had just saved, for now. The other, called the Southside Railroad, ran southwest for a few miles to a small hamlet called Black's and White's, after a pair of taverns, and then turned northwest to Farmville on the Appomattox before proceeding westward to Lynchburg and points southwest. About halfway between Black's and White's and Farmville, the Southside line crossed another railroad that ran southwest from Richmond to Danville, Virginia, and on into the Carolinas. Other than the railroad running northwestward to the Shenandoah and the James River Canal to Lynchburg, this latter was the capital's only supply line that did not pass through Petersburg. Union Brigadier General James H. Wilson was under orders to take his own and Kautz's small cavalry divisions by the shortest route directly to Burkeville, where the Danville and Southside railroads crossed, and to destroy both lines as far as possible in both directions.

Wilson was a young man for a general, as were most of the cavalry commanders of both sides. The hard riding and split-second decisions required of the breed did not come easily to older men. He was then 27 years of age and only four years out of West Point. He had served on the staffs of Hunter, when he had commanded on the South Carolina coast, of McClellan at the Antietam, and of Grant through the Vicksburg and Chattanooga campaigns. Grant and Halleck had then chosen him to briefly head the newly established Cavalry Bureau in Washington until Grant had appointed him to command the 3rd Division of Sheridan's Cavalry Corps in time for the overland campaign from the Wilderness to Petersburg. In the Wilderness he had spread his division, the smallest in Sheridan's corps, too thin and had been routed by the wily Rebel horsemen. Since then he had done better, but not spectacularly so. He had screened the army's move across the James with skill, but he had not been pressed very hard by the Confederates. This move to Burkeville would be his first test in semi-independent command.

Meade had opposed the raid, fearing that the Rebel cavalry would concentrate against it now that Sheridan was no longer threatening anything vital north of the James. Meade would have preferred to wait for Sheridan to cross the James and then send the entire Cavalry Corps together. Grant however, did not want to delay that long. Waiting until everything was just right was a sure way to give Lee a chance to get into mischief. Part of his self-appointed objective was to keep Lee too busy defending himself and the Rebel capital to launch offensives or to send help to Joe Johnston in Georgia. Besides, Hampton, with two of Lee's three cavalry divisions, was known to be north of the James watching Sheridan, and Hunter was supposedly at Lexington, tying down any Confederates in that area. Wilson, too, worried about running into a large force of Southern troopers, but he told Meade's chief of staff, Major General A. A. Humphreys, "If Sheridan will look after Hampton I apprehend no difficulty."[8] He also sought and received assurance that the Federal infantry would hold open the roads by which he would have to return to the army after his raid.

Wilson's troopers had spent all day on the 21st getting ready, while unfit men and horses had been weeded out and sent to City Point. It was midnight by the time preparations were completed and the men could settle down for a little sleep. One hour later the bugles woke them up again, and at 3 a.m. on the 22nd they rode out of camp, "more asleep than awake," as one of them remembered.[9] After leaving behind two large regiments, totaling 1,146 men, so that Grant would not be completely lacking in cavalry, Wilson had about 5,500 troopers with him, 2,400 of them in Kautz's division. Some of these men were old hands at mounted warfare, others had spent the previous day assembling their first saddles from parts that had arrived in different boxes.

By mid-morning of the 22nd, the Federals came to Ream's Station on the Weldon Railroad, described by one of the raiders as "a pretty little place. . . . The houses were inhabited, with nice yards and fruit trees around, blooming with flowers."[10] They burned the railroad station and tore up a bit of track, then marched on through a beautiful country of wheat fields and arrived at Dinwiddie Court House early that afternoon. It was then that they met their first opposition, in the form of an attack on their rear guard by a portion of Rooney Lee's Division, but it was easily fended off. Some miles farther on they came to Ford's Depot on the Southside Railroad, where there were two freight trains loaded with supplies for Lee's army. They burned the trains, the station, a woodpile and a sawmill, then followed the tracks farther west, ripping them up along the way and heating the rails and twisting them, until almost midnight. The horses were left saddled, and the men got what sleep they could while lying on the ground with their reins in their hands.

Some sixty miles to the northeast, Sheridan sent Torbert's division to secure Jones' bridge over the Chickahominy River that morning. He had received orders to break up the supply base at White House and escort the remaining wagons and troops to and over Butler's new pontoon bridge across the James at Deep Bottom. "These trains amounted to hundreds of wagons and other vehicles," Sheridan wrote, "and knowing full well the dangers which would attend the difficult problem of getting them over to Petersburg, I decided to start them with as little delay as circumstances would permit."[11] The train of wagons followed Torbert's division, while Gregg's moved along a parallel road to the west to protect it from Hampton's Rebel horsemen. Yet there was no attack on the column that day, and the wagons were safely parked south of the Chickahominy that night, under the immediate protection of the fragments of infantry from the White House base.

John Hunt Morgan officially assumed command of the Department of Southwestern Virginia and East Tennessee that 22nd day of June, while to the northeast, in the Shenandoah, Jubal Early called off the pursuit of Hunter's army. "As the enemy had got into the mountains," Early wrote, "where nothing useful could be accomplished by pursuit, I did not deem it proper to continue it farther." His men were hungry, and neither his wagons nor his artillery had caught up with his infantry yet. "I was glad to see Hunter take the route to Lewisburg," Early said, "as I knew he could not stop short of the Kanawha River, and he was, therefore, disposed of for some time."[12] The Confederate commander gave his infantry a well earned day of rest while the cavalry kept a watch on Hunter, just in case. Ramseur's Division was camped at Botetourt Springs, and his dusty, weary, footsore men took the waters with more exuberance than the little spa is likely to have ever witnessed before.

In southwestern Tennessee, the Federals had been repairing the railroad eastward out of Memphis, and on the 22nd, trains carried Mower's 1st Division of the 16th Corps to Grissom's Bridge, some forty miles or so east of the city. From the cars Mower's men exchanged good-natured ribbing with the men of Bouton's brigade of U.S. Colored Troops, who were guarding the rail line. Meanwhile, Colonel David Moore was told that the trains would be ready to start carrying his 3rd Division to the same point the next day. A. J. Smith's projected raid into northern Mississippi was almost ready to get underway.

That same day, Confederate Major General S. D. Lee, who had been left in command of the Department of Alabama, Mississippi, and East Louisiana when Polk had gone to reinforce Johnston the month before, was warning his superiors in Richmond that Smith was outfitting a "formidable expedition [to] repair the disaster of General Sturgis."[13] Indications were that Smith had twice as many men as Forrest had available to oppose him. This information did not make President Davis happy. When he had allowed Polk to reinforce Johnston in Georgia, it was in the belief that the latter would stand and fight it out around Resaca, so that, after a victory there, Polk could go back to protect his own department. Instead, Johnston had retreated, Polk was dead, and his troops were badly needed in both Georgia and Mississippi.

Over in Georgia that day, a column that Sherman had sent to try to flank Johnston out of his formidable new Kenesaw Mountain line had run into a force that the Confederate commander had sent to head it off. The Federal column consisted of Schofield's 23rd Corps, also known as the Army of the Ohio, and Hooker's 20th Corps of Thomas' Army of the Cumberland. Near the Kolb farm on the Powder Springs Road that day Williams' division of Hooker's corps was deployed on the north side of the road and Hascall's division of Schofield's corps, to the south. The Rebel blocking force was Hood's 2nd Corps, but Hood was not content to stay on the defensive. Impetuously he attacked with Hindman's Division on the north side of the road and Stevenson's Division on the south side. However, by then the Federals had entrenched and had their artillery deployed in supporting positions, and no such attack—lacking an advantage in numbers—stood much of a chance. The Union artillery shattered Hindman's advance, which was slowed by the necessity of crossing a creek, and his men broke and ran for cover. Stevenson's men drove Hascall's skirmishers from their rifle pits in the Kolbs' yard, but could advance no farther and eventually fell back.

One brigade commander in Hindman's Division didn't think much of Hood's judgment for launching this attack. "I formed my estimate of him on this occasion for the first time," the brigadier wrote, "and subsequent events only confirmed me in the opinion that he was totally unfit for the command of a corps; altho he might have deserved the reputation he had acquired as the best division commander in the Army of Northern Virginia."[14] It quite often proved true that an officer who was outstanding at one level of command was not well suited to higher duties.

A case in point, on the other side of that day's battle, was Joe Hooker. He had been an outstanding division commander in the Army of the Potomac, but a gnawing ambition had undermined his usefulness at corps command, and when he had been given the overall command of that army he had not been able to stand up to the violent combativeness of R. E. Lee. When he had been returned to corps command, now in Thomas' army, his ambition had also returned. That evening he sent a signal directly to Sherman's headquarters saying, "We have repulsed two heavy attacks, and feel confident, our only apprehension being from our extreme right flank. Three entire corps are in front of us." There were just three things wrong with that message. In the first place, Hooker should have reported to his immediate superior, Thomas, not to Sherman. In the second place, there was no need for him to worry about his right flank, as Schofield's entire corps was on Hooker's right. In the third place, there were only three corps in Johnston's entire army.

As Sherman recorded in his memoirs, "I had that very day ridden six miles of their lines, found them everywhere strongly occupied, and therefore Hooker could not have encountered 'three entire corps.'" Thomas had been complaining to Sherman that Hooker constantly tried to separate himself and his troops as far as possible from the rest of his army, in order to operate independently. "Both McPherson and Schofield had also complained to me," Sherman wrote, "of this same tendency of Hooker to widen the gap between his own corps and his proper army (Thomas's), so as to come into closer contact with one or other of the wings, asserting that he was the senior by commission to both McPherson and Schofield, and that in the event of battle he should assume command over them, by virtue of his older commission. They appealed to me to protect them."

Early the next day, the 23rd, Sherman rode down to the Kolb house, where he found Schofield's corps in place, guarding Hooker's right as ordered. "I met Generals Schofield and Hooker together," Sherman recorded. "As rain was falling at the moment, we passed into a little church standing by the roadside, and I there showed General Schofield Hooker's signal-message of the day before. He was very angry, and pretty sharp words passed between them, Schofield saying that his head of column (Hascall's division) had been, at the time of the battle, actually in advance of Hooker's line; that the attack or sally of the enemy struck his troops before it did Hooker's; that General Hooker knew of it at the time; and he offered to go out and show me that the dead men of his advance division (Hascall's) were lying farther out than any of Hooker's. General Hooker pretended not to have known this fact. I then asked him why he had called on me for help, until he had used all of his own troops; asserting that I had just seen Butterfield's division, and had learned from him that he had not been engaged the day before at all; and I asserted that the enemy's sally must have been made by one corps (Hood's), in place of three, and that it had fallen on Geary's and Williams's divisions, which had repulsed the attack handsomely. As we rode away from that church General Hooker was by my side, and I told him that such a thing must not occur again; in other words, I reproved him more gently than the occasion demanded, and from that time he began to sulk."[15]

That day, the 23rd, Sherman telegraphed a report to Halleck at Washington: "We continue to press forward on the principle of an advance against fortified positions. The whole country is one vast fort, and Johnston must have at least fifty miles of connected trenches, with abatis and finished batteries. We gain ground daily, fighting all the time. On the 21st General Stanley gained a position near the south end of Kenesaw, from which the enemy attempted in vain to drive him; and the same day General T. J. Wood's division took a hill, which the enemy assaulted three times at night without success, leaving more than a hundred dead on the ground. Yesterday the extreme right (Hooker and Schofield) advanced on the Powder Springs road to within three miles of Marietta. The enemy made a strong effort to drive them away, but failed signally, leaving more than two hundred dead on the field. Our lines are now in close contact, and the fighting is incessant, with a good deal of artillery-fire. As fast as we gain one position the enemy has another all ready, but I think he will soon have to let go Kenesaw, which is the key to the whole country. The weather is now better, and the roads are drying up fast. Our losses are light, and, notwithstanding the repeated breaks of the road to our rear, supplies are ample."[16]

At Petersburg, early on the morning of the 23rd, Birney's Union 2nd Corps moved forward and occupied the line it had been driven from the day before. At the same time, Wright's 6th Corps formed on Birney's left but facing west, toward the Weldon Railroad and about a mile and a half from it. The positions of Lee's and Grant's armies would not change substantially for several weeks, except for extensive entrenching. Although the Weldon Railroad had not yet been taken, let alone the other supply lines feeding Lee's army and the Confederate capital, the writing was visible on the wall for those who understood the situation. While Grant's men were protected by their own earthworks most of the time, he could pick his own times and places to send forays against the railroads to his west. "The position which he had secured was full of great possibilities, as yet not fully comprehended," wrote Brigadier General Porter Alexander, chief of artillery in the Rebel 1st Corps. "But already the character of the operations contemplated removed all risk of serious future catastrophe. However bold we might be, however desperately we might fight, we were sure in the end to be worn out. It was only a question of a few months, more or less. We were unable to see it at once. But there soon began to spring up a chain of permanent works, the first of which were built upon our original lines captured by the skirmishers the first afternoon, and these works, impregnable to assault, finally decided our fate when, on the next March 25, we put them to the test."[17]

Like Sherman, Grant sent his own estimate of the situation to Halleck that 23rd of June. He wanted to curb the well known tendencies of his former boss, as well as of the secretary of war, to waste forces on side shows. "The siege of Richmond bids fair to be tedious," he wrote, "and in consequence of the very extended lines we must have, a much larger force will be necessary than would be required in ordinary sieges against the same force that now opposes us. With my present force I feel perfectly safe against Lee's army, and, acting defensively, would still feel so against Lee and Johnston combined; but we want to act offensively. In my opinion, to do this effectively, we should concentrate our whole energy against the two principal armies of the enemy.

"In other words," he continued, "nothing should be attempted, except in Georgia and here, that is not directly in cooperation with these moves. West of the Mississippi I would not attempt anything until the rebellion east of it is entirely subdued. I would then direct Canby to leave [Kirby] Smith unmolested where he is; to make no move except such as is necessary to protect what he now holds. All the troops he can spare should be sent here at once. In my opinion the white troops of the Nineteenth Corps can all come, together with many of the colored troops. I wish you would place this matter before the Secretary of War and urge that no offensive operations west of the Mississippi be allowed to commence until matters here are settled." Then to make sure that he was understood, he repeated the essence of what he wanted Halleck to do: "Send the Nineteenth Corps and such other troops as you can from the Department of the Gulf to me."[18]

---

1. Porter, *Campaigning With Grant*, 212–213.
2. Catton, *Grant Takes Command*, 305.
3. Porter, *Campaigning With Grant*, 217.
4. Ibid., 218.
5. Ibid., 219–220.
6. Ibid., 222–223.
7. Basler, *The Collected Works of Abraham Lincoln*, 7:406.
8. Stephen Z. Starr, *The Union Cavalry in the Civil War* (Baton Rouge, 1981), vol. 2, p. 180.

9. Ibid.
10. Ibid., 181.
11. Sheridan, *Memoirs*, 1:430.
12. William R. Scaife, *The Campaign For Atlanta* (Atlanta, 1990), 40.
13. Early, *War Memoirs*, 378–379.
14. Bearss, *Forrest at Brice's Cross Roads*, 159–160.
15. Sherman, *Memoirs*, 2:57–59.
16. Ibid., 59–60.
17. Catton, *Grant Takes Command*, 301.
18. Ibid., 302–303.

PART TWO

WASHINGTON

"Get down, you damn fool, before you get shot!"

Captain Oliver Wendell Holmes, Jr.
to President Abraham Lincoln

CHAPTER EIGHT

Had I Lain for a Century Dead

23–26 June 1864

In southern Virginia on the 23rd, Wilson sent Kautz's division of cavalry ahead well before daylight on the road to Burkeville, where the two critical railroads crossed. Brigadier General August V. Kautz was nine years older than Wilson and had graduated from West Point eight years before him, but Wilson had received his star earlier than Kautz and so commanded the combined force. Kautz had briefly worked for Wilson before, at the Cavalry Bureau in Washington, and had succeeded Wilson as chief of that bureau before being sent to command the cavalry division of Butler's army.

While Kautz's division went on ahead, one of Wilson's brigades fought off another attack by Rooney Lee's Rebel horsemen, and the other pulled up track on the Southside Railroad, one battalion at a time, while working its way westward. Around noon Wilson's troopers reached Black's and White's Station, where they stopped for lunch. There they burned sheds full of tobacco and cotton. That afternoon the Confederate cavalry got in between Kautz's and Wilson's divisions, slowing the latter's progress considerably. But Kautz reached Burkeville before night fell, burned the depot, and tore up the track on the Richmond Danville line for several miles.

Far to the northwest, at dawn on the 23rd, Ramseur's men marched out of Boutatourt Springs on the macadamized Valley Turnpike and led Early's column north. Although Lynchburg had been saved, Jubal Early had failed to carry out the first assignment Lee had given him, which was no less than the destruction of Hunter's army. However, Hunter had prodceeded to eliminate himself and his troops, temporarily at least, both as a threat to Lynchburg and as defenders of the Union occupation of the Shenandoah Valley. This meant that Early still had a chance to carry out his second assignment, which was to move down the Shenandoah (northeast) and, if possible, threaten Washington, D.C., itself. Once before, in 1862, a similar move, conceived by Lee and executed with genius by Stonewall Jackson, had taken a good deal of the pressure of McClellan's Peninsula campaign off Richmond. Perhaps Jubal Early was no Stonewall, but he faced far less opposition. Hunter had carried off into West Virginia most of the troops who had been guarding the Shenandoah, and Grant had stripped the defenses of Washington to replace the losses in the Army of the Potomac. A threat to the almost defenseless Federal capital might loosen Grant's grip on Petersburg. The 23rd was another extremely hot day in the Valley, but by the time the Rebels stopped that night they had reached the town of Buchanon and most of Ramseur's division had crossed to the north side of the upper James River.

The same unit took the lead again on the 24th, and while the main column toiled northward, a young Marylander on Ramseur's staff, Major Henry Kyd Douglas, took time to do a bit of sightseeing. "En route I got permission to take some troops from the south several miles out of the way to see the Natural Bridge," he wrote in his memoirs. "I took several bands and have never forgotten the solemn effect of their music as it rose and swelled in volume, and filled the great arch and seemed to press against the sides of that cathedral dome, and then rolled along the high rocks that walled the ravine and died away in the widening wood."[1] The head of Early's column approached Lexington late that afternoon and his troops camped near it that night. That same evening, Hunter's Union column reached White Sulphur Springs, where it found plenty of water, although food and other supplies were still a long way off.

Far to the east, Sheridan's Federal cavalry and the immense train of wagons it was escorting resumed their march for the James that day, the 24th. Again Torbert's 1st Division formed the immediate escort for the wagons, while Gregg's 2nd Division marched along roads farther to the east. As the wagons and Torbert's men were passing through the town of Charles City Court House they ran into Lomax's Brigade of Fitzhugh Lee's Rebel cavalry division, blocking their path. Sheridan ordered the wagons diverted from their objective, Butler's new bridge at Deep Bottom, and sent to Wilcox's Landing, where the infantry of the Army of the Potomac had crossed the James the week before. At the same time, the rest of the Confederate cavalry was encountered by Gregg near St. Mary's Church, which Sheridan ordered him to hold until the wagons could get to safety. Gregg's men prepared hasty defenses, and at about 4 o'clock that afternoon Fitz Lee's division of Rebel troopers attacked Gregg's front while Chambliss' and Gary's brigades hit his left flank. They kept it up for two hours, but with only small, local successes. Gregg sent numerous appeals to Sheridan for help, but all his messengers were either killed or captured. Near dark his men were finally driven out of their defenses, and in considerable confusion they fell back about six miles. "We realized for the first time how it felt to get a good sound thrashing and then be chased for our lives," the historian of the 10th New York Cavalry wrote, "somewhat as we had served the Rebs at Trevillian Station two weeks before."[2]

Gregg's men were exhausted and some of them died of heat and over-exertion that night. But the Confederates were also worn out. They could not exploit their success, and the wagons made it safely to Wilcox's Landing. Of Gregg, Sheridan wrote, "His steady, unflinching determination to gain time for the wagons to get beyond the point of danger was characteristic of the man, and this was the third occasion on which he had exhibited a high order of capacity and sound judgment since coming under my command."[3] That night the wagons were sent back through Charles City Court House to Dothard's Landing. There, boats sent down by Meade began to ferry them to the south side of the James. Meade was beginning to worry about the safety of the Wilson-Kautz expedition, and he wanted the rest of Sheridan's cavalry south of the James as soon as possible.

After a good night's rest, at last, Wilson's division caught up with Kautz's that day, the 24th, at Meherrin Station, ten miles southwest of Burkeville, and the reunited command marched on to Keysville, where it stopped for the night. This was only the third day of the raid, but the Federals' horses were already starting to give out. It was the rear-guard's job to make sure that no broken-down animals survived to join the Rebel army, and one trooper assigned this duty estimated that "we shot on the average one horse every quarter of a mile."[4] At least half of them, the same soldier estimated, could have been saved by a few days or even a few hours of rest, but the Federals could not stand still that long.

At dawn on the 25th, the march was resumed, still following the Richmond & Danville Railroad. The track of that line was constructed with wooden rails with only a strap of iron along the top, and the Yankees found it easy to destroy "by simply laying down fence rails alongside the stringers & putting fire to it." As one of them described it, "The fire destroyed the stringers, burnt the ends of the ties off, and the iron was warped & badly twisted. .... Each Regiment was given a certain distance to burn, and when it was finished they would pass on until they again came to the front, where another distance would be allotted to them." They didn't keep it up for long, however, for "it was a most terrible hot day, and carrying fence rails & wood a distance was no desirable work."[5]

While some of Wilson's troopers took care of the track and others fought off Rooney Lee's Confederates, Kautz's men, still in the lead, burned depots, turntables, bridges, and reached the long wooden trestle across the Roanoke River that afternoon. However, that structure was guarded by a pair of earthen forts containing six cannon, plus a triple line of rifle pits manned by almost a thousand Rebel infantrymen and home guards. Kautz dismounted his men and sent them forward, one brigade to the right of the embankment carrying the track, and the other to the left. Colonel West, commanding the brigade on the right, formed an assault column "and directed it up the embankment in the hope that by a quick move . . . it might obtain posssession of the . . . bridge sufficiently long to fire it," as he reported. "The men tried repeatedly to gain a foothold on the railroad, and to advance along the sides of the embankment, but could not. The height of the railroad embankment enabled the enemy from their position down by the river's edge . . . to sweep the sides and track with a terrible fire."[6]

Kautz's men were pinned down, so Wilson sent scouts up and down the river searching for a spot where it could be crossed in order to flank the Confederate position. Still, no crossing could be found, and Rooney Lee's attacks on the rear guard continued. Wilson felt he had accomplished all that could reasonably be expected of him and that it was time to return to the main army. That, however, was now a hundred miles away. Wilson's men and horses were exhausted, and he was encumbered with about 200 wounded men in wagons, not to mention a growing number of runaway slaves. So, instead of returning along the railroad, as he had come, and where he would surely be intercepted by the Rebels, he decided to move southeast and then east until he reached the Weldon Railroad well to the south of the Federal infantry lines. The troopers began their return march about 11 o'clock that night, the 25th.

Near Petersburg that day, an interesting example of Yankee ingenuity was put in play. The place where the Union and Confederate lines were closest to each other was in the sector of Burnside's 9th Corps, where his men had crossed Poor Creek west of the Taylor house and stormed up the hill to within about 125 yards of the third Rebel line. By this time, the Federal defenses were just as strong as the Confederate works opposite them, and each side had settled down to keeping a wary eye on the other and sniping at anyone foolish enough to show himself, while mortars were brought up to occasionally hurl exploding shells high into the air so that they would fall into the enemy trenches. It was clear that neither side could successfully assault the other's defenses by conventional means, but one Union outfit had an idea for an unconventional approach.

Lieutenant Colonel Henry Pleasants' 48th Pennsylvania happened to be manning a portion of the 9th Corps defenses opposite a fort in the Rebel line that contained some brass cannon and was known on the Confederate side as Elliott's Salient. And it just so happened that the 48th had been raised in Schuylkill County, Pennsylvania, which was coal mining country. Many of its men were former miners, and Pleasants was himself a former mining and railroad engineer. Pleasants had heard one of his men, who had been studying the Southern defenses, tell a friend, "We could blow that damned fort out of existence if we could run a mine shaft under it." That set the colonel to thinking and when he got back to the bombproof dugout where he and his staff lived and worked he told his officers, "That God-damned fort is the only thing between us and Petersburg, and I have an idea we can blow it up."[7]

Pleasants told his division commander, Brigadier General Robert Potter, about his idea, and a staff officer was sent down to have a look. While Pleasants was showing this officer the Rebel fort a sniper's bullet hit the man in the face, but Pleasants drew a sketch of the terrain and forwarded it up to Potter, and a few days later Potter took him to see General Burnside. Pleasants explained to the two generals that with his regiment of coal miners he could start a tunnel at a spot forty or fifty yards behind and downhill from his lines, where the Confederates could not see what they were doing. The shaft would slant uphill, which would allow any water to drain out from the opening. When the tunnel, which would be some 500 feet long, was below the Rebel lines it could be filled with powder to blow up the Confederate fort. Burnside was impressed with the plan and said he would take it up with Meade, and that meanwhile the colonel could get started. That had been the night before, and now, on the 25th, Pleasants organized several details of coal miners and put them to work scratching out the beginnings of a mine shaft at the protected spot he had picked out. The only tools they had were bayonets, but they started hacking away at the hillside and in very little time they were working underground.

When Burnside presented the idea at army headquarters Meade's engineer officers ridiculed it. Oh, there was nothing wrong with undermining enemy positions, they said. In fact it was common practice in siege warfare. But first you had to get much closer to the enemy works than any part of the Federal army was to the Rebel defenses at Petersburg. A mine shaft that long could not be ventilated, they said, so the men working at its face would suffocate; that is, if they weren't already crushed under falling dirt. And if that was not enough, the Rebels were bound to find out about the enterprise and dig countermines to block the Federal's progress long before it could do any good. Meade, himself an army engineer before the war, tended to agree with this point of view, but seemed to feel that it would do no harm to let the amateur-soldier coal miners try. Keeping the men busy would be good for morale, and maybe they would get lucky. Anyway, nobody seemed to have any better ideas.

In the Shenandoah that morning, the 25th, General Robert Rodes' Division took the lead as Early's troops hit the road again, still heading northeast down the Valley Turnpike. As they passed through Lexington they saw the blackened ruins of Governor Letcher's house and of the Virginia Military Institute. The VMI cadets, who had been marching with the army since Lynchburg, were dropped off there to resume their studies as best they could. The column also passed—with reversed arms and in complete silence—the grave of Stonewall Jackson, the man who had created the original Army of the Valley, out of which the Rebel 2nd Corps had been formed and to which name it had now returned. Was it really only a bit over a year since he had been laid to rest? Was his spirit watching over his old army, or was it beyond caring about such earthly matters? Major Henry Kyd Douglas was reminded of some lines from Tennyson, which he paraphrased in his memoirs:

They are here my own, my own;
Were it ever so airy a tread,
My heart would hear them and beat,
Were it earth in an earthy bed;
My dust would hear them and beat
Had I lain for a century dead![8]

The next day, the 26th, Early's column reached Staunton, where the Valley Turnpike crossed the Virginia Central Railroad, the Shenandoah's connection with Richmond by way of Charlottesville and Gordonsville.

There he gave his troops another day of rest while he sorted out some administrative matters. For one thing, he sent off to the quartermaster general in Richmond a reminder of an order for shoes that he had hoped would meet him at Staunton. The macadamized turnpike was tearing up the shoes of the few of his men who still had them and the feet of those who did not, which was now almost half of them. Fortunately for the Rebels, the area was full of good things to eat. In fact, although he was exceeding his authority, Early sent home all the reserves in the Valley so that the area's crops could be properly harvested, because not only his own, but Lee's forces, too, would be dependent on that harvest to get them through the coming winter.

It had become apparent on the march north that General Elzey's physical condition was not up to hard campaigning, and he had been relieved of command of the two infantry brigades that had belonged to Breckinridge. The latter, on the other hand, was now recovered enough to return to duty, but Early wanted to give the capable and influential Kentuckian a larger command. So in addition to his own two small brigades, the former vice president was also put in charge of Gordon's Division. Rodes and Ramseur would still report directly to Early, as would Ransom, now commanding all the cavalry. The artillery was also reorganized, weeding out the poorest guns and equipment until what was left more closely matched the number of serviceable horses. In order to further improve maneuverability, stern orders were issued limiting the number of wagons allowed to accompany the little army in the future. Finally, Early sent off a message to Lee that he would continue north and cross the Potomac, unless Lee ordered otherwise.

Lee was writing to President Davis that day. "Genl Hunter has escaped Early," he reported, "and will make good his retreat, as far as I can understand, to Lewisburg. Although his expedition has been partially interrupted, I fear he has not been much punished, except by the demoralization of his troops and the loss of some artillery. From his present position he can easily be reorganized and re-equiped, and unless we have sufficient force to resist him, will repeat his expedition. This would necessitate the return of Early at Staunton. I think it better that he should move down the Valley, if he can obtain provisions, which would draw Hunter after him, and may enable him to strike Pope before he can effect a junction with Hunter." The Confederates were under the mistaken impression that Union Major General John Pope was being returned to Virginia from Minnesota to take command in the lower Shenandoah.

"If circumstances favor," Lee continued, "I should also recommend his crossing the Potomac. I think I can maintain our lines here against

Genl. Grant. He does not seem disposed to attack, and has thrown himself strictly on the defensive. I am less uneasy about holding our position than about our ability to procure supplies for the army. I fear the latter difficulty will oblige me to attack Genl. Grant in his entrenchments, which I should not hesitate to do but for the loss it will inevitably entail. A want of success would in my opinion be almost fatal, and this causes me to hesitate in the hope that some relief may be procured without running such great hazard." In other words, he was hoping that Early's movement toward Washington would be a cheaper, more certain way of defeating Grant than a direct attack on his defenses.

He then commented on a plan that Davis had in the works to free Southern prisoners being held by the Yankees at Point Lookout, Maryland, on a peninsula jutting into Chesapeake Bay. "Great benefit might be drawn from the release of our prisoners at Point Lookout if it can be accomplished," he said. "The number of men employed for this purpose would necessarily be small, as the whole would have to be transported secretly across the Potomac where it is very broad, the means of doing which must first be procured." He offered the services of all the Marylanders in his army, which he thought would be about the right number of men and appropriate units for a raid on Maryland soil. For a leader he suggested Colonel Bradley T. Johnson, also a Marylander, who was at that time reorganizing the Maryland troops up in the Shenandoah Valley. "I have understood that most of the garrison at Point Lookout was composed of negroes," Lee wrote. "I should suppose that the commander of such troops would be poor & feeble. A stubborn resistance, therefore, may not reasonably be expected."

The Marylanders should be suddenly landed on the beach and the guards overpowered, he said. Once liberated, the prisoners would be organized into infantry, cavalry and artillery units, making use of the arms, cannon and horses of their guards and whatever could be captured in the area. "Such a body of men under an able leader, although they might not be able without assistance to capture Washington, could march around it and cross the upper Potomac where fordable," he said. "Provisions, &c., would have to be collected in the country through which they pass." As for the opposition they would meet once they were freed, "at this time, as far as I can learn, all the troops in the control of the United States are being sent to Grant, and little or no opposition could be made by those at Washington."

There was one other subject which Lee commented on. "With relation to the project of Marshal Kane," he wrote, "if the matter can be kept secret, which I fear is impossible, should Genl Early cross the Potomac, he might be sent to join him."[9] Marshall George P. Kane was the former

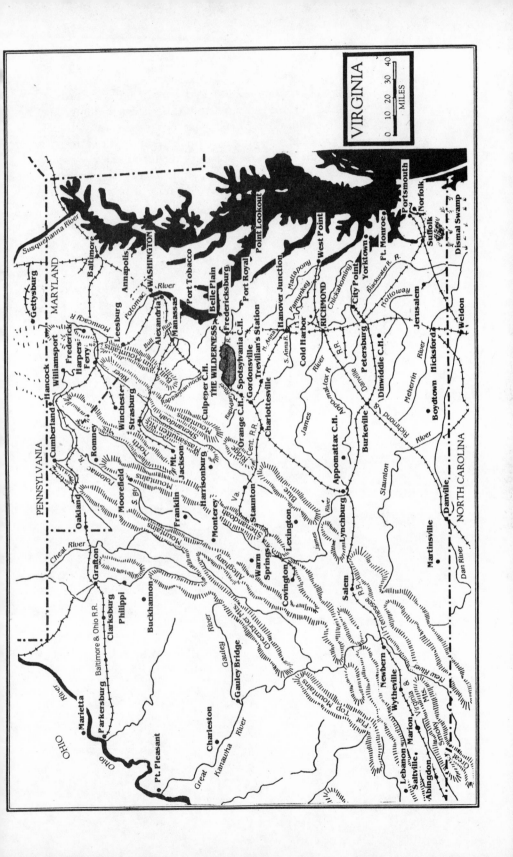

police commissioner of Baltimore. He had been working on some secret project involving Maryland with Brigadier General John Henry Winder, who was provost marshal of Richmond and superintendent of Confederate military prisons. His unnamed matter, which would indeed have been difficult to keep secret if it had actually been accomplished, was quite probably nothing less than the attempted capture of Abraham Lincoln, with the objectives of disrupting the Union war effort and possibly negotiating a favorable peace treaty, or at least trading him for a very large number of Confederate prisoners of war.[10]

---

1. Henry Kyd Douglas, *I Rode With Stonewall* (Chapel Hill, 1940), 280.

2. Stephen Z. Starr, *The Union Cavalry*, 2: 149.

3. Sheridan, *Memoirs*.

4. Starr, *The Union Cavalry*, 2: 183.

5. Ibid., 184.

6. Ibid., 191.

7. Both quotes from Bruce Catton, *A Stillness At Appomattox* (New York, 1957), 220.

8. Douglas, *I Rode With Stonewall*, 280.

9. Dowdey and Manarin, eds., *Wartime Papers of R. E. Lee*, 806–808.

10. William A. Tidwell with James O. Hall and David Winfred Gaddy, *Come Retribution* (Jackson, Miss., 1988), 275.

CHAPTER NINE

It May Be Well That We Become Hardened

26–28 June 1864

Federal wagons and cavalry continued crossing the James River that day, the 26th, while Sheridan went to City Point to report in person to Grant on his expedition to Trevilian Station and back. "He was at all times a welcome visitor at headquarters," Horace Porter wrote, "as his boundless enthusiasm, buoyant spirits, and cheery conversation were always refreshing."[1] Meade wanted the two cavalry divisions to proceed to the army's southwest flank, where they could go to Wilson's assistance, but it would be days before the men and horses could all be ferried across and then march that far. Meanwhile, Hampton's and Fitzhugh Lee's Confederate cavalry divisions were moved to Drewry's Bluff that day, so that the next morning they could set out after Wilson and Kautz.

It was on the next day, the 27th, that Hunter's Army of West Virginia was met by a train of supply wagons sent out to it from the Kanawha Valley with 70,000 rations of hardtack crackers, sugar, coffee and bacon.

Out in southwestern Tennessee that day, A. J. Smith's Federals continued to prepare for an advance against Forrest's Confederates. General
Grierson's cavalry drew its rations and pay and moved eastward along
the track of the Memphis & Charleston Railroad to the village of Saulsbury. A bridge had just been repaired across the Wolf River, allowing
the trains to run as far as that town. Smith's infantry also moved to the
east that day, to the village of La Grange. It was extremely hot and
humid, and many of the men fell behind. General Mower, bringing up
the rear, found many of them "lying by the roadside, overcome with
heat."² He got down from his horse and urged the men to move on
before they were killed or captured by roving bands of Rebels. And by
midnight most of the stragglers had caught up with their units.

General Washburn, commanding the District of West Tennessee, told
Smith that day that "you had better be in no hurry in leaving the line of
railroad with your infantry and artillery." As long as they were keeping
Forrest on the defensive instead of raiding Sherman's supply lines they
were doing good work, he said. Besides, if they could lure Forrest up
to Corinth it would be "a great deal better than to go down to Tupelo
after him."³ But Smith did not believe that Forrest would venture to
attack the Union forces until they had marched south from the railroad
for several days. Therefore he intended to do just that, as soon as he
could get ready. Unfortunately it had been discovered that about half of
his ammunition was worthless and he would have to wait for the railroad
to replenish his supply. Then he would plunge into Forrest's territory.

Sherman's advance through northern Georgia had been hampered by
rain for weeks, but finally the weather seemed to have cleared. Nevertheless, streams were still swollen, roads were still muddy, and movement
was still difficult. The nervous, energetic, red-haired Union commander
had used his larger force to maneuver Joe Johnston's Army of Tennessee
out of one strong position after another by threatening to turn his flanks
and cut his supply line. But for almost a month he had been unable to
get past the Rebels' defenses dug into the mountains and hills north and
west of Marietta. Those defenses were very strong, but at last the Northern commander had made up his mind to assault them anyway. He was
afraid that both the Rebels and his own men were beginning to assume
that he would never attack, only maneuver.

Sherman's force consisted of three armies of unequal size, each named
for a river in its original area of responsibility. Schofield's Army of the
Ohio was the smallest, consisting of only one corps, the 23rd, and
Stoneman's cavalry division. It held the Union right. Thomas' Army of

the Cumberland was the largest, consisting of the 4th, 14th and 20th Corps. It held the center. Major General James B. McPherson's Army of the Tennessee held the left. It consisted of the 15th and 17th Corps and part of the 16th (the rest was with A. J. Smith in Tennessee). This was the army that had once been Grant's and then Sherman's, and it was his favorite.

"My chief source of trouble is with the Army of the Cumberland which is dreadfully slow," Sherman had written to his old friend Grant recently. "A fresh furrow in a plowed field will stop the whole column and all begin to entrench. I have again and again tried to impress on Thomas that we must assail and not defend; we are on the offensive and yet it seems that the whole Army of the Cumberland is so habituated to be on the defensive that from its commander down to its lowest private I cannot get it out of their heads."⁴ Anyway, the recent attempt by Hooker and Schofield to get around the Confederate left had stretched the Rebel lines until they extended for almost ten miles, and Sherman reasoned that they must be thin somewhere. It was this same reasoning that had led Grant to attack Lee at Cold Harbor three weeks before.

Hood's 2nd Corps still held the left of the Confederate line, facing west. Hardee's 1st Corps held the center, also facing west. What had been Polk's Corps (or the Army of Mississippi) was now under the temporary command of Major General W. W. Loring. It held the Rebel right, running along the dual peaks of Big and Little Kenesaw mountains, facing north. The cavalry division of William H. ("Red") Jackson, technically part of the Army of Mississippi, covered the Confederate left flank, while Major General Joseph Wheeler's Cavalry Corps of the Army of Tennessee screened the right flank.

McPherson would attack the southern slopes of Little Kenesaw Mountain from the west while Thomas attacked on his right and Schofield made a feint to the south of the Rebel defenses. "Each attacking column will endeavor to break a single point in the enemy's line," said Sherman's order, "and make a secure lodgement beyond, and be prepared for following it up toward Marietta and the railroad in case of success."⁵ Details were left to the three army commanders. McPherson decided to send three brigades of Major General John A. Logan's 15th Corps against Confederate positions on Pigeon Hill at the southern end of Little Kenesaw Mountain while the other two corps demonstrated against Big Kenesaw, farther east. Thomas selected a salient in the Rebel lines about two and a half miles further south, known as Cheatham's Hill but soon to be called the Dead Angle, as the target for two brigades of the 14th Corps, and the lines just north of the salient as the objective of three brigades of the 4th Corps. Meanwhile Hooker's 20th Corps would threaten the Rebels in its front, as would Garrard's cavalry division off to the east of Kenesaw.

At 6 a.m. on the 27th the left of McPherson's line began advancing in order to tie down the units on the Confederate right. The Rebel skirmishers there were pushed back into their main works, but no real effort was made to take those. From time to time the demonstration would be renewed, and once the Federals managed to occupy the Southern skirmishers' rifle pits at the base of the mountain, but they were pushed back out again.

Pigeon Hill, just south of Kenesaw and the objective of McPherson's real attack, was held by Confederates of Major General Samuel G. French's division. French had noticed an unusual amount of activity across the way among the Federal staff officers that morning. So he and his own staff took position on the brow of the mountain, sheltered by a large rock, where they had a commanding view of the country below. "Presently as if by magic, there sprung from the earth a host of men," French reported. "In one long, wavering line of blue the infantry advanced and the Battle of Kennesaw Mountain began. We sat there perhaps an hour, enjoying a birds eye view of one of the most magnificent sights ever allotted to man—to look down upon a hundred and fifty thousand men arrayed in the strife of battle on the plain below. As the infantry closed in, the blue smoke of muskets marked out our line for miles."[6]

The two brigades of Morgan L. Smith's 2nd Division of Logan's Union 15th Corps, with Walcutt's brigade of the 4th Division, were the troops who attacked French's position. Walcutt's men advanced first because it was thought that the Confederate artillery could not be depressed enough to fire on the route chosen for them. They were slowed by swampy, heavily wooded ground just in front of their own works, then moved up the rocky and uneven slope and drove the Confederate skirmishers from their rifle pits with bayonets and clubbed muskets, capturing about 150 of them. "The Rebels fought with a desperation worthy of a better cause," a Union officer reported.

The Confederates in the main line farther up the slope rolled large stones down the hill and threw rocks at the Federals in addition to firing on them. Some of Walcutt's troops got to within about ten yards of the main Rebel line, but then they "staggered and sought cover as best they could behind logs and rocks."[7] But they were still taking too many losses, so Logan ordered the men to fall back to the protection of the captured rifle pits. Even there, all they could do was hug the ground. "It was almost sure death to take your face out of the dust," one of them remembered. "It was only necessary to expose a hand to procure a furlough," another said.[8] General French said that the Yankees "recoiled under the fire, swung around into a steep valley, where exposed to fire from right to left flank, they seemed to melt away or sink into the earth, to rise no more."[9]

Cheatham's Hill, or the Dead Angle, farther south, was manned by two Tennessee regiments. Sam Watkins was a private in one of them. For more than a week Federal artillery had been knocking down their earthworks, but they put them back together again every night. Watkins remembered that "on the fatal morning of June 27th, the sun rose clear and cloudless, the heavens seemed made of brass, and the earth of iron, and as the sun began to mount toward the zenith, everything became quiet, and no sound was heard save a peckerwood on a neighboring tree, tapping on its old trunk, trying to find a worm for his dinner. We all knew it was but the calm that precedes the storm." In the distance the Federals could be seen making their preparations. "We could hear but the rumbling sound of heavy guns, and the distant tread of a marching army, as a faint roar of the coming storm, which was soon to break the ominous silence with the sound of conflict, such as was scarcely ever before heard on earth. It seemed that the arch-angel of Death stood and looked on with outstretched wings, while all the earth was silent, when all at once a hundred guns from the Federal line opened upon us, and for more than an hour they poured their solid and chain shot, grape and shrapnel right upon this salient point, defended by our regiment alone, when, all of a sudden, our pickets jumped into our works and reported the Yankees advancing, and almost at the same time a solid line of blue coats came up the hill."[10]

These Federals were Harker's 3rd Brigade of the 2nd Division of Howard's 4th Corps, and the 2nd and 3rd Brigades of the 2nd Division of Palmer's 14th Corps. They went forward in compact columns of regiments that reached the very parapets of the Southern works. "Talk about other battles, victories, shouts, cheers, and triumphs," Watkins wrote after the war, "but in comparison with this day's fight, all others dwarf into insignificance. The sun beaming down on our uncovered heads, the thermometer being one hundred and ten degrees in the shade, and a solid line of blazing fire right from the muzzles of the Yankee guns being poured right into our very faces, singeing our hair and clothes, the hot blood of our dead and wounded spurting on us, the blinding smoke and stifling atmosphere filling our eyes and mouths, and the awfull concussion causing the blood to gush out of our noses and ears, and above all, the roar of battle, made it a perfect pandemonium."[11] Here also the Federals were repulsed, although a few reached the Rebel works. Two Union brigade commanders, Harker and Colonel Daniel McCook, were killed. The latter, one of fourteen "fighting McCook's" in the Northern army, had been Sherman's law partner before the war. The Yankees began to dig in within thirty yards of the Rebel line and even began to tunnel toward Cheatham's position, planning to blow it up in the same manner—unknown to them—that Pleasants' men planned to use at Petersburg.

A half-mile north of the Dead Angle, two brigades of Newton's 2nd Division of the 4th Corps attacked part of Cleburne's Division of Hardee's Corps, arguably the best troops in the Army of Tennessee. Gunfire set the brush on fire between the lines, threatening to roast wounded Federals where they lay. Confederate Colonel William H. Martin jumped up on the breastworks with a white flag and shouted to the Northerners that his men would hold their fire while the flames were put out. A Federal officer presented Martin with a brace of pistols for his brave and generous act. The fire was extinguished as soldiers from both sides carried and dragged the wounded men to safety. Then they went back to their previous positions and resumed killing and maiming each other. A few Northerners again reached the Rebel works, but the Union columns could not break the Southern line here either. The colors of the 27th Illinois were captured after being planted on the Confederate parapet.

By 11:30 a.m. the assaults had all ground to a halt. Watching from near the left of his line, Sherman knew that McPherson's attack had been stopped, but he was willing to order it renewed if it would help Thomas. "I will order the assault if you think you can succeed at any point," Sherman told him. But Thomas replied, "We have already lost heavily today without gaining any material advantage. One or two more such assaults would use up this army."[12] So Sherman resigned himself to a resumption of his former turning movements.

In fact, the day before the fight one brigade, Byrd's, of Schofield's small army, had crossed Olley's Creek on the Union right. Early on the 27th another brigade, Cameron's, joined it. Both were part of Jacob D. Cox's 3rd Division. Byrd's skirmishers moved northeastward, fighting with the Rebels who defended the creek in that area, while Cameron's troops went in the opposite direction and attacked the flank of a brigade of Texas cavalry defending the Sandtown Road where it crossed over the creek. Cox's remaining brigade, Reilly's, had been facing this force, but one of its regiments was sent farther southwest and took another crossing, threatening the Texans' other flank. About 8 a.m., just as the main attacks were going in farther north, the Rebel cavalrymen retreated southward down the Sandtown Road. Reilly's and Cameron's brigades followed them about a mile until they came to the valley of Nickajack Creek, where they stopped and began entrenching. This put the Federal right closer to the Chattahoochee River—the final barrier before Atlanta—than Johnston's army was, thus threatening the Confederates' lines of supply.

The day's attacks had been costly experiments in the direct assault of well-prepared field fortifications. Sherman probably lost about 3,000 men, killed, wounded and missing, while Johnston's losses were possibly 750. But both armies now knew that Sherman would fight. Joe Johnston acknowledged the courage of the Federals in his postwar memoirs: "The characteristic fortitude of the northwestern soldiers held them under a close and destructive fire long after reasonable hope of success was gone."[13] Or as Sam Watkins heard one Rebel say, "Hell had broke loose in Georgia, sure enough."[14] In his report, Sherman told Halleck, "The attack I made was no mistake, I had to do it. The enemy and our own army and officers had settled down into the conviction that the assault formed no part of my game, and the moment the enemy was found behind anything like a parapet, why, everybody would deploy, throwing up counter-works, and take it easy, leaving it to 'the old man' to turn the position."[15]

The next day, "details from both Armies were made and gathered up the dead, of which there were a great many, and at suitable places buried them," a Union private recorded. "The Confederates in one, our men in another big grave—side by side, wrapped in their blankets. Our graves were marked by a piece of board from hard tack boxes with name, Company, and Regt where we could make them out—which we could not always do. Their watches or other articles of value taken charge of by an officer to be sent home. A prayer was made by a Chaplain of either Army and the graves filled up. After this was done we filled in the rest of the time allowed with visiting between the officers and men of both Armies, all showing kindly interest in each other. When the gun was fired that announced the truce was ended we parted with expressions of good will such as:

"'I hope to miss you, Yank, if I happen to shoot in your direction,' or 'May I never hit you Johnny if we fight again.' All went back to their lines and in a short time the pickets were merrily popping away at each other."[16]

A day or so later, Sherman wrote to his wife that "it is enough to make the whole world start at the awful amount of death and destruction that now stalks abroad . . . I begin to regard the death and mangling of a couple of thousand men as a small affair, a kind of morning dash—and it may be well that we become hardened . . . The worst of the war is not yet begun."[17]

1. Porter, *Campaigning With Grant,* 228.
2. Bearss, *Forrest at Brice's Cross Roads,* 151.
3. Ibid., 152.
4. Lewis, *Sherman: Fighting Prophet,* 376.
5. James Lee McDonough and James Pickett Jones, *War So Terrible* (New York, 1987), p. 185.
6. Scaife, *The Campaign For Atlanta,* 42.
7. McDonough and Jones, *War So Terrible,* 186.
8. Ibid.
9. Scaife, *Campaign For Atlanta,* 42.
10. Sam Watkins, *Co. Aytch* (New York, 1962), 158.
11. Ibid.
12. McDonough and Jones, *War So Terrible,* 188.
13. Ibid., 190.
14. Watkins, *Co. Aytch,* 158.
15. Lewis, *Sherman's Fighting Prophet,* 378.
16. Earl Schenck Miers, *The General Who Marched to Hell* (New York, 1951), 132.
17. Lewis, *Sherman: Fighting Prophet,* 379.

CHAPTER TEN

I Shall Lose No Time

28 June–3 July 1864

At dawn on the 28th of June, Major General John B. Gordon's division, now part of Breckinridge's ad hoc corps, led Jubal Early's infantry northward out of Staunton on the Valley Turnpike. The rest followed about noon. Shoes had still not arrived from Richmond, but each man carried two days' worth of rations, and their spirits were high. They marched a mere ten miles that day, stopping at the village of Mount Sidney. The cavalry took a parallel road farther west, watching the passes through the Alleghenies just in case some of Hunter's Yankees should try to return to the Shenandoah that way.

For two days Wilson's and Kautz's troopers had been trying to get back to the safety of the Union lines near Petersburg. They had seen little of Rooney Lee's Rebels but these were known to be keeping up along parallel roads farther north. The countryside that the Federals passed through had not previously been touched by the war, so foraging was very productive and the men and horses had plenty to eat. But the heat was deadly. It was "so terrible," one trooper wrote, "that we had to move very slowly, yet fast enough to keep out of the way of the enemy." He added that "horses were continually staggering & falling with the heat." In fact, he said, "if it had not been that we were continually capturing horses fully half of the command would have been dismounted; as it was a number were now footing it." The runaway slaves who had joined the column were also getting to be a problem. "Such an army had they almost become that Wilson had appointed Officers to take charge of them, and now they were marching by fours in column," the same trooper noted.[1]

Some of these escaped slaves told Wilson that there was only a small force of Rebels at Stony Creek Depot on the Weldon & Petersburg Railroad, so he decided to take the shorter route northeastward through that point rather than continue eastward to Jarrett's Station farther south on the same line. He sent a small detachment ahead on the 28th to secure the place, and it managed to get across Stony Creek, but two miles west of the railroad, at Sappony Church, it ran into Chambliss' Brigade of Rooney Lee's cavalry, reinforced by 200 infantrymen. As his units reached the front, Wilson committed them to the attack piecemeal, but even when he had his full force in the fight, which lasted until mighnight of June 28–29, he could not budge the Confederates. Rebels taken prisoner divulged the information that Hampton's and Fitz Lee's full divisions had arrived from north of the James. Still reluctant to take the longer route farther south, at midnight Wilson ordered Kautz to march ten miles to the north and try to connect with the Union infantry, which he assumed was in the neighborhood of Ream's Station since he did not know that the infantry's move to that point had been repulsed days before. Wilson would stay at Sappony Church with his own division to delay the Southern horsemen until daylight, then would follow Kautz north.

Before dawn, word reached Wilson that the route to Ream's Station was open, so he ordered his two brigades to disengage from the enemy and to take the road north. Colonel John B. McIntosh's 1st Brigade was holding the front line, while Colonel George H. Chapman's 2nd Brigade was about 600 yards further back, behind improvised breastworks. The latter was to stay in place as a rear guard until McIntosh's men had withdrawn through its position, then to fall in behind them. McIntosh's exhausted troopers managed to pull out in fairly good order, but they made enough noise to alert the Confederates. Chambliss promptly attacked Chapman in the front, left, and rear, and drove a wedge between his brigade and McIntosh's. The Rebels also captured many of Chapman's men and separated most of the rest of them from their horses. The colonel himself had a narrow escape, and he had only 300 men still with him when they caught up with McIntosh about noon. The road was filled with stragglers, and panic was in the air. "I plainly saw that the whole Division was disorganized, one great & principal cause being the want of confidence felt in our Commanding General," one trooper wrote. "The feeling against him was bitter in the extreme."[2]

Shortly after sending Wilson the word that the road was clear to Ream's Station, Kautz discovered that the area around the station was held not by Federal infantry, but by two brigades of Mahone's Rebel foot soldiers backed up by artillery. These Confederates promptly charged Kautz's front regiment but were driven back by a skillful counter attack. However, Kautz concluded that he could not break through and that his only hope was to entrench and to try to hold out until rescued by the Army of the Potomac. Captain Edward W. Whitaker of Wilson's staff volunteered to try to get through the Rebel lines to carry word to Meade of the cavalry's predicament.

At midday, as Chapman's remnant was catching up with McIntosh, the latter caught up with Kautz in the swampy woods and fields west of Ream's Station. But the Confederate cavalry had also moved north, and the Federals found themselves surrounded on three sides. Hampton's cavalry was to the south, Mahone's infantry to the east and northeast, and Rooney Lee's and his cousin Fitz Lee's cavalry divisions to the northeast and north. Rashly, Wilson ordered McIntosh "to take the First Brigade and force the enemy's lines."[3] After a careful reconnaissance, however, McIntosh reported that an attack would be futile, and finally Wilson faced the fact that he could not get back to the army by this route and would have to retreat quickly before he was completely surrounded. To make the getaway easier, he ordered that the troops should be issued enough ammunition to fill their cartridge boxes and then the supply wagons should be burned. The ambulances and wagons full of wounded men were parked near a stream to be left, under the charge of the surgeons, to be surrendered to the Rebels.

Wilson decided to move due west about five miles to the Stage Road, then south to the Nottaway River, and then finally east by way of Jarratt's Station after all. Chapman led the way with what was left of his brigade. McIntosh was about to follow when he was attacked by the Rebel infantry, which was trying to encircle the Yankees. McIntosh left two regiments, the 2nd Ohio and 5th New York, with a battery of horse artillery, to hold what had been his front and used the other two, the 1st Connecticut and the 2nd New York, to block the Southern infantry. These latter regiments succeeded in getting away to the west with Chapman's remnant, while the other two joined forces with Kautz's division.

Kautz found he was being attacked from three directions. The only side left open "was very swampy, and any person looking at it would judge it impossible for the cavalry to push themselves through such a tangled, swampy jungle. But it was our only chance," our Union trooper noted. As the Federals entered the swamp they saw Kautz sitting with a "leg thrown over his horse's neck, and seemingly as cool as though the situation were perfectly agreeable," the trooper noted.⁴ Kautz's column got safely through the swamp, turned east around the south flank of the Rebel force, and crossed the railroad south of Ream's Station. After a seven-hour ride, with many of the men asleep in the saddle, Kautz reached the safety of the Union lines around 9:30 p.m.

Wilson's remaining command contained only two regiments that had retained their organization, the 1st Vermont and the 1st New Hampshire, and these took the lead, followed by hundreds of men on foot, stragglers, details, provost guards, and about 1,200 escaped slaves. They reached the Stage Road and marched south in a suffocating cloud of dust. As this force was crossing Stony Creek, Fitzhugh Lee's cavalry division attacked its rear. Panic struck the column, and the bridge became filled with a mass of men, black and white, mounted and afoot. Many were pushed over the sides into the stream or onto the rocks below. "It would appear," our trooper reported, "that the rebel cavalry would leave pursuing a 'Yankee' at any time for the pleasure of shooting down a negro, and our boys saw them shot down like so many mad dogs." That is, the men were shot. "The women and children were made prisoners," he said, "after being beaten & abused most shamefully; many were knocked senseless by a stroke from the back of a sabre, or a stroke from the butt of a gun."⁵ It wasn't until after midnight that Wilson was able to call a halt, having put the Nottaway and the railroad behind him. After a two-hour rest, the retreat was resumed at dawn on the thirtieth, along an obscure and hard-to-follow road through unbroken forest.

Far to the west, Hunter's small army reached Charleston, West Virginia, that day, and the Union general began to seize all the light draft transports he could find on the Kanawha River, since it s water level was low, for a trip down that river and up the Ohio in order to return to the lower Shenandoah Valley. In the Shenandoah, Gordon's Division again took the lead as Early's Army of the Valley, as he now styled it, continued its northeastward march. Early gave orders for the pace to be slackened, however. His Confederates were now approaching the part of the Valley that could be expected to contain Federal garrisons, and he didn't want to blunder into an ambush. But none were encountered, and the Rebels marched on through New Market, where Breckinridge had bested Sigel, Hunter's predecessor, six weeks before. That evening the leading units camped near Hawkinstown and the rest of the troops bivouacked two miles back, near Mount Jackson. Early sent a message to Lee saying, "If you can continue to threaten Grant I hope to be able to do something for your relief and the success of our cause shortly. I shall lose no time."⁶

Early's little army was heading straight for a weakly protected North that was already beginning to despair over the stalemate of Grant's advance against Richmond and Sherman's against Atlanta, and especially over the terrible cost of both in lives and treasure. The price of gold was at an all-time high, showing that the nation's confidence in the government's paper money, and thus in the government itself and its future, was at an all-time low. The national debt had reached $1,700,000,000; the war was costing $2,000,000 a day, and the Treasury was almost empty.

On that thirtieth day of June, the Federal secretary of the treasury, Salmon P. Chase, presented his resignation to President Lincoln. It was the fourth time he had tendered it and he probably expected that it would not be the last. But it was. To his surprise, Lincoln accepted it. The immediate cause for this latest resignation was the president's failure to back Chase on the choice of an assistant treasurer at New York. As for Lincoln's reasons for accepting it, Chase put his own theory in his diary: "I am too earnest, too anti-slavery, and, say, too radical, to make the President willing to have me connected with the Administration, just as my opinion is that he is not earnest enough, not anti-slavery enough, not radical enough."[7]

Lincoln did not particularly like the ambitious, sanctimonious Chase, whom he described as "never perfectly happy unless he is thoroughly miserable, and able to make everyone else just as uncomfortable as he is."[8] But he had often, for the good of the country, put up with many men whom he did not like personally or professionally. It was more probable that Lincoln felt the need to make some kind of change in an effort to bolster public confidence. The president named David Tod, an old Douglas Democrat and former governor of Ohio, to succeed Chase, but the Senate Finance Committee promptly protested, and Tod wired that his health would not permit him to accept.

The next morning, 1 July, when Senator William Pitt Fessenden of Maine, chairman of the Finance Committee, called at the White House to recommend someone else for the job, Lincoln smilingly informed him that he had already nominated, and the Senate had already confirmed, Fessenden himself for the position that very morning. Fessenden protested that he did not want the job, but Lincoln said he would have to refuse it in public, or not at all. The senator then hurried over to the Capitol in an attempt to withdraw his name, but he was too late, and seeing that he had been outmaneuvered, he reluctantly accepted the job. His appointment soon proved to be the most popular that Lincoln had made, with the possible exception of that of Grant to be general-in-chief. "Men went about with smiling faces at the news," one newspaper reported.[9] "It is very singular," the president observed, "considering that this appointment of F.'s is so popular when made, that no one ever mentioned his name to me for that place."[10]

The first day of July was cool and damp in the Shenandoah as Early's Army of the Valley continued its northward march. That evening his men bivouacked around Fisher's Hill, a strong defensive position just southwest of Strasburg that would become famous a couple of months later. The Confederates had still encountered no Federal opposition.

Benjamin Jeffrey Sweet was colonel of the 8th Regiment of the Veterans Reserve Corps, an organization of wounded Union soldiers who performed rear-area garrison duties so as to free able-bodied men for the front. Sweet was the commandant of Camp Douglas, a camp for Confederate prisoners of war in Chicago, and it was not an easy job. He was in charge of almost 5,000 Rebels, who were confined to an area of 70 acres surrounded only by a 12-foot-high fence made of one-inch boards, and there were too few guards. There was also too little food. Sweet was aware of this, but higher headquarters would not provide more. In fact, two dogs had recently disappeared among the hungry prisoners. Sweet's clerk informed him that some captured Texas Rangers had even put the animals' bones and hides to use in a stew.

Camp Douglas was a powderkeg just waiting to explode, and Sweet knew it. When his clerk informed him that letter-writing had suddenly picked up in the last few weeks he became suspicious, especially after he discovered that the letters were all written on long sheets of paper but had only a few lines of writing on each page. Finally he found that by holding the sheets up to the heat of his stove he could read additional lines written in invisible ink. Thus he discovered that the prisoners were all writing home to say that an uprising was planned for the Fourth of July. Under cover of the crowds drawn to the city by the Democratic party's national convention, Copperheads and Confederate agents would help the prisoners break out. Sweet asked for reinforcements but was told that none were available. So his guards took to sleeping with their rifles. Only when the Democratic convention was rescheduled for late August was Colonel Sweet able to relax—for a while.

On the first day of July, the Supreme Grand Council of the Order of the Sons of Liberty met in Chicago and conferred with the Confederacy's top secret agent, Captain Tom Hines, who had come down from Canada to meet them at the Richmond House hotel. They had been shaken by Confederate raider John Hunt Morgan's recent defeat in Kentucky—a key state in their plans. "Morgan was too soon," one of the Copperhead leaders said; "we were not ready for him."[11] Evidently they were still not ready. They asked to postpone the date of their planned uprising to 20 July, and Hines had little choice but to agree.

In the early hours of 1 July Wilson's cavalry, or such of it as remained with the general, reached Blunt's Bridge over the Big Black River. The bridge had been burned, but Wilson was a trained engineer. His hasty repairs made it usable, and by daylight the Union horsemen had crossed over. Wilson stayed until the last man had crossed and personally set fire to the span. When it was thoroughly engulfed in flames he saw a lone Confederate officer ride up to the far side. "Good-bye, boys," the Rebel shouted, "I am sorry to see you safely over."[12] Wilson waved in return and rode away. That afternoon the Federals finally came to the end of their long sojourn, and they went into camp near Fort Powhatan on the James River. For the first time in ten days the horses were unsaddled, picketed, and fed, and the men were allowed to have a full night's rest. Wilson himself fell asleep in the middle of a dispatch he was writing to headquarters to announce his safe, if harried, return. He slept for twenty hours.

Captain Whitaker of his staff had made it through Rebel lines and had reached Meade's headquarters two days before, but the rescue efforts his report had set in motion came too late to be of any help. Kautz's arrival later that same day had increased the anxiety for Wilson's remaining command but little was done to help him. When Sheridan had been urged to take the rest of his corps and save Wilson he replied, "My horses are worn out. Some of them have been without forage for forty-eight hours." He indicated that he thought it "best to keep open the roads leading to the south, so that small parties can come in as they are now doing."[13] In his memoirs, Sheridan said, "Wilson's retreat from the perilous situation at Ream's station was a most creditable performance—in the face of two brigades of infantry and three divisions of cavalry—and in the conduct of the whole expedition the only criticism that can hold against him is that he placed too much reliance on meeting our infantry at Ream's station, seeing that uncontrollable circumstances might, and did, prevent its being there."[14]

A Richmond newspaper accused Wilson's troopers of stealing not only horses and negroes on their raid, but also silverware and other private property. When Meade saw this his short-fuse temper went off and he demanded an explanation from Wilson. The cavalryman denied the charges and said he hoped Meade wasn't going to condemn him just because he had stirred up the ire of the nation's enemies. Meade eventually cooled off and accepted Wilson's explanation, but the incident brought up the subject of Meade's irrascibility at Grant's headquarters again.

Assistant Secretary of War Charles A. Dana was still with Grant, and he recorded that "there was an unusual amount of controversy going on among the officers. Smith was berated generally for failing to complete his attack of June 15th. Butler and 'Baldy' Smith were deep in a controversial correspondence; and Meade and Warren were so at loggerheads that Meade notified Warren that he must either ask to be relieved as corps commander or he (Meade) would prefer charges against him. It seemed as if Meade grew more unpopular every day. Finally the difficulties between him and his subordinates became so serious that a change in the commander of the Army of the Potomac seemed probable. Grant had great confidence in Meade, and was much attached to him personally; but the almost universal dislike of Meade which prevailed among officers of every rank who came in contact with him, and the difficulty of doing business with him, felt by every one except Grant himself, so greatly impaired his capacities for usefulness and rendered success under his command so doubtful that Grant seemed to be coming to the conviction that he must be relieved."

Dana himself did not care much for Meade. "I had long known Meade to be a man of the worst possible temper," he wrote, "especially toward his subordinates. I think he had not a friend in the whole army. No man, no matter what his business or his service, approached him without being insulted in one way or another, and his own staff officers did not dare to speak to him unless first spoken to, for fear of either sneers or curses. The latter, however, I had never heard him indulge in very violently, but he was said to apply them often without occasion and without reason. At the same time, as far as I was able to ascertain, his generals had lost their confidence in him as a commander . . . General Wright remarked confidentially to a friend that all of Meade's attacks had been made without brains and without generalship. . . . Grant expressed himself quite frankly as to the general trouble with Meade, and his fear that it would become necessary to relieve him. In that event, he said, it would be necessary to put Hancock in command."[15]

However, it was not Meade but Butler whom Grant tried to displace. He wrote a letter to Halleck that day in which he spoke of "the necessity of sending General Butler to another field of duty." Grant hoped that a suitable command might be found for him in Kentucky or Mississippi. Although Butler "has always been prompt in his obedience to orders from me and clear in his understanding of them," and although Grant "would not be willing to recommend his retirement," the man was an impediment to operations against Petersburg and Richmond.[16] The next day, 2 July, Grant received a letter from Baldy Smith asking for a brief leave. In it he also teed off on Butler, saying he could not understand "how you can place a man in command of two army corps who is as helpless as a child on the field of battle and as visionary as an opium eater in council."[17]

That same second day of July, Lee was also requesting permission to make a change in his command set-up. Since the death of his cavalry commander, Jeb Stuart, in a clash with Sheridan's troopers in mid-May, each of his three cavalry divisions had been reporting directly to headquarters. But now Lee had decided upon a successor for Stuart. "You know the high opinion I entertain of Genl Hampton," he wrote to President Davis that day, "and my appreciation of his character and services. In his late expedition he has displayed both energy and good conduct, and although I have feared that he might not have that activity and endurance so necessary in a cavalry commander, and so eminently possessed by Genl Stuart, yet should you be unable to assign anyone to the command of the cavalry in this army whom you deem possessed of higher qualifications, I request authority to place him in the command."[18]

In the Shenandoah Valley that day, a Saturday, Early's troops were on the road once more. Gordon's Division led again, moving rapidly, but Early and his staff rode on ahead. By 11 a.m. he had reached the village of Winchester, where he, and then his troops, received a royal welcome from the citizenry. At last Early received intelligence of Union forces in the area. Forty miles down the turnpike was the village of Martinsburg, and there Federal General Franz Sigel, whom Breckinridge had defeated at New Market back in May, commanded a garrison too small to stand up to Early's Army of the Valley. Another small garrison held Harper's Ferry, farther east, where the Shenandoah River empties into the Potomac. Also that day, Early received a dispatch from Lee urging him to clear the Yankees out of the lower Valley and to break the Baltimore & Ohio Railroad before crossing the Potomac into Maryland. That would cut off Hunter and any other Federal troops west of the Shenandoah and secure Early from interference from that direction once he moved on toward Washington.

Early promptly formed a plan that would take care of the railroad and Sigel as well. McCausland was called to the new headquarters in Winchester and told to take his cavalry brigade through the Allegheny Mountains into the valley of Black Creek. He was to follow the creek to where it empties into the Potomac and there to burn the bridge that carried the Baltimore & Ohio over it. Then he was to follow the tracks southeastward to North Mountain Depot, and from there to take the highway leading to Martinsburg from the north. He would then be squarely across Sigel's line of retreat, and he was to hold that road until he received further orders. Meanwhile, Early would try to see to it that Sigel would need his line of retreat in the very near future. Soon after sunset the Rebel troopers filed out of camp.

Down in Georgia that evening, 2 July, McPherson's Union Army of the Tennessee was quietly drawn out of its entrenchments on the left of Sherman's line and replaced by the dismounted troopers of Garrard's cavalry division. The three corps of infantry moved to the south behind the defenses of Thomas' Army of the Cumberland and joined Schofield's Army of the Ohio on the Federal right, south of Olley's Creek. "By this movement I think I can force Johnston to move his whole army down from Kenesaw to defend his railroad and the Chattahoochee," Sherman reported to Halleck.[19] At first light, Sherman was peering through a tripod-mounted telescope that one of his officers had set up nearby. "I directed the glass on Kenesaw, and saw some of our pickets crawling up the hill cautiously; soon they stood upon the very top, and I could plainly see their movements as they ran along the crest just abandoned by the enemy."[20] Johnston had foreseen the Federal's move and had pulled out of his Kenesaw line that same night, falling back to defenses that had already been prepared farther south at Smyrna. Now that the rains had stopped, the flanking maneuvers were in full swing again. "Sherman'll never go to hell," a Rebel prisoner brought in by the 103rd Illinois complained. "He will flank the devil and make heaven in spite of the guards."[21]

On the morning of Sunday, 3 July, more of Jubal Early's cavalry was on the move in the Shenandoah Valley. Colonel Bradley Johnson—the same Maryland officer whom Lee had mentioned as a potential commander for the raid on Point Lookout—had recently been put in charge of the brigade of cavalry that had been commanded by Grumble Jones until that general had been killed at the battle of Piedmont a few weeks before. Johnson was under orders from Early to march his brigade north, circle to the east of Martinsburg, and unite with McCausland at Hainesville, on Sigel's route of retreat to the Potomac. These two cavalry brigades would constitute the trap. Gordon's small corps of infantry would have the job of driving Sigel's Yankees into it by advancing directly up the road against their Martinsburg positions. Early himself would take the other two infantry divisions, Rodes' and Ramseur's, and follow John-

son's route to the east of Martinsburg, thus preventing Sigel from retreating eastward to Harper's Ferry instead of northward into the trap.
It was an excellent plan, worthy of Stonewall Jackson himself. There
was only one problem with it: Sigel refused to cooperate. A little after
6 a.m. Federal colonel James Mulligan, with a detachment of the 23rd
Illinois, ran into Bradley Johnson's Rebel cavalry near Leetown. When
Mulligan reported this encounter to Sigel he received orders to fall back
slowly to the east, through Kearneysville, to Shepherdstown on the Potomac. Sigel wanted Mulligan to buy time for him to concentrate his
forces and to evacuate as much as possible of the supplies stored at
Martinsburg. Then word arrived at Sigel's headquarters of the approach
of Breckinridge's infantry along the Valley Turnpike. Sigel loaded what
he could onto wagons and railroad cars and sent them, not northward
into Early's trap, but eastward toward Shepherdstown. He followed
them with his troops, about 5,000 men, leaving behind large warehouses
stacked with supplies that there had not been time to move.

It was now a contest between Mulligan's attempt to hold open the
road to Shepherdstown for Sigel and Johnson's effort to block it. Sigel
sent reinforcements of mounted and dismounted cavalry and two cannon
to help Mulligan, and with these the Union colonel not only stopped
Johnson's advance but counterattacked. The Rebel troopers broke, and
Johnson had to retreat to Leetown. There he found Ramseur's infantry
already in camp after a march of 24 miles. Their presence put an end to
Mulligan's advance, but the Federals withdrew unmolested. Early knew
his infantrymen were too exhausted after their day's march to take on
Mulligan's mixed force, so he settled down for the night at Leestown
while Sigel's wagons and troops retreated safely across the Potomac.

It fell to the lot of Gordon's Division to occupy Martinsburg. The
town's bulging warehouses, depot, and express office—Sigel's men had
been preparing for a festive Fourth of July—must have reminded the
veterans of the time they and Stonewall Jackson had captured the Federal
supply base at Manassas Junction during the Second Bull Run campaign.
However, Gordon also remembered that orgy of gluttony and its threat
to the army's discipline, and he placed guards on all the supplies. But it
was impossible to completely thwart so many wily old soldiers driven
by hunger and a long forced abstinence from such delicacies as were now
almost within reach. By the time the Rebels marched out the next
morning, much of the Union supplies had disappeared into gray-clad
stomachs.

1. Starr, *The Union Cavalry*, 2:193.
2. Ibid., 2:198.
3. Ibid., 2:199.
4. Ibid., 2:201.
5. Ibid., 2:202.
6. Vandiver, *Jubal's Raid*, 74.
7. Sandburg, *Abraham Lincoln*, 546.
8. Foote, *The Civil War*, 3:463.
9. Ibid.
10. Sandburg, *Abraham Lincoln*, 548.
11. James D. Horan, *Confederate Agent* (New York, 1954), 104.
12. Edward G. Longacre, "Wilson-Kautz Raid," *Civil War Times Illustrated*, May 1970, 42.
13. Starr, *The Union Cavalry*, 2:204.
14. Sheridan, *Memoirs*, 1:444–445.
15. Charles A. Dana, *Recollections of the Civil War* (New York, 1963), 200–202.
16. Catton, *Grant Takes Command*, 326–327.
17. Ibid., 330.
18. Dowdey and Manarin, eds., *Wartime Papers of R. E. Lee*, 813.
19. Sherman, *Memoirs*, 2:62.
20. Ibid.
21. McDonough and Jones, *War So Terrible*, 190.

CHAPTER ELEVEN

Mine Eyes Have Beheld the Promised Land

3–7 July 1864

Near Charleston, South Carolina, at dawn that third day of July, Federal troops from Morris Island, along the outer fringes of the harbor, landed from barges and assaulted Fort Johnson, which was situated on James Island along the southern shore of the harbor, between its entrance and the city. But the attack failed, and about 140 Union soldiers were captured. At the same time, about 5,000 Northerners invaded James Island from the south, but over the next two days they were driven to the banks of the Stono River under cover of the guns of the Union navy.

Down in west-central Mississippi that day, the Federal commander of the Vicksburg garrison, Major General Henry W. Slocum, crossed the Big Black River, heading east toward Jackson, the state capital, with 2,200 infantry and 600 cavalry. Here was one more problem for the outnumbered Rebels of S. D. Lee's Confederate Department of Alabama, Mississippi and East Louisiana.

In Virginia that day, Lee was writing to President Davis about the expedition to release the prisoners of war at Point Lookout, Maryland. "I send today an officer to Gen. Early to inform him that an effort will be made to release the prisoners about the 12 Inst: & if successful he will certainly know it through Northern Sources. In that event, if circumstances permit he must send down a brigade of Cavy with Genls. Gordon and Lewis to command & lead around Washington the prisoners."[1] The same day, the third, a party of about 130 Confederate marines and 150 seamen departed Richmond heading south toward the South's largest remaining port on the Atlantic coast, Wilmington, North Carolina.

Across the lines, Grant was also seeking ways to strike offensively. He asked Meade that day, "Do you think it possible, by a bold and decisive attack, to break through the enemy's center, say in General Warren's front somewhere?" But he didn't want a hasty, make-shift affair. "We would want full preparations made in advance so there should be no balk." The alternative would be another strike at the railroads. "If it is not attempted we will have to give you an army sufficient to meet most of Lee's forces and march around Petersburg and come in from above," he said. "This probably could not be done before the arrival of the Nineteenth Corps."[2] Meade looked into the possibilities, but reported that an assault in the near future was out of the question. In the longer run there was the mine that Burnside was digging, but he wasn't very optimistic about that either.

Until 3 July Grant and Meade had not realized that Early had marched down the Shenandoah Valley. They had thought the Confederate 2nd Corps had returned to Lee's army after chasing Hunter away from Lynchburg, leaving only Breckinridge's old command in the Valley. But that day word reached Grant from Washington that something was up. Rumor had it that 20,000 to 30,000 Rebels were coming down the Valley. Grant informed Halleck that if the Confederates crossed the Potomac, "I can send an army corps from here to meet them or cut off their return south."[3] Later Halleck replied that although Hunter was not yet in position to oppose the Rebel thrust, he was approaching. Halleck thought it would suffice for Grant to send to Washington all his dismounted cavalrymen, who could eventually pick up some horses while they were there. At midnight, however, Grant ordered Meade to send not only the dismounted troopers, but a good infantry division as well.

In Georgia, after seeing his men scramble up Kenesaw Mountain, Sherman rode into Marietta and found it already occupied by Thomas' infantry. He called for his cavalry to find out what had become of the retreating Confederates. "Where's Gar'd?" he roared. "Where in hell's Gar'd?" Eventually General Garrard appeared with the explanation that he had been delayed while organizing his column. "Get out of here quick!" Sherman told him. "What shall I do?" the startled cavalryman asked. "Don't make a damned bit of difference, so you get out of here and go for the rebs," came the reply. Sherman hoped to catch Johnston's army in the process of crossing the final major barrier between him and Atlanta, for "no general such as he would invite battle with the Chattahoochie behind him."[4] And he told Thomas, "We will never have such a chance again."[5] But the wily Rebel had fooled him this time, and late that day was found in his defenses at Smyrna, inviting attack. However, Sherman was not ready to repeat the carnage of Kenesaw Mountain. Sam Watkins of the 1st Tennessee said he could not remember a more severe artillery duel than the one that then commemorated the Fourth of July for both sides. But the infantry did not charge. Again Sherman moved around Johnston's flank, sending McPherson to threaten the Confederate left. That night, Johnston fell back again.

One year before, on the Fourth of July, 1863, Vicksburg had surrendered to Grant and Lee had begun his retreat from Gettysburg. But no such dramatic events marked Independence Day in 1864. In the Shenandoah, Early's Confederates moved eastward from Martinsburg through Charlestown and Halltown, and by 9 a.m. they were in sight of Bolivar Heights, a long ridge protecting Harper's Ferry on the west. Ramseur's Division deployed on the left to cut the Baltimore & Ohio Railroad, while Rodes' Division followed the road directly toward the ridge. The Federal garrison was too small to hold the heights against two full divisions, so it retired to an inner line of defenses.

The town of Harper's Ferry occupies a triangle of land with the Shenandoah River on the southeast side and the Potomac on the northeast, the two flowing together at its eastern point. When Early looked down on the village from the ridge that formed the northwestern side of the triangle, he could see not only the Union earthworks barring his path but, on the north side of the Potomac, Maryland Heights, the highest ground around, bristling with heavy Federal guns that dominated the scene for miles in all directions. Attacking such a position would be dangerous work. It required some thought.

Meanwhile, cavalry was sent to attack or harass as many Union detachments as could be found south of the Potomac so as to magnify the size of his army in Yankee eyes. Rebel guns shelled the Union earthworks protecting Harper's Ferry, and when Breckinridge's two divisions approached from Martinsburg late that afternoon the Federal commander,

Brigadier General Max Weber, decided to evacuate the town. Throughout the later part of the afternoon he sent his supplies across the Potomac, and after dark his entire garrison crossed over to Maryland Heights. The next morning, the fifth, Early discovered that another prey had slipped away from him. He sent a few skirmishers into the town, but to send a larger force—let alone to try to cross the Potomac there—would be suicide in the face of the heavy guns across the river. Orders were sent directing Breckinridge's corps to cross the Potomac farther upriver at Boteler's Ford. Once across, Gordon's Division marched downriver on the north side and camped that night near Antietam Furnace, posing a threat to the rear of the Federals on Maryland Heights. Breckinridge's old division, now under Brigadier General John Vaughn, camped that night around the battle-scarred town of Sharpsburg.

Also on the fifth, President Lincoln suspended the writ of habeus corpus in the state of Kentucky, where it was known "that combinations have been formed . . . with a purpose of inciting rebel forces to renew the said operations of civil war within the said State, and thereby to embarrass the United States armies now operating in . . . Virginia and Georgia."[6] It was now possible for the army to arrest Copperheads in Kentucky without interference from the civil courts.

That day an adjutant on General Fitzhugh Lee's staff recorded in his diary that "General Custis Lee and Colonels Wood and Cox dine with us on their way to Stony Creek."[7] Fitz Lee's cavalry division was guarding the Weldon Railroad south of Petersburg at that time. The visitors were evidently the commanders for the raid on Point Lookout, heading down the railroad for Wilmington. Brigadier General George Washington Custis Lee, generally called Custis, was the oldest son of General Robert E. Lee and a first cousin of Fitzhugh Lee. Colonel John Taylor Wood was also a commander in the Confederate navy, an Annapolis graduate, a grandson of President Zachary Taylor, and a nephew of Jefferson Davis' first wife. Both men were officers on President Davis' staff.

Down in Georgia that morning, Sherman's forces were again following Joe Johnston south. "Mine eyes have beheld the promised land," wrote Major James A. Connolly, a staff officer in the 14th Corps. "The 'domes and minarets and spires' of Atlanta are glittering in sunlight before us and only 8 miles distant . . . Generals Sherman and Thomas (who are always with the extreme front when a sudden movement is taking place) were with us on the hilltop, and the two veterans for a moment gazed at the glittering prize in silence. I watched the two noble soldiers—

Sherman stepping nervously about, his eyes sparkling and his face aglow—casting a single glance at Atlanta, another at the River, and a dozen at the surrounding valley to see where he could best cross the River, how he best could flank them."[8]

"From a hill just back of Vining's Station I could see the houses in Atlanta, nine miles distant," Sherman wrote, "and the whole intervening valley of the Chattahoochee; could observe the preparations for our reception on the other side, the camps of men and large trains of covered wagons; and supposed, as a matter of course, that Johnston had passed the river with the bulk of his army, and that he had only left on our side a corps to cover his bridges; but in fact he had only sent across his cavalry and trains."[9] It transpired that the Rebel commander had occupied another defensive position that had been prepared in advance by slave labor and "which proved one of the strongest pieces of field-fortification I ever saw," Sherman said. "We closed up against it, and were promptly met by a heavy and severe fire. Thomas was on the main road in immediate pursuit; next on his right was Schofield; and McPherson on the extreme right, reaching the Chattahoochee River before Turner's Ferry. Stoneman's cavalry was still farther to the right, along down the Chattahoochee River as far as opposite Sandtown; and on that day I ordered Garrard's division of cavalry up the river eighteen miles, to secure possession of the factories at Roswell, as well as to hold an important bridge and ford at that place."[10]

While Sherman was examining Johnston's defenses, "a poor negro came out of the abatis, blanched with fright, said he had been hidden under a log all day, with a perfect storm of shot, shells, and musket-balls, passing over him, till a short lull had enabled him to creep out and make himself known to our skirmishers, who in turn had sent him back to where we were. The negro explained that he with about a thousand slaves had been at work a month or more on these very lines, which, as he explained, extended from the river about a mile above the railroad-bridge to Turner's Ferry below, being in extent five to six miles."[11] But Sherman was well pleased with his own position relative to Johnston, for the Federals "held the high ground and could overlook his movements, instead of his looking down on us, as was the case at Kenesaw."[12] Moreover, "I knew that Johnston would not remain long on the west bank of the Chattahoochee, for I could easily practice on that ground to better advantage our former tactics of intrenching a moiety in his front, and with the rest of our army cross the river and threaten either his rear or the city of Atlanta itself, which city was of vital importance to the existence not only of his own army, but of the Confederacy itself."[13]

The city of Atlanta was only 27 years old in 1864. Back in 1836 the state of Georgia had decided to go into the railroad business, and the state's Western & Atlantic Railroad soon connected the valley of the Tennessee River, just across the northern boundary at Chattanooga, with the interior of the state. From that line's southern terminus other railroads would eventually connect with the Atlantic and Gulf coasts. In 1837, on high ground six and a half miles southeast of the railroad crossing of the Chattahoochee River, a small community grew up, calling itself simply Terminus. In 1843 it was granted a village charter as Marthasville, but in 1845 it changed its name to Atlanta (the feminine form of Atlantic), and two years later it was incorporated as a city.

By the census of 1860 Atlanta had attained a population of 10,000. Small as this may seem by our standards, it was a respectable total. In the same census Richmond had 37,910 people. By 1864 both cities had been swollen with refugees from areas overrun by the Federal armies. At the beginning of the war, Atlanta was a thriving railroad center. The Georgia Railroad from Savannah had connected with the state line in 1845, the Macon & Western in 1846, and the Atlanta & West Point in 1857. And, in the very nonindustrial South, Atlanta was second only to Richmond as an industrial center. Because of this, and especially because of the important rail junctions, Atlanta was a place the Confederacy could ill afford to lose.

General Grant responded to the growing despair among Northern civilians in a letter he wrote that day to his friend Russell Jones, U.S. marshal for Chicago. "You people up North must be of good cheer," he said. "Recollect that we have the bulk of the Rebel army, in two grand armies, both besieged and both conscious that they cannot stand a single battle outside their fortifications with the armies confronting them." A bit farther on he put his finger on the heart of the current military and political situation. "If the Rebellion is not perfectly and thoroughly crushed it will be the fault and through the weakness of the people North. Be of good cheer," he repeated, "and rest assured that all will come out right."[14]

Along the Tennessee-Mississippi border, A. J. Smith's infantry brigade commanders had their men ready to march south from the railroad that day, the fifth. But Grierson's two cavalry brigades were not ready, so the foot soldiers had to wait until late afternoon, when the horse soldiers were finally prepared to march. Meanwhile, large fatigue parties loaded supplies onto railway cars at La Grange for return to Lafayette.

Smith used the time to suggest to General Washburn at Memphis that the Rebels might block the road that Sturgis had followed from Ripley, down the Pontotoc Ridge—which is the high ground separating the streams that flow westward into the Mississippi from those that flow eastward into the Tombigbee. He asked whether, instead, it wouldn't pay for him to march eastward to Tuscumbia, Alabama, on the south bank of the Tennessee River, doing "all the mischief we can on the route."[15] From there he could reach Columbus, Mississippi, in the heart of Forrest's country, much easier than by way of the Pontotoc Ridge. Everyone was agreed at his headquarters, Smith told Washburn, that this route would permit his army to live off the country, would avoid the necessity of crossing the Tombigbee, and would draw Forrest out. Washburn, however, disapproved. He feared that it would take too long and that meanwhile Forrest would get away from him and raid Memphis. So Smith would have to follow the Pontotoc Ridge after all.

Shortly after 6 p.m. Colonel Edward F. Winslow's 2nd Brigade of Grierson's cavalry division departed Saulsbury, heading south toward Ripley. Grierson's other brigade, Colonel Datus E. Coon's 3rd, whose mission was to screen Smith's infantry, rode out of La Grange at 6:30 p.m., bound for Davis' Mills. Mower's 1st Division of the 16th Corps led the infantry column. It consisted of four brigades. Colonel David Moore's 3rd Division, consisting of three brigades, followed, and Colonel Edward Bouton's Colored Brigade marched at the rear, guarding the supply wagons. The 9th Illinois Cavalry, of Coon's brigade, was left behind to cover the army's rear. Altogether, Smith's force totaled 14,000 men and 24 field pieces. Each brigade's 26 wagons carried a reserve of 100 rounds of ammunition per man, enough food for nine days, and grain and forage for the animals for nine days. The infantry camped that night at Davis' Mills, just across the line in Mississippi.

Somewhat farther south, Slocum's small column from Vicksburg, having brushed aside troopers from Wirt Adams' Rebel cavalry division, marched into Jackson that day. This made the fourth time during the war that the capital of Mississippi had been occupied by Federal troops. After destroying the railroad bridge over the Pearl River, Slocum's troops marched back out the next day, the sixth, returning the way they had come. Wirt Adams, having assembled a sizable force from three brigades, attacked the Federal column that afternoon, but was repulsed.

Coon's cavalry brigade led A. J. Smith's main column again on the sixth, as the Federals marched from Davis' Mills toward Ripley. Confederate scouts were encountered but offered no resistance. Smith called a halt that night within fifteen miles of Ripley. Winslow's cavalry brigade joined up with Coon's troopers that day, thus uniting most of Grierson's cavalry in one spot. And the 9th Illinois Cavalry, having been relieved at La Grange by troops sent out from Memphis, marched to Davis' Mills, guarding the column's rear.

Word reached Forrest at Tupelo, Mississippi, that day that the Federals had left their camps along the railroad and were marching toward Ripley. He ordered his division and brigade commanders to prepare three days' rations and to have their men ready to march by 6 a.m. the next day.

In Georgia on the sixth, Garrard's Union cavalry captured the town of Roswell, twenty miles up the Chattahoochee from Johnston's entrenched bridgehead. There he burned a cotton mill that had been making Confederate uniforms, even though its foreign owner had sought to protect it by displaying a French flag. Sherman approved. "Such nonsense cannot deceive me," he told Halleck. "I take it a neutral is no better than one of our own citizens." To Garrard he wrote, "Should you, under the impulse of natural anger, natural at contemplating such perfidy, hang the wretch, I approve the act beforehand."[16]

Early's Rebels were on the move again on the sixth. Rodes' and Ramseur's divisions crossed to the Maryland side of the Potomac while their commander and several other top officers toured the Antietam battlefield around Sharpsburg. Less than two years before, on 17 September 1862, the Army of Northern Virginia and the Army of the Potomac had fought their single bloodiest day of battle there. Now peace lay over the East Wood, the West Wood, the Cornfield, Burnside's Bridge, the Bloody Lane. It must have seemed strange to these men, on their way to who knew what new battlefield, to thus view this old one in such quiet and repose. But more pressing matters soon occupied Early's attention. Shoes had still not arrived from Richmond. Rations were scarce and so was forage for the horses. Commissary officers and foraging parties were sent throughout the area, armed with Confederate money and certificates of impressment, to take, legally, whatever the army needed. Early issued orders reminding his men that any depredations perpetrated by them would be "summarily punished."[17]

Gordon's Division, meanwhile, was sent to probe the Union defenses on the north side of Maryland Heights. Skirmishers from both Weber's and Sigel's commands were encountered and driven into some formidable-looking works. The two Federal forces had apparently united and were intending to hold on to their position overlooking Harper's Ferry. While Gordon's men kept the Yankees busy, working parties were sent to do as much damage as they could to the Chesapeake & Ohio Canal, which paralleled the Potomac on the Maryland side. Canal boats were destroyed and locks were damaged. Meanwhile, Early continued to send his cavalry off in all directions to give the illusion of size to his force in Yankee minds.

McCausland was sent to Hagerstown, Maryland, the largest town in the area, to levy a contribution from the citizens to help pay for his foraging. Early estimated that the town could afford to pay $200,000 to avoid being damaged by the Rebels. Early's luck with his cavalry was always bad, however. Somehow McCausland dropped an important zero from the figure he demanded from the city's officials and he returned with only $20,000. Nevertheless, reports began to pour into Washington, Baltimore and the North that Confederate soldiers had crossed the Potomac and were swarming all over western Maryland, threatening, among other things, the Baltimore & Ohio Railroad. Halleck informed Grant that "the three principal officers on the line of the road are Sigel, Stahel, and Max Weber. You can, therefore, judge what probability there is of a good defense if the enemy should attack the line in force." Grant shared Halleck's low opinion of at least one of the three officers named. "All of Sigel's operations from the beginning of the war have been so unsuccessful that I think it advisable to relieve him from all duty; at least until present troubles are over," he told Halleck. "I do not feel certain at any time that he will not, after abandoning stores, artillery, and trains, make a successful retreat to some safe place."[18]

That afternoon the special courier whom Lee had mentioned to Davis on the third rode up to Early's headquarters, located in a shady orchard near Sharpsburg. He was none other than Robert Lee, Junior, youngest son of the commanding general, and brother of Custis and Rooney. He had come to inform Early of the intended raid on Point Lookout and to relay orders for the latter's part in it. Early was to send some cavalry to cooperate in the effort and to escort the released prisoners around Washington to join the Army of the Valley. Details were lacking. Early would have to rely on the Northern newspapers and Southern sympathizers among the population of Maryland for information on the success of the raid and the Federal reaction to it. He should also watch his rear, the west, from where Hunter was expected to reappear by way of the Ohio River and the Baltimore & Ohio Railroad.

If the prisoners could be freed, armed and united with his present forces, Early's strength would be doubled. He immediately abandoned any thoughts he might have had about capturing Maryland Heights. In his reply to Lee he explained that he had originally hoped to cross at Harper's Ferry, but the Federal position on Maryland Heights prevented that. Now he would do what he had already come to believe was the best alternative. He would bypass Maryland Heights, crossing South

Mountain farther north, and head for Washington, while sending some cavalry to cooperate with the Point Lookout raid.

In response to Grant's order to Meade, 4,000 dismounted cavalrymen, plus the 5,000 infantrymen of Rickett's 3rd Division of the 6th Corps, embarked on 6 July, heading north. Grant notified Halleck that these men were on the way. "We now want to crush out and destroy any force the enemy have sent north," he said. "Force enough can be spared from here to do it."[19]

Grant also wired Halleck about Butler that day. The chief of staff had informed the general-in-chief that, although he had foreseen all along that Grant would want to get rid of Butler, "on account of his total unfitness to command in the field and his generally quarrelsome character," it was not going to be easy. Sending Butler to Kentucky, he said, "would probably cause an insurrection in that state," and sending him to Missouri could do even worse damage. Now Grant took up an idea that had been proposed back in June by a pair of generals who had been sent down to inspect Butler's position at Bermuda Hundred. "Please obtain an order," Grant wrote, "assigning the troops of the Department of Virginia and North Carolina serving in the field to the command of Maj. Gen. W. F. Smith and order Major-General Butler, commanding department, to his headquarters, Fortress Monroe."[20]

Rumors and intrigue were still rife among the various Union headquarters around Petersburg. The next day, 7 July, Assistant Secretary of War Dana sent word to Secretary Stanton that "a change in the commander of the Army of the Potomac now seems probable."[21]

---

1. Tidwell, Hall, and Gaddy, *Come Retribution*, 146.
2. Catton, *Grant Takes Command*, 306–307.
3. Ibid., 310.
4. Lewis, *Sherman: Fighting Prophet*, 379.
5. McDonough and Jones, *War So Terrible*, 191.
6. Basler, ed., *The Collected Works of Abraham Lincoln*, 7:426.
7. Tidwell, Hall and Gaddy, *Come Retribution*, 147.
8. Lewis, *Sherman: Fighting Prophet*, 380–381.
9. Sherman, *Memoirs*, 2:67.
10. Ibid., 2:66.
11. Ibid., 2:66–67.
12. Ibid., 2:67.

13. Ibid., 2:67–68.
14. Catton, *Grant Takes Command*, 305.
15. Bearss, *Forrest at Brice's Cross Roads*, 153.
16. Lewis, *Sherman, Fighting Prophet*, 380.
17. Vandiver, *Jubal's Raid*, 91.
18. Ibid., 137–138.
19. Catton, *Grant Takes Command*, 310–311.
20. Ibid., 327.
21. Ibid., 331.

CHAPTER TWELVE

The War Must Halt

7–9 July 1864

The next day, Thursday, 7 July, Horace Greeley wrote a letter to President Lincoln. Greeley was the founder and editor of the *New York Tribune* and had once been described as "a self-made man who worships his creator."[1] He was an influential Republican to whom Lincoln had to pay attention. In light of the war-weariness then growing by leaps and bounds throughout the North, what he had to say was highly significant: "I venture to inclose you a letter and telegraphic dispatch that I received yesterday from our irrepressible friend, Colorado Jewett, at Niagara Falls. I think they deserve attention." Jewett's letter to Greeley stated, in part, "I have to advise having just left Hon Geo. N. Sanders of Ky on the Canada side. I am authorized to state to you—for our use only—not the public—that two ambassadors—of Davis & Co are now in Canada—with full & complete powers for a peace & Mr Sanders requests that you come on immediately to me at Cataract House—to have a private interview, or if you will send the Presidents protection for him & two friends, they will come on & meet you. He says the whole matter can be consummated by me you—them & President Lincoln."

"Of course, I do not indorse Jewett's positive averment that his friends . . . 'have full powers' from J. D. [Jefferson Davis]," Greeley wrote, "though I do not doubt that he thinks they have. I let that statement stand as simply evidencing the anxiety of the Confederates everywhere for peace. So much is beyond doubt.

"And thereupon I venture to remind you that our bleeding, bankrupt, almost dying country also longs for peace—shudders at the prospect of fresh conscriptions, of further wholesale devastations, and of new rivers of human blood. And a wide-spread conviction that the Government . . . are not anxious for Peace, and do not improve proffered opportunities to achieve it, is doing great harm now, and is morally certain, unless removed, to do far greater in the approaching Elections. . .

"I entreat you, in your own time and manner, to submit overtures for pacification to the Southern insurgents which the impartial must pronounce frank and generous. If only with a view to the momentous Election soon to occur in North Carolina, and of the Draft to be enforced in the Free States, this should be done at once.

"I would give safe conduct required by the Rebel envoys at Niagara . . . but you may see reasons for declining it. But, whether through them or otherwise, do not, I entreat you, fail to make the Southern people comprehend that you and all of us are anxious for peace. . .

"Mr. President, I fear you do not realize how intently the people desire any peace consistent with the national integrity and honor . . . With United States stocks worth but forty cents in gold per dollar, and drafting about to commence on the third million of Union soldiers, can this be wondered at?

"I do not say that a just peace is now attainable, though I believe it to be so. But I do say, that a frank offer by you to the insurgents of terms . . . will . . . prove an immense and sorely needed advantage to the national cause; it may save us from a northern insurrection. . .

"I beg you to invite those now at Niagara to exhibit their credentials and submit their ultimatum."[2]

The George N. Sanders referred to by Jewett was a member of the official Confederate circle in Canada. He was a smiling, debonair man who loved to throw lavish parties and who never lacked for money or for beautiful women. He had once been the American consul in London, and the *Times* had said of him: "He sees everybody, talks to everybody, high and low. He has little reverence for great men. He would criticize George Washington to his face if he were alive. He is one of the most adept wire-pullers in the United States."[3] The two ambassadors that Sanders had told Jewett about could be none other than Jacob Thompson and Clement C. Clay, the two senior Confederate commissioners in Canada. Sanders had great influence over Clay, and with the latter's knowledge, but without Thompson's, had approached Greeley through Jewett. William Cornell Jewett, incidentally, was an ardent advocate of a negotiated peace and was reported to have carried Confederate dispatches to Canada from England.

Early that morning, 7 July, Gordon's Division of Jubal Early's Army of the Valley drove Union defenders from one of the stronger forts guarding the northern approaches to Maryland Heights. Meanwhile, Ransom's cavalry pushed through the passes leading east through South Mountain, the Maryland extension of the Blue Ridge. Around 10 a.m. Bradley Johnson's brigade was trotting through the village of Middletown, halfway to the next ridge, Catoctin Mountain, when it was fired on by a Yankee cannon. Suddenly the Confederates were charged by a regiment of Federal horsemen, the veteran troopers of the 8th Illinois Cavalry, and Johnson's surprised Rebels retreated a half-mile before reinforcements and artillery support brought an end to their flight. They formed a dismounted line of battle and began to push the Federals back, eventually driving the smaller force back to, and then through, Catoctin Pass.

Looking down into the next valley, Johnson could see that his home town of Frederick contained an unknown number of Union infantry, backed up by at least one battery of artillery. He surveyed the terrain, checked his ammunition supply, brought up some artillery and maneuvered his men into position. Then, finally, at 4 p.m. his three cannon opened fire and his dismounted skirmishers went forward. By the time his main line became engaged with the Yankees he was able to judge that there must be at least a thousand of them, and they showed every indication of standing to fight it out. But Johnson continued to threaten their front while working other units around their flanks, and about 6 p.m. the defenders' fire began to slacken.

Just then Robert Ransom, Johnson's boss, showed up. He was not as optimistic about the way the fight was turning out as was Johnson, and after thinking it over, ordered the latter to fall back to Catoctin Mountain. They could report to Early that only small units from local garrisons blocked the roads to Washington and Baltimore. That was enough accomplishment for one day. The disgusted Johnson obeyed, disappointed to see the Yankees not only escape the trap he had been about to spring, but follow his retreat as if they had won the battle, not he.

Three miles southeast of Frederick was the little town of Monocacy Junction, where the Frederick branch of the Baltimore & Ohio Railroad joined the main line coming in from Harper's Ferry to cross the Monocacy River, a southward-flowing tributary of the Potomac. That day the sleepy village was the temporary headquarters of Union major general Lew Wallace, commander of the Middle Department. Wallace was a pre-war Indiana politician and militia officer who had been side-lined since he took a wrong road and kept his division out of the battle of Shiloh for the entire first day. In later years he would make his mark on history as the author of the famous novel *Ben Hur,* written while he was territorial governor of New Mexico. But that was yet to come on that hot July day in 1864.

Halleck did not like Wallace, nor any political general for that matter, but Lincoln had thought it safe enough to put him in command of this rear-area department, whose regular headquarters was at Baltimore. Since Lee's invasion of Maryland and Pennsylvania the summer before, West Virginia had been separated from the Middle Department as an independent command, so that what was left of it, also known as the 8th Corps, consisted only of the state of Maryland east of Harper's Ferry and Delaware. Wallace had been a good administrator of this politically divided state, but he longed to see action and perhaps gain a bit of glory.

When both Sigel and Weber were thrown out of the Shenandoah and reports started coming in of Rebel horsemen swarming over western Maryland, he saw his chance and his duty. If a large force of Confederates was north of the Potomac, as rumor maintained, poorly defended Washington was their logical objective. Should the national capital, which was also an immense supply base for both the army and the navy, be captured, he reasoned, "the war must halt, if not stop for good and all."[4] The District of Columbia was not part of his department, but the approaches to it through central Maryland certainly were. So he had come here to Monocacy Junction, where the roads to Washington and Baltimore diverged, to try to find out what the Rebels were up to. To avoid any difficulties with Halleck over this move he simply didn't tell him about it. By the seventh, he had scraped up a few odds and ends of infantry from his department and he had commandeered the 8th Illinois Cavalry, which had been sent out by Major General Christopher C. Augur, commander of the Department of Washington, also known as the 22nd Corps. Altogether he had accumulated perhaps 2,300 men, and these he sent out to find the invading Rebels.

When the Illinois troopers ran into Bradley Johnson's brigade, the sound of firing reached Wallace at his temporary headquarters, and he sent forward the infantry who defended Frederick, while holding others to defend the bridges of the Monocacy. When word reached him that Johnson was threatening the flank of the force at Frederick he had no help to send them, only encouraging news: "I have a telegram announcing veterans from Grant landing at Baltimore, and they will be up some time tonight," he said, and added, "The fellows fighting you are only dismounted cavalry, and you can whip them. Try a charge." This message reached Frederick just as the Rebels withdrew. Satisfied with what he called "the best little battle of the war," Wallace finally announced his current location to Halleck in conjunction with news of his supposed victory.[5]

It was true. The veterans of the 3rd Division of the 6th Corps had landed at Baltimore. Just over a year before, the same troops had themselves been run out of the Shenandoah Valley by Lee's army on its way to Gettysburg and had taken refuge on Maryland Heights until the Army of the Potomac had absorbed them during its pursuit of Lee's retreat. Now they were the veterans coming to fight the Rebels while other garrison troops took refuge on the hills across from Harper's Ferry.

At his headquarters in the orchard at Sharpsburg, Early paid scant attention to the report of the small fight at Frederick by one of his cavalry brigades.

Down in central Mississippi that day, the seventh, Slocum's small column beat off another attack by Wirt Adams' Confederates and safely returned to the defenses of Vicksburg. Slocum's expedition to Jackson had caused Adams to recall Gholson's Brigade, which had been slated to join Forrest, just when the latter was going to need all the help he could get in defending the northeastern part of the state from A. J. Smith. Reports reaching Forrest that day satisfied him that Smith's column was heading for Tupelo by way of Ellistown, so he ordered one of his three division commanders, Brigadier General Abraham Buford, to send a brigade, Colonel Tyree Bell's 4th, to watch the Ripley-Ellistown road. S. D. Lee, the commander of the Department of Alabama, Mississippi and East Louisiana, arrived at Forrest's headquarters at Tupelo that day, accompanied by 600 heavy artillerymen converted to infantry, from Mobile. He found that Forrest could field about 7,500 mounted men, 2,100 dismounted troopers and twenty pieces of artillery. Lee and Forrest decided it would be best to lure Smith as far south as Okolona before attacking him. Then troops could be sent quickly to reinforce Mobile, which Lee expected Canby, the Federal commander on the Gulf, to attack any day, and which was now defended by a mere 2,500 infantry plus a small fleet of gunboats.

A. J. Smith's Federals, in fact, were marching toward Ripley again that day, with the 2nd Iowa Cavalry of Coon's brigade in the lead. About 3 p.m., three and a half miles north of Ripley, Coon, with the Iowans, ran into stiff opposition from the 1st Mississippi Partisan Rangers and the 3rd Tennessee Cavalry, both under Lieutenant Colonel Samuel M. Hyams of the Partisans. The Rebels were posted on a hillside, under the cover of trees and brush, protecting the junction of two roads and the crossing of Whitten's Branch. Coon attacked with six dismounted companies of the 2nd Iowa and, after an hour of manuevering for position and the expenditure of a good deal of ammunition, charged across an open field and drove the Rebels from the hill. By then General Smith and the head of the infantry column had arrived, and a halt was called for the day, three miles northwest of Ripley.

The Federal advance continued on the eighth, with Winslow's cavalry brigade taking over the lead, and passed through Ripley and out the New Albany road. The Federal vanguard, the 10th Missouri Cavalry, fought a few skirmishes with Hyam's Rebels as they approached Orizaba. Then, to confuse the Confederates, Grierson sent the 3rd Iowa Cavalry on a reconnaissance down the Ellistown road, the very one Forrest expected Smith to take, as far as Kelly's Mill. A half-mile down the road these Federals ran into breastworks on the brow of a hill. But the Rebels, seeing that they were outnumbered and outflanked by the main column, retreated across the Tallahatchie at Kelly's Ford. The Iowans followed them for four miles before turning back and rejoining the main column where it was camped that night, a mile south of Orizaba on the road to New Albany and Pontotoc. Behind them, in Ripley, the court house, Methodist and Presbyterian churches, the Masonic and Odd Fellows' halls, several stores, and three homes had been put to the torch.

At 5 a.m. on the eighth, Bell's Confederate brigade rode out of its camp north of Tupelo. When he reached Ellistown, Bell left the 2nd and 16th Tennessee regiments there and proceeded with the 19th and 20th Tennessee to the crossings of the Tallahatchie River. Forrest learned that day of the fight between Hyam's two regiments and Coon's Yankees the day before, and that Smith's column had passed through Ripley that day. So he alerted his division commanders, Buford, James R. Chalmers and Philip D. Roddey, to have their units ready to move at a moment's notice. Also, Chalmers was to send officers "to examine the roads, creeks, and crossings on the New Albany road."[6]

Over in Georgia that day, the eighth, Sherman was working on turning Johnston out of his Chattahoochee bridgehead by finding a way to cross the river elsewhere. The stream was 150 yards wide, swollen by the recent rains, with muddy banks. "At this time Stoneman was very active on our exteme right," he wrote in his memoirs, "pretending to be searching the river below Turner's Ferry for a crossing, and was watched by the enemy's cavalry on the other side. McPherson, on the right, was equally demonstrative at and near Turner's Ferry. Thomas faced substantially the entrenched tête-du-point, and had his left on the Chattahoochee River, at Paice's Ferry. Garrard's cavalry was up at Roswell, and McCook's small division of cavalry was intermediate, above Soap's

Creek. Meantime, also, the railroad-construction party was hard at work, repairing the railroad up to our camp at Vining's Station.

"Of course," he continued, "I expected every possible resistance in crossing the Chattahoochee River, and had made up my mind to feign on the right, but actually to cross over by the left. We had already secured a crossing-place at Roswell, but one nearer was advisable; General Schofield had examined the river well, found a place just below the mouth of Soap's Creek which he deemed advantageous, and was instructed to effect an early crossing there, and to intrench a good position on the other side."[7] At 3 p.m. on the eighth, Schofield's Army of the Ohio began crossing the river. First, fifty men, selected for their height and strength, were sent across on an old fish dam, and when they met no opposition most of the brigade followed by the same route, gaining a ridge on the other side, opposed only by a few startled pickets. About an hour later 25 pontoon boats floated down Soap's Creek carrying the 12th Kentucky Infantry Regiment. This drew the fire of a single Confederate cannon, but covering fire from Union infantry and artillery north of the river soon drove the Rebel gunners away, leaving their gun to be captured. "The crossing was secured without the loss of a man," Schofield proudly reported.[8] By nightfall all of Cox's 3rd Division of the 23rd Corps was entrenched on the southeast side and a pontoon bridge had been laid across the river.

President Lincoln published a proclamation that day, 8 July. Congress had, a few days before, passed a bill outlining its own formula for the reconstruction of the Southern states. That is, it outlined the legal procedure for the seceded states to rejoin the Union. This measure, known for its sponsors in the Senate and House as the Wade-Davis Bill, was the product of the Radical Republicans. It provided that provisional governors would be appointed to take over the Southern states until the end of the war, that civil government would be restored in a state when half of the white male citizens took the loyalty oath, and that slavery would be abolished in all such states. It also provided, in Davis' words, that until "Congress recognize a State government, organized under its auspices, there is no government in the rebel States except the authority of Congress."[9] In other words, Congress was rejecting and overriding the proclamation of amnesty which Lincoln had issued some months before and his plan to let 10 percent of the registered voters of any state form a new government. Further, it was rejecting the president's right to set up any plan.

Now, on the eighth, Lincoln formally announced why he was not signing this bill, thus killing it by a pocket veto. He said he was "unprepared, by a formal approval of this Bill, to be inflexibly committed to any single plan of restoration," and that he was "also unprepared to declare, that the free-state constitutions and governments, already adopted and installed in Arkansas and Louisiana, shall be set aside and held for nought [or] to declare a constitutional competency in Congress to abolish slavery in States," although he was "sincerely hoping and expecting that a constitutional amendment, abolishing slavery throughout the nation, may be adopted." However, he said, "I am fully satisfied with the system for restoration contained in the Bill, as one very proper plan for the loyal people of any State choosing to adopt it."[10] He just was not prepared to accept it as the only plan.

In Maryland that Friday, 8 July, Union general Franz Sigel was relieved of command again, replaced this time by Brigadier General Albion P. Howe, a former division commander in the Army of the Potomac, who had been sent out to Maryland Heights with a few reinforcements from the Department of Washington, where he had been in charge of the light artillery camp of instruction. Ramseur's Confederate division took the road from Sharpsburg to Boonsboro that day, Breckinridge's corps marched from Rohrersville toward Fox's Gap and Middletown with Gordon's Division leading, and Rodes' Division marched southeast from Rohrersville through Crampton's Gap. It was uphill all the way, and the day was hot and extremely dusty. Breckinridge's and Ramseur's weary, grimy men camped that evening near Middletown, and Rodes' near Jefferson. It was all familiar territory to the veterans of the Antietam campaign of less than two years before. Early established his headquarters at the western foot of Catoctin Mountain. Ransom's cavalry still held the pass leading to Frederick, where it rained intermittently.

Bradley Johnson had fumed as the day passed without his being allowed to liberate his home town of Frederick. That night a courier brought him orders to report to Early's headquarters, where he received instructions for a special mission. He would take 800 troopers and pass north of Frederick the next day, guarding the army's left during the action which Early expected, and if all went well he would then move eastward on his own, cutting railroad and telegraph lines north of Baltimore. He was then to circle around that city, cut the Baltimore & Ohio between it and Washington, and be at Point Lookout on the night of the twelfth. Early passed on what little he knew about the planned raid on the prisoner of war camp. Johnson would take charge of the liberated prisoners and lead them to Washington, where he would find the rest of the army. The prisoners could then be armed with weapons captured there and add their strength to his forces. Johnson knew the country he would be operating in, and he said there would not be time to accomplish all that by the twelfth. It would mean covering almost 300 miles in four days, with stops to tear up railroad tracks and burn bridges. But he would do everything in his power to be at least within supporting distance of Point Lookout by the twelfth. Early said he was to move out at dawn.

Across the way, Wallace was worried by Breckinridge's position at Jefferson, from which he threatened to pass beyond his left and move directly on Washington. So he sent the 8th Illinois Cavalry to block that path. That night the rest of his force fell back from Frederick and concentrated on holding the bridges at Monocacy Junction. Rickett's division was known to be marching to join him there, which would give him a strength of 5,000 or 6,000 men. Early's strength was unknown to him but he assumed it to be considerably larger. He was determined to stand and fight the next day, whatever the odds, in order to buy time for reinforcements to reach Washington.

The advance element of Hunter's Army of West Virginia, Sullivan's 1st Infantry Division, reached Cumberland, Maryland, on the Potomac, that day, and the entire force was concentrated at Cherry Run the next day, the ninth. But Early was moving away from him, to the east. Halleck was getting worried and warned Grant that there were dreadfully few Federal forces in Washington and Maryland, and even those were poorly organized. He knew that the 19th Corps was due to start arriving from Louisiana soon and wanted to know if it could be diverted to Washington. Grant wired back on the ninth: "If you think it necessary order the Nineteenth Corps as it arrives at Fortress Monroe to Washington. About the 18th or 20th is the time I should like to have a large force here; but if the rebel force now north can be captured or destroyed I would willingly postpone aggressive operations to destroy them, and could send in addition to the Nineteenth Corps the balance of the Sixth Corps."[11] Without waiting for an answer, he ordered Wright's other two divisions to embark for Washington. That evening he wired Halleck again: "Forces enough to defeat all that Early has with him should get in his rear south of him and follow him up sharply, leaving him to go north, defending depots, towns, etc., with small garrisons and militia. If the President thinks it advisable that I should go to Washington in person I can start in an hour after receiving notice, leaving everything here on the defensive."[12]

At Wilmington, North Carolina, that day, the ninth, after delays caused by problems in finding arms to take along for the soon-to-be released prisoners, two blockade runners, the *Florie* and the *Let-Her-Be,* set sail on the expedition to capture Point Lookout, Maryland.

It was that day, the ninth, that Lincoln wrote an answer to Horace Greeley. "If you can find," he said, "any person anywhere professing to have any proposition of Jefferson Davis in writing, for peace, embracing the restoration of the Union and abandonment of slavery, what ever else it embraces, say to him he may come to me with you, and that if he really brings such proposition, he shall, at the least, have safe conduct, with the paper (and without publicity, if he choose) to the point where you shall have met him. The same, if there be two or more persons."[13]

---

1. Louis M. Starr, *Bohemian Brigade: Civil War Newsmen in Action* (New York, 1954), 4.
2. Basler, ed., *The Collected Works of Abraham Lincoln,* 7:435–436, n. 1.
3. Horan, *Confederate Agent,* 87.
4. Vandiver, *Jubal's Raid,* 99.
5. Ibid., 100.
6. Bearss, *Forrest at Brice's Cross Roads,* 164.
7. Sherman, *Memoirs,* 2:68–69.
8. McDonough and Jones, *War So Terrible,* 197.
9. Sandburg, *Abraham Lincoln,* 3:550.
10. Basler, ed., *The Collected Works of Abraham Lincoln,* 7:433.
11. Catton, *Grant Takes Command,* 311.
12. Ibid., 312.
13. Basler, ed., *The Collected Works of Abraham Lincoln,* 7:435.

CHAPTER THIRTEEN

This Ought to Immortalize You

9–11 July 1864

Saturday, 9 July, dawned a balmy, breezy, mid-summer day in Maryland. Almost immediately, firing broke out between dismounted Confederate cavalry troopers, reinforced by Ramseur's infantry, and Wallace's skirmishers. The Federals were pushed through Frederick by 8 a.m., and the Rebels followed them southeastward toward Monocacy Junction. Rodes' Division formed to support Ramseur's left flank, while Breckinridge's two divisions advanced south of Frederick. Ramseur's troops soon reported that Union resistance was stiffening and that a line of defense was drawn up on the east side of the Monocacy River. So, about 9 a.m., the Southern infantry began to deploy into lines of battle. Meanwhile, several Confederate cannon bombarded the far side of the river. A Union 24-pound howitzer and a few other guns, mostly north of the iron Baltimore & Ohio Railroad bridge, returned the fire, and thousands of Federal infantrymen could be seen deployed in line south of that bridge.

Jubal Early was busy just then in Frederick. He informed the city authorities that he would spare their town if they contributed $200,000 to the Rebel cause. The mayor protested that the city of 8,000 people could not come up with that amount of cash. But the only concession Early would allow was to give the officials time to discuss methods of raising such a sum. Then he left three officers to receive the payment while he proceeded to the front.

Some generals have a talent for quickly sizing up terrain for its advantages and uses; some don't. Early seems to have been in the latter category. Certainly on this occasion he decided to take his time and to look the situation over carefully. He found that Wallace had selected a good, two-mile-long position along a range of hills on the east side of the Monocacy, covering the railroad and the turnpikes to Washington and to Baltimore. The Union right guarded a stone bridge and the Baltimore road. The center, strengthened by a blockhouse, covered the iron railroad bridge and an old covered wooden bridge just south of it that carried the macadamized road to Washington. Early estimated that there were upwards of 7,000 Yankees blocking his route to Washington, but he assumed that most of them must be green militia or 100-days men.

Rodes' skirmishers were fighting the defenders of the stone bridge, while Ramseur's were advancing through a wheatfield into the angle between the two branches of the railroad and approaching the iron and covered bridges. But Early could see that a frontal attack would be too costly. However, Wallace obviously didn't have much of a reserve and was already covering about all the front he could manage. A flank attack seemed the natural solution, and since what Early needed most was the road to Washington, the southern flank was the obvious choice. The first step was to find a place for such an attack to cross the Monocacy.

About 11 a.m., amid oppressive heat, Early rode south to have a look, when he saw some of his own cavalry ford the river about a mile south of the wooden bridge, dismount, drive back the Union left, and capture a battery of artillery. This was McCausland's Brigade returning to the army from a raid on the railroad and telegraph between Harper's Ferry and Washington. But McCausland had bitten off more than he could chew, for he was badly outnumbered. Quickly, Early sent a courier with orders for Gordon's Division, until then uncommitted, to advance and cross the river at McCausland's ford and support the cavalry.

Gordon's men had been enjoying their role as spectators, lounging in the fields and along the road under the shade of their tents, cheering on their more active comrades, when they saw Early's courier ride up in a cloud of dust and present his dispatch to General Gordon. Soon the orders rang out down the line: "Take arms!—no time now for blankets, but get in your places at once! Right face. Forward march!"[1] The men did not so much mind being sent into the fight as they did having to leave behind their blankets, tents, etc. There was no way of knowing when, if ever, they would see them again. Grumbling, they marched toward the Confederate right, while Gordon rode ahead for a look at the ford. When the men caught up, he ordered them to cross quickly. Under the fire of Union guns and skirmishers they splashed across, covered by the high, steep, muddy east bank, which they then climbed with some difficulty. And when they reached the top of the bank they were met with a volley from the top of a ridge. They rushed into a field and fanned out into a line of battle, the brigades formed in echelon from the right. Gordon wanted to hit the extreme Federal left first and then extend the contact up the line.

Watching the Rebels form up was Union brigadier general James Ricketts, commander of the 3rd Division of the 6th Corps. He had been stunned to learn from Wallace, when he had arrived at Monocacy Junction, that Jubal Early and the 2nd Corps of the Army of Northern Virginia was approaching. As far as he had known until that moment, those troops were down at Petersburg with the rest of Lee's army. He had also been shocked to learn that, other than the 3–4,000 troops Ricketts had brought, Wallace had on hand only 2,500 men. Nevertheless, Ricketts agreed that they had to make a stand at the Monocacy to delay Early's advance. The two generals also agreed that Early would try to turn their left, and so Ricketts' veterans had been placed on that flank. Around noon he sent word to Wallace that Rebel troops were crossing the river a half-mile southwest of his flank and that he would need help. Wallace concurred, and did what little he could. He sent orders to the men holding the west end of the covered bridge to abandon and burn their blockhouse and the bridge, retire to the east bank, and go to Ricketts' support.

But more Rebels kept crossing the river and extending their front toward Ricketts' left. Then, about 1:30 p.m. several brigades of Confederates emerged from the woods about 700 yards from his left front, skirmishers out, battle flags waving, threatening to overlap his line and roll it up. He ordered his men to fall back and change front, placing the right of his division against the river bank and the rest running along the Washington pike, facing south. It was a hazardous move to perform under fire, but his men pulled it off rapidly and in good order.

The precision of this maneuver must have alerted Gordon to the fact that he was facing veteran troops. But his right-most brigade continued its advance. This was his own former brigade of Georgians, now under Brigadier General Clement Evans. However, Evans fell badly wounded in the advance. To Evans' left was the combined Louisiana brigade of Brigadier General Zebulan York, which was shaken somewhat by the Federal fire. To York's left and farther back came Brigadier General William Terry's Virginians—what was left of several veteran outfits after their terrible losses at Spotsylvania. The Southerners had to cross a field full of grain stacks and cross or knock down some fences, but about 2:30 p.m. Gordon sent him men forward, driving the Union firstline back on a second. These Federals fell back across a small stream that, Gordon noted, ran red with blood, and then they broke and ran. But Gordon came upon a third Yankee line, which was longer than his own, stretching beyond both of his flanks, and a deadly fire was hitting the Confederate left. Gordon stopped to regroup his forces and to consider his next move.

He decided that, although he appeared to be outnumbered on this front, a fresh brigade hitting the right spot would push this third Union line beyond the Washington pike, thus clearing the way for Ramseur's Division to cross the river and join the attack. So Gordon sent orders for Terry to attack on the left and put an end to that dangerous flank fire. Terry's Virginians attacked across a field of waist-high corn, taking fire from a line of Federals behind a post-and-rail fence at its far extremity. Southern casualties began to fall, but the rest moved on with a high-pitched Rebel yell, and soon the Yankees abandoned their fence and fell back.

Realizing that he needed help, Gordon sent a staff officer back across the river with a request for another brigade. Word came back that help would be sent, but would take a while to reach him. Gordon decided that he couldn't risk losing the momentum he had gained, so he ordered Terry to move even farther to the left and to attack the Northerners' right while the other two brigades assaulted their front. Terry's men filtered back across their hard-won cornfield, reformed, then marched upriver and up a hill, where they spotted Gordon sitting on his horse. When they came into view, Gordon spurred to meet them, calling, "Hurry up, boys." Then he turned and led them toward a fence. About 200 yards farther ahead was another fence, and a line of Union infantry could be seen marching along it at the double, toward the river. This sight brought a yell of "At them, boys!" from the ranks, but Gordon turned in his saddle and said, "Keep quiet, we'll have our time presently. Some of you pull down the fence, so that we may go through!" But he couldn't keep the men in check very long. Soon cries of "Charge them! Charge them!" came from the ranks,[2] and the Rebels ran forward, beating the Federals to the section of the second fence to their front, and they poured a volley into the surprised Union column that caused it to break and run.

The Virginians then crossed the fence and chased after the retreating Northerners and were soon joined by York's Louisianians on their right. Ricketts' entire line began to collapse. Soon the railroad bridge was abandoned, and Ramseur's Division united with Gordon's in pursuit of the Yankees. By hard work and bravery Ricketts and Wallace managed to keep the retreat from turning into a complete rout, and a rear guard was formed to delay the pursuit, but by 4 p.m. the battle was over and the Federals were streaming down the Baltimore pike. "It was the most exciting time I witnessed during the war," one Confederate veteran recalled.[3] "Gordon," Breckinridge told the Georgian, "if you had never made a fight before, this ought to immortalize you."[4]

Ricketts had lost almost half of his division killed, wounded and missing, and Wallace's entire force, including Ricketts', had lost 2,000 men. To Halleck, Wallace reported that he was "retreating with a foot-sore, battered, and half-demoralized column. I think the troops of the Sixth Corps fought magnificently."[5] Confederate losses were about 700. Early did not press the pursuit. The last thing he needed was more prisoners to take care of.

Word of the Union defeat quickly pried the desired $200,000 out of the city fathers of Frederick. But the important thing was that the road to Washington was now undefended, for Wallace's remnants were retreating toward Baltimore. Early's headquarters and his wagons were brought to the east side of the Monocacy, but it was too late in the day and the men were too tired to do more than go into camp. The advance on Washington would have to await the dawn. And that was Wallace's victory—his and Ricketts' and the men who had fought for them. "Whether the delay caused by the battle amounted to a day or not," Grant wrote in his memoirs, "General Wallace contributed on this occasion, by the defeat of the troops under him a greater benefit to the cause than often falls to the lot of a commander of an equal force to render by means of a victory."[6] That same day the other two divisions of the 6th Corps embarked at City Point for shipment to Washington, and Meade ordered the Army of the Potomac to begin constructing regular seige approaches to the Rebel defenses of Petersburg.

In Mississippi that day, the ninth, it was Coon's brigade's turn to take the lead in A. J. Smith's advance. The Federals' march was unopposed and uneventful. They crossed the Tallahatchie River and camped that night around the village of New Albany. Confederate colonel Tyree Bell, commander of the brigade that had been sent to Ellistown, sent the 2nd Tennessee Regiment westward from that town with orders to establish a roadblock between New Albany and Pontotoc. Meanwhile, General Buford, with the other brigade of his division, Brigadier General Hylan B. Lyon's 3rd, reached Elliston, where he was reinforced by a brigade under Colonel Hinchie P. Mabry, borrowed from Wirt Adams. There

Buford learned from Bell that the Federals were not advancing toward Ellistown as expected but down the Pontotoc ridge instead. Buford detached the 6th Mississippi from Mabry's Brigade and sent it to operate on the Yankee's flank and rear, and then marched all night with the rest of his command for Pontotoc. Forrest sent orders to his other two divisions, Chalmers' and Roddey's. The latter had been loaned to him by S. D. Lee from its usual post in northern Alabama. It was to march night and day from Corinth to Okolona. Chalmers, whose division was at Verona, between Okolona and Tupelo, was to send one brigade, Rucker's, to join the dismounted men at Tupelo and the other, McCulloch's, to Pontotoc.

The same day, the ninth, over in Georgia, Garrard's cavalry division crossed the Chattahoochee at Roswell, drove away the Rebel cavalry pickets, and held its ground until relieved by Newton's division of Howard's 4th Corps, which in turn was relieved by Dodge's Left Wing of the 16th Corps as the advance of the entire Army of the Tennessee.

On orders from Confederate president Jefferson Davis, General Braxton Bragg left Richmond for Georgia that day to find out what Joe Johnston's intentions were regarding the defense of Atlanta. However, Johnston was already being visited by a delegation of politicians from Richmond, and he readily told them what the president wanted to know. "You may tell Mr. Davis that it would be folly for me under the circumstances to risk a decisive engagement," he said. "My plan is to draw Sherman further and further from his base in the hope of weakening him and by cutting his army in two. That is my only hope of defeating him." One member of the group, a Missourian, replied that the situation required that the general strike the Federals a "crushing blow," and added that he had heard President Davis say that "if he were in your place he could whip Sherman now." Johnston replied with scorn, "Yes, I know Mr Davis thinks he can do a great many things other men would hesitate to attempt. For instance, he tried to do what God failed to do. He tried to make a soldier of Braxton Bragg, and you know the result. It couldn't be done." Just then a courier brought Johnston word that Schofield had crossed the Chattahoochee, and the general announced that since Sherman had thus divided his army, with part on the north bank and part on the south, the time had finally arrived to attack and "whip him in detail."[7]

But it just was not in Johnston's nature to make such an attack. "That night Johnston evacuated his trenches, crossed over the Chattahoochee, burned the railroad-bridge and his pontoon and trestle bridges, and left us in full possession of the north or west bank," Sherman wrote. Then he added, "I have always thought Johnston neglected his opportunity there, for he had lain comparatively idle while we got control of both banks of the river above him."[8]

Sunday, 10 July, was even hotter in Maryland than the day before. Jubal Early's Army of the Valley took the dusty road from Monocacy Junction toward Washington with McCausland's cavalry and Breckinridge's corps in the lead, followed by Rodes' Division and then Ramseur's, and by the time the Rebels went into camp they had covered about half the forty miles to the Federal capital. Union cavalry snapped at the heels of Ramseur's column, often forcing the Confederates to deploy into battle formation, so that it wasn't until about 1 a.m. that the last men went into camp. Bradley Johnson's brigade started on its way to Baltimore, while McCausland's troopers fought with outposts of the 2nd Massachusetts Cavalry, driving them beyond Rockville, within ten miles of the District of Columbia line.

News of Wallace's defeat had alarmed Baltimore, and all day people ran about town, while the bells rang out and various home guard units mustered and marched here and there. Southern sympathizers became a bit bolder, but they were far outnumbered by the loyal citizens, who breathed a collective sigh of relief when word came that the Rebels had turned toward Washington instead of coming in their direction.

The capital's defenses consisted of a 37-mile circle of the best entrenchments that the country's most expert engineers could devise, but they needed, according to a recent estimation, 25,000 infantrymen and 9,000 artillerymen to man them. All that was available, however, after deducting guards for buildings and bridges, untrained artillerists, and so forth, were 9,600 men, mostly half-trained militiamen from Ohio and semi-invalid members of the Veteran Reserve Corps. The dismounted cavalry sent from the Army of the Potomac turned out not to be complete regiments, but mostly sick and unserviceable individuals. Only about 500 of them proved of much use, mostly the troopers of the relatively green 25th New York Cavalry, who had left the defenses of Washington just the month before to serve briefly in the provost guard of Meade's army.

The city was only beginning to perceive its danger. But Secretary of War Stanton and Chief of Staff Halleck were working furiously, although often at cross purposes. "Halleck is in a perfect maze," Navy Secretary Gideon Welles recorded, "bewildered, without intelligent decision or self-reliance, and Stanton is wisely ignorant. I am inclined to believe, however, that at this time profound ignorance reigns at the War Department concerning the Rebel raid . . . that they absolutely know nothing of it—its numbers, where it is, or its destination."[9] Lincoln seemed to be perfectly calm, however. He sent a message to Grant at 2 p.m. on the tenth: "Your despatch to Gen. Halleck, referring to what I may think in the present emergency, is shown me. Gen. Halleck says we have absolutely no force here fit to go to the field. He thinks that with the hundred day-men, and invalids we have here, we can defend Washington, and scarcely Baltimore. Besides these, there are about eight thousand not very reliable, under Howe at Harper's Ferry, with Hunter approaching that point very slowly, with what number I suppose you know better than I. Wallace with some odds and ends, and part of what came up with Ricketts, was so badly beaten yesterday at Monocacy, that what is left can attempt no more than to defend Baltimore. What we shall get in from Penn. & N.Y. will scarcely [be] worth counting, I fear. Now what I think is that you should provide to retain your hold where you are certainly, and bring the rest with you personally, and make a vigorous effort to destroy the enemie's force in this vicinity. I think there is really a fair chance to do this if the movement is prompt. This is what I think, upon your suggestion, and is not an order."[10]

Grant answered at 10:30 that night: "I have sent from here a whole corps commanded by an excellent officer, besides over three thousand other troops. One Division of the Nineteenth Corps, six thousand strong is now on its way to Washington. One Steamer loaded with these troops having passed Ft. Monroe today. They will probably reach Washington tomorrow night. This force under Wright will be able to compete with the whole force of Ewell. Before more troops can be sent from here Hunter will be able to join Wright in rear of the Enemy, with at least ten thousand men, besides a force sufficient to hold Maryland Heights. I think on reflection it would have a bad effect for me to leave here, and with Genl Ord at Baltimore and Hunter and Wright with the forces following the enemy up, could do no good. I have great faith that the enemy will never be able to get back with much of his force."[11]

There were other reasons why Grant did not want to leave Petersburg to take personal command of the pursuit of Early. For one thing, it would leave the politically and administratively talented, but militarily incompetent, Ben Butler as the senior officer on that front. For another, it would put offensive operations against Lee on hold. Grant told his staff, "One reason why I do not wish to go to Washington to take personal direction of the movement against Early is that this is probably just what Lee wants me to do, in order that he may transfer the seat of war to Maryland, or feel assured that there will be no offensive operations against Petersburg during my absence, and detach some of his forces and send them against Sherman."[12] But perhaps the main reason

was Grant's lifelong abhorrence of retracing his steps. "One of my super-
stitions," he wrote in his memoirs, "had always been when I started to
go any where, or to do anything, not to turn back, or stop until the
thing intended was accomplished."[13]

Lee wrote a short note to his own president that day: "I have the
honour to send you a N.Y. *Herald* of the 8th containing some items of
interest." Both sides found enemy newspapers to be excellent sources of
military intelligence, since they were subjected to very little censorship
by either government. "You will see the people in the U.S. are mystified
about our forces on the Potomac," Lee pointed out. "The expedition
will have the effect I think at least of teaching them they must keep some
of their troops at home & that they cannot denude their frontier with
impunity. It seems also to have put them in bad temper as well as bad
humour. Gold you will see has gone as high as 271 & closed at 266 3/4.
Provisions, &c., are rising. I see also they are removing the prisoners
from Point Lookout."[14]

The two blockade runners loaded with Confederate sailors and marines on their way to liberate those prisoners had that day proceeded as
far as Fort Fisher, which guarded the mouth of the Cape Fear River
south of Wilmington, when they were signaled to stop for a message
from Davis to their commander, Colonel John Taylor Wood. "The object
and destination of the expedition have somehow become so generally
known that I fear your operations will meet unexpected obstacles," it
said. "General R. E. Lee has communicated with you and left your
actions to your discretion. I suggest calm consideration and full comparison of views with General G. W. C. Lee, and others with whom you
may choose to advise."[15] The operation was aborted.

In response to Grant's wire to Halleck of 6 July, the adjutant general's
office in Washington had drafted General Order No. 225, which said:
"The troops of the Department of North Carolina and Virginia serving
with the Army of the Potomac in the field, under Major General Smith,
will constitute the Eighteenth Army Corps, and Maj. Gen. William F.
Smith is assigned to the command of the corps. Maj. Gen. B. F. Butler
will command the remainder of the troops in that department, having
his headquarters at Fort Monroe."[16] However, this was not what Grant
had asked for. He didn't want to remove the troops of the Army of the
James from Butler's department altogether. He just wanted Butler to stay
at his headquarters and take care of the garrisons and administrative
matters while someone more competent commanded the troops at the
front. This order just aggravated the split between Smith and Butler, for

friends of the former interpreted it as a victory. Wilson, for instance, congratulated Smith because "General Butler has been relieved."[17]

Grant wired Halleck on the tenth: "I would not desire this change made, but simply want General Smith assigned to the command of the Eighteenth Corps, and if there is no objection to a brigadier general holding such position, General W. T. H. Brooks to the command of the Tenth Corps, leaving both of these corps in the Department as before, the headquarters of which is at Fortress Monroe. When the Nineteenth Corps arrives I will add it to the same Department."[18] Grant said he would suspend Order No. 225 until he got further word from Washington. Meanwhile, he wanted one man to command the 10th and 18th Corps in the field, and now he wanted that man to be Major General William B. Franklin, one of Grant's classmates and a friend of Baldy Smith. Butler talked to Grant that day and was happy with this arrangement. He wrote his wife that he was even better off than before the whole matter had come up: "From Grant's suspension of the order, and saying that he proposed to have the 19th corps added to my command, he has vindicated me and my military operations."[19]

As Butler was leaving, Smith was going in to see Grant, before departing on leave. But he made the mistake of criticizing his fellow generals once too often. This time his target was not the inept Butler but Meade, a man who stood even higher in Grant's esteem than Smith himself. Smith later told one of his friends that he "tried to show him the blunders of the late campaign with the Army of the Potomac," speaking of the great loss of life due to "a want of generalship in its present commander." Colonel Comstock, one of Grant's aides, said that Smith "finally asked the general in the most offensive way if he expected he was ever going to do anything with that man in command."[20]

A new Union expedition into Confederate territory started out on that tenth day of July. Sherman had previously ordered Major General Lovell Rousseau, commander of the District of Nashville in Thomas' Department of the Cumberland, to collect from the various units scattered around Tennessee "2,500 good cavalry, well armed, and a sufficient number of pack-mules loaded with ammunition, salt, sugar, and coffee, and some bread or flour," for a raid into Alabama. Rousseau had asked and received permission to lead the force himself, and he selected detachments from five regiments, taking horses away from other units to get them all mounted. They set out from Decatur, Alabama, on the Tennessee River at 1 p.m. under orders to strike the railroads connecting Montgomery, Alabama, with Atlanta somewhere between Tuskegee and Opelika, which would sever the connections between S. D. Lee in Alabama and Joe Johnston in Georgia. That accomplished, they should, if possible, march northeastward up the Chattahoochee, "doing all the mischief possible," to join Sherman in Georgia.[21] But if the raiders ran into trouble and couldn't turn eastward they could ride on south to Pensacola, which was in Union hands.

The raid was timed to take advantage of the fact that Forrest and his superior, S. D. Lee, would have their hands full with A. J. Smith in Mississippi. In fact, 1,500 Confederate troops under Brigadier General Gideon Pillow, who had been defending the area about to be raided, had just been sent to western Alabama to be closer to Forrest. What's more, the commander of the state's reserve and militia forces was already under orders to send them as soon as possible to Mobile, which was feared to be under threat from the Federals in Louisiana. That left only the small cavalry brigade of Brigadier General James H. Clanton, which was technically part of Joe Johnston's Army of Tennessee, far away in Georgia. Rousseau's column crossed the Tennessee River and marched seventeen miles before going into camp that night.

Over in Mississippi that day, Confederate attention was indeed focused on A. J. Smith's advance. In accordance with orders from Forrest, Buford's men left Pontotoc on the tenth and headed southeast toward Okolona, stopping about six miles down the road, where Lyon's and Mabry's brigades took a strong position behind Chiwapa Creek. Bell's Brigade, which was out of forage for its horses, went on to Pontotoc, where there were warehouses full of corn. Chalmers was told to join Buford and take charge of both divisions, but, because the latter was moving, it was after dark when Chalmers found his command post. From Buford, Chalmers learned that "the enemy was moving very slowly, and usually with a line of battle and skirmishers about one mile in length."[22]

In fact, Smith, divided his force that day in order to advance along two parallel roads as far as Cherry Creek, over half the distance from New Albany to Pontotoc. The Union cavalry proceeded due south down the road toward Pontotoc, but the infantry took a road farther east that led through the town of Plentytude. The day was hot and humid and the Federals stayed in camp until 9 a.m. The terrain was level, and the two columns were within supporting distance of each other. The 4th Iowa Cavalry led Grierson's troopers south until they ran into the 2nd Tennessee in position on a commanding ridge. But the firepower of the Federals' Spencer repeating carbines soon forced the Confederates to fall back. They then broke into individual companies or squadrons to take successive positions blocking the road, and as the Yankees advanced, each detachment in turn would fire and then fall back behind the others. These tactics soon wore down the 4th Iowa, so the 3rd was sent to take over and it eventually pushed the Tennesseans across Cherry Creek, where they were replaced by McCulluch's Brigade of Chalmer's Division. The Union infantry, which had met no opposition, soon joined the cavalry on the north bank, and the Federals went into camp there for the night.

Unlike the day before, the Federals got an early start on the eleventh. Coon's brigade of cavalry led the way across Cherry Creek that morning as the reunited army marched toward Pontotoc. It was another hot day, and sunstrokes were numerous. Nevertheless, the officers were told to keep their men closed up and ready to deploy for a fight at a moment's notice, for they were deep in Forrest's country and a little carelessness might lead to the kind of defeat so recently dealt to Sturgis. But McCulloch's Confederates offered little resistance until the town of Pontotoc was approached. The 7th Kansas Cavalry, leading the Union column, found the Rebels posted in and around the village with a reserve massed on a hill beyond town. While the Kansans skirmished with the Southerners, Grierson sent the rest of his division by side roads to approach the town from the east and Mower brought up his lead brigade of infantry, McMillen's. Badly outnumbered, and under orders not to bring on a battle, McCulloch had his men mount up and retire toward Okolona, pursued for several miles by Grierson's troopers.

Late that afternoon, Chalmers sent Lyon's Brigade to relieve McCulloch's. These Kentuckians dismounted on a hill behind a line of fence-rail-and-log breastworks blocking the road southeast to Okolona. They had Mabry's Brigade in support on their right. On their left was McCulloch's Brigade, guarding the road due south to Houston. To Mabry's right was Rucker's Brigade of Chalmer's Division, covering what was called the Cotton Gin Road. On the far right was the 2nd Tennessee, guarding the road running due east to Tupelo. Thus Chalmers had covered all the roads that the Federals might reasonably be expected to take, especially the route to Okolona. Forrest approved of these dispositions and urged Chalmers to hold the Northerners for 48 hours while S. D. Lee completed his preparations for fighting them near Okolona. And the 2nd Tennessee was to prepare for a raid on the Federal rear.

One such raid was undertaken that day by a 100-man detachment under Captain H. A. Tyler, from Buford's division. It followed the Union column but had found the infantry too vigilant to tackle. The Rebels then switched targets to Grierson's cavalry, but were attacked and driven off by a patrol from Winslow's brigade. They wound up on the road to Tupelo, where they replaced the 2nd Tennessee. That night Smith's army camped on the hills south of Pontotoc.

1. Vandiver, *Jubal's Raid*, 110.

2. Ibid., 116.

3. Ibid., 118.

4. Ibid.

5. Pond, *The Shenandoah Valley In 1864*, 59.

6. Ulysses S. Grant, *Personal Memoirs of U. S. Grant* (New York, 1886), vol. 2:306.

7. Foote, *The Civil War*, 3:413–414.

8. Sherman, *Memoirs*, 2:70.

9. Vandiver, *Jubal's Raid*, 141.

10. Basler, *The Collected Works of Abraham Lincoln*, 7:437.

11. Ibid., 7:438. Early's force was still called "Ewell's Corps," for the commander before Early, by many on both sides at that time.

12. Porter, *Campaigning With Grant*, 238.

13. Grant, *Memoirs*, 1:50.

14. Dowdey and Manarin, eds., *Wartime Papers of R. E. Lee*, 817–818.

15. Tidwell, Hall and Gaddy, *Come Retribution*, 147–148.

16. Catton, *Grant Takes Command*, 328.

17. Ibid., 329.

18. Ibid., 328.

19. Ibid., 329.

20. Ibid., 330.

21. Starr, *The Union Cavalry*, 3:462–463.

22. Bearss, *Forrest at Brice's Cross Roads*, 170.

CHAPTER FOURTEEN

But It Won't Appear in History

11–13 July 1864

With 4,000 infantry and 2,000 cavalry, Union major general Henry W. Slocum marched eastward out of Vicksburg and crossed the Big Black River again on Monday, 11 July, keeping the Confederate defenders of central Mississippi too busy to go to the aid of Forrest farther north.

In Washington that day there were still not enough troops to properly man the miles of defenses, although there was a surfeit of generals. In addition to Halleck, the chief of staff, there was Major General Christopher C. Augur, commander of the Department of Washington, and Brigadier General Montgomery Meigs, the quartermaster general, whom Secretary of War Stanton had ordered to report for field service with as many clerks and other employees as he could muster. There were also a number of unassigned generals on hand. Halleck called in one of his favorites, Major General Quincy Gillmore, only recently fired by Butler from command of the 10th Corps. Stanton's favorite was Major General Alexander McCook. He was one of the family of "fighting McCooks" of Ohio, and had recently been cleared of any wrong-doing during the defeat at Chickamauga. Until that battle he had commanded the 20th

Corps in the Army of the Cumberland, where one of his cousins still commanded a cavalry division. Now he was in command of the reserve camp on Piney Branch Creek between the capital and Fort Stevens, which was the northernmost point on the line of defenses. Even Grant had sent a favorite, Major General E. O. C. Ord. He, however, was sent to Baltimore. But generals were getting to be so plentiful that Halleck turned down one offer of service that day with the caustic remark, "We have five times as many generals here as we want, but are greatly in need of privates. Anyone volunteering in that capacity will be thankfully received."[1]

Early's men were on the road again that day, after a difficult sleep in the heat of the previous night. The day was even hotter and lacked any breeze at all. Rodes' Division was on the road about 3:30 a.m., followed by a battalion of artillery, then Ramseur's men, another battalion of artillery, Gordon's Division, the wagon trains, and finally Echols with Breckinridge's old division and the other battalion of artillery. Ransom's cavalry screened the front, but when it reached Rockville, McCausland's Brigade stayed on the main road to Tenallytown and Washington, while the rest of the army turned off toward Silver Spring. This brought them to the Seventh Street Road, where all but Colonel William Jackson's cavalry brigade turned to the right and marched due south toward Washington. Early, watching his columns march through Rockville, noted that the dust was so thick that sometimes he could barely see the men who were kicking it up. The heat, the dust and the lack of sleep were taking their toll, and straggling was worse than usual. One of Gordon's men observed that "our division was stretched out almost like skirmishers."[2] Then, around 1 p.m. the sound of heavy guns gave notice that the van had come within range of the Washington defenses.

Early resisted the urge to ride to the front. Instead he rode along the column, trying to cajole his men into closing up and making haste. He told them he would have them in the capital by dark, but even that failed to spur the jaded infantrymen. They had no reserves of energy left to call on. Finally Early gave up and galloped ahead to join his cavalry. He watched as Imboden's Brigade, temporarily under Colonel George H. Smith, drove the skirmishers of the 150th Ohio militia and the dismounted 25th New York Cavalry into the Union defenses.

Early could see that these were "exceedingly strong, and consisted of what appeared to be enclosed forts for heavy artillery, with a tier of lower works in front of each pierced for an immense number of guns, the whole being connected by curtains and ditches in front, and strengthened by palisades and abatis. The timber had been felled within cannon range all around and left on the ground, making a formidable obstacle, and every possible approach was raked by artillery. On the right was Rock Creek, running through a deep ravine which had been rendered impassable by the felling of the timber on each side, and beyond were the works on the Georgetown pike which had been reported to be the strongest of all. On the left, as far as the eye could reach, the works appeared to be of the same impregnable character. The position was naturally strong for defence, and the examination showed, what might have been expected, that every appliance of science and unlimited means had been used to render the fortifications around Washington as strong as possible."[3]

Checking a large map prepared for him by his cartographer, Early discovered that he was confronted by Fort Stevens, which stood on slightly elevated ground just to the right of the road. It appeared to be manned, but only lightly. He found Rodes leading his division down the pike and ordered him to throw out some skirmishers, deploy the rest of his men into line of battle, and see if he could take that fort. But so many of his men had fallen behind that it was about all Rodes could do to form a skirmish line. Then, about 1:30 p.m. Early noticed a cloud of dust over Washington and soon he could make out a column of Federal infantry marching out of the city to reinforce the defenses. Before long he received word from McCausland that the works near the Georgetown pike were too strongly defended to assault. To make matters worse, not a single Southern sympathizer managed to reach him with word of what was going on inside Washington.

Excitement had taken grip of the national capital that morning as refugees swarmed into the city from Rockville, Silver Spring, and Tenallytown, their wagons stacked high with as many worldly possessions as they would hold. This was no small-scale cavalry raid, the refugees had said. There were 10,000, 20,000, maybe 30,000 Rebels coming this way. Some said that Lee was coming with his entire army. General McCook had advanced his small force of militia, invalids and dismounted cavalry from the reserve camp to Fort Stevens that morning and thrown out a skirmish line to watch for and delay the approach of the Rebels. Convalescents were scoured out of the hospitals, and stragglers were rounded up and sent out toward Tenallytown. Even the president's guards were ordered to help man the defenses.

Lincoln himself had spent the morning at Tenallytown, but at midday he was driven in a coach down to the Potomac. There, at the foot of Sixth Street, he and an eager crowd watched as steamers landed at the wharf and disgorged three brigades of veteran infantrymen wearing faded blue uniforms and Greek Cross emblems on their caps and hats. "It is the old Sixth Corps!" the soldiers heard watching civilians exclaim. "The danger is over now!"[4] Quickly the new arrivals formed column and began marching up Seventh Street, although one brigade had to be recalled because it started out for the Chain Bridge over the Potomac before word arrived from Halleck to concentrate at Fort Stevens. Not far behind the men of the 6th Corps came the first few hundred men of the 19th Corps. These were sent northeastward out the Old Bladensburg Road to Fort Saratoga, where General Gilmore took charge of them.

It was not the 6th Corps troops that Early had seen filing into the entrenchments, causing him to flinch from attacking the formidable defenses. For at 4:10 p.m. Wright, the 6th Corps commander, sent a note to Augur, commander of the Department of Washington. "The head of my column has nearly reached the front," he said, "and at the suggestion of Major-General McCook I have directed them to bivouac at Crystal Spring, about half mile in rear. The enemy has been close to Fort Stevens, and although driven back is still not far distant. I believe it to be only a very light skirmish line, and with your permission will send a brigade out against it, and try to clear it out. General McCook's men are not as good as mine for this purpose." However, Augur replied that he did not think it best to advance beyond the defenses "until our lines are better established—perhaps tomorrow."[5] Halleck at first ordered that the 6th Corps troops be held in reserve, but Wright finally received permission to move to Fort Stevens, where he found the Rebels were dangerously close to taking the position. He sent three veteran Pennsylvania regiments forward as skirmishers to stabilize the situation, and that night 900 6th Corps veterans took up picket duties. As had become their habit over the past couple of months, they promptly dug themselves in.

Extra editions of the Washington papers confirmed for one and all what the sound of heavy guns had already announced: the arrival of the Confederates. And much of the population moved toward Fort Stevens by carriage, horseback or streetcar to see the expected fight. Lincoln himself rode out that way for a look, but there was little to see. Only the more influential sightseers were allowed to proceed as far as Fort Stevens, and even there nothing developed beyond a bit of skirmishing.

Early decided he could not attack until his entire army arrived and recovered from the day's march. It was 6 p.m. before the tail of the Rebel column—not counting stragglers—reached Batchelor's, two miles north of Silver Spring, and went into camp. Early rode back to Silver Spring, where the home of Francis P. Blair, Sr.—father of the Frank Blair who was then commanding the 17th Corps in Sherman's army and of Montgomery Blair, Lincoln's postmaster general—had been commandeered for his headquarters. That evening he called his senior generals together for a council of war. Breckinridge, Gordon, Ramseur and Rodes joined him in sampling Blair's wine cellar. Breckinridge had been a guest there many times before, as vice president of the United States.

Early soon got down to business, namely, deciding whether or not to attack Washington the next day. Would it be worth the risk? The presence of Rickett's division at the Monocacy proved that veterans had been sent north from the Army of the Potomac. The Confederates did not know how many others might already be ensconced behind the capital's formidable entrenchments. Or, perhaps, if they attacked immediately, they could capture the important objective before such reinforcements arrived. Moreover, Hunter's Army of West Virginia was known to be approaching from the west, and the Rebels' route back to Virginia might soon be cut off. Nevertheless, the rewards of taking Washington would be tremendous. There were immense stores of supplies, the Treasury, the Navy Yard, the members of Congress and the Cabinet that might be captured for exchange or ransom, not to mention the president himself—the arch-enemy of Southern independence. Even if the city could not be held, nor all these prizes be garnered, a temporary occupation of the Northern capital would be a terrific humiliation to the Federals and would bring great prestige to the Confederacy overseas, perhaps even recognition by Britain and France at last.

The subordinate generals were not at all agreed on the proper course, but Early's own combative spirit won out in the end. They would attack at dawn, he said, "unless some information should be received before that time showing its impractiblity."[6] It did not take long, however, for such information to arrive. It came in the form of a report from Bradley Johnson. He had not yet reached Point Lookout, but he would push on in that direction unless ordered otherwise, even though his men had been in the saddle for 67 hours. So far they had cut the Northern Central Railroad and destroyed a bridge over the Philadelphia, Wilmington & Baltimore Railroad. They had also captured several trains and prisoners, including Union major general William B. Franklin, but the latter had gotten away when his guards had fallen asleep. However, scouts who had secretly entered Baltimore had brought back word that two Federal corps were said to be reinforcing Washington.

One Union corps would be bad enough, but two would definitely be too much to tackle behind the defenses that ringed the capital city. At first light on 12 July Early was in the saddle, examining the Federal lines. As the sun climbed higher and the light grew, Early could see that the Union defenses were well manned. An attack would be too dangerous, a defeat, even a victory, too costly. He would hold his present position through the day and then retreat under cover of night before the Yankees realized just how vulnerable his little army was. Orders were sent off for

Bradley Johnson to rejoin the main army. Gordon and Rodes were told to deploy skirmishers along a two-mile front, backed up by lines of battle. Observers on the Union side noticed that the main line stayed well back, out of harm's way, lying down in some thickets and woods. Only intermittent artillery fire and occasional rifle shots from a few pickets disturbed the quiet of the sweltering morning.

Throughout the day the Rebel skirmishers gradually creeped closer to the Federal defenses, covered by the fire of sharpshooters from two houses. Generals Wright and McCook decided that those houses, and a pair of knolls overlooking a section of the Union rifle pits, had to be taken. They made careful preparations for an attack during the early afternoon, despite problems with more civilian sightseers, who again thronged out Seventh Street in hopes of getting a look at a real battle. This time there was a bit more action to see. While the troops were brought forward by Brigadier General Wheaton, temporary commander of the 2nd Division, 6th Corps, McCook and Wright went to survey the field. However, Wright soon ran into another sightseeing V.I.P. at Fort Stevens, in this case President Lincoln, who was out for another look at the Rebels despite Secretary Stanton's warning that an assassination plot was afoot. Wright asked him if he would like to view the action, "without for a moment supposing he would accept."[7] But, to the general's horror, the president joined a group standing up on the parapet of the fort.

Wright implored Lincoln to come down. The Rebel sharpshooters were still firing. If the president were killed, what would become of the Union cause? But Lincoln stayed where he was. A sharpshooter's bullet whizzed through the air and struck a surgeon from the 102nd Pennsylvania only five feet from the president. Another bullet mortally wounded another officer even closer to him, but the president remained calm and thoughtful and seemingly unaware of any danger to himself. Wright tried to order his commander-in-chief down from the parapet, but it wasn't until young staff officer Oliver Wendell Holmes, Jr., unaware of the towering civilian's identity, yelled, "Get down, you damn fool, before you get shot!" that the amused Lincoln gave in to Wright's urging and climbed down.[8] The general could now concentrate on business, but deployment of the brigade chosen to make the attack took time, and it was 6 p.m. before the signal was given to begin the advance.

The sound of firing swelled, and Lincoln popped up to peer over the parapet to see men falling in combat. Soon they were being brought past him on stretchers, those who were still alive. Before long the commander of the attacking brigade sent back a request for reinforcements because he had encountered Rodes' solid line of battle backing up the Rebel skirmishers. Supporting regiments were sent out and the Confederates gradually gave ground, but darkness soon brought the Federal advance to a halt, although intermittent firing continued until around 10 p.m.

The attack had caught the Southerners as they were preparing to withdraw, and it put a momentary scare in them, for they feared at first that it was the beginning of a major attack by the two Federal corps presumed to be on hand. "I saw it coming and thought we were 'gone up,'" wrote staff officer Henry Kyd Douglas. "But the attack proved to be little more than a heavy skirmish and was easily repulsed. . . Why the attack was made and, if made, not kept up, I cannot tell, unless it was to see if we were still there," he added.[9] That night, Early sent for Douglas to put him in charge of a rear guard of pickets that was to be left in place while the rest of the army stole away. The young Marylander found his commander with Breckinridge and Gordon. "He seemed in droll humor, perhaps one of relief," Douglas remembered, "for he said to me in his falsetto drawl:

"'Major, we haven't taken Washington, but we've scared Abe Lincoln like h———!'

"'Yes, General,' I replied, 'but this afternoon when that Yankee line moved out against us, I think some other people were scared blue as ———'s brimstone!'

"'How about that, General?' said Breckinridge with a laugh.

"'That's true,' piped General Early, 'but it won't appear in history!'"[10]

Early ordered Breckinridge to take the lead on the return to Virginia and to push his men hard. He would be followed by Ramseur and Rodes, then the 200 pickets under Douglas, with the cavalry bringing up the rear to fight off any pursuit. But very little pursuit was made. As the Confederates withdrew, somebody, without Early's knowledge or consent, set fire to the home of U.S. Postmaster General Montgomery Blair.

Grant's old friend, Assistant Secretary of War Charles A. Dana, who had returned to Washington from Petersburg the day before, wired the general-in-chief that day: "Nothing can possibly be done here toward pursuing or cutting off the enemy, for want of a commander. Augur commands the defences of Washington, with McCook and a lot of brigadiers under him, but he is not allowed to go outside; Wright commands his own corps; Gillmore has been assigned to the temporary command of those troops of the Nineteenth Corps in the city of Washington; Ord to command the Eighth Corps and all other troops in the Middle Department, leaving Wallace to command the city of Baltimore alone; but there is no head to the whole, and it seems indispensable that you should at once appoint one . . . General Halleck will not give orders, except as he receives them. The President will give none; and until you direct positively and explicitly what is to be done, everything will go on in the deplorable and fatal way in which it has gone on for the past week."[11]

At midnight, Grant sent a telegraph to Halleck that was both positive and explicit about what to do: "Give orders assigning Major-General H. G. Wright to supreme command of all troops moving out against the enemy, regardless of the rank of other commanders. He should get outside of the trenches with all the force he possibly can, and should push him [Early] to the last moment." To Dana, Grant wrote that "boldness is all that is needed to drive the enemy out of Maryland in confusion. I hope and believe Wright is the man to assure that."[12]

Early's raid may not have scared Abraham Lincoln, but it added to the general discontent in the North with the course of the war. That same day the *New York World* asked, "Who shall revive the withered hopes that bloomed on the opening of Grant's campaign?"[13]

In Richmond that day Jefferson Davis had his own problems. He had been worried for some time about Joe Johnston's inability to stop Sherman's advance in Georgia. The Federal commander had easily crossed the Chattahoochee River, the last significant barrier north of Atlanta itself, and yet he could get no assurance from Johnston that he could—or would even try to—defend the city. He wrote to Lee that day for advice. "General Johnston has failed," he said, "and there are strong indications that he will abandon Atlanta. . . It seems necessary to relieve him at once. Who should succeed him? What think you of Hood for the position?"[14] Bringing in an outsider in the middle of the campaign hardly seemed advisable. And, of the three corps commanders already with the army, Steward had only recently been promoted to replace the slain Polk. That left Hardee, who was senior in rank and had been with the army since its creation by the amalgamation of several smaller forces over two years before, and Hood, a fairly recent transfer from Lee's own army. Hood and Davis had become close friends the previous winter while the former was recuperating in Richmond from his Chickamauga wound. But the president naturally wanted his most successful general's evaluation of a former subordinate's abilities.

Lee sent a preliminary answer by telegraph, saying, "I regret the fact stated. It is a bad time to release the commander of an army situated as that of Tennessee. We may lose Atlanta and the army too. Hood is a bold fighter. I am doubtful as to other qualities necessary."

He went into more detail in a letter that night. After repeating that changing commanders was a dangerous move at that time, he added,

"Still if necessary it ought to be done. I know nothing of the necessity. I had hoped that Johnston was strong enough to deliver battle. We must risk much to save Alabama, Mobile & communication with the Trans Mississippi. It would be better to concentrate all the cavalry in Mississippi & Tennessee on Sherman's communications." There, unknowingly perhaps, he touched a sore spot. Johnston had been asking for weeks that Forrest's cavalry be sent to raid Sherman's supply line, but Davis would not agree to relinquish northern Mississippi even temporarily and continued to charge S. D. Lee and Forrest with the defense of that area. He had suggested that Johnston send his own cavalry to make a raid, but that general had insisted that his horsemen were needed with his main army.

"If Johnston abandons Atlanta," Lee continued, "I suppose he will fall back on Augusta. This loses us Mississippi and communication with Trans Mississippi. We had better therefore hazard that communication to retain the country. Hood is a good fighter, very industrious on the battle field, careless off, & I have had no opportunity of judging his action, when the whole responsibility rested upon him. I have a high opinion of his gallantry, earnestness & zeal. Genl Hardee has more experience in managing an army. May God give you wisdom to decide in this momentous matter."[15]

Out in Mississippi Forrest's cavalry was far too busy to be thinking about raiding Sherman's supply lines. A. J. Smith still refused to behave as the Confederates expected. Instead of continuing to advance toward Okolona, his main force stayed in camp that twelfth day of July, while small expeditions were sent out to find the Rebels. The 9th Illinois Cavalry, supported by the 52nd Indiana Infantry, pushed southeastward down the Okolona Stage Road and soon flushed Southern pickets from a log cabin. The Federals came to a halt, however, when they reached the brow of a ridge overlooking swampy Chiwapa Creek. On the other side and about a mile and a half away, Lyon's brigade of Rebels manned breastworks on the next hill. After studying the position through his field glasses, the commander of the Union cavalry sent one of his three battalions forward, but a close-range volley broke up the attack. The Federals fell back and notified General Grierson that the road to Okolona was well defended.

Grierson himself had accompanied another probe by the 3rd Iowa Cavalry due south down the road toward Houston. Covered by the fire of one of its battalions, the rest of the regiment crossed Calloway Creek and drove some Texans of McCulloch's Brigade from a hill on the other side. Grierson left one battalion to hold the hill and advanced with the others to a plantation road that connected with the Okolona road farther east. This they followed until they came upon Lyon's defenses. Then Grierson ordered them to return to camp by way of the Okolona road. Other Federal scouts moved eastward on the Tupelo road, advancing five miles before encountering a roadblock manned by Mississippians of Rucker's Brigade. The Confederates also made a probe of the Union position, but it was driven off by men of Bouton's Colored Brigade.

At 9 a.m. that day, Forrest was informed that Roddey's division had reached the Okolona area on its forced march south from Corinth. With the arrival of these reinforcements, he was ready to fight Smith. Chalmers was told to send one of his brigades to the rear and to let the Federals come on. But soon Forrest realized that the Northerners were not advancing into his trap—at least not right away. He even began to fear that they were about to return to Memphis without a fight. And that would not do. As long as Smith's force remained undefeated, it was a threat that could not be ignored. S. D. Lee needed to withdraw forces from northern Mississippi to reinforce Wirt Adams against Slocum's latest expedition and especially to strengthen Mobile, but he could not afford to do so until Smith was defeated and in full retreat.

It was therefore decided to accept battle with Smith wherever it could be had and to assail his column if he "attempted to retreat." Lee ordered Forrest "to move everything to the front," and an officer was sent with orders for Chalmers to stay put where he was; Lee and Forrest would join him before morning "with all the force, to give battle there." Rucker was sent north again, as were Bell's brigade, the artillery, and the small infantry force. It was well after dark when Lee and Forrest reached the Rebel defenses. There they were told by General Buford that he "had discovered no evidence of the reported demoralized condition of the enemy, but had found him ever ready for action."[16]

Rumor and intrigue continued to be rife in the Union armies at Petersburg. Hancock went to see Meade that day and said that he had heard that Meade was to be removed and that he was to replace him. Hancock refused to reveal his source but said it seemed to be reliable. He added that Grant was opposed to the move but would be overruled. Meade went straight to Grant, who said he had not heard the rumor and did not think there could be any truth in it, as he certainly would have been consulted. Meade suggested that the rumor might have arisen from speculation that Grant was going to put him in command of the troops around Washington. Grant was not convinced, for that had never been his intention. However, he did go on to say that if he had to send another corps of troops up there, he probably would send Meade with it.

Something besides rumor was also going around just then, as most of Grant's staff was sick. "The fact is," Grant wrote to his wife that day, "I am the only one at Head Quarters who has not had a day's sickness since the campaign commenced."[17]

The next day, 13 July, General Bragg reached Atlanta from Richmond. Machinery and supplies were being shipped out of town and most of the population was already gone. He reported to President Davis that "the indications seem to favor an entire evacuation of this place."[18]

---

1. Vandiver, *Jubal's Raid*, 142.

2. Ibid., 151.

3. Ibid., 154.

4. Margaret Leech, *Reveille In Washington* (New York, 1941), 339.

5. George E. Pond, *The Shenandoah Valley in 1864* (New York, 1883), 68.

6. Vandiver, *Jubal's Raid*, 156.

7. Ibid., 168.

8. Foote, *The Civil War*, 3:459.

9. Douglas, *I Rode With Stonewall*, 283.

10. Ibid., 284.

11. Pond, *The Shenandoah Valley in 1864*, 71.

12. Ibid., 71–72.

13. Foote, *The Civil War*, 3:461.

14. Steven E. Woodworth, *Jefferson Davis and His Generals* (Lawrence, 1990), 283.

15. Dowdey and Manarin, eds., *Wartime Papers of R. E. Lee*, 821–822.

16. Bearss, *Forrest at Brice's Cross Roads*, 175–176.

17. Catton, *Grant Takes Command*, 335.

18. Woodworth, *Jefferson Davis and His Generals*, 282.

PART THREE

ATLANTA

"Down through the great, open fields they were coming, thousands of them, men in gray, by brigade front, flags flying."

1st Lieutenant Stephen Pierson

Adjutant of the 33rd New Jersey

CHAPTER FIFTEEN

We Are Going to Be Badly Whipped

13–14 July 1864

In Maryland, Early's retreat continued that thirteenth day of July. Bradley Johnson's tired brigade caught up with the main column in the wee hours of the morning. The 2nd Massachusetts Cavalry harried the Confederates near Rockville, but Southern horsemen drove the Yankees off, and the Rebels marched southwestward, reaching White's Ford on the Potomac about midnight.

About noon, Halleck told Augur that Wright's two divisions of the 6th Corps ought to "immediately move out on the river road from Tenallytown, and Gillmore follow as soon as possible." By 5 p.m. the head of Wright's column, including about 750 cavalry and 650 men from the 19th Corps, had reached Fort Reno, and he sent back word to Secretary of War Stanton that his force would be "pushed to the limit of the endurance of the men. I can assure yourself and the President that there will be no delay on my part to head off the enemy."[1] About 7:30 p.m. the Federals went into camp at Offutt's Cross Roads. The 1st Division of the 19th Corps, under Brigadier General William H. Emory, landed at Washington that day and followed Wright west.

In northern Alabama late on the thirteenth, Rousseau's Union raiders reached the Coosa River at Greensport Ferry. So far they had encountered only a few Rebels, who had fired a shot or two and run. The Federals had captured a large amount of corn and other supplies, as well as a paymaster with $160,000 in Confederate money. Now they secured a ferry boat, and by dark about 200 men had crossed to the east side. Meanwhile, Rousseau and his officers weeded out several hundred men and horses who did not look capable of going on and sent them back to the Union lines along the Tennessee River. Then he issued orders for his forces on both sides of the river to move downstream the next day to Ten Islands Ford, where Andy Jackson had crossed fifty years before on his way to fight the Creek Indians at the battle of Horseshoe Bend.

Confederate brigadier general James H. Clanton, commander of the only Southern troops in the area, first learned of the Yankee raid that evening. Leaving part of his brigade to cover Jacksonville and Blue Mountain, to the east, he moved during the night to patrol the crossings of the Coosa with about 200 men of the 6th and 8th Alabama Cavalry regiments. He reached the river near Greensport Ferry about 1 a.m. and sent half of his men, under Lieutenant Colonel Henry J. Livingston, on down to Ten Islands Ford.

Horace Greeley wrote another letter to Lincoln that day. "I have now information on which I can rely that two persons, duly commissioned and empowered to negotiate peace, are at this moment not far from Niagara Falls, in Canada, and are desirous of conferring with yourself or with such persons as you may appoint and empower to treat with them," he said. "You will of course understand that I know nothing, and have proposed nothing, as to terms, and that nothing is conceded or taken for granted by the meeting of persons empowered to negotiate for peace. All that is assumed is a mutual desire to terminate this wholesale slaughter if a basis of adjustment can be mutually agreed on."[2]

Down in central Mississippi, Slocum's Union column passed through Utica that day. Meanwhile, farther to the northeast in that state, Grierson's Federal horse soldiers had gotten up early that morning. The reconnaissances of the day before had convinced A. J. Smith that Forrest's Rebels were defending the road to Okolona in strength. So, leaving one battalion of the 3rd Iowa to hold the hill on the Houston road, the rest of the cavalry started out at dawn to countermarch through Pontotoc and turn to the east toward Tupelo and the Mobile & Ohio Railroad.

Five miles down the road the head of the column ran into the 100-man detachment of Kentucky Confederates, who were beginning a re-

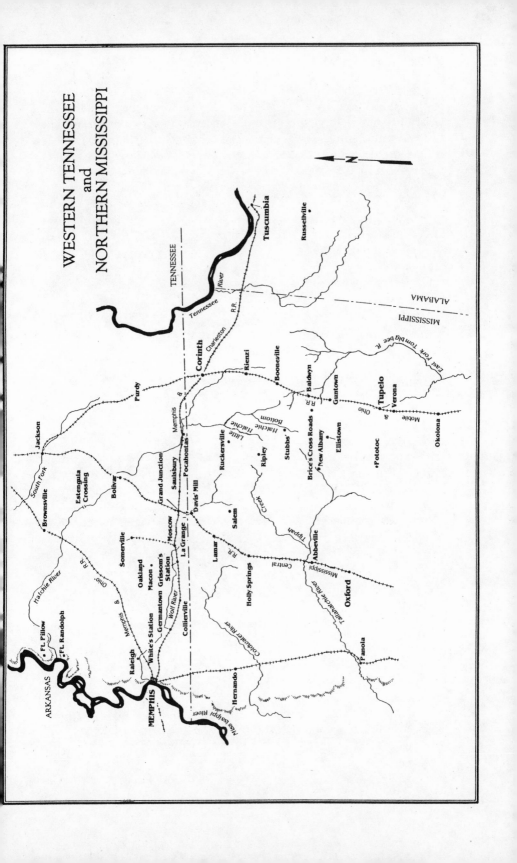

WESTERN TENNESSEE
and
NORTHERN MISSISSIPPI

connaissance of their own. Unaware of the size of the Union force, the Rebels tried to block the road, but the Yankees deployed and threatened them in front and flank simultaneously, forcing them to retreat, and the Federals chased them until the Southerners turned off the Tupelo road twelve miles east of Pontotoc and headed south toward Verona. The Union column continued on to the east, with the infantry now following the cavalry, Moore's division leading, followed by Mower's. Bouton's U.S. Colored Troops guarded the rear with the help of the 7th Kansas Cavalry and the detached battalion of the 3rd Iowa. Ward's brigade of Mower's division was split onto 25-man detachments and distributed along the southern flank of the wagon train.

Smith's sudden change of direction caught the Confederates by surprise, and their reactions were slowed by the confusion caused by their own change of plan the night before. Forrest and S. D. Lee had been so convinced that the Yankees would move southeast toward Okolona that they had practically abandoned the road eastward to Tupelo. Rucker's brigade was the nearest formation of Rebels to the Union line of march. His scouts detected the large enemy column moving along the Tupelo road, "well closed up, his wagon train well protected, and his flanks covered in an admirable manner," but he did nothing to hinder it, merely reporting this development to Chalmers.[3] The latter waited for orders from Forrest, and by the time these arrived, Grierson's troopers had covered half of the eighteen miles from Pontotoc to Tupelo.

At 6 a.m. Mabry had reported to Buford that the Federals on the Okolona road were pulling back, and his men had followed them cautiously. Before long S. D. Lee and Forrest joined them with a battery of horse artillery and Forrest's escort company. As the Confederate advance approached Pontotoc it ran into the 61st United States Colored Troops of Bouton's brigade, and as that regiment withdrew through the town toward Tupelo the Southern generals realized that Smith had stolen a march on them. After a brief discussion, Lee ordered Forrest to take Mabry's Brigade, an Alabama regiment, the battery of horse artillery, and his escort, and harass the enemy's rear. Lee would take Buford's and Chalmer's divisions and try to strike the flank of the moving column wherever it looked vulnerable. He got Buford's men moving, but it was hours before he was able to contact Chalmers, because the latter, evidently assuming that the Federal move was an attempt to get around the Confederate flank and move on Okolona, had taken it upon himself to call up Roddey's division and Rucker's brigade and to hold the crossings of Chiwapa Creek.

Forrest, on this his 43rd birthday, meanwhile, ordered Mabry's Mississippians to attack Pontotoc, supported by the Alabama regiment and the escort company, and they soon drove the 7th Kansas Cavalry and Company A of the 61st U.S.C.T. through the town. However, the commander of the Kansas regiment called on Bouton for help, and the latter told the commander of the 61st U.S.C.T. to set up an ambush. Two companies of that regiment were hidden in the brush beside the road, and after Company A and the Kansans passed by, they poured a deadly volley into Mabry's surprised troopers, throwing them into confusion. This gave the Federals time to fall back in good order, but the pursuit soon came on again.

About five miles east of Pontotoc the Rebels caught up with the tail of the Union column again. Forrest brought up a pair of 10-pounder rifled guns to shell the Federals, but Battery I of the 2nd U.S. Colored Artillery unlimbered its four guns and returned the fire while all three U.S.C.T. infantry regiments prepared to receive an attack. It took time for the Rebels to deploy enough force to challenge this formation, and in the meantime the Union wagons made it across Mubby Creek. When Bouton put two of his regiments and half of his guns back on the road to keep from getting too far behind, leaving the 59th U.S.C.T. and two guns to hold off the Rebels, the Alabama regiment and Forrest's escort company charged the 59th's left flank, but its commander brought up one of his reserve companies, which waited until the Rebels were within fifteen yards before firing. Those Confederates fell back, but then Mabry's Mississippians were seen approaching the right flank. The Federals retreated under the cover of two companies of skirmishers.

About a mile beyond Mubby Creek, Bouton deployed his brigade in line of battle again, but this time Forrest did not attack, because as far as he could tell S. D. Lee had not yet struck the Union column's flank, and he was afraid, he said, that he was driving the Yankees too fast. So he called a halt to give Lee time to attack. Bouton put his brigade back on the road.

Grierson's cavalry at the head of the Federal column met no resistance after clearing the 100 Kentuckians off the road, and about noon the 10th Missouri Cavalry and two companies of the 3rd Iowa rode into Tupelo. They were soon joined by the rest of the division, after it had stopped to feed the horses. All roads leading out of town were picketed, and battalions from the 9th Illinois and the 4th Iowa started tearing up track and burning trestles on the Mobile & Ohio Railroad.

Meanwhile Mower moved the 33rd Wisconsin to the rear of the wagon train, where it could support Bouton's troops if needed. However, this left about a fourth of the wagons without immediate escorts. Around 2 p.m., as the train was passing Burrow's Shop, where a side road came in from the south, the 14th Wisconsin was attacked by some of Rucker's Mississippians. Chalmers had finally been found by one of S. D. Lee's aides and had sent Rucker's brigade up the road that brought it to Burrow's Shop. The lead regiment, the 8th Mississippi Cavalry, broke through the 14th Wisconsin Infantry and started shooting down the mules pulling the Federal wagons. But the Union troops did not panic. The commander of the 14th got his men into line along the edge of the road facing south, and Colonel Ward, the brigade commander, called up the 33rd Wisconsin and placed it behind a rail fence facing east. From there the 33rd poured volleys into the flank of Mabry's troopers that shook them badly, and then Ward yelled for the 14th to charge. The 8th Mississippi was scattered, leaving behind its dead, its wounded, and its battle flag.

Ward had the dead mules cut out of their harnesses and several damaged wagons unloaded and set afire while the column moved on, this time with Mower's division marching behind the wagons. When the Federals were all beyond Burrow's Shop, Forrest's pursuit force linked up with Chalmers' division and the combination continued to follow and harrass Bouton's rear guard. Then Union scouts brought word of another Rebel column approaching rapidly from the southeast. This was Buford's division. When he came within sight of the Federal column, Buford ordered Bell to dismount his brigade, cross Coonewah Creek, and attack the wagons. As the 2nd Tennessee Cavalry advanced, Buford told the men, "Boys, do not kill the mules, but turn them down this way."[4]

However, capturing the wagons wasn't going to be quite as easy as he thought. The 2nd and 20th Tennessee regiments were sent forward before Bell's other two regiments were ready. The Federals of McMillen's 1st Brigade of Mower's 1st Division did not see the Rebels coming because of dense brush between the road and the creek, and were surprised by the sudden attack, but they rallied before the rest of Bell's troops caught up. The 2nd Tennessee was hit on both flanks and broke for the rear, while the rest of Bell's brigade had all it could do to hold its position while waiting for the Kentucky Brigade to come up. But the next brigade in the Union column arrived first, and Bell's troopers fell back behind Coonewah Creek after taking heavy losses. The Kentuckians arrived just in time to dismount and cover this retreat. The Federals gathered up their dead and wounded and resumed their march. They were not subjected to any more attacks, other than some sniping and artillery fire.

A. J. Smith ordered the wagons to be parked about two miles west of the railroad near the little ghost town of Harrisburg, which had been abandoned a few years before, when the railroad had been built through nearby Tupelo. Colonel Moore put his division in position south of the road, on high ground overlooking a stream called Harrisburg Branch, to cover the wagons and the arrival of Mower's and Bouton's troops. Mower's division took position about 8 p.m. on the north side of the road on high ground overlooking another stream, King's Creek. Bouton's brigade camped in the center, near the wagons. It was 9 p.m. by the time the last weary infantryman had filed into camp. The cavalry bedded down in Tupelo.

Most of Forrest's units camped about four miles west of Tupelo, but the Kentucky Brigade—now under Colonel Crossland, as Lyon had been sent to take command of the ad hoc infantry force of dismounted troopers and converted heavy artillerymen—was used to man a picket line closer to Harrisburg. Forrest himself, with one staff officer, made a personal reconnaissance, riding clear around to the rear of the Union position and getting in among the wagons. It was too dark for the Federals to notice the color of their uniforms, and they weren't challenged until they started to leave the Federal camp. Forrest bluffed his way through, and by the time the Northern pickets realized that the two were Rebels, it was too late. They fired, but missed, and Forrest got away.

He had his own men up, fed, and in ranks by 2 a.m. on the fourteenth, but it was daylight before they marched out of camp. General Lyon, with the small infantry force, had arrived by then. Buford took Mabry's and Bell's brigades eastward to Crossland's picket line about a mile and a half west of Harrisburg, where they dismounted, and every fifth man was detailed to hold the horses. Chalmers' men left their horses at the infantry camp and marched on foot to the picket line. By the time they arrived, Crossland's skirmishers were advancing against the Union pickets on both sides of the Pontotoc-Tupelo road.

Before dawn on the fourteenth, Winslow's Union cavalry brigade moved cautiously west on a reconnaissance in force along both sides of the Pontotoc road. The Federals ran into Crossland's skirmishers and pushed them back, but when Winslow saw that larger Rebel formations were coming up he sent a warning to Grierson and Smith that the Confederates were about to attack. Smith ordered Winslow to hold his ground until the Rebels were fully deployed and then to fall back behind the infantry. He then pointed out to General Mower the ground that he wanted his 1st Division to hold north of the road. Mower put Woods' 3rd Brigade on his left, part facing west, and part facing north along a section of the Pontotoc road that ran southwest to northeast. Ward's 4th Brigade was placed in Mower's center, facing northwest, just north of where the road turned back to its normal east-west alignment, and McMillen's 1st Brigade was on the right, facing to the north and northeast. Wilkin's 2nd Brigade—better known as the Eagle Brigade because of its live bald eagle mascot—was held in reserve in a sheltered position behind the center. The four guns of the 2nd Iowa Battery were placed between Woods and Ward, while the four 3-inch rifles of the 6th Indiana Battery were sited between Ward and McMillen. Two guns of Battery E, 1st Illinois, were on McMillen's right.

Colonel Moore placed Murray's 1st Brigade of his 3rd Division just south of the Pontotoc road, on Woods' left. His regiments were concealed by brush and a rail fence and faced west and southwest. One 6-pounder James rifle of the 3rd Indiana Battery was placed in the road between Woods and Murray. The other three guns of the battery occupied a knoll, with one 6-pounder James rifle covering Murray's left and two 12-pounder Napoleons, his front and right. Wolfe's 3rd Brigade of Moore's division was to Murray's left, facing south. Gilbert's 2nd Brigade constituted Smith's general reserve and was posted near the intersection of the Pontotoc and Verona roads. Bouton's brigade guarded the wagons.

Generals Forrest and S. D. Lee realized that Smith's position was a strong one, on ground that sloped up from Harrisburg Branch, and that the Confederates would have to cross several hundred yards of open ground to get at the Yankees. But there were reasons why an attack was necessary. For one, Smith had to be disposed of rapidly so that reinforcements could be sent to Mobile and to head off Slocum's raid. For another, it was necessary to get the Yankees off the Mobile & Ohio Railroad before they did it even further damage. It is also possible that the two Confederate generals underestimated the Federals' morale and cohesion. They knew that most of Grierson's cavalry and some of Smith's infantry had been with Sturgis at Brice's Cross Roads, where the Yankees had been completely routed, and they probably assumed that if the Southern forces could penetrate the Union line, panic would again set in and the Federals would again rout.

There has long been doubt about whether Forrest agreed with Lee's decision to attack. Long after the war, Lee wrote that he and Forrest "were in perfect accord as to delivering battle," but he also admitted that Forrest had "considered the Confederate troops inadequate to defeat Smith."[5] As a major on Forrest's staff later recalled, Forrest told Lee: "The enemy have a strong position—have thrown up defensive works and are vastly our superior in numbers and it will not do for us to attack them under such conditions. One thing sure, the enemy cannot remain long where he is. He must come out, and when he does, all I ask or wish is to be turned loose with my command. I will throw Chalmers' Division on the Ellistown Road, and if Smith undertakes to cross the country to Sherman, turn south to devastate the prairies, or return to Memphis, I will be on all sides of him attacking day and night. He shall not cook a meal or have a night's sleep and I will wear his army to a frazzle before he gets out of the country."[6] Chalmer's post-war recollection, however, was that "Lee, Forrest, Buford and I were riding to the front, when the battle was about to begin. Buford said to Lee and Forrest, who had spent the night and morning together in consultation: 'Gentlemen, you have not asked my opinion about this fight, but I tell you, we are going to be badly whipped.' Forrest replied sharply: 'You don't know what you are talking about; we'll whip 'em in five minutes.' Buford replied: "I hope you may be right, but I don't believe it.'"[7]

Since most of the Confederate troops on hand were from Forrest's corps, Lee offered to allow him the tactical command of the battle, but Forrest declined, saying that Lee outranked him and was his superior and that the responsibility was his. Lee then gave Forrest his choice of which wing of the army to command in the battle, and Forrest chose the right, consisting mostly of Roddey's small division, which Lee wanted to envelop the Federals' southern flank. So Lee would personally direct Buford's division, which would assault down both sides of the Pontotoc road, and Chalmers' division, which would constitute the reserve. Altogether, Lee and Forrest commanded about 9,500 effectives, but deductions for artillerymen and horse-holders left about 7,500 infantry and cavalry to make the attack. Forrest's chief of artillery suggested that all twenty Southern guns be concentrated on the Confederate left center, but Lee ordered the batteries to be parcelled out to support the various brigades.

The four 3-inch rifles and four 6-pounder guns of two Tennessee batteries would support Buford's three brigades. Mabry's Mississippians would attack just north of the Pontotoc-Tupelo road and Crossland's Kentuckians just south of it. Bell's Tennesseans would support Mabry on his left rear. Chalmers' two brigades, Rucker's and McCulloch's, were massed about 400 yards behind Crossland's. Lyon, with the dismounted cavalry and gunless heavy artillerymen, was placed even farther back. Forrest, with Roddey's two small Alabama brigades and 4-gun Georgia battery, plus one of his own 4-gun batteries, was over a mile south of Crossland's right flank. These formations were deployed under the cover of woods while the skirmishers kept the Yankees at a distance. By 7 a.m. the Confederates had pushed their way to the edge of the woods opposite Smith's position and Winslow's Federal cavalry fell back behind the infantry to guard the army's right and rear.

Lee tried, with the fire of sharpshooters and artillery, to goad the Yankees into leaving their defensive position to attack his troops, but with no success. Smith did, however, notice Roddey's division forming up to threaten his southern flank, so Wolfe's 3rd Brigade of Moore's division was advanced to a position on a commanding ridge to the left of Murray, blocking Roddey and facing southwest, with the four guns of Battery G, 2nd Illinois, inserted between his two left regiments. Bouton's brigade was deployed on Wolfe's left and rear facing south and east, blocking the road that led south to Verona, with the 59th U.S.C.T. in reserve, and Battery I, 2nd U.S. Colored Artillery holding the end of the Union line with the 9th Illinois Cavalry in support.

Lee and Forrest had synchronized their watches and arranged that the firing of a single gun on the Pontotoc road would be the signal for the attack. Shortly before the appointed time, Forrest rode off to take charge of Roddey's movement. The day was already hot at 8 a.m., when Lee gave Buford the order to advance. The two rode together to the edge of the open field which Buford's men would have to cross, and the division commander turned to Lee and said that instead of making a direct attack on the Union position, it would be better to move the majority of their army around to the Verona road and attack the Federals' left flank. But Lee considered it too late to change the plan and ordered the attack to proceed.

Crossland's Kentuckians happened to leave the cover of the woods ahead of the other two brigades. Their officers tried to get the men to advance slowly in order to allow time for Mabry's and Bell's formations to catch up, but they found that it was impossible to restrain the ardor of their men. With a shout, the Kentuckians charged forward toward Murray's position. As they advanced they obliqued slightly to their right, opening a growing gap between themselves and Mabry's brigade, which Buford ordered Bell to fill.

Murray's Federals, lying on the ground concealed by brush and corn stalks, waited until Crossland's men had advanced to within 200 yards of them, then opened a terrific fire of both rifles and cannon. The artillerymen of the battery supporting Wolfe's brigade wheeled their guns to the right and hit the Kentuckians with a deadly crossfire that, in Crossland's words, "was fatal to my men."[8] Two regiments of Wolfe's brigade poured their oblique fire into the Confederates' flank as well.

This was made possible because Roddey's men did not advance to threaten Wolfe. The Kentuckians had charged before Forrest was ready. He had been conferring with Roddey, and "after giving him the necessary orders in person I dashed across the field at a gallop for the purpose of selecting a position in which to place his troops, but on reaching the

front I found the Kentucky brigade had been rashly precipitated forward."[9] The Rebels wavered, but Crossland rode out in front of his
brigade and shouted, "Forward men; forward!", and they surged ahead
again. But when they had come to within 50 or 100 yards of the Union
line, Murray ordered his men to countercharge them. The Federals
sprang to their feet "and with a yell like that of demons" poured a volley
into the Kentuckians that decimated their ranks, and then charged.[10]
Crossland's Rebels broke and ran, pursued by Murray's regiments and
one of Wolfe's, who continued to pour volleys into their thinning ranks.
The 8th Kentucky Mounted Infantry lost half its men in those few minutes. When the Confederates reached the cover of the woods from which
they had advanced, the Northerners fell back to their original positions—
all except the 122nd Illinois on Murray's right, which took cover behind
a fence near a church in the abandoned village of Harrisburg, between
the lines.

When he saw Crossland's men retreating, Forrest rode over to rally
them. "I seized their colors," he wrote, "and after a short appeal ordered
them to form a new line."[11] After seeing what had happened to the
Kentuckians, Forrest stopped the advance of Roddey's Alabamans. He
explained that "the terrific fire poured upon the gallant Kentucky brigade
showed that the enemy were supported by overwhelming numbers in an
impregnable position."[12] Forrest sent Roddey's men to cover the Tupelo-
Verona road, except for the artillery, which dueled with the Union guns.
When Crossland's men were reformed and had rested a bit, Lee sent
them to the Verona road also.

The Kentuckians' premature advance set off a domino effect among
the Confederates. When Mabry saw that Crossland's brigade was in
trouble he hurried his own men forward without waiting for Bell's Tennesseans to catch up. But they swung far to their left and struck Woods'
and Ward's brigades of Mower's division. When the Mississippians
emerged from the cover of the woods the guns of the 2nd Iowa and 6th
Indiana batteries began to strike them, and when the Rebels closed to
within 300 yards, Ward's infantry opened a terrific rifle fire. Mabry
yelled for his men to charge, and some of them got to within sixty yards
of the Federals, but by then the brigade looked like little more than a
skirmish line. Mabry called a halt and ordered his men to take cover in
a hollow of land and behind a low fence, where they lay down and
returned the Union fire as best they could.

Then it was Bell's turn. His Tennesseans advanced to the right, or
south, of Mabry's Brigade, "yelling and howling like Comanches," as
A. J. Smith wrote, in the face of what one Rebel called the most appalling
fire of musketry and artillery that his regiment had ever faced.[13] From

its advanced position in Harrisburg, the 122nd Illinois fired into the
Confederate flank, as did the 3rd Indiana Battery from Murray's position
south of the Pontotoc road. Nevertheless, the Rebels got to within 75
yards of the ground held by the 12th Iowa and 33rd Missouri on Woods'
left. Then they too went to earth, and a great fire fight followed. When
the 12th Iowa began to run out of ammunition Woods replaced it with
the 7th Minnesota. Federal colonel Alexander Wilkin was killed by a
Rebel bullet. He was replaced in command of the Eagle Brigade by
Colonel John D. McClure.

Many of Mabry's men took advantage of the switch of Federal fire to
Bell's men to slip to the rear, and then Mabry officially ordered a withdrawal. As the Mississippians fell back they came upon Rucker's brigade
advancing in line of battle. Chalmers had been told by Forrest to move
his division to the right and support Roddey, but Lee had ordered him
to move to the left and reinforce Mabry. To make the confusion complete, Buford sent him an order, citing Lee as authority, for him to
support the center. He chose to obey his immediate superior, Forrest,
but before he got to Roddey's command post he was overtaken by Lee,
who told him to divide his division, leaving McCulloch's brigade in
reserve and sending Rucker's to the left, where it was to "charge at a
double-quick and with a shout."[14]

Chalmers went with them, riding on one flank while Rucker took the
other. The men, not used to long marches on foot, were all tired out
from marching to the right and back to the left in the July heat. Then
they had to go uphill, across plowed ground and a cornfield, causing
many of the men to faint from exhaustion. Those were the lucky ones,
because others soon began to drop from the murderous fire of Ward's
Federal infantry. Rucker himself was struck twice and carried off badly
wounded. He was succeeded by Colonel Duckworth. Bell took advantage of Rucker's advance to pull his own troops back, and when the 10th
Minnesota of McMillen's brigade rose from cover and fired a close-range
volley, Rucker's men, now Duckworth's, also fell back to the protection
of a hollow of ground. Seeing this, Mower ordered his Union brigades
to advance. Woods', Ward's and McClure's men went forward, pushing
the Rebels back into the woods, capturing a number of prisoners, including a group of sharpshooters, and the colors of the 6th Mississippi
Cavalry. Wounded Confederates were gathered up and taken to the
Union field hospital, and 270 dead Rebels were counted in front of
Mower's lines, while their rifles were collected and smashed against trees.

Seeing that Roddey's Division never advanced, S. D. Lee rode over to
his right, where he found Forrest and asked, "Why did you not carry
out the plan of attack?" Forrest explained that "Buford's right had been

rashly thrown forward and repulsed," and that "in the exercise of my discretion I did not move Roddey forward, but I have moved him to the left, and formed a new line." Lee snapped back, "In doing as you did, you failed to carry out the plan of battle agreed on."[15] It was, however, too late now and he had ordered McCulloch's men to cover the withdrawal of the four shattered brigades. Then Forrest was directed to take charge of Chalmers' and Buford's divisions and Lyon's infantry, and to put them all into defensive positions.

At about 5:30 p.m. Bouton reported that a large force of Confederates was on the Verona road. Smith therefore ordered Gilbert's brigade forward and it took position on Bouton's left, behind the crest of a high hill which commanded that part of the field. But when no attack came, Smith sent both Gilbert's and Bouton's brigades back to their camps, leaving skirmishers in place to hold the ground, and the 9th Illinois Cavalry rejoined Coon's brigade in Tupelo.

Grierson's cavalry had not been heavily engaged during the day's fight. After Winslow's brigade made the reconnaissance that discovered the Rebel build-up to the west, it had joined Coon's brigade, which had occupied Tupelo and picketed all the roads south of the Federal defenses. There was some skirmishing with the 100-man detachment of Kentuckians, who probed their positions, but no real fighting.

That afternoon, Smith asked Grierson's help in finding out where the Rebels' had gone. Grierson sent a column, consisting of a battalion each of the 3rd and 4th Iowas, two miles out the Pontotoc road, where they discovered Forrest's defenses. After a brief examination, the column returned to report, dropping off three companies of the 3rd Iowa to picket the Pontotoc road and to sound the alarm, should the Rebels advance.

At dark the Confederates were angered to see that the Yankees were burning the abandoned buildings of Harrisburg. Chalmers led McCulloch's brigade forward but found Woods' and Murray's Federals still in position on the ridge east of the town. Meanwhile, Forrest led Rucker's brigade on a similar probe of the Union left. He drove in the skirmishers left behind by Bouton's and Gilbert's brigades, but Wolfe's left-flank regiment, the 117th Illinois, stood its ground and fired volley after volley in his direction while Bouton's and Gilbert's brigades hurried forward, deploying on the run. Forrest said the enemy's fire on this occasion was one of the heaviest he had heard during the war. "There was unceasing roar of small-arms, and his whole line was lighted up by a continuous stream of fire."[16] However, due to the darkness and the fact that the Confederates were on lower ground, the Union fire passed harmlessly overhead. But, satisfied that he had stirred up the Yankees and made it hard for them to sleep, he felt he had done enough and returned to his defenses. There he ordered Buford to move his division to reinforce Roddey on the Verona road.

The four Confederate brigades that had charged piecemeal had lost a little over one-third of their troops that day, and their combat effectiveness had been destroyed. Seven of Buford's regiments had lost every officer over the grade of captain. The 2nd Tennessee was now commanded by a lieutenant. In later years, supporters of Forrest and S. D. Lee argued about who was to blame for this disaster, but the two generals remained friendly. Lee summed it up this way: "I am sure he did the best as he saw it. I am sure I did my best as I saw it."[17]

The Federal infantry rested on their arms that night and wondered whether the next day would bring another fight or a pursuit of the defeated Rebels.

----

1. Pond, *The Shenandoah Valley in 1864*, 73–74.
2. Basler, ed., *The Collected Works of Abraham Lincoln*, 7:441.
3. Foote, *The Civil War*, 3:511.
4. Bearss, *Forrest at Brice's Cross Roads*, 186.
5. Herman Hattaway, *General Stephen D. Lee* (Jackson, 1976), 120.
6. Bearss, *Forrest at Brice's Cross Roads*, 199.
7. Ibid., 199–200.
8. Ibid., 204.
9. Hattaway, *General Stephen D. Lee*, 123.
10. Bearss, *Forrest at Brice's Cross Roads*, 204.
11. Hattaway, *General Stephen D. Lee*, 123.
12. Bearss, *Forrest at Brice's Cross Roads*, 205.
13. Ibid., 207.
14. Ibid., 208.
15. Ibid., 211.
16. Ibid., 214.
17. Ibid., 216.

CHAPTER SIXTEEN

As You Have Failed to Arrest the Advance of the Enemy

14–17 July 1864

In Maryland that same day, the fourteenth of July, Wright's Union troops reached Seneca Creek. From there he sent a report to Halleck, back in Washington. "I believe that the bulk of the enemy's force has already crossed the river at Edward's Ferry," he wrote.[1] He sent out reconnaissance parties and marched his main column on as far as Pooles-ville, but his conclusion remained the same. He reported to Halleck that the Confederates had got too great a head start. There was also another problem. "I have not been able to get any intelligence from General Hunter's command, and have, therefore, for further operations only the two divisions of my corps, numbering, perhaps, 10,000, and some 500 possibly of the Nineteenth Corps, which, unless I overrate the enemy's strength, is wholly insufficient to justify the following up of the enemy on the other side of the Potomac. I presume this will not be the policy of the War Department, and I shall therefore wait instructions before proceeding farther, which I hope to receive by the time the Nineteenth Corps arrives."[2]

He was correct about the Rebels. Early had crossed the Potomac back to Virginia that morning with his wagons, the prisoners taken at the Monocacy, and large numbers of cattle and horses, and camped at Leesburg, a bit east of the Blue Ridge. To Lee he reported, "I shall rest here a day or two, and then move to the Valley, and drive from Martinsburg a body of cavalry which has returned there, and then send the cavalry to destroy effectually the Baltimore and Ohio Railroad westward, and also to destroy the coal mines and furnaces around Cumberland, unless I get different orders." Once all this was accomplished, he said, he would "retreat in forced marches by land toward Richmond."[3]

However, Wright was wrong about the policy of his superiors. Halleck's reply stated: "General Grant directed that a junction of your forces and that of General Hunter be made in the vicinity of Edward's Ferry, to cut off the enemy's retreat, if possible; if not, to pursue him South, doing him all the damage you can. He further says that you must live mainly upon the country. He does not say how far South you are to pursue, but I will get his instructions on that point and communicate them to you. You will therefore continue the pursuit till you receive further orders. In giving you the supreme command with only general indications as to what you are to do, General Grant probably intended to leave you free to exercise your own judgment. As your force, until Hunter or the Nineteenth Corps reaches you, will be inferior to the enemy, you will move with caution. Rickett's division and Kenly's brigade, under General Ord, left this morning to join you. They number about 5,000. About 4,000 of the Nineteenth Corps, under General Emory, have also left."[4]

The Union cavalry at Martinsburg that Early was concerned about was Duffié's division of Hunter's army. And Hunter, with his main force, arrived at Harper's Ferry that night. Wright sent a request that Hunter meet him at Leesburg. But Halleck wired Hunter that "General Crook would be a suitable person for the immediate command" of the troops which he would send to join up with Wright. Halleck also complained that "for the last two weeks little or nothing of a reliable character has been heard from you."[5]

Halleck had been complaining to others lately, too. Secretary Stanton referred the president to a letter which he had received from the chief of staff that day. According to Halleck, Postmaster General Blair had been heard, in speaking of the burning of his home by Early's Confederates, to say, in effect, that "the officers in command about Washington are poltroons . . . that General Wallace was in comparison with them far better as he would at least fight." As there were, Halleck said, "a large number of officers on duty in and about Washington who have devoted their time and energies night and day, and have periled their lives, in the support of the Government, it is due to them as well as to the War Department that it should be known whether such wholesale denouncement and accusation by a member of the Cabinet receives the sanction and approbation of the President of the United States. If so the names of the officers accused should be stricken from the rolls of the Army; if not, it is due to the honor of the accused that the slanderer should be dismissed from the Cabinet."[6]

In a letter that Carl Sandburg described as "peremptory, decisive, perfectly understanding and sweetly courteous," Lincoln replied that same day.[7] "Whether the remarks were really made I do not know; nor do I suppose such knowledge is necessary to a correct response," he wrote. "If they were made I do not approve them; and yet, under the circumstances, I would not dismiss a member of the Cabinet therefor. I do not consider what may have been hastily said in a moment of vexation at so severe a loss, is sufficient ground for so grave a step. Besides this, truth is generally the best vindication against slander. I propose continuing to be myself the judge as to when a member of the Cabinet shall be dismissed."[8]

Down in northern Alabama that day, the fourteenth, Rousseau's Union raiders clashed briefly with Clanton's Rebel defenders. The 200 Federals that had crossed the Coosa River the day before at Greensport Ferry ran into Clanton's own force that morning as they left the ferry to head south. After heavy skirmishing, the Confederates were driven off. Meanwhile, when Rousseau's main force reached Ten Islands Ford it was blocked by the 100 Confederates under Lieutenant Colonel Livingston whom Clanton had sent down. But then the 200 Federals on the east bank arrived and chased these Rebels away. Clanton, believing that the Yankees would move eastward toward Jacksonville and his own headquarters at Blue Mountain, withdrew in that direction, leaving the route south open to Rousseau, who got his whole force across the river and moving toward Talladega.

Confederate president Jefferson Davis telegraphed General Bragg in Atlanta that day to tell him to use his own discretion, but that if Johnston needed to be replaced and if Hardee seemed to be the right man for the job, he should "adopt advice and execute as proposed."[9] However, Bragg was not fond of Hardee. He had come to see that the senior corps commander had been responsible for much of the discontent in the Army of Tennessee that had led to his own removal from the job. He had also been subjected to Hood's own rather self-serving version of the Atlanta campaign to date, according to which Hood had always been for standing and fighting while Johnston and Hardee had always favored retreating. "If any change is made Lieutenant-General Hood would give unlimited satisfaction," Bragg replied to Davis the next day, the fifteenth. "Do not understand me as proposing him as a man of genius, or a great general," he added, "but as far better in the present emergency than any one we have available."[10]

At the same time, the Federal government was having its problems with its commander in Georgia. Sherman wired to Halleck that day about a new law that would allow state governments to send agents into the South to recruit blacks to help fill the states' quotas of new soldiers. New England manufacturers had lobbied for this bill to prevent their mill hands from being drafted into the army at a time when the demands of the war were keeping their factories humming and their profits high. Sherman told Halleck, "If State recruiting agents must come into the limits of my command under the law, I have the honor to request that the commanding officers or adjutants of regiments be constituted such agents, and that States be entitled to a credit for recruits they may enlist . . . This will obviate the difficulty I apprehend from civilian agents."[11] In a second telegram Sherman was more frank. "Before regulations are made for the States to send recruiting officers into the rebel States, I must express my opinion that it is the height of folly. I cannot permit it here and I will not have a set of fellows hanging around on any such pretenses. We have no means to transport and feed them. The Sanitary and Christian Commisions are enough to eradicate all traces of Christianity out of our minds less a set of unscrupulous State agents in search of recruits."[12]

That same day, Grant told Meade to send Sheridan's cavalry to cut the Richmond & Danville and the Petersburg & Weldon railroads, so that Lee could not send troops to Georgia to help Joe Johnston. But Meade and Sheridan replied that this would be too dangerous unless a strong force of infantry could be sent in support, so Grant put off the movement until the 6th and 19th corps were returned to him.

At Harper's Ferry that day, Hunter replied to Halleck's censure of

him the day before. He had begun to realize that he was being blamed
for Early's raid. As for not keeping Halleck informed, he said that if any
important event had occurred in his department that the War Department
wouldn't have known about earlier than he did himself, he didn't know
what it would be. He said that he "could have telegraphed many alarming
rumors every hour," but that was not his way and that at any rate, he had
been too busy trying to hurry his forces forward.[13] Then he requested to
be relieved from command. He also ordered Crook to take charge of all
the forces from his department in the field. Grant had heard that a number of accusations were being made against Hunter, and he wrote that
day to Assistant Secretary of War Dana: "I am sorry to see such a disposition to condemn as brave an old soldier as Hunter is known to be without
a hearing."[14]

Lincoln replied to Horace Greeley's latest letter regarding the Confederate commissioners that day, the fifteenth, with a telegram. "I suppose
you received my letter of the 9th," he said. "I have just received yours
of the 13 and am disappointed by it. I was not expecting you to send me
a letter, but to bring me a man, or men."[15] He concluded by saying that
he was sending his secretary, John Hay, with his answer.

In Alabama early that day, Rousseau's Union raiders entered Talladega, where they paroled 143 Confederate convalescents in the military
hospital and captured 20,000 rations of flour and bacon and 100,000 of
sugar and salt. What they didn't eat they destroyed, along with a gun-
making establishment, several railroad cars, and the depot. A few hours
later they were back on the road. Rousseau feinted to the west toward
an important bridge over the Coosa and then south toward Montgomery,
the state capital, and finally, about 5 p.m., he turned his column to the
southeast.

That morning, 15 July, General A. J. Smith received some bad news.
His staff informed him that after issuing all the reserve artillery ammunition, there remained only about 100 rounds per gun. But what was
worse, most of the hardtack crackers had spoiled, leaving only about
one day's rations on hand. This left him little choice but to return to
Memphis.

All the wounded Confederates and forty of the most serious Federal
cases were moved to Tupelo, along with two surgeons and a number
of male nurses with enough medical supplies for ten days. Meanwhile,
Winslow's troopers were sent to reconnoiter the Confederate defenses
and to bring in a disabled cannon that the Rebels had abandoned. They

drove in the Southern pickets and discovered that Mabry's Brigade and Lyon's "infantry" were still holding the same defenses as Forrest had occupied the evening before.

About noon, Smith ordered Colonel Moore to withdraw his division, march to Tupelo and turn to the northwest, up the Ellistown road. His column was to move "very slowly, the train to follow with sick and wounded, protected well on the flanks by a brigade of cavalry and in the rear by the colored brigade."[16] The division's march was uneventful, except for the heat, and the column crossed Oldtown Creek on a rickety old bridge and camped on a ridge beyond it. Meanwhile, Mower redeployed his brigades to cover the army's withdrawal.

S. D. Lee had feared that the Yankees would move south in order to lay waste to the crops of the fertile Black Prairie region, so he had massed most of his troops across the Tupelo-Verona road, three miles north of Verona. But when the Federals did not advance, Forrest sent Buford's troopers northward up the road, and they dismounted two and a half miles south of Tupelo with Rucker's brigade on the right, Crossland's in the center, and Bell's on the left. They drove in the Union pickets guarding the southern flank of Smith's force just as Bouton's brigade was ready to follow the wagons out of camp. Mower directed Bouton to hold his last two regiments, the 61st and 68th U.S.C.T., ready to meet the enemy. Bouton formed them in line of battle and advanced through some woods. When they emerged on the other side they could see Buford's Rebels, and Bouton ordered his men to charge. They surged forward with a shout, supported on their left by the 9th Illinois Cavalry and on their right by the 9th Minnesota of McClure's brigade and the 93rd Indiana of McMillen's, and four guns. The oppressive heat had already taken its toll of Buford's men, and now their skirmishers were driven back half a mile. But the Federals fell back before encountering the main line.

This threat to the Union southern flank caused Winslow's brigade to be withdrawn from the Pontotoc road and sent to join Coon's, and when Chalmers saw Winslow's troopers fall back he ordered McCulloch's brigade to mount up and follow them. But from the ridge looking down on Harrisburg Branch he soon saw that the Federal infantry was still present, so he moved to the northeast to see if he could find the Union right flank. What he saw, instead, was Moore's column moving along the Ellistown road approaching Oldtown Creek, and he rode back to the Pontotoc road to report this important development to S. D. Lee.

In the meantime, General Lyon advanced with his dismounted Rebels, covered by skirmishers from the 14th Confederate Cavalry of Mabry's Brigade, to probe the Union defenses beyond Harrisburg Branch.

Mower cautioned Woods and Ward, whose brigades were still in position, to keep their men concealed behind their breastworks and to hold their fire until the Southerners were within fifty yards. Lyon, however, suspected a trap and stopped his men 200 yards out, where they took cover and opened fire. Mower, therefore, ordered Woods' men to charge. They lept to their feet, jumped over their defenses, and ran down the hill toward the Rebels, who promptly broke ranks and ran for the rear. Woods' men chased the Confederates for half a mile but couldn't catch them, so Woods called a halt and marched them back to their breastworks. Mower then put his division on the road to follow Bouton's brigade, while Grierson, with Winslow's cavalry, screened the army's rear.

When S. D. Lee and Forrest learned that Chalmers had spotted a Federal column moving up the Ellistown road they realized that Smith was returning to Tennessee. Lee learned that day of Rousseau's raid into the eastern edge of his department, so he put Forrest in charge of the pursuit of Smith. Forrest led Roddey's division toward Harrisburg and threw its leading regiment, the 5th Alabama, against the 9th Illinois, but was unable to move it. Then Buford arrived with Bell's and Crossland's brigades and a battery of artillery, and Forrest directed him to push toward Tupelo. Mabry's Brigade was sent northwest up a road toward Chesterville to establish a roadblock, and Chalmers was to follow Buford with McCulloch's brigade.

Mower's division followed Bouton's brigade and the wagon train up the Ellistown road, and the rear brigade, McMillen's, was just crossing Oldtown Creek when Buford's division attacked the Union cavalry rear guard. Confederate cannon began to shell the wagon park as Crossland's and Bell's brigades dismounted and deployed into line. Then the Rebels advanced. Winslow dismounted the 3rd and 4th Iowa Cavalry regiments, while Smith ordered Mower and Moore to send them some help. Mower told McMillen to send his brigade back across the creek, and Moore sent first Gilbert's and then Wolfe's brigades.

The Union infantry recrossed the waist-deep stream and started up the hill occupied by Buford's men, wounding Colonel Crossland in the process. Chalmers rode up at the head of McCulloch's brigade and, in an attempt to save the situation, fed in his regiments one at a time as they came up, but to no avail, and McCulloch went down with a wound in the shoulder. Forrest also came up but was soon wounded in the foot, so he turned command over to Chalmers with orders to withdraw. Chalmers told Buford to reform his division, but the latter was only able to rally three companies. So McCulloch's troopers were remounted and used to screen a withdrawal of about a quarter of a mile. McMillen's troops were then sent back to the north side of the creek again, as Mower's division was to lead the column the next day. Gilbert's and Wolfe's brigades occupied the ridge south of the stream.

A rumor soon spread through the Confederate army that Forrest was dead. When the general heard about it, he left the field hospital at Tupelo, where he had gone to have his wound attended to, mounted his horse, and rode at a gallop along his lines, assuring his troops that it was only a minor wound and that he was still able to lead them. "The effect produced upon the men by the appearance of General Forrest is indescribable," one of his solders wrote. "They seem wild with joy at seeing their great leader still with them."[17]

Sometime that evening Forrest gave Buford an order regarding his division. "I have no division, General Forrest," Buford answered. "Where is your division?" Forrest asked. "They are dead and wounded," was the reply.[18]

By dawn of the sixteenth, Smith had his men on the road, Mower's division leading the column and Winslow's cavalry brigade bringing up the rear. They marched northwest to Ellistown and most of the men had started preparing their evening meal when cannon fire was heard from the southeast.

Due to the condition of his troops, S. D. Lee had decided not to pursue the Yankees in force. He did direct Chalmers to harass them with Roddey's Division and Rucker's brigade. They followed along behind the Federals, occasionally exchanging shots with the 7th Kansas Cavalry. Then as the Northerners settled into camp the Rebels became bolder. But when the Union pickets called for help, Moore sent Wolfe's brigade and the two guns of Battery G, 2nd Illinois Artillery. After a few rounds from the cannon and the sight of the reinforcements, Chalmers called off his troops and went into camp.

That morning, the sixteenth, Wright's troops of the Federal 6th and 19th corps crossed the Potomac at White's Ford and marched for Leesburg, where Early's Confederate Army of the Valley had been encamped for two days. Wright had been informed that part of Hunter's army, under Brigadier General Jeremiah C. Sullivan, had already crossed into Virginia a bit father west and was moving toward the same town. However, Early had also taken to the roads that day, heading west for the Shenandoah Valley by way of Snicker's and Ashby's gaps.

About noon Brigadier General George Crook caught up with Sullivan and took command of all of Hunter's troops in the area. He promptly sent cavalry patrols out in all directions searching for the Rebels. One of these located Early's wagon train moving west, and while Crook's infantry was too far away to catch it in time, Duffié sent a small cavalry brigade under Colonel William B. Tibbets, which captured 117 mules and horses, 82 wagons, and 50 or 60 prisoners for the loss of 20 men. Early hurried troops from Rodes' and Ramseur's divisions to recoup his losses, but Tibbets managed to get away with 37 loaded wagons and burned over 40 others. That night, Crook's men from the Army of West Virginia camped within six miles of Wright's force, which had stopped three miles west of Leesburg, and Crook came under Wright's orders.

That same day, Colonel Comstock of Grant's staff arrived at Washington bearing a letter to Halleck saying that "the Sixth and Nineteenth Corps should be got here without any delay, so that they may be used before the return of the troops sent into the Valley by the enemy. Hunter, moving up the Valley, will either hold a large force of the enemy, or he will be enabled to reach Gordonsville and Charlottesville. The utter destruction of the [rail]road at and between these two points will be of immense value to us." That was always one of Grant's pet objectives throughout the war. But he added, "I do not intend this as an order to bring Wright back whilst he is in pursuit of the enemy with any prospect of punishing him, but to secure his return at the earliest possible moment after he ceases to be absolutely necessary where he is." He went on to say that "if the enemy has left Maryland, he should have upon his heels veterans, militiamen, men on horseback, everthing that can be got to follow, to eat out Virginia clear and clean, as far as they go, so that crows flying over it, for the balance of this season, will have to carry their provender with them." In a letter written that same day, Grant said, "Hunter should make all the Valley south of the B. and O. road a desert, as high up as possible. I do not mean that houses should be burned, but every particle of provisions and stock should be removed, and the people notified to move out."[19]

Comstock said that Halleck greeted him with a laugh and that "his first question, in a rather sneering way, was when were we going to do something." Halleck still thought the Army of the Potomac should operate against Richmond from north of the James. Comstock noted in his diary that the chief of staff "said it was useless to talk about elements of strategy—that Lee was in a central position in reference to A. of P. and troops at Washn and could act on either at pleasure. That if Wright & 19th Corps were withdrawn Early would at once come back & play the same game over. Asked him what he supposed we could do with a siege of Richmond on North side—he said that was not for him to say—that he might return by asking what we could do by siege on S. side."[20]

Evidently Comstock reported this to Grant, who sent a new message to Halleck that day: "I want if possible to get the 6th & 19th corps here to use them before the enemy can get Early back. With Hunter in the Shenandoah and always between the enemy and Washington force enough can always be had to check an invasion until reinforcements can go from here. This does not prevent Hunter from following the enemy even to Gordonsville and Charlottesville if he can do it with his own force and such other improvised troops as he can get. But he should be cautious."[21]

This fell on deaf ears. Halleck wrote in a letter to Sherman—to whom he always felt closer than to Grant—"Entre nous, I fear Grant has made a fatal mistake in putting himself south of James river. He cannot now reach Richmond without taking Petersburg, which is strongly fortified, crossing the Appomattox and recrossing the James. Moreover, by placing his army south of Richmond he opens the capital and the whole North to Rebel raids. Lee can at any time detach 30,000 or 40,000 men without our knowing it till we are actually threatened. I hope we may yet have full success, but I find that many of Grant's general officers think the campaign already a failure."[22] Where Lee was going to get a spare 30,000 or 40,000 men Halleck didn't say.

Grant was also writing to Sherman that day. As ever, he was determined to prevent the Confederates from using their interior lines to combine forces from different points against one of the Union armies, as they had at Chickamauga. In a telegram to his old friend he warned: "The attempted invasion of Maryland having failed to give the enemy a firm foothold North, they are now returning, with possibly 25,000 troops . . . It is not improbable, therefore, that you will find in the next fortnight re-enforcements in your front to the number indicated above. I advise, therefore, that if you can get to Atlanta you set about destroying the railroads as far to the east and south of you as possible; collect all the stores of the country for your own use, and select a point that you can hold until help can be had. I shall make a desperate effort to get a position here which will hold the enemy without the necessity of so many men. If successful, I can detach from here for other enterprises, looking as much to your assistance as anything else."[23]

Lincoln's secretary, John Hay, arrived at New York that day, the sixteenth, with the president's reply to Horace Greeley: "Yours of the 13th. is just received; and I am disappointed that you have not already reached here with those Commissioners, if they would consent to come, on being shown my letter to you of the 9th Inst. Show that and this to them; and if they will come on the terms stated in the former, bring them. I not only intend a sincere effort for peace, but I intend that you shall be a personal witness that it is made."[24] Hay telegraphed Greeley's reaction as follows: "Although he thinks some one less known would create less excitement and be less embarrassed by public curiousity, still he will start immediately if he can have an absolute safe conduct for four persons to be named by him. Your letter he does not think will guard them from arrest and with only those letters he would have to explain the whole matter to any officer who might choose to hinder them. If this meets with your approbation I can write the order in your name as A A G. [assistant adjutant general] or you can send it by mail." Lincoln replied, "Yours received. Write the Safeconduct, as you propose, without waiting for one by mail from me. If there is, or is not, any thing in the affair, I wish to know it, without unnecessary delay."[25]

Far to the north, the cashier at the bank in Calais, Maine, received a message on the sixteenth from the United States' consul in St. John's, New Brunswick, British North America (now Canada). It warned that a group of twenty or thirty Confederates were planning to cross the border into Maine and to rob that bank, and it arrived none too soon. The Rebels appeared that very same day. Four of them were captured, including their leader, Captain William Collins, formerly of the 15th Mississippi Infantry. This Scots-Irishman, who had immigrated first to New Brunswick, then to New York and then to Mississippi, said he had served as a scout for the late General Polk.

Down in Georgia that day, the largest of Sherman's three armies, Thomas' Army of the Cumberland, began crossing the Chattahoochee River at two places, while Confederate Joe Johnston's Army of Tennessee waited in the outer defenses of Atlanta behind Peachtree Creek. Johnston received a telegram from President Davis that day which said, "I wish to hear from you as to the present situation and your plan of operations so specifically as will enable me to anticipate events."[26] Johnston replied that because he was so badly outnumbered, he was forced to act on the defensive and that his plan would "depend upon that of the enemy." It was, he said, "mainly to watch for an opportunity to fight to advantage."[27] He had been saying the same thing since before he retreated from Dalton. Furthermore, he now said he planned to pull his army out of the defenses of Atlanta, which he would leave to the Georgia militia, so that his veterans' "movements may be freer and wider."[28] Davis saw that as a plan to abandon Atlanta, which confirmed his worst fears.

The next day Johnston received a wire from Adjutant General Cooper: "I am directed by the Secretary of War to inform you that, as you have failed to arrest the advance of the enemy to the vicinity of Atlanta, far in the interior of Georgia, and express no confidence that you can defeat or repel him, you are hereby relieved from the command of the Army and Department of Tennessee, which you will immediately turn over to General Hood." Johnston replied that the order had been received and obeyed. "As to the alleged cause of my removal," he said, "I assert that Sherman's army is stronger, compared with that of Tennessee, than Grant's with that of Northern Virginia. Yet the enemy has been compelled to advance more slowly to the vicinity of Atlanta than to that of Richmond and Petersburg, and penetrated much deeper into Virginia than into Georgia. Confident language by a military commander is not usually regarded as evidence of competence."[29]

1. Pond, *The Shenandoah Valley in 1864*, 74.
2. Ibid., 75.
3. Ibid.
4. Ibid., 76.
5. Ibid., 78.
6. Dana, *Recollections of the Civil War*, 204–205.
7. Sandburg, *Abraham Lincoln*, 559.
8. Basler, ed., *The Collected Works of Abraham Lincoln*, 7:439–440.
9. Woodworth, *Jefferson Davis and His Generals*, 284.
10. Foote, *The Civil War*, 3:418.
11. Basler, ed., *The Collected Works of Abraham Lincoln*, 7:450.
12. Lewis, *Sherman: Fighting Prophet*, 392.
13. Pond, *The Shenandoah Valley in 1864*, 78.
14. Dana, *Recollections of the Civil War*, 206.
15. Basler, ed., *The Collected Works of Abraham Lincoln*, 7:440.
16. Bearss, *Forrest at Brice's Cross Roads*, 222.
17. Ibid., 228.
18. Ibid., 231.
19. Pond, *The Shenandoah Valley in 1864*, 76–77.
20. Catton, *Grant Takes Command*, 315.
21. Ibid.
22. Ibid., 315–316.
23. Basler, ed., *The Collected Works of Abraham Lincoln*, 7:444–445.
24. Ibid., 7:441–442.

25. Ibid., 7:443.

26. Woodworth, *Jefferson Davis and His Generals*, 285.

27. McDonough and Jones, *War So Terrible*, 203.

28. Woodworth, *Jefferson Davis and His Generals*, 285.

29. Miers, *The General Who Marched to Hell*, 135.

CHAPTER SEVENTEEN

We Are Fighting for Independence

17–19 July 1864

As the church bells rang throughout Richmond that Sunday morning of 17 July, two unofficial Northern emissaries were meeting with plump, jovial Judah P. Benjamin, the Confederate secretary of state. The Federals were Colonel James F. Jaquess and Mr. J. R. Gilmore. The latter was a New York businessman with important Washington connections, who had traveled extensively in the South before the war. The former was a Methodist minister who had raised a regiment in Illinois but had become so shocked by the horrors of war that, after Chickamauga, he had obtained an extended leave of absence to see what he could do to put an end to them. Gilmore had managed to get permission from Lincoln for their unofficial visit to Richmond in the hope of arranging some sort of armistice. Benjamin promised to set up a meeting between them and President Davis that evening.

They returned at the appointed time and found Benjamin with "a spare, thin-featured man with iron-gray hair and beard, and a clear, gray eye full of life and vigor." Jefferson Davis rose and extended his hand, saying, "I am glad to see you, gentlemen. You are very welcome to Richmond." Davis had not been able to meet with the visitors earlier because of the lengthy cabinet meeting resulting in the telegram of dismissal just sent to Joe Johnston, though he did not mention this to them. The Southern president's face "was emaciated, and much wrinkled," Gilmore recorded, "but his features were good, especially his eyes, though one of them bore a scar, apparently made by some sharp instrument. . . . His manners were simple, easy and quite fascinating, and he threw an indescribable charm into his voice."[1]

Colonel Jacquess explained that they had requested this interview in the hope that Davis could suggest how the fighting might be stopped. "In a very simple way," the president replied. "Withdraw your armies from our territory, and peace will come of itself." Jacquess began to ask if Lincoln's recent Proclamation of Amnesty would provide a place to start, but Davis cut him off. "Amnesty, sir, applies to criminals. We have commited no crime." Gilmore suggested that both sides lay down their arms and let the issues be decided by a vote of the people. "That the majority shall decide it, you mean," Davis replied. "We seceded to rid ourselves of the rule of the majority, and this would subject us to it again." So it came down to a question of union or disunion, Gilmore observed. Davis agreed, but preferred the terms, "Independence or Subjugation." He added, "We are fighting for Independence—and that, or extermination, we will have." The discussion covered numerous topics, including the military situation, which Davis professed to consider favorable to the South—and slavery, which he said was never "an essential element"—but always the sticking point was independence for the South. As the president rose to see his visitors out he said, "Say to Mr Lincoln, from me, that I shall at any time be pleased to receive proposals for peace on the basis of our Independence. It will be useless to approach me with any other."[2]

Lincoln had said in his first inaugural address that "no government proper, ever had a provision in its organic law for its own termination."[3] He had been referring at the time to the United States and the question of secession. But the same reasoning applied to the Confederate government. Once created, it could not be expected to negotiate itself out of existence. And yet, its very existence was the primary cause of the war. To Lincoln there was only one country, and it was his duty to keep it whole at all costs. To Davis there were two countries, and it was his duty to keep them distinct at all costs. Negotiation was useless. And so the war must continue.

And yet the war and its horrors weighed on the minds of both presidents. That same day Lincoln was telegraphing to Grant: "In your dispatch of yesterday to Gen. Sherman, I find the following, towit: 'I shall make a desparate effort to get a position here which will hold the enemy without the necessity of so many men.' Pressed as we are by lapse of time, I am glad to hear you say this; and yet I do hope you may find a way that the effort shall not be desparate in the sense of a great loss of life."[4]

Among Lincoln's many problems at that time was soothing the ruffled feathers of General Hunter, who had complained to him about the order to put all his troops in the field under Crook, and the apparent intention of everyone to blame him for all of Early's recent depredations. The beleaguered president took the time to reply to Hunter that day: "The order you complain of was only nominally mine; and was framed by those who really made it, with no thought of making you a scape-goat. It seemed to be Gen. Grant's wish that the forces under Gen. Wright and those under you should join and drive at the enemy, under Gen. Wright. Wright had the larger part of the force, but you had the rank. It was thought that you would prefer Crook's commanding your part, to your serving in person under Wright. That is all of it. Gen. Grant wishes you to remain in command of the Department, and I do not wish to order otherwise."[5]

Grant was writing a letter to Halleck the same day, the seventeenth, saying that "there can be no use in Wright's following the enemy, with the latter a day ahead, after he has passed entirely beyond all our communications. I want, if possible, to get the Sixth and Nineteenth Corps here, to use them here before the enemy can get Early back."[6] Halleck, in fact, was already acting on Grant's instructions of the day before by notifying Wright that he should pursue Early's Confederates only far enough to be sure they were in full retreat. At that point he should leave Crook "to continue the pursuit cautiously, under General Hunter's orders."[7]

Down in Mississippi that day, General Chalmers was still in charge of the Confederate pursuit of A. J. Smith's invaders. Assuming that the Yankees would continue to follow the same road as they had taken from Tupelo to Ellistown and on up to Ripley, they would have to cross the Tallahatchie River at Kelley's Mill. So he sent Roddey's Division to head them off there while he harassed their rear guard with Rucker's brigade. But Smith refused to cooperate. Instead of proceeding north-northwest to Ripley, the Federals marched west-northwest that day and returned to New Albany, where they crossed the Tallahatchie and went into camp. By noon Chalmers knew that he had been fooled, so he called off the pursuit and turned back.

Over in Alabama that seventeenth of July, Braxton Bragg, on his western tour, had taken charge of the defense of Montgomery. Some of the state's reserves who had been sent to Mobile were brought to the capital, and more were called up to active duty; some conscripts waiting for orders to the front were rounded up, and volunteers were organized into companies. All in all, a hodgepodge force of about 500 men was thus patched together, armed with old muskets that had been converted to rifles. Late that day Rousseau's Union raiders reached Loachapoka and the tracks of the Montgomery & West Point Railroad about forty miles northeast of the Alabama capital. After a brief rest they were put to work at tearing up the rails and burning the depot and some military supplies. But when the fire threatened to spread to the town, the Union soldiers worked to save civilian buildings from the flames. The next morning—a hot day without a breeze or a cloud—"the work of destroying the railroads began in earnest," as one Federal put it.[8] The troopers were split into four groups, distributed along thirty miles of track. The eastern-most detachment captured and destroyed a train in addition to destroying about six miles of track.

Rousseau's westernmost detachment, under Major Harlon Baird of the 5th Iowa Cavalry, was busy tearing up track when it, too, detected a train, coming up the line from Montgomery. However, the Federals' attempt to ambush it was spoiled by a nervous trooper who fired too soon. The engine screeched to a halt, and the 500 Rebels that had been scraped together at Montgomery and sent up to deal with these raiders piled off the train. They fell back a short distance and took position behind a rail fence, where they were joined by some militia cavalry that had ridden over from Tuskegee. Major Baird sent for reinforcements, and when these arrived a little after noon some of the Federals advanced directly at the Confederates to keep them pinned in place, while others swept around their left flank. The inexperienced Southerners ran for their lives—except for the eighty who were killed, wounded, or missing—and didn't stop until they reached the bridge over Ufaupee Creek, about a mile back toward Montgomery. The Northerners, who lost three killed and eight or ten wounded, went back to work on the railroad. After completing the job, Rousseau's entire force moved to the northeast along the railroad and camped that evening a few miles east of Auburn.

A little farther to the east, near Atlanta, the high command of the Confederate Army of Tennessee had been thrown into confusion by the previous day's order from Richmond for Hood to succeed J. E. Johnston. Hood recorded that the order had "so astounded and overwhelmed" him that he had "remained in deep thought throughout the night." A telegraph from Secretary of War Seddon had warned him: "You are charged with a great trust. You will, I know, test to the utmost your capacities to discharge it. Be wary no less than bold."[9] Photographs of Hood, showing a man with a long face, sad eyes, and a full beard, make it hard to realize that he was only 33 years old when he was given command of one of the South's two great field armies, with the temporary rank of full general. He was missing an arm and a leg from wounds received at Gettysburg and Chickamauga, and his heart had been captured the winter before by a Richmond belle, whom he longed to impress. But despite a burning ambition that had led him to angle for this command ever since being assigned to this army five months before, he seems to have had second thoughts when the responsibility was dropped upon him.

With the help of an orderly, the crippled young general mounted his horse before dawn and rode toward army headquarters. On the way he ran into Lieutenant General A. P. Stewart, who had commanded a division in Hood's corps until recently being promoted to replace the late Leonidas Polk in command of the corps still known as the Army of Mississippi. The two agreed that the three corps commanders should unite "in an effort to prevail on General Johnston to withhold the order and retain command of the army until the empending battle has been fought." Johnston received them courteously, but when Hood appealed to him to "pocket that dispatch, leave me in command of my corps, and fight the battle for Atlanta," the older general would not hear of it. "Gentlemen, I am a soldier," he said. "A soldier's first duty is to obey."[10]

By then Hardee had also arrived and the three corps commanders sent a joint telegram to President Davis asking that he delay the transfer of command "until the fate of Atlanta is decided." But leaving the fate of Atlanta in the hands of Joe Johnston was the one thing Davis was determined to avoid and he refused to rescind his order. Hood again appealed to Johnston to ignore the order, but to no avail. "With all the earnestness of which man is capable," he later wrote, "I besought him, if he would under no circumstances retain command and fight the battle for Atlanta, to at least remain with me and give me the benefit of his counsel whilst I determined the issue." With tears in his eyes, Johnston agreed that on his return that evening from a necessary trip to Atlanta, he would offer his young successor all the help he could. However, as Hood recorded, "he not only failed to comply with his promise, but, without a word of explanation or apology, left that evening for Macon, Georgia."[11]

So, like it or not, Hood was the new commander of the Army and Department of Tennessee. Not many Confederates seemed to like it. Hardee was resentful that the younger Hood had been promoted over him. He complained that the president was "attempting to create the impression that in declining the command at Dalton [six months before], I declined it for all future time." He asked to be transferred, and Davis was only able to talk him out of it by appealing to his patriotism.

Anyone who knew Hood knew that the army would now stop retreating and start fighting. They weren't so sure that it would start winning. Pat Cleburne, the Army of the Tennessee's best division commander, aluded to Roman strategy in the Punic Wars when he said, "We are going to carry the war to Africa, but I fear we will not be as successful as Scipio was."[12]

But the enlisted men took the change the hardest. "Great stalwart, sunburnt soldiers by the thousands would be seen falling out of line, squatting down by a tree or in a fence corner, weeping like children," wrote the historian of the 20th Tennessee. "This act of the War Department threw a damper over this army from which it never recovered, for 'Old Joe,' as we called him, was our idol."[13] It was not that they had anything against Hood, but rather that they were so fond of Johnston. As Sam Watkins of the 1st Tennessee put it: "Old Joe Johnston had taken command of the Army of Tennessee when it was crushed and broken, at a time when no other man on earth could have united it. He found it in rags and tatters, hungry and heart-broken, the morale of the men gone, their manhood vanished to the winds, their pride a thing of the past. Through his instrumentality and skillful manipulation, all these had been restored."[14]

Word of the change of commanders reached Sherman that day. "I immediately inquired of General Schofield," he said, "who was his classmate at West Point, about Hood, as to his general character, etc., and learned that he was bold even to rashness, and courageous in the extreme; I inferred that the change of commanders meant 'fight.'"[15] That suited Sherman just fine. "At this critical moment the Confederate Government rendered us most valuable service," he wrote after the war. He added that "the character of a leader is a large factor in the game of war, and I confess I was pleased at this change." He had great respect for his former antagonist. "No officer who ever served under me will question the Generalship of Joseph E. Johnston," he said. But it is interesting to note that the best commendation he could give his departing opponent was that "his retreats were timely, in good order, and he left nothing behind."[16] Whether intentional or not, this was a classic case of damning with faint praise.

Now that he had his three armies across the Chattahoochee, the Union commander sent Thomas' large Army of the Cumberland due south toward Atlanta, while Schofield's small Army of the Ohio moved down east of the city, and McPherson's Army of the Tennessee swung far to the east, to approach Atlanta along the Georgia Railroad, the city's direct link with Virginia. If Confederate reinforcements were coming from that area, as Grant had warned, they would come by that route. "I want that railroad as quick as possible," Sherman said.[17] By noon of the eighteenth Thomas' infantry had pushed Wheeler's Confederate cavalry off the high ground north of Peachtree Creek, and the Rebel horsemen had retreated to the south side of the stream, burning three bridges behind them before riding off to oppose McPherson's advancing column, east of Atlanta.

Grant was still concerned about the situation around Washington. He told Halleck that day that "to prevent a recurrence of what has just taken place in Maryland" he wanted all the little departments in that area to be merged into one big one.[18] And to command the whole he suggested his old West Point classmate Major General William B. Franklin, who was in the East on sick leave just then, after commanding the 19th Corps on the recent, unsuccessful, Red River campaign in Louisiana.

Horace Greeley had arrived at Niagara Falls to meet the Confederate commissioners about peace terms, and he sent Lincoln a telegram: "I have communicated with the Gentlemen in question & do not find them so empowered as I was previously assured they say that—

"We are however in the confidential employment of our Government & entirely familiar with its wishes & opinions on that subject & we feel authorized to declare if the circumstances disclosed in this correspondence were communicated to Richmond we would at once be invested with the authority to which your letter refers or other Gentlemen clothed with full power would immediately be sent to Washington with the view of hastening a consumation so much to be desired & terminating at the earliest possible moment the calamites of war We respectfully solicit through your intervention a safe conduct to Washington & thence by any route which may be designated to Richmond—

"Such is the more material portion of the Gentlemen's letter. I will transmit the entire correspondence if desired." Lincoln responded with a document addressed "To Whom it may concern: Any proposition which embraces the restoration of peace, the integrity of the whole Union, and the abandonment of slavery, and which comes by and with an authority that can control the armies now at war against the United States will be received and considered by the Executive government of the United States, and will be met by liberal terms on other substantial and collateral points; and the bearer, or bearers thereof shall have safe-conduct both ways."[19]

The same day, the president issued a proclamation calling for 500,000 more troops and providing that a draft would be held on 5 September to fill any quotas not yet met by volunteers. And it looked like the draft would be needed. As Halleck complained to Grant the next day, 19 July: "We are not now receiving one half as many as we are discharging. Volunteering has virtually ceased, and I do not anticipate much from the President's new call, which has the disadvantage of again postponing the draft for fifty days. Unless our governemnt and people will come square up to the adoption of an efficient and thorough draft, we cannot supply the waste of our army."[20]

This message, and word of Lincoln's proclamation, had evidently not yet reached Grant when he sent the president a telegram that day: "In my opinion there ought to be an immediate call for, say, 300,000 men to be put in the field in the shortest possible time. The presence of this number of re-enforcements would save the annoyance of raids, and would enable us to drive the enemy from his present front, particularly from Richmond, without attacking fortifications. The enemy now have their last man in the field. Every depletion of their army is an irreparable loss. Desertions from it are now rapid. With the prospect of large additions to our force the desertions would increase. The greater number of men we have the shorter and less sanguinary will be the war. I give this entirely as my views and not in any spirit of dictation, always holding myself in readiness to use the material given me to the best advantage I know how."[21]

---

1. Foote, *The Civil War*, 3:467–468.

2. Ibid., 3:468.

3. Basler, ed., *The Collected Works of Abraham Lincoln*, 4:264.

4. Ibid., 7:444.

5. Ibid., 7:445.

6. Pond, *The Shenandoah Valley in 1864*, 77.

7. Ibid., 78.

8. Richard M. McMurry, "Riding Through Alabama: Part I," *Civil War Times Illustrated* 20 (5 August 1981): 17.

9. Foote, *The Civil War*, 3:420.

10. Ibid., 3:421.

11. Ibid., 3:422.

12. Ibid., 3:423.

13. Scaife, *The Campaign For Atlanta*, 45.

14. Watkins, *Co. Aytch*, 171.

15. Sherman, *Memoirs*, 2:543–544.

16. William T. Sherman, "The Grand Strategy of the Last Year of the War," in *Battles and Leaders*, 4:253.

17. McDonough and Jones, *War So Terrible*, 209.

18. Catton, *Grant Takes Command*, 317.

19. Basler, ed., *The Collected Works of Abraham Lincoln*, 7:451.

20. Foote, *The Civil War*, 3:470.

21. Basler, ed., *The Collected Works of Abraham Lincoln*, 7:453.

CHAPTER EIGHTEEN

An Ardent Advocate of the Lee and Jackson School

19–21 July 1864

Baldy Smith returned from leave on 19 July, only to discover that he no longer had a job. As Rawlins, Grant's chief of staff, wrote to his wife: "General Grant today relieved Major General William F. Smith from command and duty in this army, because of his spirit of criticism of all military movements and men, and his failure to get along with anyone he is placed under, and his disposition to scatter the seeds of discontent throughout the army. I have never been deceived in the man since his promotion, but because of acknowledged ability have done all I could to sustain him. The action of the General is justifiable."[1]

Another of Grant's favorites, Major General E.O.C. Ord, was brought down from Maryland to command the 18th Corps, and Smith went to New York to await orders that never came. He later wrote a book claiming that, in order to keep his own job and to get rid of Smith, Butler had blackmailed Grant with evidence that the general-in-chief had been drunk on duty. As historian Bruce Catton has pointed out this is

easily refuted by the fact that six months later Grant did dismiss Butler.
But until the November election, at least, it was safer to keep such a
powerful War Democrat where he was than to have him turn his tremendous influence against the administration.

Down in Alabama, Rousseau had his Union raiders up early that day
and back at work tearing up the Montgomery & West Point Railroad. At
the town of Opelika they consumed or destroyed thousands of pounds of
bacon, sugar, flour and other supplies, as well as six railroad cars full of
leather and tools. A brigade of Confederates under Colonel Charles P.
Ball reached Montgomery from Mississippi, but by the time they had
reached the western end of the area where the railroad tracks had been
torn up, the Federals were gone, for at 10 a.m. Rousseau had decided
that enough damage had been done and had put his troopers on the
road to the northeast, moving toward Marrietta, Georgia, and Sherman's
armies.

The on-again, off-again pursuit of Early was on again that day. Crook
pushed forward with part of the West Virginia forces and crossed the
Shenandoah River where it was fordable, near Snicker's Ferry. However,
when it was learned that Early's entire force was not far away, around
Berryville, Crook put his division-sized force into a defensive position
on the west side of the river to wait for a division of the 6th Corps
that was expected to arrive soon. That afternoon Breckinridge's two
Confederate divisions attacked Crook's left and center while Rodes hit
the Union right. That flank was held by about 1,000 dismounted Federal
cavalrymen, who retreated across the river in disorder. That exposed the
flank of the Northern infantry, and they too had to fall back across the
stream. The head of the 6th Corps column had reached the east bank by
that time, but Crook ordered the combined force to fall back under the
cover of the Union artillery in order to avoid another attack, which it
could be seen that the Rebels were preparing.

However, that night Early retreated to the south, toward Strasburg,
because Averell, with a mixed Union force of cavalry and infantry, had
advanced during the day up the Valley from Martinsburg to Stephenson's
Depot, thus threatening Early's rear. To block this move and cover his
retreat, Early sent Ramseur's Division and two batteries of artillery to
reinforce Vaughn's and William Jackson's brigades of cavalry at Winchester.

The next day, 20 July, Averell continued his advance along the Valley
Turnpike, two regiments of infantry on each side of it, his artillery on
the road, and a regiment of cavalry covering each flank. Three miles

north of Winchester, the Federals came upon Ramseur's Confederates. Although his force was outnumbered about two to one, Averell unlimbered his twelve guns, opened fire, and sent his infantry forward across an open field. Ramseur thought he was faced by only a couple of regiments and had advanced with insufficient precautions. The Union charge broke Ramseur's left brigade and the panic spread. His entire force fled in confusion to Winchester, leaving four cannon and two wounded generals to be captured.

"I am greatly mortified at the result," young Ramseur confessed in a letter to his wife. "My men behaved shamefully." Later he wrote her again: "I am sure I did all that mortal man could do. Yet, newspaper editors and stay-at-home croakers will sit back in safe places and condemn me."[2] Early had to send Rodes' division to Ramseur's relief, then withdrew that night to Newtown, where his infantry halted while his wagons proceeded south. Meanwhile, Wright crossed the Shenandoah that day and marched his force to Berryville. On the way, the Federals passed the gruesome sight of heads, arms, and legs protruding from the shallow graves of the men killed in Crook's battle of the day before.

The twentieth of July was the date originally set for a Copperhead revolt in what were then known as the northwestern states. Instead, the Supreme Grand Council of the Sons of Liberty met in Chicago to review the situation. Captain Majors, a Confederate paymaster, represented the Rebel commissioners in Canada. He reimbursed the delegates for their expenses and gave each state leader a large sum to finance his military units. The meeting chose 16 August as the new date for the revolt. Armed bands would descend upon Chicago, Indianapolis and Springfield. Prisoner of war camps Douglas, near Chicago, Chase, near Columbus, Ohio, and on Rock Island, in the middle of the Mississippi, were to be seized, and their prisoners released. Arsenals would be occupied and their arms given to the released Rebels. Then all would march on Louisville. A committee was selected to go to Canada to meet with the commissioners.

Lieutenant General S. D. Lee received orders that day to leave his Department of Alabama, Mississippi and East Louisiana and report to General Hood near Atlanta. Hood had wired President Davis the day before, requesting a new commander for what had been his own corps, the 2nd of the Army of Tennessee, before his own recent promotion. Lee was one of three officers whom Hood suggested for the job, and it didn't take Davis long to make up his mind. It would be a few days before Lee could wind up his duties and reach Atlanta, but Hood did not intend to wait. In the meantime, Hood's old corps would be led by one of Hardee's division commanders, Major General Benjamin Franklin Cheatham, a pre-war Tennessee militia officer who was more famous for his ability to drink and curse than for any great skill as a general.

Hood had obviously been given command of the Army of the Tennessee because it was believed that he would put up a fight. He knew it, the people of Atlanta knew it, and even the Federals knew it. Now he had to live up to President Davis' expectations. This was fine with Hood, since he was, as he later said, an "ardent advocate of the Lee and Jackson school."[3] He called his three corps commanders together that morning and outlined his plan for an attack to be launched at 1 p.m. The general idea had been inherited from Joe Johnston: the Confederates would take advantage of the wide separation of Sherman's three armies to ambush the Federals in the woods north of Atlanta, while they were in the act of crossing Peachtree Creek. Cheatham, with the 2nd Corps, plus Wheeler's cavalry and a division of Georgia militia under Major General G. W. Smith, would take up position east of Atlanta to protect the city and the rest of the army from McPherson and Schofield long enough for Hardee and Stewart, with the 1st Corps and the Army of Mississippi, to attack Thomas' Army of the Cumberland before it could dig in south of Peachtree Creek. They were to attack in echelon from right to left and drive it to the west, away from Sherman's other two armies, and back against the Chattahoochee River, which would cut off its retreat.

This was not a bad plan, except for three things. For one, the change of command and the confusion it entailed had cost the Rebels a day, and now most of the Federals were already south of the creek. For another, the attack was aimed at the largest of Sherman's three armies. In fact, Thomas had more men in his three corps than there were in the two Confederate corps that were about to assault him. For a third, Thomas was famous for his skill and determination on defense. In fact, he has gone down in history as the Rock of Chickamauga for his stand on that occasion.

To make matters even worse, the attack did not go in on schedule. For his first battle in overall command, Hood stayed at army headquarters in Atlanta, and there he received word from Cheatham that he would have to move his corps farther south to keep McPherson from getting around his right flank. Hood authorized him to extend his line to the south by the length of one division, but Cheatham was not satisfied with that and continued to sidle to his right. Meanwhile, Hood ordered Hardee and Stewart to move a half-division to their right in order to maintain contact with Cheatham. But Hardee, who held the right of the attacking formation, eventually found that he had to move his troops two miles to the east, and Stewart had to follow suit. By the time this had been accomplished, three hours had been lost.

McPherson's Union Army of the Tennessee had swung far to the east and reached the railroad at the town of Decatur, then had turned westward, closing in on Atlanta. It was just about 1 p.m., the time for which Hood's attack was originally scheduled, when a battery of 20-pounder rifled guns in Logan's 15th Corps opened fire on the city. According to a witness, the very first shell exploded at the intersection of East Ivy and Ellis streets, killing a little girl who had been walking with her parents.

Hardee told Stewart that he was ready to attack before 3 p.m., but for some reason he didn't advance until around 4 p.m. and, in fact, Stewart's attack went forward first, over what proved to be rougher terrain than would have been found in the area originally selected. Morale was high among the Rebel soldiers, glad to finally be attacking the Yankees who had flanked them out of every position from Dalton to Atlanta in the previous two months. "Although I am not very fond of fighting," one young Tennessean wrote to his parents, "I am anxious to see the decisive battle of this campaign come off." He added that he had "no fears as to the results when it does take place [for] such soldiers as compose our army can not be whipped no matter what the odds may be."[4] He was killed in that day's battle.

Because of the dense undergrowth and the rough ground, the Federals were not aware of the Rebels' proximity. "Not a man of theirs was seen or heard in any direction," Union general John W. Geary reported.[5] Geary, commander of the 2nd Division of Hooker's 20th Corps, had posted the 33rd New Jersey and a battery of artillery 500 yards in advance of his main line. A lieutenant from that regiment was sent by his colonel "out to the open on our left. And there I saw a beautiful sight. Down through the great, open fields they were coming, thousands of them, men in gray, by brigade front, flags flying."[6]

Major General William W. Loring's division held the right of Stewart's line and was the first to go forward in the July heat. One of his three brigades had been left behind on picket duty, but the other two advanced side by side, and what the Union lieutenant saw was probably Loring's right brigade, Featherston's, advancing past the 33rd into the woods, where it veered to the east into a gap between Geary's division and Newton's 2nd Division of Howard's 4th Corps. It was soon followed by the four brigades of Maney's Division of Hardee's corps. But the Rebels were hit by a crossfire from both Union forces, and just then Ward's 3rd Division of Hooker's corps arrived to fill the gap and drove the Confederates back with severe losses. "Meeting my line of battle seemed to completely addle their brains," Ward reported. "Their first line broke, mixing up with the second line; they were now in the wildest confusion, firing in all directions, some endeavoring to get away, some undecided what to do, others rushing into our lines."[7]

Colonel Benjamin Harrison, the future president and the commander of Ward's 1st Brigade, called forward a detachment of 100 men armed with Spencer repeating rifles, who poured a deadly fire into the Southerners, and then Ward ordered his entire division to counterattack. "Our advance, though desperately resisted by the enemy, was steady and unfaltering," Harrison reported; "the fighting was hand to hand, and step by step;" by the enemy was pushed back.[8] The Rebels made what Ward called a feeble attempt to rally, but they were too badly disorganized. Featherston reported that his brigade lost half of its men that day, killed, wounded, or missing, including all but one of its regimental commanders.

Loring's other brigade, Scott's, quickly overwhelmed the 33rd New Jersey, capturing a flag and four cannon. The commander of the 33rd said that "to stand longer was madness, and I reluctantly gave the order to retire fighting." The Confederates chased them toward Geary's main line, and "as the enemy fled, the steady aim of the Mississippi, Alabama, and Louisiana marksmen of my command produced great slaughter in his ranks," Loring reported.[9] Moving on into the woods, Scott's Brigade became divided into two parts, but they both approached Geary's main line, and three Federal regiments were pushed back by their advance. Geary wrote that the Southerners charged "with more than customary nerve and heartiness in the attack." He added that he had "never seen more heroic fighting," and that it reminded him of Gettysburg.[10] Geary pulled part of his line back, where his men stood firm, and this attack was also repelled.

About 400 yards west of Loring was Walthall's Division of Stewart's corps, also with two brigades deployed side by side. O'Neal's Brigade, on the right, advanced obliquely to the northeast and struck the Union line at the junction of Geary's division with Williams' 1st Division of the 20th Corps to the west. It, too, got caught in a crossfire and took heavy losses before it could be withdrawn. The other brigade, Reynolds', ran into Williams' division deployed on a ridge concave to its advance and was also driven back after losing heavily. Two brigades of Stewart's other division, French's, started out just west of Walthall's Division, but veered to their left and advanced about 600 yards across a plantation against only light resistance from part of the 14th Corps. But when Walthall's men on their right retreated they also fell back, going about halfway to their starting point.

Hardee's 1st Corps consisted of four divisions. Cheatham's Division, now under Maney, was on the left, closest to Loring; Walker's in the center, and Bate's on the right, with Cleburne's in reserve behind Walker's. Bate's three brigades advanced first, through the brush along Clear Creek, then Walker's three, and then Maney's four brigades traversed a heavily wooded area of many small hills and ravines. Bate's Brigade threatened to turn the left, or eastern, flank of Newton's Union division—in fact, of Thomas' whole line, for the rest of Howard's corps had been sent earlier to reinforce Schofield, and Palmer's 14th Corps was on the other side of Hooker's 20th. But Newton's reserve brigade was nearby and stopped Bate's men with a heavy fire of musketry. Meanwhile, Maney, as we have already seen, came in behind Featherston's Brigade of Loring's Division and ran into Ward's Federal division. Walker's three brigades in the center of Hardee's line struck the front of Newton's division and made some progress, but were eventually driven back like all the others. Both Hardee's and Stewart's corps were then withdrawn to the outer defenses of Atlanta, thus ending the battle.

Thomas usually maintained such an air of calm that another of his nicknames was "Old Slow Trot," but the fire of battle could animate him. He was seen that day to personally apply the point of his sword to the rumps of horses in order to hurry forward more artillery. And an Indiana captain said that you could judge the progress of the battle by how Old Tom nervously fiddled with his whiskers. "When satisfied he smoothes them down," the officer noted, "when troubled he works them all out of shape." When the Rebels were finally driven back, Thomas threw his hat on the ground in exultation and shouted, "Hurrah! Look at the Third Division! They're driving them!" And the captain noted that "his whiskers were soon in good shape again."[11]

The Confederate generals promptly began to argue over who was to blame for their failure. Loring and his brigade commanders said that it was due to the delay of Hardee's attack, and especially his failure to cover their right. Hardee blamed the fact that he had to send his reserve, Cleburne's crack division, to reinforce Cheatham just as he was ready to send it into the fight. However, it was 7 p.m. by the time the order to send a division to Cheatham reached him, so it is doubtful that Cleburne could have accomplished much before dark, anyway. Hood praised Cheatham, Wheeler, and especially Stewart, but declared that Hardee had delayed the attack and had failed to push it as ordered. He said that although Hardee commanded "the best troops in the army," he had "virtually accomplished nothing," and "did nothing more than skirmish with the enemy."[12] While there was some justice in all of these complaints, there were other reasons for the failure of the attack, including the difficult terrain over which it had to advance, the determined resistance of Thomas' Federals, and the pressure of McPherson's advance from Decatur, which first caused the delay of the attack and then the diversion of Cleburne's Division.

Sherman was not much impressed by the day's fight. In fact, when he first heard about it from Thomas he replied: "I have been with Howard and Schofield today, and one of my staff is just back from General McPherson. All report the enemy in front so strong that I was in hopes none were left for you, but I see it is the same old game. . . each division commander insists he has to fight two corps."[13] That evening, as Sherman was looking over a newspaper he discovered an article announcing that A. J. Smith was retreating toward Ripley. He dashed off a telegram to Washburn at Memphis: "Order Smith to pursue and keep after Forrest all the time."[14] But he was a little late. At noon that day the advance elements of Smith's column returned to their old camps at La Grange.

Lincoln sent an answer to Grant that day about the need for more troops: "Yours of yesterday about a call for 300,000 is received. I suppose you had not seen the call for 500,000 made the day before, and which I suppose covers the case. Always glad to have your suggestions."[15] Grant asked Halleck that day what was being done about his request of the eighteenth to consolidate all the little departments around Washington under General Franklin. The next day, the 21st, Halleck replied that nothing was being done. The suggestion had been passed on to Secretary of War Stanton and there it rested. Halleck added that he felt Grant ought to know that "General Franklin would not give satisfaction."[16] Franklin was a close friend of Baldy Smith, who was busy campaigning to have Franklin given command of the Army of the Potomac. He had also been one of McClellan's favorites, which was enough to put him on Stanton's list of enemies.

Grant told Halleck that he could "retain Wright's command until the departure of Early is assured, or other forces are collected to make his presence unnecessary." But he added, "If Early has halted about Berryville, what is to prevent Wright and Hunter from attacking him?" However, Halleck also heard from Wright that day, who said: "Conceiving the object of the expedition to be accomplished, I at once started back, as directed in your orders, and tonight shall encamp on the east side of Goose Creek, on the Leesburg Pike. Two days' easy march will bring the command to Washington."[17]

Down in Georgia, Sherman had also received a telegram from Lincoln:

"I have seen your despatches objecting to agents of Northern States opening recruiting stations near your camps. An act of congress authorizes this, giving the appointment of agents to the States, and not to this Executive government. It is not for the War Department, or myself, to restrain, or modify the law, in it's execution, further than actual necessity may require. To be candid, I was for the passage of the law, not apprehending at the time that it would produce such inconvenience to the armies in the field, as you now cause me to fear. Many of the States were very anxious for it, and I hoped that, with their State bounties, and active exertions, they would get out substantial additions to our colored forces, which, unlike white recruits, help us where they come from, as well as where they go to. I still hope advantage from the law; and being a law, it must be treated as such by all of us. We here, will do what we consistently can to save you from difficulties arising out of it. May I ask therefore that you will give your hearty co-operation?"[18]

Sherman replied on the 21st, saying, "I have the highest veneration for the law, and will respect it always, however it conflicts with my opinion of its propriety. I only telegraphed to General Halleck because I had seen no copy of the law, and supposed the War Department might have some control over its operation."[19]

Sherman wrote to Halleck that he did not want to be "construed as unfriendly to Mr. Lincoln," but he had seen recruiting agents take escaped slaves back to Nashville, "where, so far as my experience goes, they disappear."[20] Earlier in the campaign he had written to Adjutant General Lorenzo Thomas, who was in charge of recruiting the regiments of U.S. Colored Troops, that it was wrong to take too many of the young black men into the army. "The first step in the liberation of the negro from bondage will be to get him and his family to a place of safety, then to provide him the means of providing for his family. . . . If you divert too large a proportion of the able-bodied into the ranks, you will leave too large a proportion of black paupers on our hands."[21]

Now he told Halleck, "If Mr. Lincoln or Stanton could walk through the camps and hear the soldiers talk they would hear new ideas. I have had the question put to me often: 'Is not a negro as good as a white man to stop a bullet?' Yes; and a sand-bag is better." However, like most whites of his day, North and South, he still had his doubts about blacks. "But can a negro do our skirmishing and picket duty?" he asked. "Can they improvise roads, bridges, sorties, flank movements, etc., like the white man? I say no."[22]

1. Catton, *Grant Takes Command*, 335.
2. Douglas Southall Freeman, *Lee's Lieutenants (New York, 1944)*, vol. 3:570.
3. Foote, *The Civil War*, 3:472.
4. McDonough and Jones, *War So Terrible*, 212.
5. Ibid.
6. Scaife, *The Campaign For Atlanta*, 48.
7. McDonough and Jones, *War So Terrible*, 214.
8. Ibid.
9. Ibid., 215.
10. Ibid., 216.
11. Lewis, *Sherman: Fighting Prophet*, 384.
12. Foote, *The Civil War*, 3:475.
13. McDonough and Jones, *War So Terrible*, 218.
14. Bearss, *Forrest at Brice's Cross Roads*, 237.
15. Basler, ed., *The Collected Works of Abraham Lincoln*, 7:452.
16. Catton, *Grant Takes Command*, 317.
17. Pond, *The Shenandoah Valley in 1864*, 85.
18. Basler, ed., *The Collected Works of Abraham Lincoln*, 7:449–450.
19. Ibid., 7:450, n. 1.
20. Lewis, *Sherman: Fighting Prophet*, 393.
21. Ibid., 392.
22. Ibid., 393–394.

CHAPTER NINETEEN

You Have Killed the Best Man in Our Army

21–22 July 1864

A. J. Smith's two infantry divisions, constituting the Right Wing of the 16th Corps, marched back into La Grange, Tennessee, that day, 21 July, while in Atlanta Hood was still determined to take the offensive against Sherman's three approaching armies. During the previous night his cavalry had brought him a more complete picture of just where the Federals were and what they were up to. Thomas' Army of the Cumberland was dug in north of the city, on the ground just south of Peachtree Creek where it had been attacked the day before. McPherson's somewhat smaller Army of the Tennessee was straddling the Georgia Railroad east of the city, facing west, and Schofield's small Army of the Ohio was northeast of the city, linking the other two, now that they had all come closer to Atlanta. Thomas had proven to be too tough a nut to crack where he was. And Schofield could only be attacked head-on, with the other two Union forces ready to pounce on the flanks of the attackers.

So that left McPherson, and he was the one now giving the Confederates the most trouble, anyway.

Cleburne's Division had arrived the night before just in time to keep McPherson's Federals from taking a treeless knob of high ground called Bald Hill, which seemed to be the key to the area east of Atlanta, and all day on the 21st Cleburne's infantry and Wheeler's cavalry were engaged in a fierce struggle to fight off repeated attacks by Brigadier General Mortimer D. Leggett's 3rd Division of Blair's 17th Corps on that position. One lucky shot from Union guns wiped out an entire company of Texas cavalry. One of Leggett's brigades lost 40 percent of its strength that day, in what Cleburne called "the bitterest" fighting of his career. Nevertheless, it "swept over the works precise as on parade" and finally took the high ground, known ever since as Leggett's Hill, and began to reconstruct the Confederate fortifications to face toward Atlanta.[1] The hill was an important capture. "If the enemy had been allowed to retain it and fortify himself securely upon it," Frank Blair wrote, "he could not only have prevented our advance, but would have made the positions previously held by the Seventeenth and Fifteenth Corps exceedingly insecure and dangerous."[2]

While Cleburne and Leggett were fighting, Hood was planning. McPherson was busy attacking, which meant that his troops probably had little in the way of entrenchments. What's more, their left, or southern, flank was unguarded. And, for icing on the cake, McPherson's huge train of supply wagons was parked behind his front, in the town square at Decatur, with very little protection. Still hoping to emulate the style, and the success, of Robert E. Lee and Stonewall Jackson, Hood planned a wide swing to the south around McPherson's left for an attack on his flank and rear. If all went well, he would roll up the Army of the Tennessee the way Jackson had the Army of the Potomac at Chancellorsville. During the night of the 21st, Hood's infantry would be withdrawn into a new, shorter line of entrenchments which his engineers had prepared. Stewart, Cheatham, and the Georgia militia would hold this line, while Hardee's corps and most of Wheeler's cavalry would march some eighteen miles that night, south and then northeast, to attack Decatur in the morning. Once the flank attack was rolling, Cheatham would assault McPherson's front while Stewart held off Thomas and Schofield.

That was the plan which Hood outlined to his corps commanders that day, but it soon began to break down. Cleburne's Division was, of course, part of Hardee's corps, but it had not been able to disengage from McPherson's attacking troops when ordered by Hardee, at 7:30 p.m., to do so. In fact, it was near midnight before Cleburne was able to withdraw by leaving his skirmishers behind to fool the Federals. Due to this delay Hood, at a second meeting with his corps commanders, apparently gave Hardee authority to shorten his turning movement and strike directly at McPherson's left flank, instead of going around it to Decatur. Or so Cheatham later claimed. Accounts by the participants differ on this point. Hardee said that Hood himself ordered the shorter move. Hood denied saying anything at all about a change of plan. At any rate, it was the early hours of the 22nd before the tail of the Confederate column left Atlanta. Many of the city's residents stood on rooftops to watch the soldiers march out. They feared that the army was retreating, and many civilians fled from the city. Others were glad to see the soldiers leave, for "a lot of cavalry robbers broke into the stores and stole everything that they took a fancy to."[3] Some of Hardee's men had not slept for two days and all of them had been fighting and digging entrenchments for most of that time. Some were short on ammunition, and delays ensued while they were resupplied. It was a hot night and the road was dusty, adding to the troops' discomfort.

The Federals were not blind to the danger of an attack on their flank. McPherson advised Blair, on the night of the 21st, to impress upon his division commanders "the importance of being on the alert at all times to repel an attack, especially about daybreak," and warned Sherman that there was no cavalry watching his left flank because it was off tearing up railroad track east of Decatur. "The whole rebel army," he reminded his commander, ". . . is not in front of the Army of the Cumberland."[4] But Sherman was feeling confident after the drubbing that Thomas had given the Rebels the day before, and Leggett's success that day. His armies would continue to close in on Atlanta and bombard the Confederates out of their defenses and the city, if Hood did not abandon it first. "I would not be astonished to find him off in the morning," Sherman said.[5]

By dawn of the 22nd, the head of Hardee's column was still six miles southwest of Decatur, and he stopped to confer with his division commanders and Wheeler. None of them knew exactly where they were in relation to McPherson, but cavalry patrols indicated that they had at least gotten behind the Federal left flank. It was near noon before all of Hardee's troops had caught up and he had his divisions deployed for the attack, fifteen miles distant from the rest of the army. Cheatham's Division, still under Maney, was on the left, while Cleburne's, Walker's and Bate's, in that order, extended to the northeast along the road from Cobb's Mill toward Decatur.

That day McPherson rode over to the house behind Schofield's lines that served as Sherman's headquarters, and the two generals sat on the steps "discussing the chances of battle, and Hood's general character,"

Sherman remembered. "McPherson had also been of the same class at West Point with Hood, Schofield, and Sheridan. We agreed that we ought to be unusually cautious, and prepared at all times for sallies and for hard fighting, because Hood, though not deemed much of a scholar, or of great mental capacity, was undoubtedly a brave, determined, and rash man."[6] Sherman had ordered McPherson not to extend too far to the south because he planned to move his Army of the Tennessee to the north and west, behind Schofield and Thomas, around to the west side of Atlanta soon.

Sherman had also ordered McPherson to use Dodge's Left Wing of the 16th Corps to "destroy every rail and tie of the railroad, from Decatur up to your skirmish line."[7] But now McPherson told him that, before receiving that order, he had already sent Dodge's two divisions along a road leading to his left for the purpose of strengthening that flank. "He said he could put all his pioneers to work, and do with them in the time indicated all I had proposed to do with General Dodge's two divisions," Sherman wrote. "Of course I assented at once." While the two generals were talking, they noticed that the sound of firing was becoming "a little more brisk," and they wondered what this meant. They consulted a compass, Sherman remembered, "and by noting the direction of the sound, we became satisfied that the firing was too far to our left rear to be explained by known facts." McPherson mounted and rode rapidly to the south with part of his staff. "McPherson was then in his prime (about thirty-four years old)," Sherman recorded, "over six feet high, and a very handsome man in every way, was universally liked, and had many noble qualities."[8] That was the last time he ever saw him alive.

Dodge's two 16th Corps divisions—minus one brigade that had been left in Decatur to guard the wagon train—were marching to the south behind Blair's 17th Corps when they learned that Confederates were approaching from the southeast. One of Dodge's brigades was quickly placed a half-mile to the rear of Blair's left, facing south. Sweeney's 2nd Division was also placed behind Blair's left, facing southeast to block the impending attack.

At noon Major General Joseph Wheeler, the 28-year-old commander of the Cavalry Corps of the Confederate Army of Tennessee, was reconnoitering the area around Decatur, which he had been ordered to attack, when he found troops of Sprague's 2nd Brigade of Fuller's 4th Division of the 16th Corps posted south of the town and supported by artillery. Wheeler ordered his two divisions to dismount.

Hood, meanwhile, watching with Cheatham's corps on the east side of Atlanta, had been waiting since dawn to hear the sound of guns out toward Decatur. Finally the sound of skirmishing could be heard to the east. At about 12:15 p.m. Walker's and Bate's divisions advanced and were soon met by Sweeney's Federals. What became known as the battle of Atlanta was on.

The three brigades of Bate's Division were deployed side by side to the east of Sugar Creek, facing northwest, while Walker's three brigades were in similar formation west of the stream, facing the same way. On the Union side, Brigadier General Thomas W. Sweeny's small 2nd Division of the 16th Corps was just going into position. It had only two brigades to meet Bate's three, because its 3rd Brigade had been left behind to garrison Rome, Georgia, a couple of months before. The 1st Brigade, under Brigadier General Elliot W. Rice, held the southeastern corner of the Federal line, and the 2nd Brigade, under Colonel August Mersy, was deployed on Rice's right. In addition, there was a battery of artillery in the middle of Rice's brigade, and another between the two brigades, posted on a commanding hill. Colonel John Morrill's 1st Brigade of Fuller's 4th Division of the 16th Corps was about 300 yards to Mersy's left, and faced Walker's Division alone.

However, Walker's advance was blocked by a pond and swampy ground around Terry's Mill on Sugar Creek. Walker who had graduated from West Point one year ahead of Hardee, appealed to the latter to allow him to change the deployment of his division in order to avoid this obstacle, but Hardee was not sympathetic. "No, sir!" the corps commander replied. "This movement has been delayed too long already. Go and obey my orders." Walker turned to a staff officer and asked, "Major, did you hear that?" His aide tried to soothe Walker's ruffled pride, but he vowed, "I shall make him remember this insult. If I survive the battle he shall answer me for it." Hardee, realizing that he had been too harsh with his touchy subordinate, sent a staff officer after him to convey his regrets for "his hasty and discourteous language."[9] But Walker would not be placated. When he finally got his men around the barrier and was approaching a ridge of high ground, Walker moved to the front, and as he raised his field glasses to study the ground ahead, he was shot dead by a Northern picket. Brigadier General Hugh Mercer assumed command of the division, and after some confusion and delay he got the attack moving again.

General Rice described what happened as his Union brigade and Bate's Confederate division collided: "The skirmish line had just arrived at the timber, 800 yards from my front when they met the enemy advancing in heavy force. The skirmish line, after exchanging a few shots with the enemy, moved by the left flank and uncovered my front . . . the enemy emerged from the woods in heavy charging column with battle flags proudly flaunting in the breeze. They burst forth from the woods in truly magnificent style in front of my right . . . Yet still my thin line stood like a fence of iron, not a man deserting his colors, which were all the time being proudly and defiantly waved in the very teeth of the enemy."[10]

An Ohio major described the Rebels' attack on Mersy's brigade: "They came tearing wildly through the woods with the yells of demons. We had an advantage in artillery; they in numbers. Their assaults were repulsed, only to be fearlessly renewed, until the sight of dead and wounded lying in their way, as they charged again and again to break our lines, must have appalled the stoutest hearts. So persistant were their onslaughts that numbers were made prisoners by rushing directly into our lines."[11] When the Confederates finally gave up and withdrew, Dodge sent three regiments forward in a counterattack which drove the Southerners off with heavy losses and captured 226 prisoners.

McPherson and his small party, riding south, came to a commanding hill behind Dodge's 16th Corps, from which they could see the attack on Rice's, Mersy's and Morrill's brigades. McPherson's chief of staff, Colonel William E. Strong, recorded the action: "The scene was grand and impressive. It seemed to us that every mounted officer of the attacking column was riding at the front of the first line of battle. The regimental colors waved and fluttered in advance of the lines, and not a shot was fired by the rebel infantry, although their movement was covered by a heavy and well-directed fire of artillery. It seemed impossible, however, for the enemy to face the sweeping deadly fire from Fuller's and Sweeny's divisions and the guns of Laird's and Welker's batteries fairly mowed great swaths in the advancing columns. They showed great steadiness, and closed up the gaps and preserved their alignment; but the iron and leaden hail that was poured upon them was too much for flesh and blood to stand, and before reaching the center of the open fields, the columns were broken and thrown into great confusion."[12]

McPherson sent Colonel Strong to check on Blair's front, and when he returned, Strong reported that a great many Confederates were advancing on Blair's position. McPherson, with his staff officers, rode forward the way Strong had just come. Meanwhile, Cleburne's Division, supported by Maney's, had advanced at about 12:45 p.m., or half an hour after Bate's and Walker's divisions, and attacked the left flank of Brigadier General Giles A. Smith's 4th Division of Blair's 17th Corps. Some of Smith's men jumped over their defenses to fight off this attack on their rear, only to be attacked by other Rebel units from the other direction. The Confederates drove both of Smith's brigades north to Leggett's Hill, capturing the entire 16th Iowa Regiment and eight pieces of artillery in the process, as well as forcing Morrill's brigade of the 16th Corps to move to the northeast, closer to Sweeny's Division. Logan had the brigade at the south end of his 15th Corps line, Walcutt's, turn to face south, and its fire and that of a pair of 24-pounder howitzers helped deflect the Confederate advance to the west, toward the rear of Blair's lines around Leggett's Hill. "We slaughtered the Rebels by the hundreds," Walcutt wrote.[13]

The Arkansans of Govan's Brigade, Cleburne's Division, crawled up on hands and knees and jumped into the Union trenches. Believing themselves to be outnumbered, the Federals surrendered, but when they realized that they were not really outnumbered, they demanded that the Rebels, instead, surrender to them. The Confederates considered this, but while the two sides were parlaying it was decided that their forces were about equal. Both surrenders were called off and they resolved to settle the issue by combat after all. Eventually the Southerners were ejected.

At 1 p.m. Wheeler's cavalry advanced against Decatur and drove Sprague's Federal brigade northward across the tracks of the Georgia Railroad to the courthouse square. The supply wagons of the Union Army of the Tennessee were in the town at the time and were Wheeler's main objective. But Sprague held the Rebel troopers off long enough for the wagon train to get away to the west and take cover behind Schofield's Army of the Ohio. Wheeler finally forced Sprague to fall back to the north by threatening his left flank, but as Wheeler was mounting a pursuit he received repeated orders from Hardee to go to the aid of the latter's infantry.

In the meantime, unaware of what had happened to Giles Smith's and Morrill's men, McPherson first ordered Colonel Strong to ride back to the north with orders for Logan to send a brigade to a good defensive position that he had spotted. Then he hurried on to find Smith, followed by a colonel, a lieutenant, and an orderly. They had gone only about 150 yards when they rode across the front of an advancing regiment of Cleburne's Division. A Rebel captain signalled with his sword for the Union general to surrender, but he "checked his horse slightly, raised his hat as politely as if he were saluting a lady, wheeled his horse's head directly to the right, and dashed of to the rear in a full gallop." The Confederate officer ordered his men to fire. A bullet struck the young general in the back and penetrated his lungs. The colonel who was with him, a brigade commander in Leggett's division, was captured when his horse was shot out from under him. The lieutenant's horse bolted with fright and slammed him into a tree, breaking his pocket watch, which showed that McPherson had been shot at 2:02 p.m. The general's orderly bent over him and asked if he was hurt. "Oh, orderly, I am," came the weak answer. His body quivered, his face fell to the side, and he was dead. Pointing to the general, the Rebel captain asked, "Who is this lying here?" With tears in his eyes the young Federal answered, "Sir, it is General McPherson. You have killed the best man in our army."[14]

Meanwhile, Blair's men who had been outflanked by Cleburne decided that they had retreated far enough and formed a new line, running eastward from Leggett's Hill. "Some general officer may have given an order to stop there," a Federal artillery officer wrote. "My own belief always has been that the boys did it of their own accord. They had been in so many fights that they did not need a general to tell them where and when to stop running and begin shooting." The Federals hurriedly threw up small breastworks of fence rails and dirt, and then Cleburne's crack troops came on, determined to regain the hill that they had lost to some of these same men the day before. "Their line well formed, they emerged from their concealment in the woods, and yelling as only the steer-drivers of Texas could yell, charged upon our division," the artillery officer recorded, ". . . but they were met by a continuous volley of musketry and shrapnel, shell and canister from our six-rifled Rodmans and Cooper's howitzers. It seemed as if no man of all the host who were attacking us could escape alive; and yet, still yelling, they persisted in their desperate undertaking. Their line was re-formed, and again they attempted the impossible,—to drive the Third Division from the line it had decided to hold. Many of the men reached our line; some got across it; many were bayonetted, many killed with clubbed muskets; hand-to-hand conflicts were frequent. But not one inch did the Third Division give way."[15]

At 3 p.m. Hood finally ordered Cheatham's corps forward from Atlanta's eastern defenses, supported on its right by the division of Georgia militia. Maney, who had been supporting Cleburne's attack, shifted his division to its left to join in Cheatham's advance. In fact, Maney attacked first, at about 3:30 p.m., followed by Cheatham at 4 p.m. Maney struck the bend in McPherson's line just south of Leggett's Hill, manned by Giles Smith's and Leggett's divisions of Blair's 17th Corps, from the southwest. But Blair's Federals were strongly entrenched and refused to budge, either for Maney or for Cheatham's right division, four brigades under Stevenson, attacking Leggett's Hill from the west.

Brigadier General Manning Force, commander of the 1st Brigade of Leggett's division, called for a flag. Some frightened young officer, thinking that it was time to give up, ran about trying to find something white to wave. "Damn you, sir!" Force exclaimed. "I don't want a flag of truce; I want the American flag!"[16] When one was found, it was planted on the highest part of the Federal works. Force was later hit by a bullet that entered his face at the outside corner of his eye, passed through his head, and came out near the base of his brain, but he survived to become a judge in Cincinnati after the war.

Cheatham's other two divisions, Clayton's on the left and Brown's just to Clayton's right, struck Logan's 15th Corps, which was just north of Blair's line. Manigault's Brigade of Brown's Division, in the center of the front line of this attack, approached the Federal line by following a deep ravine which the Georgia Railroad passed through. His advance was slowed by a battery of six guns and his formation was broken as it passed around the home of a Widow Pope. But Southern sharpshooters were placed on the second floor of the house, and under the cover of their fire Manigault's reformed brigade resumed its advance, captured four of the Union guns, and penetrated Logan's line. Swinging to his left, Manigault took the regiments of Lightburn's 2nd Brigade of Morgan L. Smith's 2nd Division of the 15th Corps in flank, one at a time, and each in turn broke and ran for the rear. Farther to the north, Manigault captured the two-story brick house of Troup Hurt and four 20-pounder rifles. Another brigade of Brown's Division, Sharp's, had been in support behind Manigault's, and now it wheeled to the right and took Martin's 2nd Brigade of Morgan L. Smith's division in the flank, capturing the other two guns near the railroad cut in the process. "I never enjoyed a thing better in my life," a member of Sharp's Brigade recorded. "We had the pleasure of shooting at Yankees as they ran without being shot at much."[17] The other two brigades of Brown's Division, on Manigualt's right, also turned to the south and drove the right two brigades of Harrow's 4th Division of the 15th Corps out of their defenses and to the southeast.

Sherman, at his headquarters, three-fourths of a mile to the northwest, saw the Confederates break Logan's line and ordered Schofield to mass all 20 of his cannon and open fire on the Confederates, and Sherman aimed the guns himself. "The shells tore through the lines or exploded in the faces of the men with unerring regularity," Manigault remembered.[18] But Sherman sent no infantry to help. In his memoirs he explained, "I purposely allowed the Army of the Tennessee to fight this battle almost unaided . . . because I knew that the attacking force could only be part of Hood's army, and that if assistance were rendered by either of the other armies, the Army of the Tennessee would be jealous. Nobly did they do their work that day, and terrible was the slaughter done to our enemy, though at sad cost to ourselves."[19] Meanwhile, Major General John ("Black Jack") Logan, as senior corps commander, had assumed command of the Army of the Tennessee. He sent word to Sherman that he was being attacked by the entire Confederate army. "Tell General Logan to FIGHT EM!" Sherman replied, "FIGHT EM LIKE HELL!"[20]

Logan ordered Mersy's brigade of the 16th Corps to hurry northward from its position on the southern front up to the Georgia Railroad to block Brown's Confederate breakthrough, and brought back the brigade of Woods' division which McPherson had earlier ordered him to send to Dodge's support. Lightburn's and Martin's reformed brigades of Morgan L. Smith's division deployed on Mersy's left in some defenses that they had occupied earlier that day. Harrow's three brigades extended this new line to the south and connected with Blair's right, while to Mersy's right were the two brigades of Woods' 1st Division of the 15th Corps. Sherman ordered Woods, "to wheel his brigades to the left, to advance in echelon, and to catch the enemy in flank."[21] They struck Clayton's Confederate division, on the left of Cheatham's corps, just north of Brown's Division. Logan rode among the men of the five brigades that had been driven back, waving his floppy hat, his long dark hair streaming behind him. "Will you hold this line with me?" he asked them. "Will you hold this line?" He was answered with cries of "McPherson and revenge!" and chants of "Black Jack! Black Jack!"[22]

The Federals then advanced to retake their lost defenses, which proved to be relatively easy, for as Manigault recorded: "A message had been sent to the Division Commander by both Sharp and myself, to say that we could make our positions good and hold them, when an order came to retire, quickly, as the enemy was moving in large masses on our left flank and rear, and to delay would cause the loss or capture of the forces engaged. There was nothing left for us to do but obey, and I never saw men obey an order so unwillingly. They were fully conscious of having distinguished themselves, and wanted to bring off the artillery they had so gallantly captured."[23]

By 5 p.m. the Union 15th Corps had regained its lost guns and entrenchments. Between 5 and 7 p.m. Maney and Cleburne attacked the 17th Corps three more times around Leggett's Hill, but only succeeded in lenghtening the casualty lists. By dark, the Confederates had retired within the defenses of Atlanta. "In the impetuosity, splendid abandon, and reckless disregard of danger with which the rebel masses rushed against our line of fire, of iron and cold steel, there has been no parallel during the war," General Giles A. Smith wrote.[24]

Again Hood had attacked and again he had failed, and with much higher losses than along Peachtree Creek two days before: about 8,000 men, compared to half that for the Federals. However, this time Hood had come much closer to victory. "Had Dodge's men not been where they were," wrote a major in Mersy's brigade, "there would have been absolutely nothing but the hospital tents and the wagon trains to stop Hardee's command from falling unheralded directly upon the rear of the XV and XVII Corps in line. Upon what a slight chance, then, hung the fate of Sherman's army that day."[25]

Hood's timing had been poor. He had expected Hardee to attack much sooner than he did, and yet he waited so long to send Cheatham's corps forward, that Hardee's attacks had about played out. Then, after Cheatham had been withdrawn, Hardee's attacks were allowed to continue. "If the enemy had concerted his attacks front, flank and rear," Blair said, ". . . it would have been extremely difficult, if not impossible, to hold our ground."[26]

That night Logan sent Dodge to Sherman's headquarters to ask for reinforcements. "He seemed surprised to see me," Dodge said, "but was cordial. I stated my errand."

"Dodge, you whipped them today, didn't you?" Sherman asked.

"Yes, sir," Dodge replied.

"Can you do it again tomorrow?"

Dodge stiffened, said, "Yes, sir," again, and went back to his command.

"The Army of the Tennessee had fought the great battle without aid," Sherman later wrote, "and, all alone, could whip Hood's whole army." His biographer, Lloyd Lewis, wrote, "He seemed as proud of that army as if every man in it had been his son."[27]

McPherson's body was recovered by Union forces before the day was over. His pockets had been emptied, but, to Sherman's relief, a notebook with McPherson's notes on Sherman's future plans was found on a Rebel prisoner. McPherson was taken to Sherman's headquarters, where he was laid out on a door supported by two chairs. His commander had lost more than a capable, trusted subordinate. "I expected something to happen to Grant and me," Sherman told a staff officer that night; "either the rebels or the newspapers would kill us both, and I looked to McPherson as the man to follow us and finish the war."[28]

Even more than that, Sherman had lost a friend. The young general had been engaged to Miss Emily Hoffman of Baltimore, who had defied her Southern-sympathizing family in agreeing to marry him. When the telegram announcing her fiancé's death reached her home she overheard one member of her family tell another, "I have the most wonderful news—McPherson is dead." She went to her room, closed her door, and spoke no more for a year. She did receive a letter from Sherman. "I yield to no one on earth but yourself the right to exceed me in lamentations for our dead hero," he told her. "I see him now, so handsome, so smiling, on his fine black horse, booted and spurred, with his easy seat, the impersonation of the gallant knight . . . Though the cannon booms now, and the angry rattle of musketry tells me that I also will likely pay the same penalty, yet while life lasts I will delight in the memory of that bright particular star."[29]

---

1. McDonough and Jones, *War So Terrible*, 219.
2. Ibid., 219–220.
3. Ibid., 224.
4. Ibid., 220.
5. Ibid., 220–221.
6. Sherman, *Memoirs*, 2:548–549.
7. McDonough and Jones, *War So Terrible*, 226.
8. Sherman, *Memoris*, 2:550.
9. McDonough and Jones, *War So Terrible*, 225.
10. Scaife, *The Campaign For Atlanta*, 53.
11. Ibid.
12. Ibid., 54.
13. McDonough and Jones, *War So Terrible*, 233.
14. Otto Eisenschiml and Ralph Newman, *The American Iliad* (New York, 1947), 621–622.
15. Henry Steele Commager, ed., *The Blue and the Gray* (New York, 1950), 945.
16. Ibid., 946.
17. McDonough and Jones, *War So Terrible*, 234.
18. Scaife, *The Campaign For Atlanta*, 57.
19. Sherman, *Memoirs*, 2:555.
20. Scaife, *The Campaign for Atlanta*, 59.
21. McDonough and Jones, *War So Terrible*, 235.

22. Ibid., 232.

23. Scaife, *The Campaign For Atlanta*, 57.

24. McDonough and Jones, *War So Terrible*, 236.

25. Scaife, *The Campaign For Atlanta*, 59.

26. McDonough and Jones, *War So Terrible*, 233.

27. Lewis, *Sherman: Fighting Prophet*, 388.

28. Ibid., 387.

29. McDonough and Jones, *War So Terrible*, 233.

CHAPTER TWENTY

It Is My Duty and I'll Perform It

22–25 July 1864

The same day as the battle of Atlanta, 22 July, Rousseau's Federal cavalrymen reached Marietta, Georgia, the end of their raid through Alabama. They had ridden 400 miles through the heart of the Confederacy, captured 60 able-bodied Rebels and paroled hundreds of sick and wounded ones, freed several hundred slaves, and put the railroad between Montgomery and Atlanta out of commission for four or five weeks. They had also demonstrated the inability of the Confederacy to protect its territory and its people. When Rousseau recounted his exploits to Sherman, he told him of one afternoon on which he and some of his staff officers had stopped at a plantation deep in Alabama. The owner had mistaken the dust-covered riders for Southern soldiers and cheerfully offered them drinks of water. Rousseau told the planter that he would have to take some of his mules, but the civilian protested that he had given ten mules to the Confederate army just the week before. Rousseau countered that both sides deserved equal treatment. "Ain't you on our side?" the Southerner asked. Rousseau said that he was a Federal general and that all the soldiers with him were Union troopers. "Great God," the planter exclaimed, "whoever would have thought that the Yankees could come way down here in Alabama."[1]

A short account of J. R. Gilmore's and Colonel Jaquess' talk with Jefferson Davis about peace appeared that 22nd day of July in the *Boston Evening Transcript,* but it was another month before the full account appeared, at Lincoln's request, in the *Atlantic Monthly.* The president wanted the people of both sides to know Davis' intransigent position.

The committee of Copperheads selected at the Chicago conclave met with the Confederate commissioners at St. Catherine's in Canada that day. They insisted that the Rebel army must cooperate with their revolt in order for it to succeed. Dr. William Bowles, head of the Sons of Liberty's military department, said that Southern forces would have to keep Union troops in Missouri and Kentucky busy, at least. To prepare the public, it was decided to replace secret meetings of the lodges and state councils with public mass meetings, which Commissioner Jacob Thompson agreed to finance. And St. Louis was added to Louisville as a rendezvous for columns of Copperheads and freed prisoners, who, when the revolt came, would march to link up with Southern armies. Thanks to a tip from Felix Stidger, a Federal spy in the Copperhead organization, Judge Joshua Bullitt, the head of the Sons of Liberty in Kentucky, was arrested at the ferry to Louisville on his way home from this meeting. He was found to be carrying incriminating checks drawn on a Toronto bank and signed by Thompson. A wave of further arrests soon followed.

In the Shenandoah Valley on the 22nd, Early's Confederate Army of the Valley reached Strasburg, while Averell and Crook united their columns from the Union Army of West Virginia at Kernstown, a little south of Winchester. Halleck wired Grant that day that Wright was on his way back to Washington: "Acting on your previous orders, he had given up the pursuit, and would reach Washington to-day. He left the enemy retreating on Front Royal and Strasburg. In my opinion raids will be renewed as soon as he leaves." Grant telegraphed to Halleck that same day: "You need not send any troops back until the main force of the enemy are known to have left the Valley. Is Wright still where he can act in conjunction with Hunter? If the two can push the enemy back, and destroy the railroad from Charlottesville to Gordonsville, I would prefer that service to having them here."[2] Conducting a campaign in the Shenandoah Valley by remote control over a telegraph wire that was subject to delays and cuts was proving to be harder for Grant than it had looked, especially with Halleck as middle man.

Sherman was having similar difficulties. Trains were already carrying A. J. Smith's troops back to their camps at Memphis that day, when Washburn finally received Sherman's telegram telling him to order Smith to keep after Forrest. Due to the circuitous route, it was taking two days for telegrams to get back and forth between Georgia and Memphis. The next day, the 23rd, Washburn sent a reply in which he pointed out that Smith had defeated Forrest and S. D. Lee and had only returned to his base due to an acute shortage of supplies. He added that he had "ordered General Smith to put his command in order to again move against Forrest. He will so move as soon as he can get ready, unless you should think he had better go to Mobile."[3] (Canby's projected move against Mobile had been on hold for lack of troops since Smith had been diverted to chase Forrest, and the 19th Corps had been sent from Louisiana to Virginia.) Meanwhile, Smith met with his two division commanders that day and instructed them to have their units—the last of which only reached Memphis that afternoon—ready to return to the field at the earliest possible moment.

Down in Georgia, at 10 a.m. on the 23rd a truce was called to allow for the recovery of the wounded and the burial of the dead of both sides. "The sight of the great number of Confederate dead in front of our lines was appalling, and never to be forgotten by those who saw it," wrote one of Sherman's aides. "Many times have I prayed," wrote an officer of the Georgia state troops, "that visions of those upturned faces, blackened and distorted, of the staring, glazed eyeballs, of the stiffened, outstretched hands, seemingly grasping for support, those rigid forms, wrapped in gray, who had met death in one of the deadliest battles in the history of the world, might be blotted forever from my recollection." The fighting had been "breast to breast," as the Georgian described it, ". . . such as seldom comes in any war." He said, "It was necessary in some places to climb over the heaps of the dead. The wonder seemed to be not that there were so many dead, but that any lived at all."[4]

Sherman and Thomas met that day at the headquarters of the 4th Corps, and their conversation revolved around the question of a permanent successor for McPherson. "General Logan had taken command of the Army of the Tennessee by virtue of his seniority, and had done well," Sherman wrote; "but I did not consider him equal to the command of three corps. Between him and General Blair there existed a natural rivalry. Both were men of great courage and talent, but were politicians by nature and experience, and it may be that for this reason they were mistrusted by regular officers like Generals Schofield, Thomas, and myself."[5] But it was Thomas, rather than Sherman or Schofield, who was not happy with the idea of having Logan as one of the three army commanders under Sherman. The previous March, Logan had been in temporary command of the Army of the Tennessee and had quarrelled with Thomas over control of the railroads through Tennessee.

"If you give it to Logan," Thomas told his old friend Sherman, "I should feel like asking to be relieved."

"Why, Thomas," Sherman exclaimed, "you would not do that?"

"No," Thomas admitted, "I would not, but I feel that army commanders should be on friendly terms and Logan and I cannot. Let the President decide it."

"No," Sherman replied, "it is my duty and I'll perform it."[6]

"We discussed fully the merits and qualities of every officer of high rank in the army," Sherman later wrote, "and finally settled on Major-General O. O. Howard as the best officer who was present and available for the purpose."[7] Howard had come west with Hooker after Chickamauga, as commander of one of the latter's two corps of reinforcements from the Army of the Potomac. When Hooker's two small corps had been consolidated into one large one as part of Thomas' Army of the Cumberland, Howard had been given command of another of Thomas' corps, the 4th. Like Hood, Howard was then 33 years of age, and he had been one class behind him, as well as McPherson and Schofield, at West Point. He had not been lucky in the East. He had lost an arm during McClellan's seven days of battle before Richmond, and he had not gotten on well with the men of the predominantly German 11th Corps that he had led at Chancellorsville and Gettysburg. Hooker blamed him, with some justice, for his defeat at the former, and in both battles his corps had been outflanked and routed.

But Meade had liked him. "He always votes to fight," he had said. And Sherman had taken a liking to him when they had served together in the relief of Knoxville, after Grant's victory at Chattanooga, "as one who mingles so gracefully and perfectly the polished Christian gentleman and the prompt, zealous and gallant soldier."[8] In fact, Howard was such a puritanical New Englander that he was known as the Christian General, and Bible-thumping Howard. General Carl Schurz remembered a cold day during the Knoxville campaign when Howard had entered a house where he, Sherman, and General Jefferson C. Davis were warming themselves. "Glad to see you, Howard," Sherman had said. "Sit down by the fire. Damned cold this morning."

"Yes, General," Howard had answered, "it is *quite* cold this morning."

At this, Sherman winked at Davis, who was as well known for his salty language as Howard was for his piety, and Davis promptly launched into the telling of a tale whose sole purpose was to give full play to his gift for profanity. "Howard made feeble efforts to turn the conversation," Schurz recorded, "but Davis, encouraged by repeated winks and sympathetic remarks from Sherman, grew worse and finally Howard, with distress all over his face, left, whereupon Sherman and Davis made the house ring with laughter." When Schurz protested this behavior, Sherman replied, "Well, that Christian-soldier business is all right in its place, but he needn't put on airs when we are among ourselves."[9]

In his memoirs, Sherman explained his choice of Howard: "I wanted to succeed in taking Atlanta, and needed commanders who were purely and technically soldiers, men who would obey orders and execute them promptly and on time; for I knew that we would have to execute some most delicate manoeuvres, requiring the utmost skill, nicety, and precision. I believed that General Howard would do all these faithfully and well, and I think the result has justified my choice. I regarded both Generals Logan and Blair as 'volunteers,' that looked to personal fame and glory as auxiliary and secondary to their political ambition, and not as professional soldiers."[10]

In Virginia that day Grant was still trying to outmaneuver Early by telegraph. He wired Halleck: "If Wright has returned to Washington, send him immediately back here, retaining, however, the portion of the 19th Corps now in Washington for further orders. Early is undoubtedly returning here to enable the enemy to detach troops to go to Georgia." Halleck replied: "General Wright in person arrived this morning, and most of his forces will encamp at an outer line to-night. The rebels generally said to the country people that as soon as they secured their plunder, they would return to Maryland and Pennsylvania for more." This caused Grant to hesitate, and the next day, the 24th, he told Halleck: "You can retain General Wright until I learn positively what has become of Early." At this, Halleck threw up his hands. He replied that night: "General Wright, in accordance with your orders, was about to embark for City Point. I have directed him to await your further orders. I shall exercise no further discretion in this matter, but shall carry out such orders as you may give."[11]

Early soon made the location of his Army of the Valley apparent, for he put it on the road heading north again that day. Halleck had been correct to assume that as soon as the Confederate commander discovered that Wright's force had withdrawn to Washington, he would turn back. At Kernstown, Crook had only the three very small divisions of infantry and two of cavalry of the Army of West Virginia, which, when he learned of Early's approach, were deployed on the same open ground as where General Shields had repulsed Stonewall Jackson 28 months before. A few miles south of Kernstown, Early sent Ramseur's Division to get around Crook's right, while the rest of his infantry threatened his front, and the Southern cavalry was split in half and sent around both sides of the town to establish a position to block the Union line of retreat.

Crook had a similar idea and ordered Averell's cavalry division to pass around Early's right and attack his wagons, but this left the Federal infantry's left flank unprotected. Early directed Breckenridge to take his old division, now under Wharton, and strike that flank. This move was "handsomely executed," as Early put it, while the rest of the Rebel infantry advanced against the Union right and center.[12] "I regret to say," Crook reported, "that the greater portion of my dismounted cavalry, along with some infantry, the whole numbering some 3,000 or 4,000, broke to the rear at the first fire, and all efforts to stop them proved of no avail."[13] The entire Union force was soon streaming down the Valley Turnpike and across the nearby fields, pursued by the Confederate infantry and artillery through and beyond Winchester. Rodes' Division carried on as far as Stephenson's Depot, six miles north, but could not catch the fleeing Federals.

Again Early's cavalry let him down. It "had not been moved according to my orders," Early wrote; "and the enemy, having the advantage of an open country and a wide macadamized road, was enabled to make his escape with his artillery and most of his wagons. General Ransom had been in very bad health since he reported to me in Lynchburg, and unable to take the active command in the field; and all of my operations had been impeded for the want of an efficient and energetic cavalry commander. I think, if I had had one on this occasion, the greater part of the enemy's force would have been captured or destroyed, for the rout was thorough."[14] One of the Rebel cavalry brigades did eventually strike the Union column on the turnpike, causing the Union teamsters to burn a number of caissons and wagons. Federal artillerymen abandoned four guns, but the infantry brought them off. At dusk the retreating Federals reached Bunker Hill, crossed Mill Creek, and bivouacked on the far side.

Colonel James A. Mulligan, commanding the small 3rd Division, which was drawn from Sigel's force that he had done so much to save the month before, was mortally wounded that day. His men were removing him from the field when he saw that their colors were about to be captured. "Lay me down and save the flag!" he shouted.[15] His men hesitated, but he repeated the order and they obeyed. Before they could get back to him, the colonel himself had been captured, and he died of his wounds three days later. As no officer above the rank of captain was now left in this entire division—which consisted of only five regiments—it was soon consolidated and became the 3rd Brigade of the 1st Division.

Trains pulled out of Tupelo, Mississippi, that day carrying Roddey's Division to Montgomery, Alabama. This was part of the break-up of the force which S. D. Lee had assembled to defend northern Mississippi now that A. J. Smith was no longer threatening it. The same day, Forrest received orders to return Mabry's Brigade to central Mississippi. The battalion of heavy artillerymen serving as infantry was returned to Mobile, and the men of various reserve units were allowed to return to their homes.

In a violent rainstorm on the 25th, Early's infantry divisions, still tired from their long march and fight of the day before, moved only twelve miles to Bunker Hill, although his cavalry continued the pursuit of Crook's still-retreating Federals. But at Martinsburg the Union rear guard turned on the Confederate troopers and drove them back a mile. After dark the Union retreat continued to the Potomac at Williamsport.

Grant took his case for combining the departments around Washington directly to President Lincoln in a letter that day. After telling him about his request which Secretary Stanton had squelched, he added: "I do not insist that the departments should be broken up, nor do I insist upon General Franklin commanding. All I ask is that one general officer, in whom I and yourself have confidence, should command the whole. General Franklin was named because he was available and I know him to be capable and believe him to be trustworthy. It would suit me equally as well to call the four departments referred to a 'Military Division' and to have placed in command of it General Meade. In this case I would suggest General Hancock for command of the Army of the Potomac and General Gibbon for command of the Second Corps. With General Meade in command of such a division I would have every confidence that all the troops within the Military Division would be used to the very best advantage, from a personal examination of the ground, and he would adopt means of getting the earliest information of any advance of the enemy and would prepare to meet it. During the last raid the wires happened to be down between here and Fort Monroe, and the cable broken [between] there and Cherrystone. This made it take from twelve to twenty-four hours each way for despatches to pass. Under such circumstances it was difficult for me to give positive orders or directions, because I could not tell how the conditions might change during the transit of despatches. Many reasons might be assigned for the changes here suggested, some of which I would not care to commit to paper, but would not hesitate to give verbally."[16] General Rawlins, Grant's chief of staff, delivered this letter in person, and no doubt passed on those reasons.

Meanwhile, since he wasn't going to be getting his 6th Corps and 19th Corps troops back for a while—in fact he now sent on to Washington a second division of the 19th Corps that had just arrived from Louisiana— Grant decided to wait no longer for their return and to get things moving again around Petersburg and Richmond. He decided that day on a plan to send Sheridan's cavalry and the 2nd Corps, under the recovered Hancock, across the James River on Butler's bridge at Deep Bottom. Hancock's infantry was to probe the defenses of Richmond to see if the Rebel capital could be taken by a quick assault. But the main object of the expedition was for the cavalry to slip past Richmond under the cover of the infantry's approach and to strike the railroads between that city and Hanover Junction. The cutting of those lines would make it difficult for the Rebels to bring supplies from the Shenandoah or for Early to return too quickly to rejoin Lee. The time for this move was set for the night of July 26.

Also on the 25th, Federal officers began a careful examination, from a newly erected signal station, of the ridge behind the Confederate lines opposite Burnside's sector, where the Pennsylvania coal-miners had completed their excavations. They wanted to determine whether, as feared, the Rebels had constructed a second line of defenses which would stop any breakthrough that might result from the explosion of the mine.

Down in Georgia that day, General Braxton Bragg, nominal commanding general of the Confederate army, returned to Atlanta, and Hardee took advantage of his presence again to ask for a transfer from the Army of Tennessee. There was also discontent among the Federal officers around Atlanta. Around the middle of the morning of the 25th, Dodge went riding along his lines to make sure that his troops were ready, in case the Rebels should attack again. He was joined on his tour by General Fuller, commander of his 4th Division, and together they rode to the headquarters tent of Brigadier General Thomas W. Sweeny, commander of the 2nd Division.

Dodge and Sweeny had never gotten along with each other. Dodge was a New England Protestant who had moved to the Iowa frontier, where he had become a railroad surveyor—engineer and banker, and he owed his high rank—he had just received his second star a few days before—at least partially to political influence. Sweeny was an Irish-born

Catholic who had lost an arm in the Mexican War and had stayed on in the regular army to become a career officer. By the accident of the seniority of his commission, Dodge had been Sweeny's boss since the fall of 1862, even though Sweeny was 11 years older and a regular. Several times the two had argued, usually when the latter's punctilious adherence to regulations conflicted with the orders and wishes of his volunteer superior. The ill feeling had grown to such a point that Sweeny had recently threatened to shoot Dodge's medical director for issuing orders to Sweeny's division surgeon without consulting Sweeny, the division commander, as regulations required. Dodge had appealed to McPherson to relieve and punish Sweeny, but McPherson had told Dodge that he should relieve Sweeny himself, "if he deems it for the best interests of the Service."[17]

So Dodge and Fuller, another volunteer general, were pleasantly surprised when Sweeny invited the two of them into the shade of his headquarters tent on that hot July day. But no sooner had the three generals seated themselves than Sweeny, whom Dodge later claimed was drunk, started complaining about the "damned political generals" who had almost led the army into disaster three days before. His own 2nd Division had fought splendidly, he said, but he claimed that Fuller's men "broke" and had to be saved by Sweeny's artillery. Dodge and Fuller said that Morrill's brigade, the only part of Fuller's division near Sweeny's that day, had found it necessary to adjust its line a few times because its right flank had been exposed, but they objected to the term "broke." Sweeny appealed to his artillery officer, saying, "Ain't I right, Welker?" That officer, a mere captain caught in an argument between generals, reluctantly sided with Sweeny.

"Fuller carried out my orders faithfully," Dodge growled, "and anybody who says differently is saying that which is not so." He stood up and glowered at Captain Welker, and Sweeny also got to his feet.

"I say so, you God-damned liar!" Sweeny yelled at Dodge. "I say so, you cowardly son of a bitch!" and added injury to insult by throwing a punch that caught Dodge in the shoulder. A swearing and slugging match followed until corps and division staff officers were finally able to separate the two generals. But Sweeny broke away from Captain Welker's grasp, shook his fist at Dodge and challenged him to a duel, saying, "Mr. Dodge of Iowa, you can fire a pistol—and so can I!"

Fuller then joined in, telling Sweeny, "You have feloniously assaulted and insulted the corps commander." Sweeny demanded to know just what "put in" Fuller had, and the latter replied that he did not want to take advantage of a one-armed man.

"Then by God, sir, why do you do it?" Sweeny yelled and hit him in the face. This started another fight, and Fuller had Sweeny down and was choking him when the staff officers managed to break them up. Sweeny now turned his anger against these underlings, particularly Captain Barnes, Dodge's adjutant general. Finally, at Dodge's order, Barnes proclaimed Sweeny to be under arrest.

"You don't know how to arrest an officer!" Sweeny shouted in derision, pointing out that the volunteer had no sword, prescribed in the regulations for such occasions. "Get out of my headquarters!" Sweeny said, rushing at the staff captain with raised fist. Barnes hurried away, supposedly to get the necessary sword, while Dodge and Fuller took advantage of this relative lull to mount up and ride off. "Go, Mr. Dodge of Iowa," Sweeny shouted after them, "you God-damned political general! I shall expect a note from you, sir!"

Dodge sent off a note all right, not a challenge to Sweeny, but a report to Logan, still in temporary command of the Army of the Tennessee, announcing that Sweeny "has been put in arrest for conduct disgraceful to a Comd'g Officer."[18] Sweeny was sent north to await court martial, which did not come until December because all the witnesses were busy fighting a war, and Sherman appointed Brigadier General John M. Corse to take command of Sweeny's division. Sweeny was eventually acquitted of all charges. But in the meantime more altercations and ill feelings among Sherman's officers would arise.

Some things were going well for Sherman that day, however. His railroad repair crews completed a bridge over the Chattahoochee River, crossing a 760-foot span 90 feet above the stream and allowing trains to deliver supplies almost to the front lines of Thomas' Army of the Cumberland. "Sherman's immense bridge across the Chattahoochee was done so quickly that he was ever afterward regarded by our boys as the champion bridge builder of the world," one Confederate recorded.[19]

The stalemate of Grant's armies before Petersburg and the inconclusive results in the Shenandoah were causing Northern hopes, and particularly those of the Republican party, to be increasingly placed on the campaign in Georgia. The Northern people were becoming weary of a war they couldn't seem to win. And the Confederates and Copperheads were doing their best to make it seem that the only obstacle to peace was Lincoln and his insistence on an end to slavery. In a letter written that day, which he evidently hoped would be shown to James Gordon Bennett, influential owner of the *New York Herald*, Lincoln said: "The men of the South, recently (and perhaps still) at Niagara Falls, tell us distinctly that they *are* in the confidential employment of the rebellion; and they tell us as distinctly that they are *not* empowered to offer terms of peace.

Does any one doubt that what they *are* empowered to do, is to assist in selecting and arranging a candidate and a platform for the Chicago convention? Who could have given them this confidential employment but he who only a week since declared to Jaquess and Gilmore that he had no terms of peace but the independence of the South—the dissolution of the Union? Thus the present presidential contest will almost certainly be no other than a contest between a Union and a Disunion candidate, disunion certainly following the success of the latter. The issue is a mighty one for all people and all time; and whoever aids the right, will be appreciated and remembered."[20]

A memorandum which Lincoln wrote at that time about Clement C. Clay and the Confederate activity in Canada shows that he well understood the Confederate strategy. "Mr. Clay confesses to his Democratic friends that he is for *peace* and *disunion;* but, he says 'You can not elect without a cry of war for the union; but, once elected, we are friends, and can adjust matters somehow.' He also says 'You will find some difficulty in proving that Lincoln could, if he would, have peace and reunion, because Davis has not said so, and will not say so; but you must assert it, and re-assert it, and stick to it, and it will pass as at least half proved.'"[21]

It was obvious that when the new draft started in September, Lincoln's popularity would plummet and would throw into doubt his reelection, unless somebody could win a spectacular victory that would demonstrate unmistakable progress toward winning the war. As Senator John Sherman, a Republican, put it in a letter then on its way to his brother down in Georgia, "We all feel that upon Grant and you . . . the fate of the country depends."[22]

---

1. Richard M. McMurry, "Riding Through Alabama: Part II," *Civil War Times Illustrated* 20:6 (October 1981): 41.

2. Pond, *The Shenandoah Valley in 1864*, 95 n. 1.

3. Bearss, *Forrest at Brice's Cross Roads*, 238.

4. Carter, *The Siege of Atlanta, 1864*, 243.

5. Sherman, *Memoirs*, 558–559.

6. Lewis, *Sherman: Fighting Prophet*, 389.

7. Sherman, *Memoirs*, 559.

8. Both quotes from Lewis, *Sherman: Fighting Prophet*, 349.

9. McDonough and Jones, *War So Terrible*, 242.

10. Sherman, *Memoirs*, 559.

11. Pond, *The Shenandoah Valley in 1864*, 94 n. 1.

12. Early, *War Memoirs*, 399.
13. Pond, *The Shenandoah Valley in 1864*, 97 n. 1.
14. Early, *War Memoirs*, 399–400.
15. Mark Mayo Boatner III, *The Civil War Dictionary* (New York, 1959), 574.
16. Pond, *The Shenandoah Valley in 1864*, 113–114.
17. Leslie Anders, "Fisticuffs at Headquarters: Sweeny vs. Dodge," *Civil War Times Illustrated* 15:10 (February 1977): 11.
18. Ibid., 13–15.
19. Lewis, *Sherman: Fighting Prophet*, 360.
20. Basler, ed., *The Collected Works of Abraham Lincoln*, 7:461.
21. Ibid., 7:460.
22. Lewis, *Sherman: Fighting Prophet*, 397.

CHAPTER TWENTY-ONE

They'll Only Beat Their Own Brains Out

25–29 July 1864

Sherman's problems with his generals continued that day, the 25th. They all began to complain when a list of newly promoted officers was published. They observed that Peter J. Osterhaus, a former division commander in the Army of the Tennessee, had been made a major general despite having been on leave for a long time, and they suspected that political influence was at work. Even more rankling had been the recent breveting to major general of A. P. Hovey, who had left the Army of the Ohio on leave in June, just as the Atlanta campaign had been heating up. Hovey was a political general who had gone off in a huff because he had not been allowed to retain command of all of the troops he had recruited. Sherman had insisted on separating the cavalry, which badly needed some training, from the infantry division that Hovey had been allowed to keep. When Hovey had departed for Indiana on leave, Sherman had broken up his division, giving one of his brigades to each of the other divisions in the 23rd Corps, and Hovey had been put in command of the District of Indiana, where he could make himself useful by fighting Copperheads.

So Sherman fired off a typically sarcastic wire to the inspector general in Washington saying that "it is an act of injustice to officers who stand by their posts in the day of danger to neglect them and advance such as Hovey and Osterhaus, who left us in the midst of bullets to go to the rear in search of personal advancement. If the rear be the post of honor, then we had better change front on Washington."[1]

But once again Sherman drew a reply straight from the president. "The point you make is unquestionably a good one," Lincoln said; "and yet please hear a word from us. My recollection is that both Gen. Grant and yourself recommended both H & O. for promotion; and these, with other strong recommendations, drew committals from us which we could neither honorably or safely, disregard. . . . I beg you to believe we do not act in a spirit of disregarding merit. We expect to await your programme, for further changes and promotions in your army. My profoundest thanks to you and your whole Army for the present campaign so far."[2]

John Wilkes Booth checked into the Parker House hotel in Boston the next day, 26 July 1864. So did four men using aliases, one giving Baltimore as his address and the other three giving various Canadian cities. There is no proof, but the odds are that these were Confederate agents, meeting with Booth to recruit him into a scheme to kidnap President Lincoln.[3]

That same morning Crook's retreating Army of West Virginia crossed the Potomac into Maryland and, at Hunter's direction, took position at Sharpsburg, except for Averell's cavalry, which was stationed at Hagerstown with pickets guarding the fords of the river. Early advanced his Army of the Valley to Martinsburg that day.

In Mississippi, with S. D. Lee on his way to take up his new duties as corps commander under Hood, Major General Dabney Maury, commander of the defenses of Mobile, was placed in temporary charge of the Confederate Department of Alabama, Mississippi, and East Louisiana that day. He wrote to Forrest the next day, the 27th: "I wish you to take charge of the defense of the northern part of Mississippi. The prairie country appears to me to be the first object of our care. I know how disproportionate the forces at present under your command are to those which we understand the enemy has, but it will be difficult for him to advance far into the country while you are before him. I would not, if I could, undertake to prescribe to you any plan of operations. I wish you to understand that I intrust to you the conduct of affairs, and desire only to be able to aid you effectively with the means of executing your own views."[4]

In Georgia on the 27th Sherman sent off an answer to Lincoln's reply about Osterhaus and Hovey: "I beg you will not regard me as fault-finding, for I assert that I have been well sustained in every respect. . . . I did not suppose my dispatches could go outside the office at the War Department. . . . Hovey and Osterhaus are both worthy men and had they been promoted on the eve of the Vicksburgh campaign it would have been natural and well accepted but I do think you will admit that their promotion coming to us when they had been to the rear the one offended because I could not unite in the same division five Infantry and five cavalry regiments; and the other for temporary sickness, you can see how ambitious aspirants for military fame regard these things; and they come to me and point them out as evidence that I am wrong in encouraging them in a silent, patient discharge of duty. I assure you that every General of my army has spoken of it and referred to it as evidence that promotion results from importunity and not from actual services. . . . I will furnish all my army and Division commanders with a copy of your dispatch, that they may feel reassured."[5]

And yet Sherman's troubles with his generals were still far from over. Howard officially assumed command of the Army of the Tennessee that same day. In a letter written to Logan that day, Sherman said, "I fear you will be disappointed at not succeeding permanently to the command of the army. I assure you in giving prejudice to Gen. Howard I will not fail to give you every credit for having done so well. . . . No one could have a higher appreciation of the responsibility that devolved on you so unexpectedly and the noble manner in which you met it."[6] Logan asked Sherman to leave him in command until the campaign for Atlanta ended, but Sherman refused.

On a visit to Sherman's headquarters General Dodge found Logan sitting on the porch. "He hardly recognized me as I walked in, and I saw a great change in him," Dodge said. ". . . As everyone knows, Logan's independence and criticism in the army was very severe, but they all knew what he was in a fight, and whenever we sent to Logan for aid, he would not only send his forces but come himself; so, as Blair said, we only knew Logan as we saw him in battle. Logan could hear every word that was said between Sherman and myself. Sherman did not feel at liberty to say anything in explanation of this change. He simply put me off very firmly, but as nicely as he could, and spoke highly of

General Howard . . . I went away . . . without any satisfaction, and when I met Logan on the outside I expressed to him my regrets, and I said to him 'There is something here that none of us understand,' and he said: 'It makes no difference; it will all come out right in the end.'"[7]

Logan was not the only officer disappointed by not receiving the job. Hooker was by far the most senior major general among Sherman's corps commanders, and if someone outside the Army of the Tennessee was to receive the command, he thought it should be himself. "General Hooker is offended because he thinks he is entitled to the command," Sherman wrote. "I must be honest and say he is not qualified or suited to it. He talks of quitting. I shall not object. He is not indispensible to our success." Hooker wrote to Thomas: "I have just learned that Major General Howard my junior, has been assigned to the command of the Department and Army of the Tennessee. If this is the case I request that I may be relieved from duty with this army. Justice and self-respect alike require my removal from an army in which rank and service are ignored." To Logan he wrote that day: "I asked to be relieved from duty with the army, it being an insult to my rank and service. Had you retained the command I could have remained on duty without the sacrifice of honor or principle."[8]

Although there is no hint of it in the records, it is possible that one reason why Howard had been chosen by Thomas and Sherman was the hope that Hooker would react in just the way that he did. Neither one of them liked Hooker. Thomas sent Hooker's application for relief from duty to Sherman "approved and *heartily* recommended."[9] And it was common knowledge that Hooker disliked Howard.

In his memoirs, Sherman wrote: "General Hooker was offended because he was not chosen to succeed McPherson; but his chances were not even considered; indeed, I had never been satisfied with him since his affair at the Kulp House, and had been more than once disposed to relieve him of his corps, because of his repeated attempts to interfere with Generals McPherson and Schofield. I had known Hooker since 1836, and was intimately associated with him in California, where we served together on the staff of General Persifer F. Smith. He had come to us from the East with a high reputation as a 'fighter,' which he had fully justified at Chattanooga and Peach-Tree Creek, at which latter battle I complimented him on the field for special gallantry, and afterward in official reports. Still, I did feel a sense of relief when he left us."[10] Hooker's place as commander of the 20th Corps was filled for a while by his senior division commander, Brigadier General A. S. Williams.

Hood was also making command changes that day. S. D. Lee, at 31 the youngest lieutenant general in the Confederate army, took command of the Confederate 2nd Corps that day, sending Cheatham back to command his own division in the 1st Corps, and Maney back to his brigade. A young artillery officer described Lee as "of medium height with dark hair, blue eyes, and affable manner." But he said that many of the veteran troops resented the displacement of that "rough and ready fighter, General Cheatham; hence he assumes command with the prejudices of the army against him."[11] Yet, Hood liked him because he shared his views about entrenchments and morale. "Troops once sheltered from fire behind works, never feel comfortable unless in them," Lee said. He felt the men's offensive spirit was affected as well. "When orders were given to attack and there was a probability of encountering works, they regarded it as reckless in the extreme . . . and therefore did not generally move to the attack with that spirit which nearly always ensures success."[12]

T. C. Hindman, a division commander in the 2nd Corps, had become ill and was replaced by J. Patton Anderson, brought up from Florida. And General Francis Shoup, the chief of artillery, was made Hood's chief of staff, to replace General W. W. Mackall, who had not only resigned but had taken all of his records with him, leaving army headquarters in a state of confusion. No suitable replacement could be found for Walker, who had been killed on the 22nd, so his division was broken up, his brigades being assigned to Hardee's other three divisions. Hood also ordered earthworks built to protect the railroad for six miles down to East Point, where the line to Alabama separated from the line to Macon.

The defenses of Atlanta were too formidable for Sherman to hope to take the city by assault and too large for him to encircle and take by siege. He therefore planned to force Hood to give up the city by severing all its connections with the outside world, namely its railroads. If food, ammunition and other supplies could not be brought into the city, the Confederate army would have to leave it. The Army of the Tennessee and Garrard's cavalry division had done a thorough job of destroying the Georgia Railroad for miles to the east of Atlanta and, of course, the railroad running north was in Union hands. Rousseau's raid had temporarily broken the line to the west, and now Sherman intended to do it even more damage by swinging the Army of the Tennessee around behind his other two forces to the west side of town. Under its new commander, this force began the move that day, with the wheels of its wagons muffled by hay and grain sacks so as not to alert the Rebels. The other armies were then to repeat the process until the remaining line running south could eventually be cut. Meanwhile, Thomas and Schofield were told to keep the Rebels' attention away from Howard by being "as bold and provoking to the enemy as possible."[13] And the division of Jefferson C. Davis, the general with the talent for swearing, was sent forward from Thomas' extreme right to clear the way for the approach of Howard's army.

But in an effort to speed the process, Sherman sent out most of his cavalry that day to strike that southern line, the Macon & Western Railroad. Brigadier General Edward McCook was to take two brigades of his 1st Division of the Cavalry Corps of the Army of the Cumberland across the Chattahoochee far to the southwest of Atlanta to strike the Macon & Western near Jonesboro, around 25 miles south of the city. His force was brought up to 3,600 men by adding Rousseau's recently arrived raiders, now consolidated into one brigade under Colonel Thomas J. Harrison. Meanwhile, Major General George Stoneman was to take his Cavalry Division of the Army of the Ohio, plus Garrard's 2nd Division of the Cavalry Corps of the Army of the Cumberland, totalling about 5,900 men, from Decatur, on the east side of the city, and meet McCook at Lovejoy's Station on the Macon & Western, a little south of Jonesboro.

Stoneman had talked Sherman into allowing him to add a second mission to his part of the raid. After tearing up the railroad, McCook and Garrard would return to the main army, but Stoneman would continue with his own small division of 2,100 men to Macon, where about 1,500 Northern officers were being held prisoner, and then on to Andersonville, where he hoped to rescue the 20,000 or more Union prisoners being held there. "This is probably more than he can accomplish," Sherman told Halleck, "but it is worthy of a determined effort." To Stoneman he wrote, "If you can bring to the army any or all of those prisoners of war, it will be an achievement that will entitle you and the men of your command to the love and admiration of the whole country."[14]

But Stoneman got so carried away with the idea of freeing the prisoners that he neglected the primary objective of the raid, to tear up the Macon railroad. He sent Garrard's division toward that goal by way of Flat Rock, where there was a ford on the South River, but he led his own division along a more easterly route, heading straight for Macon. Major General Joseph ("Fightin' Joe") Wheeler, the 28-year-old commander of the Cavalry Corps of the Army of Tennessee, learned that morning of Garrard's approach and he moved to intercept him with most of his corps.

In the Shenandoah Valley that 27th day of July, Early's Confederates began to tear up the tracks of the Baltimore & Ohio Railroad around Martinsburg. In Washington, Secretary Stanton was making his own arrangements for unifying the small departments threatened by Early's army. He instructed Halleck to "take all military measures necessary for defense against any attack of the enemy and for his capture and destruction."[15] Stanton also wired Grant to ask when the general-in-chief could meet President Lincoln at Fort Monroe for a discussion of the whole situation. Grant answered that he could not leave the front just then because pressing matters would require his personal attention.

Hancock's 2nd Corps crossed the James River over Butler's bridge at Deep Bottom in the early hours of the 27th and attacked the Confederate defenses along Bailey's Creek, driving in an advanced Rebel force and capturing four 20-pounder rifles. But then the Federals ran into unexpected opposition from Wilcox's Division of Hill's 3rd Corps and Kershaw's Division of Anderson's 1st Corps. In fact, the latter counterattacked, and Hancock could make no further progress. Kershaw had been sent to Chafin's Bluff as a precaution a few days before, and when Lee had learned that Butler was entrenching at Deep Bottom he had ordered Kershaw to drive him back and if possible to destroy his bridge. But Hancock had crossed to the north side before Kershaw had been able to comply. During the day, Heth's Division of the 3rd Corps arrived to reinforce the Rebel position.

Meanwhile, Sheridan crossed the river with two of his own divisions, Torbert's 1st and Gregg's 2nd, plus Kautz's Cavalry Division of the Army of the James. These troopers traversed an area called Strawberry Plains, advanced on Hancock's right, and also found Rebels defending the crossings of the creek. Grant arrived that afternoon and realized that he had underestimated Rebel strength north of the James. He ordered the infantry to move north and try to get around the Confederate flank the next day, so that the cavalry could set out on its raid. Grant did not want his troops to assault the formidible Confederate defenses, but the Rebel line was much longer than expected. On the 28th, Hancock left Gibbon's 2nd Division to hold his corps' original position, and led Barlow's and Mott's northward to join Sheridan.

But as soon as the Federal line was formed, the Confederate infantry advanced to attack it. The Rebels directed most of their strength against the cavalry and drove the Union troopers, still mounted, some distance over high ground. However, when the Federals reached the east side of this ridge they were ordered to quickly dismount and lie down about 15 yards from the crest. As the Confederates came over the hill, the Northern troopers opened such a devastating fire on them that they gave way in disorder. Now it was the Federals' turn to chase the Rebels across the ridge and back to their defenses. In the process they captured about 250 prisoners and two battleflags.

Rooney Lee's cavalry division then joined the Confederate infantry on the north side of the James. Mott's Union infantry division, however, was sent back south of the river that night, for by then Grant had given up the hope of achieving anything on the north side. That night he telegraphed Halleck: "We have failed in what I hoped to accomplish—that is, to surprise the enemy and get on to their roads with the cavalry near to Richmond and destroy them out to the South Anna. I am yet in hopes of turning this diversion to account, so as to yield greater results than if the first object had been accomplished."[16] That day Meade chose the morning of the 30th as the time to set off explosives in the mine dug by the 48th Pennsylvania and to assault the area thus disrupted.

In the meantime a number of ruses were employed in order to make Lee think that the main Federal effort would yet be on the north side of the James. One of the cavalry divisions was sent quietly back across the river, the bridge having been covered with hay to deaden the sound, and then marched conspicuously back again in plain view of the Confederates. Also, an empty train of wagons was sent to the north side, and steam boats were kept plying back and forth, as though ferrying troops.

Down in Georgia that morning, the 28th, Brigadier General Kenner Garrard found his Union cavalry division confronted by three divisions of Wheeler's Confederate cavalry corps. According to Garrard's report, "after being surrounded by a superior force for over twelve hours, and contending against every disadvantage, in hopes of benefiting General Stoneman in his attempt to destroy the railroad, it extricated itself from its perilous situation."[17] According to Colonel Robert Minty, one of Garrard's brigade commanders, the breakout was led by Colonel Abram Miller's crack Lightning Brigade of Illinois and Indiana mounted infantry regiments, one of the first Western outfits armed with Spencer repeaters. Garrard retreated about halfway back to Decatur, but by then Wheeler had learned about Stoneman's division heading straight for Macon, and McCook's column, which had slipped past Red Jackson's cavalry division of the Army of Mississippi on the Confederate army's left.

Wheeler left one of his division commanders, Brigadier General John H. Kelly, with one his brigades, to keep an eye on Garrard. And he sent three brigades to pursue Stoneman. These he put under one of the brigade commanders, Brigadier General Alfred Iverson, who came from the area between Atlanta and Macon and thus would be familiar with the terrain. Wheler himself took two brigades west to reinforce Jackson and deal with McCook. The latter had marched down the northwest bank of the Chattahoochee with a train of pontoons, which slowed his progress. Eighteen mules died in their harnesses hauling the heavy loads. But by that afternoon the pontoon bridge was laid, and McCook's troopers crossed to the southeast side of the river. Before the day was over they had torn up two and a half miles of track on the Atlanta & West Point Railroad.

By nightfall on the 27th Dodge's 16th Corps was in position on Thomas' right on high ground, facing east. At dawn on the 28th Blair's 17th Corps was in place to the right of Dodge, while Logan's 15th Corps marched on to the south. As the latter approached Lick Skillet Road, west of Atlanta, Confederate resistance stiffened. "About 8 o'clock Sherman was riding with me through the wooded region in rear of Logan's forces," Howard wrote, "when the skirmishing began to increase, and an occasional shower of grape cut through the tree-tops and struck the ground beyond us. I said: 'General, Hood will attack me here.' 'I guess not—he will hardly try it again,' Sherman replied. I said that I had known Hood at West Point, and that he was indomitable."[18] Sherman soon rode back to Thomas' headquarters, where he would be in position to send help if it was needed.

Howard was right. Hood was attacking again. He sent S. D. Lee with two divisions of his 2nd Corps along Lick Skillet Road to an important road junction where there was a Methodist meeting house called Ezra Church. There he was to entrench a line facing north to stop this move of Sherman's around the west side of the city. Stewart, with two divisions of the Army of Mississippi, marched down the Sandtown Road to the southwest. The plan was that Lee would block the Union progress to the south, and Stewart would move around Lee's left and strike Howard's western flank. But when Lee reached Ezra Church he found that Logan's 15th Corps of Howard's Army of the Tennessee was already in possession of the intersection. Without informing Hood of this unexpected situation or even waiting for Stewart to come up on his left, Lee attacked.

To make matters worse for Lee, he was picking on the wrong man. Logan was still smarting over losing command of the army to Howard and was determined to prove his worth to Sherman. His 15th Corps followed a curved line facing southeast on the left and southwest on the right, and his men hurriedly covered their front with logs and rails. At about 12:30 p.m. Brown's Division, on the left of Lee's line, advanced, with three brigades abreast and a fourth in reserve, against Morgan L. Smith's 2nd Division and part of Harrow's 4th Division of the 15th

Corps, 400 yards away. The Rebels came on with what Howard remembered as a terrifying yell, through thickets and fences. Brantley's Mississippi brigade, on the left of Brown's line, got around Logan's right flank and overran the hastily constructed defenses of the 83rd Indiana. But Dodge sent four regiments to the threatened point, Howard's inspector general brought over two more from Blair, both armed with repeating rifles, and his chief of artillery placed several batteries to cover the exposed flank. "These were brought in at the exact moment," Howard wrote, "and after a few rapid discharges, the repeating-rifles being remarkable in their execution, all the groups of flankers were either cut down or had sought safety in flight."[19]

The rest of Brown's Division struck the right half of Logan's line head on. "Hold 'em!" Logan roared over the noise of battle, turning back stragglers with his drawn sword, "Hold 'em!"[20] The Federals poured volley after volley into the advancing Rebels. Brown lost three of his four brigade commanders and reported that his "troops were driven back with great slaughter."[21] Clayton's Division of Lee's corps advanced on Brown's right at about 12:40 p.m. Clayton's left-most brigade, Gibson's, received confusing orders and moved out in advance of the other two brigades. It struck the part of the line held by Wangelin's 3rd Brigade of Wood's 1st Division of the 15th Corps just in front of Ezra Church, where Logan's line bent. Wangelin's men had formed a hasty barricade from the pews of the church and their own knapsacks, but seeing this lone Confederate brigade approach, these Federals counterattacked and shattered Gibson's advance.

When Sherman learned that Hood was definitely attacking, a staff officer heard him say, "Good—that's fine—just what I wanted, just what I wanted. Tell Howard to invite them to attack, it will save us trouble, save us trouble, they'll only beat their own brains out, beat their own brains out."[22] To make sure that Hood hadn't abandoned Atlanta, he ordered Thomas and Schofield to probe the defenses of the city, but these were found to be held, as Schofield reported, "in sufficient force to resist an assault."[23] Davis' division of Thomas' army was sent to try to get on the Rebels' western flank and roll them up, but he got lost and never found the battle.

At 1 p.m. Lee's men attacked again and were again driven back. "Lee looked like the God of war," a Rebel lieutenant remembered. "I can see him now, positively radiant . . . I expected to see him fall every minute."[24] Stewart, instead of turning Howard's flank, marched to the sound of guns and at about 2 p.m. his lead division, Walthall's, arrived on the scene and was inserted in the line between Brown's and Clayton's divisions. Walthall's men advanced across the same ground that Brown's had traversed, stumbling over Brown's dead and wounded, with Clayton supporting their right. This advance was a "grand display," a Union officer recorded, "as they took up their line of march down the hill, marching as cooly and as deliberately as if they were going out on battalion or grand review."[25] This attack was also repulsed, but Lee kept attacking, and when Stewart's other division, Loring's, showed up, it too went forward. However, just as it was being deployed Loring was wounded, and Stewart was struck in the forehead by a spent bullet. Finally the Confederate troops refused to advance. The Federals could see the Rebel officers trying to lead their men forward again, but the men would not follow and some began to run. "What are you running for?" a Georgia officer demanded of one of them. "Bekase I kaint fly!" came the answer.[26]

Again Hood stayed in Atlanta, where he had almost no idea of what was going on out by Ezra Church. Finally he decided to send Hardee out to take charge of the troops at the front, but by the time he arrived it was too late to affect the course of events, as the troops were already refusing to make another attack. "No action of the campaign probably did so much," Hardee wrote, "to demoralize and dishearten the troops engaged in it." That evening one of Logan's pickets called across the lines, "Well, Johnny, how many of you are left?" And one of his Confederate counterparts answered, "Oh, about enough for another killing."[27] During the night, after losing at least 5,000 men and five battle flags, the Confederates withdrew quietly into the defenses of Atlanta.

Howard stayed out of the way and let Logan have all the glory. "I never saw better conduct in battle," he wrote. "General Logan, though ill and much worn out, was indefatigable, and the success of the day is as much attributable to him as to any one man."[28] After the fighting was over Sherman came forward to compliment the men of the corps that had been his own the year before. "It was easy," they told him, pointing out the dead and wounded Confederates who lay "in windrows, sometimes two or three deep."[29]

Logan had one more duty to perform that night. He and some of his officers came across a dilapidated cabin where a young woman, whose husband had recently died in Lee's army, had just given birth to a baby girl. Logan put his officers to work repairing the cabin's roof, which had been shot away during the day's fighting. Then, while shells exploded in the woods outside, Logan took the baby in his arms as a Union chaplain performed the christening ceremony. At the mother's and grandmother's request Logan provided a name for the little girl. He named her Shell-Anna and left a gold coin with the grandmother for the child. "Put it in a safe place," he told her, "or some damned bummer will steal it in spite of everything."[30]

Sherman also had one other matter to deal with. He received a dispatch from the War Department asking him to nominate eight colonels for promotion to brigadier general. He sent a circular to his three army commanders, requesting nominations, and the next day, the 29th, he telegraphed the names to Washington, two from the Army of the Ohio and three each from the other two. "I doubt if eight promotions were ever made fairer, or were more honestly earned, during the whole war," he wrote.[31]

Before dawn, on the 29th, the 1st Tennessee Cavalry (Union), leading McCook's column, captured a train of several hundred wagons. The wagons were destroyed and the best of the horses and mules were taken, while the rest were killed by saber thrusts. At about 7 a.m. the Federals reached Lovejoy's Station on the Macon & Western Railroad. There they destroyed the depot, a large quantity of Confederate supplies, two and half miles of track, and four miles of telegraph line. But, hearing nothing from Stoneman and learning that Confederate cavalry was nearby, McCook decided to turn back, leading his column due west.

In southwestern Tennessee that day, the first brigade of A. J. Smith's force, McMillen's, was loaded onto boxcars at Memphis and taken to Grand Junction, where the east-west Memphis & Charleston Railroad crossed the north-south Mississippi Central. Smith and Washburn had decided that for the former's next expedition into Forrest's country he would use the Mississippi Central as his line of supply, so he would not have to turn back as he had been forced to do the last time. The drawback to this approach would be the necessity of repairing the rail line as they advanced. Once he got as far as Oxford, Smith would leave the railroad and head east to raid the fertile Black Prairie region, which would be certain to bring Forrest to its defense.

In the Shenandoah Valley, Early had plans to carry the war to the north again. "A number of towns in the South, as well as private country houses, had been burned by the Federal troops," he wrote. "I came to the conclusion it was time to open the eyes of the people of the North to this enormity, by an example in the way of retaliation . . . The town of Chambersburg in Pennsylvania was selected as the one on which retaliation should be made, and McCausland was ordered to proceed, with his brigade and that of Johnson and a battery of artillery, to that place, and demand of the municipal authorities the sum of $100,000 in gold or

$500,000 in U.S. currency, as a compensation for the destruction of the houses named and their contents; and in default of payment, to lay the town in ashes."[32] After Chambersburg, McCausland was to proceed to Cumberland, Maryland, on the upper Potomac, and levy contributions from that town and others, and destroy the machinery of the coal pits near there, as well as the machine shops, depots, and bridges of the Baltimore & Ohio.

On the 29th McCausland crossed the Potomac above Williamsport, while Early, with Rodes' and Ramseur's infantry divisions and Vaughan's cavalry brigade, moved to that town, driving some Union cavalry across the river. Breckinridge's two divisions remained at Martinsburg to continue the destruction of the Baltimore & Ohio Railroad. Imboden, with his own and Jackson's cavalry brigades, rode toward Harper's Ferry as a diversion. And as further cover for McCausland's raid, Vaughan crossed the Potomac at Williamsport and rode into Hagerstown, Maryland, where he captured and destroyed a train loaded with supplies. To further confuse the Federals, one of Rodes' infantry brigades was sent across the Potomac at Williamsport, but was then brought back.

On the Richmond-Petersburg front that day, more Confederates crossed to the north side of the James: Field's Division of Anderson's 1st Corps and Fitzhugh Lee's cavalry division. That left on the Petersburg front only Beauregard's two divisions, Mahone's Division of the 3rd Corps, and Hampton's cavalry division, while Pickett's Division of the 1st Corps continued to hold the defenses opposite Butler's Bermuda Hundred lines. Neither side launched a major attack, although Kautz made a feint to maintain the appearance that the Federals were up to something. But that night Hancock's 2nd Corps and Sheridan's cavalry crossed back to the south side of the James, ready to follow up any success resulting from the explosion of Colonel Pleasant's mine.

1. Basler, ed., *The Collected Works of Abraham Lincoln*, 7:463–464, n. 1.

2. Ibid., 7:463.

3. Tidwell, Hall, and Gaddy, *Come Retribution*, 262–263.

4. Bearss, *Forrest at Brice's Cross Roads*, 250.

5. Basler, ed., *The Collected Works of Abraham Lincoln*, 7:464.

6. McDonough and Jones, *War So Terrible*, 245.

7. Ibid., 243–244.

8. Ibid., 242.

9. Ibid.

10. Sherman, *Memoirs*, 560.

11. Carter, *The Siege of Atlanta, 1864*, 255.

12. Hattaway, *General Stephen D. Lee*, 126–127.

13. McDonough and Jones, *War So Terrible*, 251.

14. Both quotes from Scaife, *The Campaign For Atlanta*, 69.

15. Catton, *Grant Takes Command*, 318.

16. Ibid., 320.

17. Starr, *The Union Cavalry*, 3:467.

18. Howard, "The Struggle For Atlanta," 319.

19. Ibid.

20. McDonough and Jones, *War So Terrible*, 258.

21. Ibid., 259.

22. Lewis, *Sherman: Fighting Prophet*, 399.

23. McDonough and Jones, *War So Terrible*, 260.

24. Hattaway, *General Stephen D. Lee*, 128.

25. Both quotes from McDonough and Jones, *War So Terrible*, 259.

26. Ibid.

27. Both quotes from Scaife, *The Campaign For Atlanta*, 63.

28. Sherman, *Memoirs*, 2:564.

29. Lewis, *Sherman: Fighting Prophet*, 399.

30. Ibid., 401.

31. Sherman, *Memoirs*, 2:569.

32. Early, *War Memoirs*, 401.

PART FOUR

SUMMER OF DISCONTENT

"Everything is darkness and doubt and discouragement."

John Nicolay, one of President Lincoln's secretaries

CHAPTER TWENTY-TWO

The Saddest Affair I Have Witnessed in the War

30 July 1864

At 3 a.m. on 30 July 1864 Lieutenant Colonel Henry Pleasants, commander of the 48th Pennsylvania Volunteers, hurried through the pre-dawn Virginia darkness to the entrance of the mine that he had engineered and his men had dug. When he reached the mouth of the tunnel, hidden by bushes in a ravine just behind his regiment's earthworks east of Petersburg, he and two of his men made their way to the end of 98 feet of fuse leading to 8,000 pounds of gunpowder positioned 20 feet beneath a Confederate earthwork known as Elliott's Salient. Pleasants struck a match and lit the fuse, and after watching for a second to make sure it was burning true, the three men quickly scrambled out of the tunnel to a place of safety. If their calculations were correct, the powder would explode at 3:30 a.m., obliterating the Rebel fort, and its defenders, and opening a hole in the Confederate line through which Union troops could be poured before the enemy could stop them.

The military engineers had scoffed at Pleasants' mine and had given him no aid. "If ever a man labored under disadvantages, that man was Colonel Pleasants," a Union officer later wrote.[1] "General Burnside told me," Pleasants later explained to Congress' Joint Committee on the Conduct of the War, "that General Meade and Major Duane, chief engineer of the Army of the Potomac, said the thing could not be done—that it was all clap-trap and nonsense; that such a length of mine had never been excavated in military operations, and could not be; that I would either get the men smothered, for want of air, or crushed by the falling of the earth; or the enemy would find it out and it would amount to nothing." But the determined former mining and railroad engineer had persevered.

"At first I employed but a few men at a time," Pleasants later testified, "but the number was increased as the work progressed, until at last I had to use the whole regiment—non-commissioned officers and all." He said that his greatest problem had been getting rid of the dirt dug out of the tunnel. "I found it impossible to get any assistance from anybody; I had to do all the work myself. I had to remove all the earth in old cracker-boxes." These he strengthened with pieces of hickory and iron hoops from barrels of pork and beef issued as rations for his men. But that was hardly his only problem. To get timber to shore up his tunnel he had torn up an old bridge, and then he had found it necessary to send two companies of his regiment outside of Union lines with wagons to local saw mills. And he "had to take common army picks and have them straightened for my mining picks . . .

"Whenever I made application I could not get anything, although General Burnside was very favorable to it," he said. "The most important thing was to ascertain how far I had to mine, because if I fell short of or went beyond the proper place, the explosion would have no practical effect. Therefore I wanted an accurate instrument with which to make the necessary triangulations. I had to make them on the farthest front line, where the enemy's sharp-shooters could reach me. I could not get the instrument I wanted, although there was one at army headquarters, and General Burnside had to send to Washington and get an old-fashioned theodolite, which was given to me."[2]

The main gallery of the mine was a fraction under 511 feet long, and the army engineers had been correct that, under normal circumstances, there would not be enough fresh air for the miners to breathe at the face of a tunnel anywhere near that long. But they had not reckoned with the Yankee ingenuity of Henry Pleasants. A hundred feet inside the mine, he had installed an airtight canvas door, and just inside of that he had built a two-foot-square chimney leading to the open air 23 feet above. A fire at the base of this chimney created a draft that pulled fresh air in through a square wooden pipe that ran the length of the tunnel. At the

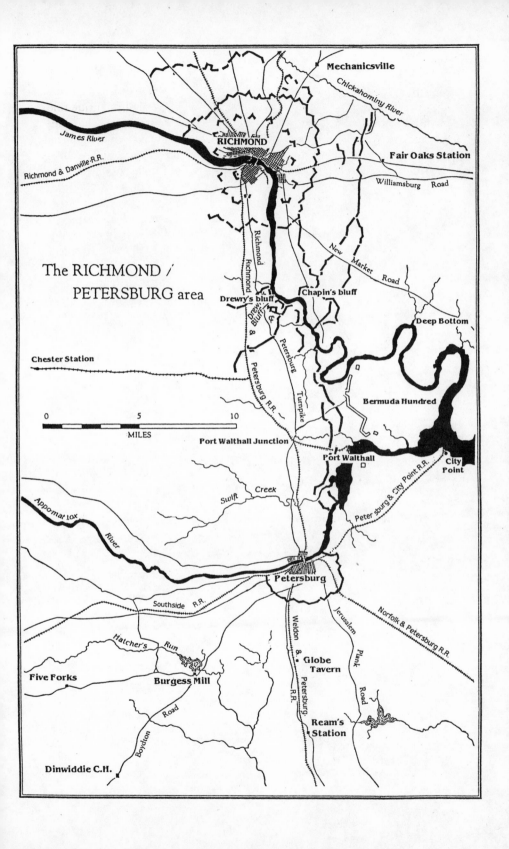

end of this main tunnel were two lateral galleries that gave the plan of the mine the shape of an elongated Y.

Despite all the experts' expectations of failure, the mine had been completed by July 23. The Confederates had become suspicious, even though all efforts had been made to keep the mine a secret, and they had tried to dig down and meet it, but had not been able to find it. It was obvious, however, that given enough time they would either dig into the mine and destroy it, adjust their line to avoid it, or construct a second line behind Elliott's Salient to prevent a breakthrough. It was feared that they had already done the latter, but what had at first seemed like a second line on high ground, called Cemetery Hill, behind the fort, turned out on closer examination to be a series of unconnected earthworks for artillery. So with Grant determined to take the offensive in order to keep Lee from sending troops to Georgia, with the move across the James stymied, and for lack of a better option, Meade was forced to make use of the "clap-trap" mine after all.

On the 26th Burnside had presented an elaborate plan for an assault to follow the explosion of the mine. He had been training Brigadier General Edward Ferrero's 4th Division of his 9th Corps for this attack for several weeks. That division had been chosen because it was comparatively fresh, having yet to see any large-scale combat. And that was because it was composed entirely of regiments of United States Colored Troops. No one quite wanted to trust these untried black soldiers with important assignments, and so, all the way from the Rapidan to the James, Ferrero's division had been used only to guard the supply wagons and lines of communication.

Meade had objected to using them for this assault because they were untried, while this was an operation that called for the very best troops. Burnside had insisted, however, so the question had been referred to General Grant. He had agreed, at the time, with Meade, but later admitted that this had been a mistake. "General Burnside wanted to put his colored division in front," he told the Congressional investigators, "and I believe if he had done so it would have been a success. Still, I agreed with General Meade as to his objections to that plan. General Meade said that if we put the colored troops in front (we had only one division) and it should prove a failure, it would then be said, and very properly, that we were shoving these people ahead to get killed because we did not care anything about them. But that could not be said if we put white troops in front."[3] But that decision had not been made until the night before, the 29th, which left no time for giving the white troops any of the special training which the black troops had received.

Up to this point the blame for any lack of success in the operation would have to be borne by Meade and Grant. But now Burnside put in his contribution. Instead of choosing the best troops and commander to lead the assault, he left the decision to pure chance by having his other three division commanders draw straws. It is seldom wise to tempt fate so flagrantly, and this case was no exception. The short straw went to Brigadier General James H. Ledlie, who had only taken over the 1st Division a few weeks before. In his memoirs, Grant wrote, "Ledlie besides being otherwise inefficient, proved also to possess disqualification less common among soldiers."[4] This was a polite way of saying the man was a coward. To further complicate matters, by the time Ledlie had been chosen it was dark and so he was unable to study the terrain, even if he had been inclined to do so.

Meade not only changed the troops chosen to lead the charge, he also changed Burnside's plan for the assault. Burnside had intended that the first units to penetrate the expected hole in the Rebel line would turn to their right and left in order to widen the breach for following units. But Meade was determined to seize the high ground behind the Confederate defenses, so he directed that the troops should push on through, for the crest of Cemetery Hill.

Shortly after midnight Ledlie's troops advanced through the covered ways behind the Union front line, which one of his staff officers, Major William H. Powell, described as being "almost as puzzling to the uninitiated as the catacombs of Rome." The men and officers, he said, were "in a feverish state of expectancy, the majority of them having been awake all night."[5] And just before dawn they were in position across from the fort that was to be blown up, with Marshall's 2nd Brigade in front and Bartlett's 1st Brigade in the rear. Behind them were the divisions of Willcox and Potter, who were to follow Ledlie's troops and protect their left and right respectively. Only then would Ferrero's black troops follow the original plan of widening the breach. Most of Warren's 5th Corps was massed on Burnside's left, ready to exploit his success, while Ord's 18th Corps, from Butler's Army of the James, was formed behind Burnside's divisions, ready to support the attack.

As it slowly began to grow light, the men became restless, Major Powell said, "with every nerve strained prepared to move forward the instant an order should be given."[6] Four a.m. arrived and still the mine had not exploded. Grant and Meade, watching from nearby, began to consider launching the attack without benefit of the mine, because the Confederates were bound to spot the preparations for the assault soon. The frantic Pleasants was about to go into the tunnel and find out what was wrong when the mine boss, Sergeant Henry Rees, beat him to it. Rees found that the fuse, which was not of the quality that Pleasants had originally requested, had burned out where two sections had been spliced together. He cut away the charred portion, and on his way out for materials was met by Lieutenant Jacob Douty, who helped him make a fresh splice. They lit the fuse again and scrambled for safety. At 4:45 a.m., an hour and fifteen minutes behind schedule, the four tons of black powder ignited with a blast "that would have done credit to several thunderstorms," as one Northern soldier put it.[7]

Grant "had been looking at his watch," Horace Porter recorded, "and had just returned it to his pocket when suddenly there was a shock like that of an earthquake, accompanied by a dull, muffled roar; then there rose two hundred feet in the air great volumes of earth in the shape of a mighty inverted cone, with forked tongues of flame darting through it like lightning playing through the clouds. The mass seemed to be suspended for an instant in the heavens; then there descended great blocks of clay, rock, sand, timber, guns, carriages, and men whose bodies exhibited every form of mutilation."[8] "It was a magnificent spectacle," Ledlie's staff officer remembered, "and as the mass of earth went up into the air, carrying with it men, guns, carriages, and timbers, and spread out like an immense cloud as it reached its altitude, so close were the Union lines that the mass appeared as if it would descend immediately upon the troops waiting to make the charge. This caused them to break and scatter to the rear, and about ten minutes were consumed in reforming for the attack. Not much was lost by this delay, however, as it took nearly that time for the cloud of dust to pass off. The order was then given for the advance."[9]

As soon as the powder exploded, 110 Union cannon and 50 mortars opened fire from commanding positions covering the ground to the right and left of the crater. Finally, Ledlie's men scrambled over their own defenses, none of which had been removed as Meade had ordered them to be. To have done so "would have been an arduous as well as hazardous undertaking," according to Major Powell.[10] Anyway, this broke the ranks of the advancing troops, who did not stop to reform but pushed ahead to the spot where the Rebel fort had been, 130 yards away. Dirt thrown up by the explosion had smoothed their path somewhat by covering the obstructions in front of the Confederate works.

The men and guns of the battery that had occupied Elliott's Salient, plus nearly 300 other Confederates, were wiped out by the explosion, which left an oblong crater 30 feet deep, 60 feet wide, and 170 feet long. What was more, the defenders for 200 yards on both sides of the crater fled in terror. "We could see the men running without any apparent object except to get away," Grant wrote.[11] Many of the Rebels were found partially buried in the debris, "some up to their necks, others to their waists, and some with only their feet and legs protruding from the earth," Major Powell recorded. "One of these near me was pulled out, and proved to be a second lieutenant of the battery which had been blown up. The fresh air revived him, and he was soon able to walk and talk. He was very grateful and said that he was asleep when the explosion took place, and only awoke to find himself wriggling up in the air; then a few seconds afterward he felt himself descending, and soon lost consciousness."[12]

"The whole scene of the explosion struck every one dumb with astonishment," Powell said, "as we arrived at the crest of the debris. It was impossible for the troops of the Second Brigade to move forward in line, as they had advanced; and, owing to the broken state they were in, every man crowding up to look into the hole, and being pressed by the First Brigade, which was immediately in rear, it was equally impossible to move by the flank, by any command, around the crater. Before the brigade commanders could realize the situation, the two brigades became inextricably mixed, in the desire to look into the hole."[13]

Nevertheless it was going to be up to the brigade commanders to sort things out. Major Powell and a Lieutenant Randall were the only members of the division headquarters who went forward with the troops. They had been informed "that the volunteer staff would remain with General Ledlie, all of whom did so during the entire engagement, in or near a bomb-proof within the Union lines."[14] Eventually Colonel Marshall yelled for his 2nd Brigade to advance, "and the men did so, jumping, sliding, and tumbling into the hole, over the debris of material, and dead and dying men, and huge blocks of solid clay."[15] Bartlett's 1st Brigade soon followed, and the men began to clamber up the opposite side of the hole, while some of them stopped to place two of the dismounted Confederate guns on the western crest of the crater. Part of Marshall's brigade passed over that crest and tried to reform its ranks on the other side, but they were struck from the rear by fire from Rebels on both sides of the breakthrough, and they withdrew to the shelter of the crater.

If Burnside's original plan had been followed, designated Union regiments would have attacked to each side and cleared those Rebels from the nearby trenches, but Meade's plan called for all of the Federals to advance straight ahead, and that they could not do while taking fire from the rear. Ledlie's two brigade commanders got their men sorted out as best they could inside the crater, but because of the steepness and depth of its sides it was difficult for their men to find positions from which they could load and fire their rifles. Meanwhile, the Confederates had brought up a battery of guns which began to sweep the crest of the crater with canister fire.

Colonel Marshall sent Major Powell to report the situation to General Ledlie. He braved the enemy canister fire, found Ledlie "ensconced in a protected angle of the works," and made his report. But all he got for his trouble was a reiteration of the order to advance. Powell returned with this message, but the firing was now so intense that it would be "as utterly impracticable to re-form a brigade in that crater," he said, "as it would be to marshal bees into line after upsetting the hive."[16]

However, that was only the beginning of the Federals' problems. Soon Brigadier General S. G. Griffin's brigade of Potter's 2nd Division of the 9th Corps advanced just to the right of the crater. But Griffin did not get far enough to the right, and two or three of his regiments joined the throng in the crater. "Those on the right passed over the trenches," Powell wrote, "but owing to the peculiar character of the enemy's works, which were not single, but complex and involuted and filled with pits, traverses, and bomb-proofs, forming a labyrinth as difficult of passage as the crater itself, the brigade was broken up, and, meeting the severe fire of canister, also fell back into the crater, which was then full to suffocation. Every organization melted away, as soon as it entered this hole in the ground, into a mass of human beings clinging by toes and heels to the almost perpendicular sides. If a man was shot on the crest he fell and rolled to the bottom of the pit."[17]

Potter also sent his other brigade, under Colonel Zenas R. Bliss, to make an attack to the right of the crater. Two of Bliss' regiments moved to the crater and then turned right, sweeping down the Confederate lines, while the rest of the brigade assaulted them from the front. By these tactics they captured 200 or 300 yards of the Rebels works, and one of Bliss' regiments got to within twenty or thirty yards of the battery whose fire was pinning down the troops in the crater, but that was as far as these Federals could go, and they fell back to the enemy's entrenchments. Potter sent a dispatch to Burnside saying that, in his opinion, too many men were being piled into this one point, that the men were in confusion, and that what was needed was an attack made on some other part of the Confederate works to divert the enemy's attention. But he received no answer, while he, Ledlie, and Willcox received repeated orders to push their men forward as fast as possible.

When the situation was reported to Meade he sent Burnside a note saying: "Do you mean to say your officers and men will not obey your orders to advance? If not, what is the obstacle? I wish to know the truth." The normally amiable Burnside, no doubt frustrated at seeing his attack falter, and no doubt feeling it was all Meade's fault, took exception to his commander's tone. "I have never, in any report, said anything different from what I conceive to be the truth. Were it not insubordinate, I would say that the latter remark of your note was unofficerlike and ungentlemanly."[18]

Again Powell left the crater and appealed to Ledlie, sitting in a bombproof dugout, to try to have something done on its right and left. He reported that every man who got into the Rebel trenches used them as a means of escape from enemy fire into the crater itself, and that the Confederates were then reoccupying their works. Again Ledlie's only answer was an order to go back and tell his brigade commanders to press forward to Cemetery Hill. Shortly thereafter, Willcox advanced with his 3rd Division and attacked the enemy defenses to the left of the crater. He was able to carry the entrenchments for about 150 yards, but could not hold them for long.

"When it was found that the troops were accomplishing so little," Horace Porter recorded, "and that matters were so badly handled, General Grant quickly mounted his horse, and calling to me, said, 'Come with me.'" The two, plus one orderly, rode forward, and at about 5:30 a.m. they came upon a brigade of Ferrero's black troops lying upon their arms. "Who commands this brigade?" Grant called out. "I do," replied Colonel Henry G. Thomas. "Well, why are you not moving in?" Grant asked. "My orders are to follow that brigade," the colonel replied, pointing to the brigade in front of his. Then he asked, "Will you give me the order to go in now?" But Grant declined to interfere with the chain of command to that extent. They passed other troops and as they approached the fighting Porter managed to convince the general that they should dismount. Turning their horses over to the orderly, they continued to make their way forward on foot. "The general had by this time taken in the situation pretty fully," Porter wrote, "and his object was to find the corps commander, to have him try to bring some order out of the chaos which existed . . .

"General Grant now began to edge his way vigorously to the front through the lines of the assaulting columns as they poured out of the rifle-pits and crawled over the obstructions. It was one of the warmest days of the entire summer, and even at this early hour of the morning the heat was suffocating," Porter remembered. Grant was dressed in an ordinary private's uniform except for his shoulder straps bearing three stars each, and nobody paid him much attention as he hurried past and they shoved and crowded toward the front. Finally Grant and Porter spotted some officers in an earthwork up ahead where Burnside was presumed to be. "To reach them by passing inside of our main line of works would have been a slow process," Porter wrote, "as the ground was covered with obstacles and crowded with troops; so, to save valuable time, the general climbed nimbly over the parapet, landed in front of our earthworks, and resolved to take the chances of the enemy's fire. Shots were now flying thick and fast, and what with the fire of the enemy and the heat of the midsummer Southern sun, there was an equatorial warmth about the undertaking. The very recollection of it, over thirty years after, starts the perspiration."[19]

Sometimes at a fast walk, sometimes at a dog-trot, Grant and Porter made their way to the earthwork where Burnside was watching the action. The latter was "not a little astonished to see the general approach on foot from such a direction, climb over the parapet, and make his way to where the corps commander was stationed. Grant said, speaking rapidly: 'The entire opportunity has been lost. There is now no chance for success. These troops must be immediately withdrawn. It is slaughter to leave them here.'"[20] Grant and Porter then made their way, "with no little difficulty," back to their horses and returned to where he and Meade had been watching.

Nevertheless, at about 7 a.m. General Ferrero received orders from Burnside to advance his division past the white troops and to carry the crest of Cemetery Hill at all hazards. Ferrero told Colonel Loring of Burnside's staff that he did not think this was advisable. Loring suggested that Ferrero wait until he could report this to Burnside, but Ferrero did not think he could do that. So Loring wrote out an order, in Burnside's name, to halt without passing over the Union works and then went off to report to the corps commander. He came back to report that the latter's order was peremptory for the 4th Division to advance. As they were moving forward a white sergeant, who was being carried to the rear with his leg shot off, called out, "Now go in with a will, boys. There's enough of you to eat 'em all up."[21] But a black sergeant replied that he and his men did not have just the best of appetites that morning. Ferrero did not choose to go forward with his men, but joined Ledlie in the safety to the bomb-proof dugout.

The black troops advanced "under a most galling fire, passed around the crater on the crest of the debris, and all but one regiment passed beyond the crater," Major Powell wrote. "The fire upon them was incessant and severe, and many acts of personal heroism were done here by officers and men. Their drill for this object had been unquestionably of great benefit to them, and had they led the attack, fifteen or twenty minutes from the time the debris of the explosion had settled would have found them at Cemetery Hill, before the enemy could have brought a gun to bear on them. The leading brigade struck the enemy's force . . . in front of the crater, and in a sharp little action the colored troops captured some two hundred prisoners and a stand of colors, and recaptured a stand of colors belonging to a white regiment of the Ninth Corps. In this almost hand-to-hand conflict the colored troops became somewhat disorganized, and some twenty minutes were consumed in re-forming; then they made the attempt to move forward again. But, unsupported, subjected to a galling fire from batteries on the flanks, and from infantry fire in front and partly on the flank, they broke up in disorder and fell back to the crater, the majority passing on to the Union line of defenses, carrying with them a number of the white troops who were in the crater and in the enemy's intrenchments."

"Had any one in authority been present when the colored troops made their charge," Powell said, "and had they been supported, even at that late hour in the day, there would have been a possibility of success; but when they fell back and broke up in disorder, it was the closing scene of the tragedy. The rout of the colored troops was followed up by a feeble attack from the enemy, more in the way of a reconnaissance than a charge; but the attack was repulsed by the troops in the crater and in the intrenchments connected therewith, and the Confederates retired."[22]

At about 9:30 a.m. instructions were repeated by army headquarters for Burnside to withdraw his troops, but he came to Meade in person and insisted that his men could not be safely withdrawn from the crater because Confederate fire now covered the only escape route. He wanted a passageway to be dug to protect them. Meade quickly unleashed his famous temper, and Horace Porter said that "the scene between them was decidedly peppery, and went far toward confirming one's belief in the wealth and flexibility of the English language as a medium of personal dispute."[23]

General Lee and his staff, north of the Appomattox, had heard the sound of the mine's detonation that morning, but it was 6:10 a.m. before a galloping officer had arrived from Beauregard's headquarters with word of what had happened. Lee sent Colonel Venable of his staff to General Mahone, who was holding the right end of the Confederate lines at Petersburg, to tell him to pull two of his brigades out of his defenses without the enemy seeing them, and to hurry them to a position in rear of the Union breakthrough. Then Lee rode alone to A. P. Hill's headquarters. There he found Colonel Palmer of Hill's staff, who said that Hill had already gone to get Mahone, but Lee decided to go on himself, to hurry them along. Before reaching Mahone's headquarters he encountered his troops marching toward the threatened point. He

then rode to where he could see the break in his lines and asked Palmer
to count the Union flags on the works. Eleven was the answer, which
indicated that roughly one division of Federal troops was in position.

After checking on the progress of Mahone's two brigades, Lee rode
over to General Bushrod Johnson's headquarters near the cemetery that
gave the hill its name. There he found Beauregard, and the two of them
went forward to a house which was only about 500 yards from the crater.
From its upstairs windows they had an excellent view of the situation.
Lee could see thousands of enemy soldiers crowded into the crater. He
also saw that they held about thirty yards of the defenses to his right
(their left) of the crater, about 200 yards to his left (their right), and part
of a second Confederate line.

He learned that most of Elliott's Brigade of Johnson's Division was
holding on in the ditches and traverses on the left side of the Union
break-in and that the rest of Elliott's men, supported by Wise's Brigade,
held a sector on the right from which they could fire into the crater and
cover the field leading to it. One cannon on Wise's front was able to
bear on the Federals, while on the left a battery of light 12-pounders on
a hill was firing into the crater at almost point-blank range. The gunners
serving these pieces were firing as fast as they could, despite the shells
from enemy guns across the lines that were bursting all around them.
Another battery, due west of the crater, was firing on the Federals in the
second line, while some nearby mortars were dropping shells among the
Yankees.

Besides the two brigades that Mahone was bringing onto the field even
then, there was one more on the way. One regiment of Hoke's Division
was also coming, and a few of Elliott's men were sheltering in a ravine
a couple of hundred yards west of the crater, out of sight of the numerous
Union guns. Mahone was told to file his men into this same ravine and
then to charge the enemy as soon as possible. While this was being done,
Lee gave directions for the placement of the reserve artillery of the 3rd
Corps, which was then arriving. Fourteen Federal flags could now be
seen, as well as Union officers standing on the parapet of the second line,
waving their swords and urging their men forward. Then one could be
seen to seize a flag, call to his men, and spring down from the parapet
on the Confederate side. That was Lieutenant Colonel John A. Bross of
the 29th U.S. Colored Troops. "He had hardly reached the ground outside the works before he fell to rise no more," Colonel Henry wrote.[24]
But the black men continued to clamber out of the Rebel works until
about 200 of them, from three regiments, were assembled, and with a
thin little cheer they came on in a ragged line.

One of Mahone's staff officers called out, "General, they are coming!"[25] At that same moment Mahone's old brigade of Virginians, under its senior colonel, Weisiger, plus part of Wright's Georgia brigade, and a few of Elliott's men, advanced from the ravine, under orders not to fire until they were on the enemy. The Confederates drove the advancing blacks back to the crater and the nearby trenches, but the right part of the Georgia brigade had not advanced, and Mahone's front was too short to cover the entire line occupied by the Federals. In fact his right was about 100 yards to the left of the crater, but he retook most of the defenses in that area. The remainder of the Georgians were then ordered to advance and retake the second line just behind the crater, and they went forward at 10:30 a.m. But they were met by such a heavy fire that they drifted to their left and joined the rest of Mahone's troops in the defenses already retaken. However, the combined force steadily drove the Federals back along the lines until they were almost to the edge of the crater, while Wise's Brigade on the other side pushed right up to its very rim.

Mahone's third brigade, Saunders' Alabamans, arrived at 11 a.m. and formed line in the ravine. They were told to stoop low until they got far enough up the slope to see the enemy. Then they were to break into the doublequick and not stop until they reached the crater. Meanwhile the artillery and the troops on each side, including Colquitt's Brigade on the right end of Johnson's line, were to provide fire support. Lee sent a message to Saunders that his Alabamans were the last troops available to seal this breach in the line. The rest of the line had been stripped of every available man. On Mahone's original front there was now only one man for every twenty paces of defenses. If Saunders' men did not take the crater in their first attempt, Lee said, he would lead them in person for a second try.

At 1 p.m. they began to creep up the hill from their ravine as artillery shells screamed over their heads. With them went the 61st North Carolina from Hoke's Division and the 17th South Carolina of Elliott's Brigade. Enemy fire was taking its toll, but on they went, over the second line, abandoned by the Federals, and straight for the crater. Some of the Yankees raised a white flag and surrendered, while others continued to fight. Some of the Rebels raised their hats on their ramrods over the crest of the crater, and when a Federal volley tore these to shreds they sprang over the edge before the defenders could reload. They were soon followed by men from the other Rebel brigades, and a desperate hand-to-hand fight ensued. The sight of the black troops seemed to throw the Southerners into a frenzy. "Take the white man—kill the nigger!" someone cried.[26]

The crater and the adjacent trenches were so crowded with Union troops that most of them could not fight back. Some said they were packed in so tightly that they literally could not raise their hands. "The loss of life was terrible," a Pennsylvania captain wrote. "There was death below as well as above ground in the crater. It seemed impossible to maintain life from the intense heat of the sun."[27] More and more Federals surrendered, while thousands ran across the open ground toward their own lines, preferring to risk being shot to spending the rest of the war in a Southern prison.

"Thus ended an operation conceived with rare ingenuity, prepared with unusual forethought, and executed up to the moment of the final assault with consummate skill," Horace Porter wrote, "and which yet resulted in absolute failure from sheer incapacity on the part of subordinates."[28] He didn't mention the part played by headquarters in failing to provide needed materials, nor in changing a good plan at the last moment. About 1,500 Union soldiers were captured, including brigade commanders Bartlett and Marshall, along with twenty flags. About 3,500 were killed or wounded. Most of these losses occurred after Grant and Meade had told Burnside to call off the attack. The Confederate casualties totalled about 1,500, including those blown up with the mine.

"I expected to write to you of one of the most glorious victories that was ever won by this army," a member of Pleasants' 48th Pennsylvania wrote to his sister, "but instead of victory I have to write about the greatest shame and disgrace that ever happened to us. The people at home may look at is as nothing but a mere defeat, but I look at it as a disgrace to our corps." Colonel Pleasants had watched all the planning and hard work done by himself and his men turned to nought by the bungling of others. A member of his regiment recorded that "Pleasants was awful mad when he saw how things were going on." He stormed and swore and told Burnside that he had "nothing but a damned set of cowards in his brigade commanders."[29]

A matron at Chimborazo Hospital in Richmond wrote that until that battle, the sick and wounded Confederate soldiers under her care had never seemed to be bitter toward their enemies. "They fit us, we fit them," seemed to be their attitude. But from then on there was a change. They considered the explosion of the mine a "mean trick" and the use of black troops, even worse. "Eyes gleamed, and teeth clenched as they showed me the locks of their muskets, to which the blood and hair still clung, when, after firing, without waiting to reload, they had clenched the barrels and fought hand to hand."[30]

Riding back to his headquarters at City Point with his staff that day, Grant was even quieter than usual, Horace Porter noted, attributing it to his aversion to criticizing others. Finally he said, "Such an opportunity for carrying a fortified line I have never seen, and never expect to see again." He did not mention Burnside or Ledlie by name but remarked, "If I had been a division commander or a corps commander, I would have been at the front giving personal directions on the spot. I believe that the men would have performed every duty required of them if they had been properly led and skillfully handled."[31] But to Halleck he revealed a bit more of his feelings when he wrote him that what came to be known as the Battle of the Crater was "the saddest affair I have witnessed in the war."[32]

Never one to dwell on a disappointment, Grant ordered Meade to put the cavalry and one corps of infantry on the road for the southern flank at dawn the next morning, before Lee could get all his forces back from north of the James. But that night Grant received word that Early was heading north again. He cancelled the move south and directed Meade to send a division of cavalry to Washington instead. He also wired the president that he was free to meet him at Fort Monroe the next day.

---

1. William H. Powell, "The Battle of the Petersburg Crater," in *Battles and Leaders*, 4:545.

2. Ibid., 545–546.

3. Ibid., 548.

4. Grant, *Memoirs*, 2:313.

5. Powell, "The Battle of the Petersburg Crater," 549–550.

6. Ibid., 550.

7. George F. Skoch, "Thunder From Below," *America's Civil War* 1:2 (July 1988): 31.

8. Porter, *Campaigning With Grant*, 263.

9. Powell, "The Battle of the Petersburg Crater," 551.

10. Ibid.

11. Grant, *Memoirs*, 2:315.

12. Powell, "The Battle of the Petersburg Crater," 551.

13. Ibid.

14. Ibid., 549–550, note.

15. Ibid., 551.

16. Ibid., 553.

17. Ibid., 553–554

18. Porter, *Campaigning With Grant*, 267–268.

19. Ibid., 266.

20. Ibid., 267.

21. Ibid., 268.

22. Powell, "The Battle of the Petersburg Crater," 556–557.

23. Porter, *Campaigning With Grant*, 267.

24. Henry Goddard Thomas, "The Colored Troops at Petersburg," in *Battles and Leaders*, 4:565.

25. Douglas Southall Freeman, *R. E. Lee (New York, 1935)*, vol. 3, 474.

26. Catton, *A Stillness At Appomattox*, 251.

27. Ibid., 252.

28. Porter, *Campaigning With Grant*, 268–269.

29. Both quotes from Catton, *A Stillness At Appomattox*, 252.

30. Freeman, *Lee's Lieutenants*, 3:544.

31. Porter, *Campaigning With Grant*, 269.

32. Catton, *A Stillness At Appomattox*, 252.

CHAPTER TWENTY-THREE

I Had Only to Obey

30 July–4 August 1864

Down in Georgia, in the midst of the only campaign that still seemed to be going well for the Union cause, Sherman took time out on that thirtieth day of July to write to the numerous state recruiting agents who had arrived at Nashville. They had asked him where they could go to start recruiting escaped slaves. In reply he named eight cities, all deep in Confederate territory.

Stoneman's small cavalry division approached Macon that day, the first time it had come anywhere near the railroad on the raid that was supposed to make the line its primary target. There he hoped to release several hundred Union officers from a small prisoner of war camp. Instead, he found Major General Howell Cobb and about 1,500 Georgia militia and citizen volunteers, with artillery support, drawn up on high ground east of the Ocmulgee River. Stoneman had just decided to bypass this unexpected opposition and move on to Andersonville when he received a false report, planted by the Confederates, that 1,800 Rebel cavalrymen were entering Macon. This was enough to cause him to give up hope of getting through to Andersonville, and to turn back to the north without having accomplished any of his objectives.

Meanwhile, McCook's division was having problems with real Confederates. Those Federals were riding westward, trying to get safely back across the Chattahoochee, but Wheeler was hard on their heels and Ross' Brigade of Texas cavalry from Jackson's Division attacked the northern flank of the rear brigade, Croxton's. "The light of the morning disclosed the enemy in every direction, and swarming about us, seemingly as numerous as the vandals that pillaged Rome," wrote Lieutenant Granville West, commanding the 4th Kentucky Cavalry in Croxton's Brigade. The Confederate commander yelled, "Surrender, you damn Yankee!" but West told him to "go to Hell!" and led his men in a charge. "It was a reckless move," West conceded, "but the effect was instantaneous. A convulsive tremor, a rush, and, in defiance of a chorus of demands to surrender, we were out, and away, and gone."[1]

There followed a running fight all the way to the town of Newnan on the Atlanta & West Point Railroad, where McCook hoped to take refuge. But when he got there, he found the town already occupied by 550 men of Roddey's Division, recently arrived from Alabama. The Federals bypassed the town to the south and headed southwest toward Philpot's Ferry on the Chattahoochee. Wheeler sent part of Ashby's Brigade through Newnan and down a road that would intercept the head of McCook's column, while he attacked their flank with Ross' Brigade and part of Harrison's. Ashby's attack scattered Torrey's 2nd Brigade, which was leading McCook's column. McCook's two artillery pieces managed to check the Confederate advance for a while, but when their supply of canister and shells ran out they had to be abandoned. The gunners spiked the vents and chopped the spokes of the wheels with axes, then cut the harnesses, mounted the mules that had pulled the guns, and fled to the south.

At the same time, Croxton's 1st Brigade, now in the center of McCook's column, was attacked by Ross' Texans again. Worried that he would lose contact with Torrey's brigade, McCook sent the 8th Iowa to break through the Rebel lines. This they did, and, in fact, the Iowans captured General Ross himself, but they were soon cut to pieces by a counterattack that also freed Ross. Another of Croxton's Union regiments, the 1st Tennessee, charged around the dismounted Texans' flank and got between them and their horses, but Ross turned his men around, and after a bitter fight they retrieved their mounts.

Colonel Thomas J. Harrison, commanding the veterans of Rousseau's raid at the rear of the Federal column, left his 8th Indiana as a rear guard and sent the 4th Tennessee and 5th Iowa, dismounted, against Wheeler's skirmishers to his right. But soon he found that the Confederates had him almost surrounded and he was forced to surrender. In desperation, McCook gave orders for each brigade to break out on its own. Major George H. Purdy led a sizable remnant of Torrey's and Croxton's brigades, first to the south and then northwest. Colonel James Brownlow led the 1st Tennessee and part of the 4th Kentucky of Croxton's brigade northwest to Moore's Bridge on the Chattahoochee. Croxton himself was cut off and hid in the woods to avoid capture. Colonel Fielder A. Jones led the 8th Indiana, 5th Iowa, and part of the 4th Tennessee, all of Harrison's brigade, to the south and then the west and linked up with McCook and another remnant of his division. They managed to get to Philpot's Ferry and crossed the Chattahoochee there, covered by volunteers from the 2nd and 8th Indiana regiments, who fought until they had used up all their ammunition. "History contains no nobler example of devotion," McCook wrote of these men.[2] In all, the Confederates captured about 950 men, two brigade commanders (Torrey and Harrison), 1,200 horses, and the two guns—a heavy price to pay for tearing up five miles of railroad track. Two days later the Confederates had the damage repaired enough to get trains through to Atlanta.

Western Maryland and southern Pennsylvania were in a panic that day, as word spread that Confederate cavalry was north of the Potomac again. Appeals for protection poured into Washington from civilians as far west as Pittsburg and Wheeling, and the governor of Pennsylvania called out 30,000 militiamen. To heighten the excitement, Lieutenant Colonel John S. Mosby's Confederate guerrillas crossed the Potomac and captured half a dozen pickets of the 8th Illinois Cavalry after killing and wounding an equal number. Meanwhile, McCausland, with his two brigades and four guns, rode for Chambersburg. Averell, whose headquarters were at Hagerstown, began to concentrate his scattered units, and kept pace with the Rebels on a parallel course to the east. Vaughn's Brigade of McCausland's force entered Hagerstown after the Federals left it, and destroyed a train loaded with government supplies that had been left behind. Early's main force, however, marched back to Martinsburg on the 30th.

Soon after dawn that day, McCausland rode into Chambersburg with 400 of his men, rounded up about 40 citizens, and presented them with Early's demand for $100,000 in gold or $500,000 in greenbacks. This was greeted with incredulity. Gold was out of the question, they said, and added that there was probably not one-tenth of that amount of currency on hand. "The policy pursued by our army on former occasions had been so lenient that they did not suppose the threat was in earnest this time," Early wrote, "and they hoped for speedy relief."[3] That was not an unreasonable hope. McCausland's scouts brought him word that Averell was rapidly approaching. So, at about 9 a.m., after he had finished his breakfast at the hotel, McCausland ordered the 3,000 inhabitants to be evacuated and the town burned. Colonel William E. Peters of the 21st Virginia Cavalry refused to obey the order and was placed under temporary arrest. The job was then given to Major Harry Gilmor, commander of the Maryland troops. In the meantime, some of the Southern troopers got out of hand and plundered businesses and private homes, although one elderly woman saved her house by whacking a Rebel with her broom.

"Deeply regretting that such a task should fall upon me," Gilmor wrote, "I had only to obey." He added that he "felt more like weeping over Chambersburg, although the people covered me with reproaches, which all who know me will readily believe I felt hard to digest; yet my pity was highly excited in behalf of these poor unfortunates, who were made to suffer for acts perpetrated by the officers of their own Government." The weather was hot and dry, and when torches were applied to a warehouse, the courthouse, and the city hall the flames spread rapidly. "Dense clouds of smoke rose to the zenith, and hovered over the dark plain," Gilmor wrote. Leaving the town in flames, McCausland led his force westward and camped that night at McConnellsburg, about twenty miles away, leaving behind what Gilmor described as "groups of women and children exposed to the rays of a burning sun, hovering over the few articles they had saved, most of them wringing their hands, and with wild gesticulations bemoaning their ruined homes!"[4] About two-thirds of the town was destroyed.

Averell's Federals were so hot on his heels that McCausland decided to forego a planned move westward to Bedford in favor of heading back to the Potomac at Hancock, which was reached by noon on the 31st. There his artillery chased off a train carrying an ironclad car and he burned buildings belonging to the Baltimore & Ohio. But soon Averell attacked, and the Union guns made it dangerous for the Rebels to try to ford the river, so they turned westward along the old National Road toward Cumberland, Maryland.

Down in Georgia it was the Union cavalry that was running from pursuers. Survivors of McCook's flight began to reach Marietta that day. But in Stoneman's case, the Federals were actually running into their pursuers. His lead brigade, Colonel Horace Capron's 3rd, found itself confronted by Rebel horsemen that morning. They were drawn up on a ridge across the road near Sunshine Church. These were the three brigades under Iverson, who had been chasing Stoneman's column, and by turning back to the north the Federals had run smack into them. Iverson, who was from nearby Clinton, had chosen his position well. He had his men placed in a V-shaped formation that would funnel the Yankees toward the center, where he had placed some of his artillery. Other guns were placed on the flanks, and the dismounted troopers were protected by barricades of trees and fence rails.

At 9:30 a.m. Stoneman advanced with Colonel Silas Adams' Independent Brigade on the left, or west, Capron's on the right, and Colonel James Biddle's 2nd Brigade in reserve. Confederate fire forced the Northerners back, but Stoneman reformed them, bringing Biddle's brigade up on the left of his line, and they charged on foot again at 1 p.m. But the Rebels counterattacked, throwing the Federals into confusion. In the meantime, Iverson sent small mounted forces around the Union flanks, and these then charged back to the north through the enemy lines, yelling and firing and spreading more confusion. Stoneman assumed that these were the 1,800 Confederate cavalry he had been led to believe had reinforced Macon the day before, causing him to think that he was surrounded by superior numbers.

Just then Adams' men, now in the Union center, broke and ran for their horses. "The sudden retreat of Adam's Brigade opened a wide gap in our line," Colonel Capron reported, "through which the enemy plunged in a wild rush toward the rear, where our horses were. The men of my brigade for a few minutes maintained their alignment, meanwhile casting wistful glances toward their horses." But the Rebel threat to their mounts was more than they could stand. When each Federal trooper "reflected that he was a hundred miles in rear of the enemy's lines, with an immense army interposed between him and freedom, he wanted his horse," Capron explained, "and many a man lost his life in trying to get one." For, as he put it, "a foot race and a rough and tumble fight ensued."[5]

Believing his little division to be outnumbered, when in fact his was the larger force, Stoneman informed his brigade commanders that he would remain in place with Biddle's brigade and hold the Rebels long enough for Capron and Adams to get away. He would then surrender. The two escaping units fled to the east and then turned north again. And Stoneman did surrender, with about 500 of his men, including Colonel Biddle, and a runaway slave named Minor, who had been the Federals' guide since he had joined the column a couple of days before. The Rebels promptly hanged Minor from the nearest tree and were about to do the same to Stoneman when some Confederate officers stopped them. Stoneman and his officers soon reached the prisoner of war camp at Macon and his enlisted men the one at Andersonville, but not in the manner originally intended.

That same, final day of July, the day after the dismal Battle of the Crater, General Grant took a steamboat down the James River to meet with Lincoln at Fort Monroe. Neither man ever said very much about what they discussed that day, but on the back of the telegram which the president had received from Grant the day before, he had written: "Meade & Franklin/McClellan/Md. & Penna."[6] Evidently Lincoln wanted to explain in person why he did not consider Franklin suitable for the command of the unified departments in the Maryland/D.C. area.

Quite possibly he told Grant that Meade would not be acceptable either. Meade had been half hoping for the job as a chance to regain his independence from Grant, although the thought of having to deal directly with Halleck and Stanton again did not appeal to him. But Lincoln may have described for Grant the disappointment that Meade had given him the year before with his timid pursuit of Lee after Gettysburg, and might have expressed a desire that he not be trusted to do any better with Early. Besides, there had also been a considerable amount of politicking by Baldy Smith and others lately to have Meade replaced by Franklin, or anyone, and to move Meade now would give the appearance that Lincoln and Grant were giving in to that pressure.

That McClellan's name appears on Lincoln's notation is very intriguing. Some prominent Republicans had been advancing the idea of giving General McClellan some such command as that now under consideration, primarily to prevent him from becoming the Democrats' candidate for the presidency in November. But it is hard to believe that Lincoln could have seriously considered putting McClellan in such a position. If Meade's caution had been a trial for the president the previous summer, it was nothing compared to the frustration Lincoln had suffered in trying to get McClellan to accomplish something as commander of the Army of the Potomac. Nor is it likely that Grant would have cared for the idea either.

More likely, Lincoln and Grant found that they both wanted one thing from whomever they chose to command around Washington, and that was the kind of killer instinct of which neither Meade nor McClellan had ever shown the slightest hint. It seems very likely that they agreed on the best man for the job. At any rate, after conferring for five hours, they returned to Washington and City Point.

The next day, 1 August, Grant told Meade, "I see the artillery belonging to the cavalry division is being shipped first; my instructions were that the cavalry should be got off first. The enemy's cavalry is now in Pennsylvania, and it is important that we should get a mounted force after them. If Sheridan is able for duty, I wish you would send him to me in person. I shall send him to command all the forces against Early."[7] Grant then informed Halleck: "I am sending General Sheridan for temporary duty whilst the enemy is being expelled from the border. Unless General Hunter is in the field in person, I want Sheridan put in command of all the troops in the field, with instructions to put himself south of the enemy and follow him to the death. Wherever the enemy goes let our troops go also. Once started up the Valley they ought to be followed until we get possession of the Virginia Central railroad. If General Hunter is in the field give Sheridan direct command of the Sixth Corps and cavalry division. All the cavalry I presume will reach Washington in the course of to-morrow."[8]

Halleck replied that "if Sheridan is not placed in general command, I think he should take all the cavalry, but not the Sixth Corps; to make that and the cavalry a single and separate command will, in my opinion, be a very bad arrangement. If Sheridan is placed in general command, I presume Hunter will again ask to be relieved."[9]

In Maryland that first day of August, McCausland's Confederate raiders approached Cumberland, but found it defended by Brigadier General B. F. Kelley, who had been warned by Halleck that the Rebels were headed his way. The Union commander had taken position three miles east of the town with his garrison troops. The Southern artillery engaged these Federals but could not dislodge them. About the middle of the afternoon, fearing that Averell must be getting close, McCausland attacked, but still the Northerners held. He continued to skirmish with them until dark, and then retreated by way of an obscure mountain road toward Oldtown on the Potomac, leaving behind thirty dead and wounded men, as well as two caissons, some wagons, and ammunition.

At daylight on the 2nd, McCausland reached the Potomac and found the ford guarded by a garrison of hundred-days men from Ohio, who drove his skirmishers back. But when he dismounted three regiments and sent them forward between the river and the Chesapeake & Ohio Canal, the Federals fell back across the river to Green Springs Run Station on the Baltimore & Ohio Railroad, where there was a blockhouse and a train whose cars had been strengthened with crossties. One of Johnson's Confederate regiments attacked, but was driven back after losing a dozen men. Under a flag of truce, a demand was sent to the blockhouse for the Federals to surrender, otherwise no quarter would be given. The eighty Ohioans in the blockhouse, who were nearing the end of their enlistments, surrendered on condition that they would be paroled. The rest of the Northerners escaped to Cumberland. McCausland then destroyed the train and moved on nine miles to Springfield, where he crossed the South Branch of the Potomac, burning the bridge behind him.

Down in Georgia on 2 August, Sherman put Garrard's cavalry division, which had done nothing since escaping from Wheeler, in the trenches east of Atlanta. It was there to replace Schofield's two infantry divisions, which filed to the north and west behind Thomas' and Howard's armies, to extend Sherman's right down to Utoy Creek.

Before dawn the next day, the third, Colonel Capron's brigade of Stoneman's division was surprised by a party of 85 Confederates. These were men who had been chosen from among the pursuing Rebels for having the freshest horses, and had been sent ahead under Lieutenant Richard Bowles. "I had scarcely lost consciousness in sleep," Capron later reported, "when I was suddenly aroused by the most unearthly yells and screams, mingled with pistol shots." The Rebels charged through a bunch of runaway slaves, who were camped next to the Union troopers, making directly for the sleeping Federals, bivouacked by Mulberry Creek.

"Every darkey, mule, horse and donkey were driven pell-mell upon our poor, worn out troops," Capron said. "The result may be imagined, but it is indescribable. Men leaped to their feet in utter bewilderment, without arms and bare-headed, and not waiting to mount their horses, many of them burst through the fences and ran frantically through the fields, anywhere to get away from the yells and volleys of musketry. Brave men as ever drew a sabre in battle ran past their officers in a confused, frenzied mass towards the bridge . . . As the crowd poured upon it, the bridge gave way with a crash, followed by the cries of the wounded men . . . Then commenced another haphazard ride, which not only tried the mettle of our steeds, but our own nerves as well. Ditch after ditch, fence after fence, was scaled, thickets of briers and scrubby trees were brushed through at breakneck speed, while now and then a rifle ball cut the branches from around us, but the thoughts of the terrible suffering in a rebel prison-pen had by far the most powerful influence to stimulate us to renewed exertion."[10] The pre-dawn attack by the small band of Rebels netted them 430 Union prisoners.

A new front was opened on 3 August. The long-delayed campaign against Mobile was finally getting under way. Grant and Banks had wanted to take it the year before, after they had captured Vicksburg and Port Hudson, to clear the Mississippi. But Halleck, who had been the general-in-chief at the time, had ruled otherwise. Grant's army had been split up and sent off in several directions, and Banks had been sent up the Red River in an attempt to gain a foothold in Texas. When Grant had become general-in-chief he had revived the idea, but by then Banks was well on his way up the Red. His subsequent defeat and the problems of getting the accompanying fleet of gunboats back down the unseasonably low river had led to more delays, and by then Grant had decided to bring part of Banks' army, two divisions of the 19th Corps, to Virginia, while the troops under A. J. Smith, which had been borrowed from Sherman, were sent to Memphis.

Meanwhile, Major General E. R. S. Canby had been given command of a new Military Division of West Mississippi, which combined Banks' Department of the Gulf with the Department of Arkansas under Frederick Steele. To Canby had fallen the job of providing the army's part in the campaign against Mobile and he assigned the job to Major General Gordon Granger. The campaign began on that third day of August, when a force of 1,500 men landed on the western end of Dauphine Island, the eastern end of which was the site of one of the two forts that guarded the main entrance to Mobile Bay.

Halleck wired Grant on 3 August: "General Sheridan has just arrived. He agrees with me about his command, and prefers the cavalry alone to that and the Sixth Corps. How would it do to make a Military Division of Departments of Pennsylvania, Washington, Maryland, and West Virginia, and put Sheridan in command, so far as military operations are concerned? Only about three regiments of Sheridan's cavalry have arrived, and he thinks it will not all be here for several days. It is important to hurry it up, for if the enemy should make a heavy cavalry raid toward Pittsburg or Harrisburg, it would have so much the start that it would do immense damage before Sheridan could possibly overtake it. He thinks that for operations in the open country of Pennsylvania, Maryland, and Northern Virginia, cavalry is much better than infantry, and that the cavalry arm can be much more effective there than about Richmond or south. He therefore suggests that another cavalry division be sent here, so that he can press the enemy clear down to the James River." Grant's reaction was an order to Meade to "send another division of cavalry to Washington at once."[11]

Meanwhile, President Lincoln saw Grant's 1 August wire to Halleck and also sent a telegram to City Point: "I have seen your despatch in which you say 'I want Sheridan put in command of all the troops in the field, with instructions to put himself South of the enemy, and follow him to the death. Wherever the enemy goes, let our troops go also.' This, I think, is exactly right, as to how our forces should move. But please look over the despatches you may have receved from here, even since you made that order, and discover, if you can, that there is any idea in the head of any one here, of 'putting our army South of the enemy' or of 'following him to the death' in any direction. I repeat to you it will neither be done nor attempted unless you watch it every day, and hour, and force it."[12]

The phrase "I repeat to you" shows that the rest of the sentence summarized part of the discussion between the president and the general-in-chief at Fort Monroe. Lincoln had told Grant that the situation along the Potomac required his personal attention. The fact that Lincoln made no comment in this message on the selection of Sheridan is good evidence that it came as no surprise and thus had probably already been decided on, at Fort Monroe.

At noon the next day, 4 August, Grant replied to Lincoln: "Your dispatch of 6 p.m. just received. I will start in two hours for Washington & will spend a day with the Army under Genl Hunter."[13] After ordering a dispatch boat to get up steam, he wrote a note to Ben Butler: "I find it necessary to go to Washington for a day or two to give direction to affairs there. In my absence remain on the defensive, notifying General Meade that if attacked he is authorized to call on such of your troops as are south of the Appomattox. Only expecting to be gone three days I will not relinquish command. But being senior you necessarily would command in any emergency. Please communicate with me by telegraph if anything occurs where you wish my orders."[14] He also pointed out that he was leaving most of his staff on duty at City Point, and that Butler could communicate with him through them. His personal chief of staff, Rawlins, however, was not among them. He had been given a leave of absence due to ill health and would be away for a couple of months.

The source of Grant's current problems, Early, moved his main force from Martinsburg back to the Potomac that day, "in order to enable McCausland to retire from Pennsylvania and Maryland, and to keep Hunter, who had been reinforced by the 6th and 19th corps, and had been oscillating between Harper's Ferry and Monocacy Junction, in a state of uncertainty," as Early put it.[15] At the same time, he sent Imboden's cavalry to threaten Harper's Ferry. McCausland moved west that day from Romney to New Creek, on the Baltimore & Ohio Railroad. He found it strongly garrisoned by Federal troops, however, and after a stubborn fight of several hours, he withdrew to the south to Moorefield, West Virginia, where the South Fork joins the South Branch of the Potomac. The same day Averell's Union cavalry crossed to the south side of the Potomac at Hancock.

Down in Mississippi that fourth day of August, the Federals reopened the Mississippi Central Railroad from Grand Junction to Holly Springs, where most of A. J. Smith's troops had assembled for their second expedition against Forrest. Rumor had it, however, that Forrest had contracted lockjaw from his recent wound and had died.

Over in Georgia that day, Colonel Silas Adams and 490 men of Stoneman's scattered division reached the safety of Federal lines at Marietta. "I now became satisfied that cavalry could not, or would not, make a sufficient lodgment on the railroad below Atlanta," Sherman wrote, "and that nothing would suffice but for us to reach it with the main army."[16] He therefore ordered Schofield, now on the right, or southern, end of his line, to "make a bold attack on the railroad, anywhere about East Point."[17] To strengthen the little Army of the Ohio for this move, Sherman ordered what was left of McCook's cavalry division and Palmer's 14th Corps of Thomas' Army of the Cumberland to report to Schofield. "General Palmer was a man of ability, but was not enterprising," Sherman said. "His three divisions were compact and strong, well commanded, admirable on the defensive, but slow to move or to act on the offensive. His corps . . . had sustained, up to that time, fewer hard knocks than any other corps in the whole army, and I was anxious to give it a chance."[18]

But Sherman's problems with his generals were not yet over, and this time interfered directly with his operations. Back came a note from Palmer, a pre-war politician and post-war governor of Illinois, that said, "I am General Schofield's senior. We may cooperate but I respectfully decline to report to or take orders from him."[19] Schofield argued that he was senior to Palmer "first, because I have the senior commission, and, second, because I am by the President's order commander of a separate army."[20] While this argument raged, very little was accomplished on the field. One brigade of Palmer's corps attacked, driving in some Confederate skirmishers, but the fire from the main Rebel line was so severe that the Federals, lacking support on their flanks, retreated to their starting position.

Sherman examined the dates of Schofield's and Palmer's commissions, heard their arguments, and then replied to Palmer: "From the statements made by yourself and General Schofield to-day, my decision is, that he ranks you as a major-general, being of the same date of present commission, by reason of his previous superior rank as brigadier-general. The movements of to-morrow are so important that the orders of the superior on that flank must be regarded as military orders, and not in the nature of cooperation. I did hope that there would be no necessity for my making this decision; but it is better for all parties interested that no question of rank should occur in actual battle. The Sandtown road, and the railroad, if possible, must be gained to-morrow, if it cost half your command. I regard the loss of time this afternoon as equal to the loss of two thousand men."[21]

But even this did not settle the matter. That night Palmer wrote to Sherman, "I am unable to acquiesce in the correctness of the decision that Major-General Schofield legally ranks me," and cited dates of promotion and appointment. He ended with the request that he be allowed to resign the command of his corps. Years after the war he wrote, "It was the idea of the regular army men that they ranked all volunteer officers."[22]

"Nothing accomplished today," a dispatch from Sherman's chief telegrapher said that evening, "movements having been brought to deadlock by squabble about rank between Schofield and Palmer, which at this hour is unsettled. Hope to do something tomorrow but cannot say exactly what."[23]

Judge David Davis, who had been Lincoln's campaign manager in 1860, wrote to his brother that day about a discouraging trip that he had just made to Chicago, sounding the political climate. "People are getting tired of the war," he said. "Some of them can't see a ray of light. I am speaking of good men. Two years ago I succeeded in raising 1,300 men in this country. It took about ten days. There in no note now of any volunteering." He added that "there is faith in the administration, and yet you will hear whispering inquiries as to whether the plan they are pursuing is the best."[24]

---

1. Scaife, *The Campaign For Atlanta*, 72.
2. McDonough and Jones, *War So Terrible*, 253.
3. Early, *War Memoirs*, 404.
4. Pond, *The Shenandoah Valley in 1864*, 103.
5. Scaife, *The Campaign For Atlanta*, 76.
6. Basler, ed., *The Collected Works of Abraham Lincoln*, 7:470, n. 1.
7. Pond, *The Shenandoah Valley in 1864*, 114.
8. Basler, ed., *The Collected Works of Abraham Lincoln*, 7:476, n.1.
9. Pond, *The Shenandoah Valley in 1864*, 115.
10. Scaife, *The Campaign For Atlanta*, 77–78.
11. Both quotes from Pond, *The Shenandoah Valley in 1864*, 115–116.
12. Basler, ed., *The Collected Works of Abraham Lincoln*, 7:476.
13. Ibid., 7:476, n. 1.

14. Catton, *Grant Takes Command*, 344.

15. Early, *War Memoirs*, 402.

16. Sherman, *Memoirs*, 2:572.

17. Ibid., 2:573.

18. Ibid., 2:572–573.

19. Scaife, *The Campaign For Atlanta*, 87.

20. McDonough and Jones, *War So Terrible*, 265.

21. Sherman, *Memoirs*, 2:573.

22. McDonough and Jones, *War So Terrible*, 266.

23. Ibid.

24. Sandburg, *Abraham Lincoln*, 3:575.

CHAPTER TWENTY-FOUR

Damn the Torpedoes

5 August 1864

Joseph J. Bingham was a member of the Copperhead organization, but only because he had been persuaded against his better judgment to join it the year before. He was also proprietor of the *Indiana State Sentinel* newspaper and chairman of the Democratic State Committee in Indiana. When Harrison H. Dodd, Sons of Liberty Grand Commander for Indiana, asked him to announce a great mass meeting of Democrats in Indianapolis on 16 August, Bingham naturally asked for details, and when he learned that the meeting was a cover for a revolt planned not just for Indianapolis but for the entire Northwest, he was aghast.

Bingham had sense enough to know that any such uprising was very unlikely to succeed. He also knew that the attempt would ruin the Democrats' considerable hopes for political success in Indiana that year. This illustrates the horns of the Copperheads' dilemma. If they openly revolted against the government, they would ruin their chances of a peaceful political victory. But if they waited for the election and lost, it might then be too late to revolt. Anyway, Bingham quickly called together a group of leading Democrats in the state and told them what the Copperheads were planning. One of them, a Congressman, said that rumors of such a revolt were already circulating and that many Copperhead farmers were selling their crops for cash, some at considerable loss, to prepare for action. The assembled politicians called in Dodd on 5 August and demanded that he cancel the revolt, which he did. The Copperheads could not afford to cross the leadership of their own party.

The Republicans were having their own intra-party problems just then. In the *New York Tribune* of 5 August Senator Benjamin F. Wade and Congressman Henry Winter Davis answered President Lincoln's proclamation of 8 July, in which he had given his reasons for not signing their bill that would have set up a program for reconstructing the seceded states. It was addressed "To the Supporters of the Government." In it, they said that they had "read without surprise, but not without indignation" the president's proclamation. And they maintained that it was their right and their duty "to check the encroachments of the Executive on the authority of Congress, and to require it to confine itself to its proper sphere." They were unhappy that "the President persists in recognizing those shadows of governments in Arkansas and Louisiana, which Congress formally declared should not be recognized—whose representatives and senators were repelled by formal votes of both Houses of Congress." These state governments, they said were "the mere creatures of his will," and he held "the electoral votes of the rebel states at the dictation of his personal ambition." They said that Lincoln must understand "that the whole body of the Union men of Congress will not submit to be impeached by him of rash and unconstitutional legislation: and if he wishes our support he must confine himself to his executive duties—to obey and to execute, not make the law."[1]

Lincoln remarked to members of his cabinet that he had not read this Wade-Davis Manifesto, and probably should not. To one visitor the president said, "It is not worth fretting about; it reminds me of an old acquaintance, who, having a son of a scientific turn, bought him a microscope. The boy went around experimenting with his glass on everything that came in his way. One day, at the dinner-table, his father took up a piece of cheese. 'Don't eat that, father,' said the boy; 'it is full of wrigglers.' 'My son,' replied the old gentleman, taking, at the same time, a huge bite, 'let 'em wriggle; I can stand it if they can.'"[2]

Down in Georgia that day, General McCook finally reached Federal lines with remnants of Torrey's brigade, Harrison's brigade, and his mule-mounted artillerymen. In the meantime, Sherman's problems with General Palmer continued. The latter suggested that, while he would not personally take orders from Schofield, whom he still insisted was his junior in rank, Schofield could issue his orders to Palmer's senior division commander, Brigadier General R. W. Johnson. This was tried, but at day's end Schofield reported to Sherman that he had "totally failed to make any aggressive movement with the Fourteenth Corps." Sherman complained to Thomas, who had been that corps' commander before being promoted to command the entire Army of the Cumberland. "I would prefer to move a rock than to move that corps," he said. Thomas expressed surprise, saying that he had always found it "prompt in executing any work given to it." But, he said, "If General Palmer is an obstacle to its efficiency, I would let him go." One Federal officer wrote home, "I'm glad I'm not a general, to be quarreling with my companions about questions of rank, like a bunch of children quarreling about their painted toys." Not that anybody really needed the generals. "If they had happened to be killed the army would go along just the same," he said.[3]

The Federal advance was also hindered by a lack of cavalry to scout for Schofield's advance, for the troopers who had survived the recent raids were still recuperating. Meanwhile, Hood's scouts had brought him word of the Union advance, and he had a new line entrenched along the Sandtown Road, with its left pulled back along some high ground overlooking Cascade Springs. That night Bate's Division of Hardee's Corps filed into these defenses.

Rodes' and Ramseur's Confederate divisions crossed the Potomac at Williamsport on 5 August as part of Early's effort to keep the Federals in a state of uncertainty regarding his intentions. Vaughn's Brigade of Rebel cavalry also crossed and rode as far as Hagerstown. Breckinridge, with his two infantry divisions plus Jackson's cavalry brigade, crossed the river at Shepherdstown and advanced as far as Sharpsburg. There they could be seen by the Union troops on Maryland Heights and some Northern cavalry was sent out to reconnoiter, but was driven off by Gordon's infantry.

At 5:45 on the morning of 5 August, the attack signal went up on the USS *Hartford*, the flagship of Admiral Farragut's fleet off Mobile, Alabama. Before the war, Mobile had been second only to New Orleans as a port for exporting cotton, but, of course, New Orleans had been in Union hands for over two years. Now it was second only to Wilmington, North Carolina, as a haven for blockade runners. Between the city and the Gulf of Mexico lay a thirty-mile-long bay, and between the bay and the open sea there were narrow passes.

The more westerly of these, Grant's Pass, between the mainland and Dauphine Island, was too shallow for Farragut's warships. The main entrance to the bay was farther east, a three-mile stretch of water between Dauphin Island and a narrow, sandy peninsula called Mobile Point. It was guarded by two forts. Fort Gaines was a pentagonal brick structure at the eastern tip of Dauphine Island, and it contained sixteen guns. Fort Morgan was a similar but larger structure at the western tip of Mobile Point. It contained forty heavy guns, and seven more were placed in a water battery on the beach near the northwest face of the fort.

The western two-thirds of this main pass had been closed by pilings driven into the bottom and protected by the guns of Fort Gaines. Most of the remaining gap had been sewn with a triple line of mines—called torpedoes in those days—anchored just far enough below the surface to make them almost invisible. The eastern limit of the torpedoes was marked with a red buoy to keep blockade-runners out of danger. The remaining 200 yards of the entrance was all within point-blank range of the guns of Fort Morgan, but for Farragut's fleet, it was the only way into Mobile Bay.

Farragut had wanted to take Mobile ever since he ran the defenses of the lower Mississippi and captured New Orleans in April 1862, but he and his ocean-going fleet had been sent up the Mississippi instead. And by the time he got back to the Gulf, the Rebels had not only strengthened their forts but added another deadly element to the defense of the bay, an ironclad ram. This was the CSS *Tennessee,* and she was said to be the most formidable Confederate ship ever built. She was over 200 feet long and followed the usual Rebel design, a sloping casement being the only part showing above the waterline, and that covered by six inches of iron, backed by two feet of solid oak and pine. She carried 7-inch Brooke rifles at both ends, mounted on pivots so that they could fire to the sides or abeam, backed up by two 6.4-inch rifles on each side. Farragut had seen first-hand what a ship like that could do when the *Arkansas* had steamed through the middle of his fleet, as well as the river gunboats and rams, on its way to Vicksburg the year before. Moreover, the *Tennessee* and her three unarmored consorts were commanded by the South's foremost admiral, Franklin Buchanan, the former commander of the *Merrimack-Virginia.* It was feared that the *Tennessee* would soon come out and attempt to lift the blockade of Mobile by sinking or scattering the Union fleet.

Against such a vessel, Farragut knew he would need some ironclads of his own, much as he disliked the newfangled vessels. And he asked the Navy Department for at least a pair of monitors. "If I had them," he said, "I should not hesitate to become the assailant instead of awaiting the attack."[4] But the monitors were all busy elsewhere, and so was the army, whose help he needed to take the forts. Four monitors were promised, but the first did not arrive until 20 July. That was the USS *Manhattan.* She had ten inches of iron on her revolving turret and carried two 15-inch smoothbore guns. On the thirtieth, a second, shalower-draft ironclad arrived, the USS *Chickasaw*, which had two turrets with a pair of 11-inch guns in each, and the next day the identical *Winnebago* arrived. A fourth monitor arrived on 4 August, the *Tecumseh*, a sister ship of the *Manhattan*. The *Tecumseh* arrived none too soon, for Farragut was ready to proceed without her.

David Glasgow Farragut had been in the navy since 1810, when, at the age of nine, he had become a midshipman and was virtually adopted by Commodore David Porter. Although originally from Tennessee, he had remained loyal to the Union cause. His conquest of New Orleans in April 1862 had made him the premier officer of the U.S. Navy. And yet he longed for a different kind of glory. After the *Kearsarge* sank the *Alabama* he wrote, "I would sooner have fought that fight than any ever fought on the ocean."[5] A young army signal officer, Lieutenant John C. Kinney, who was aboard the *Hartford* at the battle of Mobile Bay, later gave this description of the admiral: "He was sixty-three years old, of medium height, stoutly built, with a finely proportioned head and smoothly shaven face, with an expression combining overflowing kindliness with iron will and invincible determination, and with eyes that in repose were full of sweetness and light, but, in emergency, could flash fire and fury."[6] Asked, the night before going into Mobile Bay, if he would allow his men a glass of grog to fortify their courage for the coming battle, he replied: "No sir. I never found that I needed rum to enable me to do my duty. I will order two cups of good coffee to each man at 2 o'clock, and at 8 o'clock I will pipe all hands to breakfast in Mobile Bay."[7]

Fog delayed the start, but shortly after dawn, all was ready. The four monitors led the way in single file, followed by the seven large wooden ships, each of which had a smaller wooden gunboat lashed to its port side, protected from the guns of Fort Morgan by the larger ship, but ready to pull the big ship along if it became disabled by Confederate fire. The admiral had intended to lead the wooden squadron in his flagship, the USS *Hartford*, a 1,900-ton, steam-powered, wooden sloop-of-war carrying 22 nine-inch guns. But his captains pleaded that he should not place himself in such danger, for his death or disablement would jeopardize the entire operation. So he let the similar *Brooklyn* take the lead, partly because she carried a device on her bow for fishing out torpedoes, and also because she carried four guns that were capable of firing forward.

As Lieutenant Kinney, the army signal officer, noted: "The primary objects of Admiral Farragut in entering the bay were to close Mobile to the outside world, to capture or destroy the *Tennessee*, and to cut off all possible means of escape from the garrisons of the forts. Incidentally, also, he desired to secure the moral effect of a victory, and to give his fleet, which had been tossed on the uneasy waters of the Gulf for many months, a safe and quiet anchorage. There was no immediate expectation of capturing the city of Mobile, which was safe by reason of a solid row of piles and torpedoes across the river, three miles below the city. Moreover, the larger vessels of the fleet could not approach within a dozen miles of the city, on account of shallow water. But the lower bay offered a charming resting-place for the fleet, with the additional attraction of plenty of fish and oysters, and an occasional chance to forage on shore."[8]

Aboard the *Tennessee*, Buchanan got word that the Federals were coming within minutes of their start. He hurried on deck in his underwear for a look at them, and while he dressed he gave orders for the ironclad and her three attendant, unarmored gunboats to take up position across the main channel, just behind the inner line of torpedoes. Then he assembled the crew of the *Tennessee* and made a brief speech: "Now, men, the enemy is coming, and I want you to do your duty. You shall not have it said when you leave this vessel that you were not near enough to the enemy, for I will meet them, and you can fight them alongside of their own ships. And if I fall, lay me on the side and go on with the fight."[9]

At 6:47 a.m. the *Tecumseh* opened fire on Fort Morgan with its 15-inch guns, and the battle was on. The fort did not reply, however, until the wooden ships had closed to within a mile, and then, shortly after 7 a.m. opened fire. A young surgeon on one of the Union ships described what it was like to be fired on: "First you see the puff of white smoke upon the distant ramparts, and then you see the shot coming, looking exactly as if some gigantic hand has thrown in play a ball toward you. By the time it is half way, you get the boom of the report, and then the howl of the missile, which apparently grows so rapidly in size that every green hand on board who can see it is certain that it will hit him between the eyes. Then, as it goes past with a shriek like a thousand devils, the inclination to do reverence is so strong that it is almost impossible to resist."[10]

The line of monitors, *Tecumseh, Manhattan, Winnebago,* and *Chickasaw,* moved in close to Fort Morgan, pounding it with their heavy guns, while the wooden ships, moving more rapidly, closed up behind them. As they approached, the *Tennessee* and the three wooden, sternwheel Confederate gunboats steamed out from behind the fort and fired broadsides into the approaching Federals. There was scant breeze, and the smoke of the guns and engines soon obscured the scene. Farragut therefore climbed the ratlines on the port side to a point from which he could communicate with the *Hartford*'s pilot, up in the maintop, and the captain of the *Metacomet*, the wooden gunboat lashed to the *Hartford*'s port side. But soon the smoke drove him even higher, until, almost level with the pilot, he clung to the shrouds with one arm and held his binoculars with his other hand. The captain of the *Hartford* sent a seaman up to lash him to the rigging, so that a lurch of the ship could not send the admiral overboard.

The army signal officers were on board so that the ships could, once they got into the bay, communicate with General Granger's soldiers, who had moved up to besiege Fort Gaines on Dauphin Island. The two soldiers on the *Hartford* were sent below to help the surgeons until they should be needed, but a few minutes later, as Lieutenant Kinney remembered, an officer shouted down the hatchway: "Send up an army signal officer immediately; the *Brooklyn* is signaling." When he got up on deck he discovered that an army signal officer on the *Brooklyn*, at the head of the line of wooden ships, was signaling, "The monitors are right ahead; we cannot go on without passing them." Kinney sent Farragut's reply: "Order the monitors ahead and go on."[11]

But the *Brooklyn* reversed power and came to a stop, for the *Tecumseh*, afraid of running aground in shallow water near the fort, was veering across the path of the wooden ships. In fact, she went so far to the west that she ran past the buoy marking the minefield. Suddenly the ironclad reeled to one side and began to sink bow first, her stern rising out of the water with her screw spinning helplessly in the air. She went to the bottom in about two minutes, taking with her the captain and 93 officers and men out of a crew of 114. Captain Tunis A. M. Craven might have made it to safety, but at the foot of the ladder leading to the top of the turret, the only avenue of escape, he met the pilot, John Collins. "After you, pilot," he said. "But," Collins wrote, "there was nothing after me. When I reached the upmost round of the ladder, the vessel seemed to drop from under me."[12] Cheering spread from one Union ship to another, for the Federal sailors thought at first that it was the *Tennessee* that had been sunk.

The Union ships were thrown into great confusion when the *Brooklyn* came to a halt. They were right under the guns of Fort Morgan, and their losses from the Confederate fire were heavy. Twenty-five men were killed on the *Hartford* alone. "Shot after shot came through the side," Lieutenant Kinney wrote, "mowing down the men, deluging the decks with blood, and scattering mangled fragments of humanity so thickly that it was difficult to stand on the deck, so slippery was it . . . A solid shot coming through the bow struck a gunner on the neck, completely severing head from body. One poor fellow . . . lost both legs by a cannonball; as he fell he threw up both arms, just in time to have them also carried away by another shot." Kinney said the mast upon which he was perched was struck twice, the second time by a shell from a heavy gun on the Rebel gunboat *Selma*. He could see the projectile coming, but only had time to take a firmer grip on the mast. "Fortunately the shell came tumbling end over end," he said, "and buried itself in the mast, butt-end first, leaving the percussion-cap protruding."[13]

Another signal from the army officer on the *Brooklyn* told of the sinking of the *Tecumseh*, and the reply, "Go on," was sent, but not obeyed. "What is the matter with the *Brooklyn*?" Farragut shouted to the *Hartford*'s pilot. "She must have plenty of water." The pilot answered, "Plenty, and to spare, Admiral; but her screw is moving." By this they could tell that the *Brooklyn* was under power. What they could not tell was that her engines were in reverse. And to make matters worse, the *Brooklyn* slewed around until she was broadside to the channel, further blocking the narrow stretch of deep water. Farragut, in after years, told his son that at that moment he prayed for guidance: "O God, who created man and gave him reason, direct me what to do. Shall I go on?" It seemed to him, he said, that he heard a voice commanding, "Go on!" To the pilot he said, "I will take the lead," and he ordered the *Hartford* to pass the *Brooklyn* on the port, or west, side.[14]

As they passed, the sailors on the flagship ran to the starboard railing and shouted insults at the *Brooklyn* and at her captain, who the year before had been among those who failed to run the guns at Vicksburg when Farragut had done so with the *Hartford* and others. In passing the *Brooklyn*, the *Hartford* had to steam through the edge of the minefield that had been the doom of the *Tecumseh*, and it was at this point that, according to legend, Farragut called to Captain Alden of the *Brooklyn*, "What's the trouble?" On being told, "Torpedoes!", he supposedly gave the famous reply, "Damn the torpedoes! Go ahead!"[15] Lieutenant Kinney wrote that "there was never a moment when the din of the battle would not have drowned any attempt at conversation between the two ships, and while it is quite probable that the admiral made the remark it is doubtful if he shouted it to the *Brooklyn*."[15] Whether he said it or not it sums up his attitude and his bravery. Men below decks could hear the bottom of the ship scraping against the deadly torpedoes and even the snap of their primers, but not one of them exploded. "The ships followed on," Farragut later reported, "their officers believing that they were going to a noble death with their commander-in-chief."[17]

But no more ships were sunk, although those toward the end of the line took a terrific beating from the guns of the fort, as the Union fire was diminished by the head of the line moving on into the bay. The

Oneida, at the end of the line, was struck in the boiler by a 7-inch shell and her firemen were scalded by the escaping steam. Another hit cut the ropes that connected her wheel to the rudder. She would have drifted, powerless and out of control, under the guns of the fort had it not been for Farragut's foresight in having smaller ships lashed to the port sides of the larger ships. The *Oneida*'s consort brought her safely past the fort and into the bay. The *Hartford*'s consort, the *Metacomet,* dispatched a boat to pick up survivors of the *Tecumseh* swimming in the area. The commander of Fort Morgan, Brigadier General Richard L. Page, ordered his men not to fire on the boat. "She is saving drowning men," he said.[18]

Meanwhile, the *Hartford,* a mile ahead of the other Federal sloops, encountered the Confederate ships. The three unarmored Rebel gunboats managed to stay about a thousand yards ahead of the Federals for a while, firing their small broadsides into the Union ship, which could only reply with its bow gun, which was soon knocked out by a shot from the *Selma.* Another shell penetrated the Hartford's hull, killing ten men and wounding five more. But the Federals came on, avoiding an attempt by the slow and clumsy *Tennessee* to ram the flagship. "I took no further notice of her than to return her fire," Farragut later remarked.[19]

Admiral Buchanan pursued the *Hartford* for a while, still hoping to ram her, but she was easily able to outdistance the clumsy ironclad. After a while he gave up and turned back to take on the other six sloops, just coming up, and the *Tennessee* passed down the line of wooden ships. Two of her shots penetrated the *Brooklyn,* but two others missed the *Richmond.* Both ships returned full broadsides, which had absolutely no effect on the ironclad. Buchanan then passed the *Lackawanna* and made for the *Monongahela.* This was the fastest of the Union sloops. She had been strengthened with an artificial iron prow, and was expected to act as a ram if the opportunity arose. "After passing the forts I saw the rebel ram *Tennessee* head on for our line," the captain of the *Monongahela* reported. "I then sheered out of the line to run into her, at the same time ordering full speed as fast as possible. I struck her fair, and swinging around poured in a broadside of solid 11-inch shot, which apparently had little if any effect upon her."[20] The Federal ship lost her first lieutenant, however, both of whose legs were shattered.

The *Tennessee* continued down the line of Union ships. Two shells from the Confederate ironclad penetrated the *Ossipee* and then the unlucky *Oneida,* at the tail of the column, suffered the loss of its after pivot gun, and her skipper, the loss of an arm. Finally the *Tennessee* passed the three remaining monitors, which were just catching up, doing them no more damage than they did to her, and then pulled up under the protection of the guns of Fort Morgan.

When the *Hartford* was able to bring its broadsides to bear on the wooden Confederate gunboats, they were quickly driven to seek the protection of shallow water, where the *Hartford* could not follow. But one of them, the *Gaines,* was holed and sinking, causing her crew to abandon her, after setting her on fire. Then the *Metacomet,* the fastest of all the Union ships, was cast loose to chase them. Under the cover of a brief, light rain another of the Rebel gunboats, the *Morgan,* made it safely to the protection of the guns of Fort Morgan. The *Selma,* however, was chased eastward across the shallows of the bay. On the bow of the Union ship, a seaman used a line with a lead weight to measure the depth of the water, and soon he was indicating a foot less than the *Metacomet* drew, as she scraped through the mud of the bottom. "Call the man in," her captain told his first officer. "He is only intimidating me with his soundings."[21] The captain's courage and persistence paid off, for the *Selma* was overtaken, losing eight killed and seven wounded before she hauled down her flag in surrender.

In the meantime the rest of the Federal ships anchored a few miles inside the bay, while their crews began to clear away the blood and debris on their decks. By then it was 8:30 a.m. and, only a half-hour late, Farragut ordered breakfast prepared for his men. Captain Drayton, commander of the *Hartford,* approached Farragut on the poop deck and said, "What we have done has been well done, sir; but it all counts for nothing so long as the *Tennessee* is there under the guns of Morgan." The admiral replied, "I know it, and as soon as the people have their breakfasts I am going for her."[22] But Buchanan saved him the trouble. At 8:50 a.m. came a cry from aloft, "The ram is coming!" Soon the Rebel ironclad could be seen from the deck, steaming directly for the Union fleet. "I did not think Old Buck was such a fool," Farragut remarked.[23]

In fact, some of Buchanan's officers had advised him against making this second attack, but he replied, "No; I will be killed or taken prisoner; and now I am in the humor, I will have it out."[24] The Confederate soldiers crowded the ramparts of the forts, now out of range, to watch the *Tennessee,* considered the most powerful vessel then afloat, take on the entire Federal fleet. Farragut used the army signal officers to order the sloops *Monongahela* and *Lackawanna* to "run down the ram," and then the order was repeated to the monitors.[25] The *Monongahela* took the lead, as she had not even anchored yet. The Confederate ironclad fired on these two Federal attackers, but steered straight for the *Hartford.* When the *Monongahela* rammed the *Tennessee* at full speed amidships, her iron prow was torn away and she was badly damaged by the collision. It was "a blow that would have sunk almost any vessel of the Union navy," Lieutenant Kinney wrote, "but which inflicted not the slightest damage on the solid iron hull of the ram." The *Lackawanna* followed closely and delivered a similar blow with her wooden bow, which only caused the Rebel ram to lurch to one side slightly. As she then swung alongside, the ironclad sent two shots through her and held her course straight for the *Hartford*.

And the Union flagship headed straight for the iron monster. "But for the two vessels to strike fairly, bows on," Lieutenant Kinney wrote, "would probably have involved the destruction of both, for the ram must have penetrated so far into the wooden ship that as the *Hartford* filled and sank she would have carried the ram under water. Whether for this reason or for some other, as the two vessels came together the *Tennessee* slightly changed her course, the port bow of the *Hartford* met the port bow of the ram, and the ships grated against each other as they passed."[26] The *Hartford* fired a point-blank broadside, but the 9-inch-diameter, solid iron balls only dented the ironclad's casemate and bounded into the air. The *Tennessee* tried to return the favor, but defective primers prevented all but one gun from firing. That one sent a shell through the berth deck, killing five men and wounding eight.

Captain Drayton of the *Hartford* saw Buchanan sticking his head out of the *Tennessee* to have a look around. Lacking any better weapon, Drayton took the binoculars that were hanging around his neck and flung them at the Confederate admiral, whom he called, "You infernal traitor!"[27] Farragut jumped up on the port-quarter rail, holding to the mizzen-rigging, to watch as the other Union ships now closed in, pounding the *Tennessee* with their guns and trying to run her down. A lieutenant, "who knew better than to consult him before acting," as Kinney put it, slipped a rope around him and secured it to the rigging so that he wouldn't be knocked overboard.[28] That was fortunate, for as the *Hartford* turned around for another try at the ironclad she collided with the *Lackawanna*, causing considerable confusion and consternation on both ships. For a while it was thought that the flagship was sinking, and cries of "Save the admiral!" rang out.[29] The port lifeboats were lowered, two of them landing upside down and floating away. But Farragut looked over the starboard side and saw that the hole caused by the collision was a few inches above the water line. He ordered full speed and continued heading for the *Tennessee*.

Meanwhile the *Lackawanna* had rammed the ironclad and was maneuvering for another try when she almost collided with the *Hartford* again. "And now the admiral became a trifle excited," Kinney said. Farragut turned to him and asked, "Can you say 'For God's sake' by signal'" Kinney said that he could. "Then say to the *Lackawanna*, For God's sake get out of our way and anchor!" Kinney tried to comply, but "in my haste to send the message," he said, "I brought the end of my signal flag-staff down with considerable violence upon the head of the admiral, who was standing nearer than I thought, causing him to wince perceptibly."[30] Kinney finally got the message sent, but the army signal officer on the *Lackawanna* missed the end of it, because the wind happened to wrap her American flag around him just then.

But before either ship could ram the Confederate again, the united fire of the Federal fleet finally began to take effect. The monitor *Chickasaw* managed to get in close astern, pounding away with the 11-inch guns in her forward turret "like pocket-pistols," as the *Tennessee*'s pilot put it.[31] One of these shots jammed the iron cover of the stern gunport on the *Tennessee,* which meant that the after 7-inch rifle could not be run out to fire. Buchanan sent below for a machinist to come and back out the pin so the cover could be removed, but while this was being done another shot struck the edge of the port cover just where the machinist was sitting. "His remains had to be taken up with a shovel, placed in a bucket, and thrown overboard," the *Tennessee*'s captain recorded.[32] The same shot sent splinters flying around inside the Rebel ship, one of which killed a seaman, and another broke Admiral Buchanan's leg below the knee. He sent for Captain James D. Johnston and told him, "Well, Johnston, they've got me. You'll have to look out for her now."[33]

The *Tennessee*'s flag staff was shot away and her smokestack, after being riddled with holes, also disappeared, leaving her engines without enough power to oppose the tide, then running out at over four miles an hour. At 15-inch shot from the *Manhattan* smashed her casemate between her two port-side 6.4-inch rifles, knocking a hole through the armor and its wooden backing, leaving on the inside a mass of oak and pine splinters projecting about two feet into the ship. Then a shot from the *Chickasaw* broke the chain that connected the *Tennessee*'s wheel with her rudder and ran unprotected from the casemate across her afterdeck. "Realizing the impossibility of directing the firing of the guns without the use of the rudder, and that the ship had been rendered utterly helpless," Captain Johnston wrote, "I went to the lower deck and informed the admiral of her condition, and that I had not been able to bring a gun to bear upon any of our antagonists for nearly half an hour, to which he replied: 'Well, Johnston, if you cannot do them any further damage you had better surrender.'"[34]

The *Ossipee* was just about to ram her when Johnston came out on the top of the shield and displayed a white flag. The Federal ship reversed engines and bumped the ironclad harmlessly while the thunder of guns was replaced by wild cheering from the entire Union fleet. It was then just 10 a.m. The commander of the *Ossipee* was an old friend of Johnston's and hailed him in friendly terms, sent a boat over to fetch him, and gave him some ice water and navy sherry. Buchanan surrendered his sword to a lieutenant from the *Ossipee* who was sent to take charge of the Rebel ironclad with a guard of marines. On meeting Buchanan, the Marine Corps captain could not resist informing the admiral that they had met before under different circumstances. The marine had been aboard the frigate *Cumberland* when Buchanan had sunk her with the *Merrimac/Virginia* in Hampton Roads. "Within an hour after I was taken on board the *Ossipee* Admiral Farragut sent for me to be brought on board his flag-ship," Johnston wrote, "and when I reached her deck he expressed regret at meeting me under such circumstances, to which I replied that he was not half as sorry to see me as I was to see him."[35]

That afternoon the monitor *Chickasaw* shelled Fort Powell, a small work that guarded the shallow Grant's Pass entrance to Mobile Bay, and at 10 p.m. it was evacuated, its garrison escaping to the mainland in the dark. The Confederate gunboat *Morgan* also escaped that night, crossing the shallow end of the bay and going upriver to Mobile.

That night Farragut wrote to his wife: "The Almighty has smiled upon me once more. I am in Mobile Bay. It was a hard fight, but Buck met his fate manfully. After we passed the forts, he came up in the ram to attack me. I made at him and ran him down, making all the others do the same. We butted and shot at him until he surrendered."[36]

---

1. Sandburg, *Abraham Lincoln*, 552–553.
2. Ibid., 553.
3. All these quotes from McDonough and Jones, *War So Terrible*, 266.
4. Foote, *The Civil War*, 3:494.
5. Macartney, *Mr. Lincoln's Admirals*, 23.
6. John Coddington Kinney, "Farragut at Mobile Bay," in *Battles and Leaders*, 4:383.
7. Foote, *The Civil War*, 3:498.
8. Kinney, "Farragut at Mobile Bay," 385.
9. Foote, *The Civil War*, 3:498–499.
10. Ibid., 3:499.
11. Kinney, "Farragut at Mobile Bay," 387–388.
12. Macartney, *Mr. Lincoln's Admirals*, 67–68.

13. Kinney, "Farragut at Mobile Bay," 389–390.

14. Macartney, *Mr. Lincoln's Admirals*, 68.

15. Ibid., 68, n. 14. There are several versions of the second sentence, but all agree that the first was, "Damn the torpedoes!"

16. Kinney, "Farragut at Mobile Bay," 391.

17. Macartney, *Mr. Lincoln's Admirals*, 70.

18. Joseph Bough, "Iron Versus Wood," *America's Civil War* 1:4 (November 1988): 48.

19. William M. Fowler, Jr., *Under Two Flags: the American Navy in the Civil War* (New York, 1990), 242.

20. Kinney, "Farragut at Mobile Bay," 394.

21. Foote, *The Civil War*, 3:502.

22. Macartney, *Mr. Lincoln's Admirals*, 70.

23. Joseph Marthon, "The Lashing of Admiral Farragut in the Rigging II," in *Battles and Leaders*, 4:407.

24. Macartney, *Mr. Lincoln's Admirals*, 70.

25. Kinney, "Farragut at Mobile Bay," 395.

26. Ibid., 396.

27. Macartney, *Mr. Lincoln's Admirals*, 72.

28. Kinney, "Farragut at Mobile Bay," 396.

29. Ibid., 397.

30. Ibid.

31. Ibid, 398, note.

32. James D. Johnston, "The Ram 'Tennessee' at Mobile Bay," in *Battles and Leaders*, 4:404.

33. Ibid.

34. Ibid.

35. Ibid.

36. Foote, *The Civil War*, 3:506.

CHAPTER TWENTY-FIVE

Grant Now Runs the Whole Machine

5–8 August 1864

General Grant arrived at Monocacy Junction, Maryland, on that fifth day of August. He did not stop in Washington to see Halleck or Stanton, nor even Lincoln, but proceeded directly to the camp of General Hunter, where the forces of Crook and Wright spread over the fields and along the banks of the Monocacy River. There he found many hundreds of railroad cars and locomotives belonging to the Baltimore & Ohio, which had been brought there to keep them safe from the Rebels. Grant asked Hunter where Early's army was, and the latter confessed that he did not know. "He said the fact was," Grant wrote in his memoirs, "that he was so embarrassed with orders from Washington moving him first to the right and then to the left that he had lost all trace of the enemy."[1]

Grant replied that he would find out where the enemy was, and he proceeded to do so in a typically straight-forward way. He ordered "steam got up and trains made up," he said, "giving directions to push for Halltown, some four miles above Harper's Ferry, in the Shenandoah Valley. The cavalry and the wagon trains were to march, but all the troops that could be transported by the cars were to go in that way. I knew," Grant explained, "that the valley was of such importance to the enemy that, no matter how much he was scattered at that time, he would in a very short time be found in front of our troops moving south."[2]

Grant then wrote out instructions for Hunter's guidance. After directing him to concentrate near Harper's Ferry and telling him the whereabouts of the cavalry that was coming to reinforce him, he got down to the heart of the matter. "In pushing up the Shenandoah Valley, where it is expected you will have to go first or last, it is desirable that nothing should be left to invite the enemy to return. Take all provisions, forage, and stock wanted for the use of your command; such as cannot be consumed, destroy. It is not desirable that the buildings should be destroyed—they should rather be protected; but the people should be informed that, so long as an army can subsist among them, recurrences of these raids must be expected, and we are determined to stop them at all hazards.

"Bear in mind, the object is to drive the enemy south; and to do this, you want to keep him always in sight. Be guided in your course by the course he takes.

"Make your own arrangements for supplies of all kinds, giving regular vouchers for such as may be taken from loyal citizens in the country through which you march."[3]

Grant suggested that Hunter establish his headquarters at Cumberland, Baltimore, or wherever he liked and give Sheridan command of the troops in the field. Hunter replied that he thought it would be better if he were relieved of his command. "He said that General Halleck seemed so much to distrust his fitness for the position he was in that he thought somebody else ought to be there," Grant wrote. "He did not want, in any way, to embarrass the cause; thus showing a patriotism that was none too common in the army. There were not many major-generals who would voluntarily have asked to have the command of a department taken from them on the supposition that for some particular reason, or for any reason, the service would be better performed."[4]

"Very well then," Grant said, and did not try to argue him out of resigning, since it cleared the way for what he wanted: Sheridan in command.[5] Instead, he telegraphed immediately for Sheridan to come to Monocacy from Washington, saying he would wait there until he arrived.

Sheridan went with Secretary of War Stanton to call on the president before leaving Washington, and Lincoln told the general that Stanton had objected to his assignment to this command because he thought him to be too young, and that he had concurred with the secretary. But now that Grant had "ploughed round" the difficulties by putting him in command of "the boys in the field" he was satisfied and "hoped for the best." Sheridan noted that "Mr. Stanton remained silent during these remarks, never once indicating whether he, too, had become reconciled to my selection or not; and although, after we left the White House, he conversed with me freely in regard to the campaign I was expected to make, seeking to impress on me the necessity for success from the political as well as from the military point of view, yet he utterly ignored the fact that he had taken any part in disapproving the recommendation of the general-in-chief."[6]

Grant's comments on the personalities of Lincoln and Stanton in his memoirs are interesting in this regard: "They were the very opposite of each other in almost every particular, except that each possessed great ability. Mr. Lincoln gained influence over men by making them feel that it was a pleasure to serve him. He preferred yielding his own wish to gratify others, rather than to insist upon having his own way. It distressed him to disappoint others. In matters of public duty, however, he had what he wished, but in the least offensive way. Mr. Stanton never questioned his own authority to command, unless resisted. He cared nothing for the feelings of others. In fact it seemed to be pleasanter to him to disappoint than to gratify. He felt no hesitation in assuming the functions of the executive, or in acting without advising with him. If his act was not sustained, he would change it—if he saw the matter would be followed up until he did so.

"It was generally supposed that these two officials formed the complement of each other. The Secretary was required to prevent the President's being imposed upon. The President was required in the more responsible place of seeing that injustice was not done to others. I do not know that this view of these two men is still entertained by the majority of the people. It is not a correct view, however, in my estimation. Mr. Lincoln did not require a guardian to aid him in the fulfillment of a public trust.

"Mr. Lincoln was not timid, and he was willing to trust his generals in making and executing their plans. The Secretary was very timid, and it was impossible for him to avoid interfering with the armies covering the capital when it was sought to defend it by an offensive movement against the army guarding the Confederate capital. He could see our weakness, but he could not see that the enemy was in danger. The enemy would not have been in danger if Mr. Stanton had been in the field."[7]

Sheridan arrived at Monocacy Junction on the sixth, by which time Hunter and his staff, and Grant and one or two members of his staff, were about all of the army that remained there. Grant met Sheridan at the station and gave him a quick rundown of what had been done and what he wanted him to do, giving him the instructions which he had written out for Hunter. Within two hours Grant was on a train heading east to Washington and Sheridan was on another, heading west to Harper's Ferry. One of Grant's aides, Major Joe Bowers, wrote to one of Grant's military secretaries that Grant had told Sheridan "to drive Early out of the Valley and to receive orders from no live man but Grant himself."[8]

It was probably no coincidence that Early took his infantry back across the Potomac to Virginia that day, heading toward Martinsburg after loading his wagons with wheat from the farms around Sharpsburg. In West Virginia that day, Averell was in hot pursuit of McCausland's raiders. Unaware of the command changes in his department, he reported to Hunter that he had lost 100 horses the day before and was down to only 1,600 mounted men, but he added that he would "follow and fight" the Rebels "if it kills every horse and man in the command."[9]

Reflecting on the public's great longing for peace negotiations that summer, *Leslie's Weekly* commented that day that "peace must come through the powerful negotiations of Gens. Grant and Sherman."[10]

In Richmond that day, General Lee and President Davis were discussing the situation in northern Virginia. They knew that Grant had been sending more troops down the James, presumably to reinforce Hunter. They did not, of course, know that these troops were cavalry, nor that a new commander had been sent as well. But they were concerned that Grant had now fortified his infantry and artillery so thoroughly that he could afford to send off more troops against Early and still hold his lines around Petersburg. They came to the conclusion that they should also send more troops to northern Virginia and decided to send General Anderson with Kershaw's infantry division of his own 1st Corps and Fitzhugh Lee's cavalry division. They would not join Early, however, at least not at first. They would proceed to Culpeper Court House, where they would be a menace to the flank of any Union force in the Shenandoah Valley, or could go on to reinforce Early if necessary, and yet not have so far to go if Lee should need to recall them quickly. They were trying, bit by bit, to transfer the seat of the war in the East from Richmond's back door to Washington's side yard. The troops marched that day.

Also on the sixth, another Confederate commerce raider began her career. Like the *Florida,* which was the only raider then still afloat, and the *Alabama* before her, this one had been built in Britain. Unlike them, she was converted from a blockade runner and manned by a real Confederate crew instead of one recruited in England. She had a twin-engine, twin-screw system which enabled her to turn on her center, and she carried a 100-pounder rifle as well as two smaller guns. She was skippered by Commander John T. Wood, the man who had been selected to lead the expedition to Point Lookout, Maryland. When that project had been aborted he had stayed on at Wilmington and had been given command of the converted blockade runner that he was about to make famous as the CSS *Tallahassee*.

After running aground a couple of times due to the ship being overloaded with extra coal, Wood waited until the moon went down on the night of the sixth and steamed cautiously out the southern outlet of the Cape Fear River. The *Tallahassee* grazed the bar but did not stick, and Wood turned to his chief engineer, John W. Tynan. "Open her out, sir," he said, "but let her go for all she is worth."[11] Almost immediately the *Tallahassee* was in the midst of the Union blockaders, and flame from her smokestacks soon gave away her presence. Wood ignored signals from two of them, and they both opened fire. The Rebel raider did not answer but slipped between the two Federals and soon was out of range of their rockets and calcium searchlights. She passed three more Union ships, unobserved.

Down in Georgia, Bate's Confederate division occupied the new line of entrenchments at the far left of Hood's Army of Tennessee by dawn of that sixth day of August. The 2nd Brigade of Georgia Militia was on Bate's right, connecting him with the main Confederate defenses. Ross' Brigade of Texas cavalry guarded his left. On the Union side, during the early morning hours Schofield shifted the two divisions of his own 23rd Corps to the right of Palmer's 14th Corps. Then he ordered one of them, Cox's 3rd Division, to advance to the south, attack and, if possible, turn the Rebels' flank. The other division, Hascall's 2nd, was ordered to cover Cox's flank, while the 14th Corps was to support the attack with skirmishers and artillery fire. That was evidently about all that Schofield thought he could get out of it.

At about 10 a.m. Cox sent one of his four brigades forward on a reconnaissance in force, and it drove in Bate's skirmish line. But as the Federals struggled through the entanglements in front of the Confederate defenses, the main Rebel line opened a deadly fire upon them at a range of only 25 or 30 yards. "They were plucky fellows," one Confederate wrote, "and charged to within a few yards of our works, paying dearly for their courage and temerity."[12] The attack came to a halt. The brigade commander brought up his reserve regiment and tried again, but with no more success. Finally, after losing over 300 men and two flags, the attackers withdrew.

Meanwhile, Thomas accepted Palmer's formal resignation of his command of the 14th Corps that day, and he and Sherman sent their recommendation to the War Department that the corps' senior division commander, Brigadier General Richard W. Johnson, be made Sherman's chief of cavalry, and that Jefferson C. Davis, complete with his talent for profanity, be given command of the 14th Corps. Until approval of this plan was received, Johnson continued as acting commander, for only the president could appoint the commander of an army or a corps. The 14th Corps made a general advance that afternoon, but was no more successful than Cox had been.

Finding Cox's path solidly blocked, Schofield sent Hascall's division on an attempt to outflank the Southern defenses, or at least find a more weakly defended section. Late that afternoon the Federals did manage to drive back the Rebel flank slightly, but darkness and a rain storm put an end to the Union advance. The position gained, however, would allow the Northerners to enfilade Bate's line, so that night, at Hood's direction, he pulled back to the main line of Rebel works covering the railroad to East Point.

Sherman told Schofield that night, "There is no alternative but for you to continue to work on that flank with as much caution as possible, and it is possible the enemy may attack us, or draw us out. He must defend that road," Sherman said, meaning the railroad to and beyond East Point. "We are working hard for the big road," Schofield replied. "The ground is very rough. I am confident of getting the road, but doubt my ability to either reach the enemy's left or break his lines, but will give it a fair try."[13]

The next day, the seventh, Schofield advanced against the main line of Confederate defenses protecting the railroad to East Point and engaged in what Sherman called a "noisy but not a bloody battle." Schofield reported that "it was ascertained that the enemy's line, strongly fortified and protected by abatis, extended . . . far beyond the reach of a single corps, unless it were detached to an unsafe distance from the main army."[14] Sherman told him to suspend the offensive and to dig in. "I do not deem it prudent to extend any more to the right," Sherman told Halleck that day.[15] He was bringing down more heavy guns with which to bombard Atlanta, but, he told Halleck, "I am too impatient for a siege, and don't know but this is as good a place to fight it out on, as farther inland. One thing is certain, whether we get inside of Atlanta or not, it will be a used-up community when we are done with it."[16]

That same day, Sherman received a dispatch from Washburn, at Memphis, saying that the latter had received a report that Forrest had died of lockjaw several days before. "Is Forrest surely dead?" Sherman responded. "If so, tell General Mower I am pledged to him for his promotion, and if Old Abe don't make good my promise then General Mower may have my place."[17]

By then most of Mower's division of A. J. Smith's force was gathered at Waterford, the new Union railhead on the Mississippi Central Railroad a few miles south of Holly Springs. And Grierson's cavalry, recently reorganized into a corps of two divisions, reached Holly Springs that day. The rest of Smith's infantry would arrive in the next 24 hours. Meanwhile, Smith sent a small force ahead about ten miles to the Tallahatchie River to clear the way for his pioneers to repair the railroad and build a bridge there. The force consisted of the 35th Iowa and 7th Minnesota infantry regiments and the 12th Missouri Cavalry, and it was commanded by Colonel Sylvester G. Hill of the 35th Iowa.

The Federals marched south at 2 p.m. on the seventh, and about a mile and a half north of the river the cavalry, which had the lead, was fired on by dismounted troopers of the 18th Mississippi Cavalry Battalion. Colonel Hill sent Company B of his 35th Iowa to support the Union cavalry. These foot-soldiers soon drove off the Rebels and chased them as far as the Tallahatchie, where they found that the flooring of the railroad bridge had been removed, but they captured a flatboat which the Confederates had been using as a ferry. One company from each infantry regiment was soon ferried over to the south bank to establish a bridgehead on that side of the river before darkness put an end to the day's activity. The rest of the Union force went into camp three-quarters of a mile north of the river.

Colonel William B. Wade, commander of the 2nd Brigade of Chalmer's Division, was in charge of the Confederate defense of the Tallahatchie. When word reached him that Yankees had crossed the river he immediately organized a counterattack. Two guns of an Arkansas battery were put into position under cover of darkness, while dismounted troopers of the 1st Mississippi Partisan Regiment crept forward toward the two Federal companies. At 11 p.m. the two cannon fired several rounds into the bridgehead and the main camp on the north bank, and then the Mississipians charged. They were met by a hail of bullets that drove them back. They reformed and tried again, but with the same result. Meanwhile, Colonel Hill sent a courier galloping for Waterford with an urgent request for Union artillery.

Off the coast of North Carolina the CSS *Tallahassee* spotted two more Federal blockaders soon after daylight on the seventh, but the sleek raider eventually outran them. Later, another gave chase but was also outdistanced. That night she almost blundered into yet another, and it managed to get off one shot when her signal was not answered, but the

Confederate ship soon got away. Wood intentionally held his fire during all these encounters so that the Federals would not know that his ship was anything but an unarmed blockade runner, and thus would not know that their own unarmed merchant ships were in danger.

Copperheads met with Confederate commissioners at London, Upper Canada, again that day. Their revolt was now set for Chicago on 29 August, the first day of the rescheduled Democratic national convention. The Copperheads told the Rebels that unsupported uprisings at Indianapolis and Springfield were too risky. "You underrate the condition on things in the Northwest," the Copperheads said. "By patience and perseverance in the work of agitation, we are sure of a general uprising which will result in glorious success. We must look to bigger results than the mere liberation of prisoners. We should look to the grand end of adding an empire of Northwestern States."[18] The Confederates insisted that this must be the last change of date.

In West Virginia, in the wee hours of 7 August, two men in gray uniforms rode up to a picket of Bradley Johnson's brigade of McCausland's Confederate raiders, bivouacked near Moorefield. When they were challenged they said they were scouts from the 8th Virginia Cavalry. After exchanging a word or two more, one of the scouts rode back to pick up something lost from his saddle, but he returned with twenty other men, who captured the entire picket post. When these twenty encountered the reserves for the Rebel pickets, they told them they were relief pickets from the 8th Virginia. "Get your horses, you are relieved," they said. "Thus scout, picket, and reserve were captured by the enemy uniformed as Confederates," Colonel Johnson reported, "who then rode in my camp without giving any alarm." A captured Union sergeant later told a staff officer that "a man who had been in camp to have a stolen horse restored had guided them to the picket and my headquarters," Johnson said.[19]

These Federals were from Averell's cavalry, which had been pursuing McCausland's raiders, and as soon as they had cleared the way, one Union brigade launched a surprise attack on Bradley Johnson's Confederate troopers, and drove them through the South Branch of the Potomac and into the camp of McCausland's own brigade. Then another brigade of Averell's division charged across the stream under fire and routed McCausland's troopers before they could get organized. And as the Rebel force fled, it was struck in the flank by a battalion of the 22nd Pennsylvania Cavalry that Averell had sent the day before by another road.

All told, Averell captured all four of McCausland's artillery pieces, all but one of his caissons, all of his wagons, over 400 horses, three battleflags, and 420 prisoners, including 38 officers. Bradley Johnson was captured, but escaped. A reporter for the *Richmond Whig*, who was present, wrote that Johnson's and McCausland's brigades were "stampeded and routed," their "men scattering in wild disorder and confusion and running in different directions."[20] What was left of the Confederate raiders eventually made their way back to Early's army in the Shenandoah Valley.

"This great disaster would have at once been retrieved," Bradley Johnson reported, "but for the insufficient armament of the command. Besides the First and Second Maryland and a squadron of the Eighth Virginia there was not a saber in the command." During the course of the war, the Confederates had found that, in the wooded country of eastern and southwestern Virginia where they usually operated, the saber was an unnecessary encumbrance. Since most of their fighting was done on foot, they had come to rely on rifled muskets. However, the Federals had followed the standard manuals on cavalry and had not only retained their sabers but had become quite proficient in their use over the years. "In that open country, perfectly level," Johnson continued, "the only mode to fight charging cavalry was by charging, and this the men were unable to do. The long Enfield musket once discharged could not be reloaded, and lay helpless before the charging saber."[21] Johnson also blamed the lack of discipline under McCausland's command and the many lawless acts that the men had been allowed to engage in on their raid. "Had there been less plunder there would have been more fighting at Moorefield," he said.[22]

"This affair," Early wrote, "had a very damaging effect upon my cavalry for the rest of the campaign."[23]

In Washington, on his way back to City Point on the seventh, Grant conferred with Lincoln, Stanton and Halleck. Just what was said is not known, but when it was over orders were issued to create the Middle Military Division, a command comparable to those held by Sherman and Canby, and consisting of the Middle Department and the departments of Washington, of the Susquehanna, and of West Virginia. Sheridan was named temporary commander of the new organization. Major Joe Bowers of Grant's staff wrote to Rawlins, the ailing chief of staff, that Grant "has settled Halleck down to a mere staff officer for Stanton. Halleck has no control over troops except as Grant delegates it. He can give no orders and exercise no discretion. Grant now runs the whole machine independently of the Washington directory. I am glad to say he is fully

himself, works vigorously, and will soon devise another plan for discom-
fiting all the enemies of the country."[24]

Grant wrote to Sheridan that day: "Do not hesitate to give commands
to officers in whom you repose confidence, without regard to claims of
others on account of rank. If you deem Torbert the best man to command
the cavalry, placed him in command and give Averell some other command, or relieve him from the expedition, and order him to report to
General Hunter. What we want is prompt and active movements after
the enemy in accordance with instructions you already have. I feel every
confidence that you will do the very best, and will leave you as far as
possible to act on your own judgment, and not embarass you with orders
and instructions."[25]

The next day Sheridan did appoint Torbert to be his chief of cavalry.
Meanwhile, the Union officers and men were already noticing a change
under their new commander. "Everything is in chaos here," wrote Colonel Charles Russell Lowell, commanding a brigade of cavalry in the
Valley from the Department of Washington, "but under Sheridan is rapidly assuming shape. It was a lucky inspiration of Grant's or Lincoln's
to make a Middle Military Division and put him in command of it . . .
It is exhilarating to see so many cavalry about and to see things going
right again."[26]

On that next day, 8 August, down in Mobile Bay, Fort Gaines surrendered to the Federal Forces on Dauphine Island investing its landward
side. But the larger Fort Morgan, on the other side of the main entrance
to the bay, continued to hold out.

Down in Mississippi that morning, at the first light of dawn, Colonel
Hill, commander of the Union forces at the Tallahatchie, decided to pull
the two companies of infantry out of their bridgehead on the south bank.
Reinforcements were soon on the way from Waterford, one brigade plus
one regiment of infantry and a battery of artillery. And Brigadier General
Edward Hatch, commander of the 1st Division of Grierson's Cavalry
Corps, was already headed south from Holly Springs with his own divi-
sion and Colonel John W. Noble's 2nd Brigade of Colonel Edward F.
Winslow's 2nd Division.

Meanwhile the Confederate commander, Colonel Wade, placed the 1st
Mississippi Partisan Regiment and the 18th Mississippi Cavalry Battalion
on a low ridge in the edge of some woods half a mile from the river.
They quickly threw up a line of defenses constructed of felled timber
and fence rails. When General Hatch arrived at the front at about 10
a.m., Colonel Hill pointed out the Rebel defenses and said that all the

evidence indicated that the Confederates were determined to resist another crossing.

Hatch ordered Hill to move his infantry into the woods on the north bank of the river, and from there they began to fire on the Confederates across the way. Under the cover of this fire and that of a pair of 6-pounder guns, Colonel Noble dismounted two of his regiments, the 3rd Iowa and the 10th Missouri, and sent them forward in a double line of battle toward the damaged railroad bridge. Meanwhile, infantrymen of the 35th Iowa were ferried across the river on the flatboat, covered by the troopers of the 1st Brigade of Hatch's division. On the south side, the Iowans deployed as skirmishers and prepared to attack the Confederate breastworks, but the Rebels saw this coming and pulled back to the ridge overlooking the valley of the Tallahatchie, blocking the road south to Abbeville.

Dismounted troopers of the 3rd Iowa then crossed the river on the stringers of the bridge, and Hatch put his pioneers to work building a crude floating bridge out of driftwood secured to the supports of the railroad bridge. By 5 p.m. it was finished, and Hatch sent a brigade of cavalry across it to replace the 3rd Iowa. A strong line of outposts was established covering the approaches to the bridgehead. Meanwhile, the 7th Indiana Cavalry had been sent from Holly Springs at dawn to Toba Tubby Ferry, about ten miles downstream, or west, on the Tallahatchie, where it skirmished with troopers of the Confederate 10th Missouri across the river.

An editorial in the *Richmond Sentinel* newspaper that day suggested that the war was nearly over. The Northern leaders were not yet willing to admit defeat, it said, but there was little more they could do to hurt the South.

---

1. Grant, *Memoirs*, 2:319.
2. Ibid.
3. U.S. War Department, *The War of the Rebellion: A Compilation of the Official Records of the Union and Confederate Armies* (Washington, 1893), vol. 43, part I: 57–58.
4. Grant, *Memoirs*, 2:320.
5. Ibid.
6. Sheridan, *Memoirs*, 1:463–464.
7. Grant, *Memoirs*, 2:536–537.

8. Catton, *Grant Takes Command,* 349.

9. Starr, *Union Cavalry in the Civil War,* 2:224.

10. Sandburg, *Abraham Lincoln,* 566.

11. Royce Gordon Shingleton, "Cruise of the CSS Tallahasee," *Civil War Times Illustrated,* 15 (2 May 1976): 32–33.

12. Scaife, *The Campaign For Atlanta,* 89.

13. McDonough and Jones, *War So Terrible,* 267.

14. Albert Castel, "Union Fizzle at Atlanta: the Battle of Utoy Creek," *Civil War Times Illustrated,* 16 (10 February 1978): 30.

15. McDonough and Jones, *War So Terrible,* 268.

16. Miers, *The General Who Marched to Hell,* 164.

17. Bearss, *Forrest at Brice's Cross Roads,* 245–246, n. 14.

18. Milton, *Abraham Lincoln and the Fifth Column,* 298.

19. *Official Records,* 43:I:6.

20. Ibid., 43:I:991.

21. Ibid., 43:I:6.

22. Ibid., 43:I:8.

23. Pond, *The Shenandoah Valley in 1864,* 107.

24. Catton, *Grant Takes Command,* 348.

25. *Official Records,* 43:I:719.

26. Starr, *Union Cavalry,* 2:256–257.

CHAPTER TWENTY-SIX

Our Enemy Would Hold Fast

9–12 August 1864

Grant was back at City Point on the morning of 9 August, from his trip to Monocacy Junction and Washington. Sitting in front of his tent with several staff officers, he heard the assistant provost marshal general report that he thought that there were spies in the headquarters camp. No sooner had that officer departed after outlining plans for detecting and capturing these enemy agents than, at about 11:40 a.m., a terrific explosion shook the earth with a roar that vividly reminded everybody present of the Petersburg mine.

Two Confederate agents had indeed entered the huge Federal supply base at City Point that day with what they called a horological torpedo, a box containing a clockwork detonator and twelve pounds of gunpowder. They watched the busy wharf for a while, and when the captain of an ordnance barge went ashore they saw their chance. One of the agents, John Maxwell, described by his superior as "a bold operator," calmly carried his box full of explosive out to the barge and told the sentry that it was something which the captain had ordered.[1] The sentry let him on board, where Maxwell set the timer on his bomb and gave it to a deckhand, saying that the captain wanted it stowed below decks. Then he walked away, without anyone challenging his presence or purpose on the wharf. The two Rebels retired to a supposedly safe distance and awaited events.

When the bomb went off, so did the barge's supply of gunpowder, artillery shells, and rifle ammunition. A shower of shells, bullets, boards, and fragments of iron and of timber rained down on the wharf, the nearby warehouses, and the headquarters tents on the bluff above. Down on the docks 42 men were killed and 122 wounded. Maxwell was temporarily in shock, and his companion was permanently deafened by the explosion. A Confederate prisoner of war was among the killed. The rifle of one of the guards was found a half-mile away, sticking bayonet-first in the ground.

Up on the bluff, Lieutenant Colonel Babcock of Grant's staff was wounded in the hand, a mounted orderly and several horses were killed, and three orderlies wounded. "The general was the only one of the party who remained unmoved." Horace Porter wrote, "he did not even leave his seat to run to the bluff with the others to see what had happened. Five minutes afterward he went to his writing-table and sent a telegram to Washington, notifying Halleck of the occurance."[2] He told Halleck that "every part of the yard used as my headquarters is filled with splinters and fragments of shell."[3] It wasn't until the war was over that the Federal authorities were able to confirm their suspicions that Rebel agents had caused the explosion.

"This occurrence set the staff to thinking of the various forms of danger to which the general-in-chief was exposed," Horace Porter wrote, "and how easily he might be assassinated; and we resolved that in addition to the ordinary guard mounted at the headquarters camp, we would quietly arrange a detail of 'watchers' from the members of the staff, so that one officer would go on duty every night and keep a personal lookout in the vicinity of the general's tent. This was faithfully carried out. It had to be done secretly, for if he had known of it he would without doubt have broken it up and insisted upon the staff-officers going to bed after their hard day's work, instead of keeping these vigils throughout the long, dreary nights."[4]

Getting back down to business, Grant sent a telegram to Sheridan at noon: "Information derived from deserters, refugees, and a man sent from here to Richmond, all corroborating, locate every division and brigade of Hill, Longstreet, and Beauregard's forces. Not one brigade has been sent from here. I shall endeavor to hold them, and rather create a tendency to draw from your front than allow them to re-enforce."[5] Anderson's move north had gone undetected.

Down in Georgia that day the Federals delivered even more explosives to the defenders and inhabitants of Atlanta, but by more conventional means. General Hood wrote that "the 9th was made memorable by the most furious cannonade which the city sustained during the siege."[6] For, on that date the 200-plus Federal guns fired an estimated 5,000 shells at the city and its defenses. A young civilian called it "that red day in August, when all the fires of hell, and all the thunders of the universe seemed to be blazing and roaring over Atlanta." He looked up and saw that a "great volume of sulphorous smoke rolled over the town, trailing down to the ground, and through this stifling gloom the sun glared down like a great red eye peering through a bronze colored sky."[7]

Down on Mobile Bay that ninth day of August, General Granger's troops were ferried from Dauphine Island to Mobile Point, where they began to invest the landward side of Fort Morgan, the only remaining Confederate work. While this was going on, two monitors, three sloops and a few gunboats fired on the fort to keep it busy, but with little damage to either side. Farragut and Granger sent a note to the fort under a flag of truce: "To prevent the unnecessary sacrifice of human life which must follow the opening of our batteries, we demand the unconditional surrender of Fort Morgan and its dependencies." The fort's commander, Brigadier General Richard L. Page, a first cousin of General R. E. Lee, replied: "I am prepared to sacrifice life, and will only surrender when I have no means of defense."[8] All day the Federal soldiers labored under a sun that one of them said was hot enough to roast potatoes, digging entrenchments and hauling big guns and ammunition into position just a mile east of the fort. Meanwhile the navy towed the captured *Tennessee* into position, and at nightfall the guns, the ironclad, the monitors, the sloops and the gunboats all began to fire shells and heated solid shot at the fort, literally shaking it, but still Page refused to consider surrendering.

In the Shenandoah Valley that ninth day of August, Torbert's 1st Division of the Cavalry Corps of the Army of the Potomac reached Halltown. In addition, Sheridan now had Wright's 6th Corps, one division and part of another of the 19th Corps, under Brigadier General William H. Emory, the two infantry divisions of the Army of West Virginia, under Crook, and a cavalry brigade from the Department of Washington, under Colonel Charles Russell Lowell. Wilson's 3rd Division of the Cavalry Corps was on the way. Averell's 2nd Cavalry Division of the Army of West Virginia had still not returned from chasing McCausland's raiders, while Duffié's small 1st Cavalry Division, the rest of the second division of the 19th Corps, and various garrisons were scattered throughout the four departments of Sheridan's Middle Military Division. Sheridan issued orders for the force at Halltown, soon to be known unofficially as the Army of the Shenandoah, to advance the next day.

Down in Mississippi on the ninth, General Hatch began crossing his men over the Tallahatchie on the flatboat ferry at 2 a.m., and four hours later all were across, including the 7th Indiana Cavalry, which had been demonstrating the day before down at Toba Tubby Ferry. Hatch put the infantry of McMillen's 1st Brigade of Mower's division in a column two companies wide, then deployed the dismounted 7th Indiana on their right and two other dismounted cavalry regiments on their left, with the 3rd Iowa still mounted behind one of those. As soon as the Union force came within range of the Southerners on their ridge two miles south of the river, their four pieces of artillery opened fire. The Federals responded as best they could with their two rifled 6-pounders, and although they were losing the artillery duel General Chalmers, who was now personally in command of the Confederate defense, could see that the Northerners overlapped both of his flanks. At about 11 a.m. the Rebels withdrew, screened by a strong rear guard.

Leaving the infantry to hold the bridgehead south of the Tallahatchie, Hatch pursued with Noble's brigade of cavalry, but the Confederates managed to set fire to the railroad bridges and trestles and retire across Hurricane Creek. Despite the fire of the four Rebel guns, Noble dismounted the 3rd Iowa and the 10th Missouri, and they went forward with a cheer. When the Southerners found that they could not stop this advance, they mounted up and rode off in disorder. Noble had the 7th Indiana still mounted and was about to send it forward to complete the rout and perhaps capture those bothersome guns, but just then Colonel Winslow, commander of Grierson's 2nd Division, to which the 7th Indiana belonged, rode up, and he countermanded the order to charge.

Chalmers fell back to Oxford, where he reformed his command. Hatch brought up another cavalry brigade, Herrick's, and continued the pursuit. When the Federals approached Oxford they were again met with fire from those four guns. Several little Union mountain howitzers were unlimbered and they began to bombard the town while Coon's 2nd Brigade of Winslow's 2nd Division was dismounted and massed in support. Calculating that this would absorb the Rebels' attention, Hatch sent two of Herrick's regiments to circle around to the west of the town for a flank attack. Chalmers detected this move and withdrew his men from Oxford, leaving one gun and a small rear guard to cover the retreat. When he saw this, Hatch sent Coon's dismounted troopers forward, but the Confederates got away, although the Federals did capture three caissons, quite a bit of camp equipment and, of course, the town.

Chalmers dropped off his 2nd Missouri Cavalry two miles south of Oxford to keep an eye on the Yankees and retreated with the rest of his command to Taylor's Station, nine miles down the railroad, where he camped for the night. When word of the day's events reached Forrest, he was convinced that the Union advance would follow the Mississippi Central Railroad south, and he ordered Neely's 1st Brigade and another battery to march to reinforce Chalmers.

Colonel Bouton's brigade of U.S. Colored Troops escorted the Union train of supply wagons forward that day from Holly Springs to Waterford, and General Mower, on orders from A. J. Smith, established his headquarters at Abbeville, a little south of the Tallahatchie. He inspected and approved Hatch's dispositions of his infantry in the bridgehead, but was disappointed to learn that efforts to restore service on the railroad south of Waterford were not going well. Recent heavy rains had washed out several bridges and had caused landslides which had blocked the tracks. Also, Southern partisans had attacked various Union detachments guarding the railroad between Grand Junction and Holly Springs. Patrols from the 72nd Ohio captured 29 Rebel raiders who tried to burn a bridge that day. Another group of guerrillas attacked a Federal outpost near Holly Springs that night and killed one Union trooper.

With his own three brigades tied up guarding the bridgehead south of the Tallahatchie and the railroad between Waterford and the river, Mower asked for reinforcements. A. J. Smith ordered Colonel William T. Shaw, the new commander of the 3rd Division of the 16th Corps, to send one of his brigades forward, and the next day, the tenth, Colonel Edward Wolfe's 3rd Brigade marched from Holly Springs to Waterford.

Chalmers learned, on the morning of the tenth, that the recent rains had swollen the Yacona River just south of his position at Taylor's Station. He did not think it prudent to leave his force between the aggressive Hatch and this swollen stream, with his line of retreat consisting of two narrow bridges. So, leaving only the 2nd Missouri on the north bank to keep an eye on the Federals, he took his men across and put them in position to defend the two bridges. That night he was reinforced by the weary troopers of Mabry's Brigade, who had marched up from Grenada.

Hatch, however, decided that he had accomplished his mission of pushing the Rebels beyond Oxford and led his men north to Abbeville that day. There was very little destruction or plundering at Oxford, with one notable exception. Hatch had made his headquarters at the home of former U.S. Secretary of the Interior Jacob Thompson, who was then the top Confederate commissioner in Canada. In the eyes of many Federals, Thompson was a traitor, and they felt free to help themselves to his property. When Mrs. Thompson appealed to Hatch for protection, the general told her "that his men could take anything they might wish, except the chair on which he was then seated."[9] However, Hatch himself seems to have garnered the lion's share, for when the Union cavalry departed at dusk his headquarters wagon was loaded with paintings, china, and glassware.

At about the same time as the Federals were going into camp at Abbeville that night, General Forrest rode into Oxford with Neely's Brigade of Chalmer's Division, Bell's Brigade of Buford's Division, and a battery of artillery, the last two of which he had brought over from Pontotoc by forced march. Buford, with his other brigade and another battery, had been left behind to protect the Black Prairie region, just in case A. J. Smith made another of his unexpected changes of direction. As soon as Forrest arrived at Oxford, he sent a staff officer south to order Chalmers to join him there with his command.

Over in Georgia on that tenth day of August, Sherman telegraphed Grant: "Since July 28 Hood has not attempted to meet us outside his parapets. In order to possess and destroy effectually his communications, I may have to leave a corps at the railroad-bridge, well intrenched, and cut loose with the balance to make a circle of desolation around Atlanta. I do not propose to assault the works, which are too strong, nor to proceed by regular approaches. I have lost a good many regiments, and will lose more, by the expiration of service; and this is the only reason why I want reenforcements. We have killed, crippled, and captured more of the enemy than we have lost by his acts."[10]

Sherman received two 30-pounder rifles, larger than any of his field guns, that day. "For a couple of days we kept up a sharp fire from all our batteries converging on Atlanta," Sherman wrote in his memoirs, "and at every available point we advanced our infantry-lines, thereby shortening and strengthening the investment; but I was not willing to order a direct assault, unless some accident or positive neglect on the part of our antagonist should reveal an opening. However, it was manifest that no such opening was intended by Hood, who felt secure behind his strong defenses. He had repelled our cavalry attacks on his railroad, and had damaged us seriously thereby, so I expected that he would attempt the same game against our rear."[11]

And he was right. Hood decided that the recent decimation of Sherman's cavalry presented him with a chance to detach his own horsemen to raid Sherman's much longer, and therefore supposedly more vulnerable, supply line. It did not look like Forrest was ever going to be available to do the job. So Joe Wheeler departed that day with all eight brigades of his Cavalry Corps, leaving Red Jackson's large division to perform scouting and screening duties for the army. Wheeler was to cut the Western & Atlantic Railroad between Atlanta and Chattanooga and then cross into Tennessee and raid the lines running from Nashville to Chattanooga. He was then to leave 1,200 men for further operations in Tennessee and return to Georgia with the rest.

Sheridan's Army of the Shenandoah began its advance toward Winchester that day. As the Federals marched through Charlestown, where John Brown had been hanged in 1859 after his unsuccessful attempt to capture the arsenal at Harper's Ferry and start a slave revolt, their bands played "John Brown's Body Lies A-mouldering in the Grave, But His Soul Goes Marching On," which Julia Ward Howe had already rewritten into the Battle Hymn of the Republic. "The men joined in singing the hymn," noted Captain Elisha Hunt Rhodes, "much to the disgust of the people."[12]

But Early detected the Union move and marched south to take up a position covering Winchester. That same day he got a new chief of cavalry for his Army of the Valley. Robert Ransom had not been well for some time and he was now replaced by Brigadier General Lunsford Lomax, sent over from Fitzhugh Lee's division, now operating under Anderson around Culpeper Court House.

By the next day, the eleventh, Lee was aware that Sheridan was in command of Federal forces in the Valley and that much of his cavalry had been sent there. So he ordered Wade Hampton to take his cavalry division to Culpeper, where he would report to Anderson. "The object," he said, "is to threaten the enemy's flank and rear should he move across the Blue Ridge into the Valley, and to retain his forces about Washington for its protection. It is desirable that the presence of the troops in that region be felt, and should the enemy move up the Potomac, leaving his capital uncovered, that the cavalry cross the Potomac if practicable east of the Blue Ridge. Should the enemy's cavalry be concentrated in the Valley, ours must meet it, if it cannot cause its withdrawal by other operations."[13]

The same day, the eleventh, Grant recommended some promotions. "I think it but a just reward for services already rendered," he told Halleck, "that General Sherman be now appointed a major-general, W. S. Hancock and Sheridan brigadiers in the Regular Army. There are three vacancies for major-generals and one for brigadier-general and Sherman's promotion would make the second. All these officers have proven their worthiness for this advancement. I would also recommend the promotion of Brigadier-General Mower to fill the vacant volunteer major-generalship that would thus be created."[14] So, in a sense, Mower did get Sherman's "place," as Sherman had promised.

Sherman himself was writing to a friend that day, a prominent Kentucky Democrat who had protested the turn that the war had taken toward the devastation of private property. Sherman said that the Confederates had started it, "and did they not begin to burn the houses of Union men in Kentucky and carry off the slaves of Union men in Kentucky, when I, poor innocent, would not let a soldier take a green apple, or a fence rail to make a cup of coffee? Why! we have not yet caught up with our friends of the South in this respect for private rights." Sherman is best known today as the man who carried the war to the civilians of the South with a will, in his famous march to the sea, but he was at heart very fond of the South and Southerners. It was secession that he hated. "I pledge my honor," he told his friend, "when the South ceases its strife, sends its members to Congress and appeals to the courts for its remedy and not to 'horrid war,' I will be the open advocate of mercy and a restoration to home, and peace, and happiness of all who have lost them by my acts."[15]

The CSS *Tallahassee* had been following the gulf stream north since escaping the Union blockaders. Captain Wood had hailed several ships flying British flags and had boarded some, but their papers had appeared authentic. On the morning of the eleventh, however, the Confederate raider came across a coastal merchant vessel, the *Sarah A. Boyce*, off Long Branch, New Jersey. Wood's normal procedure was to show a United States flag until his victim was within close range, but the master of this ship seemed to sense that something was wrong and tried to flee. An hour's chase and a musket shot finally brought him to a stop.

A second ship was taken off Long Island, the pilot boat *James Funk*. Mistaking the Rebel for a Yankee ship making for New York, the master sent a pilot over in a small boat. As he stepped on board the Confederate flag was run up and he was informed that his ship was a prize. Most captures were scuttled or burned, after their crews were removed, but Wood kept the *James Funk* as a tender, putting two officers and twenty men aboard, and she was used to lure Northern ships to the *Tallahassee*.

When the pilot boat brought the schooner *Carroll* to him late that afternoon, Wood allowed her captain to bond her for $10,000 so he could take the forty prisoners captured so far into New York. Many of the Northern seamen were happy to sign paroles, for they were thus protected from the draft. Seven prizes were taken that day, the final one being another pilot boat, the *William Bell,* which tried to get away. But the chase was soon ended by three shots from the raider's bow gun, and after the crew was taken off the ship was burned, including her mahogany berths, rosewood paneling, and expensive carpets.

Wood tried to get one of the captured pilots to lead him through the East River, where there were bound to be many rich merchant ships, and out Hell Gate into Long Island Sound. But none of them could be bribed or coerced into doing it. Meanwhile, the *Carroll* and the prisoners taken into New York raised the alarm. "Pirate off Sandy Hook capturing and burning," the commandant of the Brooklyn Navy Yard telegraphed to Washington.[16]

Down in Mississippi on the eleventh, A. J. Smith received a telegram from Washburn at Memphis informing him that, according to questionable sources, Forrest, who evidently was not dead after all, and Lieutenant General Richard Taylor were moving toward La Grange and Smith's supply line with 20,000 men. Smith was a cautious man, and he decided to hold a large strategic reserve at Holly Springs until the report could be checked out. He therefore recalled Murray's 3rd Brigade of Shaw's 3rd Division, which had left for Abbeville a short time before. Two of Murray's regiments were put on a train and rushed to La Grange. And at Smith's direction, Grierson ordered Winslow to collect Noble's cavalry brigade and to return to Holly Springs. In the meantime Winslow's other brigade, Kargé's 1st, scouted the area east of the railroad to see if there was any truth to the rumored Confederate advance, but they found no evidence of it.

When Chalmers joined him at Oxford that morning, Forrest moved the four brigades and two batteries forward to Hurricane Creek, about halfway between Oxford and Abbeville. There he had a good position on a pine-covered ridge overlooking the stream that wandered through a narrow bottom, and outposts were established near the Union defenses at Abbeville.

Up in the Shenandoah Valley of Virginia on the morning of 11 August, Sheridan's Federals were advancing toward the fords of Opequon Creek on their way to Winchester. Early, however, was also on the move, heading south up the Valley toward Strasburg. When Torbert's cavalry detected this move, Sheridan ordered the horsemen to harass the Rebels' march while the Union infantry continued marching south on the right bank of the Opequon. Some of the Federal troopers drove Imboden's and Vaughn's Confederate cavalry toward Newtown, but Gordon's infantry then fought them off. General Weber, commanding the garrison at Harper's Ferry, sent Sheridan a message at noon saying he had information, "from a source always found reliable, that re-enforcements under Hill and Longstreet are within five day's march of Early's present position, moving up the Valley; that, if attacked, Early proposes to show fight and retire until a junction can be formed with the advancing forces. Mosby is already between Harper's Ferry and your command, and last night captured and paroled the *Tribune* correspondent, as he reports."[17]

The next day, the twelfth, Early's march continued. He crossed Cedar Creek and took position on Hupp's Hill on the southern bank. But that evening most of the Confederates were pulled back to a stronger position on Fisher's Hill, two miles south of Strasburg, with their right covered by the north fork of the Shenandoah River and Massanutten Mountain, and their left, by Little North Mountain. Sheridan followed, taking position on the north bank of Cedar Creek. From there he sent a report to Halleck, in which he complained that the rest of the 19th Corps should have been sent to him instead of being held in the defenses of Washington. He had planned for it to escort a train of supply wagons coming to him. "General Duffié has not yet joined me," he added, "nor has General Averell or General Wilson. Generals Wilson and Duffié should have been here by this time, particularly the latter." He added that he had received two reports that Anderson's corps (still known as Longstreet's for its original commander, who was wounded in the Wilderness) was in the Valley and heading his way. "I am exceedingly anxious to hear whether Longstreet has left to come here or not."[18]

That same day, Grant was wiring Halleck: "Inform Sheridan that it is now certain two divisions of infantry have gone to Early and some cavalry and twenty pieces of artillery. This movement commenced last Saturday night. He must be cautious and act now on the defensive until movements here force them to detach to send this way. Early's force, with this increase, cannot exceed 40,000, but this is too much for Sheridan to attack. Send Sheridan the remaining brigade of the Nineteenth Corps. I have ordered to Washington all the 100 days' men. Their time will soon be out, but for the present they will do to stand in the defenses."[19]

Down in Georgia on the twelfth, Sherman was cheered by news of Farragut's victory at Mobile Bay seven days earlier. He also learned that he had been commissioned a major general in the regular army, "which was unexpected, and not desired until successful in the capture of Atlanta." He added that this news "did not change the fact that we were held in check by the stubborn defense of the place, and a conviction was forced on my mind that our enemy would hold fast, even though every house in the town should be battered down by our artillery."[20]

The CSS *Tallahassee* continued to capture Union shipping off Long Island on the twelfth, taking six more prizes. One of these was a large packet ship, the *Adriatic,* carrying 170 passengers, mostly German immigrants. Captain Wood thought at first that he would have to bond the ship rather than destroy it, because he did not want to be burdened with so many prisoners, but just then the captured *James Funk* showed up with a prize of her own, the *Suliote.* Wood bonded the latter and sent her with his prisoners on to New York. Then the *Adriatic* was burned and the *Tallahassee,* with the *James Funk* in tow, headed up the coast toward Boston. Wood felt that the waters around New York had been "sufficiently worked, and the game was alarmed and scarce."[21] At 5 p.m. that day word of the Southern raider finally reached Secretary of the Navy Gideon Welles, who immediately ordered all available vessels to pursue her, although with little idea of just where she might be.

That same day, Thurlow Weed, long-time Whig and Republican bigwig in New York State, told Abraham Lincoln that his reelection was an impossibility.

---

1. Catton, *Grant Takes Command,* 350.
2. Porter, *Campaigning With Grant,* 274.
3. Tidwell, Hall and Gaddy, *Come Retribution,* 163.
4. Porter, *Campaigning With Grant,* 275.
5. *Official Records,* 43:I:737.
6. McDonough and Jones, *War So Terrible,* 275.
7. Ibid., 275–276.
8. Foote, *The Civil War,* 3:506.
9. Bearss, *Forrest at Brice's Cross Roads,* 268.
10. Sherman, *Memoirs,* 2:102.
11. Ibid.
12. Robert Hunt Rhodes, ed., *All For the Union: the Civil War Diary and Letters of Elisha Hunt Rhodes* (New York, 1985), 178.
13. Dowdey and Manarin, eds., *Wartime Papers of R. E. Lee,* 832–833.
14. *Official Records,* 43:I:767.
15. Lewis, *Sherman: Fighting Prophet,* 398.
16. Foote, *The Civil War,* 3:509.

17. *Official Records*, 43:I:772.

18. Ibid., 43:I:18–19.

19. Ibid., 43:I:775.

20. Sherman, *Memoirs*, 2:102–103.

21. Shingleton, "Cruise of the CSS Tallahassee," 34.

CHAPTER TWENTY-SEVEN

As Simple As a Schoolboy's Fight

13–15 August 1864

At 7:30 on the morning of 13 August, Phil Sheridan wired Grant that he "was unable to get south of Early, but will push him up the Valley. Reports from citizens here, Washington, and Harper's Ferry report Longstreet's corps coming this way from Staunton, but I still rely on your telegram that it is not so. There is nothing in the Valley but wheat and a few fine mules. The sum total of all Early's transportation is 250 wagons. He has not sent off or accumulated any supplies. He was simply living off the country."[1]

Early did receive reinforcements that day. What was left of McCausland's two brigades of cavalry returned from their circuit through Maryland, Pennsylvania, and West Virginia. But of far more importance was the arrival of Anderson with Kershaw's Division of infantry, Fitz Lee's division of cavalry, and Cutshaw's battalion of artillery, all of which came by way of Chester Gap to guard the Luray Valley, between Massanutten Mountain and the Blue Ridge.

At 10 that night Sheridan wired Grant again to let him know that the latter's warning about Anderson's corps going to the Valley had been received. "I was making preparations to attack them when your dispatch arrived. It did not appear as though they would make a stand, and looked more like an invitation for me to follow them up. I did not think it best to do so, and have taken position on the south side of Cedar Creek. All the reports that I hear, and have been hearing for some days, confirm your telegram that Longstreet is in the Valley, and that Fitz Lee's cavalry is making its way up the country and when last heard from was at Orange Court House." Then he took up Grant's instruction to go on the defensive. "So far as I have been able to see, there is not a military position in this Valley south of the Potomac. The position here is a very bad one, as I cannot cover the numerous roads that lead in on both of my flanks to the rear. I am not aware that you knew where my command was when you ordered me to take up the defensive. I should very much like to have your advice." In closing he noted that "Mosby attacked the rear of my train this morning, en route here from Harper's Ferry, and burned six wagons."[2]

Halleck sent word to Sheridan that same day that Wilson's cavalry division from the Army of the Potomac had finally begun its march from Washington to the Valley the night before, and that the 2nd Division of the 19th Corps would start out that day.

Down in Georgia, Sherman was getting impatient. He ate little and smoked constantly. Unlike many officers of both sides, he led a Spartan existence in the field. One of his officers recalled, "He ate hardtack, sweet potatoes, bacon, black coffee on a rough table, sitting on a cracker box, wearing a gray flannel shirt, a faded old blue blouse, and trousers he had worn since long before Chattanooga."

By now Sherman had decided that his artillery could not blast the Confederates out of Atlanta, and yet the defenses were too strong to assault. "It was evident that we must decoy him out to fight us on something like equal terms," he later wrote, "or else, with the whole army, raise the siege and attack his communications. Accordingly, on the 13th of August, I gave general orders for the Twentieth Corps to draw back to the railroad-bridge at the Chattahoochee, to protect our trains, hospitals, spare artillery, and the railroad-depot, while the rest of the army should move bodily to some point on the Macon Railroad below East Point." But before this move could get underway he changed his mind. "Luckily, I learned just then that the enemy's cavalry, under General Wheeler, had made a wide circuit around our left flank, and had actually reached our railroad at Tilton Station, above Resaca."[4] Sherman felt that this development might provide him with a better move. His men did not know what his plan was, but they had supreme confidence

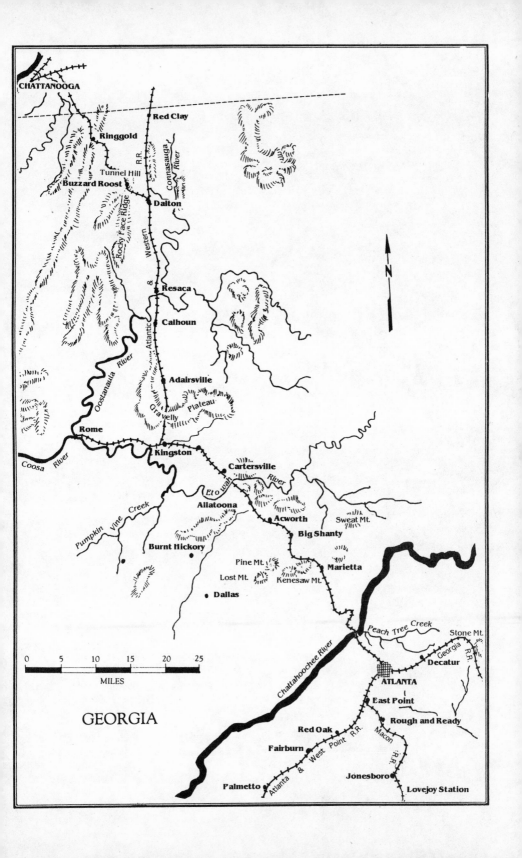

CHATTANOOGA

Red Clay

Ringgold

Tunnel Hill

Buzzard Roost

Dalton

Connasauga River

R.R.

Western

Rocky Face Ridge

Resaca

Calhoun

&

Atlantic

Oostanaula River

Adairsville

Gravelly Plateau

Rome

Coosa River

Kingston

Cartersville

Etowah River

Allatoona

Pumpkin Vine Creek

Acworth

Big Shanty

Sweat Mt.

Burnt Hickory

Pine Mt.

Lost Mt.

Kenesaw Mt.

Marietta

Dallas

Peach Tree Creek

Stone Mt.

Chattahoochee River

Decatur

Georgia R.R.

ATLANTA

East Point

Rough and Ready

Red Oak

Macon R.R.

Fairburn

West Point R.R.

Jonesboro

Atlanta & West Point R.R.

Palmetto

Lovejoy Station

N

0   5   10   15   20   25

MILES

GEORGIA

in him. "It will take a smarter man than General Hood," they said, to hold Atlanta against "Old Tecumseh."[5]

Over in Mississippi that day, General Mower decided that it would be dangerous to allow Forrest to remain in his new Hurricane Creek position and continue to strengthen its defenses. So at about noon on Saturday, 13 August, Hatch's cavalry division, reinforced with five regiments of infantry and a battery of artillery, marched out of Abbeville, easily pushing aside a number of small Rebel patrols. A few miles north of Hurricane Creek, Hatch stopped and deployed his division while giving his assignments to his subordinates. Colonel Starr was sent with his 6th and 9th Illinois Cavalry regiments to ford Hurricane Creek two miles west of where it was crossed by the road, and turn the Confederate left. Starr's other regiment, the 2nd Iowa, would continue down the road to screen the advance of the infantry, and Herrick's brigade was sent two miles in the other direction, to ford the creek and attack the Rebel right.

A mile north of the creek the Federals encountered strong dismounted Confederate detachments, and it took three hours for Starr to force Mabry's Brigade, reinforced by the 18th Mississippi Cavalry Battalion, to fall back across the stream, where the Rebels took shelter in rifle pits which had been dug earlier. Herrick's brigade encountered less opposition and thus reached the creek sooner, but was stopped by the fire of one of the three Southern batteries. At the same time, a thunderstorm roared over, almost drowning out the sound of the guns.

The leading elements of the 2nd Iowa, preceding the infantry, were momentarily disrupted by an ambush, but the regiment's commander sent the rest of his men forward dismounted and drove the Rebels across the creek. There Forrest's other two batteries opened fire on the Iowans and drove them to cover. Mower then brought up his infantry and artillery, the four Union guns dueling with the eight Confederate pieces while the foot soldiers deployed for an attack. However, the two Illinois cavalry regiments under Colonel Wolfe struck first, crossing the creek, and driving Mabry's men out of their rifle pits. In the meantime a sergeant and four men of the 7th Kansas Cavalry in Herrick's brigade discovered a gap between the Confederate right and center. The five Federals dismounted, crossed the creek, and came up on the left rear of McCulloch's Brigade, holding the Rebel right. When they opened fire, McCulloch thought he was outflanked and also fell back.

With both of his flanks collapsing, Forrest had no choice but to order up the horse-holders, mount his men, and fall back. When Mower saw the Rebels preparing to pull out, he ordered three of his infantry regiments to charge, but by the time they had crossed the rain-swollen creek the Confederates were mounted and retreating. The Union infantry followed the Rebels about half a mile, but darkness soon put an end to their pursuit. Then, satisfied with having broken up the Hurricane Creek defensive position, Mower put his men back on the road north, and they were back in their camps by 11 p.m. Forrest, meanwhile, stopped a short distance down the road and established a new line of defense on the Isham plantation, four miles north of Oxford.

In southern Virginia the fighting around Petersburg and Richmond flared up again that day. Grant wanted to do something to draw Confederate attention, and troops, away from the Shenandoah Valley. Since Anderson's 1st Corps seemed to be gone, it was logical to assume that Rebel defenses north of the James must have been weakened. So on the night of 13–14 August the troops of the Union 10th Corps in Butler's bridgehead at Deep Bottom were reinforced by the rest of that corps, now commanded by Major General David B. Birney, formerly a division commander in the 2nd Corps. Also sent across the bridge was Gregg's division, which was all that was left of the Cavalry Corps of the Army of the Potomac, and the artillery of Hancock's 2nd Corps. Hancock's infantry units boarded transports at City Point in the hope of making the Confederates believe that they were being sent to join Sheridan, but in fact they were ferried over to the north bank of the James. Difficulties in unloading these troops until after 9 a.m. delayed an attack scheduled for dawn.

The plan was that the 10th Corps would break through the Rebel defenses opposite Deep Bottom and advance toward Chafin's Bluff. Mott's 3rd Division of the 2nd Corps would advance up the New Market Road on Birney's right, while Barlow, with the other two divisions of the 2nd Corps, would advance on Mott's right to attack Southern defenses near Fussell's Mill. Gregg's cavalry, on the extreme Union right, was to make a dash for Richmond once the infantry had broken through the Confederate defenses. Hancock was in overall command. The objective of the whole operation was to turn the Confederates out of their formidable defenses at Chafin's Bluff.

The Rebels were in greater strength north of the James than the Federals expected, however. Mott's division soon ran into Field's Division of the 1st Corps entrenched along Deep Run, supported by Wilcox's Division of the 3rd Corps. Barlow's attack near Fussell's Mill was late and not very effective, but it did draw Rebel forces away from Birney's front, and he was able to make some progress. Furthermore, Gregg managed to break through and advance far up the Charles City Road toward Richmond. Before the day was over the Confederates were reinforced by

Mahone's Division of the 3rd Corps, and Rooney Lee's and Hampton's cavalry divisions, the latter having to be recalled by Lee before it had gone very far toward northern Virginia. That afternoon, what Lee called a "sweet rain" fell. "More water has fallen than at any point I have been since I left Orange," he wrote to his wife. "I trust it will revive vegetation."[5]

That night Grant wired Sheridan: "I moved Hancock's corps, Gregg's division of cavalry, and part of the Tenth Corps to the north side of the James last night to surprise the enemy and prevent him from sending troops away. We captured six pieces of artillery and prisoners from four different brigades of Field's division, Longstreet's corps. This is a division I supposed had gone to the Valley. It is now positive that Kershaw's division had gone, but no other infantry has. This re-enforcement to Early will put him nearer on an equality with you in numbers than I want to see, and will make it necessary for you to observe some caution about attacking. I would not, however, change my instructions, further than to enjoin caution."[6]

Down in Mississippi on the fourteenth, Colonel Winslow, commander of the 2nd Division of Grierson's cavalry corps, in accordance with instructions from A. J. Smith, sent out more reconnaissance patrols from Holly Springs to search for the phantom Confederate column supposedly heading for La Grange. That same day, General Buford met with the colonels of the 3rd and 7th Tennessee Cavalry regiments, which had been left behind at Pontotoc when Neely's Brigade had gone to reinforce Chalmers. Buford instructed the two regiments to raid A. J. Smith's supply line by cutting the Mississippi Central Railroad between Holly Springs and Grand Junction, and the Memphis & Charleston between Grand Junction and Memphis.

The two regiments rode north as far as New Albany, where Colonel Duckworth of the 7th Tennessee decided to call a halt, but Colonel Kelley of the 3rd, known as the Fighting Preacher, pressed on. At Salem, farther north, the Rebels were able to pick up some sledgehammers and crowbars for use against the railroad tracks and learned that the Union garrison had been withdrawn from Lamar, a nearby town on the Mississippi Central. The Confederates reached Lamar shortly after dark, but only slightly ahead of a 33-man patrol of the 7th Indiana Cavalry under a young lieutenant.

As the Federals rode into town the lieutenant spotted a dozen men in shirtsleeves hanging around the depot with four wagons. Figuring that they were guerrillas, he sent four of his men to cut off their retreat, and to cover this move he had one of his men fire a shot. Some of the Rebels panicked, and Colonel Kelley galloped forward to restore order. Seeing some men on the horizon, he shouted for them to rally to him, but these turned out to be the Union patrol. When a cloud suddenly moved out of the way of the moonlight, Kelly saw his mistake and ordered his men to charge. On the other hand, the Federals, now seeing that they were outnumbered, managed to get away in the confusion and the dark. Kelley put his men back to work at tearing up the railroad tracks, until he learned from friendly civilians that Winslow's whole division was stationed only 10 miles away at Holly Springs. Then he called a council of war. The Confederate officers did not think they could do very much damage to the railroad and voted to return to their base. Before daylight they were back on the road to New Albany.

A secret movement was afoot among Republicans that summer to dump Lincoln as their nominee for president in order to avoid what seemed to be certain defeat in November. One of many conferences among Republicans took place that fourteenth day of August in New York. Among the two dozen or so leaders present were Henry Winter Davis, of the Wade-Davis Manifesto, and Horace Greeley of the *New York Tribune*. Those assembled agreed that a committee should ask Lincoln to withdraw his candidacy. The majority of them hoped to replace him with Grant, and they prepared a call for a new convention to be held in Cincinnati on 28 September. "Mr. Lincoln is already beaten," Greeley wrote to a prominent Republican who had not been present. "We must have another ticket to save us from utter overthrow. If we had such a ticket as could be had by naming Grant, Butler, or Sherman for President, and Farragut as Vice, we could make a fight yet."[7]

Lincoln, meanwhile, had other problems on his mind, such as the recent fate of Chambersburg, Pennsylvania. He telegraphed Grant that day: "The Secretary of War and I concur that you better confer with Gen. Lee and stipulate for a mutual discontinuance of house-burning and other destruction of private property. The time and manner of conference, and particulars of stipulation we leave, on our part, to your convenience and judgment."[8]

The best response could have been found in a letter that Sherman was writing to a civilian friend that day: "War is the remedy our enemies have chosen . . . and I say let us give them all they want; not a word of argument, not a sign of let-up, no cave in till we are whipped or they are . . . The only principle in this war is, which party can whip. It is as simple as a schoolboy's fight and when one or the other party gives in, we will be the better friends."[9]

Wheeler, with some of his Confederate cavalry, attacked Sherman's railroad lifeline north of Resaca on the fourteenth, after capturing a herd of 1,000 cattle intended as fresh beef for Federal soldiers. Then the Rebel raiders demanded the surrender of the Union garrison at Dalton. But General John E. Smith, commander of the 3rd Division of the 15th Corps, which had been guarding the railroad throughout the campaign, scraped up a couple of thousand men from around Kingston, loaded them onto railroad cars, and got to Dalton in time to scare Wheeler off. On the fifteenth the Confederates continued northward toward Cleveland, Tennessee, and Knoxville, which took them away from Sherman's supply line.

Lieutenant General Richard Taylor was assigned command of the Confederate Department of East Louisiana, Mississippi, and Alabama on 15 August. He was the son of Zachary Taylor, twelfth president of the United States, and brother-in-law to Jefferson Davis. Without prior military service, he had been commissioned colonel of the 9th Louisiana at the beginning of the war and, promoted to brigadier general, had commanded a brigade in Ewell's Division in Stonewall Jackson's Shenandoah Valley campaign of 1862 and Lee's Seven Days battles around Richmond. He had then been promoted again and sent back to his home state to command the District of Western Louisiana in Kirby Smith's Trans-Mississippi Department. For his victory at Sabine Cross Roads, which put an end to Banks' Federal advance up the Red River in April, he had been promoted to lieutenant general. But he had quarrelled with Kirby Smith over the latter's overall conduct of that campaign and had asked to be relieved. So he would be brought east of the Mississippi to replace S. D. Lee. Once Taylor arrived to take over, Maury, who had temporarily commanded the department after Lee had been sent to command a corps under Hood, would resume his previous position as commander of the defenses of what little of the Gulf coast east of the Mississippi was still held by the Confederacy.

Up in the Shenandoah Valley on the fifteenth, Torbert's division of Union cavalry, now under its senior brigadier, Wesley Merritt, was sent to Front Royal to protect the left flank of Sheridan's army from any move by Anderson's Confederates. There was sharp skirmishing that afternoon by the infantry pickets of both sides as the 6th Corps was withdrawn to the north side of Cedar Creek, "where it would be in a position enabling me either to confront Anderson or to act defensively as desired by General Grant," Sheridan wrote. "To meet the requirements of his instructions I examined the map of the valley for a defensive line—a position where a smaller number of troops could hold a larger number—for . . . information led me to suppose that Early's force would greatly exceed mine when Anderson's two divisions of infantry and Fitzhugh Lee's cavalry had joined him. I could see but one such position, and that was at Halltown, in front of Harper's Ferry. Subsequent experience convinced me that there was no other really defensive line in the Shenandoah Valley, for at almost any other point the open country and its peculiar topography invites rather than forbids flanking operations."

He considered, also, that retiring down the Valley would allow him to meet Grover's 2nd Division of the 19th Corps and Wilson's division of cavalry that much sooner. Both were marching from Washington via Snicker's Gap. "After fully considering the matter, I determined to move back to Halltown," Sheridan wrote, "carrying out, as I retired, my instructions to destroy all the forage and subsistence the country afforded."[9] That night the 1st Division of the 19th Corps was put on the road to Winchester, as the start of a general withdrawal that Sheridan did not want Early to know about.

The CSS *Tallahassee* was off New England by then. She had taken two more prizes on the thirteenth, one on the fourteenth, and took six that day, the fifteenth. The only serious opposition Captain Wood had run into was from the wife of a retired sea captain who had been on one of the ships he had captured. He said that she was a real shrew who "came on board scolding and left scolding," adding that "when she left to take passage in a Russian bark, she called down on us all the imprecations that David showered on his enemies. And as a final effort to show how she would serve us, she snatched her bonnet from her head, tore it to pieces, and threw it into the sea."[10]

---

1. *Official Records*, 43:1:783.
2. Ibid.
3. McDonough and Jones, *War So Terrible*, 279.
4. Sherman, *Memoirs*, 2:103.
5. Dowdey and Manarin, eds., *Wartime Papers of R. E. Lee*, 837.
6. *Official Records*, 43:1:791–792.
7. Sandburg, *Abraham Lincoln*, 576.
8. Basler, ed., *The Collected Works of Abraham Lincoln*, 7:493.
9. Sheridan, *Memoirs*, 1:483–484.
10. Shingleton, "Cruise of the CSS Tallahassee," 34–35.

CHAPTER TWENTY-EIGHT

Hold on with a Bulldog Grip

15–17 August 1864

"Right in the midst of all these embarrassments," Grant wrote—an interesting and revealing turn of phrase—"Halleck informed me that there was an organized scheme on foot in the North to resist the draft, and suggested that it might become necessary to draw troops from the field to put it down." There had been extremely bloody draft riots in New York City the summer before, and veteran troops from the Army of the Potomac had to be sent to put them down. "He also advised taking in sail, and not going too fast."[1] Grant replied on the fifteenth: "If there is any danger of an uprising in the North to resist the draft or for any other purpose our loyal Governor's ought to organize the militia at once to resist it. If we are to draw troops from the field to keep the loyal States in harness it will prove difficult to suppress the rebellion in the disloyal States. My withdrawal now from the James River would insure the defeat of Sherman. Twenty thousand men sent to him at this time would destroy the greater part of Hood's army, and leave us men wherever required. General Heintzelman can get from the Governors of Ohio, Indiana, and Illinois a militia organization that will deter the discontented from committing any overt act. I hope the President will call on Governors of States to organize thoroughly to preserve the peace until after the election."[2] (Heintzelman, a former corps commander under McClellan, was the commander of the Northern Department, consisting of the states named by Grant, plus Michigan.)

The next day, the sixteenth, Grant wrote to Congressman Washburne, his political sponsor: "I state to all Citizens who visit me that all we want now to insure an early restoration of the Union is a determined unity of sentiment North. The rebels have now in their ranks their last man. The little boys and old men are guarding prisoners, rail-road bridges and forming a good part of their garrisons for intrenched positions. A man lost by them cannot be replaced. They have robbed the Cradle and the grave equally to get their present force. Besides what they lose in frequent skirmishes and battles they are now losing from desertions and other causes at least one regiment per day. With this drain upon them the end is visible if we will be true to ourselves. Their only hope now is in a divided North. This might give them reinforcements from Tenn. Ky. Maryland and Mo. whilst it would weaken us. With the draft quietly enforced the enemy would become dispondent and would make but little resistance."

In what followed, Grant showed that he understood Jefferson Davis and the Southern aristocracy very well: "I have no doubt but the enemy are exceedingly anxious to hold out until after the Presidential election. They have many hopes from its effects. They hope for a counter revolution. They hope for the election of the peace Candidate. In fact, like McCawber, they hope something to turn up.

"Our peace friends, if they expect peace from separation, are much mistaken. It would be but the beginning of war with thousands of Northern men joining the South because of our disgrace allowing separation. To have peace 'on any terms' the South would demand the restoration of their slaves already freed. They would demand indemnity for losses sustained, and they would demand a treaty which would make the North slave hunters for the South. They would demand pay or the restoration of every slave escaping to the North."[3]

The Union troops north of the James had not been seriously engaged on the fifteenth. Birney had made a wide circuit in search of the Confederate left flank, but had failed to find it in time to attack before dark. Although Grant noted to Washburne that the weather was so hot that "marching troops is nearly death," on the sixteenth an attack by part of Birney's 10th Corps and one brigade of the 2nd succeeded in overrunning Field's position at Fussell's Mill and capturing 300 prisoners and three battleflags. "Not only the day but Richmond seemed gone," Field wrote.[4] But the Confederates later counterattacked and managed to restore their line by nightfall, killing the commander of the 2nd Corps brigade.

Gregg's cavalry, supported by a brigade of the 2nd Corps, again attacked up the Charles City Road and got as far as White's Tavern, only seven miles from the Confederate capital, killing Brigadier General John Chambliss, one of Rooney Lee's brigade commanders, in the process. Then Hampton's cavalry reached the battlefield and helped Rooney Lee drive Gregg's Federal troopers back behind Deep Creek. Rooney's father, R. E. Lee, was personally directing the pursuit of the Federals when he was interrupted by a Yankee prisoner, who boldly approached him to complain that a Confederate soldier had stolen his hat. Lee stopped what he was doing, had the offending Confederate pointed out, and saw that the prized hat was returned, just as though recovering stolen hats was part of the commanding general's routine duties.

That night the Union transport boats were brought up to Deep Bottom in an attempt to fool the Rebels into believing that the Federals were withdrawing, thus luring them into a costly attack, but they did not fall for the ruse.

August 16, the date set for the Copperhead uprising, passed quietly in the North except that a steamer on the Ohio was seized by a Confederate colonel Johnson at Shawneetown, Illinois. Down in Mississippi on the sixteenth, the Federals had the Mississippi Central Railroad running from Grand Junction all the way to the Tallahatchie River. So A. J. Smith ordered Colonel Shaw to concentrate his 3rd Division of the 16th Corps at Abbeville. Meanwhile, the CSS *Tallahassee* took five more prizes off New England that day, and down in Georgia a detachment of Wheeler's Rebel cavalry appeared in force about Allatoona and the bridge over the Etowah, convincing Sherman that "Hood had sent all of his cavalry to raid upon our railroads. For some days our communication with Nashville was interrupted by the destruction of the telegraph-lines, as well as railroads."[5]

Rumors began to reach Hood's army that Wheeler was playing havoc with the Union line of communications, but in truth it was so well protected with garrisons, blockhouses, and patrols, and Sherman's repair crews were so numerous, skilled, and well prepared, that little damage was actually done. The Federals even had prefabricated duplicates of many of their trestles, ready to put in place whenever the originals were destroyed. The Rebels had great respect for the Yankees' capabilities in this regard, as is illustrated by a story that made the rounds. One Confederate, it was said, when told that Wheeler had blown up the railroad tunnel through Tunnel Hill near Dalton, replied, "Oh hell! Don't you know that old Sherman carries a duplicate tunnel along with him?"[6]

"I at once ordered strong reconnoissances forward from our flanks on the left by Garrard, and on the right by Kilpatrick," Sherman later wrote. Kilpatrick had only recently returned to duty as commander of one of the three cavalry divisions of Thomas' Army of the Cumberland, after being severely wounded at Dalton back in May. As usual, Sherman was dissatisfied with Garrard's performance, saying that he "moved with so much caution that I was displeased; but Kilpatrick, on the contrary, displayed so much zeal and activity that I was attracted to him at once. He reached Fairburn Station, on the West Point road, and tore it up, returning safely to his position on our right flank. I summoned him to me, and was so pleased with his spirit and confidence, that I concluded to suspend the general movement of the main army, and to send him with his small division of cavalry to break up the Macon road about Jonesboro', in the hopes that it would force Hood to evacuate Atlanta, and that I should thereby not only secure possession of the city itself, but probably could catch Hood in the confusion of retreat; and, further to increase the chances of success, I ordered General Thomas to detach two brigades of Garrard's division of cavalry from the left to the right rear, to act as a reserve in support of General Kilpatrick. Meantime, also, the utmost activity was ordered along our whole front by the infantry and artillery."[7]

In the Shenandoah Valley on the sixteenth, Sheridan prepared to continue his retreat toward the defensive position at Halltown. As part of his preparations he sent the following order to Torbert, his chief of cavalry: "In compliance with instructions of the lieutenant-general commanding, you will make the necessary arrangements and give the necessary orders for the destruction of the wheat and hay south of a line from Millwood to Winchester and Petticoat Gap. You will seize all mules, horses, and cattle that may be useful to our army. Loyal citizens can bring in their claims against the Government for this necessary destruction. No houses will be burned, and officers in charge of this delicate, but necessary, duty must inform the people that the object is to make this Valley untenable for the raiding parties of the rebel army."[8]

"The 17th of August will be remembered," wrote the chaplain of the 1st Rhode Island Cavalry, "as sending up to the skies the first great columns of smoke and flame from doomed secession barns, stacks, cribs and mills, and the driving into loyal lines of flocks and herds. The order was carefully yet faithfully obeyed," he said, and "led to the destruction of about 2,000 barns, 70 mills, and other property, valued in all at 25 millions of dollars." He felt that the order was justified, saying, "The time had fully come to peel this land and put an end to the long strife for its possession."[9]

In his memoirs, Sheridan explained this order: "During his visit to General Hunter at the Monocacy, General Grant had not only decided to retain in the Shenandoah Valley a large force sufficient to defeat Early's army or drive it back to Lee, but he had furthermore determined to make that section, by the destruction of its supplies, untenable for continued occupancy by the Confederates. This would cut off one of Lee's mainstays in the way of subsistence, and at the same time diminish the number of recruits and conscripts he received; the valley district while under his control not only supplying Lee with an abundance of food, but also furnishing him many men for his regular and irregular forces. Grant's instructions to destroy the valley began with the letter of August 5 to Hunter, which was turned over to me, and this was followed at intervals by more specific directions, all showing the earnestness of his purpose. He had rightly concluded that it was time to bring the war home to a people engaged in raising crops from a prolific soil to feed the country's enemies, and devoting to the Confederacy its best youth. I endorsed this programme in all its parts, for the stores of meat and grain that the valley provided, and the men it furnished for Lee's depleted regiments, were the strongest auxiliaries he possessed in the whole insurgent section. In war a territory like this is a factor of great importance, and whichever adversary controls it permanently reaps all the advantages of its prosperity. Hence, as I have said, I endorsed Grant's programme, for I do not hold war to mean simply that lines of men shall engage each other in battle, and material interests be ignored. This is but a duel, in which one combatant seeks the other's life; war means much more, and is far worse than this. Those who rest at home in peace and plenty see but little of the horrors attending such a duel, and even grow indifferent to them as the struggle goes on, contenting themselves with encouraging all who are able-bodied to enlist in the cause, to fill up the shattered ranks as death thins them. It is another matter, however, when deprivation and suffering are brought to their own doors. Then the case appears much graver, for the loss of property weighs heavy with the most of mankind; heavier often, than the sacrifices made on the field of battle. Death is popularly considered the maximum of punishment in war, but it is not; reduction to poverty brings prayers for peace more surely and more quickly than does the destruction of human life, as the selfishness of man has demonstrated in more than one great conflict."[10]

At 3:30 that afternoon a staff officer came galloping up to Brigadier General George Armstrong Custer to report that a large body of Confederate cavalry was approaching Crooked Run from the direction of Front Royal. Custer was in temporary command of Devin's 2nd Brigade as well as his own 1st Brigade of what was now Merritt's division of cavalry. While his men saddled their horses, Custer borrowed an orderly's mount and rode toward the sound of battle. From the top of a high hill he soon saw a brigade or more of Rebel horsemen in column of fours preceded by a dismounted skirmish line pushing the Union pickets across the creek. Behind the cavalry came a very large force of infantry, and as Custer watched he saw a smaller force split off to the left.

Hurrying back to his own brigade, Custer brought his four Michigan regiments to a high ridge facing Crooked Run, where he positioned his battery of four guns in the center, so that it had a clear field of fire and no shortage of targets. One battalion of the 6th Michigan was sent to reinforce the picket line while the rest of the brigade was drawn up just behind the crest of the ridge, where it was protected from the fire of the eight Confederate guns which were now firing on the Union battery, and from the sight of the Rebel cavalry and infantry.

For three-quarters of an hour little happened, other than the continuing artillery duel and some sniping by pickets and skirmishers, although Custer did send the rest of the 6th Michigan to the skirmish line. Then the Confederates, stung by the fire of the Union guns and the repeating carbines of the Federal skirmishers, launched a charge. That was just what Custer had been waiting for. The 6th Michigan rapidly mounted and, along with the 4th and 6th New York regiments of Devin's brigade, countercharged. At the sight of the three mounted regiments pounding down upon them, sabers swinging, the Rebels bolted and ran for Crooked Run, leaving their dead, wounded, two battle flags, and a large number of prisoners behind.

Then, while the battle again degenerated into an artillery duel, Custer took two of his four guns downstream where a staff officer had observed the divergent column of Rebels making its covert way toward a crossing of Crooked Run. He also brought the 5th Michigan, along a route screened from the Confederates by hills, to a ravine behind the ridge where he had placed the two guns, and had the troopers dismount out of sight. The Southerners, galled by the fire of the guns, but thinking that they had no supports, quickly formed line and charged with a yell.

Watching from beside the guns, Custer gave a signal and the troopers of the 5th Michigan charged up the reverse slope and arrived at the crest of the ridge just seconds ahead of the Rebels. There the Federals poured a storm of lead into the Confederates with their Spencer repeating carbines, and as the Southerners broke and ran back down the ridge, Custer and his bugler hurried along the crest to the center of the 5th. Every Rebel still carrying a gun seemed to take aim at the young general but they all missed except one, whose bullet clipped a lock of Custer's long blond hair from his temple.

Waving his hat, the general ordered the Michiganders to advance, and they bounded forward with a cheer. The Confederates fell back, but reinforcements were hurrying to them from the ford over Crooked Run. Custer sent back for a battalion of the 1st Michigan and sent it on a mounted charge past the 5th, cutting the Rebels off from the ford and pushing them into a bend of the creek. A group of mounted Confederates tried to force their way across the ford to aid the infantry, but Custer sent the rest of the 1st Michigan and all of the 7th charging into them just as they cleared the ford, pushing them back into the water. Panic swept the ranks of the Southern infantry. Many of the Rebels threw away their rifles and leapt into the stream, and about 150 surrendered. Darkness soon put an end to the battle, except for sporadic picket firing far into the night.

That afternoon Sheridan was heading for Winchester, where he could better supervise the withdrawal of his forces. "As I was passing through Newtown," he recorded, "I heard cannonading from the direction of Front Royal, and on reaching Winchester Merritt's couriers brought me word that he had been attacked at the crossing of the Shenandoah by Kershaw's division of Anderson's corps and two brigades of Fitzhugh Lee's cavalry, but that the attack had been handsomely repulsed, with a capture of two battle-flags and three hundred prisoners. This was an absolute confirmation of the despatch from Grant, and I was now more than satisfied with the wisdom of my withdrawal."[11] That night he ordered the secret retreat of the 6th Corps and Crook's Army of West Virginia. (To avoid the confusion of an army within an army, the latter was sometimes called the 8th Corps, although technically it had been separate from that organization since the Department of West Virginia had been formed out of the Middle Department the summer before, during Lee's invasion of Pennsylvania.)

"On the morning of the 17th," Early wrote, "it was discovered that the enemy was falling back, and I immediately moved forward in pursuit, requesting General Anderson, by signal, to cross the river at Front Royal and move towards Winchester."[12] The Union infantry marched on toward Berryville that day, but Torbert was left at Winchester to cover the withdrawal and was joined there by Wilson's 3rd Division of cavalry, finally arriving from Petersburg via Washington. Wilson's division and Lowell's brigade of cavalry, reinforced with a small brigade of New Jersey infantry from the 6th Corps, formed the rear guard of the army. They held Early's cavalry at bay all afternoon, and only when the Confederate infantry arrived and attacked in force was the Union line broken. More than 350 Federals were captured, mostly from the infantry.

The CSS *Tallahassee* took three more prizes off New England that day.

At City Point on the seventeenth, Grant was telegraphing to President Lincoln: "I have thought over your dispatch relative to an arrangement between Gen. Lee and myself for the suppression of insidiaryism by the respective Armies. Experience has taught us that agreements made with rebels are binding upon us but are not observed by them longer than suits their convenience. On the whole I think the best that can be done is to publish a prohibitory order against burning private property except where it is a Military necessity or in retaliation for like acts by the enemy. When burning is done in retaliation it must be done by order of a Dept. or Army Commander and the order for such burning to set forth the particular act it is in retaliation for. Such an order would be published and would come to the knowledge of the rebel Army. I think this course would be much better than any agreement with Gen. Lee. I could publish the order or it could be published by you. This is respectfully submitted for your consideration and I will then act as you deem best."[13]

Republican leaders continued to worry about the ability of Lincoln to lead them to victory in the coming fall elections. Ben Butler, the quintessential political general, was among those being considered as a replacement for Lincoln, and his chief of staff, Colonel Shaffer, was in New York sounding out the possibilities. He wrote to Butler that day that "the country has gone to hell unless Mr. Lincoln can be beat by a good loyal man." He said that if the Democrats should nominate a peace candidate at their late August convention, the Republican leaders would want a new candidate. Lincoln, they felt, was too warlike for the peace-minded and too forgiving for the warlike. Colonel Shaffer said that Thurlow Weed, Republican boss of New York state, "thinks Lincoln can be prevailed upon to draw off." The leading Republicans agreed, he said, that Lincoln should withdraw as soon as the Democrats made their choice. "Nearly all speak of you as the man," he told Butler, "but I studiously avoid bringing your name in."[14]

The actor John Wilkes Booth was in Baltimore around the middle of August, where he had a room at Barnum's Hotel. While there, he met with two boyhood friends. Both were former members of the 1st Maryland infantry battalion in Lee's army. Over brandy and cigars the three discussed old times, and then Booth got down to business. The Confederacy was running out of men and Grant refused to exchange prisoners. But if they could capture Lincoln, he could be traded for any number of privates or officers. During the summer months Lincoln lived at the Soldier's Home on the outskirts of Washington, to avoid the heat and humidity near the Potomac. Booth pointed out that the president often traveled unguarded, so his capture should prove easy. His two friends, Michael O'Laughlen and Samuel B. Arnold, agreed to the plan.

Also around the middle of August a guard, John W. Nichols, on duty at the large gate to the Soldier's Home grounds, heard a rifle shot in the direction of the city about 11 one night, and then the sound of hoofbeats coming closer and closer. Soon President Lincoln arrived, riding rapidly all alone, and without his ubiquitous stove-pipe hat. "He came pretty near getting away with me, didn't he?" Lincoln asked. "He got the bit in his teeth before I could draw rein." The guard asked the president about his missing hat, and he replied that someone had fired off a gun down at the bottom of the hill, causing his horse to bolt and his hat to fall off.

After seeing the president safely into the Soldier's Home and taking care of his horse, the guard and a corporal went in search of the missing hat. They found it where the driveway intersected the main road. "Upon examination," Nichols said, "we discovered a bullet-hole through the crown. We searched the locality thoroughly, but without avail. Next day I gave Mr. Lincoln his hat, and called his attention to the bullet-hole. He made some humorous remark, to the effect that it was made by some foolish marksman and was not intended for him; but added that he wished nothing said about the matter. We all felt confident it was an attempt to kill the President, and after that he never rode alone."[15]

"On the evening of August 17," Horace Porter wrote, "General Grant was sitting in front of his quarters, with several staff-officers about him, when the telegraph operator came over from his tent and handed him a despatch. He opened it, and as he proceeded with the reading his face became suffused with smiles. After he had finished it he broke into a hearty laugh." Although Grant possessed a dry sense of humor he was seldom known to laugh out loud, so naturally the staff officers were curious to know what was so funny. The general glanced over the telegram again and said, "The President has more nerve than any of his advisers." Then he read them Lincoln's reply to his own answer to Halleck's suggestion that he take in sail: "I have seen your despatch expressing your unwillingness to break your hold where you are. Neither am I willing. Hold on with a bulldog grip, and chew and choke as much as possible."[16]

1. Grant, *Memoirs*, 2:323.
2. Basler, ed., *The Collected Works of Abraham Lincoln*, 7:499, n. 1.
3. Catton, *Grant Takes Command*, 354–355.
4. Freeman, *R. E. Lee*, 3:588.
5. Sherman, *Memoirs*, 2:103.
6. McDonough and Jones, *War So Terrible*, 287–288.
7. Sherman, *Memoirs*, 2:103–104.
8. *Official Records*, 43:1:43.
9. Catton, *A Stillness at Appomattox*, 285–286.
10. Sheridan, *Memoirs*, 1:488.
11. Ibid., 488–489.
12. Early, *War Memoirs*, 407–408.
13. Basler, ed., *The Collected Works of Abraham Lincoln*, 7:493, n. 1.
14. Catton, *Grant Takes Command*, 339–340.
15. Sandburg, *Abraham Lincoln*, 669–670.
16. Porter, *Campaigning With Grant*, 279.

CHAPTER TWENTY-NINE

This Road Was Very Important to the Enemy

18–20 August 1864

On the eighteenth of August the CSS *Tallahassee* put into Halifax, Nova Scotia, a neutral British colony northeast of Maine. Captain Wood was forced to make this stop because of his vessel's need for coal. He had captured a ship full of coal off the Maine coast a few days before, but the sea had been so rough that it had been impossible to transfer the coal to the *Tallahassee*. All that Wood was able to do was to use the prize to tow his raider and thus save what was left of her own coal. Then he had sunk the prize and run into Halifax. The prize he had previously been using as a tender, the *James Funk*, had already been scuttled.

At the British port, a throng of a thousand or more crowded the docks to see the now-famous raider. In the town, Wood saw Northern newspapers for the first time and was able to read how much consternation he had brought to the northeastern seaboard and that the prisoners he had paroled were charging him with inhumane treatment. The United States Consul, of course, wired Secretary of the Navy Welles as soon as the *Tallahassee* appeared. Wood sent his paymaster to buy coal, a new mast to replace one that had been damaged when he collided with the *Adriatic*, and provisions. The crew was given a month's pay to buy clothes, and Wood put on his best uniform for a call upon the local British naval commander, Vice-Admiral Sir James Hope.

The latter, who had not made the customary call on a newly arrived ship, "did not rise from his seat, nor shake hands, nor offer me a seat," Wood reported. "I mention this to show his animus."[1] The admiral informed Wood that, according to the Queen's neutrality proclamation, he had use of the port for only 24 hours. The lieutenant governor of Nova Scotia seemed friendlier, but repeated the 24-hour rule and added that Wood could only take on enough supplies to allow him to reach the nearest Confederate port, which was Wilmington. He was therefore allowed only 100 tons of coal, although he was given an extra 12 hours to replace his mast.

Down in Mississippi, Forrest learned from his scouts on the morning of the eighteenth that the Federals had trains running on the Mississippi Central Railroad as far south as the Tallahatchie River, and that A. J. Smith was in the process of concentrating his troops and supplies at Abbeville. Forrest knew the Union force was too large for him to stop with the troops he had available, but the unseasonal rain that had been falling since the tenth had swollen the streams and turned the roads to quagmires, and that would slow the Federal advance. He decided, therefore, to seize the initiative while the Yankees were floundering in the mud.

After conferring with Chalmers he issued orders for colonels Neely, Bell, and Wade to have picked units from their brigades at Forrest's headquarters in Oxford at 5 p.m. Forrest would lead these troops, plus the four 3-inch guns of Morton's Tennessee Battery, on a raid around Smith's western flank, Chalmers would remain at Oxford with the dregs of these commands, the other two batteries, and the 3rd and 7th Tennessee, which were ordered to join him there. Also, General Buford was directed to move to Oxford from Pontotoc with Faulkner's Brigade and another battery.

The units designated for the raid packed their gear, drew 80 rounds of ammunition per man, and reported as ordered. Forrest inspected them and culled out all men and horses that did not appear able to make the difficult search. A bit after 5 p.m. the remaining 2,000 troopers mounted up, and the column took to the road in a driving rain, heading almost due west toward Panola on the Tallahatchie. They marched on through the night, swimming their horses across several swollen streams, pulling the accompanying guns, caissons, and ambulances across by hand. Their objective was Memphis itself.

There was no rain in Georgia on the eighteenth, for it was a "bright, beautiful moonlight night" when Kilpatrick's Union cavalry division marched out of Sandtown, west of Atlanta, headed for Hood's railroad lifelines. With him went four guns, plus two brigades of Garrard's division, but without Garrard. As Sherman told Thomas: "I am willing to admit that General Garrard's excessive prudence saves his cavalry . . . but though saved, it is as useless as so many sticks. Saving himself, he sacrifices others operating in conjoint expeditions. I am so thoroughly convinced that if he can see a horseman in the distance . . . he will turn back, that I cannot again depend on his making an effort, though he knows a commander depends on him. If we cannot use that cavalry now, when can we?" Sherman put Colonel Eli Long, "a hard-working and worthy cavalry officer," in charge of the two brigades sent to reinforce Kilpatrick and recommended his promotion to brigadier general of volunteers as a permanent replacement for Garrard.[2]

In southern Virginia, Grant unleashed the second blow of his one-two punch against Richmond and Petersburg. Now that the move of the 2nd and 10th corps and Gregg's cavalry division had pulled Confederate reinforcements to the north bank of the James, he ordered Warren's 5th Corps to move out at 4 a.m. on the eighteenth from the left flank of the Army of the Potomac's Petersburg lines to make a reconnaissance in force toward the Weldon Railroad near Globe Tavern and there to destroy as much track as possible. Spear's brigade of Kautz's cavalry division of Butler's Army of the James was temporarily loaned to Warren for this move. Calculating that there were probably only two or three divisions of infantry left in the Confederate defenses of Petersburg, Meade wanted Warren to attack the southern sector of those entrenchments, but Grant did not want to take the risk. His hope was to cut one of Lee's supply lines. "I want, if possible," Grant said, "to make such demonstrations as will force Lee to withdraw a portion of his troops from the Valley, so that Sheridan can strike a blow against the balance."[3] In his memoirs he wrote, "This road was very important to the enemy. The limits from which his supplies had been drawn were already very much contracted, and I knew that he must fight desperately to protect it."[4]

Although it was raining, the heat was intense, and the area was so drenched that the fields were almost impossible for artillery. Spear's cavalry brigade and Griffin's 1st Division had the lead and they met Rebel pickets of Dearing's cavalry brigade of Beauregard's department about a mile from the railroad. Griffin deployed his skirmishers, advanced in column of brigades to the tracks near Globe Tavern, and turned to the south and west. The 2nd Division, commanded by Ayres, came next, and it turned north, toward Petersburg, with Crawford's 3rd Division in column on its right. Cutler's 4th Division was in reserve.

After advancing a mile, Ayres found his left flank attacked by two brigades of Heth's Division of A. P. Hill's 3rd Corps, which had been sent down by Beauregard upon hearing from Dearing of this latest Yankee move. The Maryland Brigade of Ayres' division was driven back and Ayres had to retreat a short distance to keep his left flank from being turned. But a brigade from Cutler's division was brought up to help out, and the Federals attacked and drove Heth from his position, although at the cost of almost a thousand Union casualties. The Union advance continued, but Crawford's division could not keep up because its path led through thick woods and swampy ground, cut up with ravines, so Warren called a halt a mile or two short of the road intersection that Meade had hoped Warren would gain. He was happy enough, however, with what had been achieved and ordered Warren to hold onto his position on the railroad "at all hazards."[5] The troops began to build breastworks and dig trenches.

North of the James, at 5 p.m. that day, the Confederates attacked the Union position at Fussell's Mill, but the 1st Division of the 2nd Corps, now commanded by Brigadier General Nelson Miles, counterattacked the Rebels' northern flank and drove them back with heavy losses. Meanwhile, Lee ordered his son's cavalry division across the James to help cover the southwestern flank of the Petersburg line. That night Mott's 3rd Division of the Federal 2nd Corps was sent back to the south side of the James and used to extend the Union line toward Warren's new position, while allowing most of the 9th Corps to be withdrawn from the defenses.

Burnside was no longer with that corps. Because of his role in the disastrous battle of the Crater, he had been replaced by Major General John G. Parke, who had been his chief of staff, off and on, since late 1862 and who had previously commanded the corps while Burnside had commanded first the Army of the Potomac and then the Army of the Ohio. Ledlie was also gone, replaced by Brigadier General Julius White. Willcox's 3rd Division was the first to arrive on the morning of the nineteenth and it was ordered to bivouac near Globe Tavern, where Warren had his headquarters. White's 1st Division was the next to arrive and was posted farther to the right. Potter's 2nd Division was not sent to join Warren until later.

Also on the morning of the nineteenth, Brigadier General Edward S.

Bragg's Iron Brigade of Cutler's division was sent to Crawford's right, where it was spread out in a long skirmish line to connect it with the main Union defenses. It was not an easy job, for the country between the two corps was covered with dense woods and underbrush, and the roads in the area were mere cart tracks and completely unknown to the Federals.

Beauregard also sent out reinforcements that morning. These consisted of three brigades of infantry under Mahone, plus Rooney Lee's cavalry and several batteries of artillery, all under the command of General A. P. Hill. Beauregard sent word to Lee, still north of the James, that the "result would be more certain with a stronger force of infantry," but he did not directly ask for more reinforcements.[5] Heth was to attack Ayres' left again while Mahone, who knew this area well, would move under the concealment of the woods beyond Crawford's right, break through Bragg's skirmish line, and take Crawford in the rear. Rooney Lee's cavalry would move to the south and try to get around Griffin's flank. At about 4:30 p.m., in a driving rain, Mahone, with his command formed in columns of fours, broke through the Iron Brigade's skirmish line, faced to the west and advanced rapidly against Crawford's flank, whose skirmish line fell back in great confusion, blocking the fire of the main line and forcing it also to fall back, along with a part of Ayres' division. "For a short time chaos and confusion reigned," General Willcox remembered. "Crawford fighting on all sides, and pieces of artillery of both armies pouring their fire into the intermingled mass of friend and foe—ranks there were none."[7] Crawford himself was captured, but he soon escaped in the confusion. About 2,700 other Federals were not so fortunate.

Meanwhile, Heth attacked Ayres, but with no success. Hearing this battle, Willcox at first marched his two brigades toward Ayres' left, but when stragglers and wounded men came streaming back from Crawford's front, Willcox changed his course for Crawford's right. His lead brigade, Hartranft's 1st, ran into Clingman's Brigade of Mahone's force and drove it back. Twice the Rebels rallied and counterattacked, but were driven back again both times. Just as his other brigade, Humphrey's 2nd, was coming up, Willcox received orders from Warren to send a brigade to the point where Ayres' right joined Crawford's left, so Humphrey's was sent. He soon ran head-on into another of Mahone's brigades. Both sides stopped advancing and started firing, but the Confederates soon fell back to the defenses they had captured. Humphrey then reformed his brigade and charged, driving the Rebels from the works and capturing a battleflag and a number of prisoners.

Warren soon reformed the broken units of Crawford's and Ayres' divisions and counterattacked, regaining the rest of the lost ground and capturing two Rebel flags, while White's division formed facing to the Union right, driving Colquitt's Brigade back and wounding General Colquitt.

Heth had assaulted Ayres' left twice, and just before dark he made a third attack, but with no more success. Far to the south, Spears brigade of Union cavalry, supported by the far left of Griffin's infantry line, fought off all of Rooney Lee's attempts to turn that flank. That night Spear reported that he had driven Lee to within a mile of Reams' Station. "There was much jubilation in our camps that night," Willcox recorded. Meade sent his congratulations to Warren, by the field telegraph, for his victory. "It will serve greatly to inspirit the whole army," he said, "and proves that we only want a fair chance to defeat the enemy. I hope he will try it again." Willcox said, "Well did that army need cheering up, for it had been under a black cloud ever since the fatal mine affair, and felt the long strain of the trenches on its nerves."[8]

When Grant heard of Warren's success he sent a wire to Meade's headquarters, now connected with his by military telegraph: "I am pleased to see the promptness with which General Warren attacked the enemy when he came out. I hope he will not hesitate in such cases to abandon his lines and take every man to fight every battle, and trust to regaining them afterward, or to getting better." He told his staff, "Meade and I have had to criticize Warren pretty severely on several occasions for being slow, and I wanted to be prompt to compliment him now that he has acted vigorously and handsomely in taking the offensive."[9]

Lee responded to the defeat by sending back to the Petersburg front all of the infantry which he had sent to the north side to meet Hancock's threat.

In the Shenandoah Valley that day, the nineteenth, Early advanced his infantry to Bunker Hill as he followed up Sheridan's withdrawal, while his cavalry reconnoitered to Martinsburg and Shepherdstown. Anderson was left behind to guard Winchester. Sheridan had his forces, which now included the other division of the 19th Corps and Wilson's cavalry, in position around Charlestown, and Averell's cavalry was now covering the crossings of the Potomac upstream from Harper's Ferry.

Down in Mississippi that day, A. J. Smith finally had his entire field force assembled at Abbeville. They had overcome the rain and mud, although they were on half rations due to the transportation problems. At dawn, about 5 a.m., Hatch's cavalry division, reinforced by Wolfe's brigade of infantry and the pioneers from both Mower's and Shaw's divisions, marched southward through a pelting rain, headed for Hurricane Creek, where they would build a bridge. Due to the mud, it was 2 p.m. before these Federals reached the creek, and when the condition of the road was reported, Smith suspended the march of the rest of his force.

As soon as the bridge was completed, Hatch's cavalry crossed to the south side, and soon they ran into Wade's Brigade of Confederates, dismounted and deployed in the edge of some trees overlooking a field just north of the Isham plantation. The Southerners held their fire until the dismounted Union skirmishers were within a hundred yards, but when they pulled their triggers, few of their rifles would fire. Five days of heavy rain had ruined their ammunition, and they had to retreat. Unaware that Forrest had left with a sizable portion of his command, Hatch decided that it would not be safe to advance any farther without infantry support, so he established a strong line of pickets and let his men bivouac for the night. Meanwhile, Wolfe's infantry had crossed the new bridge and had begun to dig in on the ridge just south of the creek. That evening Buford rode into Oxford with Faulkner's Brigade.

At 7 a.m. Forrest and his 2,000 raiders reached Panola after riding 40 miles. There he was informed that many of the artillery horses were breaking down and would not be able to continue. So he decided to send half the battery and his ambulances south to Grenada and to put ten good horses on each of the other two guns. He also inspected his cavalry and found about a hundred mounts that did not look like they could go much farther, so those men were left at Panola. The rest of the column crossed the Tallahatchie on a pontoon bridge at about 10 a.m. and marched northward on the muddy roads as the skies finally began to clear. It was dusk before Forrest reluctantly called a halt at Senatobia, about 20 miles north, and let his men bivouac for the night.

Over in Georgia that day, the nineteenth, skirmishing and bombarding continued while Sherman and Hood awaited the results of their cavalry raids against each other's communications. General Grenville Dodge, commander of the Left Wing of the 16th Corps, was severely wounded that day. He was replaced by Brigadier General T. E. G. Ransom, who had commanded the 13th Corps on Banks' recent unsuccessful expedition up the Red River in Louisiana. In another command change, General Richard Johnson was made chief of cavalry of Thomas' Army of the Cumberland that day, thus clearing the way for Jefferson C. Davis to take over the 14th Corps that Palmer had quit.

At daylight on the nineteenth, Kilpatrick's Union cavalry reached the Atlanta & West Point Railroad near Fairburn. From there the two brigades from Garrard's division took over the lead and drove Ross's brigade of Jackson's Confederate cavalry from a series of barricades to the Flint River, where they found that the bridge had been partially dismantled and that there were Rebels in a strong position on the far bank. But the fire of the Union guns and a charge by dismounted troopers drove them off. The bridge was soon repaired and the Federal troopers crossed over, driving the Confederates, now joined by Jackson's other two brigades, to Jonesborough, less than five miles away, on the Macon & Western Railroad.

There Kilpatrick found the track and the depot protected by a fort made of cotton bales. But shells from his guns soon set the cotton, the depot, and other buildings on fire, and the Rebels pulled out. For the next five hours Kilpatrick's own troopers worked at tearing up about two miles of track while Long, with his own brigade, held off the Confederates south of town and his other brigade, Minty's, guarded the north end of town. "It was a wild night and a most graphic scene," the historian of one of Long's regiments recorded. "The sky lit up with burning timbers, buildings and cotton bales, the continuous bang of carbines, the galloping of staff officers and orderlies up and down the streets . . . the terrified citizens, peering out of their windows, the constant marching of troops changing position, Kilpatrick's headquarters band discoursing national airs, with the shouts of the men—all made a weird scene never to be forgotten."[10]

Colonel Long informed Kilpatrick that there was Confederate infantry moving up from the south of town, so he withdrew to the east and then swung back to the railroad again farther south, about a mile north of Lovejoy's Station, arriving at mid-morning on the twentieth. But on the way, his two leading regiments were ambushed and cut up pretty badly, and before his men could start tearing up the track he found out that he was completely surrounded by Rebels. There was a division of infantry moving up on his right, a brigade of infantry to his front and left, and Jackson's three brigades of cavalry coming up behind him. The 4,500 Union troopers were confronted by about 12,000 Confederates.

Where other commanders might have surrendered or ordered their men to break up into small groups and try to escape, Kilpatrick was determined to break out. He assembled his own division on the left of the road, facing east, and Long's two brigades to the right. Those who no longer had horses, plus ambulances filled with wounded men, the artillery, ammunition wagons and pack mules brought up the rear, while the rest formed in columns of regiments, mounted with drawn sabers. When all were ready, they charged over an old, deserted plantation, across ground cut up by ditches and washouts and two or three lines of fences.

To their left, on the north side of the road, there was Rebel infantry "formed in three lines," one of the Union regimental historians wrote, "about fifty yards apart, in double rank; the first and second lines with fixed bayonets and the third line firing; in both the first and second lines the front rank knelt on one knee, resting the butt of the gun on the ground, the bayonet at a 'charge.'" But on the south side of the road, Minty's brigade struck the Confederate cavalry, who "broke and fled in the wildest panic."[11] Then Minty's and Long's brigades turned to their left and took the infantry in the flank, riding the Rebels down and sabering them until the road was cleared for Kilpatrick's own troopers. The Federals then marched eastward in a torrential rain and soon outdistanced the pursuing Southern infantry. After a short rest at McDonough, they rode on, this time heading north.

In southern Virginia on the twentieth, Warren was sure that the Confederates would again try to drive him away from the Weldon Railroad. So he fell back a mile or two and entrenched in more open ground around Globe Tavern, which was more favorable for the use of his artillery. With the Federals blocking the railroad from there to Reams' Station, Lee had to organize convoys of wagons to haul supplies twenty miles from Stony Creek Depot to Petersburg. That night the Union troops north of the James were withdrawn to their former positions on the south side.

In Indianapolis on 20 August General Henry Carrington, commander of the District of Indiana, sent soldiers to search the private office of H. H. Dodd, Copperhead commander for Indiana, and found boxes containing about 400 navy revolvers and 135,000 rounds of ammunition, a supply of Sons of Liberty rituals, and a list of members of that organization in Indianapolis.

At 1 a.m. on the twentieth the CSS *Tallahassee* steamed out of Halifax on a high tide, after having been in port for forty hours. Fearing that Union cruisers were already waiting for him outside, Wood employed one of the port's most skillful pilots and utilized the maneuverability of his twin-screw craft to steer through a narrow, shallow, unlighted channel east of the island that divided the harbor. At 6:15 a.m. the USS *Pontoosuc*, the first Federal warship to arrive, steamed into Halifax. The U.S. consul informed her captain that Wood had been heard to say that he would steam to the Gulf of St. Lawrence to attack the Northern fishing fleet. So the *Pontoosuc* steamed after her, ignoring the neutrality rule that required the pursuing vessel to stay in port for 24 hours. But, as the *New York Tribune* observed: "It would be just like the insolent Rebel not to be found when sought for in the place to which he gave out he was going."[12]

---

1. Shingleton, "Cruise of the CSS Tallahassee," 38.
2. Starr, *The Union Cavalry*, 3:476.
3. Andrew A. Humphreys, *The Virginia Campaign of '64 and '65* (New York, 1883), 273.
4. Grant, *Memoirs*, 2:324.
5. Orlando B. Willcox, "Actions on the Weldon Railroad," in *Battles and Leaders*, 4:568.
6. Freeman, *R. E. Lee*, 3:485.
7. Ibid., 569.
8. All three quotes from Ibid., 570–571.
9. Both quotes from Porter, *Campaigning With Grant*, 280–281.
10. Starr, *The Union Cavalry*, 3:478.
11. Ibid., 479.
12. Shingleton, "Cruise of the CSS Tallahassee," 38.

CHAPTER THIRTY

General, They Are After You

20–21 August 1864

Despite the heavy rains in Mississippi, A. J. Smith sent another brigade of infantry, from Colonel Shaw's 3rd Division, to Hurricane Creek on the twentieth of August. The men carried three days' rations in their haversacks to save the muddy roads from more vehicular traffic. They left Abbeville early that afternoon, but it was 8 p.m. by the time they bivouacked on the muddy ridge south of the creek.

There were several sharp clashes of patrols from both sides near the Isham house that day, and Chalmers was worried about his position. There were only two bridges still standing across the swollen Yacona River behind him, the terrain between that stream and the Tallahatchie was almost all open, without any commanding hills or ridges, and there were numerous roads that would lead around the flanks of any position that he decided to take. To be on the safe side, he decided to send his supply wagons south of the Yacona. "I have sent off everything I can spare," he said in a midday telegram to Maury, who remained in charge of the department until Taylor arrived, "and am prepared for light travel." In another wire at 4 p.m. he said, "My situation here is critical. Yockeney rising behind me and may become impassable, and when the enemy discovers the absence of General Forrest and my weakness he may press me." An hour later, after conferring with Buford, he told Maury that he had decided to pull back across the Yacona that night. But at around 6 p.m. he received Maury's answer: "Don't yield ground to enemy unnecessarily until he forces you. When he finds Forrest in his rear he will not be apt to advance, and the weather is unfavorable to him."[1] Chalmers replied that he did not agree, but he would stay north of the Yacona as long as he could.

At Senatobia, Forrest learned that morning that Hickahala Creek, normally a placid stream a mile north of the town, was impassable. But he sent patrols out through the surrounding area to rip up flooring from every gin-house and cabin and bring it to the bank of the roaring stream, where a small flatboat had been found. There he had his men fashion two strong cables from vines, which were stretched across the creek between the stumps of two trees by using the flatboat as a raft. Then, using the flatboat and a number of telegraph poles that they cut down, his men built a floating bridge out of more poles and the flooring planks and secured it to the cables. In this way a 60-foot bridge was built in less than an hour, and the Confederates soon crossed over, leading their horses and carrying their cannon.

Six miles farther north they came to the raging Coldwater River. Forrest discovered, to his disgust, that the small ferryboat there could not carry more than four horses at a time, which would make the crossing far too slow for his purposes. Again he put a detail of men to work fashioning cables from grapevines while another constructed pontoon rafts from cypress logs. Using the ferryboat as the center section, telegraph poles as stringers, and flooring torn up from more cotton gin houses, the Rebels built another bridge, twice the length of the first. The guns were rolled across by hand, and the wagons full of unshucked corn for the horses were unloaded, pulled across, and then reloaded on the north side. Forrest set an example by carrying across the first armload himself, despite his still-injured foot. In less than three hours the head of the column began to cross. "I never saw a command more like it was out for a holiday," one of the Rebels later wrote, while Forrest complained afterward that he "had to continually caution the men to keep quiet. They were making a regular corn shucking out of it."[2]

Eight miles farther on they stopped for a rest at Hernando, where Forrest had once lived and still had many friends. There he was met by several spies who had left Memphis earlier that day. They reported that the Yankees still had no idea of his approach and gave him information on the positions and strengths of Union units in the city. After a few hours, the weary troopers were back on the road again, but their fatigue and the clinging mud slowed their pace. As they crossed into Tennessee, some ten miles south of Memphis, they were met by sympathetic residents of the city, who gave Forrest more information about the garrison, as well as the locations of the quarters of the three Union generals stationed there. Four miles south of Memphis, at the crossing of Nonconnah Creek, more scouts reported in, bringing further information on the exact location of various Federal detachments which were guarding the entrance to the city via the road from Hernando.

Since Forrest knew the city well, he soon put together a mental picture of the Federal defenses from all these sources of information. Contrary to what he had previously thought, the city was not fortified. There was an earthwork called Fort Pickering on the Mississippi riverbank south of town, but the rest of the eight- to ten-mile circuit of the city was protected only by a picket line. Since the garrison, composed mostly of 100-days' men and recently recruited former slaves, numbered only about 5,000 men, it had to be a pretty thin line.

Forrest ordered his men to close up and his principal subordinates to join him at the head of the column so that he could give them their assignments without stopping. They reported that more horses had given out and that there were then about 1,500 men left in the column. The general ordered his brother, Captain William H. Forrest, to take the lead with his 40 scouts, surprise and capture the Federal outpost on the Hernando road, and then gallop to the Gayoso House hotel to capture General Stephen Hurlbut, former commander of the Union district, who was known to be living there while awaiting further assignment. To another brother, Lieutenant Colonel Jesse Forrest, went the job of taking a picked detachment to capture the current district commander, General C. C. Washburn, who was living in a commandeered private home. Lieutenant Colonel Thomas H. Logwood, with the 12th and 15th Tennessee of Neely's brigade, was to follow Captain Forrest to the Gayoso House and set up roadblocks at two key intersections, as well as occupy the steamboat landing and capture any transports tied up there. Neely would lead the rest of his brigade in an attack on the camp of the 100-days' men near the Hernando road. The three regiments of Bell's brigade that had been brought on the raid, as well as the two guns, would be held in reserve.

Forrest sent his subordinates to join their respective commands with an injunction to observe strict silence until they reached the center of the city, in order to ensure surprise. The officers formed the men into columns of fours, and at 3:15 a.m. on Sunday, 21 August, Captain William Forrest and his scouts led the way toward the sleeping city. The captain himself and ten picked men were about 60 paces out in front, as the point of the entire column. It was still dark at that hour—a hot and humid night—and a dense fog not only helped to reduce visibility but muffled sounds as well.

All was quiet until the Confederates were within two miles of Court

Square. Then a Union sentry called out, "Who goes there?" Captain Forrest replied, "A detachment of the 12th Missouri with rebel prisoners." The sentry gave the expected command to "dismount and come forward alone and on foot." The captain said, "All right," but did not dismount.[3] Instead, he rode forward until he could see the dim shape of the sentry, then he charged him and knocked him down with a blow from his revolver. His men followed right behind him and captured the dozen men of the 137th Illinois stationed at this outpost with only one shot being fired.

A quarter of a mile farther on another outpost of the same Union regiment was encountered, but the captain was not able to bluff these Federals. The shot had aroused their suspicions, and they greeted the Rebels with a volley. However, in the fog their shots went wild. The Confederates charged and scattered the Northerners. But, in the excitement of the moment they forgot General Forrest's admonition to maintain silence and let out a Rebel yell that was taken up by the rest of the column. The sun was now coming up and through the fog they could see the tents of the main camps of the 137th Illinois, 3rd Illinois Cavalry, and 61st U.S. Colored Troops on both sides of the road. So, the general ordered his bugler to sound the charge and the units galloped off to perform their various tasks.

About 900 yards beyond the Union infantry and cavalry camps, Captain Forrest and his scouts came to the encampment of the 7th Battery of Wisconsin Light Artillery. They scattered the startled gunners before they could get any of their guns into action, killing four, wounding two, while the rest sought shelter in nearby houses. Moving on to the Gayoso House, the captain rode his horse right into the lobby of the hotel and ordered his men to block all exits. Then they began a search for General Hurlbut and his staff. Lieutenant Colonel A. H. Chalmers of the 18th Mississippi, who was along for some reason, bashed in the door of the general's room, but he was not there. He checked other rooms, and in one of them "he was met by a beautiful damsel with dishevelled locks and becoming dishabille, who threw her arms about his neck, imploring his protection, which he claimed he was only too glad to give if she would not take up her arms until regularly exchanged as a prisoner of war."[4] Several other Union officers were staying in the hotel, however, and, awakened by the noise, rushed out of their rooms with drawn pistols. A gun fight ensued through the halls of the hotel, in which one Federal was killed and several others captured.

Lieutenant Colonel Jesse Forrest entered the city close behind his brother and, guided by a scout who knew the city, reached the address on Union Street where Washburn had his headquarters. But the general had been warned just minutes before and had fled out the back door in his nightshirt, heading for Fort Pickering, a half-mile away. In his hurry to escape, however, the general gave no instructions for dealing with this raid. Several members of Washburn's staff were captured, as were his uniform and his personal effects, which were delivered to General Forrest as trophies of war. "They removed me from command because I couldn't keep Forrest out of West Tennessee," Hurlbut later complained, "and now Washburn can't keep him out of his own bedroom."[5]

Lieutenant Colonel Logwood's two regiments were next in the Confederate column, but in the few minutes since General Forrest's two brothers and their special detachments had gone by, the officers of the 137th Illinois had begun to form their men in line of battle east of the road, and they were soon firing on the Rebels, if somewhat raggedly. Logwood told his men to ignore these Yankees and press on into the city as ordered. However, not much farther up the road they came to a detachment of Federals in position across the road, which was blocked on one side by a fence and on the other by a ditch. Since these Yankees could not be ignored, Logwood ordered a charge, and with a wild Rebel yell they smashed through the road block, using their carbines as clubs, since they did not carry sabers. Soon they came to the camp of the 7th Wisconsin Battery, whose officers had just restored some order, but they still had not loaded their guns, and they were scattered again by this even larger force of Rebels. Riding on into the city, Logwood dropped off detachments at the key intersections which Forrest had designated and proceeded to the Gayoso House.

From there he sent a detachment to release the Confederates in the Irving Block Prison and to capture the other Union general in Memphis, Brigadier General Ralph P. Buckland, commander of the District of Memphis. But this general was also warned of the Rebels' coming. A sentry pounded on his door and yelled, "General, they are after you." Running to his window, he asked, "Who are after me?" and the sentry answered, "The rebels."[6] Just then the sound of firing reached his ears, so he hastily dressed and ran for the nearby barracks of a detachment of the 8th Iowa, whom he found milling around in the street. He ordered them into line and then went on to the headquarters of the 2nd Regiment of the local militia of loyal citizens to make sure that the alarm gun was fired. When Logwood's detachment showed up at Buckland's headquarters a few seconds later and demanded his surrender, they were fired upon, losing one horse. So they moved on to the prison, but this was defended by a detachment of the 113th Illinois and a few men from the 8th Iowa, who fought them off.

Colonel Neely with the rest of his brigade was next in the Confederate column, but one of his regiments became entangled with part of Logwood's command, and by the time he got it sorted out and advanced on the Union camps the 137th Illinois had gotten itself organized. Neely's men were met with several well-aimed volleys that brought their advance up short. The detachment of the 61st U.S. Colored Troops that had been left behind by Colonel Bouton to guard his brigade's camp was not so well prepared, however, and Neely's troopers overran it and captured its camp. Only a few of the men put up any resistance. Two who did were a lieutenant and a sergeant, who loaded one of the guns of Battery I of the 2nd U.S. Colored Artillery. They waited until the Rebels were within 30 yards of the muzzle and then blasted them with cannister, escaping in the resultant confusion.

General Forrest, observing the stiff resistance that Neely's command was receiving from the 137th Illinois, placed himself at the head of Bell's Tennesseans and led them forward at a trot to Neely's right. Riding over fences and through several gardens, they soon reached the camp of the 3rd Illinois Cavalry, and after a brief struggle captured 28 men and scattered the rest. They also captured all of the Federals' horses. Neely's men went forward again, as well, and this time they managed to dislodge the 137th Illinois, which, with the 3rd Illinois Cavalry and a detachment of the 6th Illinois Cavalry, took refuge in the large brick building of the nearby State Female College. Forrest then called up his two guns to blast the Federals out of this impromptu fortress while he deployed a number of his troopers as dismounted skirmishers. But he soon decided that it would cost him too many casualties to take the college.

At the wharf, the hospital boat *Red Rover* got up steam when word was received that the Confederates were raiding the city. She pulled up alongside the ironclad *Essex*, whose engines were being repaired, ready to tow her out into the river if necessary.

Colonel George B. Hoge of the 113th Illinois was in charge of a number of men on detached duty, casuals, supply people, and 100-days' men, and he ordered them to meet at the camp of the 120th Illinois at the intersection of Poplar and Alabama streets, because he thought that Forrest would probably go by it on his way out of town. One of the units that gathered there was Battery G of the 2nd Missouri Artillery, and Hoge ordered its commander to site a couple of his guns to cover Poplar Street and the other two to cover Alabama Street. Then Hoge posted a line of outposts to watch the various streets and roads in the area and waited for Forrest to blunder into his ambush. Another Union commander intended to wait for the Rebels to come to him. He was Colonel

Edwin L. Buttrick, whose brigade was camped near the Hernando road. He put his three regiments in line of battle and waited.

Meanwhile, General Buckland managed to get the signal gun loaded and fired and was joined by Colonel Charles W. Dustan, commander of the militia, Colonel Matthew H. Starr, commander of the 6th Illinois Cavalry, and Lieutenant Colonel William B. Bell, commander of the 8th Iowa. Soon about 150 men had also reported. Starr told Buckland that he thought that Washburn had been captured, and if this was true, Buckland was now in command. So he and Bell took 70 of the latter's Iowa infantrymen down Third Street to attack the Rebels who were said to be barricaded in Washburn's headquarters, while Dustan was to take a detachment of the Block Prison guards and 20 of his militiamen and set up a roadblock on Main Street, a block farther east. But they found Washburn's headquarters deserted by both sides. Unable to obtain any information about Washburn's fate, Buckland returned to his own headquarters, from which he sent one staff officer to scout out the situation on the Hernando road and another to Fort Pickering to confer with its commander. The latter brought back word that Washburn was at the fort, and Washburn himself soon came to Buckland's headquarters and took command, sending Buckland to the Hernando road area to take charge there. But by the time he arrived there, the Confederates were gone.

Colonel Logwood had ordered a thorough search of the Gayoso House in the hope of turning up General Hurlbut, but to no avail. He was also trying to round up his scattered troopers, for many of them had decided to take an hour or two off from the war to visit friends and relations in the city or to search for plunder or horses. At the Eclipse Stable they found several mounts and quickly drafted them all into the Confederate service. By the time he had rounded up his wayward men, Logwood had received orders from General Forrest to evacuate the city. He soon joined up with Jesse Forrest's detachment and together they began to move rapidly back the way they had come.

Unknown to them, the Iowans under Lieutenant Colonel Bell were paralleling their march one street over, and both groups reached the outskirts of the city at about the same time. The Federals then fired a volley into the Rebels that felled a captain and several men. This threw the Confederates into confusion, and the Iowans took advantage of it to get ahead of them and set up a roadblock on the Hernando road. When Logwood discovered this, he ordered a company of the 15th Tennessee to break through, but it was repulsed. A second company did break through, however, and the Rebels were able to rejoin General Forrest, who was still with Tyree Bell's command near the State Female College. Then the entire force fell back slowly, maintaining a threatening posture.

By then Colonel Hoge had discovered that he had guessed wrong, and that the Rebels were not going to walk into his trap. Hurriedly he marched his men over to the camp of the 7th Wisconsin Battery on the Hernando road, and there, at about 9 a.m., he took command of all the troops in the area, including Bell's Iowans, the Illinois troops still holding out in the State Female College, and Buttrick's three regiments. But since he feared that the Confederates were regrouping for another dash into the city, he deployed his troops in defensive positions rather than attacking. By then the fog had finally lifted, so he did, at least, have Battery G of the 2nd Missouri Artillery open fire on the Rebels with their 20-pounder rifles. Colonel Starr, with a detachment of cavalry, had meanwhile chased some Rebel stragglers out of the city, and now he was determined to attack some Confederates who were plundering the camp of the 137th Illinois. He ordered the Union guns to hold their fire and then the troopers charged. But Forrest saw this and led his 2nd Missouri Cavalry in a countercharge that mortally wounded Starr and drove the Federals off.

Forrest then retreated about a mile before stopping to allow about 300 of his men to exchange their worn-out mounts for horses captured in the city. A check with his units disclosed that he had about 400 Union prisoners, some still in their night clothes and many others without shoes. At about noon he stopped again at Crane Creek. By then it was obvious that many of the prisoners could not walk much farther, so he sent Major Anderson of his staff back toward Memphis to offer an immediate exchange of prisoners "as an act of humanity."[7] Certain that he held more Federals than they did Confederates, he offered to parole the rest, provided that General Washburn would accept that arrangement as binding. If the Federals would not swap prisoners, Anderson was to tell them that Forrest would stop at the crossing of Nonconnah Creek and wait there for them to bring clothing for his captives.

Buckland had by then arrived at the Hernando road battle area and fearing, like Hoge, a renewal of the Confederate attack he ordered the troops to be deployed to meet an assault from any direction. He was apparently unhappy with Hoge's efforts, however, for he put Colonel Edwin Moore in command of the infantry and artillery in the area. Colonel Winslow, who had been commander of the 2nd Division of Grierson's cavalry until his horse had fallen on him a few days before, put Lieutenant Colonel George W. Duffield in charge of the cavalry in the city, and the latter rounded up about 650 troopers and took off in pursuit of the retreating Rebels. Not far from Nonconnah Creek they encountered Major Anderson coming out with Forrest's offer under a flag of truce.

It was around 2 p.m. when Anderson returned to Forrest with Washburn's reply. The Union commander said that he did not have the authority to recognize the parole of Federal prisoners, but that he would send clothes and shoes for them. Duffield's troopers pulled back to the perimeter of Memphis while both sides waited for the clothing to arrive. When it finally came, Forrest had the prisoners examined and separated into two groups. The sick, injured, and civilians were released on their promise not to take up arms against the Confederacy until properly exchanged and allowed to make their way back to Memphis. The able-bodied Union soldiers were mounted on led horses so that they could be taken with the Rebel column. Learning from his commissary officer that the heavy rains of the past day or two had ruined most of his rations, Forrest told the Federal officers who brought the clothing that if Washburn would not receive the prisoners on parole, he should at least send rations for them to Hernando. The Confederate column pulled out at about 5 p.m., reached Hernando by dusk, and stopped there for the night.

At about the same hour Duffield received permission to call off his pursuit. Washburn had at first told Winslow that he wanted the cavalry to hound the Rebel retreat, but Duffield soon discovered that many of his men and horses had not eaten for 24 hours. He passed this information back to Winslow and continued to follow the Confederates cautiously until a message finally caught up with him about dusk to fall back and meet food and forage that were being sent out for him. At 11 p.m. the wagons full of rations for the prisoners passed through Duffield's lines, and he learned from the officers in charge of these that the drivers of the wagons with his own supplies had returned to Memphis because they refused to bring them forward without an escort.

A. J. Smith was happy to see the 21st dawn bright and clear, as it augured well for better roads. He marched out of Abbeville that morning with the 2nd Division of cavalry, now under Colonel Joseph Kargé, plus Mower's 1st Division of the 16th Corps, Gilbert's brigade of the 3rd, Bouton's brigade of U.S. Colored Troops, and the supply wagons of the expeditionary force. Not long after the tail of the column left it, the town went up in flames, thanks, no doubt to vindictive Union stragglers. Meanwhile Hatch decided to make room for newcomers by expanding the bridgehead south of Hurricane Creek. He sent the two infantry brigades of the 3rd Division along both sides of the road to Oxford, with their skirmishers out front and mounted patrols from his own 1st Division of cavalry covering the flanks. At about 11 a.m., near the Isham house, they ran up against a couple of Chalmers' regiments, but these, seeing the size of the Federal column, soon mounted up and moved off. Not far south of Isham's, Hatch called a halt at a favorable camp site in order to keep his advanced force from getting too far ahead of Smith's main column, which reached the bridgehead at noon and went into camp there.

Chalmers received an alarming report at about 11 a.m. that a large force of Union cavalry was heading for College Hill to cut his line of retreat to the Yacona. Without verifying the report, which turned out to be false, he wired the information to Maury, who authorized him to retreat. Chalmers therefore ordered his men to break contact with the Federals and fall back across the Yacona. This was done easily enough, since Hatch had put his men into bivouac near Isham's by then. In fact, one Confederate regiment did not get the word and stayed put until dusk, when it withdrew unmolested. A few scouts were left behind on purpose, as was an officer with a telegraph key, to keep Chalmers posted.

---

1. Bearss, *Forrest at Brice's Cross Roads,* 303–304.
2. Foote, *The Civil War,* 3:516.
3. Bearss, *Forrest at Brice's Cross Roads,* 286.
4. Ibid., 288.
5. Ibid., 289.
6. Ibid., 291.
7. Ibid., 295.

CHAPTER THIRTY-ONE

His Re-election Was an Impossibility

21–23 August 1864

In the Shenandoah Valley on that 21st day of August, the Confederates moved in pursuit of Sheridan's withdrawing Federals. Early's forces passed through Smithfield toward Charlestown, while Anderson's command took the direct road through Summit Point. Sheridan's army was encountered at Cameron's depot, about three miles from Charlestown, in a position he was already starting to entrench. Early sent Rodes' and Ramseur's divisions to the front to skirmish with Wright's 6th Corps, and a sharp little fight developed, but he made no real attack, preferring to wait for Anderson to join him. However, that general ran into Merritt's cavalry at Berryville and Wilson's at Summit Point, where dusk caught up with him, so he went into camp there.

"It seems that General Early thought I had taken position near Summit Point," Sheridan wrote, "and that by moving rapidly around through Smithfield he could fall upon my rear in concert with an attack in front by Anderson, but the warm reception given him disclosed his error, for he soon discovered that my line lay in front of Charlestown instead of where he supposed."[1] At midnight, Sheridan pulled in his cavalry and fell back to Halltown, near Harper's Ferry, where, with the Potomac covering one flank and the Shenandoah the other, he had a compact line of strong entrenchments and the backing of the heavy guns on Maryland Heights.

In southern Virginia that morning Lee, satisfied that the Federal attacks north of the James were over, ordered Hampton to take his cavalry division to the south side of the Appomattox, and later in the day he told Field to send two of his infantry brigades there also. Meanwhile, A. P. Hill, with his own corps, part of Hoke's Division, and Rooney Lee's cavalry, attacked Warren's position around Globe Tavern. He started with a bombardment by 30 guns against Warren's front and right and then assaulted both areas with infantry, but, as General Willcox wrote, "Hill's long, serried lines were smashed by our guns before they got within reach of our musketry."[2]

Later Mahone attacked the Union left, but fell into a trap. It may have only been a lucky break for the Federals, but was deadly for the Rebels, nevertheless. Warren's line ran east to west until it was about 450 yards west of the Weldon Railroad. Then it turned south, paralleling the tracks until almost even with Globe Tavern. There the line of the 1st Division of the 5th Corps began, but it was about 200 yards closer to the railroad than was the main line, leaving what military engineers called a *reentrant* in the line.

The Confederates were evidently not aware of this second line and thought that the end of the main line was the Union left flank. They emerged from the woods into a cornfield and advanced into this indentation in the Northern defenses, with the evident intention of rolling up the Federal main line. Instead, the Rebels ran into an unexpected crossfire from the 1st Division that proved nothing short of wholesale slaughter. It was, as a modern historian of one Union regiment put it, like firing lengthwise down a sidewalk crowded with people. One Federal wrote that "our men enjoyed it very much, for they remembered how often we had been obliged to charge upon their lines, and be shot down by thousands, while they were screened from our fire, and we now rejoiced that for once the tables were turned, and that to our advantage."[3]

The Southerners were thrown into utter confusion. Some of them falling dead or wounded, some running back toward the woods, some rushing blindly into the angle between the two Union lines, and some running toward the Federals with their hands raised in token of surrender. "We then had them between two fires," one Northerner remembered, "and could have slaughtered them like sheep in the shambles, but our men instinctively forebore to again fire upon them after they had given this indication of a surrender."[4] A mounted Confederate general led a dash for freedom and got away, but many of his men did not. Hagood's Brigade of Hoke's Division had 681 men when it went into this attack and it came back with only 274 of them. Harris' Brigade went in with 450 and came back with 196. The Federals captured 517 officers and men plus six battleflags. General John C. Sanders, commander of a brigade in Mahone's Division, was among those killed. "Besides all the wounded," Willcox wrote, "over two hundred Confederates lay dead upon the field in front of our defenses—a sad sight, for, enemies as they were, they were bone of our bone and flesh of our flesh."[5]

The last two divisions of the Union 2nd Corps returned to their old camps on the south side of the James early that morning, after what Hancock described as one of the most fatiguing and difficult marches of the entire campaign. They got little enough rest, however, for they were soon ordered out again to take position behind Warren's corps.

Down in Georgia at daylight on the 21st Kilpatrick's Union cavalry, heading northeast from McDonough, came to the Cotton River, "swollen to an enormous height" by the recent rains.[6] The raging water had swept away the bridge, but the Federals swam their horses across. One man and fifty horses were lost, as were almost all of the pack mules of Minty's brigade. By the 22nd Minty's and Long's men were back in their own camps, after completely circling Atlanta in five days, and Kilpatrick's own brigades had ridden half the circuit. The young cavalry general reported to Sherman that he had destroyed three miles of railroad track and three Confederate cannon, while bringing another back with him as a trophy of war, along with three captured battleflags and seventy prisoners. That same day Sherman finally put Jefferson C. Davis in command of the 14th Corps as the permanent replacement for Palmer.

Over in Mississippi, the Northern truce team reached Hernando at dawn on the 22nd with the rations for Forrest's prisoners, and when each of them had been given enough to last them for two days there was enough left over to feed all of Forrest's own men for one day. As soon as the Northern wagons left, at about 9 a.m., the Confederates resumed their march, reaching Panola at 10 that night. Due to the delay over their own rations, Duffield's pursuers did not reach Hernando until five hours after the Rebels left it. Learning from local civilians that the Confederates were far ahead of them and heading for the Tallahatchie, and recognizing that the area had been thoroughly stripped of food and forage, Duffield gave up the chase and turned back for Memphis.

A. J. Smith was happy on the morning of the 22nd because it had not rained for 36 hours. He had heard a rumor of Forrest's raid on Memphis but gave it little credence. He rode out of the Hurricane Creek bridge-head that morning with Mower's division and Bouton's brigade, and as they passed the camp of Shaw's division those three brigades joined the column. One of Kargé's cavalry regiments screened the advance, while the rest of the cavalry covered the flanks by taking roads parallel to that being followed by the infantry. At 8 a.m. the Union cavalry entered Oxford from all three directions, and within an hour the head of Mower's division marched in. Smith had Shaw's division halt a mile north of the town. Hatch was instructed to take his cavalry division westward to Panola, where he would turn to the south, destroying the tracks of the Mississippi & Tennessee Railroad as he marched.

Not long after Hatch departed, an officer brought Smith three dis-patches from Washburn, all dated the 21st and giving him the first reliable information about Forrest's raid. The first of these ordered Smith to send half his cavalry to Panola—which he had just done—and the other half to Abbeville. The second message gave the reasoning behind this order: "I am at a loss to know whether he means to cross at Panola, or go via Holly Springs. With a force to dispute the Panola crossing, and another force crossing at Abbeville, and moving toward him until they strike his trail, and then following him until overtaken, he may be captured."[7] The third message said that Rebels captured during the raid believed that Forrest would retreat by way of Holly Springs. The officer who brought the dispatches also informed Smith that part of the Union pontoon bridge across the Tallahatchie had been washed away by the swollen river.

Taking the third message as overriding the other two, Smith told Kargé to turn around and march to Abbeville, and then sent a staff officer galloping after Hatch to tell him also to turn back to Abbeville. The two divisions would cross to the north side of the river and proceed immediately to New Albany to intercept Forrest, who would presum-ably go through there on his way to Tupelo, Okolona, or Pontotoc. Kargé's troopers were back on the road by 11:30 a.m. and they reached Abbeville at 6 p.m., only to find that the troops left to guard the pontoon bridge had made no effort to repair the damage done by the swollen river. So Kargé put some of his own tired troopers to work on the job.

Forced to send off all his cavalry, worried about the lack of forage for his draft animals, and concerned about the condition of the roads and his bridge over the Tallahatchie, Smith decided to take his infantry back to Abbeville. Orders were given to destroy all public buildings in Oxford and all unoccupied private dwellings. One of the five private homes destroyed was definitely not unoccupied. It was the home of Jacob Thompson, whom Hatch had visited two weeks before. Smith sent a staff officer to oversee the destruction, and he gave Mrs. Thompson

fifteen minutes to save her personal effects. However, as fast as her valu-
ables were carried out of the house, they were stolen by Union soldiers.
Many homes that were not burned were broken into and robbed or
vandalized. Some of the junior officers tried to put a halt to this activity,
but none of the senior officers made any effort to stop it. In addition to
the five homes, 34 stores and businesses, two large brick hotels, several
carpenters' and blacksmiths' shops, and the Masonic Hall were burned.
As one Federal wrote, "The public square was surrounded by a canopy
of flame; the splendid courthouse was among the buildings destroyed,
with other edifices of a public character. In fact, where once stood a
handsome little country town, now only remained the blackened skele-
tons of the houses, and the smouldering ruins that marked the track of
war."[8] The Federals never commented much on the destruction of Oxford, either to deny it or justify it. Years later, one Union regimental
historian wrote that Southern newspapers they captured that day were
bragging about McCausland's burning of Chambersburg, Pennsylvania.
He said that Oxford was burned in retaliation.

"When, ten or eleven days since, I told Mr. Lincoln that his re-election
was an impossibility," New York political boss Thurlow Weed wrote to
Secretary of State Seward on the 22nd, "I also told him that the information would soon come to him through other channels. It has doubtless,
ere this, reached him. At any rate, nobody here doubts it; nor do I see
any body from other States who authorises the slightest hope of success.
Mr. Raymond [editor of the *New York Times*], who has just left me,
says that unless some prompt and bold step be now taken all is lost. The
People are wild for Peace. They are told that the President will only
listen to terms of Peace on condition Slavery be 'abandoned.' Mr. Swett
is well informed in relation to the public sentiment. He has seen and
heard much. Mr. Raymond thinks commissioners should be immediately
sent, to Richmond, offering to treat for Peace on the basis of Union.
That something should be done and promptly done, to give the Administration a chance for its life, is certain."[9]

It was during these dark days of the summer that, on a carriage ride
to the Soldiers' Home with Republican leader and brigadier general Carl
Schurz, Lincoln reacted to all the criticism that had been heaped upon
him by his own party. "They urge me with almost violent language to
withdraw from the contest, although I have been unanimously nominated," he complained. And he went on, more to himself than to Schurz:
"God knows, I have at least tried very hard to do my duty, to do right
to everybody and wrong to nobody. And now to have it said by men
who have been my friends and who ought to know me better, that I have

been seduced by what they call the lust of power, and that I have been doing this and that unscrupulous thing hurtful to the common cause, only to keep myself in office! Have they thought of that common cause when trying to break me down? I hope they have."[10]

Two prominent Republicans from Wisconsin paid a visit to the president at the Soldiers' Home. They saw Lincoln enter the room with inclined shoulders, rapid gait, "and shuffling, ample understandings with large slippers, and Briarian arms, a face radiant with intelligence and humor." He told them, "There are now between 1 & 200 thousand black men in the service of the Union . . . There have been men who have proposed to me to return to slavery the black warriors of Port Hudson and Olustee to their masters to conciliate the South. I should be damned in time and eternity for so doing. The world shall know that I will keep my faith to friends and enemies, come what will. My enemies say I am now carrying on this war for the sole purpose of abolition. It is & will be carried on so long as I am President for the sole purpose of restoring the Union. But no human power can subdue this rebellion without using the Emancipation lever as I have done . . . My enemies condemn my emancipation policy. Let them prove by the history of this war, that we can restore the Union without it."[11]

Jefferson Davis had his own problems just then. Lee wrote him a letter that day which showed that he understood what Grant was up to. "I think it is his purpose to endeavor to compel the evacuation of our present position by cutting off our supplies, and that he will not renew the attempt to drive us away by force." He also painted a grim picture of the consequences. "As I informed Your Excellency when we first reached Petersburg, I was doubtful of our ability to hold the Weldon road so as to use it. The proximity of the enemy and his superiority of numbers rendered it possible for him to break the road at any time, and even if we could drive him from the position he now holds, we could not prevent him from returning to it or to some other point, as our strength is inadequate to guard the whole road." Yet he was guardedly optimistic. "I shall do all in my power to procure some supplies by the Weldon road, bringing them by rail to Stony Creek, and thence by wagons. One train has already been sent out, and others are prepared to go. I think by energy and intelligence on the part of those charged with the duty, we will be able to maintain ourselves until the corn crop in Virginia comes to our relief, which it will begin to do to some extent in about a month." He closed with a personal appeal: "I trust that Your Excellency will see that the most vigorous and intelligent efforts be made to keep up our supplies, and that all officers concerned in the work, be required to give their unremitting personal attention to their duty."[12]

Grant also knew what Lee was up to. He knew that Warren's grasp on the Weldon Railroad at Globe Tavern did not prevent Lee from using wagons to bypass the Union position and reach the tracks farther south. But if he could destroy the track as far south as Rowanty Creek, thirteen miles beyond Warren's left, the Confederates would have to haul their supplies by wagon at least thirty miles from Stony Creek Depot to Dinwiddie Court House. So Hancock was sent south down the rail line on the 22nd with two divisions of his 2nd Corps to accomplish this task, while Gregg's cavalry division kept an eye out for the enemy.

Down on Mobile Bay, Fort Morgan continued to hold out, but Granger's Union forces had worked to within 200 yards of her glacis. "The topography of the country afforded the enemy great advantages," wrote the Confederate commander, General Page, "and they made a steady advance, covering it with an irregular fire from the batteries already in position, and lining their works with sharp-shooters to pick off our gunners. At daylight of the 22nd the fleet was reported moving up and encircling the fort, the iron-clads and the captured *Tennessee* included, and shortly its guns and all the batteries on land opened a furious fire, which came from almost every point of the compass, and continued unabated throughout the day, culminating in increased force at sundown; after which the heavy calibers and mortars kept it up during the night."[13]

Page was unable to return fire because the Union sharpshooters could pick off his gunners whenever they appeared at their guns. The walls of the fort were partly breached in several places "cutting up the fort to such an extent as to make the whole work a mere mass of debris," Page said.[14] In addition, all but two of the Confederate guns were disabled. Early in the night the woodwork of the citadel was set on fire by shells from Northern mortars, which Page said were particularly accurate, and when the Federals saw the flames they increased their rate of fire. Page ordered the powder brought out and flooded and had all the unserviceable guns spiked. With great efforts the Rebels were able to put out the fire before it could spread to the magazines.

"At daybreak on the 23rd," Page wrote, "accompanied by the engineer, I inspected the fort to determine its condition for further defense. The report was made by some of the company captains that of the casemates, which had been made as safe for the men as my means allowed, some had been breached, others partly so, and that another shot on them would bring down the walls. A resumption of the fire would thus inflict heavy loss of life, as there was no bomb-proof in the fort. The enemy's approach was very near the glacis, my guns and powder were destroyed, the citadel had been set on fire the second time and entirely consumed; the commissariat and quartermaster's stores had been destroyed by the shells of the enemy. It was evident that 'I had no means left of defense,' and that under a renewed bombardment unnecessary loss of life would result." At 6 a.m. the white flag went up over the fort, and by 2:30 p.m. the surrender was completed. "I am proud to say," Page wrote, "that throughout this severe test the garrison behaved like brave men."[15] The Federals took about 500 prisoners and 50 guns, bringing the total for the operations in the bay to 1,464 prisoners and 104 guns.

By dawn of the 23rd Duffield's Union cavalry was back in Memphis. At about 10 a.m. a rumor that Forrest had returned started a panic among the civilians and the Northern forces. Alarm bells rang, the loyal militia was turned out, and hundreds of former slaves were armed. "It was the most disgraceful affair I have ever seen," one staff officer wrote, "and proves that there is demoralization and want of confidence by the people in our army, and our army in some of its officers."[16] Washburn asked the local navy commander to send the ironclad *Carondolet* down the Mississippi on a reconnaissance, but it found nothing. Also that day, Washburn received a dispatch from Sherman, dated four days earlier, saying he wanted A. J. Smith and his old division, now commanded by Colonel Shaw, to join his armies before Atlanta.

Chalmers Confederates broke camp at dawn that day and crossed to the north side of the Yacona at two places. They found the inhabitants of Oxford so destitute that Chalmers had to give them rations from his supplies. At around 2 p.m. the Rebel vanguard approached Abbeville and ran into a Union patrol. The sound of gunfire alerted the two Union brigades still in the bridgehead and these soon attacked the Southerners, who had been trying to surround the outnumbered patrol. Before long the Confederates found that a Federal force was moving to block their retreat and that they were almost surrounded themselves. They escaped just in time, covered by the fire of their four guns, and rejoined the rest of Chalmers' command behind Hurricane Creek.

Over in Georgia that day—the day after Kilpatrick returned from his raid, reporting that it would take the Rebels ten days to repair the damage he had done to their railroads—the Federals saw trains coming into Atlanta from the south. "I became more than ever convinced," Sherman wrote, "that cavalry could not or would not work hard enough to disable a railroad properly, and therefore resolved at once to proceed to the execution of my original plan. Meantime, the damage done to our own railroad and telegraph by Wheeler, about Resaca and Dalton, had been repaired, and Wheeler himself was too far away to be of any service to his own army, and where he could not do us much harm."[17]

In Washington that day, President Lincoln received a letter from Henry J. Raymond, owner and editor of the *New York Times* and chairman of the Republican National Executive Committee. "I feel compelled to drop you a line concerning the political condition of the country as it strikes me. I am in active correspondence with your staunchest friends in every state, and from them all I hear but one report. The tide is setting strongly against us." Things were so bad, Raymond said, that if the election were to be held the next day, New York would be lost by 50,000 votes, and several other important states also. "Nothing but the most resolute action on the part of the government and its friends can save the country from falling into hostile hands," he said. The form of action he had in mind was another peace offer to the South. "In some way or other the suspicion is widely diffused that we can have peace with Union if we would. It is idle to reason with this belief—still more idle to denounce it. It can only be expelled by some authoritative act, at once bold enough to fix attention and distinct enough to defy incredulity and challenge respect."[18]

At a cabinet meeting that day, Lincoln passed around a sheet of paper that was so folded and pasted as to conceal what was written on it. He asked each member of the cabinet to sign his name on the back of the sheet, which they did without knowing why. It was a memorandum: "This morning, as for some days past, it seems exceedingly probable that this Administration will not be re-elected. Then it will be my duty to so co-operate with the President elect, as to save the Union between the election and the inauguration; as he will have secured his election on such ground that he can not possibly save it afterwards."[19]

---

1. Sheridan, *Memoirs*, 1:491.

2. Willcox, "Actions on the Weldon Railroad," 571.

3. John J. Pullen, *The 20th Maine* (New York, 1957), 229–230.

4. Ibid., 230.

5. Willcox, "Actions on the Weldon Railroad," 571.

6. Starr, *The Union Cavalry*, 3:480.

7. Bearss, *Forrest at Brice's Cross Roads*, 306.

8. Ibid., 309.
9. Basler, ed., *The Collected Works of Abraham Lincoln*, 7:514–515.
10. Sandburg, *Abraham Lincoln*, 577.
11. Ibid., 577–578.
12. Dowdey and Manarin, eds., *Wartime Papers of R. E. Lee*, 842–843.
13. R. L. Page, "The Defense of Fort Morgan," in *Battles and Leaders*, 4:410.
14. Ibid.
15. Ibid.
16. Bearss, *Forrest at Brice's Cross Roads*, 297.
17. Sherman, *Memoirs*, 2:104.
18. Foote, *The Civil War*, 3:549–550.
19. Basler, ed., *The Collected Works of Abraham Lincoln*, 7:514.

CHAPTER THIRTY-TWO

I Will Move With the Balance of the Army

24–27 August 1864

Washburn forwarded Sherman's request for Shaw's division to A. J. Smith on the 24th. This, coupled with the loss of all his cavalry as it rode off in search of Forrest, and the fact that a small party of Rebel raiders had burned five small trestles and bridges on the Mississippi Central, made Smith decide to retire to Holly Springs as soon as his bridge over the Tallahatchie was repaired. Meanwhile, Chalmers was also worrying about his situation. His men and his horses were very tired, he was finding it difficult to supply his command from the area north of the Yacona, and the recent rains had ruined much of his ammunition. Chalmers reported to Forrest that Abbeville residents had heard Smith's Federals deprecate the raid on Memphis as being unimportant. Anyway, he asked permission to fall back to "where the duty will not be so heavy and await developments."[1] Forrest told him to fall back behind the Yacona again but to leave scouts behind to keep an eye on the Yankees. He also ordered Colonel Bell to reinforce Chalmers.

Over in Georgia that day, Sherman heard about Forrest's raid on Memphis and telegraphed to Washburn to "send word to Forrest that I admire his dash but not his judgment. The oftener he runs his head against Memphis the better."[2] Sherman rode down to the big Chattahoochee bridge that day, "to see in person," as he wrote, "that it could be properly defended by the single corps proposed to be left there for that purpose, and found that the rebel works, which had been built by Johnston to resist us, could be easily utilized against themselves." When he got back to his camp that evening, he telegraphed Halleck: "Heavy fires in Atlanta all day, caused by our artillery. I will be all ready, and will commence the movement around Atlanta by the south, to-morrow night, and for some time you will hear little of us. I will keep open a courier line back to the Chattahoochee bridge, by way of Sandtown. The Twentieth Corps will hold the railroad-bridge, and I will move with the balance of the army, provisioned for twenty days."[3]

If the cavalry could not, or would not, do enough damage to the railroads south of Atlanta, the infantry would have to do it. So Sherman was taking the entire army, except for the 20th Corps. These men from the East would be given the job of holding the bridgehead south of the Chattahoochee while Sherman took his old reliable Westerners to do the work and the fighting.

Up in the Shenandoah Valley that day, Sheridan dismounted most of Duffié's 1st Cavalry Division of the Department of West Virginia so that the horses could be used to completely mount two of his regiments, which were then reassigned. The next day, the 25th, Colonel N. P. Chipman, Stanton's aide, sent a long report to his boss, showing that he was much impressed with Sheridan, his army, and his position. "The advantages are now all with Sheridan, as they were all with Early at Cedar Creek," he observed, after recounting the reasons for Sheridan's retreat from there. "Early cannot cross the Potomac at Shepherdstown into Pennsylvania, as its proximity would enable Sheridan to strike his column in flank at a moment of his own choosing. He will not attempt a like movement at Williamsport, as Sheridan could immediately put his army in their rear and close all lines of communication south, and, with such aid as could be readily given him, annihilate the enemy. He cannot pass through Snicker's Gap toward Washington without his movement being known in six hours from its commencement; he would enter a country lately made desolate and wholly incapable of subsisting an army, and could not reach Washington so soon as could Sheridan by the north side. It was necessary for Early, designing either of these objects, to have first eaten Sheridan, and at least temporarily to have rendered his army powerless. This he has failed to do, and it is no longer possible for him to do it."

Chipman predicted that Early would soon have to retreat. "Sheridan's army is in splendid condition," he said, "well in hand and manifesting the greatest anxiety for a fight. There is a feeling of entire confidence in their leader, and regiments talk about being able to whip brigades. Sheridan really has a very fine army here, and the universal good spirits that prevail and anxiety to fight manifested would make it a hard army to compete with."[4]

However, Early was not yet ready to retreat. In order to keep up the fear of an invasion of Maryland and Pennsylvania, he sent Fitz Lee's cavalry division northward to Williamsport that day, while marching his infantry and artillery to nearby Shepherdstown. Both were sites of major fords on the Potomac. Anderson, with Kershaw's infantry and McCausland's cavalry, was left to face Sheridan's Halltown lines. Near Kearneysville, Early's infantry ran into Torbert with Merritt's and Wilson's divisions of cavalry. Not realizing the size of the Rebel force, Torbert attacked and drove the leading troops back in confusion for three-quarters of a mile. But as the rest of the Southern infantry came up, the Union horsemen gave way. The Reserve Brigade of Merritt's division formed the rear guard, but the Southern infantry advanced so quickly that it was in danger of being cut off. Torbert sent Custer's brigade to the rescue.

"Custer accomplished his object with his usual magnificent dash," one of Torbert's aides wrote, "but going too far to the rear was himself cut off with his whole command from the rest of the corps." Neither Torbert nor anyone else seemed to worry very much about Custer's situation, however. As a Baltimore newspaper correspondent noted, "those who knew him better, and were acquainted with his dashing qualities as a cavalry leader, made up their minds he would cut his way out in some way or other."[5] Custer formed his brigade in a horseshoe formation with his back against the river as if preparing to fight to the death, but while the Confederates were conferring on how to wipe out his brigade with a minimum of losses to themselves he slipped one regiment at a time across the ford. And when the Rebels advanced they found the last of Federals riding up the hill on the Maryland side. Some of the Southerners actually cheered Custer's audacity and cleverness.

Sheridan sent Wilson's division across the Potomac at Harper's Ferry to hold the crossings of Antietam Creek in case the Rebels crossed into

Maryland. But Fitz Lee found Averell's Union cavalry guarding the fords at Williamsport and could not cross, and Early, realizing that his move had been discovered, did not take his infantry across either.

In Washington that day, Lincoln met with Henry J. Raymond of the pro-administration *New York Times*. "Hell is to pay," one of Lincoln's secretaries, John Nicolay, wrote to another. "The New York politicians have got a stampede on that is about to swamp everything. Raymond and the National Committee are here to-day. R. thinks a commission to Richmond is about the only salt to save us; while the Tycoon [Lincoln] sees and says it would be utter ruination. The matter is now undergoing consultation. Weak-kneed damned fools . . . are in the movement for a new candidate to supplant the Tycoon. Everything is darkness and doubt and discouragement."[6]

Later in the day Nicolay felt better about the visit, for the idea of sending a peace offer to Richmond had been squelched. In his private notebook, he wrote that Lincoln "and the stronger half of the Cabinet, Seward, Stanton, and Fessenden," showed Raymond that they had thoroughly considered his idea of a peace offer to Richmond. "He very readily concurred with them in the opinion that to follow his plan of sending a commission to Richmond would be worse than losing the Presidential contest—it would be ignominiously surrendering it in advance. Nevertheless the visit of himself and committee here did great good. They found the President and cabinet much better informed than themselves, and went home encouraged and cheered."[7]

In southern Virginia on the 25th, Hancock's Federals had torn up the track of the Weldon Railroad as far as three miles south of Reams Station. The night before, Hancock had received a warning from Meade that Confederate forces were heading his way. So he placed his men in the entrenchments that had been built around Reams Station two months before, when the Union 6th Corps had been there. These defenses formed three sides of a square, with each side about 1,000 yards long, and the east end open. Hancock put his 1st Division, under Brigadier General Nelson A. Miles, on the northern and western sides, and Gibbon's 2nd Division on the south. These units had been sadly depleted by casualties and expiring enlistments, so that they now totaled only about 6,000 men, mostly recent recruits and draftees received as replacements. Many of their officers also were new, or newly promoted. In addition, Hancock had with him 16 guns and about 2,000 cavalrymen from Gregg's division and Spear's brigade of Kautz's division.

Gibbon's division was about to proceed down the track to continue its work of destruction when, at about 8 a.m., three brigades of Confederate cavalry attacked Spear's Union troopers. Gregg went to Spear's support, but another brigade of Rebel horsemen made a wide circuit that took it around to the east of the Federal infantry, where it attacked Gregg's picket line, which ran from the Reams Station defenses to the Jerusalem Plank Road. These Southerners soon ran into stiffer opposition and circled back to rejoin the main body of Hampton's cavalry, but when Hancock reported this attack to Meade, the latter jumped to conclusions. Two northern-born boys had recently come into Union lines from Petersburg and had told of a rumor spreading in the city, that Early's and Anderson's forces had returned from the Shenandoah for an attack on Meade. And, after all, Grant's strikes north of the James and against the Weldon Railroad had been launched for the very purpose of bringing at least some of the Confederates back from the Valley. Two years before, Lee had brought Stonewall Jackson down from the Shenandoah for the attack on McClellan that had driven him away from Richmond.

Meade's primary fear was that the Rebels would interpose between Warren and Hancock. So he sent two brigades from the 3rd Division of the 2nd Corps from the main Union defenses to guard the intersection of the Jerusalem Plank Road and the road to Reams Station, four miles east of Hancock's position, which he considered vital to the safety of his army's rear. Later he ordered Willcox's 3rd Division of the 9th Corps sent to the same place from Globe Tavern. Both forces were in position to support either Hancock or Warren. White's division of the 9th Corps and Crawford's of the 5th were held in reserve at Globe Tavern, ready to counterattack any force that moved between Warren and Hancock.

Early and Anderson were, of course, still in the Valley, but the Rebels were massing what force they could manage in order to try to drive Hancock from the railroad. A. P. Hill was again in command, and he had with him a total of eight brigades of infantry—one from Field's Division, two from Mahone's, two from Heth's, and three from Wilcox's—as well as all five brigades of Hampton's Cavalry Corps, for a total of 5,000 infantry, 5,000 cavalry, and 20 guns. At around noon, Confederate major general Cadmus Wilcox, no kin to the Union brigadier general Orlando Willcox, sent two battalions of sharpshooters forward as skirmishers and drove in the Federal pickets, and next came two brigades of Rebel infantry, who assaulted Miles' defenses at around 2 p.m. One of the brigades approached through woods and underbrush and got all the way to the Union breastworks, but the other came to an open field, and when it saw the well-manned Northern defenses beyond, it stopped. This caused Willcox to withdraw the more successful brigade.

Still worried about the army's rear, Meade, who by then was at Globe

Tavern, authorized Hancock to withdraw from Reams Station if he thought it necessary, but Hancock felt that he was too closely engaged to withdraw before dark. Instead, he asked for the Union Willcox to bring his small 9th Corps division of 2,000 men to join him. From Globe Tavern to Reams Station was a distance of five miles, but Meade sent Willcox by way of the Jerusalem Plank Road because of his fear that the Rebels would be moving in force between Warren and Hancock, and to his concern for the Union rear, and this increased the march to twelve miles. Meade evidently considered a direct assault on Hancock's position at Reams Station to be the least dangerous contingency he faced.

Nevertheless, at about 5 p.m. the Confederate artillery began to bombard Hancock's defenses. Not many Federals were hit, but the effect on the morale of the inexperienced troops was considerable, especially in Gibbon's division, which was enfiladed. After about 15 minutes of this, four brigades of Rebel infantry advanced against Miles' defenses through a thunderstorm. Major General Henry Heth led the Rebel attack. He wanted to carry the flag of the 26th North Carolina in the charge, but the color bearer twice refused to yield it to him. "Come on then," Heth said, "we will carry the colors together."[8] This time all of the Confederate infantry reached the Union works, all that survived the advance at least. Many of the green Federals were firing too high, but others took a deadly toll of the attackers.

A Rebel captain was one of the first Southerners to reach the Union defenses, and he found them still fully manned. "Yanks," he yelled, "if you know what is best for you, you had better make a blue streak toward sunset." And many of them did. A Confederate major said that the Northerners "did not show the determination which had generally marked the conduct of Hancock's Corps." He said that the Federal infantry "seemed to be dazed by the vehemence of the attack, and made a very feeble resistance after their ranks were reached."[9] The Union artillerymen, however, fought to the last, and some of the infantry stayed long enough to use their bayonets. But a brigade of Gibbon's division that was in reserve refused to either advance or fire when Miles ordered it to counterattack. Hancock ordered others of Gibbon's units to retake the lost positions, but they made only token attempts. Miles led a counter attack by the 61st New York that recaptured some lost ground and a battery of guns and even threatened the Confederate rear, but his force was too small and had to withdraw.

When he heard Hill's infantry charge with a Rebel yell, Hampton sent his dismounted cavalrymen forward to attack Gibbon's position from the south. Gibbon's men soon found themselves caught between the Confederate infantry pouring through Miles' defenses on the right and the Rebel cavalry charging their front, and they moved back and forth from one side of their breastworks to the other, trying to find cover. To make matters worse for them, some of the Southern infantry turned captured Union guns their way. Gibbon's men were soon driven from their defenses into the woods to the east. Gregg's dismounted Union cavalry checked the Confederate advance for a while, but they, too, were soon driven back to the new line that Gibbon was forming in the woods. Miles blocked every attempt by the Rebels to advance any farther, and both Miles and Gregg offered to retake their lost positions, but Gibbon did not think his men could, or would, retake theirs. Hancock decided that such an attack would not be worth the losses that it would incur, anyway. No further destruction to the railroad could be accomplished in the presence of so large a Confederate force.

After dark the Federals fell back toward the junction with the Jerusalem Plank Road, meeting along the way Willcox's 9th Corps division coming from there. "Had our troops behaved as they used to, I could have beaten Hill," Hancock told Willcox. "But some were new, and all were worn out with labor."[10] Later Meade ordered Crawford's and White's divisions to join Hancock also.

The Rebels did not pursue. Hampton's cavalry occupied the Union entrenchments, and Hill's infantry returned to the defenses of Petersburg. The Southerners had captured between 1,750 and 2,150 prisoners, 9 guns, 12 flags and 3,100 small arms. News of the victory at Reams Station set off a round of rejoicing throughout the Confederacy and added to the feelings of frustration and hopelessness throughout the North. Angered and embarrassed by the behavior of his men, Gibbon submitted his resignation but was persuaded to withdraw it. The defeat also had a profound effect upon Hancock. "The agony of that day never passed from that proud soldier," his adjutant later wrote, "who for the first time, in spite of superhuman exertions and reckless exposure on his part, saw his lines broken and his guns taken."[11]

The CSS *Tallahassee* outran two Union blockading ships as she approached the North Carolina coast on the 25th. At sunset she moved toward the New Inlet off Wilmington under the cover of a haze. Another blockader, the USS *Monticello*, challenged the raider and she veered seaward. Soon two other blockaders joined the *Monticello* and opened fire. Commander Wood responded with all three guns and made for the inlet. More blockaders soon came up and one received slight damage to its starboard paddle box from a Confederate shell, but no other ships were hit. Guided by lights set out by the Southern garrison of Fort Fisher, the *Tallahassee* made it safely across the bar and under the protection of the guns of the fort. At 10:30 p.m. she dropped anchor, and Wood read prayers of thanks for their safe return before the mustered crew.

"The reason we have not more cruisers afloat is a deficiency of Wood suitable for naval purposes," the *Charleston Courier* quipped; "such as John Taylor Wood, for instance." Others in the South were not so happy about the *Tallahassee*'s cruise, however. "There is a thundering blockade off here now," the Wilmington *Daily Journal* complained. "All credit is mainly to the real or supposed presence of the *Tallahassee* and sundry other mysterious sea monsters."[12] General Chase Whiting, Confederate commander in the Wilmington area, complained to the secretary of the navy that because the raider had taken all the hard coal in the port, the blockade runners had been forced to use soft coal, which not only caused them to show black smoke from their stacks, but also cut their speed in half. As a result, seven of the fastest had recently been caught by the Federals.

In Mississippi, at dawn of the 25th, A. J. Smith's force began to cross back to the north bank of the Tallahatchie River, and by 8 a.m. both of Grierson's cavalry divisions were across. He took Kargé's division and rode to Holly Springs, which he reached at 2 p.m. There he was informed that it would be three or four days before service could be restored on the Mississippi Central Railroad. Hatch's division guarded the left flank of the infantry column and stopped for the night at Waterford. The recent unseasonal rains had been replaced by a scorching sun, and Smith's wagons were soon full of infantrymen who had collapsed from heat exhaustion. Many members of Bouton's brigade of U.S. Colored Troops were longing for the good old days when they had been slaves instead of soldiers.

General Washburn wrote a letter to his brother, Congressman Elihu B. Washburne, that day about Forrest's raid on Memphis: "We had a big thing here on Sunday morning, and ran a very narrow escape, indeed it was almost a miracle that I was not either killed or captured. One main drive . . . was to catch me. Forrest fooled A. J. Smith very badly, leaving his immediate front at Oxford and making a dash at Memphis without Smith knowing it, tho he had 4,500 cavalry with him. Had not Smith disregarded my orders he would have caught Forrest on his retreat. The whole [raid] was barren of fruit. They were in so great hurry to get away that they carried off hardly anything. I lost two fine horses, which is about the biggest loss of anybody."[13]

Over in Georgia on the night of the 25th, Sherman began moving his armies around the west side of Atlanta, toward the city's railroad lifelines. Slocum's 20th Corps marched north and took up position in the defenses on the south end of the Chattahoochee bridge. Stanley's 4th Corps closed up on Davis' 14th near Utoy Creek, and Garrard's cavalry division took over the vacated entrenchments. As all this took place during the hours of darkness, it was not immediately detected by the Confederates. With Wheeler still off on his fruitless raid, the Rebels were short on cavalry for reconnaissance, but they knew something was up, for the shelling of Atlanta had stopped. On the 26th, Hood's chief of staff, General Francis Shoup, recorded that "the prevailing impression of the scout reports thus far indicated the enemy were falling back across the Chattahoochee."[14] That night, in a driving rain, Howard's Army of the Tennessee drew out of its trenches, marched around behind Thomas' troops, and came up on the right of the 14th Corps along Utoy Creek, facing south. "The enemy seemed to suspect something that night," Sherman wrote, "using his artillery pretty freely; but I think he supposed we were going to retreat altogether."[15]

Up in the Shenandoah Valley on the 26th, Sheridan sent orders to Averell, whose cavalry division was already on the north side of the Potomac, to unite with Wilson's, which had been sent across the day before. Together they should be strong enough to stop any Rebels who crossed the river until reinforcements could be sent from Halltown by way of Harper's Ferry. Then Crook's infantry was sent forward to reconnoiter Anderson's lines and it not only broke through the Rebel skirmish line but, aided by a mounted charge by Lowell's cavalry brigade, drove two Confederate brigades from their entrenchments. Meanwhile, finding it impossible to assault Sheridan's lines and too dangerous to cross the Potomac, Early decided to fall back to his old position around Bunker Hill and he put his infantry on the road that day, while Anderson withdrew that night to Stephenson's Depot.

Sheridan reported to Grant that day: "The movement of the enemy toward Shepherdstown yesterday amounted to nothing. It did not disturb me nor cause me to make any changes, except to send one division of cavalry to Antietam Creek, on the north side . . . I think I can manage this affair. I have thought it best to be very prudent, everything considered."[16]

This crossed with a wire from Grant to Sheridan: "I now think it likely that all troops will be ordered back from the Valley except what they believe to be the minimum number to detain you. My reason for supposing this is based upon the fact that yielding up the Weldon road seems to be a blow to the enemy he cannot stand. I think I do not overstate the loss of the enemy in the last two weeks at 10,000 killed and wounded. We have lost heavily, mostly in captured, when the enemy gained temporary advantages. Watch closely, and if you find this theory correct push with all vigor. Give the enemy no rest, and if it is possible to follow to the Virginia Central road, follow that far. Do all the damage to railroads and crops you can. Carry off stock of all descriptions, and negroes, so as to prevent further planting. If the war is to last another year, we want the Shenandoah Valley to remain a barren waste."[17]

Over in Mississippi the Federals really were retreating, not because of Forrest's raid on Memphis, but because their railroad supply line had been cut and Sherman wanted part of Smith's infantry over in Georgia. After leaving two regiments to garrison Waterford, A. J. Smith marched his infantry and Hatch's cavalry to Holly Springs. That same day, Forrest received a message from Chalmers reporting that the Yankees had retreated across the Tallahatchie the day before. The elated Forrest, convinced that the threat to his district had ended, issued orders dispersing his units to various staging areas, where they would be easier to supply while still within supporting distance of each other. The next day, the 27th, Forrest asked for permission to go on sick leave until his foot was healed. Smith received instructions from Washburn that day to evacuate Holly Springs and return to Memphis with his infantry. He was to be sent to join Sherman with one division, and Mower would be held in Memphis with the other, ready to go down to reinforce Canby in case the latter decided to attack Mobile. Grierson's cavalry was to return to its camps along the Memphis & Charleston Railroad, and Bouton's brigade would rejoin the city's garrison.

---

1. Bearss, *Forrest at Brice's Cross Roads*, 313.

2. Foote, *The Civil War*, 3:518.

3. Sherman, *Memoirs*, 2:104.

4. *Official Records*, 43:1:907.

5. Both quotes from Gregory J. W. Urwin, *Custer Victorious* (East Brunswick, N.J., 1983), 176.

6. Sandburg, *Abraham Lincoln*, 580.

7. Ibid., 581.

8. John Horn, "Charge of the Tarheel Brigades," *Civil War Times Illustrated*, 29 (6, January–February 1991): 49.

9. Ibid.

10. Willcox, "Actions on the Weldon Railroad," 573.

11. Foote, *The Civil War*, 3:547.

12. Both quotes from Shingleton, "Cruise of the CSS Tallahassee," 39–40.

13. Bearss, *Forrest at Brice's Cross Roads*, 317.

14. Thomas Lawrence Connelly, *Autumn of Glory: The Army of Tennessee, 1862–1865* (Baton Rouge, 1971), 459.

15. Sherman, *Memoirs*, 2:105.

16. *Official Records*, 43:I:21.

17. Ibid., 43:I:916–917.

CHAPTER THIRTY-THREE

After Four Years of Failure

27–31 August 1864

Down in Georgia on the 27th of August, where rain continued to fall, Major General Henry W. Slocum assumed command of the 20th Corps of Thomas' Army of the Cumberland. He had come west from the Army of the Potomac with Hooker, whom he detested and vice versa. But when his 12th Corps had been consolidated with Howard's 11th to form the new 20th Corps, Slocum had been given command of the District of Vicksburg, which kept him away from Hooker. Now, with Hooker gone, Slocum had been given the corps, and the task of holding the bridgehead on the Chattahoochee.

Also on 27 August, two days before the Democratic national convention was to open, the *Chicago Tribune* noted that the city was "full to overflowing already with the gathering clans of Copperheads, Butternuts, O.A.K.'s, Sons of Liberty, original peace men, gentlemen from Canada, Fort Lafayette graduates, and border rebels under military parole."[1]

On the night of the 28th, Confederate agents met with the officers of the Sons of Liberty to see how the planned uprising was going. Captain

Hines reported that the prisoners inside Camp Douglas were organized and ready to attack their guards as soon as they heard the Sons of Liberty attack from outside. But the Copperheads had to report that they were still not ready. Their lodges had not been alerted, and the men they had brought to Chicago were not organized or prepared to take the initiative. It was also revealed that Vallandigham would not be able to take over the Democratic convention. He might be able to force a peace plank onto the platform, but he could not control the nomination. This was expected to go to either General McClellan or Governor Seymour of New York, and neither would go along with a northwestern confederacy.

It was also learned that Camp Douglas had suddenly been reinforced with several regiments of veteran soldiers. In fact, 3,000 Union troops had marched into Chicago in response to appeals from the commander of Camp Douglas, Colonel Sweet. Unknown to any of those present, an agent of the U.S. Secret Service had ridden to Chicago on the same train with several of Hines' men. Hines told the Copperheads that they should tell their followers that the troops were there to interfere with the Democratic convention. "We emphasized that any arrest would mean violent interference with the rights of the people," another Confederate agent, Captain Castleman, remembered. "We knew that an arrest by the troops was our best hope and it mattered little who was arrested. In other words an inflammable mob might thus be led beyond retreat."[2]

At 7 a.m. on the morning of the 28th Sheridan began to advance up the Shenandoah Valley again, heading for Charlestown without opposition. He was moving back to the Clifton-Berryville position, from which he could threaten an advance on Winchester and Early's lines of communication. Meanwhile, Averell's cavalry crossed to the south side of the Potomac at Williamsport and advanced toward Martinsburg, while Wilson crossed at Shepherdstown and Custer at Harper's Ferry. Merritt's division moved west and encountered Rebel cavalry at Leetown, near Kearneysville, and drove it across Opequon Creek.

Grant, who was not yet aware of this move, nevertheless would have agreed with it, for he telegraphed Sheridan that afternoon: "If you are so situated as to feel the enemy strongly without compromising the safety of your position, I think it advisable to do so. I do not know positively that any troops have returned yet from the Valley, but think you will find the enemy in your immediate front weaker than you are. We are quiet here, the enemy having abandoned the idea of driving us from the Weldon road, at least with his present force."[3]

Down in Georgia on the 28th of August, Sherman's three armies reached the Atlanta & West Point Railroad. Schofield's Army of the Ohio held the left near East Point. Thomas' Army of the Cumberland was in the center around Red Oak, and McPherson's Army of the Tennessee extended down to Fairburn. The rain had stopped as the Federals began to tear up the track. "You can't do too much of it," Sherman told Howard. "I don't think the enemy yet understand our movement. They have made no effort to stop us, only cavalry holding the road."[4]

The Confederates had been confused about Sherman's intentions since his current move began. At first they thought he was retreating. Then they found out that he had moved to the west of Atlanta. That day, Hood learned that at least part of Sherman's forces were on the West Point Railroad. Perceiving that the Federals' next objective would be the Macon Railroad, the last lifeline of Atlanta, but not anticipating the boldness of Sherman's maneuver, Hood sent two brigades of infantry and a regiment of cavalry down to Jonesboro to protect against raids. Three other infantry brigades, under General John C. Brown, were sent to Rough and Ready, about halfway between Atlanta and Jonesboro, while Hardee's corps was stationed at East Point, and Jackson's cavalry division was sent to probe west of there in an attempt to find out what the Yankees were up to.

Thomas' and Howard's Union armies spent the next day, the 29th, continuing to break up the West Point Railroad. "The track was heaved up in sections the length of a regiment," Sherman wrote, "then separated rail by rail; bonfires were made of the ties and of fence-rails on which the rails were heated, carried to trees or telegraph-poles, wrapped around and left to cool. Such rails could not be used again; and, to be still more certain, we filled up many deep cuts with trees, brush, and earth, and commingled with them loaded shells, so arranged that they would explode on an attempt to haul out the bushes. The explosion of one such shell would have demoralized a gang of negroes, and thus would have prevented even the attempt to clear the road."[5]

The trans-Mississippi region had been fairly quiet since Banks' unsuccessful Red River campaign. General Edmund Kirby Smith, the Confederate commander in the area, had tried to send two divisions east of the Mississippi, but the river was too well patrolled by the Federals. So, after abandoning that effort, Smith decided to try an invasion of Missouri, a state of deeply divided loyalties. For this purpose, all the cavalry he could scrape up was assembled at Princeton, Arkansas, south of Little Rock, halfway to Camden. There Major General Sterling Price, a former governor of Missouri, assumed command of the expedition that day, 29 August.

In the Shenandoah Valley that day, Early sent two divisions of infantry to drive Merritt's cavalry away from a bridge from which it threatened to interpose between his right and left flanks. After a severe fight the Union cavalry was forced to retreat. Sheridan sent Ricketts' 3rd Division of the 6th Corps to their aid, however, and they soon reestablished their control of the bridge.

The Democratic national convention finally opened on 29 August in Chicago, at a huge temporary structure known as the wigwam, like the one where the Republicans had gathered four years before to nominate Lincoln. The convention had originally been scheduled for 4 July, but the peace Democrats had managed to have it postponed on the theory that their influence would wax as the North's fortunes of war waned that summer. They were not entirely wrong, but they still could not control the convention. Lincoln was one of the few Republicans who saw that the better the Democrats' prospects became, the deeper would be the divisions in their party. In 1860 they had split over the question of slavery, nominated two different candidates, and thus allowed Lincoln to win the election. Now they would have to avoid splitting over the question of war and peace, or they would give him the election again. "They must nominate a Peace Democrat on a war platform, or a War Democrat on a peace platform," he had told newspaper reporter Noah Brooks a few days before; "and I personally can't say that I care much which they do."[6]

Thousands of spectators jammed the building, and trains on the nearby Lake Shore line filled the building with smoke and cinders and added to the cacophony. National chairman August Belmont, whom Brooks described as "pale, sleek-headed, dapper and smooth," predicted that the reelection of Lincoln would mean "the utter disintegration of our whole political and social fabric." He was followed at the rostrum by temporary chairman William Bigler, former governor of Pennsylvania, who declared that the land was "literally drenched in fraternal blood." Then Governor Horatio Seymour of New York, "smooth, oily, dignified, and serene," as Brooks described him, took the gavel as the permanent chairman of the convention.[7] He told the delegates and spectators that "the administration cannot save the Union. We can." This was greeted with loud applause. "Mr. Lincoln views many things above the Union. We put the Union first of all," he said. "He thinks a proclamation more than peace. We think the blood of our people more precious than edicts of the President."[8]

A number of resolutions were introduced: one suggesting a convention of the states, one for a demonstration in favor of the freedom and purity of the elective franchise, one suggesting that a committee immediately proceed to Washington to demand that President Lincoln suspend the draft until after the election. Samuel ("Sunset") Cox of Ohio moved that all resolutions should be referred to the proper committees without debate, but he was hissed by the spectators with cries of, "Get down, you War Democrat!"[9]

Captains Hines, the Confederate secret agent, met with the Copperhead leaders again that afternoon and asked about their readiness for the attacks on Camp Douglas and Rock Island. "The excuses of our comrades made evident a hesitancy about the sacrifice of life," Hines recorded.[10] That night he called a final meeting, but many did not attend. He asked for 500 men he could lead against Rock Island but was given only more excuses. He then asked for 200, half to go with Captain Castleman to Rock Island, half to stay with him to attack the city. The Copperheads promised to return with the men in a few hours. They came back with 25. Hines gave up.

On the 30th, the platform committee, known formally as the Committee on Resolutions, presented its work for the convention's approval. This was the moment of triumph for Clement Vallandigham. He had gained control of the subcommittee that actually wrote the platform and had rammed through a plank which maintained that "after four years of failure to restore the Union by the experiment of war, during which, under the pretense of a military necessity or war power higher than the Constitution, the Constitution itself has been disregarded in every part . . . the public welfare demands that immediate efforts be made for a cessation of hostilities with a view to an ultimate convention of the States, or other peaceable means to the end that at the earliest practicable moment peace may be restored on the basis of the Federal union of the States."[11]

The platform went on to pledge that, as soon as the party came to power, the armies would be disbanded and sent home and the Southern states would then be asked to join a convention for the restoration of the Union. Many observers were stunned when the platform passed with only four dissenting votes. McClellan's supporters had tried to substitute a plank that would have made the restoration of the Union a precondition to peace, "but it would have involved a fight & probably a rupture," as one of them explained. The one thing that had to be avoided was splitting the party again, and Vallandigham was threatening just that. As he wrote to McClellan a few days later, "If any thing implying war is presented, two hundred thousand men in the West will withhold their support, & many go further still."[12]

Next came the nomination of candidates, which included McClellan, L. W. Powell of Kentucky (who declined), Thomas H. Seymour of Connecticut, and former-president Franklin Pierce. Everyone assumed that McClellan, with the support of the War Democrats of the populous northeastern states, would receive the nomination. Then 37 years old, he was still known as the Young Napoleon. He had graduated second in the West Point class of 1846, three years behind Grant, and had gone immediately into the Engineers, always the elite branch of the pre-war regular army. He served with distinction in the Mexican War and gained an over-blown military reputation as an official observer of European military methods during the Crimean War. He had resigned his commission in 1857 and had soon become the vice-president of the Illinois Central Railroad.

At the outbreak of the war he had been put in charge of all of Ohio's volunteers, had been made a major general in the regular army, and had conducted a campaign that liberated most of Union-sympathizing West Virginia. Following the Federal disaster at Bull Run he had been called to Washington to bring order out of chaos, which he had done very well. He had soon maneuvered old Winfield Scott into retiring and took his place as general-in-chief, but when, after months of inactivity, he had taken his Army of the Potomac to the Virginia Peninsula east of Richmond, he had been reduced to the command of that army only. He had led it to within sight of the steeples of the Confederate capital, but when Lee attacked him, he lost his nerve and retreated to the James River and the protection of the navy's gunboats. By then Lincoln had tired of his caution and insubordination, but his strong political support and his popularity with both the officers and men of the army had made in risky to remove him. He had been given one more chance when Lee invaded Maryland. McClellan had attacked the Southerner, who had eventually retreated back to Virginia, but McClellan had been extremely slow about following him. As soon as the elections of November 1862 were past, Lincoln had fired him, and he had been sitting on the shelf ever since.

Now Congressman B. G. Harris of Maryland took the convention floor and tried to make an anti-McClellan speech. Chairman Seymour at first ruled him out of order, but "he went on shrieking and vociferating," as Noah Brooks put it, "denouncing McClellan for his so-called arbitrary arrests in Maryland, and saying that he had initiated tyranny and oppression before Lincoln had." The spectators rose in support of Harris, and Seymour let him come up to the platform and continue his tirade against McClellan. "Will you vote for such a man?" he asked. "I never will!" At this, several War Democrats protested that if he would not promise to support the nominee of the convention he was not fit to be a member of it, let alone address it. He was then ruled out of order again, and as he took his seat a New York delegate called him a traitor. "Harris promptly struck his defamer, and for a time there was a scene of general uproar and riotous confusion," Brooks said. General George Morgan, a delegate from Ohio, began a defense of McClellan's conduct in Maryland, but it caused such an outburst in the Maryland delegation that he changed the subject. Congressman Alexander Long, an ardent Peace Democrat, then rose to say that McClellan was "the worst and weakest man" who could be chosen and he begged the convention to nominate Governor Seymour of New York, or Vallandigham, or anybody but "this weak tool of Lincoln's." Both sides argued back and forth for so long that there was no time left to vote on the candidates, so that was put off until the next day. "Chicago was wild that night with brass bands and cheering Democrats," Brooks wrote, "who visited the different hotels, and insisted upon speeches from prominent delegates."[13]

Early on the morning of the thirtieth, after thoroughly wrecking the Atlanta & West Point Railroad, Sherman's armies began to march eastward, heading for the Macon & Western line. Logan's 15th Corps headed straight toward Jonesboro, where Kilpatrick had struck the week before, with Ransom's 16th and Blair's 17th corps on Logan's right. To the left were the 4th and 14th corps of Thomas' Army of the Cumberland. "I was with General Thomas that day," Sherman wrote, "which was hot but otherwise pleasant. We stopped for a short noon-rest near a little church . . . the infantry column had halted in the road, stacked their arms, and the men were scattered about—some lying in the shade of the trees, and others were bringing corn-stalks from a large corn-field across the road to feed our horses, while still others had arms full of the roasting-ears, then in their prime. Hundreds of fires were soon started with the fence-rails, and the men were busy roasting the ears. Thomas and I were walking up and down the road which led to the church, discussing the chances of the movement, which he thought were extra-hazardous, and our path carried us by a fire at which a soldier was roasting his corn. The fire was built artistically; the man was stripping the ears of their husks, standing them in front of his fire, watching them carefully, and turning each each little by little, so as to roast it nicely. He was down on his knees intent on his business, paying little heed to the stately and serious deliberations of his leaders. Thomas's mind was running on the fact that we had cut loose from our base of supplies, and that seventy thousand men were then dependent for their food on the chance supplies of the country (already impoverished by the requisitions of the enemy), and on the contents of our wagons. Between Thomas and his men there existed a most kindly relation, and he frequently talked with them in the most familiar way. Pausing awhile, and watching the operations of this man roasting his corn, he said, 'What are you doing?' The man looked up smilingly: 'Why, general, I am laying in a supply of provisions.' "That is right, my man, but don't waste your provisions.' As we resumed our walk, the man remarked, in a sort of musing way, but loud enough for me to hear: 'There he goes, there goes the old man, economizing as usual.'"[14] Sherman laughed at Thomas for economizing on corn, which cost only the labor of gathering it and roasting it, and for his worries about lines of supply when the fields were full of ripe corn. He told Thomas, "I have Atlanta as certainly as if it were in my hand!"[15]

Kilpatrick's Union troopers scouted in front of the moving infantry columns and covered their right. All morning they faced what Howard called an "endless plague" of Confederate cavalry backed up by artillery, but, with the help of two regiments of Howard's infantry, the Federals managed to convince the Rebels to "keep traveling." By noon the resistance had stiffened, forcing the Army of the Tennessee to stop, deploy into combat formations, and chase off the defenders. "Every half mile the operation was repeated," Howard recorded, "till everybody became weary and impatient."[16]

At 1 p.m. Hood told Hardee that he did not think it would be necessary to reinforce Jonesboro that day, but he did tell him to take whatever measures he might think necessary to hold that town and Rough and Ready. Later Hood told him to take command of all forces from East Point to Jonesboro, but he sent no forces south of Rough and Ready.

By 3:30 p.m. Howard's army had reached its objective for the day, Renfro Place. With plenty of daylight left, and lacking water, he pushed on six miles, with Sherman's permission, to the Flint River. There infantrymen from Hazen's division and dismounted troopers from Kilpatrick's division raced each other for the burning bridge. They extinguished the fire, and by dusk Logan's corps had established a bridgehead on a ridge east of the river, where it began to entrench. Kilpatrick rode on to Jonesboro, but was then driven back to the bridgehead by its defenders. One Confederate defender of Jonesboro remembered wishing, "Oh! that Hardee or night would come."[17]

That evening, when he finally learned that the Federals had reached the Flint River, Hood called for Hardee and S. D. Lee to join him at his headquarters. There Hood told Hardee to take both corps to Jonesboro that night and to attack Logan at dawn. Hood planned to follow that up the next day by bringing Lee's corps up to Rough and Ready, where it would be joined by Stewart, with Polk's old corps, and the Georgia militia, both sent down from Atlanta, for an attack down the west bank of the Flint River which he hoped would destroy Howard's army.

Up in Chicago the next day, the 31st, the Democratic National Convention finally got down to the business of selecting a presidential candidate. It did not take long, once the delegates got to it. Only 151 votes were needed to secure the nomination, and on the first ballot McClellan received 150, while Thomas H. Seymour received 43, and Horatio Seymour 7. Then the Missouri delegation switched 7 of its 11 votes from Thomas H. Seymour to McClellan, putting him over the top amid loud cheering. Everyone then rushed to get on the bandwagon by switching their votes until the tally finally stood at 202½ for McClellan and 23½ for Thomas Seymour. "Instantly the pent-up feelings of the crowd broke forth in the most rapturous manner," Noah Brooks recorded: "Cheers, yells, music, and screams indescribable rent the air, and outside the wigwam a park of cannon volleyed a salute in honor of the nominee. The long agony was over, and men threw up their hats, and behaved as much like bedlamites as men usually do under such circumstances." Vallandigham then rose, mounted the rostrum, and moved that the nomination be made unanimous. "His appearance on the platform, bland, smiling, and rosy, was the signal for a terrific outburst before he could open his mouth; and when his little speech was done, another whirlwind of applause greeted his magnanimous motion in favor of a war candidate."[18]

Several names were placed in nomination for the vice-presidential candidacy, but George H. Pendleton, a Peace Democrat from Ohio, won when the New York delegation threw its support behind him at a crucial point. Charles A. Wickliffe of Kentucky informed the convention that he and his colleagues in the West were "of the opinion that circumstances may occur between now and March fourth [inauguration day] which will make it proper for the Democracy of the country to meet in convention again." Brooks wrote that "although the real motive for this proposed action was not apparent to anybody, so far as I could learn by talking with the delegates afterward, Wickliffe's suggestion was received with a shout of boisterous applause. Mystery characterized many of the proceedings of the convention, and the mysteriousness of this proposition appeared to be significant to the delegates. It was taken as a warning that the managers of the party expected something extraordinary to happen, and were determined to be ready for any emergency that might arise; so the convention accordingly adopted a resolution to 'remain as organized, subject to be called at any time and place that the Executive National Committee shall designate.' It is a matter of history, however, that the convention never was called together again, and the reason for this cautious anchor to windward has never been disclosed."[19]

Before Captain Hines left Chicago for a tour through Ohio and Indiana, the Copperheads told him they had prepared for a new military establishment within the Sons of Liberty, under Jim Barrett and Dr. Bowles. The date for "positive action" had been postponed to election day in November. "We doubted this," Captain Castleman wrote.[20]

---

1. Milton, *Abraham Lincoln and the Fifth Column*, 302.
2. Horan, *Confederate Agent*, 129–130.
3. *Official Records*, 43:I:939.
4. McDonough and Jones, *War So Terrible*, 293.
5. Sherman, *Memoirs*, 2:106.
6. Noah Brooks, *Washington In Lincoln's Time* (New York, 1958), 164.
7. All three quotes from Allan Nevins, *The War For the Union: The Organized War to Victory 1864–1865* (New York, 1971), vol. 4, 98.
8. Foote, *The Civil War*, 3:551.
9. Brooks, *Washington In Lincoln's Time*, 166.
10. Horan, *Confederate Agent*, 130–131.
11. Earl Schenck Miers, *The Last Campaign: Grant Saves the Union* (Philadelphia, 1972), 137.
12. Both quotes from Stephen W. Sears, *George B. McClellan: The Young Napoleon* (New York, 1988), 373.
13. All these quotes from Brooks, *Washington In Lincoln's Time*, 168–169.
14. Sherman, *Memoirs*, 2:108.
15. Foote, *The Civil War*, 3:523.
16. McDonough and Jones, *War So Terrible*, 298.
17. Ibid., 299.
18. Both quotes from Brooks, *Washington In Lincoln's Time*, 170.
19. Ibid., 171.
20. Horan, *Confederate Agent*, 131.

CHAPTER THIRTY-FOUR

And Fairly Won

31 August–3 September 1864

At 3 a.m. on the 31st, down in Georgia, the head of Hardee's column, marching south from East Point, ran into Union pickets, and rather than reveal their movement by attacking, the Confederates detoured to the east. At about the same time, Hood was writing a nagging dispatch to Hardee, saying, "You must not fail to attack the enemy so soon as you can get your troops up." Ten minutes later a staff officer followed this with another: "General Hood desires you to say to your officers and men that the necessity is imperative. The enemy must be driven into and across the river."[1] Hardee stepped off a train at Jonesboro at dawn, ready to lead two-thirds of Hood's army against Logan's single corps, only to find that the troops had not yet arrived. He could not even find anyone who knew where they were. The detour had greatly lengthened the march, and the men were out of shape. General Patton Anderson said there was "a degree of straggling which I do not remember to have been exceeded in any former march of the kind." He added that the night march was very exhausting "to troops who had not been out of the trenches for thirty days."[2]

It was 9 a.m. before Hardee's corps was in position near Jonesboro, and S. D. Lee's men were still on the road even then. At 10 a.m. another prod came from army headquarters: "General Hood desires the men to go at the enemy with bayonets fixed, determined to drive every thing they may come against."[3] It was 11 a.m. before the bulk of Lee's corps arrived, and the last units did not get into position until 1:30 p.m. Hardee had everybody ready a half-hour later, and yet it was almost 3 p.m. before he launched the attack, nine hours behind schedule. In fact, on Howard's orders, Logan was just about to probe Hardee's position when the Confederates finally advanced.

While waiting for the others, the first Rebel units to arrive had spent the time digging in and watching Logan's Federals doing the same on high ground overlooking their own defenses and within rifle range of them. Meanwhile, Howard had sent Corse's 2nd Division of the 16th Corps across the Flint to take up position on Logan's right, facing southeast and south across a swampy ravine and extending westward to the river. To Corse's right, on the other side of the Flint, facing east, was Fuller's 4th Division of the same corps. To Corse's left were Harrow's 4th and Hazen's 2nd divisions of Logan's 15th Corps, with Osterhaus's 1st Division in reserve 500 yards behind them. Blair's 17th Corps was farther back, by the bridge over the Flint,

Hardee deployed S. D. Lee's corps on the right of his line, facing Logan, with Hindman's Division, under Patton Anderson, on the right, Stevenson's on the left, and Clayton's in reserve behind Anderson. Hardee's own corps, under the temporary command of Patrick Cleburne, his best division commander, was on Lee's left, with Bate's Division, temporarily commanded by Brown, next to Stevenson; Cleburne's, under Mark Lowrey, to Brown's left; and Cheatham's Division, under Maney, in the second line. Having so many units under temporary commanders did not help the efficiency of the attack. Hardee's plan was for Cleburne to wheel to the north and attack Logan's right, and then, when that was well under way, S. D. Lee would attack the Federals' front.

However, Lowrey's left-most brigade, Granbury's, ran into the dismounted cavalrymen of Kilpatrick's division on its left flank, and these troopers, with the help of their horse artillery, drove the Rebels back twice before retiring westward across the Flint River. Then, instead of turning north as planned, the Confederates followed the Union troopers to the west and across the river. Lowrey's own brigade, and Mercer's as well, moved in the same direction in an advance that Lowrey termed "impetuous and against orders."[4] Howard was delighted with this development: "Nothing, even if I had planned it, could have been better done to keep an entire Confederate division away from the main battlefield."[5]

This Southern advance in the wrong direction opened up a space between Lowrey's division and Brown's, which was moving to the northwest as planned, so Lowrey's reserve brigade, Govan's, had to be inserted into the gap. Maney's reserve division followed Brown's and tried to align with it, but Brown was repulsed so quickly by Corse's entrenched Federals that there was not enough time for that. "Their batteries opened on us by the dozen," one Confederate wrote, "with grape and cannister shot and shell. The face of the earth was literally torn to pieces, and how any of us escaped is yet a mystery."[6] Another Rebel remembered that "the air seemed literally swarming with screaming and bursting shells."[7] The chaplain of the 10th Tennessee was decapitated by one Union projectile as he knelt to comfort the dying colonel of a South Carolina regiment. It was a bad day for men of the cloth, for the chaplain of the 4th Kentucky (Confederate) lost his head in the same way, carried off by a cannon ball as he lifted his hands in prayer over a wounded soldier.

When S. D. Lee heard the noise of Granbury's fight with the dismounted Union troopers he assumed that Cleburne's attack on Corse was under way, so he sent his men forward against Logan. They overran the rifle pits of the Northern skirmishers and then approached the main line of defenses. The Federals held their fire until the Rebels were almost on top of them, then tore huge holes in the attacking formations with what Logan called the "most terrible and destructive fire I ever witnessed." "Many fell," a Union officer reported, "but with a stubborness and determination that showed no value was attached to human life, the gaps were soon closed, as if by magic."[8] But the Confederates could advance no further, and it was almost as dangerous to fall back. Many of them raised their hands in surrender and ran for the cover of the Federal lines, rather than fall back across the bullet-swept field. Clayton's reserve division, along with the reserve brigades of the other two divisions, then advanced and attacked Logan's line, but they were also repulsed. Late that afternoon Hardee pulled both corps back into the defensive line that had been dug near the railroad tracks just north of Jonesboro. Several Confederates braved the waning Union fire to go to the aid of their wounded comrades, and when the Federals realized what these men were doing they held their fire and gave them a cheer for their bravery.

One Union officer thought that the Confederates' attack had not been up to their old standards. "Besides losing a host of men in this campaign," he wrote, "the Rebel Army has lost a large measure of vim, which counts a good deal in soldiering." One Southern regimental commander seemed to agree, for he found his men were "possessed of some great horror of charging breastworks, which no power, persuasion, or example could dispel." General Clayton was not unhappy with his men's elan, just with their results. "Never was a charge begun with such enthusiasm terminated with accomplishing so little," he said.[9] Hood applied his standard yardstick for measuring offensive spirit to this attack, writing twenty years later that "the general attack . . . must have been rather feeble, as the loss incurred was only about fourteen hundred in killed and wounded—a small number in comparison to the forces engaged."[10]

At about the same time as this battle raged just northwest of Jonesboro, Stanley's 4th Corps of Thomas' army and Schofield's 23rd Corps reached the Macon & Western tracks just south of Rough and Ready, routing a force of dismounted Rebel cavalrymen who were dug in there. During this battle a train came steaming down the track, but when the engineer saw what was going on he backed his engine all the way to Atlanta, where he reported that Union troops were advancing upon the city from the south. Fearing an attack on the city by the still-unlocated forces of Thomas and Schofield, Hood ordered Hardee to send S. D. Lee's corps back to Atlanta. But Sherman was not turning toward Atlanta. Not yet. "Don't get off the track," he told Schofield; "hold it fast. We will get our whole army on the railroad as near Jonesborough as possible and push Hardee and Lee first, and then for Atlanta."[11]

That night Hood learned that Sherman's troops had cut his last railroad at Rough and Ready and several other places, and when S. D. Lee arrived at East Point at dawn he reported that Schofield's and Thomas' armies were both blocking the tracks in force. Hood realized that he could not hold Atlanta any longer, and after putting his staff to work at evacuating as much of his supplies as possible, he concentrated on trying to save his army. He now realized that most of Sherman's forces were not only sitting on his final lifeline, but were interposed between Hardee and the rest of his army. If the Federals concentrated against that one corps they might destroy it before he could come to its aid. Therefore, he decided to rush to Hardee's rescue with Lee's and Stewart's corps. Sherman saw the same possibility for ganging up on Hardee. He ordered Howard to send his entire army plus Kilpatrick's cavalry across the Flint to pin Hardee in place, while Thomas and Schofield were to turn to the south toward Jonesboro, tearing up track as they went.

The morning was cool for a change, a hint of the coming autumn in the air, but by afternoon the heat had returned. Hardee spent the time arranging his three divisions and improving the defenses just north of the little village of Jonesboro. Cheatham's Division, still under Carter, held the left, facing west, with three brigades on the front line and two more in reserve. Brown, still in command of Bate's Division, held the center, with three of his brigades on the line extending to the north and one in reserve. Cleburne held the right, with three of his brigades extending the line and Govan's Brigade facing north at the right end of the line to protect the flank. The reserve brigade of Bate's Division, Lewis', was soon sent to extend Govan's line to the east, and as these Kentuckians were beginning to dig in, Howard's artillery began to bombard them. One Rebel, who had just filled his canteen when a shell landed next to him, calmly poured the water on its sputtering fuse and put it out before it could explode. At about 1 p.m. Hardee sent one of Cheatham's reserve brigades, Gist's, to extend the east-west line even farther east. The area to Gist's front was covered by a dense stand of small trees, and the men were sent to bend them down, cut them off, and form an abatis of interlaced limbs to cover the brigade's entire front.

Meanwhile Thomas' army moved in slowly from the north. Jefferson C. Davis' 14th Corps was the first to arrive, coming in on Logan's left at about 3 p.m. Behind it, Stanley's 4th Corps lost its way and was on the wrong road, while Schofield's 23rd Corps, still tearing up track, brought up the rear. By 4 p.m. the 4th and 23rd Corps had still not arrived when the Union attack went in. Logan's three divisions advanced against the main Confederate line, while Davis, holding one division in reserve, sent his other two against the point where the Rebel line turned toward the east. Davis' men were slowed up by thick underbrush and sharp-barbed blackberry vines and then hit by the rapid fire of Cleburne's men, which drove them back. But they came on again, and this time Morgan's 2nd Division charged right over the works of Govan's Brigade, capturing General Govan, about 600 of his men, and eight pieces of artillery. "They ran over us like a drove of Texas beeves, by sheer weight of numbers," one of Govan's Arkansans remembered.[12] "They're rolling them up like a sheet of paper," Sherman exulted.[13]

Cheatham's other reserve brigade was brought over from the other end of the line, and with its help, and that of Granbury's men to their left, Govan's survivors and Lewis' Brigade managed to hold on until dark, although the fighting was fierce. "The troops met were confessedly among the best of the rebel army," a Union brigade commander wrote of Lewis' Kentuckians. "They fought with the greatest desperation."[14] Absalom Baird, commander of Davis' reserve division, reported that "on no occasion within my knowledge has the use of the bayonet been so general."[15]

"Being on the spot," Sherman wrote, "I checked Davis's movement, and ordered General Howard to send the two divisions of the Seventeenth Corps (Blair) round by his right rear, to get below Jonesboro', and to reach the railroad, so as to cut off retreat in that direction. I also dispatched orders after orders to hurry forward Stanley, so as to lap around Jonesboro' on the east, hoping thus to capture the whole of Hardee's corps." First he sent a captain, then a colonel, and finally he sent General Thomas himself to find Stanley and hurry him into position. "And that is the only time during the campaign I can recall seeing General Thomas urge his horse into a gallop," Sherman said.[15]

It was past 5 p.m. when Stanley's 4th Corps, with two divisions in the front line and the other in reserve, finally advanced against Gist's Brigade. "This delay," Stanley wrote, "which was fatal to our success, was in part owing to the very dense nature of the undergrowth and further to the slow progress the skirmishers made in pushing back those of the enemy." The commanders of the two Union brigades that actually faced Gist's defenses both reported that "they could not carry the position in their fronts owing to the perfect entanglement made by cutting down the thick undergrowth in front of the barricade the rebels had hastily thrown up. Newton's Division had a much longer circuit to make, and, when moved forward, the right brigade found no enemy in front but received a fire from their right flank. The flank of the enemy had been turned, but it was now pitch dark and nothing more could be done."[17] Sherman later complained that Stanley should not have stopped to deploy his troops into line of battle. "Had he moved straight on by the flank," he wrote, "or by a slight circuit to his left, he would have inclosed the whole ground occupied by Hardee's corps, and that corps could not have escaped us; but night came on, and Hardee did escape."[18]

It was a Union victory nevertheless, and a decisive one at that. A Federal major remembered finding himself "in a tangled lot of soldiers, on my horse, just against the enemy's log breastworks, my hat off, and tears streaming from my eyes, but as happy as a mortal is ever permitted to be. I could have lain down on that blood-stained grass, amid the dying and the dead and wept with excess of joy. I have no language to express the rapture one feels in the moment of victory, but I do know at such a moment one feels as if the joy were worth risking a hundred lives to attain. Men at home will read of that battle . . . but they can never feel as we felt, standing there quivering with excitement, amid the smoke and blood, and fresh horrors and grand trophies of that battlefield."[19]

That night Hardee retreated six miles down the railroad to Lovejoy's Station, while Hood marched southward with the rest of his army to link up with him. The Confederates left Atlanta "almost in a state of anarchy," as one journalist put it.[20] With all the railroads cut their ammunition train could not escape. Five locomotives, 81 cars, 13 pieces of heavy artillery, and large quantities of other supplies and equipment were destroyed, along with the roundhouse of the Western & Atlantic Railroad, a cannon foundry, a rolling mill, and the Atlanta Machine Company. Flames shot hundreds of feet into the air while explosions shattered windows and rocked houses all over the city. "It was a hot, stifling night," the journalist recorded, "and the people found it impossible to sleep. Shortly after dark the streets resounded with the heavy tread of marching soldiers . . . It soon became evident that they were moving out of the city."[21]

"That night I was so restless and impatient," Sherman wrote, "that I could not sleep, and about midnight there arose toward Atlanta sounds of shells exploding, and other sound like that of musketry. I walked to the house of a farmer close by my bivouac, called him out to listen to the reverberations which came from the direction of Atlanta (twenty miles to the north of us), and inquired of him if he had resided there long. He said he had, and that these sounds were just like those of a battle. An interval of quiet then ensued, when again, about 4 a.m., arose other similar explosions, but I still remained in doubt whether the enemy was engaged in blowing up his own magazines, or whether General Slocum had not felt forward, and become enganged in real battle."[22]

That same first day of September, the *Richmond Examiner* reported on the convention in Chicago. The Democrats' platform, it said, "floats between peace and war; being constructed in such a way as to drift to either side, and settle down next March in a war or peace policy as circumstances may require. Armistice will certainly be a feature in the new policy; armistice with a view to negotiation."[23] Southern independence would be secure if a Democratic administration negotiated with the Richmond government, the editor thought, but if it negotiated with the individual states, he was not so sure. In either case, he thought a negotiated peace would mean the preservation of slavery.

But the next day, 2 September, Lee wrote a very gloomy letter to President Davis outlining the predicament in which Grant had placed him. "As matters now stand," he said, "we have no troops disposable to meet movements of the enemy or strike where opportunity presents, without taking them from the trenches and exposing some important points. The enemy's position enables him to move his troops to the right or left without our knowledge, until he has reached the point at which he aims, and we are then compelled to hurry our men to meet him, incurring the risk of being too late to check his progress and the additional risk of the advantage he may derive from their absence. This was fully illustrated in the late demonstration north of the James River, which called troops from our lines here, who if present might have prevented the occupation of the Weldon Railroad. These rapid and distant movements also fatigue and exhaust our men, greatly impairing their efficiency in battle." He went on for most of the rest of this long letter to appeal for more men, especially the reserves of both Virginia and North Carolina. These were old men and young boys, who were normally only called out in the event of a local and temporary emergency. "I need not remind Your Excellency that the reserves are of great value in connection with our regular troops to prevent disaster, but would be of little avail to retrieve it," he said. "For this reason they should be put in service before the numerical superiority of the enemy enables him to inflict a damaging blow upon the regular forces opposed to him. In my opinion the necessity for them will never be more urgent, or their services of greater value than now."[24]

Down in Georgia at dawn on 2 September, Sherman sent his troops in pursuit of Hardee's corps. They soon found the woods south of Jonesboro to be full of Confederate stragglers and wounded men, while the roads were jammed with abandoned ambulances and burned wagons. That afternoon they found Hardee's troops behind formidable intrenchments, which looked to Sherman to be "as well constructed and as strong as if these Confederates had a week to prepare them." Other than a tentative probe that was violently repulsed, Sherman ordered no attack. "I do not wish to waste lives by an assault," he told Howard. He was still worried about Slocum and the sounds that he had heard the night before, perhaps indicating a battle. "Until we hear from Atlanta the exact truth," he told Thomas, "I do not care about your pushing your men against breastworks." But no word came. "Nothing positive from Atlanta," he told Schofield shortly before midnight, "and that bothers me."[25]

Slocum had heard the noises from Atlanta the night before even more clearly than had Sherman, since he was closer, and the next morning he sent his men cautiously toward the city to find out what they had meant. A few miles down the road the advance detachment discovered the mayor and city council coming out to meet them, and by noon a written surrender had been forwarded to the commander of the leading division. By 1 p.m. word had reached Slocum, and he fired off a telegram to the War Department in Washington. "General Sherman has taken Atlanta," he said, giving credit where it was due without trying to grab any of the glory for himself. Soon Slocum's men marched into the city and raised the Stars and Stripes over the courthouse. Then, as one witness remembered, "such a cheer went up as only a conquering army, flushed with victory, can give."[26] A 10-year-old girl living in Atlanta told her diary that "the cavalry came dashing. We were all frightened. We were afraid they were going to treat us badly. But when the infantry marched in they were orderly and behaved very well, I think I shall like the Yankees very much."[27]

Late that night Sherman's mind was finally put at ease when a courier rode up with a message from Slocum, telling him what had happened. "General Thomas's bivouac was but a short distance from mine," Sherman wrote, "and, before giving notice to the army in general orders, I sent one of my staff-officers to show him the note. In a few minutes the officer returned, soon followed by Thomas himself, who again examined the note, so as to be perfectly certain that it was genuine. The news seemed to him too good to be true. He snapped his fingers, whistled, and almost danced, and, as the news spread to the army, the shouts that arose from our men, the wild halooing and glorious laughter, were to us a full recompense for the labor and toils and hardships through which we had passed in the previous three months."[28]

A courier line from the Lovejoy Station position to Atlanta was soon organized, and from there to the telegraph line at the Chattahoochee bridgehead. And Sherman sent off a wire to Halleck: "So Atlanta is ours, and fairly won. Since May 5, we have been in one constant battle or skirmish, and need rest."[29] Back came a message that said: "The national thanks are rendered by the President to Major-General W. T. Sherman and the gallant officers and soldiers of his command before Atlanta, for the distinguished ability and perservance displayed in the campaign in Georgia, which, under Divine favor, has resulted in the capture of Atlanta. The marches, battles, sieges, and other military operations, that have signalized the campaign, must render it famous in the annals of war, and have entitled those who have participated therein to the applause and thanks of the nation." It was signed "Abraham Lincoln, President of the United States." The next day Sherman's old friend Grant sent a less formal message: "I have just received your dispatch announcing the capture of Atlanta. In honor of your great victory, I have ordered a salute to be fired with shotted guns from every battery bearing upon the enemy. The salute will be fired within an hour, amid great rejoicing.[30]

---

1. Both quotes from McDonough and Jones, *War So Terrible*, 300.
2. Ibid.
3. Ibid.
4. Scaife, *The Campaign For Atlanta*, 92.
5. Both quotes from McDonough and Jones, *War So Terrible*, 301.

6. William C. Davis, *The Orphan Brigade: the Kentucky Confederates Who Couldn't Go Home* (Garden City, N.Y., 1980), 232.

7. McDonough and Jones, *War So Terrible*, 302.

8. Ibid., 301.

9. Ibid., 302.

10. Ibid., 303.

11. Ibid., 304.

12. Ibid., 306.

13. Ibid.

14. Davis, *The Orphan Brigade*, 235.

15. McDonough and Jones, *War So Terrible*, 305–306.

16. Sherman, *Memoirs*, 581.

17. Scaife, *The Campaign For Atlanta*, 94.

18. Sherman, *Memoirs*, 581.

19. Miers, *The General Who Marched to Hell*, 179.

20. McDonough and Jones, *War So Terrible*, 307.

21. Ibid., 308.

22. Sherman, *Memoirs*, 582.

23. Nevins, *The War for the Union*, 4:101.

24. Dowdey and Manarin, eds., *Wartime Papers of R. E. Lee*, 847–850.

25. All three quotes from Foote, *The Civil War*, 3:529.

26. Both quotes from McDonough and Jones, *War So Terrible*, 310.

27. Ibid., 312.

28. Sherman, *Memoirs*, 582.

29. Scaife, *The Campaign For Atlanta*, 95.

30. Both messages in Sherman, *Memoirs*, 583.

EPILOGUE

The capture of Atlanta sharply contradicted the Democratic party's contention that the war was a failure. And in the new mood of cautious optimism that followed Sherman's victory, the North suddenly remembered Farragut's closing of Mobile Bay and recognized it as another important nail in the Confederacy's coffin. When Sheridan soon added a string of victories in the Shenandoah Valley, Lincoln's reelection began to look like a distinct possibility, although by no means a certainty even then.

The next volume in this series will detail those victories in the Shenandoah, as well as more battles around Richmond and Petersburg in which Grant extended his death grip on the railroads; also the election, more plots by Copperheads and Confederate agents, and Sherman's march across Georgia, plus Hood's invasion of Tennessee and defeat at Nashville. The fourth, and final, volume will then carry the narrative on through Sherman's march through the Carolinas, the fall of Richmond, Lee's surrender at Appomattox, Wilson's raid through Alabama, the capture of Mobile, the assassination of Lincoln, and the capture of Jefferson Davis.

Appendix A

Cast of Characters

The principal characters mentioned in this book are listed here alphabetically, with a brief description of their place in the scheme of events. Those who have only minor roles in the text, and are not likely to be confused with others, are not listed.

Abbreviations used below:
CSA—Confederate States Army
CSN—Confederate States Navy
USA—United States (regular) Army
USMA—United States Military Academy (given with class)
USN—United States Navy
USV—United States Volunteers

ADAMS, Wirt—Brigadier General, CSA. Commander of the District of Central Mississippi in S. D. Lee's Department of Alabama, Mississippi and East Louisiana.

ANDERSON, J. Patton—Major General, CSA. Succeeded Hindman in command of a division in S. D. Lee's 2nd Corps of Hood's Army of Tennessee.

ANDERSON, Richard H. ("Dick")—Major General, CSA (USMA 1842). Commander of the 1st Corps of Lee's Army of Northern Virginia.

AUGUR, Chrisopher C.—Major General, USV (USMA 1843). Commander of the Department of Washington.

AVERELL, William Woods—Brigadier General, USV (USMA 1855). Commander of the 2nd Cavalry Division of Hunter's Department of West Virginia.

AYRES, Romeyne B.—Brigadier General, USV (USMA 1847). Commander of the 2nd Division of Warren's 5th Corps in Meade's Army of the Potomac.

BABCOCK, Orville—Lieutenant Colonel, USA (USMA May 1861). Aide on Grant's staff.

BANKS, Nathaniel P.—Major General, USV. Commander of the Department and Army of the Gulf. Prominent Republican politician before the war.

BARLOW, Francis C.—Brigadier General, USV. Commander of the 1st Division of Hancock's 2nd Corps in Meade's Army of the Potomac.

BATE, William B.—Major General, CSA. Commander of a division in Hardee's 1st Corps of Johnston's (later Hood's) Army of Tennessee.

BEAUREGARD, P. G. T.—General, CSA (USMA 1838). Commander of the Department of Southern Virginia and North Carolina, which included Petersburg but not Richmond.

BELL, Tyree H.—Colonel, CSA. Commander of the 4th Brigade in Buford's 2nd Division of Forrest's District of Northern Mississippi and West Tennessee in S. D. Lee's Department of Alabama, Mississippi and East Louisiana.

BELL, William B.—Lieutenant Colonel, USV. Commander of the 8th Iowa Volunteer Infantry Regiment in Buckland's District of Memphis in Washburn's District of West Tennessee in Howard's Department of the Tennessee in Sherman's Military Division of the Mississippi.

BENJAMIN, Judah P.—Secretary of State in Jefferson Davis' cabinet.

BIRNEY, David B.—Major General, USV. Commander of the 3rd Division of Hancock's 2nd Corps in Meade's Army of the Potomac. Temporarily replaced Hancock when the latter was incapacitated by an old wound. Later commander of the 10th Corps in Butler's Army of the James (Dept. of Va. and N.C.).

BLAIR, Francis P. ("Frank"), Jr.—Major General, USV. Commander of the 17th Corps in McPherson's (Later Howard's) Army of the Tennessee in Sherman's Military Division of the Mississippi. Simultaneously a member of Congress. Brother of Montgomery Blair.

BLAIR, Montgomery—Postmaster General in Lincoln's cabinet (USMA 1835). Brother of Frank Blair.

BOUTON, Edward—Colonel, USV. Commander of a brigade of U.S. Colored Troops in Washburn's District of West Tennessee of McPherson's (later Howard's) Department of the Tennessee in Sherman's Military Division of the Mississippi. Attached to A. J. Smith's force.

BRAGG, Braxton—General, CSA (USMA 1837). Nominal general-in-chief of the Confederate army. Former commander of the Army of Tennessee.

BRECKINRIDGE, John C.—Major General, CSA. Commander of the Department of Southwestern Virginia. Former vice-president of the United States. Presidential candidate of the Southern wing of the Democratic party in 1860.

BROOKS, W. T. H.—Brigadier General, USV (USMA 1841). Commander of the 1st Division of W. F. Smith's 18th Corps in Butler's Army of the James (Dept. of Va. and N.C.).

BROWN, John C.—Brigadier General (Major General as of 4 August 1864), CSA. Commander of a division in Hood's (temporarily Cheatham's, later S. D. Lee's) 2nd Corps of Johnston's (later Hood's) Army of Tennessee.

BUCKLAND, Ralph P.—Brigadier General, USV. Commander of the District of Memphis in Washburn's District of West Tennessee in Howard's Army of the Tennessee in Sherman's Military Division of the Mississippi.

BUFORD, Abraham—Brigadier General, CSA (USMA 1841). Commander of the 2nd Division of cavalry in Forrest's District of Northern Mississippi and West Tennessee in S. D. Lee's Department of Alabama, Mississippi and East Louisiana.

BURNSIDE, Ambrose E.—Major General, USV (USMA 1847). Commander of the 9th Corps in Meade's Army of the Potomac. Had been commander of the Army of the Potomac, then Schofield's predecessor as commander of the Army of the Ohio.

BUTLER, Benjamin Franklin—Major General, USV. Commander of the Department of Virginia and North Carolina and the Army of the James. Prominent Democratic politician before the war.

CANBY, Edward R. S.—Major General, USV (USMA 1839).

Commander of the Military Division of Western Mississippi, consisting of Steele's Department of Arkansas and Banks' Department of the Gulf.

CHALMERS, A. H.—Lieutenant Colonel, CSA. Commander of the 18th Missouri Cavalry Battalion in Rucker's 6th Brigade, later transfered to Wade's 2nd Brigade, of General James Chalmers' 1st Division of Forrest's District of Northern Mississippi and West Tennessee.

CHALMERS, James R.—Brigadier General, CSA. Commander of the 1st Division of cavalry in Forrest's District of Northern Mississippi and West Tennessee in S. D. Lee's Department of Alabama, Mississippi and East Louisiana.

CHEATHAM, Benjamin F.—Major General, CSA. Commander of a division in Hardee's 1st Corps of J. E. Johnston's (later Hood's) Army of Tennessee. Temporarily succeeded Hood as commander of the 2nd Corps, until S. D. Lee arrived.

CLAY, Clement C.—Commissioner of the Confederate government in Canada.

CLAYTON, Henry D.—Major General, CSA. Commander of a division in Hood's (briefly Cheatham's, later S. D. Lee's) 2nd Corps of Johnston's (later Hood's) Army of Tennessee.

CLEBURNE, Patrick R.—Major General, CSA. Commander of a division in Hardee's 1st Corps of Johnston's (later Hood's) Army of Tennessee.

COON, Datus E.—Colonel, USV. Commander of the 3rd Brigade in Grierson's Cavalry Division of the 16th Corps in Washburn's District of West Tennessee, later the 2nd Brigade of Winslow's 2nd Division of Grierson's Cavalry Corps.

CORSE, John M.—Brigadier General, USV (USMA 1857). Inspector general on Sherman's staff. Appointed to replace Sweeny as commander of the 2nd Division of the 16th Corps in Dodge's Left Wing of that corps in Logan's (later Howard's) Army of the Tennessee in Sherman's Military Division of the Mississippi.

COX, Jacob D.—Major General, USV. Commander of the 3rd Division of the 23rd Corps in Schofield's Army of the Ohio of Sherman's Military Division of the Mississippi.

CRAWFORD, Samuel W.—Brigadier General, USV. Commander of the 3rd Division of Warren's 5th Corps in Meade's Army of the Potomac.

CROOK, George—Brigadier General, USV (USMA 1852). Commander of the 2nd Infantry Division of Hunter's Department of West Virginia.

CROSSLAND, Edward—Colonel, CSA. Succeeded Lyon in command of the 3rd (Kentucky) Brigade in Bell's 2nd Division of Forrest's District of Northern Mississippi and West Tennessee in S. D. Lee's Department of Alabama, Mississippi and East Louisiana.

CURTIN, John I.—Colonel, USV. Commander of the 1st Brigade of Potter's 2nd Division of Burnside's 9th Corps in Meade's Army of the Potomac.

CUTLER, Lysander—Brigadier General, USV. Commander of the 4th Division of Warren's 5th Corps in Meade's Army of the Potomac.

DANA, Charles A.—U.S. Assistant Secretary of War. Sent by Lincoln to accompany Grant and report on the general's progress.

DAVIS, Jefferson—(USMA 1828). First and only president of the Confederate States of America.

DAVIS, Jefferson C.—Brigadier General, USV. Commander of the 2nd Division of Palmer's 14th Corps of Thomas' Army of the Cumberland in Sherman's Military Division of the Mississippi. Later succeeded Palmer in command of the corps.

DODGE, Grenville M.—Brigadier General, USV. Commander of the Right Wing of the 16th Corps, part of McPherson's Army of the Tennessee in Sherman's Military Division of the Mississippi.

DOUGLAS, Henry Kyd—Major, CSA. Officer on the staff of Major General Dodson Ramseur.

DUCKWORTH, W. L.—Colonel, CSA. Commander of the 7th Tennessee Cavalry Regiment. Succeeded Rucker as commander of the 6th Brigade in Chalmers' 1st Division of Forrest's District of Mississippi and West Tennessee in S. D. Lee's Department of Alabama, Mississippi and East Louisiana.

DUFFIÉ, Alfred N.—Brigadier General, USV. Commander of the 1st Cavalry Division of Hunter's Department of West Virginia.

DUFFIELD, George W.—Lieutenant Colonel, USV. Commander of the 3rd Iowa Cavalry Regiment in Noble's 2nd Brigade in Winslow's (later Kargé's) 2nd Division in Gierson's Cavalry Corps of Washburn's District of West Tennessee. In charge of the pursuit of Forrest after his raid on Memphis.

EARLY, Jubal Anderson—Lieutenant General, CSA (USMA 1837). Commander of the 2nd Corps of Lee's Army of Northern Virginia, renamed the Army of the Valley when detached to the Shenandoah.

ELZEY, Arnold—Major General, CSA (USMA 1837). Commander of a division composed of two infantry brigades that Breckinridge had brought from his Department of Southwestern Virginia to Lynchburg.

EMORY, William H.—Brigadier General, USV (USMA 1831). Commander of the 1st Division of the 19th Corps, sent to Washington from Louisiana. Then commanded all 19th Corps troops in Sheridan's Army of the Shenandoah (Middle Military Division).

EWELL, Richard S. ("Dick")—Lieutenant General, CSA (USMA 1840). Commander of the Department of Richmond. Early's predecessor in command of the 2nd Corps of Lee's Army of Northern Virginia.

FIELD, Charles W.—Major General, CSA (USMA 1849). Commander of a division in Anderson's 1st Corps of Lee's Army of Northern Virginia.

FORREST, Jesse—Lieutenant Colonel, CSA. Commander of a picked detachment of men sent to capture General Washburn. Brother of General Nathan B. Forrest.

FORREST, Nathan Bedford—Major General, CSA. Commander of Confederate forces in northern Mississippi and western Tennessee.

FORREST, William H.—Captain, CSA. Commander of a company of scouts under his brother General Nathan B. Forrest.

FRANKLIN, William B.—Major General, USV (USMA 1843). Recuperating from a wound received while commanding the 19th Corps in Banks' Red River campaign, he was briefly captured by Bradley Johnson's cavalry near Baltimore. Grant first considered placing him in charge of the Army of the James while confining Butler to administering the Department of Virginia and North Carolina, then nominated him to command the combined forces confronting Early.

FRENCH, Samuel G.—Major General, CSA (USMA 1843). Commander of a division in Polk's (later Stewart's) Corps (Army of Mississippi) in Johnston's Army of Tennessee.

FULLER, John W.—Brigadier General, USV. Commander of the 4th Division of the 16th Corps in Dodge's Left Wing of that corps in McPherson's (later Howard's) Army of the Tennessee in Sherman's Military Division of the Mississippi.

GARRARD, Kenner—Brigadier General, USV (USMA 1851). Commander of the 2nd Cavalry Division of Thomas' Army of the Cumberland in Sherman's Military Division of the Mississippi.

GEARY, John W.—Brigadier General, USV. Commander of the 2nd Division of Hooker's 20th Corps in Thomas' Army of the Cumberland in Sherman's Military Division of the Mississippi.

GIBBON, John—Brigadier General, USV (USMA 1847). Commander of the 2nd Division of Hancock's 2nd Corps in Meade's Army of the Potomac.

GILBERT, James I.—Colonel, USV. Commander of the 2nd Brigade of Moore's 3rd Division of the 16th Corps in A. J. Smith's Right Wing of that corps.

GILLMORE, Quincy A.—Major General, USV (USMA 1849). Former commander of the 10th Corps in Butler's Army of the James (Dept. of Va. and N.C.), put in temporary command of the troops of the 19th Corps as they arrived in Washington.

GILMORE, J. R.—New York businessman who met with Jefferson Davis about terms for peace.

GORDON, John B.—Major General, CSA. Commander of a division in Early's 2nd Corps of Lee's Army of Northern Virginia and Early's Army of the Valley.

GRANGER, Gordon—Major General, USV (USMA 1845). Commander of army forces in Mobile Bay from Canby's Military Division of West Mississippi.

GRANT, Ulysses Simpson—Lieutenant General, USA (USMA 1843). General-in-chief of the United States Army.

GREELEY, Horace—Founder and editor of the *New York Tribune*. Influential Republican.

GREGG, David McMurtrie—Brigadier General, USV (USMA 1855). Commander of the 2nd Division of Sheridan's Cavalry Corps of Meade's Army of the Potomac.

GRIERSON, Benjamin H.—Brigadier General, USV. Commander of the 1st Cavalry Division of the 16th Corps (later upgraded to a Cavalry Corps) in McPherson's (later Howard's) Department of the Tennessee in Sherman's Military Division of the Mississippi. Attached to A. J. Smith's force.

GRIFFIN, Charles—Brigadier General, USV (USMA 1847). Commander of the 1st Division of Warren's 5th Corps in Meade's Army of the Potomac.

GRIFFIN, Simon—Brigadier General, USV. Commander of the 2nd Brigade of Potter's 2nd Division of Burnside's (later Parke's) 9th Corps in Meade's Army of the Potomac.

GROVER, Cuvier—Brigadier General, USV (USMA 1850). Commander of the 2nd Division of Emory's 19th Corps in Sheridan's Army of the Shenandoah (Middle Military Div.).

HALLECK, Henry Wager—Major General, USA (USMA 1839). Grant's predecessor as general-in-chief and former boss in the trans-Allegheny West. Named by Grant as the chief of staff of the U.S. Army to take care of the paperwork in Washington while he ran the armies from the field.

HAMPTON, Wade—Major General, CSA. Commander of the Cavalry Corps of Lee's Army of Northern Virginia.

HANCOCK, Winfield Scott—Major General, USV (USMA 1840). Commander of the 2nd Corps in Meade's Army of the Potomac.

HARDEE, William J.—Lieutenant General, CSA (USMA 1838). Commander of the 1st Corps of J. E. Johnston's Army of Tennessee.

HARROW, William—Brigadier General, USV. Commander of the 4th Division of Logan's 15th Corps in McPherson's (later Howard's) Army of the Tennessee in Sherman's Military Division of the Mississippi.

HASCALL, Milo S.—Brigadier General, USV (USMA 1852). Commander of the 2nd Division of the 23rd Corps in Schofield's Army of the Ohio in Sherman's Military Division of the Mississippi.

HATCH, Edward—Brigadier General, USV. Commander of the 1st Division of Grierson's Cavalry Corps of Howard's Department of the Tennessee in Sherman's Military Division of the Mississippi. Attached to A. J. Smith's force.

HAZEN, William B.—Brigadier General, USV (USMA 1855). Succeeded Morgan L. Smith in command of the 2nd Division of Logan's 15th Corps in Howard's Army of the Tennessee in Sherman's Military Division of the Mississippi.

HETH (pronounced heath), Henry—Major General, CSA (USMA 1847). Commander of a division in A. P. Hill's 3rd Corps of Lee's Army of Northern Virginia.

HILL, Ambrose Powell—Lieutenant General, CSA (USMA 1847). Commander of the 3rd Corps of Lee's Army of Northern Virginia.

HILL, Daniel Harvey—Major General, CSA (USMA 1842). Without assignment, due to a quarrel with President Davis over the latter's withdrawal of his promotion to lieutenant general.

HINCKS, Edward W.—Brigadier General, USV. Commander of a division composed entirely of regiments of U.S. Colored Troops in W. F. Smith's 18th Corps in Butler's Army of the James (Dept. of Va. and N.C.).

HINDMAN, Thomas C.—Major General, CSA. Commander of a division in Hood's (later S. D. Lee's) 2nd Corps of Johnston's (later Hood's) Army of Tennessee.

HINES, Thomas—Captain, CSA. The Confederacy's top secret agent working out of Canada.

HOKE, Robert F.—Brigadier General, CSA. Commander of a division in Beauregard's Department of Southern Virginia and North Carolina.

HOOD, John Bell—Lieutenant General (later temporary General), CSA (USMA 1853). Commander of the 2nd Corps of J. E. Johnston's Army of Tennessee and Johnston's successor as commander of that army.

HOOKER, Joseph—Major General, USV (USMA 1837). Commander of the 20th Corps in Thomas' Army of the Cumberland in Sherman's Military Division of the Mississippi. Had been commander of the Army of the Potomac between Burnside and Meade. Came west with reinforcements after Chickamauga.

HOWARD, Oliver O.—Major General, USV (USMA 1854). Commander of the 4th Corps in Thomas' Army of the Cumberland in Sherman's Military Division of the Mississippi. Succeeded McPherson as commander of the Army of the Tennessee.

HUMPHREY, William—Brigadier General, USV. Commander of the 2nd Brigade of Willcox's 2nd Division of Burnside's (later Parke's) 9th Corps in Meade's Army of the Potomac.

HUMPHREYS, Andrew A.—Major General, USV (USMA 1831). Chief of staff of Meade's Army of the Potomac.

HUNTER, David—Major General, USV (USMA 1822). Commander of the Department of West Virginia.

HURLBUT, Stephan A.—Major General, USV. Former commander of

the 16th Corps, Department of the Tennessee, headquartered at Memphis.

IMBODEN, John D.—Brigadier General, CSA. Commander of a brigade of cavalry stationed in the Shenandoah Valley.

JACKSON, Thomas J. ("Stonewall")—Lieutenant General, CSA (USMA 1846). Late commander of the Army of the Valley, and of the 2nd Corps of the Army of Northern Virginia. Mortally wounded at the battle of Chancellorsville in May 1863.

JACKSON, William H. ("Red")—Brigadier General, CSA (USMA 1856). Commander of a division of cavalry in Polk's (later Stewart's) Army of Mississippi in Johnston's (later Hood's) Army of Tennessee.

JACKSON, William L.—Colonel, CSA. Commander of a brigade of cavalry in the Shenandoah Valley area.

JAQUESS, James F.—Colonel, USV. Former minister who met with Jefferson Davis about terms for peace.

JOHNSON, Bradley T.—Colonel (later Brigadier General), CSA. Commander of Maryland units in the Shenandoah Valley. Later commander of a brigade of cavalry in Early's Army of the Valley.

JOHNSON, Bushrod R.—Brigadier General, CSA (USMA 1840). Commander of a division of infantry in Beauregard's Department of Southern Virginia and North Carolina.

JOHNSON, Richard W.—Brigadier General, USV (USMA 1849). Commander of the 1st Division of Palmer's 14th Corps in Thomas' Army of the Cumberland in Sherman's Military Division of the Mississippi. Later, made Sherman's chief of cavalry in order to clear the way for Jefferson C. Davis to succeed Palmer in command of the corps.

JOHNSTON, Joseph Eggleston—General, CSA (USMA 1829). Commander of the Army of Tennessee, defending Georgia.

KAUTZ, August V.—Brigadier General, USV (USMA 1852). Commander of the Cavalry Division of Butler's Army of the James (Dept. of Va. and N.C.).

KELLY, John H.—Brigadier General, CSA (USMA June 1861). Commander of a division in Wheeler's Cavalry Corps of Johnston's (later Hood's) Army of Tennessee.

KERSHAW, Joseph B.—Major General, CSA. Commander of a division in Anderson's 1st Corps of Lee's Army of Northern Virginia.

KILPATRICK, Hugh Judson—Brigadier General, USV (USMA 1861). Commander of the 3rd Cavalry Division of Thomas' Army of the Cumberland in Sherman's Military Division of the Mississippi.

LEDLIE, James H.—Brigadier General, USV. Commander of the 1st Division of Burnside's 9th Corps in Meade's Army of the Potomac.

LEE, Fitzhugh ("Fitz")—Major General, CSA (USMA 1856). Commander of a division in Hampton's Cavalry Corps of R. E. Lee's Army of Northern Virginia. Nephew of R. E. Lee.

LEE, George Washington Custis—Brigadier General, CSA (USMA 1854). Aide on President Davis' staff. Eldest son of R. E. Lee.

LEE, Robert Edward—General, CSA (USMA 1829). Commander of the Army of Northern Virginia.

LEE, Samuel P.—Rear Admiral, USN. Commander of the North Atlantic Blockading Squadron, which included the Union ships in the James River.

LEE, Stephen Dill—Major General, CSA (USMA 1854). Commander of the Department of Alabama, Mississippi and Eastern Louisiana. Later sent to command the 2nd Corps of Hood's Army of Tennessee. Only very distantly related to the Virginia Lees.

LEE, W. H. F. ("Rooney")—Major General, CSA. Commander of a division in Hampton's Cavalry Corps of R. E. Lee's Army of Northern Virginia. Second son of R. E. Lee.

LEGGETT, Mortimer D.—Brigadier General, CSA. Commander of the 3rd Division of Blair's 17th Corps in McPherson's (later Howard's) Army of the Tennessee in Sherman's Military Division of the Mississippi.

LINCOLN, Abraham—Sixteenth president of the United States.

LOGAN, John A.—Major General, USV. Commander of the 15th Corps in McPherson's (later Howard's) Army of the Tennessee in Sherman's Military Division of the Mississippi.

LOMAX, Lunsford L.—Brigadier General (Major General as of 10 August), CSA (USMA 1856). Commander of a brigade in Fitzhugh Lee's division of Hampton's Cavalry Corps of Lee's Army of Northern Virginia. Succeeded Robert Ransom as chief of cavalry in Early's Army of the Valley.

LONGSTREET, James—Lieutenant General, CSA (USMA 1842).

Anderson's predecessor in command of the 1st Corps of Lee's Army of Northern Virginia, wounded at the battle of the Wilderness.

LORING, William W.—Major General, CSA. Commander of a division in Polk's (later Stewart's) Corps (Army of Mississippi) in Johnston's (later Hood's) Army of Tennessee.

LYON, Hylan B.—Brigadier General, CSA (USMA 1856). Commander of the 3rd (Kentucky) Brigade in Buford's 2nd Division of Forrest's District of Northern Mississippi and West Tennessee in S. D. Lee's Department of Alabama, Mississippi and East Louisiana. Put in temporary charge of an "infantry" force composed of dismounted cavalrymen and gunless heavy artillerymen.

MABRY, Hinchie P.—Colonel, CSA. Commander of a brigade of cavalry attached to Buford's 2nd Division of Forrest's District of Northern Mississippi and West Tennessee from Adams' District of Central Mississippi, both in S. D. Lee's Department of Alabama, Mississippi and East Louisiana.

MAHONE, William ("Billy")—Brigadier General, CSA. Commander of a division in the 3rd Corps of Lee's Army of Northern Virginia.

MANEY, George E.—Brigadier General, CSA. Commander of a brigade in Cheatham's Division of Hardee's 1st Corps of Johnston's (later Hood's) Army of Tennessee. Took temporary command of the division while Cheatham was in temporary command of what had been Hood's 2nd Corps.

MARTINDALE, John H.—Brigadier General, USV (USMA 1835). Commander of the 2nd Division of W. F. Smith's 18th Corps in Butler's Army of the James (Dept. of Va. and N.C.).

MAURY, Dabney H.—Major General, CSA (USMA 1846). Commander of the District of the Gulf in S. D. Lee's Department of Alabama, Mississippi and East Louisiana. Left in temporary command of the department when Lee was sent to command a corps in the Army of Tennessee.

McCAUSLAND, John—Brigadier General, CSA. Commander of a brigade of cavalry in the Shenandoah Valley area.

McCLELLAN, George B.—Major General, USA (USMA 1846). Founder of the Army of the Potomac. Halleck's predecessor as general-in-chief of the U.S. Army. Democratic candidate for president in 1864.

McCLURE, John D.—Colonel, USV. Commander of the 47th Illinois

Volunteer Infantry Regiment. Succeeded to command of the 2nd ("Eagle") Brigade of Mower's 1st Division of the 16th Corps in A. J. Smith's Right Wing of that corps in Washburn's District of West Tennessee.

McCOOK, Alexander M.—Major General, USV (USMA 1852). Former commander of the 20th Corps in the Army of the Cumberland. Put in command of the reserve forces in Washington during Early's raid.

McCOOK, Edward M.—Brigadier General, USV. Commander of the 1st Cavalry Division of Thomas' Army of the Cumberland in Sherman's Military Division of the Mississippi. Cousin of Alexander McCook. One of 17 McCook brothers, sons and cousins who served in the Union army.

McCULLOCH, Robert—Colonel, CSA. Commander of the 2nd Brigade of cavalry in Chalmers' 1st Division of Forrest's District of Northern Mississippi and West Tennessee in S. D. Lee's Department of Alabama, Mississippi and East Louisiana.

McMILLEN, William L.—Colonel, USV. Commander of the 1st Brigade of Mower's 1st Division of the 16th Corps in A. J. Smith's Right Wing of that corps in Washburn's District of West Tennessee.

McPHERSON, James B.—Major General, USV (USMA 1853). Commander of the Department and Army of the Tennessee, part of Sherman's Military Division of the Mississippi.

MEADE, George Gordon—Major General, USV (USMA 1835). Commander of the Army of the Potomac.

MERRITT, Wesley—Brigadier General, USV (USMA 1860). Commander of the Reserve Brigade in Torbert's 1st Division of Sheridan's Cavalry Corps. Succeeded to command of the division when Torbert became chief of cavalry in Sheridan's Army of the Shenandoah (Middle Military Division).

MILES, Nelson A.—Brigadier General, USV. Commander of the 1st Brigade of Barlow's 1st Division of Hancock's 2nd Corps in Meade's Army of the Potomac. Succeeded to command of the division on 29 July. He was later the general-in-chief of the U.S. Army, during the Spanish-American War.

MOORE, David—Colonel, USV. Commander of the 3rd Division of the 16th Corps, part of A. J. Smith's Right Wing of that corps in Washburn's District of West Tennessee in McPherson's (later Howard's) Department of the Tennessee in Sherman's Military Division of the Mississippi.

MORGAN, John Hunt—Brigadier General, CSA. Commander of a small division of Kentucky cavalry in the Department of Southwestern Virginia. Recently defeated during a raid into Kentucky.

MOSBY, John Singleton—Lieutenant Colonel, CSA. Commander of a battalion of partisan rangers in northern Virginia.

MOTT, Gershom—Brigadier General, USV. Commander of the 3rd Brigade of Birney's 4th Division of Hancock's 2nd Corps of Meade's Army of the Potomac. Succeeded to command of the division when Birney succeeded Hancock in command of the corps.

MOWER, J. A.—Brigadier General, USV. Commander of the 1st Division of the 16th Corps, part of A. J. Smith's Right Wing of that corps, in Washburn's District of West Tennessee in McPherson's (later Howard's) Department of the Tennessee in Sherman's Military Division of the Mississippi.

MURRAY, Charles D.—Colonel, USV. Commander of the 1st Brigade of Moore's 3rd Division of the 16th Corps in A. J. Smith's Right Wing of that corps in Washburn's District of West Tennessee.

NEELY, James J.—Colonel, CSA. Commander of the 1st Brigade of cavalry in Chalmer's 1st Division of Forrest's District of Northern Mississippi and West Tennessee in S. D. Lee's (temporarily Maury's) Department of Alabama, Mississippi and East Louisiana.

NEILL, Thomas H.—Brigadier General, USV (USMA 1847). Commander of the 2nd Division of Wright's 6th Corps in Meade's Army of the Potomac, later in Sheridan's Army of the Shenandoah.

NEWTON, John—Brigadier General, USV (USMA 1842). Commander of the 2nd Division of Howard's (later Stanley's) 4th Corps in Thomas' Army of the Cumberland in Sherman's Military Division of the Mississippi.

ORD, Edward O. C.—Major General, USV (USMA 1839). Briefly assigned to command the Middle Department, then succeeded W. F. Smith as commander of the 18th Corps in Butler's Army of the James (Dept. of Va. and N.C.).

OSTERHAUS, Peter J.—Major General, USV. Commander of the 1st Division of Logan's 15th Corps in Howard's Army of the Tennessee in Sherman's Military Division of the Mississippi. His promotion while on extended leave caused Sherman to protest the unfairness of such promotions.

PAGE, Richard L.—Brigadier General, CSA. Commander of outer defenses of Mobile Bay. First cousin of R. E. Lee.

PALMER, John M.—Major General, USV. Commander of the 14th Corps in Thomas' Army of the Cumberland in Sherman's Military Division of the Mississippi.

PARKE, John G.—Major General, USV (USMA 1849). Burnside's successor as commander of the 9th Corps in Meade's Army of the Potomac.

PICKETT, George E.—Major General, CSA (USMA 1846). Commander of a division in Anderson's 1st Corps of Lee's Army of Northern Virginia.

PLEASANTS, Henry—Lieutenant Colonel, USV. Commander of the 48th Pennsylvania Volunteer Infantry Regiment (1st Brig., 2nd Div., 9th Corps), which captured Battery No. 15 at Petersburg and dug the mine that provoked the battle of the Crater.

POLK, Leonidas—Lieutenant General, CSA (USMA 1827). Commander of a force known as the Army of Mississippi, or Polk's Corps, that had been brought from the Department of Alabama, Mississippi and Eastern Louisiana to reinforce J. E. Johnston's Army of Tennessee in Georgia. Former Episcopal bishop of Louisiana.

POLK, Lucius E.—Brigadier General, CSA. Commander of a brigade in Cleburne's Division of Hardee's 1st Corps of Johnston's (later Hood's) Army of Tennessee.

PORTER, Horace—Lieutenant Colonel, USA (USMA 1860). An aide on Grant's staff. His book *Campaigning With Grant* is frequently quoted in these pages.

POTTER, Robert B.—Brigadier General, USV. Commander of the 2nd Division of Burnside's 9th Corps in Meade's Army of the Potomac.

PRICE, Sterling—Major General, CSA. Commander of Confederate forces in Arkansas. Former governor of Missouri.

RAMSEUR, Stephen Dodson—Major General, CSA (USMA 1860). Commander of a division in Early's 2nd Corps of Lee's Army of Northern Virginia (later the Army of the Valley).

RANSOM, Matthew W. ("Matt")—Brigadier General, CSA. Commander of a brigade of North Carolina infantry in the Department of Richmond. Brother of Robert Ransom.

RANSOM, Robert, Jr.—Major General, CSA (USMA 1850). Former commander of the Department of Richmond, sent to command all the cavalry in the Shenandoah Valley area. Brother of Matt Ransom.

RANSOM, Thomas E. G.—Brigadier General, USV. Succeeded Dodge as commander of the Left Wing of the 16th Corps in Howard's Army of the Tennessee in Sherman's Military Division of the Mississippi.

RAWLINS, John A.—Brigadier General, USV. Grant's chief of staff and former neighbor in Galena, Illinois.

RICKETTS, James B.—Brigadier General, USV (USMA 1839). Commander of the 3rd Division of Wright's 6th Corps in Meade's Army of the Potomac, later Sheridan's Army of the Shenandoah.

RODDEY, Philip D.—Brigadier General, CSA. Commander of the District of Northern Alabama in S. D. Lee's Department of Alabama, Mississippi and East Louisiana.

RODES, Robert Emmett—Major General, CSA. Commander of a division in Early's 2nd Corps of Lee's Army of Northern Virginia (later the Army of the Valley).

ROSSER, Thomas L.—Brigadier General, CSA (USMA May 1861). Commander of a brigade of Virginia cavalry (known as the Laurel Brigade) in Hampton's (Butler's) Division of Hampton's Cavalry Corps of Lee's Army of Northern Virginia. Close friend of Union general George A. Custer.

ROUSSEAU, Lovell H.—Major General, USV. Commander of the District of Nashville in Thomas' Department of the Cumberland in Sherman's Military Division of the Mississippi. He led a cavalry raid through eastern Alabama to join Sherman in Georgia.

RUCKER, Edmund—Colonel, CSA. Commander of the 6th Brigade of cavalry in Chalmer's 1st Division of Forrest's District of Northern Mississippi and West Tennessee in S. D. Lee's Department of Alabama, Mississippi and East Louisiana.

SANDERS, George N.—One of the Confederate commissioners in Canada.

SCHOFIELD, John M.—Major General, USV (USMA 1853). Commander of the Army of the Ohio (also known as the 23rd Corps) in Sherman's Military Division of the Mississippi.

SEDDON, James A.—Secretary of War in Jefferson's Davis' cabinet.

SEMMES, Raphael—Commander, CSN. Commander of the commerce raider CSS *Alabama*.

SEYMOUR, Horatio—Governor of New York and prominent Democrat.

SHAW, William T.—Colonel, USV. Succeeded Moore as commander of the 3rd Division of the 16th Corps, in A. J. Smith's Right Wing of that corps, in Howard's Department of the Tennessee in Sherman's Military Division of the Mississippi.

SHERIDAN, Philip Henry—Major General, USV (USMA 1853). Commander of the Cavalry Corps of the Army of the Potomac. Later commander of the Middle Military Division and of the Army of the Shenandoah.

SHERMAN, William Tecumseh—Major General, USV (USMA 1840). Grant's favorite subordinate and his successor in command, first of the Army of the Tennessee, and then of the Military Division of the Mississippi.

SIGEL (rhymes with regal), Franz—Major General, USV. Commander of the Reserve Division of the Department of West Virginia. Hunter's predecessor in command of the department until defeated at New Market in May 1864. Prominent leader of the German-American community, which was very important to the Republican party.

SLOCUM, Henry W.—Major General, USV (USMA 1852). Commander of the District of Vicksburg in McPherson's Department of the Tennessee in Sherman's Military Division of the Mississippi. Later made commander of the 20th Corps in Thomas' Army of the Cumberland.

SMITH, Andrew Jackson—Brigadier General (later Major General), USV (USMA 1838). Commander of the Right Wing, 16th Corps, Army of the Tennessee, just returned from Banks' Red River campaign.

SMITH, E. Kirby—General, CSA (USMA 1845). Commander of the Trans-Mississippi Department.

SMITH, Giles A—Brigadier General, USV. Commander of the 4th Division of Blair's 17th Corps in McPherson's (later Howard's) Army of the Tennessee in Sherman's Military Division of the Mississippi.

SMITH, Gustavus W.—Major General of Georgia Militia (USMA 1842). Commander of a division of Georgia Militia attached to Johnston's (later Hood's) Army of Tennessee.

SMITH, John E.—Brigadier General, USV. Commander of the 3rd Division of Logan's 15th Corps in Howard's Army of the Tennessee in Sherman's Military Division of the Mississippi. He and his division protected the railroads in northern Georgia throughout the Atlanta campaign.

SMITH, Morgan L.—Brigadier General, USV. Commander of the 2nd Division of Logan's 15th Corps in McPherson's Army of the Tennessee in Sherman's Military Division of the Mississippi.

SMITH, William Farrar ("Baldy")—Major General, USV (USMA 1845). Commander of the 18th Corps in Butler's Army of the James (Dept. of Va. and N.C.).

STANLEY, David S.—Major General, USV (USMA 1852). Commander of the 1st Division of Howard's 4th Corps in Thomas' Army of the Cumberland in Sherman's Military Division of the Mississippi. Succeeded to command of the corps when Howard succeeded McPherson in command of the Army of the Tennessee.

STANTON, Edwin McMasters—Secretary of War in Lincoln's cabinet.

STEELE, Frederick—Major General, USV (USMA 1843). Commander of the Department of Arkansas.

STEWART, Alexander P.—Major General, CSA (USMA 1842). Commander of a division in Hood's 2nd Corps of Johnston's Army of Tennessee. Succeeded Polk in command of the Army of Mississippi, or Polk's Corps, in Johnston's (later Hood's) Army of Tennessee.

STEVENSON, Carter—Major General, CSA (USMA 1838). Commander of a division in Hood's (later S. D. Lee's) 2nd Corps of Johnston's (later Hood's) Army of Tennessee.

STONEMAN, George—Major General, USV (USMA 1846). Commander of the Cavalry Division of Schofield's Army of the Ohio in Sherman's Military Division of the Mississippi.

STURGIS, Samuel D.—Brigadier General, USV (USMA 1846). Former chief of cavalry of McPherson's Department of the Tennessee in Sherman's Military Division of the Mississippi. Soundly defeated by Forrest at Brice's Cross Roads, Mississippi.

SULLIVAN, Jeremiah C.—Brigadier General, USV. Commander of the 1st Infantry Division of Hunter's Department of West Virginia.

SWEENY, Thomas W.—Brigadier General, USV. Commander of the

2nd Division of the 16th Corps in Dodge's Left Wing of that corps in McPherson's (later Howard's) Army of the Tennessee in Sherman's Military Division of the Mississippi.

TAYLOR, Richard ("Dick")—Lieutenant General, CSA. Commander of Confederate forces in western Louisiana. Son of former U.S. president Zachary Taylor. Succeeded S. D. Lee as commander of the Department of Alabama, Mississipi and East Louisiana.

TERRY, Alfred H.—Brigadier General, USV. Commander of the 10th Corps in Butler's Army of the James (Dept. of Va. and N.C.).

TERRY, William—Brigadier General, CSA. Commander of a brigade of Virginia infantry in Gordon's Division of Early's Army of the Valley.

THOMAS, George H.—Major General, USV (USMA 1840). Commander of the Department and Army of the Cumberland, the largest force in Sherman's Military Division of the Mississippi.

THOMPSON, Jacob—The senior Confederate commissioner in Canada. Former secretary of the interior in the Buchanan administration.

TORBERT, Alfred T. A.—Brigadier General, USV (USMA 1855). Commander of the 1st Division of Sheridan's Cavalry Corps of Meade's Army of the Potomac. When Sheridan was given command of the Middle Military Division, he named Torbert his chief of cavalry.

VALLANDIGHAM, Clement L.—Former Ohio Congressman who had been arrested by General Burnside for anti-war speeches and banished by Lincoln to the Confederacy. From there he went to Canada and became the head of the Sons of Liberty, the latest in a string of anti-war secret societies whose members were known collectively as Copperheads.

VAUGH, John C.—Brigadier General, CSA. Commander of a brigade of cavalry in the Shenandoah Valley area. He briefly succeeded Elzey in command of the two infantry brigades Breckinridge had brought to that area from southwestern Virginia.

WALLACE, Lewis—Major General, USV. Commander of the Middle Department.

WALKER, William H. T.—Major General, CSA. Commander of a division in Hardee's 1st Corps of J. E. Johnston's Army of Tennessee.

WALTHALL, Edward C.—Major General, CSA. Commander of a division in Stewart's Corps (or Army of Mississippi) in Hood's Army of Tennessee.

WARD, Lyman M.—Colonel, USV. Commander of the 4th Brigade of Mower's 1st Division of the 16th Corps in A. J. Smith's Right Wing of that corps in Washburn's District of West Tennessee.

WARREN, Gouverneur Kemble—Major General, USV (USMA 1850). Commander of the 5th Corps in Meade's Army of the Potomac.

WASHBURN, Cadwallader Colder—Major General, USV. Commander of the District of West Tennessee in McPherson's (later Howard's) Department of the Tennessee in Sherman's Military Division of the Mississippi. Brother of Congressman Elihu Washburne *(sic)*.

WASHBURNE, Elihu—United States Congressman from Galena, Illinois. Grant's political sponsor. Brother of Cadwallader C. Washburn *(sic)*.

WEBER, Max—Brigadier General, USV. Commander of the garrison at Harpers Ferry in Hunter's Department of West Virginia.

WELLES, Gideon—Secretary of the Navy in Lincoln's cabinet.

WHEELER, Joseph—Major General, CSA (USMA 1859). Commander of the Cavalry Corps of J. E. Johnston's Army of Tennessee.

WHITE, Julius—Brigadier General, USV. Succeeded Ledlie as commander of the 1st Division of Parke's (previously Burnside's) 9th Corps in Meade's Army of the Potomac.

WILCOX, Cadmus Marcellus—Major General, CSA (USMA 1846). Commander of a division in A. P. Hill's 3rd Corps of Lee's Army of Northern Virginia.

WILKIN, Alexander—Colonel, USV. Commander of the 2nd ("Eagle") Brigade of Mower's 1st Division of the 16th Corps in A. J. Smith's Right Wing of that corps in Washburn's District of West Tennessee.

WILLCOX, Orlando B.—Brigadier General, USV (USMA 1847). Commander of the 3rd Division of Burnside's 9th Corps in Meade's Army of the Potomac.

WILLIAMS, Alpheus S.—Brigadier General, USV. Commander of the 1st Division of Hooker's 20th Corps in Thomas' Army of the Cumberland in Sherman's Military Division of the Mississippi. Temporarily commanded the corps after Hooker resigned until Slocum arrived from Vicksburg.

WILSON, James Harrison—Brigadier General, USV (USMA 1860).

Commander of the 3rd Division of the Cavalry Corps of the Army of the Potomac.

WINSLOW, Edward F.—Colonel, USV. Commander of the 2nd Brigade of Gierson's Cavalry Division of the 16th Corps in Washburn's District of West Tennessee. Later commander of the 2nd Division in Grierson's Cavalry Corps of Howard's Department of Tennessee in Sherman's Military Division of the Mississippi.

WINSLOW, John A.—Captain, USN. Captain of the USS *Kearsarge*, which sank the CSS *Alabama*.

WISE, Henry A.—Brigadier General, CSA. Commander of a brigade in Beauregard's Department of Southern Virginia and North Carolina. Former governor of Virginia.

WOLFE, Edward H.—Colonel, USV. Commander of the 3rd Brigade of Moore's 3rd Division of the 16th Corps in A. J. Smith's Right Wing of that corps in Washburn's District of West Tennessee.

WOOD, Fernando—Congressman and former mayor of New York. Influential Peace Democrat.

WOOD, John Taylor—Colonel, CSA, and Commander, CSN. Aide on the staff of President Davis and commander of the CSS *Tallahassee*. Grandson of President Zachary Taylor.

WOOD, Thomas J.—Brigadier General, USV (USMA 1845). Commander of the 3rd Division of Howard's (later Stanley's) 4th Corps in Thomas' Army of the Cumberland in Sherman's Military Division of the Mississippi.

WOODS, Charles R.—Brigadier General, USV (USMA 1852). Commander of the 1st Division of Logan's 15th Corps in McPherson's (later Howard's) Army of the Tennessee in Sherman's Military Division of the Mississippi.

WOODS, Joseph J.—Colonel, USV (USMA 1847). Commander of the 3rd Brigade of Mower's 1st Division of the 16th Corps in A. J. Smith's Right Wing of that corps in Washburn's District of West Tennessee.

WRIGHT, Horatio G.—Major General, USV (USMA 1841). Commander of the 6th Corps in Meade's Army of the Potomac. Later sent to defend Washington from Early's invasion.

Appendix B

Military Organizations (mid-June 1864)

UNITED STATES ARMY:

Commander-in-Chief—President Abraham Lincoln
Secretary of War—Edwin McMasters Stanton
General-in-Chief—Lieutenant General Ulysses S. Grant
Chief of Staff—Major General Henry W. Halleck
Quartermaster General—Brigadier General Montgomery C. Miegs

ARMY OF THE POTOMAC:

Commanding General—Major General George Gordon Meade
Chief of Staff—Major General Andrew A. Humphreys
Chief of Artillery—Brigadier General Henry J. Hunt
Chief Engineer—Brigadier General Henry W. Benham
Provost Marshal General—Brigadier General Marsena R. Patrick

2nd ARMY CORPS: Major General Winfield S. Hancock

1st Division: Brigadier General Francis C. Barlow
  1st Brigade: Brigadier General Nelson A. Miles
  2nd ("Irish") Brigade: Colonel Patrick Kelly
  3rd Brigade: Colonel Clinton D. McDougall
  4th Brigade: Colonel James A. Beaver

2nd Division: Brigadier General John Gibbon
  1st Brigade: Brigadier General Byron R. Pierce
  2nd Brigade: Colonel John Fraser
  3rd Brigade: Colonel Thomas A. Smythe
  4th Brigade: Colonel J. P. McIvor

3rd Division: Major General David B. Birney
  1st Brigade: Colonel Thomas W. Egan
  2nd Brigade: Colonel Thomas R. Tannatt
  3rd Brigade: Brigadier General Gershom Mott
  4th ("Excelsior") Brigade: Colonel William R. Brewster

Artillery Brigade: Colonel John C. Tidball

5th ARMY CORPS: Major General Gouverneur K. Warren

1st Division: Brigadier General Charles Griffin
  1st Brigade: Brigadier General Joshua L. Chamberlain
  2nd Brigade: Colonel Jacob B. Sweitzer
  3rd Brigade: Brigadier General Joseph J. Bartlett

2nd Division: Brigadier General Romeyne B. Ayres
  1st Brigade: Colonel Edgar M. Gregory
  2nd ("Maryland") Brigade: Colonel N. T. Dushane
  3rd ("Heavy Artillery") Brigade: Colonel J. H. Kitching

3rd Division: Brigadier General Samuel W. Crawford
  1st Brigade: Colonel Peter Lyle
  2nd Brigade: Colonel James L. Bates
  3rd Brigade: Colonel James Carle

4th Division: Brigadier General Lysander Cutler
  1st ("Iron") Brigade: Brigadier General Edward S. Bragg
  2nd Brigade: Colonel John W. Hofmann

Artillery Brigade: Colonel Charles S. Wainright

6th ARMY CORPS: Major General Horatio G. Wright

1st Division: Brigadier General David A. Russell
  1st Brigade: Colonel William H. Penrose
  2nd Brigade: Brigadier General Emory Upton

3rd Brigade: Lieutenant Colonel Gideon Clarke
4th Brigade: Colonel Nelson Cross

2nd Division: Brigadier General Thomas H. Neil
1st Brigade: Brigadier General Frank Wheaton
2nd ("Vermont") Brigade: Brigadier General Lewis A. Grant
3rd Brigade: Colonel D. D. Birdwell
4th Brigade: Colonel Oliver Edwards

3rd Division: Brigadier General James B. Ricketts
1st Brigade: Colonel William S. Truex
2nd Brigade: Colonel Benjamin Franklin Smith

Artillery Brigade: Colonel Charles H. Tompkins

9th ARMY CORPS: Major General Ambrose E. Burnside

1st Division: Brigadier General James H. Ledlie
1st Brigade: Colonel J. P. Gould
2nd Brigade: Colonel E. W. Pierce
3rd Brigade: Colonel Elisha G. Marshall

2nd Division: Brigadier General Robert B. Potter
1st Brigade: Colonel John I. Curtin
2nd Brigade: Colonel Simon G. Griffin

3rd Division: Brigadier General Orlando B. Willcox
1st Brigade: Colonel John F. Hartranft
2nd Brigade: Colonel Benjamin C. Christ

4th (U.S.C.T.) Division: Brigadier General Edward Ferrero
1st Brigade: Colonel Joshua K. Sigfried
2nd Brigade: Colonel Henry G. Thomas

CAVALRY CORPS: Major General Philip H. Sheridan

1st Division: Brigadier General Alfred T. A. Torbert
1st ("Michigan") Brigade: Brigadier General George A. Custer
2nd Brigade: Colonel Thomas C. Devin
Reserve Brigade: Brigadier General Wesley Merritt

2nd Division: Brigadier General David McMurtrie Gregg
1st Brigade: Brigadier General Henry E. Davies, Jr.
2nd Brigade: Colonel J. Irvin Gregg

3rd Division: Brigadier General James H. Wilson
1st Brigade: Colonel John B. McIntosh
2nd Brigade: Colonel George H. Chapman

DEPT. OF VIRGINIA AND NORTH CAROLINA (ARMY OF THE JAMES):

Commanding General—Major General Benjamin F. Butler
Chief Engineer—Brigadier General Godfrey Weitzel

10th ARMY CORPS: Brigadier General Alfred H. Terry

1st Division: Brigadier General Robert S. Foster
   1st Brigade: Colonel Joshua B. Howell
   2nd Brigade: Colonel Joseph R. Hawley
   3rd Brigade: Colonel Harris M. Plaisted

18th ARMY CORPS: Major General William F. ("Baldy") Smith

1st Division: Brigadier General William T. H. Brooks
   1st Brigade: Brigadier General Gilman Marston
   2nd Brigade: Brigadier General Hiram Barnham
   3rd Brigade: Colonel Guy V. Henry

2nd Division: Brigadier General John H. Martindale
   1st Brigade: Brigadier General George J. Stannard
   2nd Brigade: Colonel Griffin A. Stedman, Jr.

3rd Division: Brigadier General Adelbert Ames
   1st Brigade: Colonel William B. Barton
   2nd Brigade: Colonel Newton M. Curtis
   3rd Brigade: Colonel Louis Bell

Provisional Brigade: Colonel A. A. Rand

U.S.C.T. Division: Brigadier General Edward W. Hincks
   1st Brigade: Brigadier General Edward W. Wild
   2nd Brigade: Colonel Samuel A. Duncan

Naval Brigade: Brigadier General Charles K. Graham

Cavalry Division: Brigadier General August V. Kautz
   1st Brigade: Colonel Simon H. Mix
   2nd Brigade: Colonel Samuel P. Spear

Independent (U.S.C.T.) Cavalry Brigade: Colonel Robert West

District of St. Mary's: Colonel Alonzo Granville Draper

District of North Carolina: Brigadier General Innis N. Palmer
   Subdistrict of the Albemarle: (unknown)
   Subdistrict of Beaufort: Colonel James Jourdan
   Defenses of New Berne: Colonel Thomas J. C. Amory

District of Eastern Virginia: Brigadier General Israel Vodges

DEPARTMENT OF THE SOUTH:

Commanding General—Major General John G. Foster

Northern District: Brigadier General Alexander Schimmelfennig
    Folly Island: Colonel L. von Gilsa
    Morris Island: Colonel William Gurney

District of Beaufort, S.C.: Brigadier General Rufus Saxton

District of Hilton Head, S.C.: Brigadier General J. P. Hatch

District of Florida: Brigadier General William Birney

DEPARTMENT OF WASHINGTON (22nd ARMY CORPS):

Commanding General—Major General Christopher C. Augur

District of Alexandria: Brigadier General John P. Slough

District of Washington: Colonel Moses N. Wisewell
    1st Brigade: Colonel R. H. Rush

Light Artillery Camp: Brigadier General Albion P. Howe

Independent Cavalry Brigade: Colonel Charles Russell Lowell, Jr.

Cavalry Division, Camp Stoneman: Colonel William Gamble

Defenses North of the Potomac: Lieutenant Colonel J. A. Haskins
    1st Brigade: Colonel W. H. Hayward
    2nd Brigade: Colonel J. M. C. Markie
    3rd Brigade: Lieutenant Colonel J. H. Oberteuffer

Defenses South of the Potomac: Brigadier General G. A. DeRussy
    1st Brigade: Colonel John C. Lee
    2nd Brigade: Colonel W. S. Irwin

MIDDLE DEPARTMENT (8th ARMY CORPS) (Maryland and Delaware):

Commanding General—Major General Lew Wallace
    1st Separate Brigade: Brigadier General Erastus B. Tyler
    2nd Separate Brigade: Brigadier General William W. Morris
    3rd Separate Brigade: Brigadier General John R. Kenly

DEPARTMENT OF WEST VIRGINIA:

Commanding General—Major General David Hunter

1st Infantry Division: Brigadier General Jeremiah C. Sullivan
    1st Brigade: Colonel George D. Wells
    2nd Brigade: Colonel Joseph Thoburn

2nd Infantry Division: Brigadier General George Crook
  1st Brigade: Colonel Rutherford B. Hayes
  2nd Brigade: Colonel Carr B. White
  3rd Brigade: Colonel Jacob M. Campbell

1st Cavalry Division: Brigadier General Alfred N. Duffié
  1st Brigade: Colonel William B. Tibbets
  2nd Brigade: Colonel J. E. Wynkoop

2nd Cavalry Division: Brigadier General William W. Averell
  1st Brigade: Colonel John H. Oley
  2nd Brigade: Colonel J. M. Schoonmaker
  3rd Brigade: Colonel William H. Powell

Reserve Division: Brigadier General Benajmin F. Kelley

NORTHERN DEPARTMENT:

Commanding General—Major General Samuel P. Heintzelman

DEPARTMENT OF THE EAST:

Commanding General—Major General John A. Dix

DEPARTMENT OF MISSOURI:

Commanding General—Major General William S. Rosecrans
District of Southwest Missouri: Brigadier General John B. Sanborn
District of St. Louis: Brigadier General Thomas Ewing, Jr.
District of Rolla: Brigadier General O. Guitar
District of Central Missouri: Brigadier General E. B. Brown
District of Northern Missouri: Brigadier General C. B. Fisk

DEPARTMENT OF KANSAS:

Commanding General—Major General Samuel R. Curtis
District of Nebraska: Brigadier General Robert B. Mitchell
District of Colorado: Colonel J. M. Chivington

DEPARTMENT OF THE NORTHWEST:

Commanding General—Major General John Pope

DEPARTMENT OF NEW MEXICO:

Commanding General—Brigadier General James H. Carleton

DEPARTMENT OF THE PACIFIC:

Commanding Officer—Colonel George Wright

MILITARY DIVISION OF WEST MISSISSIPPI:

Commanding General—Major General Edward R. S. Canby

U.S. Forces, Texas: Major General Francis J. Herron
    1st Brigade: Colonel William M. Dye
    2nd Brigade: Colonel John McNulta
    Colored Brigade: Colonel Justin Hodge
    Cavalry Brigade: Colonel Edward J. Noyes

DEPARTMENT OF THE GULF:

Commanding General—Major General Nathaniel P. Banks

19th ARMY CORPS: Brigadier General William H. Emory

1st Division: Brigadier General James W. McMillan
    1st Brigade: Colonel George L. Beale
    2nd Brigade: Colonel Henry Rust, Jr.
    3rd Brigade: Colonel George M. Love

2nd Division: Brigadier General Cuvier Grover
    1st Brigade: Brigadier General Franklin S. Nickerson
    2nd Brigade: Brigadier General Henry W. Birge
    3rd Brigade: Colonel Jacob Sharpe

Cavalry Division: Brigadier General Richard Arnold
    1st Brigade: Colonel Charles Everett
    2nd Brigade: Colonel John G. Fonda
    3rd Brigade: Lieutenant John M. Crebs
    4th Brigade: Colonel Edmund J. Davis
    5th Brigade: Colonel Oliver P. Gooding

Engineer Brigade: Colonel Joseph Bailey

Defenses of New Orleans: Major General J. J. Reynolds

District of West Florida: Brigadier General Alexander Asboth

District of Key West and Tortugas: Brigadier General D. P. Woodbury

District of Baton Rouge: Brigadier General William P. Benton

District of Port Hudson: Brigadier General John McNeil

CORPS DE AFRIQUE:

1st Division: Brigadier General Daniel Ullman

1st Brigade: Colonel William H. Dickey
2nd Brigade: Colonel John F. Appleton
2nd Brigade, 2nd Division: Colonel J. C. Clark
District of La Fourche: Brigadier General Robert A. Cameron

DEPARTMENT OF ARKANSAS (7th ARMY CORPS):

Commanding General—Major General Frederick Steele

1st Division: Brigadier General Frederick Saloman
   1st Brigade: Colonel Charles E. Saloman
   2nd Brigade: Colonel Adolph Engelman
   3rd Brigade: Brigadier General Cyrus Bussey

2nd Division: Brigadier General Joseph R. West
   1st Brigade: Colonel W. H. Graves
   2nd Brigade: Brigadier General Christopher C. Andrews
   3rd Brigade: Colonel W. F. Geiger

Independent Brigade: Colonel Robert R. Livingston

Independent Cavalry Brigade: Colonel Powell Clayton

District of Eastern Arkansas: Brigadier General Napoleon B. Buford

District of the Frontier: Brigadier General John M. Thayer
   1st Brigade: Colonel John Edwards
   2nd Brigade: Colonel Charles W. Adams
   3rd Brigade: Colonel E. Lynde
   Indian Brigade: Colonel William A. Phillips

MILITARY DIVISION OF THE MISSISSIPPI:

Commanding General—Major General William Tecumseh Sherman
Chief of Artillery—Brigadier General William F. Barry

DEPARTMENT AND ARMY OF THE CUMBERLAND:

Commanding General—Major General George H. Thomas

Chief of Artillery—Brigadier General John Milton Brannan
   Reserve Brigade: Colonel Joseph W. Burke
   Engineer Brigade: Colonel W. B. McCreary

4th ARMY CORPS: Major General Oliver O. Howard

1st Division: Major General David S. Stanley
   1st Brigade: Brigadier General Charles Cruft
   2nd Brigade: Brigadier General W. C. Whitaker

3rd Brigade: Colonel William Grose

2nd Division: Brigadier General John Newton
   1st Brigade: Brigadier General Nathan Kimball
   2nd Brigade: Brigadier General George D. Wagner
   3rd Brigade: Colonel Charles G. Harker

3rd Division: Brigadier General Thomas J. Wood
   1st Brigade: Colonel William H. Gibson
   2nd Brigade: Brigadier General William B. Hazen
   3rd Brigade: Colonel Frederick Knefler

14th ARMY CORPS: Major General John M. Palmer

1st Division: Brigadier General Richard W. Johnson
   1st Brigade: Brigadier General William P. Carlin
   2nd Brigade: Colonel William L. Stoughton
   3rd Brigade: Colonel Benjamin Franklin Scribner

2nd Division: Brigadier General Jefferson C. Davis
   1st Brigade: Brigadier General James D. Morgan
   2nd Brigade: Colonel John Grant Mitchell
   3rd Brigade: Colonel Daniel McCook

3rd Division: Brigadier General Absalom Baird
   1st Brigade: Brigadier General John B. Turchin
   2nd Brigade: Colonel Ferdinand Vanderveer
   3rd Brigade: Colonel George Peabody Este

20th ARMY CORPS: Major General Joseph Hooker

1st Division: Brigadier General Alpheus S. Williams
   1st Brigade: Brigadier General Joseph F. Knipe
   2nd Brigade: Brigadier General Thomas H. Ruger
   3rd Brigade: Colonel James Sidney Robinson

2nd Division: Brigadier General John W. Geary
   1st Brigade: Colonel Charles Candy
   2nd Brigade: Colonel Patrick Henry Jones
   3rd Brigade: Colonel D. Ireland

3rd Division: Major General Daniel Butterfield
   1st Brigade: Brigadier General William T. Ward
   2nd Brigade: Colonel John Coburn
   3rd Brigade: Colonel James Wood, Jr.

CAVALRY FORCES: Brigadier General W. L. Elliott

1st Division: Brigadier General Edward M. McCook
   1st Brigade: Colonel J. B. Dorr
   2nd Brigade: Lieutenant Colonel J. W. Stewart
   3rd Brigade: Colonel Louis D. Watkins

2nd Division: Brigadier General Kenner Garrard
   1st Brigade: Colonel Robert H. G. Minty
   2nd Brigade: Colonel Eli Long
   3rd ("Lightning") Brigade: Colonel Abram O. Miller

3rd Division: Colonel William W. Lowe
   1st Brigade: Lieutenant Colonel Robert Klein
   2nd Brigade: Colonel C. C. Smith
   3rd Brigade: Colonel Eli H. Murray

Post of Chattanooga: Colonel Timothy R. Stanley

District of Nashville: Major General Lovell H. Rousseau

Post of Nashville: Brigadier General John F. Miller

4th Cavalry Division: Brigadier General Alvan C. Gillem
   1st Brigade: Lieutenant Colonel D. G. Thornburg
   2nd Brigade: Lieutenant Colonel George Spalding
   3rd Brigade: Colonel J. K. Miller

District of North Alabama: Brigadier General R. S. Granger

DEPARTMENT AND ARMY OF THE TENNESSEE:

Commanding General—Major General James B. McPherson

15th ARMY CORPS: Major General John Logan

1st Division: Brigadier General Peter J. Osterhaus
   1st Brigade: Brigadier General Charles R. Woods
   2nd Brigade: Colonel James A. Williamson
   3rd Brigade: Colonel Hugo Wangelin

2nd Division: Brigadier General Morgan L. Smith
   1st Brigade: Brigadier General Giles A. Smith
   2nd Brigade: Brigadier General Joseph A. J. Lightburn

3rd Division: Brigadier General J. E. Smith
   1st Brigade: Colonel J. I. Alexander
   2nd Brigade: Colonel Green B. Raum
   3rd Brigade: Colonel J. Banbury

4th Division: Brigadier General William Harrow
   1st Brigade: Colonel Reuben Williams

2nd Brigade: Colonel Charles C. Walcutt
3rd Brigade: Colonel John M. Oliver

LEFT WING, 16th ARMY CORPS: Major General Grenville M. Dodge
2nd Division: Brigadier General Thomas W. Sweeney
  1st Brigade: Brigadier General Elliott W. Rice
  2nd Brigade: Colonel August Mersy
  3rd Brigade: Colonel M. M. Bane
4th Division: Brigadier General James C. Veatch
  1st Brigade: Colonel John W. Fuller
  2nd Brigade: Colonel John W. Sprague
  3rd Brigade: Colonel John H. Howe

17th ARMY CORPS: Major General Francis P. Blair
3rd Division: Brigadier General Mortimer D. Leggett
  1st Brigade: Brigadier General Manning F. Force
  2nd Brigade: Colonel Robert K. Scott
  3rd Brigade: Colonel Adam G. Malloy
4th Division: Brigadier General Walter Q. Gresham
  1st Brigade: Colonel W. L. Sanderson
  2nd Brigade: Colonel Benjamin Dornblaser
  3rd Brigade: Colonel William Hall
District of West Tennessee: Major General C. C. Washburn
1st Cavalry Div., 16th Corps: Brigadier General Benjamin Grierson
  1st Brigade: Colonel George E. Waring, Jr.
  2nd Brigade: Colonel Edward F. Winslow
  3rd Brigade: Colonel H. B. Burgh
District of Memphis: Brigadier General R. P. Buckland
  1st Colored Brigade: Colonel Edward Bouton
  2nd Brigade: Colonel George B. Hoge

RIGHT WING, 16th CORPS: Brigadier General A. J. Smith
1st Division: Brigadier General J. A. Mower
  1st Brigade: Colonel William L. McMillen
  2nd Brigade: Colonel Lucius F. Hubbard
  3rd Brigade: Colonel J. J. Woods
  4th Brigade: Colonel Jonathan B. Moore
3rd Division: Colonel David Moore

1st Brigade: Colonel Charles D. Murray
2nd Brigade: Colonel James I. Gilbert
3rd Brigade: Colonel Edward H. Wolfe

District of Vicksburg: Major General Henry W. Slocum
Maltby's Brigade: Brigadier General J. A. Maltby

1st Division, 17th Corps: Brigadier General E. S. Dennis
1st Brigade: Colonel Frederick A. Starring
2nd Brigade: Colonel James H. Coates

1st Division, U.S. Colored Troops: Brigadier General J. P. Hawkins
1st Brigade: Brigadier General Isaac F. Shepard
2nd Brigade: Colonel Hiram Scofield
Cavalry Brigade: Colonel Embury D. Osband

DEPARTMENT AND ARMY OF THE OHIO (23rd ARMY CORPS):

Commanding General—Major General John M. Schofield

2nd Division: Brigadier General Milo S. Hascall
1st Brigade: Brigadier General Joseph A. Cooper
2nd Brigade: Colonel John R. Bond
2nd Brig., 1st Div.: Colonel P. T. Swayne

3rd Division: Brigadier General Jacob D. Cox
1st Brigade: Colonel James W. Reilly
2nd Brigade: Colonel Daniel Cameron
3rd Brigade: Colonel R. K. Byrd
1st Brig., 1st Div.: Colonel R. F. Barter

Cavalry Division: Major General George Stoneman
1st Brigade: Colonel James Biddle
Independent Brigade: Colonel Alexander W. Holeman

4th Division (E. Tenn.): Brigadier General Jacob Ammen
1st Brigade: Colonel W. Y. Dillard
2nd Brigade: Brigadier General Davis Tillson
3rd Brigade: Lieutenant Colonel M. L. Patterson

District of Kentucky (5th Div.): Brigadier General S. G. Burbridge

1st Division: Brigadier General Edward H. Hobson
1st Brigade: Colonel Simeon B. Brown
2nd Brigade: Colonel C. J. True
3rd Brigade: Colonel C. S. Hanson
4th Brigade: Colonel J. M. Brown

2nd Division: Brigadier General Hugh Ewing

1st Brigade: Lieutenant Colonel T. B. Farleigh
2nd Brigade: Colonel Cicero Maxwell
1st Cavalry Brigade: Colonel Israel Garrard
3rd Cavalry Brigade: Colonel Horace Capron

CONFEDERATE STATES ARMY:

Commander-in-Chief—President Jefferson Davis
Secretary of War—James Alexander Seddon
Commanding General—General Braxton Bragg
Adjutant and Inspector General—General Samuel Cooper

ARMY OF NORTHERN VIRGINIA:

Commanding General—General Robert Edward Lee
Chief Engineer—Major General Martin L. Smith
Chief of Artillery—Brigadier General William N. Pendleton

Hoke's Division: Major General Robert F. Hoke
   Clingman's Brigade: Brigadier General Thomas L. Clingman
   Colquitt's Brigade: Brigadier General Alfred H. Colquitt
   Hagood's Brigade: Brigadier Johnson Hagood
   Martin's Brigade: Brigadier General James G. Martin
   Artillery Battalion: Major John P. W. Read

1st Cavalry Division: Major General Wade Hampton
   Young's Brigade: Brigadier General Pierce M. B. Young
   The Laurel Brigade: Brigadier General Thomas L. Rosser
   Butler's Brigade: Brigadier General Matthew C. Butler

2nd Cavalry Division: Major General Fitzhugh Lee
   Lomax's Brigade: Brigadier General Lunsford Lomax
   Wickham's Brigade: Brigadier General Williams C. Wickham

3rd Cavalry Division: Major General W. H. F. ("Rooney") Lee
   Chambliss' Brigade: Brigadier General John R. Chambliss
   Barringer's Brigade: Brigadier General Rufus Barringer

Horse Artillery: Major R. P. Chew

1st ARMY CORPS: Lieutenant General Richard H. Anderson

Kershaw's Division: Major General Joseph B. Kershaw
   Kershaw's Brigade: Colonel John W. Henagan
   Wofford's Brigade: Brigadier General William T. Wofford
   Humphrey's Brigade: Brigadier General Benjamin Humphreys

Bryan's Brigade: Colonel James P. Simms

Field's Division: Major General Charles W. Field
   Bratton's Brigade: Brigadier General John Bratton
   Law's Brigade: Colonel William F. Perry
   Anderson's Brigade: Brigadier General George T. Anderson
   The Texas Brigade: Brigadier General John Gregg
   Benning's Brigade: Colonel Dudley M. DuBose

Pickett's Division: Major General George Pickett
   Terry's Brigade: Brigadier General William R. Terry
   Barton's Brigade: Brigadier General Seth M. Barton
   Hunton's Brigade: Brigadier General Eppa Hunton
   Corse's Brigade: Brigadier General Montgomery D. Corse

Artillery: Brigadier General E. Porter Alexander

2nd ARMY CORPS: Lieutenant General Jubal A. Early

Early's Division: Major General Stephen D. Ramseur
   Pegram's Brigade: Brigadier General Robert D. Lilley
   Johnston's Brigade: Brigadier General Thomas F. Toon
   Hoke's Brigade: Brigadier General William G. Lewis

Gordon's Division: Major General John B. Gordon
   Evans' Brigade: Brigadier General Clement A. Evans
   Terry's Brigade: Brigadier General William Terry
   The Louisiana Brigade: Brigadier General Zebulon York

Rodes' Division: Major General Robert E. Rodes
   Grimes' Brigade: Brigadier General Bryan Grimes
   Doles' Brigade: Colonel Philip Cook
   Ramseur's Brigade: Brigadier General William R. Cox
   Battle's Brigade: Brigadier General Cullen A. Battle

Artillery: Brigadier General Armistead A. Long

3rd ARMY CORPS: Lieutenant General Ambrose Powell Hill

Mahone's Division: Major General William Mahone
   Sanders' Brigade: Brigadier General John Calhoun Sanders
   Harris' Brigade: Brigadier General Nathaniel H. Harris
   Mahone's Brigade: Colonel David A. Weisiger
   Wright's Brigade: Brigadier General Ambrose R. Wright
   The Florida Brigade: Brigadier General Joseph Finegan

Heth's Division: Major General Henry Heth
   Davis' Brigade: Brigadier General Joseph R. Davis

Cooke's Brigade: Brigadier General John R. Cooke
Kirkland's Brigade: Brigadier General William MacRae
Fry's Brigade: Brigadier General Birkett D. Fry

Wilcox's Division: Major General Cadmus M. Wilcox
Lane's Brigade: Brigadier General James H. Lane
Scales' Brigade: Brigadier General Alfred M. Scales
McGowan's Brigade: Brigadier General James Conner
Thomas' Brigade: Brigadier General Edward L. Thomas

Artillery: Colonel R. Lindsay Walker

DEPARTMENT OF SOUTHWESTERN VIRGINIA:

Commanding General—Major General John C. Breckinridge
Echols' Brigade: Brigadier General John Echols
Wharton's Brigade: Brigadier General Gabriel C. Wharton

Ransom's (cavalry) Division: Major General Robert Ransom
McCausland's Brigade: Brigadier General John McCausland
Imboden's Brigade: Brigadier General John D. Imboden
Jackson's Brigade: Colonel William Jackson
Vaughn's Brigade: Brigadier General John C. Vaughn

Morgan's (cavalry) Division: Brigadier General John Hunt Morgan
Morgan's (cavalry) Brigade: Brigadier General John Hunt Morgan
Giltner's (cavalry) Brigade: Colonel Henry L. Giltner
Cosby's (cavalry) Brigade: Colonel George B. Cosby

DEPARTMENT OF RICHMOND:

Commanding General—Lieutenant General Richard S. Ewell
Ransom's Brigade: Brigadier General Matthew W. Ransom
Cavalry Brigade: Brigadier General Martin W. Gray
Artillery Defenses: Lieutenant Colonel John C. Pemberton

DEPARTMENT OF SOUTHERN VIRGINIA AND NORTH CAROLINA:

Commanding General—General Pierre Gustave Toutant Beauregard

Johnson's Division: Major General Bushrod R. Johnson
Johnson's Brigade: Colonel John S. Fulton
Gracie's Brigade: Brigadier General Archibald Gracie
Elliott's Brigade: Brigadier General Stephen Elliott
Wise's Brigade: Brigadier General Henry Wise
Cavalry Brigade: Brigadier General James Dearing

DEPARTMENT OF SOUTH CAROLINA, GEORGIA AND FLORIDA:

Commanding General—Major General Samuel Jones

District of South Carolina: Brigadier General Roswell Ripley

District of Georgia: Major General Lafayette McLaws

District of Florida: Major General James Patton Anderson

DEPARTMENT AND ARMY OF TENNESSEE:

Commanding General—General Joseph Eggleston Johnston
Chief of Artillery—Brigadier General Francis Asbury Shoup

1st ARMY CORPS: Lieutenant General William J. Hardee
Cheatham's Division: Major General Benjamin F. Cheatham
  Maney's Brigade: Brigadier General George E. Maney
  Wright's Brigade: Colonel John Carpenter Carter
  Strahl's Brigade: Brigadier General Otho French Strahl
  Vaughn's Brigade: Brigadier General Alfred J. Vaughn, Jr.
Cleburne's Division: Major General Patrick Cleburne
  Polk's Brigade: Brigadier General Lucius E. Polk
  Lowrey's Brigade: Brigadier General Mark Perrin Lowrey
  Govan's Brigade: Brigadier General Daniel C. Govan
  Granbury's Brigade: Brigadier General Hiram B. Granbury
Walker's Division: Major General William H. T. Walker
  Jackson's Brigade: Brigadier General John K. Jackson
  Gist's Brigade: Brigadier General States Rights Gist
  Stevens' Brigade: Brigadier General Clement H. Stevens
  Mercer's Brigade: Brigadier General Hugh W. Mercer
Bate's Division: Major General William Brimage Bate
  The Orphan Brigade: Brigadier General Joseph H. Lewis
  Tyler's Brigade: Colonel Thomas B. Smith
  Finley's Brigade: Brigadier General Jesse J. Finley
Artillery: Colonel Melancthon Smith

2nd ARMY CORPS: Lieutenant General John Bell Hood
Hindman's Division: Major General T. C. Hindman
  Deas' Brigade: Brigadier General Zachry C. Deas
  Manigault's Brigade: Brigadier General A. M. Manigault
  Tucker's Brigade: Colonel Jacob H. Sharp
  Walthall's Brigade: Brigadier General Edward C. Walthall
Stevenson's Division: Major General Carter L. Stevenson

Brown's Brigade: Brigadier General John C. Brown
Cumming's Brigade: Brigadier General Alfred Cumming
Reynolds' Brigade: Brigadier General A. W. Reynolds
Pettus's Brigade: Brigadier General Edmund W. Pettus
Stewart's Division: Major General Alexander P. Stewart
  Stovall's Brigade: Brigadier General Marcellus A. Stovall
  Clayton's Brigade: Brigadier General Henry D. Clayton
  Baker's Brigade: Brigadier General Alpheus Baker
  Gibson's Brigade: Brigadier General Randall L. Gibson
Artillery: Colonel Robert F. Beckham

CAVALRY CORPS: Major General Joseph Wheeler
Martin's Division: Major General William T. Martin
  Morgan's Brigade: Brigadier General John T. Morgan
  Iverson's Brigade: Brigadier General Alfred H. Iverson
Kelly's Division: Brigadier General John H. Kelly
  Allen's Brigade: Brigadier General William W. Allen
  Dibrell's Brigade: Brigadier General George G. Dibrell
  Hannon's Brigade: Colonel Moses W. Hannon
Humes' Division: Brigadier General William Y. C. Humes
  Humes' Brigade: Colonel Henry M. Ashby
  Harrison's Brigade: Colonel Thomas H. Harrison
  Grigsby's Brigade: Colonel J. Warren Grigsby
Horse Artillery: Lieutenant Colonel Felix H. Robertson

1st Division, Georgia Militia: Major General Gustavus W. Smith
  1st Brigade: Brigadier General Reuben W. Carswell
  2nd Brigade: Brigadier General Pleasant J. Phillips

ARMY OF MISSISSIPPI: Lieutenant General Leonidas Polk
Loring's Division: Major General W. W. Loring
  Featherston's Brigade: Brigadier General W. S. Featherston
  Adams' Brigade: Brigadier General John Adams
  Scott's Brigade: Brigadier General Thomas M. Scott
French's Division: Major General Samuel G. French
  Ector's Brigade: Brigadier General M. D. Ector
  Cockrell's Brigade: Brigadier General F. M. Cockrell
  Sears' Brigade: Colonel W. S. Barry
Cantey's Division: Brigadier General James Cantey
  Quarles' Brigade: Brigadier General William A. Quarles
  Reynolds' Brigade: Brigadier General D. H. Reynolds

Cantey's Brigade: Colonel V. S. Murphey
Artillery: Lieutenant Colonel S. C. Williams
Cavalry Division: Brigadier General W. H. ("Red") Jackson
    Armstrong's Brigade: Brigadier General Frank C. Armstrong
    Ross's Brigade: Brigadier General Lawrence Sul Ross
    Ferguson's Brigade: Brigadier General Samuel W. Ferguson
    Horse Artillery: Captain John Waties

DEPARTMENT OF ALABAMA, MISSISSIPPI AND EAST LOUISIANA:

Commanding General—Major General Stephen Dill Lee
District of Mississippi and W. Tennessee: Major General N. B. Forrest
1st (cavalry) Division: Brigadier General James R. Chalmers
    1st Brigade: Colonel James J. Neely
    2nd Brigade: Colonel Robert McCulloch
2nd (cavalry) Division: Brigadier General Abraham Buford
    3rd Brigade: Colonel Hylan B. Lyon
    4th Brigade: Colonel Tyree H. Bell
6th (cavalry) Brigade: Colonel Edmund W. Rucker
Artillery Battalion: Captain John W. Morton
District of Central Mississippi: Brigadier General Wirt Adams
    Mabry's (cavalry) Brigade: Colonel Hinchie P. Mabry
    Scott's (cavalry) Brigade: Colonel John S. Scott
    5th (cavalry) Brigade: Brigadier General Samuel Gholson
District of Northern Alabama: Brigadier General Philip D. Roddey
    Johnson's (cavalry) Brigade: Colonel William A. Johnson
    Patterson's (cavalry) Brigade: Colonel Josiah Patterson
District of Central Alabama: Brigadier General Gideon Pillow
District of the Gulf: Major General Dabney H. Maury
District of S.W. Mississippi & E. Louisiana: Brigadier General George B. Hodge

TRANS-MISSISSIPPI DEPARTMENT:

Commanding General—General Edmund Kirby Smith
District of West Louisiana: Lieutenant General Richard Taylor
District of Arkansas: Major General Sterling Price
District of Texas: Major General John Magruder

Bibliography

BOOKS

Basler, Roy P., ed. *The Collected Works of Abraham Lincoln*. 8 vols. New Brunswick, N.J., 1953–1955.

Bearss, Edwin C. *Forrest at Brice's Cross Roads and in North Mississippi in 1864*. Dayton, 1979.

Boatner, Mark Mayo, III. *The Civil War Dictionary*. New York, 1959.

Brooks, Noah. *Washington In Lincoln's Time*. New York, 1958.

Carter, Samuel, III. *The Last Cavaliers*. New York, 1979.

————. *The Siege of Atlanta*. New York, 1973.

Catton, Bruce. *Grant Takes Command*. Boston, 1968.

————. *A Stillness At Appomattox*. New York, 1957.

Commager, Henry Steele. *The Blue and the Gray*. New York, 1950.

Connelly, Thomas Lawrence. *Autumn of Glory: The Army of Tennessee, 1862–1865*. New York, 1971.

Dana, Charles A. *Recollections of the Civil War*. New York, 1963.

Davis, William C. *The Orphan Brigade: the Kentucky Confederates Who Couldn't Go Home*. Garden City, N.Y., 1980.

Douglas, Henry Kyd. *I Rode With Stonewall*. Chapel Hill, 1940.

Dowdey, Clifford. *Lee's Last Campaign*. New York, 1960.

———— and Louis H. Manarin, eds. *The Wartime Papers of R. E. Lee*. New York, 1961.

Dyer, Frederick H. *A Compendium of the War of the Rebellion*. 3 vols. New York, 1959.

Early, Jubal Anderson. *War Memoirs*. Bloomington, Ind., 1860.

Eisenschiml, Otto and Ralph Newman. *The American Iliad*. New York, 1947.

Faust, Patricia L., ed. *Historical Times Illustrated Encyclopedia of the Civil War*. New York, 1986.

Foote, Shelby. *The Civil War: A Narrative*. 3 vols. New York, 1958–1974.

Fowler, William M., Jr. *Under Two Flags: The American Navy in the Civil War.* New York, 1990.

Freeman, Douglas Southall. *Lee's Lieutenants.* 3 vols. New York, 1942–1944.

———. *R. E. Lee.* 4 vols. New York, 1934–1935.

Fuller, J. F. C. *Grant and Lee: A Study in Personality and Generalship.* Bloomington, Ind., 1957.

Grant, Ulysses S. *Personal Memoirs of U. S. Grant.* New York, 1886.

Hattaway, Herman. *General Stephen D. Lee.* Jackson, Miss., 1976.

Horan, James D. *Confederate Agent.* New York, 1954.

Howe, Thomas J. *Wasted Valor: The Petersburg Campaign June 15–18, 1864.* Lynchburg, 1988.

Humphreys, Andrew A. *The Virginia Campaign of '64 and '65.* New York, 1883.

Leech, Margaret. *Reveille In Washington.* New York, 1941.

Lewis, Lloyd. *Sherman: Fighting Prophet.* New York, 1932.

Long, E. B. *The Civil War Day By Day: An Almanac, 1861–1865.* New York, 1971.

Macartney, Clarence Edward. *Mr. Lincoln's Admirals.* New York, 1956.

McDonough, James Lee, and James Pickett Jones. *War So Terrible.* New York, 1987.

Miers, Earl Schenck. *The General Who Marched to Hell.* New York, 1951.

———. *The Last Campaign: Grant Saves the Union.* New York, 1972.

Milton, George Fort. *Abraham Lincoln and the Fifth Column.* New York, 1942.

Nevins, Allan. *Ordeal of the Union.* 2 vols. New York, 1947.

———. *The War For the Union.* 4 vols. New York, 1959–1971.

Pond, George E. *The Shenandoah Valley in 1864.* New York, 1883.

Porter, Horace. *Campaigning With Grant.* New York, 1897.

Pullen, John J. *The 20th Maine.* New York, 1957.

Rhodes, Robert Hunt, ed. *All For the Union: The Civil War Diary and Letters of Elisha Hunt Rhodes.* New York, 1985.

Sandburg, Carl. *Abraham Lincoln: The War Years, 1864–1865.* New York, 1926.

Scaife, William R. *The Campaign For Atlanta.* Atlanta, 1990.

Sears, Stephen W. *George B. McClellan: The Young Napoleon.* New York, 1988.

Sheridan, P. H. *Personal Memoirs.* New York, 1888.

Sherman, William T. *Memoirs of Gen. W. T. Sherman.* New York, 1891.[1]

Starr, Louis M. *Bohemian Brigade: Civil War Newsmen in Action.* New York, 1954.

Starr, Stephen Z. *The Union Cavalry in the Civil War.* 3 vols. Baton Rouge, 1979–1985.

Tidwell, William A., with James O. Hall and David Winfred Gaddy. *Come Retribution.* Jackson, Miss., 1988.

Urwin, Gregory J. W. *Custer Victorious.* East Brunswick, N.J., 1983.

U.S. War Department. *The War of the Rebellion: A Compilation of the Official Records of the Union and Confederate Armies.* Vol. 43, Part I. Washington, 1893.

Vandiver, Frank E. *Jubal's Raid: Early's Famous Attack on Washington in 1864.* New York, 1960.

Watkins, Sam. *Co. Aytch.* New York, 1962.

Woodworth, Steven E. *Jefferson Davis and His Generals.* Lawrence, Kansas, 1990.

ARTICLES

Anders, Leslie. "Fisticuffs at Headquarters: Sweeny vs. Dodge." *Civil War Times Illustrated.* February 1977.

Beauregard, G. T. "Four Days of Battle at Petersburg." In *Battles and Leaders of the Civil War,* edited by Robert Underwood Johnson and Clarence Clough Buell, vol. 4. New York, 1887.

Bough, Joseph. "Iron Versus Wood." *America's Civil War.* November 1988.

Browne, John M. "The Duel Between the 'Alabama' and the 'Kearsarge.'" In *Battles and Leaders,* vol. 4. See Beauregard.

Horn, John. "Charge of the Tarheel Brigades." *Civil War Times Illustrated.* January–February 1991.

Howard, Oliver O. "The Struggle For Atlanta." In *Battles and Leaders,* vol. 4. See Beauregard.

Johnston, James D. "The Ram 'Tennessee' at Mobile Bay." In *Battles and Leaders,* vol. 4. See Beauregard.

Kell, John McIntosh. "Cruise and Combats of the 'Alabama.'" In *Battles and Leaders,* vol. 4. See Beauregard.

Kinney, John Coddington. "Farragut at Mobile Bay." In *Battles and Leaders,* vol. 4. See Beauregard.

Longacre, Edward G. "Wilson-Kautz Raid." *Civil War Times Illustrated.* May 1970.

Marthon, Joseph. "The Lashing of Admiral Farragut in the Rigging, II." In *Battles and Leaders,* vol 4. See Beauregard.

McMurry, Richard M. "Riding Through Alabama." *Civil War Times Illustrated.* August and October 1981.

Page, R. L. "The Defense of Fort Morgan." In *Battles and Leaders,* vol. 4. See Beauregard.

Powell, William H. "The Battle of the Petersburg Crater." In *Battles and Leaders*, vol. 4. See Beauregard.

Sherman, William T. "The Grand Strategy of the Last Year of the War." In *Battles and Leaders*, vol. 4. See Beauregard.

Shingleton, Royce Gordon. "Cruise of the CSS Tallahassee." *Civil War Times Illustrated*. May 1976.

Skoch, George F. "Thunder From Below." *America's Civil War*. July 1988.

Thomas, Henry Goddard. "The Colored Troops at Petersburg." In *Battles and Leaders*, vol. 4. See Beauregard.

Willcox, Orlando B. "Actions on the Weldon Railroad." In *Battles and Leaders*, vol. 4. See Beauregard.

---

1. Three editions of Sherman's memoirs were consulted, depending on which was available at the time. All combine the orginal two volumes into one. Two use separate page-number sequences for the two volumes while the other does not. Page numbers cited in the notes refer to the specific edition consulted at the time.

Index